More Praise for *The Long Night*

"Sensual, tender, painful in its friendships and expansive in its memory . . . With a wealth of startling detail, [Goldman] gives us a world that feels as if it could almost be touched." —*San Francisco Chronicle*

"It takes one's breath away. . . . Goldman pulls together the threads of the story brilliantly, moving back and forth in time like a nimble Mayan weaver creating an elaborate *huipil*." —*Los Angeles Times Book Review*

"Beautiful . . . A meditation, investigation, and chronicle written in a lyrical, evocative English." —*The Boston Globe*

"A tale that sensitively depicts the very best of human dignity and love . . . Brilliantly crafted . . . with great skill and poetic beauty . . . [*Chickens*] has the ability to captivate the reader with its powerful descriptive voice." —*The Christian Science Monitor*

"What Francisco Goldman has created is a masterpiece. . . . Combining American optimism, Latin illusion and Russian angst, his remarkable first novel magically explores life, love, death, politics, intrigue, and obsession in a bicultural plot twisting from here to Guatemala. . . . Infinitely satisfying." —*The Philadelphia Inquirer*

"This book is a jewel. . . . It is an insistent story, filled with characters who keep whispering to us long after we've put the book down. . . . A book about the many faces of truth, full of love and humor . . . Playing with time and reality and the idea that beauty and evil are inextricably linked could be dangerous for a first novelist, but Goldman pulls it off." —*The New York Observer*

"Goldman has synthesized the literary traditions of two continents in one of the most ambitious literary debuts in years. Funny and sad, wise and wide-eyed, *Chickens* is a richly layered, genre-busting novel that shuttles between suburban Boston and Guatemala City and devours everything in its path." —Jay McInerney

"A splendid first novel . . . Fashions a surfeit of intelligent detail about its protagonist's two countries into a fascinating study of cultural contrasts." —*USA Today*

"A beautiful story of national identity and love . . . Roger might be either the native son in search of his roots, or Holden Caulfield on a brief trip to hell. . . . With García Márquez, Goldman shares a love of narrative abundance, a profusion of character and detail that accrues to a rich whole. . . . Illuminated by innumerable small moments of humor, beauty and power." —*The Bookpress*

"The novel, like Roger himself, stands between two worlds—in part a personal story of love and coming of age, it is also a grand historical assault in the tradition of Joseph Conrad and Graham Greene."
—*Vanity Fair*

"An enthralling first novel . . . Passionate, romantic, and grimly witty . . . Subtle and tender." —*The Evening Standard* (London)

"Dazzling . . . Blending Yankee can-do intellectualism with Latin myth-making." —*The Plain Dealer* (Cleveland)

"Leaves the reader pondering the complications of vulnerable hearts and ravenous desires." —*Post-Bulletin* (Rochester)

"*The Long Night of White Chickens* is an exceptional novel that gently forces us to acknowledge and truly listen to voices from beyond our borders which have been hidden for too long." —Ariel Dorfman

"Extraordinary . . . A consummate storyteller . . . The novel's triumph is Flor, a heroine as complex and fragile as the society she inhabits."
—*The Boston Review*

"A remarkable novel . . . Accruing vivid new details at every turn, Roger's account gives the reader the most immediate possible sense of a country and its people, the comic and appealing as well as the horrific."
—*The Times Literary Supplement*

The
LONG
NIGHT
of WHITE
CHICKENS

Also by Francisco Goldman

The Ordinary Seaman
The Divine Husband
The Art of Political Murder
Say Her Name

The
LONG
NIGHT
of WHITE
CHICKENS

Francisco Goldman

Grove Press
New York

Published simultaneously in Canada
Printed in the United States of America

Library of Congress Cataloging-in-Publication Data

Goldman, Francisco.
    The long night of white chickens / Francisco Goldman.
    I. Title.
    PS3557.0368L66   1992   813'.54—dc20   91-44318
    ISBN 978-0-8021-4460-7

Grove Press
an imprint of Grove/Atlantic, Inc.
841 Broadway
New York, NY 10003
Distributed by Publishers Group West
www.groveatlantic.com

13 14 15 16   10 9 8 7 6 5 4 3 2 1

For Bert and Yoli, my parents,

and Barbara, my sister

PART ONE

GUATE
NO EXISTE

y bajo la ventana de mi Bella-Durmiente,
el sollozo continuo del chorro de la fuente
y el cuello del gran cisne blanco que me interroga.

and beneath the window of my Sleeping Beauty,
the continuous sobbing of the running fountain,
and the neck of the great white swan that questions me.

Yo persigo unaforma . . .
RUBÉN DARÍO

ONE

When I was five years old, and still in quarantine for the case of tuberculosis I'd picked up in Guatemala the year before, Abuelita, that is my mother's mother, sent us an orphan girl to be our maid, and this was Flor de Mayo Puac. Her passport and working papers said she was sixteen, but she was pretty positive she was thirteen. In the Guatemala City convent orphanage where Flor had lived since she was six (pretty positive of being six), the nuns had let her celebrate her birthday every May 10, the anniversary of her baptism there, which might actually have been her second baptism, though her father, when he was alive, had never once taken her into a church that she could remember. But the date seemed accurate enough, and not only because of the evidence provided by her name. She'd lived with her father in the department of Chiquimula, on the desert side of the mountains there where the first of the year's two or three heavy rains usually fell in April or May, inciting the locusts' racket, and it was always around that time that her father would suddenly change her age, saying, "Now you are five, *mijita,*" and then, "Now you are six." Flor lived in the convent orphanage for seven years, and then one day my grandmother came and picked her.

What had happened was that my mother had left my father when I was one and had taken me back to Guatemala, where I was going to grow up as a rich person, as she had, which is, of course, just one way of putting it. But then I caught TB from one of our maids and we went back to Massachusetts for the better hospitals in Boston, and also because Abuelita had my mother convinced that my illness was punishment from God for having abandoned my father up there, for three years, in the little suburban ranch house

3

on Codrioli Road in Namoset that my mother had never really liked. My father was still living there, alone, when we came home. Me, tubercular, browned by three years of tropical sun and then yellowed by illness, speaking no English, but still—his son. Abuelita, being a devout and ebulliently authoritarian Catholic, was against divorce, but she'd been just as against the marriage. My father is Jewish, and seventeen years older than my mother. He was raised in the poorest Jewish immigrant neighborhoods of Boston.

And because he was never comfortable with the idea of having a maid in the first place, and did not think a thirteen-year-old girl should spend all day housecleaning in a house where there wasn't all that much to clean, my farther decided that Flor should go to school. We were enrolled in the first grade together at the beginning of the next school year, and Flor eventually graduated from Namoset High four years ahead of me, in 1972. After that she won a full scholarship to Wellesley College, which is in the town of the same name, right next to Namoset.

But in 1979 Flor ended up back in Guatemala City, where she was eventually hired to be director of a private orphanage and malnutrition clinic called Los Quetzalitos. On the seventeenth of February, 1983, towards the end of General Rios Montt's highly successful counterinsurgency campaign, which according to what I've read in the papers and elsewhere added tens of thousands of new orphans to Guatemala's already huge orphan population, Flor was found murdered. She was discovered by some of her orphans lying on her bed in her room at the orphanage just before six in the morning, wearing pajamas, and dead from a single deep knife gash in her throat.

And the very next day the two major Guatemala City dailies came out saying that just two days previous the National Police had uncovered a clandestine safe house for hiding babies—also

4

called a *casa de engordes,* or fattening house—many of them not even orphans but illegally purchased and even stolen babies, and that they were being kept there until their illegal adoptions could be arranged. That is, until they could be sold to childless couples in Europe and the United States, this apparently being a highly profitable and widespread business in Guatemala and elsewhere in Central America—"a business angle to civil war and violent repression," as one human rights publication I read phrased it. The newspapers ran photographs of a house full of crowded cribs. And close-up shots of the frightened face of a captured *niñera,* or nursemaid, who was quoted as saying that her employer, or rather one of her employers but the only one who ever came to the safe house in person, was Flor de Mayo. And the newspapers and police theorized that behind this lay the probable motive for the murder, since Flor couldn't have run that kind of business all alone: so that it must have been her partners, tipped off somehow about what the *niñera* had said, who had silenced Flor forever, before the police had been able to procure the order for her arrest. The police said they were searching for these anonymous partners and that justice would be done, not just for the crime of an internecine murder but for the defamation and disgrace that all such baby-selling rings brought upon the *patria.*

They said that Flor's job as director of a legal orphanage had merely served her as a front, and as her introduction into the whole business of adoptions. And, as one newspaper put it, it was people like Flor, "a woman of *pocos escrúpulos,*" few scruples, who were "*desprestigiando,*" "de-prestiging, the entirely honorable and necessary occupation of taking care of orphans and legally finding them loving homes abroad. The newspapers highlighted Flor's beauty, though not to any specific purpose. And they made very much of the fact that, although she was Guatemalan born, this alone could not account for her corruption as she was a United

States citizen who had spent more than half her life in her adopted country and had graduated from one of its most elite colleges for women. Direct U.S. military aid to the Guatemalan military government had been cut off by Congress since 1978 because of the human rights violations, considered the most excessive in the hemisphere, and no one since in Washington who had tried had succeeded in coming up with the right words to persuade Congress to fully turn it back on. But the military, and many in the Guatemalan press, and many Guatemalans who considered themselves patriots, such as my relatives, liked to think of that cutoff as a kind of blanket violation of all Guatemalans' human rights and as a new and hypocritical form of imperialism, and now the newspapers posed Flor's case as another form of hypocrisy and imperialism: a highly educated U.S. citizen selling, for personal profit, the surviving victims of the *alleged* human rights atrocities that North Americans professed to be so concerned about.

It was into that scandal that my father and I flew together, to bring Flor's body home for burial.

It is something of a long story, what happened those two days in Guatemala, and I will come to it. But I will say that nothing happened to convince us that what the papers and authorities were saying about Flor wasn't true. Nothing. And it is what I'd more or less believed since, for over a year, about Flor, until the day just over a month ago when Luis Moya Martinez looked me up in Brooklyn, New York, where I was living.

I'd known Moya when I was of elementary school age, from all the summers that my mother and I spent back in Guatemala visiting Abuelita. (Flor stayed home in Namoset all but one of those summers and wanted to, or at least pretended to want to, not that Abuelita would have offered to pay her airfare too. Abuelita had her own maids, no need to bring ours and so on—Except my father had made Flor *not* just a maid.) Because Guatemalan schoolchildren don't get their long vacation until October and my mother had her own idea about why attending a Guatemalan private school would be a great thing for me, I was enrolled every summer in the Colegio Anne Hunt, the school that all my cousins have gone to. Moya— and even then everyone but the teachers called him nothing but that—was one of a handful of scholarship students there.

But since then I'd only seen him twice. The summer after my junior year in college I drove down to Guatemala by myself in a Ford Mustang that belonged to my roommate, who was in Italy, where his girlfriend had gone to study art history. He'd told me I could use his car while he was away, though of course taking it down to Central America wasn't what he'd meant. But he wasn't the type ever to even notice the mileage on his odometer, and when I got back in August, just days ahead of him, I took it to the car wash and then in our driveway used a sponge and his portable blow-dryer to steam the Mexican tourist stickers off the windows and he never noticed a thing. I'd taken that car for the crazy adventure of it, because I was infatuated then with what just this degree of recklessness might mean about me (though if it meant anything of value, I can't say I've lived up to it since). But mainly I'd gone down to visit Flor. And on the unforgettably chaotic day that the government reversed the direction of all the major one-way avenues in Guatemala City, I ran into Moya in the cake shop–café called Pastelería Hemmings. He was still a university student himself then, studying to be a lawyer at San Carlos, the public university.

Then I saw Moya again, even more briefly, outside La Verbena morgue, where my father and I, accompanied by U.S. Consul Joseph Simms, had gone to claim Flor's body.

* * *

7

But when my mother phoned to say that at a Latin American Society of Boston event she'd met a young Guatemalan man who was studying at Harvard now and who said he'd known me at the Colegio Anne Hunt, it didn't even cross my mind at first that she could mean Moya. I thought I knew what he was doing now: he'd become not a lawyer but a Guatemala City newspaperman. And though I'd never read anything of his and didn't even know which paper he was working for, my experience of the newspapers there in general, which have to be read to be believed, made it impossible for it even to occur to me that anyone from that background could get accepted into any kind of program at Harvard. Not that I could imagine anyone from Anne Hunt being at Harvard, certainly not any of the boys. (I might as well admit now that Harvard has always been a somewhat touchy subject with me, given my father's long obsession with the idea that his son should go there, a cause I did not help along very much by graduating from Namoset High with a 62 average, which placed me near the top of the bottom fifth of my class.) The Colegio Anne Hunt is a rich kids' school, but not one of the very best ones. It isn't like the American School or even the Colegio Maya, where they have teachers from the States and you have to take an aptitude test to get in or else have parents with enough *cuello* or pull, something like a supersignificant last name, to buy you in anyway. And of course I remembered that among the boys at Anne Hunt it had always been such a point of privileged macho pride to do badly that most never even graduated unless they went back during the school break to take the special and expensive course that allowed them to. (And allowed Anne Hunt to design her school's annual graduation ceremony to be as feminine, delicate, and expressive of the same values as high society coming out balls.) So who, in all that crowd of Anne Hunt *cabroncitos* was at Harvard now? And why would he remember me and be asking my mother for my telephone number?

8

"A very charming young man, *muy elegante, muy bien educado*" is how my mother described him over the phone, though I guess she'd say the same about Porky Pig if he was a Latin American at Harvard. She is the vice president of the Latin American Society of Boston this year, which has a floor of a brownstone on Newbury Street as its headquarters, and she told me how she'd met this elegant young "stranger" when, during the milling round over coffee and pastries following a Venezuelan diplomat's lecture on the intellectual history of Latin America, he'd approached her to ask, completely out of the blue, what had ever happened to the antique electric train that for years had decorated a window of Arrau, our family department store in Guatemala City, at Christmas time. My mother's laugh over the phone must have matched the one she'd given the stranger then, full of pleasure and surprise over having her family's business prominence so unexpectedly evoked within earshot of so many of the society's patrons—real Boston blue bloods, she has often reminded me. Which gave her the chance to recite for the stranger the cheerful and nostalgic homage I of course know by heart: . . . Well yes, *claro,* that wonderful toy train, her father used to say the elves made it to escape Switzerland, where they'd been enslaved for centuries in an underground cuckoo clock factory. Because it was a Swiss toy train, you see, though her father bought it in a Hong Kong market during his buying trip through the Orient in 1932. Back then Arrau's toy department must have been the equal of any in the world! General Ubico had no children, of course, but he used to walk over from the National Police just to say hello to her mother and look at the toys. Yes, of course, Ubico was a dictator and that is wrong but the times were so different then and he *was* a friend of her mother. But that train was special, her father wouldn't sell it, not even to Ubico. Though unfortunately it ceased to exist the day the Arrau store in Quezaltenango caught fire, she's sure it was an accident

9

because, you know, why would anyone? caught fire during a student riot coincidentally soon after that train had been brought up there for a special window display of antique toys in honor of Children's Week in Quezaltenango. *Ay no,* the treasures, the *absolute treasures* that were lost in that fire . . . ! Though of course at Christmas you *can* still hear the tape recording her father made, the one with bells from Tchaikovsky's something or other and the Negro opera singer from Belize with a deep, deep voice who her father hired to do the voice of Santa Claus, you can still hear him! The Guatemalan stranger would have nodded with enthusiasm here, would have known of the annual event if not the actual history, would have known that my mother's brother, Jorge Arrau, still plays that recording over the loudspeakers at Christmas while the little man who plays the part of Santa Claus stands on the store balcony pantomiming along to the Belizean's operatic and Caribbean *ho ho hos* and throwing candy to the children below, always so many children that the police have to close Sexta Avenida to traffic.—That recording is nearly forty years old! And do you know that little man who plays Santa is the very same man who has been doing it now for nearly forty years? (the stranger gapes in astonishment, he'd never realized) He must be able to act along to that recording in his sleep! Two hours of ho *ho hos* and *Feliz Navidades* and if you watch you'll see that he never misses a single *ho,* he opens his mouth for every single *ho!* Which just proves that any job worth doing is worth doing *well,* my dear! (Later Moya confessed to me that while his inquiry about the train had been an effective conversation opener, he really had madly desired that train as a boy and had even fantasized about talking me into stealing it for him.)

". . . Well, tall, dark, about six feet, I think," said my mother, trying to describe the elegant young stranger.

"Oh good, *tall,* when I haven't seen this guy in like twelve years probably. Brown eyes too I bet. Speaks good Spanish I bet. This is helpful, Mom."

But she couldn't remember his name because she'd assumed that if he'd gone to the Colegio Anne Hunt then she would at least know his mother, but of course she didn't because Moya's mother has never been anything, or rather anybody, more illustrious than Anne Hunt's seamstress, and back then when we were in school his father was an officers' mess waiter on a cargo ship owned by the Somoza family of Nicaragua.

"Well, he said he knew Flor de Mayo too," said my mother. "Of course I didn't tell him that you are working in a restaurant, my dear. I told him you are applying to graduate schools. Have you? Are you?"

" . . ."

Nervousness can bring out a breezy petulance in my mother's voice, as well as suddenly make her native accent much stronger, and the more or less native attitudes she reverts to when she is feeling like that can seem malicious, though they really aren't meant to be, though they can certainly be irritating. I mean, no, I hadn't applied to anything, and was pretty much paralyzed by the whole idea, and she knew that.

But just mentioning Flor makes her nervous now, and so she can't bring herself to very often, and I know that makes her feel as if she is somehow failing me, as if somehow I've needed nothing more than to pour my heart out to her about Flor and to hear all that she might have to say. When really she isn't failing me at all, because I've tried not to mention Flor either, very often, not to my mother. (Though maybe Moya is right, and I *do* need to pour my heart out about Flor, to hear all that *I* might say.) But she thinks that I am only being vengeful and stubborn in some unnecessarily private way, and that I just won't understand that Flor, her death and everything, truly shamed her, and stripped her of so many of her most necessary illusions. For she even thinks that Flor has made it impossible for her to go back to Guatemala again, partly because of the way the publicity surrounding the murder must have concentrated the sharpest scrutiny on my mother's life among her relations and lifelong acquaintances and friends, who, of course, a few initial condolences aside, never mention Flor de Mayo to her in any of their correspondences.

Mirabel Arrau was sent to America by her mother—I know she imagines them thinking and gossiping all over the place—for reasons well known and embarrassing enough, and look, there she married a much older man, a Jew and not even one with money and after she left him for the first time and then went back to him because her little son contracted tuberculosis, her mother sent her a *muchacha,* a servant, a maid. And her husband put that maid in school and treated her like a daughter. And her son made her his sister and something more, yes, something more, don't you think? Because when Mirabel's son came down here, remember?—that same year that that *muchacha* came down and took over that orphanage, that son practically ignored his own family and spent all his time with that—they ran around like a pair of—and were seen several times drunk together, disoriented together—That girl who had been their maid and who was of course corrupt in who knows how many ways and then, *por Dios,* without honor or shame, her husband and son came down to take her body back and were shown treating our poor little news reporters so crudely, so offensively on television and with no respect for this country at all or for Mirabel's good family name and then, but *no, ay no,* would you believe that they took her back and buried her in their own family plot! And now Mirabel has left her husband again! Living on her own, without help, a mature woman, living on her own like some poor little student in Boston! But I will say this we will all say this *Gracias a Dios que bendiga* that neither Mirabel's father, Don Rogerio, nor her mother, *la santísima* Doña Emilia, lived to witness any of this because *ay no* . . .

Guatemala, in so many ways the Kingdom of my mother's Pride when I was growing up, her Empire of Beautiful Nostalgia, has become, she thinks, because of Flor and only because of Flor, a place where her name only provokes gossip and condemnation or searing pity and silence. She really believes that. And I have wanted to tell her that this can't possibly be true, that she must be exaggerating, that her old-fashioned Guatemala, Abuelita's socially rigid Guatemala, probably doesn't even exist anymore, that even Uncle Jorge's family has suffered their own little scandals and, look, aren't they doing more or less fine? But I can't. How am I supposed to bring it up if she admits nothing? says nothing? True, there were a few remarks to her from Uncle Jorge and Aunt Lisel complaining about my behavior and casual dress that one summer, and they at least pretended to be a bit offended that I had chosen to sleep on a couch in Flor's apartment rather than in the guest room at their house (they should have known my mother would blow their comments all out of proportion, Aunt Lisel probably *did* know). But I've lived long enough now with my mother's Pride and Nostalgia that it doesn't take any special insight or powers of divination to know the rest.

Instead she has taken as her rhetorical escape the very sense of responsibility I have to admit I'd long urged on her. Because in Boston she often acts as if she has turned on Guatemala now because of the other things happening there, which I'd been telling her about for years, though I absolutely stopped mentioning it after Flor died. She is hardly a political person but I guess you don't need to be, she can read the *Boston Globe,* has heard my father angrily recite what he has read there in recent years, both of us reciting what we've read there or elsewhere with, at times, the most unjust belligerence, as if partly blaming her. For so many years my mother considered it one of the great offenses of life in the United States that even the plumber might assume she was Puerto Rican or, even more grating to my mother, Cuban, and so think that he could treat her as a social equal or even inferior. But now she often acts as if she prefers even that to being identified as a Guatemalan by even the most perfunctory of newspaper readers, who usually associate her country's name now only with such things as death squads, torture, disappearances, the most horrific and widespread massacres. And on days during the past year when the news from Guatemala has been especially shocking (the bayoneting of Indian babies and pregnant mothers by government soldiers) I've even heard her speak of renouncing her Guatemalan citizenship, which she has held on to all these years. My mother is not insincere, but I know that Flor came first, that the hurt Flor caused us has opened her mind, her emotions, to what has seemed like a fuller acknowledgment of these crimes.

So I didn't doubt that she'd resolved not to mention Flor at all on the phone that day, but then had finally felt obligated to. I do think I understand her. And I also felt a need to protect myself from Flor. I let a silence run between us before I finally said:

"He said he knew Flor? From when she was at Wellesley or what?"

"I, I really don't know, he didn't say, he just said he'd known her and that, you know, of course . . ." She sighed, flustered. "He offered his condolences is all. Are you taking good care of yourself at least, Sweet Pea?"

"Uh-huh," I said.

"I had dinner with your father a few days ago, by the way. He's reading *Don Quixote,* and now is full of the idea that he should visit Spain this summer. *Don Quixote,* can you imagine? He never showed an interest in things like that all the years we were married, he never even learned Spanish . . ."

But then I was barely listening. She went on about things related to their separation, and then about how much harder it was to get to work on time now that she had to drive all the way from Boston to Shreve Hall, the girls' boarding school in Dover where she teaches Spanish, she'd already been late for her first morning class three times after fifteen years of only having been late once . . . While I thought, Well, any one of them might have known Flor, even through the orphanage but more likely through the night life in La Zona Viva. I ran through that gargoyle gallery of all my old schoolmates again, and even considered Moya. He'd grown tall. He was dark. But Flor had never mentioned him to me, and I didn't link him to any boyhood obsession with that train.

"But you know," said my mother, when I'd pressed her again for a more distinguishing description, "his hair is starting to turn white. It looks fine on him but he is young for that, poor fellow."

His hair was turning white. I dismissed the possibility of Moya. I didn't know that, in fact, his hair *was* turning white. That day, over a year ago, outside La Verbena morgue, when Moya suddenly appeared, I hadn't been interested in any detail so fine as the premature silvering of his hair, certainly under way by then. I did notice the size of his hands, one of his hands, the way his long, livid fingers lightly cradled a small reporter's notebook and a tape recorder held together with tape; he'd walked towards me holding these objects a few inches in front of a bleached white shirt pocket loaded with pens. And then I'd noticed his expression, tremulously wide-eyed and miserable with what I took to be shame and a sensible fear of me. I'd thought, How dare he be here? and had only wanted to hate him . . .

Later Moya would tell me that in Cambridge he'd gone to see a doctor who told him that his "premature aging symptoms" (there were others less noticeable than his hair: inexplicable bouts of heavy fatigue, throbbing aches in the external parts of his ears) were a physiological reaction to constant anxiety and fear. He'd always understood this as the cause of an occasional tic in his right eye and the fragility of his stomach, but he'd never connected it to the other things. So he was relieved, even hopeful. Anxiety and fear might go away one day. And then maybe it will be like rain after a long drought? He'll shave his head and watch it grow back black?

Moya met my mother in April, but I wouldn't actually hear from him until May, and I wouldn't go back to Guatemala until June.

Which is where I am now sitting, in fact, in Pastelería Hemmings, up on the mezzanine, at the very same table by the window where I was sitting five years ago when Moya spotted me on the day they reversed the direction of the one-way traffic, when he said, *"Guatemala no existe . . ."* and so on. Which I kind of came to think of as his refrain, recalling it just like that even years later in Brooklyn (months before that April afternoon when my mother phoned) on the winter day that I first saw the Guatemalan knish vendor's truck parked right in front of my building on Eastern Parkway, a refurbished ice-cream truck with a man sitting inside and looking right at me with eyes that were two black, narrow stones of Indian seriousness and gravity set into a fat, round face; the truck's panel decorated with the too familiar symbols of Guatemalan kitsch: cartoony quetzal birds in unfurled flight, a grape purple volcano, a Maya pyramid, and the painted letters "KNISHES CHAPÍN"—*chapín* being Central American slang for Guatemalan. A post-Maya *chapín* selling Jewish knosh food in Brooklyn. I tried to stay away from that truck as if it were a joke aimed just at me, would literally cross the street to avoid it whenever I ran into it around my neighborhood in the year plus after Flor's death. "Guatemala doesn't exist"—I couldn't have wished more that it were true.

It's raining outside, though not heavily. Half an hour ago it was torrential, a delicious reverberation that seemed to come from the earth instead of the sky, going right through me. I'm drinking coffee, smoking filterless Payasos (a white-faced clown with the smile of a lighthearted idiot waving from every poinsettia red, thirty-five-*centavo* square little pack); I have a copy of yesterday's *New York Times,* purchased this morning for the equivalent of two bucks at Palacio de las Revistas, the Palace of Magazines, just down the block, and this notebook in which I am trying to commence this chronicling of the investigation into Flor's life and death that Moya and I have agreed to collaborate on. Moya already refers to this place as my *oficina,* though I sit nearly as often in the Picadilly on *La Sexta*—Sixth Avenue—or at the table closest to the sidewalk in the Fo Lu Shu. Moya and I met here in the *pastelería* this morning. Just a touch patronizingly, he warned me about government informers, who are everywhere, including, of course, his own newspaper office, too many of them eager and ignorant enough to misunderstand any kind of conversation. *Orejas,* they're called—*ears.* I'm supposed to act from now on as if even the old women sitting at the next table—one of them plaintively monologuing, ". . . he's a good son, a good son, he adores his mother, *la adora,* he puts his mother above everything"—might be *orejas* too. I'm to be a *tumba:* our secrets sealed inside me as if inside a tomb.

I yawn like crazy. This constant fact of paranoia, no matter how abstractly abided, tires me, 1 think. Every afternoon I feel just sapped. But it must be the altitude too and all the unfiltered motor fumes in the air and probably gastrointestinal germs working as silently inside me as this blend of excitement and fear and other more familiar emotions, which I try not to let my expression betray. (yawn, drink coffee, smoke, read newspaper, scribble in notebook, keep a quietly watchful eye, a tuned-in ear . . .) And the rain, and the afternoon light that looks washed through ashes. Guatemala City is a mountain city, and during the rainy season especially the sky couldn't feel closer or heavier.

Across the street the dim blue neon is on in the window of a shoe store, spelling out LE PETIT CHALET. And just the dimmest hue of blue neon suffuses the soft rain and the drifting mists in front of the big, wet, black granite blocks of another building, and suffuses as well the drenched blue shirts of a trio of policemen walking by, their high black boots and sharp-featured Indian faces shiny from the rain. Bumper-to-bumper traffic, cars, Jeeps, vans, many with windows polarized black so you can't see in and probably bullet-proofed too; schoolgirls in drably colored uniforms hurrying down the flooded sidewalk, books clutched to their chests or held over their hair, on their way to the avenues where the buses run; a peasant woman from the *altiplano,* the highlands, the woven colors and patterns of her traditional Indian *traje* darkened by rain, grime, and wear, her *traje*-wrapped torso immobile but her bare feet lightly trotting along under the ragged, soaked hem, an eye like a frightened bird's peering out from under the lumpy cloth bundle she carries on her head. All of this, and something else absorbed like a mood along with just what you see—La Merced Cathedral's dome and cross against the fuming sky and a shabby high rise of rust-streaked concrete; and even the tattered art deco furnishings of Pastelería Hemmings's mezzanine here inside, the weak light from the electric candelabras set into the dull crimson walls and the dusty plastic plants in urns, the odors of cheap, rain-soaked fabrics, the elephant-footed old women sitting four to a table and the middle-aged clerk expressionlessly reading a newspaper while he waits for his plump and adulterous lover, the five-year-old girl in her yellow street urchin's dress who has snuck up the stairs to beg from table to table with the melancholy, spurned self-possession of a veteran gypsy—all of this makes me think that Guatemala City, especially downtown in Zona 1, really must be something like Prague, the way you might imagine Prague if you've never been there, just what you might know and feel about Prague watching any random downtown street corner from a cake shop like this one on a rainy afternoon, people going about their subterranean business in the urban capital of a well-entrenched police state.

Now a short, portly man, his black hair gleaming with brilliantine and rain, is walking hurriedly down the sidewalk holding a flimsy umbrella, and under one arm he carries a long, rectangular photograph, wrapped in transparent cellophane, of a sweetly smiling young girl, dressed and crowned in immaculate white, kneeling to receive her First Communion.

That day five years ago, when the government changed the direction of the one-way traffic on the city's major avenues, Moya was right here in Pastelería Hemmings, sitting at a table with three other student types, two guys and a girl, and they were huddled over a copy of the afternoon daily (the very same afternoon paper, *El Minuto,* that in less than two years Moya would find himself working for) that had just hit the streets, its headline announcing that so far that day ten people had died, either in traffic accidents or from getting run over. I hadn't realized he was Moya yet—he would recognize me first—but I could hear them talking about it as I stared out the window, heard a bitterly deadpan voice (his) from their table saying in Spanish, *Permit me to say that as a way of relieving traffic congestion I find this not bad. Eliminate the drivers, eliminate the pedestrians.* And then the girl's voice petulantly saying, *Permíteme decir que no es cosa para chistes, vos,* it isn't anything to joke about . . .

About a week later my favorite cousin, Catalina, Catty to all of us, then a senior at the Colegio Anne Hunt, would tell how a teacher who had been particularly affected by the chaos of the traffic change that day, one of the perpetually young Señorita Something teachers, said, "This proves the government doesn't care about the people." Anne Hunt might have fired her for getting political in class that way, if it had gotten back to her. But what made Catty's story funny was that this teacher was practically obsessed with her car, a brand-new red Toyota she'd won in a raffle only months before. Catty said this teacher couldn't have been more *exagerada* in her pride over this car if she'd tried, always telling her class things like "Imagine how it improves the psychology to drive a car with all the windows down in the morning instead of riding the bus, to breathe fresh morning air instead of bus exhaust and the smells of all the people pressed against you, so many of them, let's face it, very poor and unhygienic people." Or she'd leave books and papers behind in the car just so she could make a show of saying, "Will someone volunteer to go out to my car and get them? It's a red Toyota, and today it is parked just down the block, on the left side, right under that jasmine tree. If it rains today my car will be covered with jasmine blossoms, and if I drive home with the windows down, I'll smell jasmine all the way!"

But this teacher had been so traumatized by the chaotic traffic that day that she'd started leaving her car at home and riding the bus, and in the days since had turned into a real *melancólica* in class, listless and distracted and constantly sipping hot lettuce tea from a thermos for her nerves. All of which culminated in the scene out in front of the school just after the siesta break one afternoon when a young lower-class man accosted this teacher as she came walking down the sidewalk from the bus stop. Through eavesdropped snatches of his tormented shouting and the teacher's pleading whispers, Catty and her friends were able to piece together a puzzle revealing that for months her teacher and this man had been meeting in her parked Toyota during the siesta, but only when it rained and rained hard, which at the height of the rainy season was just about every afternoon, to kiss and maybe even make love with the rain protecting them from the danger of curious passersby, a curtain of rain closing them off from all the world in their cozy, black vinyl, made-in-Japan love nest. But this love affair was over now that the *señorita* felt too afraid to drive her car anymore. And how could it ever be resumed now that her lover's outraged and indiscreet tantrum had let the students in on their secret? *"Pobrecita,"* poor thing, lamented my cousin Catty, while she sat facing me on the piano stool in Uncle Jorge's study, where she was waiting with placid impatience for her boyfriend's daily evening visit and telling me this story. "Why couldn't he have waited? calmed her? helped her to feel confident about taking her *carrito* out in traffic again? But that's how men are, *verdad?* They take everything personally! *Pues sí.*"

And later that same evening of the day they changed the direction of the traffic, when I went back to the furnished apartment in Zona 10 that Flor was already renting, carrying my own copy of *El Minuto* and its TEN DEAD headline, Flor had just washed her hair, had it turbaned in a towel, and was sitting on the couch, doing absolutely nothing apparently, which was not characteristic. ("You won't believe who I ran into in Pasteíería Hemmings. Moya! Remember Moya?"—it didn't mean much to her, no reason that it should have then.) But it's amazing how easy it is just to sit around doing nothing in Guatemala, or anywhere in the tropics perhaps—it isn't the heat, because Guatemala City isn't especially hot and in November, December it even gets cold. But day after day you can just sit around doing nothing and it doesn't feel particularly wrong or even tedious. Back then I thought several times that maybe this was the reason Flor had returned here and seemed interested in staying awhile: that after so many years of balancing heroic over-achieving with the more banal but just as constant demands of housework and, more recently, earning a living, not to mention what seemed to me years of unbroken and rather obsessive social-izing, that Flor was finding it pleasurable to sit around being lazy and anonymous; that she even felt a perverse and paradoxically self-negating attraction to a place—her native country!—where every-where you looked hard work seemed only one more aspect of a general futility it was easiest to escape by just not doing anything, but only if you could afford to, and she could. (But then, within two months, she would throw herself into her new job running Los Quetzalitos, and for the next three years plus work harder than she ever had before.) Anyway, I handed Flor the newspaper and she snapped it open like it was just what she'd been waiting for all day. And then seconds later tossed it aside on the couch and said sleepily and in her eternally childlike voice, "Oh well. Let them eat cake."

Because what were ten more dead people that summer?

It was the General Lucas García regime, recently embarked on its own three-year reign of unprecedented bloodiness. And it was just beginning to dawn on people that they were really into something now, that this was going to be quite a bit stranger and so much more horrific than even the previous twenty-five years of bloody enough military rule had been. But the guerrillas were strong then too, in the Indian highlands, the jungles of the Petén, and even in the cities, where businessmen were often targeted for kidnappings. Uncle Jorge would phone home just before leaving his office to alert the maids, and when he turned into the top of the street he'd honk three times and the maids would swing the steel-fortified double doors open so that he could glide the car in without having to stop, and then they'd pull the doors shut behind him. One of Catty's Colegio Anne Hunt schoolmates was ambushed coming out of a party: he'd just gotten into his car and then he refused to come out and be kidnapped. He threw it into forward and slammed into his assailants just as they'd begun to unload their machine guns into his windshield. He ran right over them, killing two guerrillas, but he died too. Which was stupid, I think. He could have had a chance to live. His family could have paid the ransom. Instead he became a Colegio Anne Hunt martyr and a year later Anne Hunt's husband, Scobie, became another. Everyone with money wanted to get their kids out of the country, and even my aunt and uncle sent Catty away to college in Montreal, Canada, that following winter, where, despite her little college being all women and Catholic, she ended up marrying the very first guy who set eyes on her. Literally, pretty much the very first one. He worked as a skycap at Dorval Airport, a half French-Canadian, half-Italian guy named Ronnie. It was love at first sight, for him anyway. He loaded Catty and Aunt Lisel's luggage onto his cart and flirted Catty up all the way out to her taxi and learned where they were going from the driver, and then he really chased her. He was more than just a skycap, of course, I mean he had other ambitions. And Catty loved him. But it ended very badly, and now Catty is living in Guatemala again, in her parents' house, with her two-year-old twin daughters, Rosie and Paloma.

Of course the people who the army and the police took or killed were rarely given the option of paying ransoms. And they took or killed thousands upon thousands.

The head of the National Police was named Chupina. One joke going around was, Did you hear Chupina had a twin brother in the womb?—Yes, stillborn, showing signs of torture and a *tiro degracia,* a coup de grâce, in the head.

And in another Chupina and General Lucas are fishing, and Lucas catches a tiny fish and he's about to toss it back but Chupina says, Wait, give it to me, and he takes the fish in one hand and starts pummeling its head with the other, saying, OK, talk, where are the big ones?

(In New York I worked as a bartender, a temperamentally good-natured if not particularly joky one. For years, whenever customers told jokes at the bar and etiquette seemed to require that I tell one too, these were the only ones that came to me.)

That was the summer that the Sandimsta revolutionaries took Managua. Or, according to Uncle Jorge and many who agree with him, the summer that U.S. President "Jimmy Castro" let the Sandinistas have it. But in Guatemala, world-wandering international hippies were still filling all the two-dollar-a-night hotel rooms in Panajachel, the tourist town up on the volcano-ringed lake, and ordering the legendary or maybe apocryphal psilocybin mushroom omelets in the Café Psicodélico; you could always tell the Germans because they were the ones who most liked to show their esteem and solidarity with the culture by going around dressed up in Indian *traje,* much of it too small for them, chubby blond calves protruding like slabs of hairy suet from beneath striped Indian britches. Young summer travelers still crowded into Livingston's reggae bars on the Caribbean coast and danced the night away under the bent palms on the pig-shit- and fish-stinking, dark dirt beach, while the black Carib kids living in the shrimpers' huts grouped around, jumping up and down and chanting "Sandinista!" to win the pretty European girls' attention.

That afternoon in Pastelería Hemmings, at a table of people from the States, a man was waving a copy of that *El Minuto* with its TEN DEAD headline and yelling, in English, "I don't believe it! The monkeys! What a bunch of monkeys! Does this say it all or what? I'm going to take this home and have it framed!"

People heard him, and some were offended. Heads turned. Guatemalans take offense easily and viscerally—you can feel it in a room, sense their breathing quickening, their tempers rising, sense a blackening rage even, when it's really bad, when they're about to lose it, utterly.

That's when I noticed the guy who turned out to be Moya staring at me.

I looked away, out the window. Honest to God, chaos was as tangible as if the whole city had just been flipped upside down and back over again. Guatemalan traffic can terrify me even on slow Sundays, but that day, all over the place, people were turning the wrong way down one-way avenues. People were looking the wrong way as they stepped off curbs. Truckers were trying to bash their way through directionless traffic jams anyway. Bus drivers were slipping confusedly back into the routes they'd been follow-ing for years. People were being injured and killed. Guatemala City, a flat plateau city in the Valley of the Virgin, was echoing with bleating car horns. Not even the birds could have felt safe; they must have stayed up in the air. And the usual traffic sounds, ranging from the high, beady spitting of mufflerless motorbikes to the wall-shaking thunder of mufflerless buses, from the iron gnashing of ancient gearboxes to the smooth-shifting hum of ex-pensive imports, the clanging of so many flimsy body parts as shockless '59 Pontiacs and trucks that are nothing more than loose piles of junk go banging over potholes and bumps, the artillery of so many backfires far away and nearby—all these sounds were accelerated and amplified that day; it sounded as if everybody was trying to get out, to flee the city all at once.

One thing I know about Guatemala now is that little of this sort happens here, no matter how shocking or outrageous, without a reason, without actual people sitting down somewhere and deciding that it should happen. Though sometimes their reasoning can seem just as outrageous or bewildering as the thing done. The new traffic ordinance was meant to improve the traffic flow, and in that way was even linked to a promised improvement in the economy. Because the perpetually jammed up traffic at certain transit points in the city's layout was responsible for making people late for work, for wasting gasoline and diesel, and that affected, among other things, the profitability of buses, as did the slow traffic, which also hindered truckers passing through downtown on their way to the highways leading to the coastal ports, and time is money. It was especially supposed to improve the traffic flow through the crucial maze of rotaries, underpasses, and switchbacks down at one end of Zona 1, suturing together downtown's old, dense grid of straight, narrow streets and the wide boulevards and expressways of the newer residential and industrial zones beyond. This area, during the rush hours, was usually impassable. My other uncle, Dr. Nelson Arrau, warned ahead of time that the whole thing might be a scam anyway, a contract awarded by government or city officials to some self-made urban planner in return for a payoff, resulting in an essentially berserk and thoughtless recommendation. And though the government had announced the new ordinance days ahead, Uncle Jorge predicted the disaster, and he's an *ultra* patriot. It's not like everybody reads the papers, he said. And of course they don't, not in a country of rampant illiteracy where much of the Indian population, at least half the national population, doesn't even speak Spanish. And it's not like *everybody* listens to the radio, paying special attention to every government public service announcement or motivational message, of which there are many. And of course people are going to get confused, or just forget. It wouldn't even take that many to screw it all up.

In the end traffic flow *was* actually improved a little (though now, five years later, it's as bad as it ever was). By that night the number of fatalities reached thirteen. It's the kind of thing that could happen in any small, poor country, you were supposed to say. Or else, *"Guatemala no existe . . ."* et cetera—So claimed Moya that afternoon in Pastelería Hemmings, reciting the speech that was in fact the opening paragraph of a French thriller he'd read in translation—something about a philosophical Gallic trucker and his hair-raising drive across Guatemala transporting a dangerous cargo, various native and foreign malevolents in pursuit—which ended with the line "Guatemala doesn't exist, and I know, because I have been there."

Moya loved that; still does, still trots it out now and then and always as if for the first time. And I carried it around with me all these years, always hearing it in his dramatic and particularly Moya voice: almost too mannishly resonant to be believed, his vibrating *r*'s rolled off his tongue in such a way that he did seem suited to play the part of Count Dracula, which is what he was actually doing then, in a homespun version of *Dracula* that his little theater group was putting on—the very production that must have caused him a batch, maybe even his very first batch, of barely discernible white hairs. Because in Brooklyn I mentioned it and he recalled that the play had had a short-lived success, well attended by university students and other sophisticates who found in it the illicit thrills of an obliquely rendered political satire, until the first wave of death threats shut it down. A few anonymous notes delivered backstage promising God's vengeance against the enemies and defamers of Guatemala were all it took. Then, to be extra prudent, his theater group promptly took out an ad in a newspaper pleading that their production had been meant as nothing more than a faithful retelling of the famous Transylvanian tale, and that they'd only dressed the count's peasant victims in the native *traje* of the Indians because it had seemed most convenient, if, of course, they now realized, insensitive to the point of unintended blasphemy to do so.

What happened that day in Pastelería Hemmings—while outside the demolition derby of the damned went on, a whole city of poor people's vehicles lurching around to the deliberate rhythm of car horns bleating near and far through the demonic whine of sirens—is that Moya left his table and came up behind me and spoke my name, and I whirled around and saw this tall, very black-haired (then) and frightened-looking (I thought) person standing there, and I saw his friends watching from their table. Their expressions were solemn, suspenseful. They looked like serious university types. Even the girl, her gaze aimed too directly at me from between sharp brows and a small, shinily upturned nose, seemed devoid of youthful frivolity: dressed in plain gray blouse and jeans, wearing no makeup, no feminine embellishment other than a thin, limp ribbon of Indian-woven threads dangling in her hair like a colorful shred of *traje* torn on a thorny bush. Which is to say they looked political as hell. That they knew my name utterly panicked me, blinded me from any possibility of recognition. It's supernatural, almost, the way Guatemala infests you. I don't think I'd ever given it deep thought, exactly, but now I suddenly knew that the worse nightmares the country has to offer could begin just like this, with a seemingly chance encounter, a name spoken inquiringly, and all the years you were going to have left to live vanishing right in front of you, draining from the room like a sudden hush in the idle chatter of a cake shop's crowded mezzanine—four sets of eyes absorbing you, the last eyes you'll ever see . . .

"Rogerio Graetz? *Verdad?*" this person had said to me, though not even my mother called me Rogerio anymore, and I'd completely forgotten that at Anne Hunt I'd sometimes been called that. (I'm Roger, a name Guatemalans tend to smudge into *Rohyyer.*)

He struck me as frightened looking because, of course, I knew nothing yet of the expressive if limited plasticity of the adult Moya's face, which even in repose is like one you might see jumping out at you amidst the medieval gloom of a Spanish Inquisition painting: the somberly composed face of an intrepid young Moor, long and full lipped, but his eyes staring out as if to pass, in the split second between blinks, a frightful message to a secret coconspirator. But then, suddenly, Moya's big, lustrous eyes go even wider and his mouth hangs open goofily, exposing blunt white teeth (the teeth of a cartoon horse, almost), and his long ascetic's frame seems to just breathlessly dangle there. Though all this usually looks something like *total alarm,* I've since learned that it can mean just about anything: astonishment, ardor, anger, elation coming on, yet another of his seizures of insight or truth.

In that electrified posture Moya stood over me, having spoken my name. Now I was trying to get a grip, to reason through my panic. Enough seconds, only seconds, had passed for me to realize that if anyone was in immediate danger it was probably these people, not me. Then I thought: Jesus, what's Flor gotten mixed up in now? They could only know of me through her, I thought, though she'd said nothing of connections to student revolutionaries. They're in trouble, I thought, and they're going to ask me to get a message to her, and then she's going to be in trouble . . .

"Luis Moya Martínez," he said, extending his hand.

"Cómo no," I said, still gaping, recognizing but not quite grasping, and then it hit me. "Holy shit, I don't believe."

"I know your face," he said, grinning his big-toothed, cheek-crunching grin. "You look like your cousin but different. Yes, I knew it was you"—at Anne Hunt half the classes were conducted in English, and Moya, always a good student, if secretly so, was nearly fluent even then, long before his six-month sojourn to Harvard, though his own accent is so strict he sounds as if it must ache his jaw to speak

29

it—"It is he, my old friend Rogerio," he announced, turning towards his friends. *"Verdad que les dije?"* (Didn't I tell you?)

And now the girl smiled at me, and they all chimed in with the usual *holas* and *mucho gustos,* bobbing their heads. Moya said they'd all just come from their theater group rehearsal. The girl was transformed now, her dimpled face brightening as she pertly lowered her lips to the pink straw standing in the fluted glass filled with her pastel *licuado,* and soon her eyes were flicking happily back and forth between the guys sitting on either side of her, who seemed to be competing to make her laugh and having no trouble getting her to . . .

"I'm amazed you recognized me," I said, when Moya had sat down.

"But you look like your cousin Freddie."

"Sort of."

"But yes! The eyes," and he slashed in brows, Arrau brows, over his own with his finger. "And the nose, still the same."

"Oh well," I said, feeling a little taken aback over how excited and happy he seemed to be at having found me. "Anne Hunt."

His laugh was a deep, uproarious giggle. "Yes, Anne Hunt. She is still living."

Then for a moment neither of us seemed to know what to say. Moya's eyebrows jumped gleefully. I was having trouble connecting the intense little poor boy who had been Moya at Anne Hunt with the hyper, friendly university student who faced me now. And while I had memories of Moya as a schoolboy, none of these seemed like particularly winning reunion anecdotes. We'd actually had a friendship at Anne Hunt, but the truth is it had ended badly, ended in fact the very day we had tried to seal it.

At the *colegio* we'd both been outsiders, Moya simply because he was poor, secretly studious, too inwardly intense for a little boy, a strange bird; his mother, a seamstress, made all his clothes but always made them the same, as if she just didn't quite get that the Colegio Anne Hunt didn't require uniforms because all the other students had the means to dress differently each day. By the time I arrived every June, well into their school year, Moya's annual pair of gray woolen pants and white shirts had always been so overwashed, scrubbed week after week with gritty soap against the sides of his mother's stone sink and hung out to dry, that they'd turned almost the same color and texture, the soft, smolderingly opaque, sun-whitened gray of an overcast high noon in the tropics. Wrapped in this garb, Moya, skinny like a palm sapling trunk, eyes burning, looked like some impoverished Arab holy man's son.

The Guatemalan rich have a style of their own: most Anne Hunt boys were really just tiny versions of the men they would grow into, fanatically fastidious in appearance, shoes always blazingly shined, shirt cuffs rolled crisply back to expose expensive, gold-banded scuba diver's and astronaut's wristwatches, boys pampered into an effeminateness contradicted by their obstinately extroverted, boisterous, violent-gestured personalities. Nothing could harm them outside the magic ring of their tight-knit family clans, nothing else really existed. Most, if their families owned plantations and established businesses, would never feel a pressure to become particularly good at anything. So that, in this world, even liking sports was looked down on. (I mean the usual team sports, because waterskiing, then hang gliding and motor-cross rallies, polo, anything smacking of a playboy's uncontroversial adventures, were somewhat popular and still are.) But it was seen as somewhat of "Indian" ambition just to want to kick a *fútbol* around . . . I remember my father complaining to his brother, my uncle Herbert, who played football at Harvard, about why he did not especially care for the kinds of people he was introduced to the two times he'd accompanied my mother to Guatemala: "To me, Ted Williams is a hero. Here's a man who could do things no other man on earth could do, a man who thrilled millions with his wonderful, wonderful skills. To him, hitting a baseball was a *science*. But to these Guatenialans he's just a bum! Talk about Ted Williams to them, and they get embarrassed, actually embarrassed for you, Herbert, and they wonder how the hell Mirabel could have married some guy who goes on about this bum."

So there I was at Anne Hunt, a middle-class American kid, Little League and Squirt League hockey despite my beginnings as a tubercular child invalid who'd emerged from a year's quarantine clinging desperately to Flor's spiritedly sallying-forth legs. It was Flor who had finally spent hours in the backyard teaching me to catch a baseball after my father had given up in exasperation over my fear of the ball and meek determination. I knew how to act, eventually, as if I wasn't afraid of a fight; became a Red Sox, Bruins, Harvard football fanatic and thought all of this meant a lot. And I believed glory and a true measure of oncoming maturity lay in the ability to endure all manner of anguish while you patiently tended and molded both sides of your crush on some oblivious girl until finally you got your chance to lure her into the woods or onto a couch at a party in a basement with the lights turned down—not that I'd yet succeeded at any of that—while quite a few of these Colegio Anne Hunt boys, by the time they were thirteen or so, had already visited a bordello or matter-of-factly molested and even impregnated a family maid or said they had.

I was American, wanted to be regarded as nothing other than Gringo American those summers at Anne Hunt. I wanted them to know it was just this weird accident of family fate that caused me to be among them at all. Wanted them to get the idea that, in the tough playgrounds and swamps and factory dumps of Namoset, none of them could have survived two seconds.

Which meant that I was flabbergasted and enraged by all these imperturbable Guatemalan kids who thought themselves frankly superior to me, even racially superior! They were richer, most were even *whiter.* In my face the lightly mestizo features of the Arraus, some of whom are actually green-eyed and blondish *chelitos,* have been made even more pronounced, somehow, by the side of me that is Jewish. This hooking triangle of a Maya nose—my mother's is a much daintier version—that, seen from the front, looks almost flat and bull-nostriled, these slashing brows and eyes that, caught in a camera's flash gleam like black diamonds or like the eyes of a demonic dog's, are regular Arrau features. But my father is actually much darker than my chestnut-haired mother, and from him I inherited this complexion and a slightly wavy mop of thin black hair.

So for a time, at Anne Hunt, I was called *"Indio."*

And: "My grandfather is British," said Vinicio Lange to me at school one day. "That makes me more gringo than you."

Comments like that, endlessly—they knew how to torment me. They knew about Flor too; many of them had gotten a glimpse of her that one summer that she did accompany my mother and me down from Namoset, when she would pick me up from school. "Hey Indio, you flick that *puta muchacha* of yours yet?" some of the older boys would say, though I was still too young that summer to know very much about it. "C'mon, Indio, so what if she's like your sister, since when do *indios* not fuck their sisters? We told you how to do it, just knock on her door some night after she's gone to bed, sniffle and tell her your tummy aches, and once you're in that bed, *cabrón,* don't hesitate, spring your little pigeon right on her!"

Another thing about Guatemalan rich kids—it's considered fair to kick during a fight, kick you in the face, in the balls, with those sharp-toed, hard-heeled Continental loafers and ankle-high zip-up boots they all liked to wear, and any number against one, that's fair too. And when you come up battered and shoe shredded, you want to run to the bathroom, to wash away not just the blood but the sickening scent of their hair creams and colognes.

In the Colegio Anne Hunt library there was a section of paperback novels from the United States and England, and on the other side of the room, two short, segregated shelves designated "Jewish" and "Negro," where you'd find Bellow and Singer, Wright and Baldwin. Maybe, as my mother said when I went home and told her about it, this was all just plain naïveté and Irish ignorance on Anne Hunt's part. After all, there weren't any "Negroes" at the school to insult—Moya was probably the darkest kid there, but they had that and a world of things to insult him about. Still, you didn't expect such meanness in a library. I was no precocious reader—fantasized about reading much more than I actually did so—but I liked libraries: Namoset's red-brick colonial-style one, with its fireplace-furnished reading room and framed N. C. Wyeth paintings and prints on the walls or preserved under the glass tops of the long reading tables, his original illustrations for *Treasure Island, Robinson Crusoe, Sinbad the Sailor,* his World War I recruiting posters and misty, gray etchings of colonials trapping muskrats from canoes in the Concord swamps. And the library of our elementary school, which was brand new the year that fifteen-year-old Flor and I were transferred into it, when I was in the second grade and she'd already been jumped ahead to start the year in the third grade, though within a few months she'd be in the fifth: every student was given a blank ceramic tile to fill in with paint and gluable colored sand, and then two walls of the library were tiled over with these, so that to this day you can go in and see Flor's rendition of a wickedly wrenched cactus in the Chiquimula-Zacapa desert, a blue volcano on the flaming horizon and a cowboy-hatted man, drawn all in black and from behind, gazing out at it, a red machete in his hand.

Anne Hunt's maiden name was Dwyer, she came from Philadelphia, and with her dowdy corona of tightly coiled, rust-colored
hair, chill blue eyes, pallid, perfectly round face, rouge clouding
across her puffy cheeks like artificial food coloring dropped in
milky water, she did resemble my father's version of the Wicked
Witch of the East, Congresswoman Louise Day Hicks, the genteel-
prole hatemonger and segregationist who ran for mayor of Boston and almost won. Her husband, Scobie, was from Philadelphia
too—he owned shares in some of the country's major hotels, in the
city and out at the tourist sights, and I don't know what else, but
in Guatemala he'd become a multimillionaire, a friend of presidents and generals. (Well, all the presidents were generals.) Their
radiantly pretty daughter Jessica was a classmate of my cousin
Catty, and here's a clue to the nature of her upbringing in the home
of that expatriate Minerva, who owned our school and taught
American history in it too: In '79 I sometimes went to watch the
Saturday broadcasts of major league baseball games from the States
in Uncle Jorge's study, and the afternoon that Jessica was there
visiting Catty she dropped in to take a diffident look at what I was
getting so worked up over in there, shouting away at the Guatemalan announcer who howled, *"Ave María Purrrísima"* through an
echo chamber after even insignificant plays, and who switched on
the very same disco song after every out or base-on-balls, as if the
few static seconds it took for a man to trot down to first or back to
the dugout were just unbearable without a chorus of women
vampily blasting, *"You set me on fire fire ooo ooo ooo . . ."* Well, I
discoursed with heartfelt bitterness against this moron for several
minutes, and it did not seem to offend Jessica's nationalism, if she
had any then, since she probably considered herself more Philly
than Guat anyway—in fact she laughed delightedly, while I melted
under her sparkling, near-violet gaze. Then she asked me which
team I was for. It was somebody against the Pirates, the "We Are

35

Family" team led by Willie Stargell that went on to take the series. I said the Pirates. And she widened her eyes at the screen like an astonished southern belle and said blithely, in her lightly accented English, "How can you be for that team? They're all *neegers!*"

Jessica dated the Colegio Anne Hunt's golden boy, stocky, blond, beachboy-faced Arturo Lange, Vinicio's younger brother. They were a very public couple, seemingly chaste, frigidly superior when they were together, invited to every party. But what mysterious nuttiness they must have been brewing in private! Because after their graduation they scandalized the universe by forgoing college abroad—Jessica, who'd graduated number one from her Anne Hunt class, had been accepted to Cambridge in England—to get married and move to Quezaltenango, the highland city, to teach in a Montessori school for poor Indian kids that some bohemian couple from Italy had founded. But it was the worst possible year to suddenly start dabbling in having a social conscience, 1980, and two of the Montessori faculty members were disappeared within days of each other, and it was also the year that Jessica's father was kidnapped—by guerrillas or by profiteers, often off-duty cops posing as guerrillas, you could never be sure—and killed, supposedly after the two-million-dollar ransom had been paid. Scobie Hunt's body was found tied to the hood of a car that had been dumped in Lake Atitlán. Jessica and Arturo's marriage dissolved. Arturo joined the Hare Krishnas, who had a handful of members in Guatemala then, though he is said to be the last still practicing—he owns a Hare Krishna vegetarian restaurant in Panajachel, his head shorn but for a shaving brush of golden hair protruding from the back of his skull. Catty still sees him sometimes, when he comes into the capital to do his banking. Jessica went to Italy to become an Opus Dci numerary, and Catty has heard that she never even leaves the grounds of her convent and sleeps on the floor at night without even sheets or a blanket. All of this, of course, is said to have shaken Anne Hunt badly. But she still has three sons, and loads of money, and, of course, her school.

It really wasn't always unbearable there: a shimmering rain falling, the breeze bouncing the geraniums hung in pots from the eaves of the covered passageway outside the Colegio Anne Hunt classrooms, which were like fancy horse stalls, each room with a wide, paneless window facing a lushly overgrown courtyard. The passageway walls were hung with framed photographs of Anne Hunt girls who had triumphed in beauty contests: several Miss Lions Clubs, Miss Club Montana, a Coffee Queen, one runner-up Miss Guatemala. It was always the rainy season. You smelled soaked earth, bark and leaves, the morning sweetness of engorged blossoms. Moya and I sat in the back together, I with a comic book or sports magazine hidden in my notebook, Moya muttering and sighing in ever quickening impatience over the idiotic proceedings of each class. You didn't have to worry about being called on because whenever you were it was the adamandy macho thing to just shrug, flap your hand in a laconic gesture of dismissal, chuckle maybe, and not say anything. If the homework was to memorize a poem, even Moya would pretend he hadn't, while girl after girl would rise to recite in prettily piping monotones.

Then outside Moya and I would be walking to the bus stop, and suddenly he'd stop and fix me with a significant look, one finger over his lips, and then he'd fling that finger skyward and lower it slowly as the day's poem flowed dramatically from his lips. His voice had a mannish timbre even back then, his poetry recitals propelled by an unnervingly passionate tone of gypsy lament that was only occasionally apt to the words he was speaking:

Quiero, a la sombra de un ala,
contar este cuento en flor:
La niña de Guatemala,
la que se murió de amor . . .

(But when the poem was something like Darío's *"Y dijo la paloma*
¡*Yo soy feliz! . . ."* adolescent girls chanting like kindergartners
about the happy pigeon was apter.) When he was fmished he'd
stiffen, his closed lips twitching a little as the emotion drained. I'd
wait in embarrassed silence to move on. He wasn't the kind of kid
I was used to hanging around with.

Our ephemeral friendship was based on encouraging each
other's dislike of nearly everybody and everything at Anne Hunt,
assuring each other of our own indistinct superiority while con-
ceding none of our failings, and walking to the bus stop together.
Back then the school was in quiet, upscale, mainly residential
Zona 9. (Now it's located atop a walled-in grassy hill near Colonia
Miraflores and the golf course, a glassy, modem complex; widowed
Anne Hunt had her new house built there too, with an indoor pool
and a temperature-controlled greenhouse enclosing an oversized
sponge of highland cloud forest where she grows orchids.) I was
living with my mother and grandparents in Zona 1, the same house
I'm living in now, and Moya lived farther out, at the far end of
Zona 6 in a barrio called La Pedrera for the cement factory there.
And though for lunch and the siesta hours I usually went to my
cousins' house, walking distance from the school, Moya and I always took the bus together after the evening sessions.

But we'd never even invited each other home. And I don't
think I'd ever mentioned him in front of my mother; I stubbornly
wanted her to believe that I had no friends at all at Anne Hunt.
We were both fourteen, and I didn't know it yet, but this would
be my final summer at that school. The next three I'd spend in a

mandatory Namoset public schools' program for underachievers, going on all manner of field trips or being taught to cook vegetarian lasagna in the home ec room of our otherwise deserted high school, anything to distract us and catch us off guard while grad student hippie psychologists snuck around conspiring to trick us into soul-baring conversations about parents, drugs, and why we hadn't tried hard during the school year since "Gee, you're doing a great job with that lasagna, Roger. Don't you find it kind of rewarding?"

That year Moya's father had temporarily retired from the sea, or else he wasn't being hired anymore, I don't know which. He'd taken a job as a waiter in a seafood restaurant and had dragged Moya into part-time work as a dishwasher there. Also, Moya claimed to have found a girlfriend, Maritza, from his barrio, older, a whole year older than him. Suddenly, at fourteen, Moya had brand-new records to drop the needle of his garrulity down on— a more complicated life was erupting all around him, turning him into a hilariously deadpan raver. The kid was all over the place! He was confused, aghast, furious, over his father's return after so many years: that diminutive and wiry sea dog had stormed the tranquillity of Moya's upbringing in a maternally doting seamstress's house like some raging, impulsive giant. Now Moya was spending some twenty-five gruesome hours a week gagging over a sink full of lukewarm soapy water and fish offal, risking hepatitis, he was sure, every time he plunged his hands in, waiting in chronic anguish for his eyeballs to turn yellow. Now he was head over heels for some pretty *patoja* who was driving him up a wall mainly because he hardly ever got to see her: she went to a public school, had her own group of friends, she was a *coqueta,* a flirt—one of those brown and shiny-eyed, notebook-clutching girls in school uniforms, black shoes, and droopy white socks you saw moving in packs with symmetrical steps down La Sexta in the afternoons, crowding into booths at McDonald's to giggle over the boys and their nervously boastful come-ons. He really was in a torment of disbelief over her liking him, and often she acted as if she didn't anyway:

"*Ay no. Pero qué bárbaro! Qué noche de la gran puta, vos . . . !*" raved Moya on our way to the bus stop, his widened eyes aimed straight ahead, his lower lip drooping in monkey-faced stupor over this latest humiliation. It was a Monday, and over the weekend Maritza had invited him to another girl's *quinceañera*. Saturday Moya had washed dishes well into the evening and then, hanging around waiting for his father to show up for his waiter's shift, had descended into a furious foreboding. When he finally left it was past nine, and the manager had fired his truant father. But that wasn't the problem. The problem was that Moya and his father now shared many of the same clothes, and in some ludicrous arrangement of fo'c'sle fairness the old man had dreamt up, the pants were kept in one compartment and the shirts were hung in the other of a single, wooden, stand-up wardrobe, and Moya had been entrusted with the key to the pants, his father with the key to the shirts. When he got home his father was still out, vanished, bingeing somewhere, passed out over a bottle-stacked table in any of the sticky, sewage-fumed little cantinas that in this city are as numerous as crab holes on a jungle beach and that constitute the repository of so many gloomily and furiously sought oblivions. Somewhere out there, in a damp pocket of his drunken father's pants, lay the stolen key to happiness. Moya's shirt was marshy with the stench of sweat and fish, and there wasn't another clean, dry one to be had in the house. For a frantic moment he even considered taking a machete to the locked shirt door . . .

"*Puchiiiis,*" growled, whined Moya, lifting his gaze to the dark, clouded-over sky. "I shouldn't have gone, *vos,* should have faked a flu or I don't know, what an idiot I am, I just didn't think, *vos,* I was in such a rush. I change my pants my socks my underwear and I go to the party, where Maritza is waiting, waiting for me, *vos,* a party in a rented hall, *vos,* everyone dressed in their best and dancing close, *vos,* and my shirt stinks worse than low tide in Champerico, *vos.* Maritza looks at me like I'm the walking dead, *vos,* and says only one *word—cochino!* (pig!). And then, there she goes! Right over to Hipólito Mercado, *vos,* she spends the night dancing with that *cerote,* that little piece of shit, Hipólito, *vos. Pero mierda! Puta! Qué pendejada, vos!"*

My notebook had fallen to the sidewalk, and I was slumped against a wall, laughing. Moya watched me with a befuddled expression for a moment, which made me laugh even harder, and then, suddenly, he grinned.

"You could have phoned me, man," I gasped. "I would have lent you a shirt!"

"We don't have a phone," he shouted gleefully.

"What happened when your father came home?"

"He hasn't yet. Maybe I'll get fired too!"

"Well, that'd be good. Wouldn't it?"

"Yes, starving to death will be a good way to forget that . . . *ayyy no,* Maritza, *vos.* Would you really have lent me a shirt?"

"Claro." Of course.

"Qué amigazo! What a great friend!"

That evening in Zona 9, where there are trees, as opposed to Zona 1, where only the sad little parks have them, the cool, blue-green air was full of the jungle chatter of grackles. Tall pines, cypresses, eucalyptuses, and all kinds of other not as ubiquitous trees rose up from behind the long, high walls wealthier people live behind, and others grew along the streets, their roots buckling the sidewalks and their bowering limbs shedding a constant confetti of pine needles, petals, and leaves. The tops of the walls were strung with barbed wire, inlaid with bristling rows of jaggedly broken bottle and window glass that glimmered with furtive light from the houses inside, or even with moonlight when the sky was clear. Sometimes you'd hear a chain dragged along the top of any flat-roofed garage, and, looking up, see a straining watchdog's glowing eyes through overhanging branches, hear its low, mesmerized growl. Or dogs would erupt into crazed barking and even fling themselves against resounding, sheet-metaled gates as Moya and I hurried past. (Nowadays people are even more security conscious, and sophisticated electronic alarm and surveillance systems have replaced, or complement, watchdogs, who have proven all too vulnerable to intruders armed with silencer-accessoried weapons or even a deftly wielded machete or knife—the late Blacky and Brownie, Uncle Jorge's two machete-decapitated Dobermans, being a case in point, though all those burglars made off with was a big, ancient Maya urn hoisted from the garden.) So it was always a bit unnerving, walking down those walled streets at night, even when "safety"—not that we were specifically scared of anything but the dogs—was just a few blocks farther on: marked against the sky by the beacon-capped spire of La Torre, the imitation Eiffel Tower spanning the busy commercial avenue where the fume-spewing buses ran.

I'd picked up my notebook, and Moya and I were walking along, flush with *amigazo* good feeling. What happened next happened spontaneously; I'd certainly never thought of trying it before. On our way to the bus stop we always passed this one odd house that had nothing more than a rusted, vine-braided chicken-wire fence, about eight feet high, running around it, and, inside, in the yard, lived Guatemala's most demented and overwrought German shepherd. Approaching that property, I'd cringe in anticipation, but the sudden explosion of barking so close by always made me jump out of my skin anyway, and we'd find ourselves speeding up our steps as the dog chased the length of its territory, shadowing us, roaring, crashing its head and forepaws through the tangled tropical shrubbery growing along the inside, making the shabby fence jingle and bend. Moya always said he was sure that dog's brain was being eaten by pig-shit worms.

"Let's seal it, Moya," I said suddenly. "Let's climb the fence, jump down, and climb out as fast as we can and we'll be best friends forever!"

"*Estás loco, vos.*"

"No, Moya. We get in and out so fast the dog doesn't know *who* to hit. He thinks he's seeing double."

The dog was in a state all right. Moya looked slowly from me to the rabid uproar in the greenery as if following and carefully considering the thread of my logic. When he turned back to me, he was wild eyed.

"It's a test," I said. I felt surprised that he seemed to be taking my proposition so seriously, but, seized by the power of my dare and my own onrushing adrenaline, I persisted: "That's how we do it in the States all the time. It'll make us like brothers."

He nodded vigorously and looked at me with such ridiculous emotion that I suddenly felt sad.

"But we have to jump down at the exact same time and then get out as fast as we can," he said.

"Well *I'm* getting out as fast *I* can," I said.

"*Bueno, vos . . .*"

He threw his notebook down. I did the same. And before I knew it we were scrambling up the fence, both of us giggling as the dog raised its demented howl several decibels. I reached the top first, a second or two ahead of Moya, clamped my elbows over it, hoisted myself up for the vault, and stared into the spacious, shadow-blackened yard, first at the old Swiss chalet–style house glowing like a fairy-tale cottage back in the trees and then, directly beneath me, at the German shepherd as it took two, three delicate steps backwards, its blazing eyes and head lifted as it let out a throbbing roar through distinctly bared fangs.

Moya was beside me, blinded by the glory of our friends-forever infantry charge.

"When I count to three!"

The more or less assenting sound that came from my throat was a high-pitched, two-syllable chipmunk's chatter.

"Uno Dos Tres Ya!"

Moya plummeted straight down and landed on his feet amidst cracking branches, stunning the dog into a few seconds' silence. Against the black-green dark, frantically treading his arms through the rain-soaked jungle that came up to his chest, he looked clad in sugary white. I had one leg dangling over the fence, and in that position I'd frozen forever.

The rest of it, all that jumping and thrashing around and the dog howling like it was in a fight to the death, happened quickly. Moya got himself turned around, fell forward, and grabbed the fence, his legs tangled up in the growth and kicking furiously while the dog barked barked barked, dodged forward, stopped, ducked under Moya's feet, and slithered lightning fast into the bush. Moya looked up at me with the expression of a terrified boy overboard. But he'd managed to free one foot and had it drawn under him, and with all his might he hopped against the fence and slid back down, landing right in front of the dog as it recoiled after its own mistimed, snarling lunge, and then Moya jumped again, hitting the fence so hard he jolted me into realizing what I'd done, but this time he stuck to it.

"*Ya!*" he yelled in triumph, hanging on. And he started to climb just as the dog, peeled-back snout fangs flashing, rose up again.

Moya screamed, "*Yaaaa . . .*"

And the dog landed on its side, writhing as if netted by the branches, while Moya pulled himself up in a few swift steps of the hands and rolled over the fence in one motion. He hit the sidewalk laterally, with a bag of cement's thudding slap. Then he lay there with his face in the leaves, one hand clutching the bottom of the fence like it was a blanket he wanted to tug over himself. His white sock was bloodstained and pulled down around his heel, which was missing a shoe.

I climbed down, stood over him. My chest was pounding as if it were me who'd been in a fight to the death. Moya sat up slowly, not looking at me. He drew up his knee and groped around his ankle and heel, finding the bloody patch where the dog had managed just a small tear in his skin—

Then he stood up quickly and as erectly as a proud soldier and glared at me, his chest rising and falling.

"Go get my shoe," he said.

The dog was still barking, attacking the fence and branches as if mad with grief over its missed opportunity for slaughter.

"Forget it," I said, my voice breaking childishly.

And he bent to pick up his notebook with shaking hands, and then, with his foot that still had a shoe, he gave my notebook a vicious kick, sending it fluttering out into the street.

"Gringo de mierda," he said.

He limped away down the dark, walled street, maintaining his erect and rigid dignity despite his one-shoed gait. I waited until he was a faraway figure in glowingly pale clothes fading into the exhaust-clouded light of the avenue where the buses ran, several long blocks away. Then I picked up my notebook and started home again, the dog's ceaseless barking scalding me.

Gringo de mierda—those were the very last words he spoke to me until some eight years later in Pastelería Hemmings, when he came up from behind and said my name. So sure, that incident shamed me, became one of those that, recalled spontaneously and unwillingly over the years, evinces a face-burning shudder of self-recrimination and doubt. I remember when I came home to Namoset that fall and told Flor about it, her face turned nearly as red as mine, she shuddered and squealed in embarrassment for me. But she got a kick out of *gringo de mierda,* and for a couple of weeks went around calling everybody in Namoset that, even the cops, who didn't know what she was saying and thought she was just being flirty and nice.

But that happened in the permissive remoteness of childhood, when our characters are still hopefully somewhat fluid, change-able, or at least improvable. And Moya certainly didn't seem to be holding it against me then and there, that afternoon in Pastelería Hemmings. Was he even remembering it?

I broke what had been a brief, shy silence: "I'm in Guatemala for a month."

"Ah bueno . . ."

"Almost over now."

"Are you taking a vacation?" he asked.

"Yeah, guess so. I'm visiting Flor, she's here now. I have to be back in time for college, you know . . . It's been some day, huh?"

"Some day?"

"The traffic."

"Puta, vos, yes. Some day!" he said, reacting as if I'd just made the most stunning observation. "Well, that's one way to solve the problem of traffic jams, yes? Eliminate the drivers, eliminate the pedestrians," he deadpanned grandly, again.

When I laughed, his smile broadened, and then he gave me one of his significantly shocked, wide-eyed looks and said, *"Ay no, Rogerio, pero qué país, no?* What a country. Guatemala, *puta, vos, mira, vos—"* And that was when he launched into his recitation about Guatemala not existing, him knowing because he's been there.

46

And when it was over I laughed again, quietly and a bit uneasily, and said, "That's pretty good."

"Yes," he said with a nod. "Pretty good!"

Then we talked about Dracula, and how he was studying to be a lawyer, and a little bit about Flor, and a little bit about the situation in Guatemala—which made him suddenly reticent—before I finally said, "Remember that with the dog?"

He slouched in his chair, looked at me meaningfully. "You were not a good friend that day, Rogerio."

For which I apologized, feeling foolish.

"*Gringo de mierda, sí pues,* I remember," he said musingly.

"I felt guilty about it for years," I said, exaggerating somewhat, of course. "I never did anything like that again."

"Still, I would not want you on my side in a combat," he said, jokingly enough.

"Yeah, yeah," I said, forcing a laugh.

"Should we go and try again?"

"You'd trust me?"

"Would you trust me!"

"Hah! We'd both stay on top. Well, that's smarter anyway. So let's not waste our time."

"It is a deal," he said.

And we laughed and talked a bit more and that was that—

I didn't see Moya again until that day, some four years later, outside La Verbena morgue, when he was there as a newspaper reporter.

I saw him for maybe less than a minute that time, because my father and I and U.S. Consul Joseph Simms were leaving, heading for the embassy car, the consul holding up his hands and saying, "No interviews, no interviews please," to all the Guatemalan press gathered there, and the next day they said in the papers that we had violated the human rights of all Guatemalans by refusing to comment publicly on the case—meaning that we'd violated their freedom of press and information. They really did that, hyped it up like it was another big hypocritical *yanqui* fuck you to Guatemala. (*"Dos yanquis más contra Guatemala"* read one newspaper subheading.) But it didn't even occur to me to wonder then about why they were actually doing it, going so overboard, trying to whip up this endless indignation over Flor, the Moral Monster of the Western World.

Moya emerged from the ugly swarm of Guatemalan television, radio, and newspaper reporters outside the morgue, calling my name, gingerly cradling his tape recorder and notebook in one long-fingered hand—I was stunned that he'd dare approach me.

We'd just visited Flor's body, laid out on a concrete slab amidst some other bodies in there. I wasn't crying now. My eyes, like my mouth and throat, felt dry as sand. But my father, who can seem to tower over me though he is only one inch taller, and whose shoulders can seem twice as wide as my own though mine are not especially narrow—rage can make him *seem* gigantic, and his face, big, old, rough, heavy featured, looks angry even when he is serene—my father *was* still crying, his face was drenched, but he was looking around glaring and daring. "Look at this goddamned slime," he went. "What about the other people in there, don't give a fuck about them, do you!" He meant—I was shocked not only to hear him cursing at the Guatemalan press but also that he'd noticed, I mean registered and drawn that conclusion so quickly, about the other two dead young men and the Guatemalan press's disinterest in them. (His old policeman's eye, I think, because in the army he'd served in the military police, so that later when that one American wire service reporter came to interview us in our hotel room he was able to concisely state what he'd seen and asked *her* why nobody cared about those men, just about Flor—and she, just a little older than I, with a gentle gravity and trying to show she was uncontaminated by the same indifference and yet no longer shockable at least outwardly, and there to talk about Flor not torture victims anyway, she said, *Well yes, you know it's like that in there almost every day and the press here, you know, they're not exactly antiestablishment and even if they are, there's all that fear . . .* And I said, *My old friend Moya was one of them,* and she said, *Luis Moya, you know him then?* and I said, *Yeah, he was there,* sort of too angrily and defiantly and she started to say something but just nodded, you could see her thoughts working, a kind of tiredness with the failure of her enterprise—particular or general, I don't know—but she was realizing we had nothing newsworthy to tell her about Flor and she was tired of bothering us, tired of our innocence too perhaps . . .) Stretched out on slabs, skinny but pigeon chested, their open eyes, like Flor's, full of the empty, astounded, fed-up stare of the dead or maybe that stare only belongs to the just murdered dead. Both of them had horribly battered faces but one hadn't been washed off yet, his face was a mask of not yet completely congealed blood, he was still bleeding a little, I think—and his lower lip looked just torn off. And the other had a cleaned-out gunshot wound in his temple and a clean-looking slice where his penis had been. Both of them were speckled with what I now realize must have been cigarette burns. I'd barely glanced, but even in my dizziness, spaciness, the nausea of the heaviest rage . . . I took it in. That carnage a contrast to the clean, nearly pristine, unbearable visage of Flor's nakedness, the slash in her throat cleaned and neatly stitched—so cleanly, precisely, delicately stitched that it smacked of her own fastidiousness, as if she'd sewn up her own mortal wound in defiance of the many forced indecencies of death (I mean, here we were, looking at her). The floor was tiled in pale colors, wet, blood sheened, here and there petaled with blood, and there was a drain in the middle and a hose coiled in the corner. I remember that, looking at it and thinking, A hose for hosing blood. And a blandly delicate Arabic-looking man in a lab coat was there, speaking quietly with Consul Simms. All three of them, Flor and the other two that were dead, had their mouths open a little, and flies flew in and out of them from one mouth to the other, not preferring any mouth to the others, lightly touching down and riding up. (The soul leaves through the mouth? . . . it takes a long time to leave and flies impartially love it, they play in that slow exhalation like dolphins in waves.) Unbearable, I mean everything there, it was Flor except she wasn't there. I looked and looked and looked (just as I look now, with a certain tremulous modesty and willed detachment, refusing that most blatant and final look—and recalling now as I recalled then, like a cold drop of anguished premonition recalled, that famous nineteenth-century explorer's description of a young and beautiful Indian girl's funeral—she'd died of heartbreak and he wrote that in death she had a sweetness of expression, as if forgiving the callous boy who had abandoned her, and you could tell the explorer was falling in love with her face, either as he watched the funeral or as he wrote about it later, and he described the dirt slowly covering up her face as the Indians buried her . . .). The wide arching brows, the wide Asiatic cheeks, the haughty Maya Princess nose, the feral brown skin with its tropical rainwater sheen, plush lips no lipstick long lashes traces of eye makeup wide-open eyes and *no sign of life in death* just as there had never been any sign of death in life in that face so far as I knew . . . She had a sweetness of expression, but such were her features, there was no new proof of innocence in it, she almost always had a sweetness of expression. She told me once about some old boyfriend of hers (which one?), about him laughing because he'd never realized, never thought that an angel could be brown, *My brown angel, qué pasó?*

—and her fingers, so tapered and womanly and brown and somehow always so much more long-lived looking than the rest of her, with a darker hued brown, like melted chocolate, in all the creases—They're *like monkey fingers,* she used to say, *the fingers of a hairless monkey!* but I didn't think so; and her nails, perfect in death, painted a soft pink; and her tawny palms, which always astonished palm readers, professionals as well as amateurs, because one palm was nearly smooth and the other so filled with criss-crossed wrinkles as to be indecipherable, as if clutching there as loosely as a handful of fine sand the layered, lacy palimpsests of all her lived lives: one palm told no story at all and the other held the record of three lives for every century going back to the beginning of time and who could find the future in that muddle?

What can I tell you? That I held Flor's smooth hand while my father held the other, and that we wept and brushed ffies away. And that we were in there with her for about half an hour, while the consul and little coroner politely waited outside. And that the worst feeling ever was the decision to leave.

Outside, Consul Simms, a man of light and athletic movement, Ivy League–seeming though a graduate of the University of Utah, heard my father's outburst and took his arm and said, "Mr. Graetz, the car is this way." Consul Simms seemed really to care for my father, and several times, during the time we all spent together, I had the impression that they would have enjoyed talking to each other under different circumstances.

But my father and I, we'd both stopped moving.

My father has always had mixed feelings about Guatemalans anyway—except for those few he absolutely adored, including Flor of course, and of course there were many sorts of Guatemalans he'd never met. Now his face was wet and furious, his lips sullenly pinched like he wanted to spit. He faced down that stunted, poly-ester mob—stunted, ignorant, venal-looking men, so many of them in the Guatemalan press (or was it just the *hate?*), and their equally sullen, jagged faces glared back, while their mouths emit-ted hysteria-strained voices, their eyes growing wild in their own agitation and rancor over my father's blatant and visceral con-tempt. Jew and mestizos hating each other—the chemistry, at that moment, felt horribly unique; it changed the air, made it unfit to breathe. My father had already made up his mind not to believe a word of what they wrote or said, no matter what Consul Simms and others, later, usually with so much appropriate though un-appeasing delicacy, implied about Flor.

But there was Moya.

"Not now, Luis," said the consul.

And Moya, of course, looked scared.

"Rogerio," he said, stepping right up to me, in a single mo-tion patting my shoulder and dropping his hand down to take mine. "I am so sony."

Now I was trying to counterbalance my father's rage with as dazed a poise as I could bring off. I was conscious of the image we made.

"You're a reporter?" It was all I could manage.

"Yes, but . . ."

"Qué quieres."

"Nothing, Rogerio," he said. "I—"

"She didn't do it," I blurted, because I could still make myself believe that, we hadn't even gotten Consul Simms's lowdown yet. I was looking away, at the dirty, bile yellow wall outside the morgue.

"This is very ugly here," I heard him say. "But that is the way they are here."

"You're here, aren't you?" I shot back, glaring at him now, while other Guatemalan reporters elbowed each other, crowding in, trying to hear what we were saying. One of them was pulling on my sleeve with rapid little tugs and repeating in an absurd dwarf's voice the "information" that the "deceased" had grown up in my house—I jerked my arm away.

Moya didn't say anything. He was looking around at his colleagues as if truly astonished to see them there.

I said, *"Sí pues."*

And I hurried away, falling in step behind Consul Simms and my father, who walked, I remember, with the lopsided, heavy-footed gait of an utterly exhausted and defeated athlete leaving the playing field, his hands loosely fisted at his sides.

"Rogerio," I heard Moya call after me. "I have no part in this."

TWO

The first time I ever saw You: My father must have left early from work for the airport, and it wasn't until much later, on an afternoon the dimming color of gray slush and a new snow falling through it like millions of fuzzy little light bulbs, that he came home with you, Flor. This was in 1963, during the year of my quarantine, I was five. My quarantine room was the living room and I was supposed to stay there, on the sofa mainly, avoiding excitement and drafts.

But I was in the kitchen, waiting. So where was Mrs. Olafson, the elderly Swedish lady who came in the days to baby-sit? Drably unaffectionate Mrs. Olafson. She wasn't a cleaning lady. She only cooked lunch, watched television for hours, looked after me. I remember her gray Swedish meatballs much more distinctly than I do her face. In fact I don't place her in this memory at all, though she must have been there because my parents wouldn't have left me home alone. My mother was at college in Boston.

My lungs were still healing, but I was past the danger point in my illness—it had been months since Mrs. Olafson had had to wear a surgical mask—so maybe I'd begun to wander the house a little. And Mrs. Olafson, knowing she wasn't going to be working for us anymore, probably wasn't even trying to keep me quiet and confined—better to let me wait in the kitchen, daring the coming breezeway draft.

You were coming to be our maid! We were going to have a *muchacha!*

And I'd been indoors, stuck in a living room, for the better part of a year already—nearly a quarter of my life so far! So I very well might have been beside myself waiting there, thrilled and anxious and praying that you would be young and pretty, not old and mean.

And my memories of the *muchachas* who lived in my grandparents' house in Guatemala City must have been bewilderingly and vividly present: bewildering because how could I, at that age, have understood how and why two places could be as different as my grandparents', where nothing was drab, and this little house on Codrioli Road, where I spent much of my time alone, or practically alone, staring out the picture window at a plain little house that mirrored our own, or amusing myself with toys on a sofa? That sofa's coarse evergreen-and-blue weave still colors my consciousness of those days the way the ocean must a sailor's after he's been on it at least a hundred days.

Indian girls, those *muchachas* who worked for my grandparents, with long black hair, gleaming eyes, and quick, fleshy smiles. They plucked chickens in the courtyard; helped me lure my fat pet palomino rabbit out from under the oversized sepulchral furniture; propped me in the seat of a big, grilled window to watch the street for the passing of the urban goat-herds and the donkey-drawn yellow cart of the trashman; rubbed a juicy Lime on my ankle after an insect bite while I sat against a tree, sobs subsiding, on the rich, machete-mowed lawn of our lakefront cottage. I craved, demanded their attentions endlessly. They wore the native skirts and *huipil* blouses of the Indians, thick cloth so colorfully and intricately woven and embroidered, patterned with birds, flowers, *animalitos* . . . corn smelling, smoky, rain-and-mud smelling. They'd stand at the outdoor sinks in the mornings washing their hair with black soap, wringing out the long wet coils with both hands, then brushing luxurious straight black hair with long downward strokes, talking and laughing together in the clucking singsong of an Indian dialect. Even Chayito, old even then, the one maid who was old, had that hair, though gray streaked—when she let it hang loose she looked like a witch-hag in a fairy tale. Her eyes were bothered black slits in a wrinkled leather mask. She had the lumpy bare feet of a troll. Abuelita was almost submissive only to her, and it was only Abuelita whom Chayito treated with the doting, stern attentiveness that was her brand of affection. She did my grandmother's hair every morning and evening and was literate in Spanish and would put on her pink-plastic-frame eyeglasses and read out loud to Abuelita, whose eyesight was already failing, from translated Zane Grey cowboy novels before they went to bed at night. But once, when I must have been bugging her, she threatened to scorch me with her iron, hatefully jabbering at me in an incomprehensible tongue.

From one of those maids, I'd contracted tuberculosis.

I wonder what our Codrioli Road neighbors were thinking of us? Here was this suburban, barely middle-class street of new yards, new trees, new little ranch houses, a neighborhood of almost entirely Irish and Italian working people who had left the ethnic enclaves of Boston behind, many of them so full of the pretension that this meant everything that they started voting Republican, even against the Kennedys. There was not, at that time, a single black family living in Namoset. So it was bad, or rather disconcerting enough that a Jewish man was living on Codrioli Road with a vain Latin Catholic wife much younger than he and who'd left him and then come back three plus years later with a sick little boy (what I had was kept from the neighbors), who often sat for hours like a house cat in a picture window, wanly watching *them.* And now these people were getting a live-in maid? And was she really going to be some jungle-reared Indian in *National Geographic* getup? They knew all about it, as Mirabel Graetz, who still signed her name Mirabel Arrau de Graetz, was not above bragging about how she'd grown up like a queen in her far-off, crummy, Communist-ridden country. As if she already wasn't ridiculously superior-acting enough: the neighborhood's first two-car family, because her mother had bought her the Plymouth so that she could drive in to Boston to finish her college degree at Simmons, which her mother was paying for too—leaving her sick little boy at home so that she could go to college, and for *what?* And refusing even to attend church with them in Namoset, driving off every Sunday in her car to attend mass at the cardinal's cathedral in Boston!

In Namoset, before she learned to drive, my mother had to have felt like a prisoner in the little house that she never learned to like much anyway. In Guatemala City she would have been content to be a housewife, surrounded by servants, absorbed in the city's endless upper-class social whirl of baby showers and baptisms and afternoon teas and evening galas. But for friends in Namoset she had Girlie O'Brien, who lived across the street, and Mary Codrioli, next door. Girlie worked as a police lady at school crossings. Mary Codrioli, married to a laborer-cousin of the Codrioli developer who'd built our neighborhood, did beautician work at home. Once Mary Codrioli asked my mother if my father worshiped a Golden Calf like other Jews. And Girlie saw a television show about Guatemala and told all the neighbors that my mother had grown up bathing naked in dirty rivers.

Waiting at the gray Formica table, I must have heard the car pull up, footsteps on the frozen wooden planks of the breezeway, but all I remember is the door opening and an icy draft swooping in on wings and my father standing in the doorway in a state of great excitement, a shopping bag from Calvert's under each arm. What was I doing in the kitchen? he wanted to know. Just as a small cardboard suitcase appeared in the space between his leg and the doorframe, and was set down on the floor and then pushed from behind into the kitchen. You were dressed in fire engine red—the winter coat my father had just bought at Calvert's, the discount outlet in Namoset Square. "Oh Roger, she was so cold, imagine! They sent her up with just a sweater!" He stepped aside, unveiling you. "C'mon, Flor de Mayo"—he pronounced it "Floor de Mayo" as in "mayonnaise"—"C'mon in and meet your new family."

You didn't wipe your feet at all, but took a few wet steps in your brand-new rubber boots onto the kitchen linoleum and stood staring over my head through the den into the pale, motley light of the living room. I don't think you even looked thirteen. Your hair was black and not quite straight, a soft, viny cascade failling around your slim shoulders, an uneven bang over your startled eyes. Years later my father would recall that it was days before you changed the expression you'd worn from the moment you got off the plane, stepping into a gale of harbor winds and snow, panic ringing inside you like a bell. Your timidity and fright over the strangeness of all that was happening to you went right through me then. I loved you from that instant on, loved you almost as if not for yourself at all but as if you were a girl in a storybook that we both had a part in, a sweet pretty orphan girl who'd come to live with us, a scrawny little thing with a doll's wide-open eyes and pert little nose and a sad little girl's mouth poised on the edge of a bereft pout, your skin brown and suffused with faraway sunshine. It was an ideal and lyrical beginning—the other kind or kinds of love came later but were often hard to distinguish from the first. After all, our lives, mine and yours, needed a shape that we could express. A yearlong quarantine is an eternity at that age, and I must have grasped the ghoulish reality that I'd had something more than just a brush with death, survived, and had been transferred to this strange new place too, where I was spending a year being orphaned from a normal little boy's life. When I'd be able to go outside again, in the spring, it would be alongside you, Flor. Until then I hardly had any idea of where we lived. I didn't even know that Codrioli Road ran through a cozy valley, and that the steep incline behind the O'Briens' house had a cemetery at the top (where my parents had resolved their religious differences by buying a family plot so that none of my father's relatives could ever even entertain the notion that my mother might end up among them one day in the Jewish cemetery in Roxbury . . . this new family plot where Flor, twenty years later . . .). So the world that I still live in begins for me then and there, with you stepping in from the breezeway so that we could be infiltrated into it together.

My father is not even conversational in Spanish: "Tell Floor de Mayo to take her coat off, Rog."

He was all worked up, grinning around like a happy frog puppet. He was already acting as if he'd brought a daughter home, not a maid. My Spanish, at that time, was much better than my English. I often didn't know what my father was saying.

"Take off your coat, but take off your gloves first," I said, in Spanish.

Actually, you were wearing mittens, but I'd have to run to a bilingual dictionary right now to know the Spanish for mittens (I just did: *zolapas*). You looked at me, startled. But you must have felt relieved that I spoke your language. Slowly, watching your own hands as if giving it a great deal of thought, you pulled off your mittens. My father took them from you, laid them on the table. Then he helped you off with your coat. Underneath you were wearing your convent orphanage uniform, the eternal school uniform, indistinguishable in style from those girls wear even now, two decades later: dull blue-and-gray plaid skirt, white blouse, droopy navy blue sweater, white knee socks. It was about two sizes too big for you even then, and for years it was what you would put on after school for comfort and warmth when you had laundry to do in the cold part of the basement, a flannel shirt and sometimes two worn instead of the white blouse.

What terrified you most of all that day was being shown to your bedroom—having to descend into a basement for the first time in your life, and then having to sleep there. A room recently paneled with finished plywood, and narrow, rectangular windows at the top of the walls, partly blocked by snow and wind-trembled shrubbery, the suburban glow of streetlights projecting trembling shadows into the room.

Houses in Guatemala generally don't have basements. It's an earthquake country, so people aren't going to rest an entire house over an abyss. During the rainy season basements would flood. In Guatemala City's General Cemetery even the dead are buried aboveground, the rich in mausoleums and the poor in long, high walls, coffins slid into them like cabinets, decorated with flowers and wreaths, Indian boys running around with rickety wooden ladders they rent for ten *centavos* to mourners who need to reach the top rows.

So that late at night, after we'd all gone to bed, I think I sensed your fear. Or maybe I heard you coming up the stairs into the kitchen. Something made me get up from my bed on the sofa and go to the kitchen. You'd left the refrigerator door open to throw a little light into the room, and you were sitting at the table in your pajamas and your sweater, your eyes glowing like a frightened forest animal's, devouring, as if it were a candy bar, a whole bar of butter.

THREE

How could my father believe it? His own and only, practically raised by him, taught by him, Guatemalan, overachieving, sweetheart, All-American Ivy League girl—a baby seller? He's *never* believed it. He won't hear of it, he just paws the hair with a disgusted swipe. That's how he's been ever since that day in Consul Simms's office at the embassy when the consul gave us his lowdown. Until Moya visited me in New York, and we took the Amtrak together to Boston and went to see my father in Namoset and so on. Small comfort we gave him even then, it being true that Moya's "information" clouded as much as it clarified. Only my own excitement must have seemed really new to him, but even then my decision to return to Guatemala struck him, I think, as belated, as too much too late.

Flor was thirteen when she came to us, though her passport said she was three years older, but I'm not sure my father ever thought anything she learned before that was of any real worth. Or let's say of any practical use to her in America and the path she was setting out on. A hindrance, a set of complexes to overcome, is more how he saw it. Well, he'd had humble beginnings too, and realized he'd let it keep him back. He'd settled for too little. By the time we were old enough to notice, he was edging past middle age, and had come to terms with his disappointments, though there had been years of anguish and bitterness over them before.

But my father knew what he'd helped to make you into, knew he'd taken this poor, pretty waif into his home and heart and treated her like a daughter. His own family was not uncolorful, but it had never produced a base moral criminal, not that he knew of, not even back in Russia! Flor became the daughter of a tough old bird, of a moral as hell Boston Russian immigrant's son Jew (though only a sporadically practicing Jew), and she fulfilled his every dream, every ambition he'd had for her, almost—Though don't ever even imply that Flor was anything like an experiment to him, because although in moments of banal cruelty certain family members have been known to suggest such a thing, they're wrong. Because, how like an experiment? Where's the original hypothesis? the proud scientific vanity? His decision to send her to school, saving her from a suburban maid's life and God knows what after? Hardly atom-smashing, gene-recombining Nobel Prize stuff, that, except maybe in Guat. The Dr. Frankensteinian thing to do, I know my father thought, would have been to *not* put Flor in school. Denying her this, condemning her to suffocation, that was how to produce a monster!

My father can be pretty heavy handed. The pressures that buried me somehow lifted Flor up. When she was seventeen and weeping with rage and frustration over the endless humiliation of being stuck in school with eleven-year-olds, my father would remind her that by the time she reached Radcliffe or Wellesley she would be in her twenties. As soon as she entered college, she'd meet seniors and grad students practically her own age. The exalted normalcy of that beckoned like a fairy-tale paradise. Do everything right in school, Flor! Keep getting jumped ahead a grade! Paradise is coming closer! Heeding my father's exhortations was Flor's only ticket out of the absurdity he'd plunged her into.

One ambition she didn't fulfill though: Flor didn't end up marrying the Cuban and that was good, Antonio Toño Tony the *good for nuthin* who was her boyfriend for years, but my father would have loved to have seen her married to some serious Ivy League kind of guy—once she was through with her understandable paying back the home country and Guatemalan "roots" thing. (Though really why so understandable? Moya has called this the fundamental mystery of the mystery of *You:* "Why if Flor had it made in the States did she ever come back to Guatemala in the first place, *vos?*") Dad never believed that you might actually reverse the whole remarkable direction of your life and choose to stay on in Guatemala forever. He knew you'd come home and resume, embark on your own serious career, marry, and then have children, his "grandchildren." My father *is* getting up there, close to his seventies now, and he'd give anything for grandchildren. And he knew he was probably going to get them from you before me. Well, you were quite a bit older, for one thing.

Remember how he roared with laughter at the dinner table the Sunday afternoon that twenty-two-year-old freshman Flor— a happy New England college girl glow in her brown cheeks and eyes and dressed appropriately, having shed her eccentrically Frenchified late high school styles for what must have seemed the delicious conformity of sweater, jeans, and penny loafers— when Flor at the table recited that little ditty a Harvard boy had taught her?:

"Lesley to bed, Wellesley to wed, and Radcliffe girls to talk to."

It was kind of like my father had been waiting all his adult life for the insider's kick of hearing one of his children say something specifically like that; he beamed at the head of our often pretty dismal (especially when Flor wasn't there) dinner table like a proud patriarch-progenitor of champion scalers of the learning curve. Not since I was getting over TB and rather comically and belatedly learning to speak English had I made him laugh with such simple fatherly joy in a "talented" kid. But I did not feel particularly jealous and was never made to feel that way, because my father did not treat or disregard me in the particular ways that might have forced me to, or else he sometimes did and I'd made myself immune, or in memory have done so, or perhaps have long ago forgiven it. If anyone was jealous of Flor it was my mother, and this hardly crippled her. My own relationship with Flor was too complicated, too riddled by confounding depths, too friendly, yet I have to admit one-sidedly fevered by my perpetual enthrallment, to be set out in some leaky old rowboat of a word like *jealous.*

Wellesley was just the next town over from Namoset, so Flor, if it wasn't too cold, rode back and forth from the campus on her bicycle when she visited. My father, of course, wanted to drive her and the bicycle back, he didn't want her riding home in the dark. But Flor insisted. I can still see her smiling that new college girl smile, contrived and charming, and getting goofy: "Exuberance . . . !" had something to do with it. She was reading William Blake in college and went on about her new philosophy of exuberance, which meant pedaling wildly back to Wellesley through the burnt-leave-smelling dark thinking about how Blake had painted the ghost of a flea—

"Of a flea!" said my father. "How do you like that!"

"See?" she said, turning on her bicycle lamp and giggling, waving her hand in front of the dim glow it sent into the dusk. "Doesn't it look like the ghost of a flea? Though of course Blake's was really this insectoid, gorgeously monstrous, diaphanously blue and gold man. Is *insectoid* a word?"

"Oh Flor, you mean you're at Wellesley and you don't know that?" chortled my father. "It's insectial."

"Insectial!" said Flor. "Where did you get such a good vocabulary, Ira?" she asked him for about the millionth time. But my father even remembers Latin, from when he had to study it at Boston English, his high school.

So there I was, standing in the front yard to say good-bye, my hair falling over my eyes, my fmgertips and army surplus fatigue jacket smelling perpetually if faintly of marijuana, with my D-minus average, my summers of forced attendance in the Namoset school system's special program for underachievers and emotional retards, listening to her and trying to grasp the elusive magic of higher education.

"But I like anthropology best, so far," she was saying now, standing beside her kickstanded bike, one hand rested on the domed lamp. "My professor's young, and kind of shy, he kind of seems to be lecturing down his own shirt collar. But you want to write down everything he says. He tasted human flesh once, in Africa! . . ."

You were good at it, acting eighteen and all of life suddenly opening up to you when really you were twenty-two and had lived quite a bit already and had even devoured your share of human flesh all right, though not, of course, literally.

The trees my father had rather obsessively planted throughout our childhoods had all grown pretty huge and leafy, making our yard stand out like a forested autumnal island in the gloomy Atlantic dusk of meagerly treed and shrubbed Codrioli Road. Our house was painted happy tropical shades of sky blue and yellow, and because my mother had placed scrolled Spanish iron grillwork under the windows and the actual heavy, baroque iron door knocker from her childhood home in Guatemala on our flimsy hollow-core front door, and had similarly decorated the inside with many Spamsh-Guatemalan kitschy flourishes, and of course because my mother and Flor lived there, our house was known to everybody at Namoset High as the Copacabana.

"Well, I better get going . . ." And then, kissing me good-bye, you put your face against mine and your arm around my shoulder, and suddenly I was as moved as if you were going somewhere far away and for a very long time. Flor had abundant, flowing, and fine black hair, as soft against my face as summer's cool, floppy leaves. "Yeah, see you later," I mumbled—it was just the smell of you, in part, I guess, so sudden and provoking in the chill October air that was like an echo chamber for smells. Because embedded in those sisterly yet always vaguely anguishing scents, as familiar to me since childhood as the smell of my own bedroom, of your bedroom in the basement, of our kitchen and garage and everything domestic and private, were more difficult matters, of course, that usually lay safe and undisturbed in the frank aroma of a much loved kin.

We were going to live apart from now on. And of course you felt much readier for that—completely ready, in fact—than I. Set to mount your bicycle and pedal off from the Copacabana, you were pulling out onto a superhighway, that's how it seemed. You were a victorious orphan, running off with your greedily, secretively possessed prize. So why did I feel stolen from? Or left behind with a secret version of the past that would come to seem as if it had never actually happened? Or one where what had never actually happened came to seem as real as what had?

You couldn't have looked lovelier.

"'Bye you guys," said Flor the Wellesley Girl, getting on her bicycle, her nearly black eyes shining with a happy integrity, a gleaming inside joke she'd been speechlessly cooing to herself ever since she became an orphan child, uprooted from the Chiquimula desert—

Dad was chortling. Ho ho ho. "'Bye, *Floorie,* you kid you. Knock 'em dead."

Standing over her seat, giving her hair a toss, she rode away, the yellow safety reflectors on her pedals bobbing up and down, the bicycle lamp projecting a dim, chalky (ghost flea) beam ahead. My father had to feel a bit tender and generous to me then, and he gave me a brief, one-armed squeeze around the shoulders, and said something about what a good job I'd done raking the leaves that morning, and that there was still time to catch the last quarter of a football game on TV. My mother had stayed inside, finishing up cleaning the kitchen, though Flor and I had rinsed the dishes and put them in the dishwasher and washed the pots and pans together.

* * *

"... The embassy never hands out judgments, oh no. Just riddles," and I remembered Flor's soft laugh, the striking, insider's delight she seemed to take in saying it. That was during one of her last visits to New York. She knew what went on in the U.S. embassy in Guatemala, or had an idea about it anyway. Often she had to go there to arrange the papers for adoptions to the States. It even turned out that she'd known Consul Simms—socially, as he put it.

We'd driven there directly from the morgue. We had to make arrangements for flying Flor's body home, and the consul was going to tell us what he knew. The embassy, on Avenida La Reforma in Zona 10, looks more like some sixties-style elementary school in the suburbs, a massive one, with a high steel fence and concrete barricades out front; Consul Simms's office was on the third floor, at the end of a long, cream-colored corridor lined with rooms full of Americans busy, all in their own specialized ways, with Guatemala. No one even glanced up at us as we passed by the open doors, but I couldn't help thinking that Flor was the problem at least some of them were working on that day, her murder and instant notoriety and its possible local consequences at least. It surprised me and made me feel incredibly apprehensive, the rarefied laboratory silence in that corridor, that atmosphere of trained meditations and calculations—made me remember "riddles" and what Flor had meant by that. So that it was as if I suddenly understood, or if I couldn't really understand then suspected or felt, that here in the embassy Flor's case was already being quietly and inexorably dissolved into a larger design that was all about rendering such shocks, any and all shocks, survivable by never forcing them or even allowing them to come to a definitive end—by processing them into "riddles." Right from the start, it felt like a horrible place to have to come to for a revelation about a person you loved.

The consul's office was small, cramped, rectangular, with just one sealed, oblong window full of limpid sky. Consul Simms took off his blazer and hung it on the back of his desk chair, undid his tie, then turned the chair towards us and sat down, his long, summer-flannel-clad legs extended so far into the room that he had to tuck his crossed ankles under the coffee table. My father was sitting in the couch on one side of the table, his rump sunk in soft leather cushions, bringing his knees up too high, his hands clamped over his knees. In this ludicrous posture he had to look up, like a penitent child, at Consul Simms. I was in the stiff-backed armchair. There were magazines in two neat stacks on top of the coffee table, and a glass ashtray with an inlaid ace of diamonds. I didn't ask if anybody minded before lighting a cigarette, though it felt somewhat shabby to do that, like smoking in a doctor's waiting room. But the formaldehyde-carrion stench of the morgue was with me now in a way I hadn't quite noticed before—in my nostrils, on my tongue. And I could feel my heart beating as if it was a labor now to keep the drained, frightened rest of me going.

Consul Simms was about forty, with the face of an adult cherub, handsome but infiltrated by mundane decay beneath his tan-drenched complexion: curly golden hair, blue eyes, pomular cheeks hard and sagging at once. Career foreign service. A consul, charged with, among other things, the often ambiguous business of looking after Americans in one kind of trouble or another. Flor wasn't his first dead American.

"Mr. Graetz, Roger," began Consul Simms. "Often people have the impression, the mistaken impression I'm afraid, that we here in the embassy somehow know everything that goes on in Guatemala, that we have some kind of direct pipeline into the Security Forces, the National Police, and so on. But it just isn't that way . . ."

He proceeded then to invoke the autonomous, sovereign nature of Guatemala's military government and security institutions, and then he recapped the details of Flor's case as presented by the National Police spokesman, as published in the Guatemalan press, though without any echo of their malignant hysteria. It didn't even occur to us to ask him why he thought the press was being that way, because my father and I, of course, thought Flor's death was every bit as significant as they were making it out to be, despite the angle they were taking.

But Consul Simms's voice had a still youthful resonance in it, and his eye contact was earnest and surprisingly baleful at once. After a while he reminded me of one of those moderators or journalists you see on public television sometimes: serious-minded, professional, every word carefully chosen, but not at all indifferent. Their messages always get through, and so did Consul Simms's— something in his subtle shifts of tone and expression more than what he actually said. But these messages of the consul's had a delayed effect, and, because they were usually hard ones, when they did finally kick in it was awful. I'd sit there feeling like I was drowning, while the consul just tacked on. If these were riddles, they weren't the kind I'd braced myself for.

I think he was affecting my father in much the same way. Because when the consul paused in his narration, we sat in stunned silence for a moment, though he'd said nothing we hadn't already heard. And then my father looked up at him from the couch, and said, with a wincing note behind his deliberate pronunciation:

"And is that what *you* think, Consul? That Flor was murdered by these so-called partners of hers."

Consul Simms said, "Mr. Graetz, I can't say with any certainty that I *do* know who was responsible," and then he shifted, briefly, his truthful blue gaze from my father to me. "There *will* be a police investigation, and hopefully some arrests, trials, and we will monitor all of that closely. Though, of course, we don't ordinarily interfere in the Guatemalan judicial process, such as it is."

Then there was a silence. But for me it was an unbearable one, and finally I blurted: "You think she was selling babies."

My father's expression cleared—he looked at me, appalled.

"Well," said Consul Simms calmly, puffing his legs in then, sitting up straight. For a long moment he seemed to be thinking hard.

"You know," he finally said, "Americans working with NGOs in Guatemala are here as private citizens, and—"

"NGOs?" I interrupted.

"Sorry," he said. "Nongovernmental organizations, which Flor's orphanage, loosely defined, is. We don't interfere, which isn't to say we aren't interested in the work they do, or that we don't think it very important. But we don't have many official dealings with them.

"Now it so happens that I was quite aware of Flor's orphanage. And, of course, in every evident way she was running an excellent program, what with the infant malnutrition clinic, the health care abroad project, and even the legal adoptions she was doing. I *knew* Flor, Mr. Graetz, Roger, I think you should know. I, and my wife, knew Flor and liked her very much. I had a lot of respect for the work Flor was doing, I thought it was important work. In fact, less than a year ago we had a problem here concerning an American child, a little girl abandoned here in Guatemala, and I had to place her in an orphanage for a while . . ."

And he'd placed her with Flor, because he'd thought that Flor would treat her just great, and she did. Flor had written to me about that girl, Belinda Towne was her name, and her father, some incredibly irresponsible hippie drifter type, had abandoned her up in Panajachel, and then she'd stayed with Flor a couple of months—

"And that little girl was *sold,* I take it?"—just a stupid fucking remark to make, because of course she hadn't sold her, not that *one.* Oh man! But I didn't feel like listening to the consul go on

about how much he'd liked Flor, and how great she'd been with
some little girl.

My father was looking at me now with total dismay, and the
consul was looking at me too. Then, "No," said the consul, a soft
and matter-of-fact, kind of rising, two-syllable *no*. So subtle then,
the tiny shift in the consul's eyes as he decided to absolve me; a very
professional little absolution there. Consul Simms, remember, was
familiar with overwrought family members. And I'm sure he'd
heard even more annoying remarks than mine before: grief—
muddled relatives automatically and bitterly implicating the U.S.
government in their loved one's death—when the poor, romanc-
ing gringo fool had really been killed by some love-struck *puta*'s
jealous pimp-boyfriend, and if that young pimp had an uncle who
was a magistrate and got him off for a supposed lack of evidence,
even though the pimp's own horrified mother had turned him in
and later recanted—as in one case Flor had told me about—well
then, what was the embassy supposed to do about it? Bring all diplomatic relations to a halt?

But there have been other cases too, to tell the truth, where
family members might have had good reason to think that the
embassy had decided against putting the Guatemalans in an embarrassing position. The priest from Oklahoma is one that everybody talks about—soldiers went into his rectory one night and put
a bullet in his head. Nothing was done about that. It occurred soon
after the shift in administrations, and the Republicans had come
in eager to repair relations that had been damaged by all the harp-
ing on human rights and the military aid cutoff, and were trying
to get their whole Central American hard line in place. And it may
have been Consul Simms who'd had to deal with *that* family.

But I did eventually feel that Consul Simms, in his own way,
was being pretty straight with us. It didn't even enter my mind that
the embassy could have a political motive for hiding anything from

us. Flor, after all, had been murdered with a knife, maybe even a common carving knife, gashed just once, if deeply and with improbable effectiveness, across the throat, and everyone said and they still say that that is just not the army's or any other death squad's way of doing it. So you'd have to get pretty elaborate in your paranoia to think they'd change their whole modus operandi just for Flor.

"I'm sorry," said my father, apologizing for that remark of mine. "This is very tough stuff for us, Consul."

"Of course," said Consul Simms.

"It was a stupid thing to say," I said quietly. "I apologize."

"Really, I understand."

"Flor wrote to me about that little girl," I said. "Her name was Belinda, right?"

"Yes, Belinda," said the consul, and he told us that Belinda had finally been placed in a foster home in Texas, and that then her father had turned up in Guatemala again, with a new wife, and had been surprised not to find Behnda being cared for by *somebody* in the Panajachel expatriate community, many of whom had cleared out in the past year, when the war had begun to affect even that town.

"Well, the long and short of it," said the consul, "is that her father went up to Texas too, and they're going to court for custody with the claim that it was really some other foreigner they'd left Beinda with who abandoned her. Flor, as I understood it, was thinking of going up there to testify for the state."

"That's pathetic!" I said, part of me honestly astounded, the other part trying to win points of ambiguous significance with Consul Simms. "I bet they'll win too."

And the consul shrugged slightly, as if in resigned agreement with my indignation.

"Consul, well then," blurted my father, "couldn't there be a motive there, a possible motive?"

"Oh no, I don't think so," he said. "Her testimony might not have been crucial, and I'm not even sure they even knew she might go up. I really don't see it, Mr. Graetz."

My father waved his hand in disgust. "You reach for straws," he said.

"Excuse me," I said. "But the way we got into this, about Belinda, is that we were talking about . . ." I couldn't even say it now.

"About Flor," said Consul Simms, with a nod. "I'm going to tell you the little that I do know. But I want you to know, also, that no hard evidence regarding her . . . alleged involvements ever reached us here. But I'm not sure what that evidence, to be actually incriminating, would have to be even if it *did* exist. Apart from a directly involved witness, like that girl the police arrested at the house, the one who did supposedly mention Flor. This so-called illegal adoption business, at least by Guatemalan legal standards, often turns out to be more a matter of ethically disturbing activities, say, than an actual violation of the laws here, because those laws just *aren't* very clear.

"But I do have to tell you, Mr. Graetz, that we *had* received inquiries, and in some cases allegations, about Flor, from people in Guatemala and sometimes from prospective adopting parents and even adoption agencies abroad. Usually it was just, you know, to adopt a child legally Flor, in the name of Los Quetzalitos, of course charged a fee. Not more than fifteen thousand dollars, I think, and sometimes even less, which supposedly included legal costs and other things. So some people just wanted to know where, exactly, their money was going. Supposedly it was going back into the general operations of the orphanage. That's what we'd tell them, that the orphanage was registered at the embassy and entitled to arrange adoptions to the States and that if Flor said that about the fee, then that was all we knew about it. Now, I don't know what kind of accounting Flor kept. I guess that's something the police will be looking into. Though none of this, the fee, though somewhat high, was exceptional here, or in itself illegal; there's nothing on the Guatemalan books that says a person isn't allowed to profit from a legally processed adoption. But naturally some of the people who pay those fees just want to be sure everything is aboveboard. Probably they've heard things about the adoption racket here and elsewhere in Central America, about people just pocketing the fees or, much more troubling of course, about stolen infants and others who've been bought cheaply, infants who are not actually orphans being illegally processed for adoption with the complicity of the courts and lawyers here.

"And often people, particularly here in Guatemala," he went on, "just like to talk. Rumors here carry substantial weight; they are like another kind of media that everyone finds themselves plugged into. So a number of the allegations we received about Flor struck me as just that kind of talk. Certain people here feeling offended or even shamed by illegal adoptions and Guatemalan involvement in that business, and wanting to implicate Flor if only because she was a U.S. citizen. And some even feeling a resentful envy towards her just because she was a Guatemalan who'd gotten away and really come up in life.

"But, Mr. Graetz, the persistence of these rumors was troubling enough that we did discuss looking into it, before finally deciding that it wasn't our jurisdiction . . . And, I don't know, I guess I wish now that we hadn't made that decision."

Then Consul Simms sighed, and ran his hand back through his hair. He wanted us to see that he did not feel at all indifferently about what had happened to Flor, and I believed that he didn't.

"What were these rumors?" I asked.

74

"Well, I never put much stock in them, and I don't think you should either."

My father said, "I'd rather hear them from you than elsewhere, Consul."

That issued in a pretty extraordinary litany. one it obviously pained the consul to deliver: telling us how not only Guatemalans but Americans too were rumored to have been going up into the war-torn highlands to buy hungry and endangered infants from families in dire conditions; and that others were said to have been paying juvenile delinquents to snatch healthy, lighter-skinned, and thus much more valuable babies from their mothers' arms on the streets of Guatemala City.

"I'm afraid to say there actually has been a rash of that kind of thing here," said the consul. "Those children are being sold to *somebody.* So you can see how someone like Flor might have been vulnerable to certain kinds of rumors?

"My God," he went on, "there's even been one going around, not only about Flor but about *anyone* doing adoptions to the States, that children are actually being sold to hospitals there so that their organs can be used in medical transplants. The one rumor we *never* heard, though, was that she was involved with a clandestine house. Though there are said to be not a few of those places."

As inwardly foul as the last cigarette had made me feel, I lit another. My father was staring down at his lap, one of his hands slowly fisting and unfisting on his knee. Consul Simms watched him for a moment, and then, with a change in his voice that was almost electrifying compared with the wary monotone he'd just been using, he spoke up again:

"Despite everything else, whether Flor was doing anything wrong or not, none of this should distract from the fact that her death was a crime. That's *primary.*"

"She was murdered by people much worse than her," I answered, unpremeditatively and not really knowing what I meant. "It was a terrible, terrible waste," said the consul, dropping his voice into a tone more intimate and grave. "She was a very remarkable person in lots of ways, I know that."

"She was," I said.

"And if you'll forgive me for thinking out loud like this," said the consul, "but I've served in Guatemala for some time now, and maybe, Mr. Graetz, Roger, some of what I have to say can be helpful to you."

He went on: Guatemala, three decades of war, the overall effects of that, a pretty lawless place where all sorts of ordinarily questionable acts might seem justified by practical necessity—

"And someone like Flor," he said, "working with victims all the time, might be especially vulnerable in just this way. Because let's face it, orphans, abandoned and displaced children, war refugees, never mind just plain poor children, don't ordinarily have much of a future here. Many people overseas want children. But the paperwork, even in an otherwise legal adoption, can move very, very slowly, so there must be quite a bit of corruption in that process by now, to expedite it, get it moving faster. And so you can get into all kinds of gray areas, as far as motivations and justifications are concerned. Flor was an orphan herself, and she certainly benefited from getting out of Guatemala; it's not hard to see why she might have wanted to do the same for others, no matter what that took . . . Well, I'm not a psychologist or ethical philosopher or anything like that.

"But my wife and I, we did admire Flor. We saw her on social occasions. For so long, we just didn't believe a thing of what we sometimes heard—I'm not saying that we do now. But no matter what else, Mr. Graetz, Roger, Flor accomplished good things here. Kids, dozens, hundreds, owe their lives to her. People brought her children all the time, some of them really at death's door, the severely malnourished ones, and she always took them right in no matter how hopeless their condition. That had to be tough. And even the ones who survived, so many of them have lived through horrors. But maybe that's where Flor was especially effective, with kids like that. I remember the day that Sue, my wife, came back from visiting Flor at Los Quetzalitos, where she'd gotten the whole tour. What Sue said was that Flor was just a natural empathizer. If you spoke to some of the others who work with children in this country, they'd still say Flor was pretty exemplary—creative, imaginative. The way she got really ill children treated abroad for free for example. That was unprecedented here."

"It *was*," said my father, tears brimming in his eyes now. "She was very excited when she began that program, I remember that, Consul."

And then we all fell silent again. The consul's speech had been too much for me to take in all at once, in all its seeming implications, though just trying to follow it had, for a while, detached me from my own devastation, had made me listen almost as if to the interesting case history of someone I didn't know. But now that the consul was done, the final fact of her death had flooded back, that horrendously heavy flood. I did feel convinced that something had gone terribly wrong with Flor, that she was "guilty" of something—but that conviction felt as far away, as irrelevant yet as unavoidable as the clear tropical sky in the office window, the same color, almost, as Consul Simms's watery eyes.

Suddenly my father, with something fierce and final in his voice, blasted us from our ruminations: "Well I am surprised, I'm damned surprised, Consul!"

". . . I'm sure you are, Mr. Graetz," said Consul Simms, quickly recovering his professional tone, but betraying, I thought, just a bit of weariness now.

"*She's not like that,*" said my father—speaking of you then as his *daughter,* though he never actually adopted you, as his very own and only, thoroughly known only to *him,* daughter. "This is a girl, Consul Simms"—A girl! You were thirty-three!—"who always had her head on straight. Who *knew* right from wrong, a very moral, thoughtful, wonderful girl. Educated at one of the very best colleges. She started out in this life with everything going against her and she made it into the *elite,* but, oh, modest as can be, so down to earth. I never saw her treat anybody badly, not gratuitously, ever! Never saw an ounce of cruelty in her. Everyone who came in contact with her, her teachers, her professors, knew this about her."

I knew her differently, of course, than a professor or even a parent could know her, but there still was some bit of truth in what my father was saying.

"So I'm sure you did like and admire Flor, Consul, and I would have been very surprised to hear that you did not. But I have to—no disrespect intended, believe me—I have to wonder if you really did know her well, to be able to imply even the *possibility* of such things about her."

"Well, I didn't know her all that well, Mr. Graetz," said the consul. "I didn't mean to give that impression, or that I absolutely *do* know what happened. Of course I don't."

But there was no stopping my father now, and he went on in the terrible cadences of a blue-collar Boston rabbi wronged by heaven.

"You have been very straightforward with us, Consul. I appreciate that. You have made my son and me feel your concern. I feel reassured to know that there are young men of your qualities in our diplomatic corps, I honestly do. And as I go along weighing the evidence in this case, I will consider, strongly and openly, what you've said to us here today, and I know that you will be a happy man when this is finally all cleared up. Because, rumors or motivations or whatever, I just cannot believe a word of it."

My poor father—there wasn't going to be any contradictory evidence to weigh, all we were going to do was talk to a few more people whose testimonies were going to be no more comforting, and then go home.

"I, and I think many people here, would be very moved, Mr. Graetz, if Flor were to be completely exonerated," said Consul Simms. "And I appreciate your kind words. They're important to me."

"Call it a gut hunch if you want," said my father. "But I did some police work myself once, long ago, back when I was in the service. And two of my brothers have been district attorneys in Boston, and one is now a judge. And I will tell you this, no one who knows about police work will disregard a gut hunch just like that, no matter what the evidence to the contrary looks like. In a courtroom you learn that the truth does ring true."

And my father pronounced these last words almost in the tone of blessing and benediction. And I could see, as he sat back in the couch now, one arm hoisted up over the armrest, that it really was as if he'd established her innocence to himself and felt relieved to have done so. He was getting ready to fight that good fight on Flor's behalf—the fight he wasn't even going to get a chance at.

"Now," said Consul Simms, "we've received a number of inquiries from Guatemala City funeral homes, addressed to you. You're not planning a funeral here, are you? Or any kind of service? I, frankly, wouldn't recommend it, Mr. Graetz, circumstances being what they are."

"No," said my father. "We will take her home with us, Consul."

"I see, then—"

"But we'd like to set something up so that donations can be sent in her memory to . . . well, to the orphanage. Maybe you can advise me. How could I let that be known down here?"

"Through the newspapers, Mr. Graetz, for one . . . Did she belong to any one church in Guatemala, do you know?"

"No I, ah, don't. Roger, do you?"

"I guess you'd have to call her a lapsed Catholic," I said. "Even though she used to go to church sometimes, but that was mainly to take her orphans there."

"There *is* an organization here called Republicans Abroad," said the consul. "They put out a newsletter that's widely distributed among the American community here. That would be a place to mention it."

"No . . . a Republican paper, did you say? No, something attached to the Republican party like that, no offense intended, Consul, but it just wouldn't be appropriate. She had strong—Flor would not have wanted that."

"Well, it isn't . . . Republicans Abroad does fund it, Mr. Graetz, but it really is just a community newsletter, not much more than that," said Consul Simms, maintaining an unruffled demeanor. "It isn't ideological, really. It's given out for free in American-owned restaurants, places like that. If you have a car to sell or . . . It's useful for what you have in mind, Mr. Graetz, that's all I mean."

"To be truthful . . . ," said my father, looking a bit confused now. "—We'll talk it over, my son and I . . . Maybe we should look at a copy."

"Isn't there a Democrats Abroad?" I asked, in as normal a tone as I could manage.

"No," said Consul Simms, and for the briefest moment, I thought, he wanted to smile. "No, there really isn't anything like that in Guatemala."

* * *

Oh well, let's not forget Democrat too, a word that means something, probably quite a bit too much nowadays, to people like my father, raised in the working-class, immigrant wards of Boston. Flor became the daughter of a Depression-era, FDR-era immigrant's son who always votes Kennedy "because with a Kennedy at least you always know what you're getting, *just look at their voting records!*" There's such a thing as Men of Harvard too and my father is one, though he never actually got to go there. Flor and I were raised in the shadows of such idealizations—Harvard, the Kennedys even (not to mention the Empire of my mother's Nostalgia, a whole other fairy tale), in the saturating fairy-tale shadows of this tangible yet hard to espouse sense of . . . the thirties and forties, of the Depression and the War . . . of what good character and good education and good politics meant, or were supposed to have meant, to my father, his brothers, and their circle of lifelong pals—none more devout later on than my father when it came to taking his son and Straight-A Guatemalan "daughter" to Harvard Stadium on Saturdays and on weekend pedagogical trips all over the Northeast to watch the Harvard football team. And those trips did influence his children's lives, perhaps even more so than they would have had he actually gone to Harvard.

My father always had it a little tougher than his brothers and friends, and I guess they all thought of him as the one who'd had the least luck. Because Harvard really had wanted him once. He was invited to a spring banquet honoring Boston's top schoolboy athletes and encouraged to apply. But, for one thing, there was always the problem of his own father, who'd fled the czar way back when in order to realize the American Dream of becoming head of the Dorchester Jewish Socialist Bakers' Union, working as a baker a hundred hours a week and dreaming of a return to Soviet Russia—now there's a dream within a dream—and who just didn't understand things like Harvard and sports. The family was always moving from one ramshackle dwelling to the next, but my father and his brothers always found a place where they could hide their athletic gear before coming indoors. Apparently my father's father was so fanatically thrifty that, no matter what the family's actual financial situation at the time, all the guy needed was to hear of a cheaper apartment, even—it is now probably exaggeratedly claimed—just a couple of dimes a month cheaper, and he'd move his wife and six kids and his barrels of souring pickles and green tomatoes and so on into that cheaper place in about two seconds flat. It was as if he conceived the American saying of a penny saved being a penny earned as being as indisputable as a czarist decree.

"Your father's father's idea of upward mobility was to keep moving down down downward," my mother used to say, fed up with a decade of still living on Codrioli Road. "Now does that make any sense? No wonder we are not going anywhere. Your father feels just fine having stopped the slide." But he hardly ever felt just fine. Money worries could make my father pace the house late at night like a wounded, groaning bear.

With the Depression at its peak, when my father could have gone to Harvard, he had five younger siblings to support. And though he did manage to squeeze in a staggered education at Boston University between his employments—"where once," Flor, here, might have felt compelled to add, "Ira walked onto a track meet that Harvard runners were in too, and he won the 440 race *going away* in his street clothes!" And he was damned lucky to have found that traveling salesman's job. The company provided him with a car, and he sold key-making machines throughout the Northeast, and was even based out of New York City for a while, where he lived in a rooming house at the edge of Times Square. I don't know what my father was actually planning, or thought was actually happening to him during those years. He acts as if he has

82

forgotten them—there is only the implicit and terrible lesson of an unfulfilled, thwarted youth. But who's to say that he wasn't blind to that then, that he wasn't having a swell enough time? I think he might have been a bit more reckless and, in his own way, stylishly self-regarding during those years than he ever wanted me, or Flor, to believe.

Because when the War came my father, nearly thirty, enlisted in the army, and served as an M.P. detective with the rank of lieutenant. Only he didn't get to go to Europe like his youngest brother, Herbert, who was in the Normandy Invasion and fought his way to Paris in the Shrub Wars, but was stationed at a base in the Deep South, where he lived the most adventurous, heroic, and bizarre episode of his life, one that seems all the more mysterious for the fact that he really went looking for it. It's no surprise that he doesn't like to talk about that much either. But the rest of his family and old pals certainly do. In fact, I can only recall hearing him tell this story from beginning to end once, the day of Aunt Beth's funeral almost ten years ago, when his cousin Maxie coaxed it out of him:

The story of Dad hunting the perverted Cracker Colonel through the bayou, and facing him off at gunpoint in a redneck bar. Colonel Culgin had fought heroically in the South Pacific, but when he came home it was with a twelve-year-old Oriental girl that he kept as some kind of sex slave in a cabin hidden somewhere. Other officers at the base would speculatively talk about it because Colonel Culgin, drunk, had himself once, but no one had any idea where the cabin was, or any proof that it actually existed. Everyone did know that the colonel, an unmarried man, left the base nightly in his private car and then was not seen at any of the drinking spots around there. And my father began to investigate this. He didn't try to hide it, he let it be known that he was investigating, asking questions around the base and even confronting the colonel himself more than one time. But the colonel was arrogant and just laughed in his face, and my father began to feel that he was having the first of his detective's gut hunches. For one thing, he thought the guy just smelled like a pervert, that is, he gave off a smell that was both sweet and sour: "like cabbage soup," said my father, "mixed with baby powder or something like that."

Gut hunch or no, my father must have been possessed of some angry, righteous, or glory-seeking high spirits back then to have pursued this case the way he did. Because he began getting threats— from Colonel Culgin's friends, anonymous threats, threats from the base's secret chapter of the Ku Klux Klan. His investigation of the colonel and then its aftermath aroused a good deal of anti-Semitic indignation, it seems. Many of my father's friends at the base advised him that it was probably a good idea to just lay off. But these threats, by their nature and vitriol, had convinced him of the colonel's probable guilt. He could have just let the colonel, who might have become psychologically imbalanced by the horrors of a war my father hadn't himself experienced, alone with his one little POW. Instead he decided that Colonel Culgin represented the enemy at home.

He finally tracked him to a roadside bar in a remote town, which he guessed must be the same town that the cabin was in. And he went into the bar and found the colonel drinking with some locals. And he told the colonel—And here, the one time I heard my father tell it, saw him act it out, he did seem to travel back in time, becoming someone I'd never seen before: his whole face seemed to tighten and pale with a street fighter's methodical rage, he cocked his head and sneered his upper lip and, his Boston accent suddenly thicker than Tip O'Neill's (and it is always pretty thick), he barked, he rhythmically barked, "Colonel, you know what I'm here for. So why don't you just step outside with me right now and tell me about it, because I'm going to find out anyway." This Hollywood stuff, my father! And Colonel Culgin said (and here my father did not even attempt to imitate a southern accent),

"Listen, Yid, you no good Yid. You must know you ain't gonna live through this. I could blow your Yid head off right here and who'd ever know or say."

And then some of the rednecks had their pistols out, but my father had his out just as fast, had it pointed at the colonel's heart, and just like that he backed out of the bar and got in his car and drove away. But not too far away, taking advantage of the time he had left as an unknown in that town to ask around. A steamy, unlit, swampy, venomous southern town of the sort I have never been to and am not sorry to have missed. It was at a closed general store with a gasoline pump out front that he found a young Negro man who would tell. The Negro had a terrible stutter, he was almost unintelligible, but he mapped out the way to the cabin by drawing with his finger on the grime-coated gas pump.

A couple of days later my father went back to that town, parked his car in a place it might not be noticed, and found the cabin in the swamp. The blinds were down over the windows and there was a common padlock over the front door. My father knocked, called "Hello? Hello?" and the ensuing silence filled him with a certainty even stronger than a hunch. He hid outside in the trees, enduring the bugs and rationing out the three cigarettes he had left over several hours. Colonel Culgin arrived at the cabin on foot, carrying a little bag of groceries. When the colonel put his key in the padlock and turned it, my father drew his pistol and crept up behind him. The colonel spun around, froze. My father disarmed him and then pushed the door open with his foot. Inside he saw the Oriental girl sitting on a stool at a table by a small shaded lamp. She was wearing a yellow dress and was looking at rather than reading—since the subsequent trial revealed that she spoke only a few words of English—a Babar the Elephant book.

It caused an ugly uproar. Local newspapers and many soldiers at the base were outraged by this northern Jew who was not even a war veteran who was trying to ruin the career and reputation of a lonely Southern War Hero just for illegally keeping a "war orphan" at home—in a cabin that wasn't actually his home, out in the bayou. There was a court-martial. The Oriental girl wouldn't speak, then finally did. And then she recanted and ceased to speak. The army had to provide my father with anned protection. Though the trial was inconclusive, Colonel Culgin was found guilty of violating immigration laws, and discharged. The girl was taken in by nuns in New Orleans. And my father was transferred to what amounted to a security guard's job at an armaments plant in Delaware.

I suppose this tells a thing or two about my father (the man who was sitting there listening to Consul Simms suggesting that his murdered "daughter" might have been selling babies). It's one thing to say that he's a moral man, but plenty of people would be outraged by a war hero colonel enslaving a little foreign girl. But not many people ever get the chance to find out if they are willing to go to such extremes to expose and condemn another man's evil and betrayal of the standards by which the American community is proud to live. (I don't say that with much irony—many Guatemalan military officers have done much worse to little orphan girls, but this seems to outrage no one who matters down here.) I believe that, after that one time, my father had had enough of it. I think he hated being temporarily in the spotlight like that, the witness and target of so much human ugliness. Which isn't just to say that he lacked the temperament, finally, to be something like a prominent Nazi hunter. But he had wanted to be an M.P. detective, and he'd wanted to be a lawyer too, like his brothers—but district attorneys have to do that all the time, stand up in public and accuse others of heinous crimes.

After all that he was tired, I think. And he settled into his happy decade of Boston bachelorhood, living a bit over his head.

He sold insurance in a small firm that his friend Eddie Rosenberg had started, but he dined at Locke-Ober's. Became a Massachusetts Class B squash champion, defeating a future governor of the state in the finals. Bridge at the Cavendish Club, dancing at the Copley Plaza, vacations in Havana. He took his nephews and friends' children to Harvard football games. He was just past forty when he met my mother—but he was fit, he was a squash champion, he looked kind of like Dean Martin and had the good manners of a professional bachelor. They married a year later, in 1956. She was twenty-four, and Catholic, and came from a wealthy Guatemalan family. She'd gone to a Catholic women's junior college in New Orleans, and then had come to Boston. Her mother wasn't going to let her come home to Guatemala until she was ready to renounce forever the handsome, blond and blue-eyed, and utterly penniless Italian who'd come to Guatemala by boat to seek his fortune and walked into the family store on Sexta Avenida one day and stolen my mother's heart, my mother pale as Snow White with her chestnut-colored hair worn in the style of Rita Hayworth, and big, honey brown, gold-flecked eyes, and the daydreamy pink and opulent lips of a lighthearted *niña indígena*. The Italian eventually married the daughter of an illustriously surnamed German-Guatemalan coffee planter, the same year that my mother fell in love with my father. Then my father moved my then pregnant mother from the small but swankily situated apartment on Commonwealth Avenue near the Public Garden in Boston, where they'd spent the first eighteen months of their marriage, to Codrioli Road in Namoset, which she hated.

It was Uncle Herbert who got to go, before the War, to Harvard, where he became a second-string tailback. Uncle Josh, my father's other younger brother, avoided the War because of flat feet and nearsightedness and went on to Suffolk Law, and was, for a while, an assistant D.A., but then became co-owner of a big hardware store out in Framingham before making a killing with his partner in North Shore real estate. Uncle Herbert eventually became Judge Herbert Graetz of the Massachusetts Appellate Court. He and Aunt Milly never had kids of their own. But Uncle Herbert could get us tickets to any Harvard game, even against Yale, and often sat with us at home games and took us into the alumni tents, and sometimes accompanied us on the road.

So we, for and I, my father, sometimes Uncle Herbert and some of their old neighborhood pals, strolled Ivy League campuses as if on inspirational tours of my and Flor's bright future destinies; we ate corned beef on bulky roll sandwiches on the steps of every Ivy League library—Flor liked to have premonitions, and once on the library steps at Dartmouth she turned to me and announced that one snowy night far in the future I'd ask a girl to marry me "on this very spot" and then a few years later had the exact same premonition all over again on the library steps at Princeton; sat in bone-chilling stadium shadows under blankets, squeezed between broad, overcoat-clad shoulders, while the grown-ups bit into unpeeled oranges and even into onions like apples and passed the whiskey flask, their talk arcing through half a century of Russian Jewish immigrant boys' tales; Flor memorized every Ivy League fight song, dreamt of being in one of those exuberantly irreverent marching bands; we stood feeling small and isolated in the parking lots of highway motels while my father napped, gaping at the late-afternoon sun on the flaming mountains, wandered into the woods to see who could find the reddest leaf, and were terrified by the war movie Nazi specter of a small German immigrant town in upstate New York (Flor saying, "They're Americans now, Americans. Just like me, just like my friend Ingrid," but her German friend Ingrid lived in Namoset and spoke English and Flor

sounded like Dorothy going "Lions and tigers and bears, oh my!").
Harvard at Columbia brought us to New York City, where we
always stayed at the Howard Johnson's Motor Lodge on Eighth
Avenue (it was there that my father had his 2:00 A.M. gallbladder
attack and had to be hospitalized in New York City for more than
a week, but that's another story); Radio City Music Hall, *Mame* on
Broadway, numbingly long drives through old Jewish neighborhoods now mainly populated by blacks and Puerto Ricans in search
of dairy restaurants my father half-remembered and could never
find, and following Flor around in Central Park while she retraced
Holden Caulfield's footsteps: the merry-go-round, the duck pond . . .

No other kids in school got to do this, year after elementary
school year and even into junior high, getting released early from
class on Fridays to go pilgrimaging around after the Harvard football team. We were children, and eager and defenseless before the
lessons my father infiltrated into his great, mystical, culminating
lesson of Harvard. (But imagine how paralyzed I was becoming—
a mediocre third-grade report card and my well-meaning but
hopelessly heavy-handed father telling me I could just about forget about getting into Harvard; well, after that the report cards got
even worse.) Then I was still pretty much "children" when
Straight-A Flor really wasn't, though she could pack that all away
in a second when it came time to hit the road with our old man.
She was fiercely loyal to him, knew just what he wanted. It was
me who tired of those trips, becoming embarrassed, inwardly defeated by them.

In the consul's office we were discussing the nitty-gritty now, the
conversation proceeding pointedly, minimally, through the awful
vacuum of there being nothing pertinent left to say about the living Flor. According to Guatemalan law, we should have had

twenty-four hours to transport the deceased out of the country, but the consul had managed to get this extended for us by a day. Which funeral parlor should prepare her for the flight to Boston, the costs, the U.S. Customs details, et cetera—all this was the worst. But my father and I were taking it now like a couple of— Maybe I shouldn't say this. So OK, please don't construe the slightest disrespect. Maybe we all have our own names for the standards we are taught to live by in childhood, and because these standards are taught to children they all sound embarrassingly silly later on, even if we do still think we at least privately understand, translate, and carry the truth they hold.

Almost twenty years ago, on a bright, sunny Saturday afternoon in Harvard Stadium, the Dartmouth football team routed Harvard 48–0, and I, frenzied beyond belief with humiliation and frustration and cringing already against the taunts I would undoubtedly be facing on the school playground on Monday, stood up and shouted, "Harvard! You stink!" shouted it so loudly that alumni heads turned throughout our section to look at me. Flor gasped my name. And my father slapped me across the face with his heavy gloved hand and said:

"That's not how a Harvard Man acts."

We walked back to our hotel, just a few blocks down the Avenida La Reforma from the embassy. The cool, high-elevation air of Guatemala City felt buoyant, alive, spicy with fresh and coniferous scents. The brightness puzzled my eyes, as if I'd just come out from years in a cave. The Avenida La Reforma is a broad, European-style boulevard (inviting to fast drivers), lined with eucalyptuses, cypresses, long-needled pines, palms, *fuego del bosque* trees with their big, flaring orange blossoms; it has a wide, grassy divide. Along the sidewalks Indian women were selling gladiolus—magenta, vermilion, brightest pale yellow—wrapped in newspapers. We were walking in silence; my father's bent forward stride looked angrily purposeful.

Then, a few blocks down from the embassy—and another block away from the military base farther on that looks just like a Disneyland castle with its bright gray castellated walls, turreted towers, drawbridgelike entrance, and antique cannons positioned outside—we passed through a tree-shaded grove of pedestaled statues like something out of Imperial Rome: huge, black, cast-iron statues of ferociously muscular beasts. Here we had to cross the avenue. My father was about to step blindly out into the traffic, and I grabbed his elbow, said, "Dad." With both hands on his arm, I felt his unsteadiness—he seemed almost to leave his feet, bobbing back onto the grassy curb with the lightness of a tugged balloon. Still, he said nothing. We waited to cross (this is always a difficult avenue to cross and sometimes I wonder how people who can't run manage to ever cross it without waiting hours), and I looked up at the statues: two boars in a back-biting fight to the death; a virile stag; a night-stalking puma; a densely maned allegorical lion with one conquering paw planted over the snout of a baffled crocodile; and, stomping atop its high, wide pedestal in the middle of the intersection, a massive bull. But the bull's member, and it is far from small or discreet, was painted a bright subversive red (it always is—they restore the bull's dick to black, someone comes along and reddens it again, over and over). And I was recalling that a few years back my cousin Freddie (Fernando) had totaled his car against the bull statue one drunken night and that shortly after Uncle Jorge sent him to a technical college in Florida to get him away from the wild *finqueros'* and generals' sons he was running with . . . when I noticed that the smell, the one that had been trailing us around all day, that smell of the morgue like an infection in my nostrils had grown weirdly stronger, much stronger, as if it wasn't merely some understandably lingering olfactory trauma of our own but had suddenly been blown into our faces by a rising wind, only there was no wind, just the smell, all around us, as if it didn't come from us but from the statues or the military base or from a nearby ditch filled with rotting ravens that we couldn't see or from somewhere ... I wanted to gag. I felt scared. (And I've been back to that spot since, and I smelled *nothing*.) My father's eyes met mine dartingly, and we both looked away. He could smell it too. We didn't dare say it.

But it stayed with us. Because when we got back to our two-room suite on the ninth floor of the Cortijo Reforma, my father decided he wanted a scotch and soda and a cigar. Our room came supplied with two-ounce bottles of Johnnie Walker and Chivas, a box of Honduran cigars, and the square little refrigerator was filled with bottles of Gab beer, Pepsis, and *agua mineral*. But we couldn't find the bottle opener. After a while I went to find a chambermaid, and when I came back with her my father was out on the little balcony with his cigar, looking back into the room through the open sliding doors as if there was something he'd wanted to get away from in there. And the chambermaid, a plumpish Indian girl with platinum blond dyed hair, glanced around, her nearly black eyes suddenly bright and round with consternation, she could smell it too. She found the bottle opener chained to the inside of a cabinet and instantly fled the room. And my father and I just looked at each other.

FOUR

Guatemala is small and the world is huge, *not* the other way around, that's what I went around telling myself during the year plus after Flor's murder. I needed to pound my planet back into perspective.

But I never put away the framed picture of Flor in my bedroom, which she'd mailed to me with her next-to-last letter. It was a picture of her, not of Guatemala, even though it was taken down here: Flor, one of her Scandinavian volunteers, and a half-dozen orphan girls—including temporarily orphaned Belinda, the abandoned little Texan—on an outing to the Guatemala City Zoo. Actually they're posed at the zoo's rear entrance, on a dark-dirt boulevard lined with the whitewashed trunks of eucalyptuses and brightly painted food kiosks; in the background are the hangarlike corrals and arena where the ranchers' livestock shows and the occasional rodeo are held, walls emblazoned with the black, gold-eyed rooster head of the Gallo beer logo; a giant Marlboro Man stands up against the sky.

Five of the six orphan girls, including Belinda, are wearing bright red jeans that must have arrived as a single orphanage donation. The sixth girl is wearing a yellow dress and holding her arms out to the photographer as if beckoning a hug. The others look straight at the camera, saying "cheese," or glance back over their shoulders at Flor, their mouths open as if they are laughing or gleefully shouting something. The Scandinavian volunteer, a girl in her twenties, is having a closemouthed giggle over whatever it is Flor has just said.

Because it must have been Flor's joke, hers is that kind of smile. She has one hand perched on her hip and her head turned just so, her hair dangling in a few loose tendrils over the corner of one mischievously gleaming eye and flowing over one shoulder, sweeping under her chin, her hair providing a frame within a frame for a face that couldn't look more remote from trouble, so full of Flor's own wild and particular joy and even innocence. She's on an outing with her orphans, they're going to look at farmers' prize cows and hogs, then into the zoo to sip *aguas* in the shade by the towering nets of the aviaries and a garden full of rain forest and elephant ear fronds, surrounded by monkey and bird chatter and the bass purr of jaguars.

Whenever people see that picture—Well, actually, when my mother saw it, when Flor was still alive, she said Flor hadn't aged a day. *"Ay Florcita,"* and she chuckled with flustered affection. You can follow the arch of her shoulders and slender back, the shape of her fill, changeless breasts in the vertical patterns of the boldly checked red and black shirt she has on, the sleeves rolled up to her elbows, her brown skin so smooth and satiny it shines along the outer curve of her visible forearm.

For a while Flor liked to put a single plaited braid into her hair along the side, though you can't see it in the picture. But if you look closely you can see that the girls—rounded Indian faces and Kewpie doll eyes, straight black hair—and even brunette Belinda have put braids into their hair in imitation of Flor. I think that's my favorite thing about that picture, which I left up on my wall, and took with me to Guatemala later.

Of course I kept her letters and postcards too, the thirteen she mailed to me during her four years in Guatemala. I must have written to her three times as frequently but she was the one living far away and through extraordinary times—running an orphanage in the middle of an all-out orphan-generating war—and was experiencing, I was always sure, significant personal changes because of that. So I imagined that the regularity and friendly mundanity of my letters pleased Flor, and helped her to keep up with herself a bit by reminding her of who she, at least in part, remained.

What I always tried to do was show her that I understood what she must be living through in Guatemala. I knew it bored her to be asked for extended explanations. When we were together I thought I was as intuitively quick with her as she could want, and left it at that. I thought Flor had transformed herself into a kind of heroine in Guatemala, one who was usually beguilingly serene about how this had actually happened to her.

About twice a year she'd find some free time, or rather it would seem to find her, lifting her and her luggage up like a wind and dropping her in New York—these visits were never prearranged or announced, suddenly she would just be there. Then she'd stay a week or less. In the middle of it she'd hop a morning shuttle to Boston, perhaps lunch with some old friend there, spend the evening with my father, and be back in New York in time to go out late that night. Sometimes she would have been in the city a couple of days already before I even knew about it, or could fix the days off from work so that I could spend all the time I wanted with her. Or her telephone would be busy for hours. Many of these calls were orphanage related—in her room I'd see papers out, documents with photocopied orphans' faces and fingerprints, and "home studies" that told in a stack of pages everything that social workers had been able to uncover about a prospective adopting family.

And she had a few old friendships to keep up, from her two plus years of living in New York City, having been hired right out of Wellesley to work in media relations at UNICEF, a job she kept about a year, when she was still planning to go to law school. After that, she'd made a friend on Wall Street—a black gay guy named Cal who'd gone to Columbia, and who she'd met in some nightclub—and for another year she worked with him as a commodities trader, of all things. (There's maybe a sad joke in that, but I don't want to make it.) But then that job suddenly ended, I never really knew why, when she'd already been saying for months that, although she was dissatisfied with it, she figured she'd hang on for another year because law school was going to be so expensive even with the scholarships she counted on getting. I was in college in upstate New York, following this from afar, and staying with her whenever I came to visit in the one-bedroom apartment on West Sixty-sixth she'd sublet from a former UNICEF colleague who'd been transferred to Bangladesh. She took her LSATs, was pleased by her scores, and then never gave a reason for not going on, for not even applying. Suddenly, just after she'd turned twenty-nine, she took off for Guatemala in the spring of '79, her first visit in years, and everyone, including her, I think, believed she'd just be staying there through the summer at most.

We were in her hotel room in the Penta, across the street from Madison Square Garden, sitting on separate beds, passing a joint, MTV on with the sound low, Flor's last visit, October of '82:

"*Oy vay, vos!* They all go around with their shirts and flies open!" She giggled sleepily. Then putting on the eagerly measured-out drawl of some midwestern Peace Corps volunteer with just a month or so of Spanish, said, "*Com-pren-do kay yo kyero de-seer ca-ra-jo?*"

Because I'd asked her if she was going out with any Guatemalan guys.

I laughed, said, "Shirts and flies open, Jesus. *Com-pren-do, nee-ña.*"

"No! They manufacture terrible zippers down there, it's hard to keep them closed, y'know?"

"Underdeveloped zippers. Well, that's an excuse."

"As if they need excuses."

She had a really funny voice. She just did. It had hardly changed at all from the day she'd arrived in Namoset to be our maid, still had the same assertive, almost childishly piping pitch, though supplemented as she grew older by an adjustable breathiness that ranged from a confidingly whispered huskiness coming from somewhere damp between her chest and throat to the hilariously evaporating squeal of her singing along with the radio, trying to hit the high notes. And when she was angry or excited you could just about feel it yourself—feel her trying to blast air into her words, the frayed, thin reed of her voice bleating. Though her accent gave her English a lilting rhythm, counterpointed by occasional echoes of my father's Bostonese and words she consistently mangled in her own particular way ("I gardner what you're trying to say," meaning "garner" of course, but who uses *garner* like that in normal conversation anyway?), her convent and higher-education formality often mixed with the slang and even illiterate vulgarity of the Chiquimula desert and a Namoset adolescence.

Flor, obliviously watching television, lightly ran two fingers down the shiny, thin braid in her hair.

"I don't know, some of them are OK." She sighed. "But they have this tendency, you know, through sheer persistence and this awful, maddening, wholehearted generosity, to trap you into thinking that actually you're rather sweet on them. When really you're not! You're just dazed. Like a boxer! Punched so much you just want to hug and lean on the man doing it so the fight can stop."

"What? You mean rich guys?"

"Uh-huh. I mean some of them try, you know. I'm *so* exotic to them, a *morenita* peasant with too much education, *imaginate?*" Now she stubbed out the joint, lit a cigarette. "Then there are the guys who have something that isn't money to be generous with.

In fact usually they don't have any—money. That's the kind I really used to fall for. Until I realized the ones who seem to want to flatter you most with it are the ones who don't actually have it for real, you know?"

"Have what?"

". . . Ohhhhh. Beards, sad eyes, a master plan. They *are* the master plan." She lightly shrugged it off. I hardly had any idea of what she was talking about, though 1 think I do now.

"Course you can't forget the place is basically the capital of motherfuckers," she said.

"Yeah. I know."

"Not that even they, at times . . ."

"Flor."

She laughed softly. "But to tell you the truth, sometimes it seems like all I do lately is hang out with little kids. And nuns."

"You hang out with nuns?"

". . . Well, not quite."

Then, in a sprightly unfolding of denim-clad legs, she was off the bed and at the window, looking out at New York. Coming from far below, the traffic sounded like an unbroken momentum of wheels tearing through puddles, though in reality the day was dry; the incremental pulsing of car horns evoked traffic lights changing from red to green all the way up a long, hazy avenue as far as the mind's eye could follow. Flor's luggage, a full suitcase open on each bed and the empty one she always brought for shopping on the floor, had the smell I'd associated since childhood with the visits of Guatemalan relatives to Namoset: mothballs and mildew and the cakelike sweetness of unvarnished tropical lumbers from closet storage during the rainy season. Even her sweaters had that smell, along with faint perfumes and smoke (I'd lifted a sleeve to my face): cigarette smoke and the copal incense and woodsy smoke of Indian towns, the tart dirt and damp grime of the highlands. It's just about impossible to find a warm shower or bath in those towns, and so cold she would have slept with the sweater on in whatever dingy, bedbug-ridden cot she'd found herself spending the night in.

I looked over at her, standing at the window with her arms crossed, in tight jeans and an untucked shirt, the air between us painted with tobacco and marijuana fumes.

I knew from previous conversations with Flor that nuns sometimes had something to do with keeping war orphans out of the hands of the army and out of the strategic hamlets—model villages, they're called—that Indian refugees displaced by the counterinsurgency campaigns are herded into. But they are not temporary, these model villages; the people are supposed to live in them from now on, even though they might originally be from different mountain areas, different tribes speaking different dialects, with different customs. It's been one of the army's masterstrokes: shatter and reorganize the hermetic patterns of four hundred years of post-Conquest highland life, bringing it all under military control. Or sometimes they take kids and keep them in their garrisons, dressing the boys in uniforms, little military mascots cleaning the latrines and growing up callous towards prisoners languishing in the tiger pits, screaming their last screams in the interrogation cells, raising the girls as military laundresses and even military whores. Or officers take them back to the capital to keep as their own children, or to sell them to other orphanages and baby-selling rings, a racket that Flor, of course, wasn't supposed to have a thing to do with, though she did do legal adoptions. She'd told me that sometimes there were children whom the nuns wanted her to take, hiding them in their rural convents until Flor got there, driving her orphanage van into the death-scorched mountains. Or sometimes some anonymous Indian woman would just turn up unannounced at

Los Quetzalitos with a kid or two in tow and a greeting from Sister Whoever.

On one of her previous visits to New York Flor had said, ". . . An Ixil Indian girl, the army brought her down from the mountains. What happens sometimes is that until they get assigned to whatever model village they're going to, the nuns in Huehue or Nebaj or wherever get put in charge of the children that get brought down; they feed them, try to treat their illnesses as well as they can, try to make them feel less afraid. And sometimes, well, now and then some of these kids end up with me, it's kind of a mystery why, I mean I'm not the one who chooses. Anyway, I didn't know much about this little girl, she'd just been dropped off at my door one day. So one afternoon I hear her singing, *La bandera que llevamos, qué roja con sangre está*. The flag we carry, how red with blood it is? Well, a guerrilla anthem, obviously. Obviously! So I take her aside and ask, Manuela? Who taught you that? I mean an Ixil girl, she barely spoke Spanish, and so she says, Padre Javier. Padre Javier! When? And she says, Oh, a few months ago. And I thought, Jesus. Padre Javier. He's kind of famous. He's this guerrilla priest who went up into the mountains ages ago but for a year I'd been hearing he was dead, even from the nuns."

"And now this girl's in your orphanage."

"Uh-huh."

"Wow."

"She's eleven," she said. "And there's a family from Stockholm just dying to adopt her. Father's this pretty big-time sculptor, mother's a surgeon. Pretty perfect, you know? But she doesn't have any papers, no paper proof that her parents are actually dead, nothing. So for now, she stays, what can I do? I guess that's OK. I mean, I always feel kind of bad about sending off a girl like that one anyway, one who has definitely seen a lot, is old enough not to forget it, and seems to be pretty well in control of herself besides. I mean,

I'm very aware of the argument that a girl like that should stay, so long as I can make sure she goes on in her studies and everything. But who's to say it isn't the other way around? That's a tough one, you can argue it both ways. You know, she stays, grows up, eventually becomes competent and probably outspoken in some way, and maybe is killed for it, or else leads a life of total frustration and near poverty *anyway*. Or she grows up in another country, gets to have loving parents, goes to university, becomes supercompetent at something, doesn't face the same kind ofprejudice she would as an educated Indian woman here, but maybe she faces other prejudices there or other pressures and she has certain memories that complicate *everything* for her . . . Of course she's bright and old enough to decide for herself, that one, Manuela. Though in her case it isn't going to happen no matter what, not without a paper saying she's really an orphan. Which I can maybe get, if I do the footwork, if I go up to her native village and try to find out or whatever. Which is just what I have to do sometimes. A lot, actually."

"It's like being a detective," I said.

"Yeah. Sometimes it really is."

And that's really the only full conversation we ever had on the subject of War Orphans, Guerrillas, and Nuns.

But back then I was full of certainties. I thought Flor's orphanage must be fill of little girls like that one, forgetting about all the children orphaned by the more mundane calamities of poverty and urban life. The Orphanage of the Revolution. Crazy. But I fantasized it. Nuns rescuing children who were in some kind of danger, because they were the offspring or siblings of guerrillas or union leaders or university students murdered or gone underground, and so they needed protection and a special environment to grow up in where they wouldn't be given away for adoption. And one day, who knew, in a Revolutionary Guatemala, they might even be reunited with their parents and relatives, or, if actually orphaned, then adopted by their parents' old comrades in arms. Well even now, though it actually makes my ears burn a bit to say it, I wonder if some of it might not have been true anyway, believing it more than likely that Flor could have gone along mixing all sorts of brave and generous impulses and calculations in with whatever it was that finally brought her down. Nuns trusted her, I guess, and maybe she never gave them any reason not to.

"Who would have thought," said Flor, "that after all these years I'd end up such a champion of nuns. But they're the only competent people in that country, I swear!"

Minutes later the phone sounded, and when she'd crawled across the bed to answer and knew who it was, she laughed, and her piping voice said, *"Cabrona!"* So that I knew this was obviously a Guatemalan friend, a woman she must know awfully well to use a greeting like that, probably not a nun. *"Aquí estoy con mi hermanito, vos, parrandeando."* She was with her little brother, screwing around, getting stoned on his *mota,* just like old times. He was looking at her bare brown feet curled under her thigh-swelled denim, a smooth, solid anlde, her tawny, potato-hued sole. She listened awhile, said she'd talk to her later, and when she hung up I asked, "A friend here in New York?"

"Calling from Miami," she said, and yawned

And she said later, suddenly, when we'd just been sitting quietly together on the same bed, a suitcase pushed all the way to the end and our feet propped against it, the television still on, the chilled bottle of white wine we'd ordered almost polished off:

"Why is it always like this, Rog? I come back, and all the time I've been in Guatemala, it all suddenly seems like just some movie I saw."

"Whenever you come to New York?"

"Uh-huh."

"Because it's so different here. And you fall back into it so quickly."

She nodded just once, her expression perfectly still. And she kept on staring blankly at the screen, hardly ever having seen MTV before.

"Now I am feeling too depraved," she said. "I think maybe it is time to go buy some toys."

So we went to Macy's, just down the block from her hotel. It felt like a staged adventure just getting there: navigating the crowded sidewalk without a word; riding the escalator up when suddenly Flor turned to me and listlessly remarked that she had no idea what floor toys were on; riding down and drifting around in the cosmetics aisles until we bumbled into the information desk; the elevator kept filling up with people we didn't feel like being crowded in with, so we rode the escalator again.

She was thinking ahead to Christmas in Los Quetzalitos. Of course she annually solicited toys from Guatemala City's more prosperous stores, though not from Uncle Jorge's Zona 1 department store. Flor preferred to avoid that sum zero equation: me Uncle Jorge's nephew, she my "sister," she his *nada*. My other uncle, Dr. Nelson Arrau, the one really open-minded Arrau, has always been something of a solitary outside his consuming medical duties and, since the stroke he'd suffered in 1978, hardly socialized at all. He'd married late in life, to a widow with grown children who is even more closed-minded than Aunt Lisel.

So I think it's fair to say that, on the whole, the Arraus have always found Flor too straining a phenomenon to deal comfortably with. And it wasn't lost on Flor that during her first months in Guatemala they never once invited her to dinner, though she'd politely phoned them a few times, and occasionally ran into Uncle Jorge during his punctual morning coffee breaks in Pastelería

Hemmings, and they kept saying they were going to invite her. But it wasn't until I came down that summer that Uncle Jorge and Aunt Lisel finally did.

In a sentimental way, Flor owed everything to my grandmother, simply because she'd turned up one day at the Hermanas del Espíritu Santo convent orphanage on the Avenida Simeón Cañas and picked an orphan to be our maid in Namoset. At dinner that night Flor was suddenly seized by a desire to pay homage to that fact, saying to my uncle, "If it hadn't been for your mother, Jorge, why, who knows what would have become of me?"

Frozen smiles at the adult ends of the long table, and my girl cousins peering wonderingly at her from heads bent over their soup bowls, and Cousin Freddie with a flat, idling look of goatish rutting in his eyes—What were they supposed to say, that maybe she would have ended up working in the family store? or else gone back to Chiquimula to marry the widowed Chinaman who owned the general store and who used to buy eggs from her and cacklingly give her arm a pinch?—the sort of story that always incited delighted smiles when she'd told it in the States, but which earlier at dinner had only put closemouthed, priggish expressions on Aunt Lisel and Mercedes and caused a green-eyed gape in Catty, seventeen then (entering her last year at the Colegio Anne Hunt) because she'd certainly never heard a "first-person" story about a little egg girl and a predatory Chinaman at the family table before.

Now it was Catty who broke the tongue-tied silence, innocently and matter-of-factly reasoning, "Well, you probably would still be in Guatemala, *verdad?* Like you are now." And everybody laughed, Flor most of all, as the irrefutable logic of Catty's answer sank in.

Flor's accomplishments did not especially impress my relatives, though even they must have realized that, theoretically at least, it had so far been an impressive life. But to find success in the United States was the reason poor people flocked there—they assumed that for many the dream came true, or else why did they keep going? Unless a fantastic amount of money had been made, it wasn't anything they especially admired or were even interested in, especially in a woman. A footloose brown girl-woman with a funny voice, an ex-servant, unmarried, inexplicably hanging around in Guatemala now, who'd so far gotten to live an eccentrically and remotely fortunate life thanks to her extremely coincidental connection to Mirabel Arrau de Graetz's equally eccentric and remote and not so fortunate (they surely thought) existence in a United States becoming so undone now by rampant libertinism that they wouldn't even *think* of sending their own daughters to study there (Mercedes never went anywhere, but the next year Catty would go to college in Canada and look what happened to her even there! She married the first guy who set eyes on her!)— that's all they really saw. The only tangibly remarkable result being that now Flor was dining at the Arrau table and not in the kitchen with the other servants who had to come running in every time Aunt Lisel gave her little gold antique bell a shake. They didn't at all begrudge it. They are friendly people, and appreciated that life sometimes turns out kind of cute that way. They made amusing small talk and tried with some success to keep attitudes they knew could offend Flor, and me, in check. And their familial affection for me was so obviously and spontaneously warm that I had no trouble at all returning it.

Afterwards Flor felt a little depressed by it all. But we went to the Tropical Room, a small discotheque in Zona 4 that still stayed open late and was always crowded despite the escalating violence in the streets during those months, and she forgot all about the dinner in two seconds flat. People danced until dawn there as if they really feared they might *not* make it home alive, and I held Flor's waist in a rowdy conga line that didn't seem to want to ever stop.

Anyway—Guatemala City stores usually donated cartons of cheap little toys manufactured in the Orient. Too many of these came with sharp tin edges, so that Flor couldn't give them out anyway, not with so many orphans who were prone to hitting each other over the head with whatever might be at hand. Or else they donated more expensive and even absolutely marvelous toys that had arrived in port absolutely too damaged to sell. Which she said was fine, because the orphans broke everything anyway and always had too many jealous and smaller orphans swarming all over them to be able to muster the patience and concentration necessary for figuring out the workings of elaborate toys. But Flor always tried to arrange it so that each child received at least one nice, well-suited, brand-new toy for Christmas. And it was always important to have brightly colored, new-looking Fisher-Price crib toys in the infant wards, not just because it created a happy environment and what she called brain aerobics for babies who often arrived already well lost in the fatal fogs of severe malnutrition and who sometimes never made it out, but because it impressed foreign adult visitors and potential aid donators, giving the infant ward a well-cared-for look, dispelling some of the miniature barracks gloom of so many cribs laid end to end, the low-tide odors of unhealthy bowels, the cries and shrill screams, the grim distraction of harried nurses, *niñeras,* and Scandinavian volunteers rushing around on urgent missions of medicine and diaper changing. And of course it was cheaper to buy these toys in New York than in Guatemala, what with the import duties and the additional markups caused by the high bribes merchants usually have to pay just to get their shipments out of customs.

Flor was matching toys to invisible little personalities, her mind and hands busy. It took concentration. We moved up and down the aisles at a steady pace, Flor deftly plucking toys from the shelves and dropping them into either of the two Macy's shopping bags I was carrying—some store detective might have had an astounded secret eye on us, but of course Flor was going to pay. A big rubber spider. The wrapper said that if you pressed the spider's belly it would light up with glow-in-the-dark colors, so she did, and the spider did.

"*You* would have liked this, *mijito,*" she said, smiling at me with her eyes as she dropped it into a bag. I would have? "Remember," she said, her gaze drawing another quick line along the shelves, "when we used to walk to Woolworth's and I'd buy you some little toy like that? Or a bag of penny candy?"

I was five, six, and she'd had no one else other than herself to spend her Guatemala-scale salary on (it became an "allowance" later). The walk to Namoset Square used to seem like such a long and meandering excursion out of reality, though it was a walk an adult could do in twenty minutes: out of Codrioli Road, past the cemetery, and then the march all the way up Nassawan Avenue, through the shade of the town's oldest trees, past many big, white, black-shuttered houses bearing Historical Society plaques, past the private horse farm and the turnoff to the Girl Scout camp on the wooded side of Sarah Hancock Pond, where Flor spent two bewildered weeks during her second summer with us, when my father enrolled her there so that she could have the chance to meet American girls her own age, which of course she couldn't at school; that was where she made friends with Ingrid Klohse, whose family had just moved to Namoset from West Germany, and who was just as ostracized at that camp as Flor.

When we reached the square we'd buy a toy at Woolworth's and then snack at the food counter, or sit with ice-cream cones on a bench on the common in front of the Town Hall, where teenagers parked their motorcycles and souped-up cars while they lounged around in the grass by the drinking fountain or strutted their big stupid mouths, some of them stealing brazen looks at the suddenly timid and unprecedentedly brown girl sitting there in one of the funny dresses my mother used to pick out for her at Calvert's or Filene's Basement, taking little rabbit licks around the edges of her slowly twirled ice-cream cone, which was how an elderly French Espíritu Santo nun had taught her was the ladylike way to do it.

"I remember the first time I ever managed to drink down a whole large Coke at Woolworth's," I said. "Remember? I'd been trying for ages. And when we got home you announced it. And Mom said *that* wasn't the kind of goal and achievement I should be proud of, and Dad said it was a *great* achievement, and they had a big fight about it."

Flor widened her eyes, and with cheerfully mock servility said, "Oh! Doña Mirabel, *disculpe!*"

One question that occasionally occurred to me but never when Flor was actually right there to answer was how did she know, or how and when was it decided, that she could stop calling my mother *"Doña"*? She called my father Ira, always, because he wasn't having any of the *Don* thing right from the start, and eventually she just started calling my mother Mirabel. Though she never addressed my mother in the familiar *tú,* not to mention the even more familiar *vos,* when they spoke in Spanish—a "custom" that evaded my father's egalitarian and monolingual ear.

"Who I'm having lunch with the day after tomorrow in Boston by the way," said Flor. "The agenda, I'll bet anything, is *you,* Rogerio, Rogito, *Roger-oger.* What the heck, it'll be great to see her. We're meeting at that little place on Newbury Street, where else, that those two Hungarian Gaborish crones own."

"Why am I the agenda?"

"Because you're so much *fun* to talk about."

". . . I make more money than Dad used to, you know. Well, maybe not if you figure in cost of living and everything. The same, anyway."

"Yeah, but you're a laborer, practically a servant."

"—A G.I. Joe doll?"

"*Cómo no,* five G.I. Joe dolls. There has been a change in policy." She was dropping boxed G.I. Joes into the bags one by one. "They're just *leetle meeleetary* toys. They can pull off their arms and legs and melt their heads over the stoves, I don't care. No, seriously. It is an armed country, is it not? A society of soldiers and guns. So what's the point of trying to keep it from them after all? I don't know, maybe it'll help."

It had previously been Flor's policy not to have war toys in the orphanage, for the obvious reason that so many of the orphans there had been so severely traumatized that just the sight of military trucks passing in the street could make them break out in tears, wails, hives. And stopped at any ordinary military checkpoint when they were, say, driving in the orphanage van on an outing to the beach, there were always at least a few orphans who'd start shrieking, "Don't kill me! Don't kill me!" and try to hide on the floor between the seats, spreading their panic to the others. Flor, driving, would try to roll her eyes in mock my-kids-are-such-comedians exasperation and smile winningly at the soldiers and hope they'd just let her pass without spending half an hour in the infernal coastal heat fumbling moronically over her passport and papers and a riled-up van's worth of orphans' identification cards. She had to laugh telling that story. But in the next moment, one that I imagined matched the moment when, driving off from the checkpoint, she returned her gaze to the heat-hazed highway, her expression became very quiet and her eyes shimmered over with what seemed a liquid spreading of her black pupils. With a toss of her head and a few blinks it went away.

"Mirabel says that you were born to happiness, that it's your one true gift," said Flor, sitting at one end of the long bar where I worked, leaning towards me with a teasing smile, both her hands wrapped around the scotch on the rocks I'd poured her. She'd flown to Boston that morning and lunched with my mother on Newbury Street, sharing tea and dessert with the two sisters from Hungary who own the place and had become my mother's friendly accomplices in Empire of Beautiful Nostalgia maintenance. And in the evening she'd dined at Durgin-Park with my father and Judge Herbert, who gave them his season tickets to the Celtics for the night. From Boston Garden she'd gone directly to Logan Airport, and it wasn't even midnight when I'd suddenly heard the diffuse murmur of a slow night scattered by her happily pitched "*Cabrón!*" and, looking up from behind the bar, where I'd been washing glasses with my head down, saw her standing there with her hands in the pockets of her leather jacket and her shoulders lifted up, her eyes giddy with amusement—she was really getting some kick out of seeing me at work for the first time. Though I'd been tending bar at the Regina Bar & Grill on Houston Street for more than two years, she'd never come in while I was on before.

"I thought my one true gift was the triple jump," I said.

She laughed and rubbed her eyes. "Well, that too, Roger. But a lot of good it's doing you now."

I smirked and, moving off down the bar to pour some drinks, shuffled my feet in a miniature version of that marginal track and field event, also known as the hop, step, and jump. To my customers it must have looked as if I was just doing a little dance in place. They couldn't have known that the first time I'd ever swung my legs into that motion has to count as one of the two or three pivotal moments of my life, which I might as well tell about now: It happened one early spring day when I was in the tenth grade, at a preseason track meet at the Perkins School for the Blind when the coach of our League Champ team tossed me into the triple jump along with all other kids who weren't supposed to be particularly good at anything. I'd only come out for track to please my father a little bit and to avoid feeling pressured to take an after-school job and to fill in some of the emptiness of not having Flor living at home anymore, since that was the year she was a fresh-man at Wellesley, only to find myself spending afternoons feeling like an anonymous ghost condemned to spend eternity running laps and wind sprints, appalled at the meaningless drudgery of it all.

Of course one of the many adjustments made that day at the Perkins School for the Blind, along with running the sprints down lanes divided by waist-high wires, which both the sightless and the seeing had to keep one hand on as they ran, was that the triple jump was performed from a standing position. Basketball players tend to excel at this event, having long, springy legs that are easily ac-customed to the three synchronized leaps from all those bound-ing, airborne lay-ups, but I was a spas at basketball. So I stood off to the side watching our varsity jumpers warm up, absorbing the footwork, and having no presentiments at all that these would be the last moments of an adolescence so muddled by routine failure that even Flor, visiting on weekends, had fallen into the habit of excessive flattery if I so much as mowed the lawn without being asked twice.

I ended up beating everybody, even the blind, undefeated, number-one seed, who had long, hairless antelope legs and special jumping cleats with thick rubberized soles, and who couldn't be-lieve it. But who could? Coach took me aside, had me execute a triple jump with a running start in the grass. At the end of it I fell flat on my back on the hard ground, but I'd gone far, and was as-tonished at the natural combination of rhythm and power my legs had just shown me. I came back grinning foolishly, and Coach just nodded once in his curt, ant-headed way and said, "Well, Roger, we're a triple jumper." And he spent the next three years feeling vaguely infuriated by my inexplicable talent and utterly lackadaisical training regimens.

I spent the next hour or so in a lonely trance, aware of the alarmed looks of curiosity and acknowledgment I was getting from the team's significant athletes, the looks of dispossessed envy and excruciated wonder from my former comrades in dinky anonymity, while I shivered in my sweats more from excitement than from the cold, watching the garrulous blind shot-putter whose eyes were grotesque webs of skin from a shotgun having exploded in his hands while he was bird hunting with his cousins in Texas years before; the pounding legs of the grunting blind sprinters, their eyes like hard-boiled eggs in the furious strain of their races; an extraordinarily pretty blind girl in neat blazer and plaid skirt, her perfect rich girl's cheeks flushed as she cheered the blind runners on, jumping up and down and clapping her hands with the starter's gun, and then smilingly asking everyone, "Who won? Who won?" with her fists pressed together under her chin and her thrilled breath puffing in the cold air.

The final event that afternoon, with dusk approaching and a light March snow falling, was the tandem distance run, and I hooked arms with the still incredulous blind boy whose undefeated reign I'd ended to run a mile and a half through the winding, wooded drives and grassy glades of that school that resembled an Ivy League campus in every way but for the absence of bicycles. I despised distance running and so did my new blind friend, who was telling me all about the triple jump and world record holders as we panted along on our prize legs, going as haughtily slowly as possible, until only twinned shot-putters lumbering along like fat drunken sailors on shore leave were near us.

"You obviously have a gift, Roger," said the blind boy.

"Thank you," I said. I had the wondrously silly sensation of running along arm in arm with an angel, a lost best friend returned to earth. The wet snow turned his pale, translucent skin a glass-sheened pink. He ran with his eyes wide open, and I could easily imagine a snowflake landing on each eye and not melting, and felt half convinced that it had happened.

It's no exaggeration to say that no one had ever suggested so adamantly that I was "gifted" before, but it couldn't have been more true. The triple jump and nothing else ended up getting me into a decent and tradition-rich and not too academically demanding college in upstate New York that happened to be big on track; and during my high school jumping career provided me with several euphoric moments in the clutch that gave me a taste of heroic predestination completely unsupported by anything else, and certainly helped me to gain the confidence to have a girlfriend for a while; and even just the other day in Pastelería Hemmings filled me with a chilling sense of my own mortality or something like that, because I was reading every inch of an imported *New York Times* as has become my expensive and somewhat homesick habit, when in the obituary of a minor Albany politician I came across the line "in high school he excelled at the pole vault." And I *swear*— well, it was a weird moment, that's all.

But I didn't go out for track in college, and there wasn't a thing anybody could do about it because I was already in, and my grades were suddenly fine, and Abuelita was helping to pay my way. And this has guaranteed me at least the chance of going on to some estimable profession in life, which was why my mother had had that conversation with Flor in the Hungarian café and more like it with me, and why Flor was teasingly and playfully repeating it now.

So I'd moved down the bar, done my little dance, poured out a round of customers' drinks, given change, selected a new tape for the stereo system and plugged it in, poured myself a bourbon, sipped it, stashed it under the counter, and gone back to Flor, where, not missing a beat, I said, "Born to happiness, huh?"—though I'd certainly heard that one before, my famous, happy-go-lucky, just wait around for something good to happen nature. "It's not such a terrible thing!" said Flor. "At least Mirabel has decided that really she should not worry so much about you since, you see, you will end up happy no matter what, Roger."

"Well that's good news."

"Exactly," said Flor. "And so Mirabel thinks that maybe you should own your *own* restaurant. That that's a good profession for a *happy* man."

"Sounds like you two had quite a lunch."

"We four, you mean. Because *Las Hermanas Húngaras* say they would be glad to advise you. Old World Budapestilent goulash secrets? I don't know, Rogerio, sounds *moocho bwayno* to me."

"Can we please stop having this conversation? I mean I can't stand it."

She giggled, sipped her drink.

"How's Dad?"

"He wants me to come back."

"No kidding!"

"Still the same, still gets *peesed* if you talk about anything during the game except the game except he's the one who changes the subject and then, 'Oh *Floor!* You're making me miss the game!'"

". . . So it's playing in Guatemala three days only. Zeffirelli's *La Traviata*. A rare thing, right? Yes, opera, I am thinking, I remember what this is, so I snuck away for the afternoon show at the Cine Lux, one of those great old art deco–ish theaters we have downtown, cavernous, like an ocean liner, and wouldn't you know it? The only ones there are this couple snuggling and one of those glue-sniffing street kids who's probably been sitting there since yesterday. Well this is great, my own private theater just about—there are people who know me just as the lady who is always coming in late for *Planet of the Bad News Muppets* with twenty or so not always well-behaved orphans in tow. So the lights go down, the movie comes on, and there they are, evidently singing opera, you can see their mouths opening and all the gestures, but the sound is so low, it's like when you hear music coming from someone else's Walkman, you know? So I went back to the projection booth to complain and there's the usual *indito* in there with his stocking cap pulled down over his ears, guess what he said?"

"What?" said Cathy Miller breathlessly—Cathy was a waitress I'd been seeing pretty regularly, and now that the kitchen was closed she'd come over to have some drinks and to talk to Flor, whom of course I'd told her plenty about.

"He said, 'But, *seño!* It's subtitled!'"

"Oh my God." Cathy laughed. "It's a sin."

"It's Guatemala. Isn't that Guatemala, Roger?"

"That's the nicer side," I said.

"Yes," said Cathy, primly folding her hands on the bar, her thin, pretty, doe-eyed face suddenly graver. "Roger tells me all about what you do down there. I . . . I just can't imagine it. I admire you so much."

"Well, thanks," said Flor. "It's a living. But I know Roger likes to think I'm Mother Teresa."

"Well not exactly." Cathy laughed.

"Hey, Mother Teresa's salt of the earth," I said—but I felt the instant panic of Cathy's being on the verge of inadvertently exposing something I suddenly felt extremely shy about.

"I don't know a thing about politics," said Cathy, who usually had an attractively fey way about her, working her tables like a balletic sleepwalker, but now she seemed reverted to the too eager pixie of her American heartland upbringing. "I know it shouldn't be, but it's all just so far from my thinking, and I feel so stupid sometimes when Roger tells me things and it's like, What side are we on again? Oh yeah."

"I can tell you one thing," said Flor, pleasantly and matter-of-factly enough, "when it comes to Guatemalan politics you're not missing a thing, believe me."

"I don't know, I just didn't picture you being . . . so cheerful and funny."

"Oh!" said Flor. "Not always."

"I guess it's just that everybody has to find the thing that fulfills them," said Cathy, and, though I sympathized with her, I was really beginning to wish she'd stop. "For me, it's acting. Acting lessons, dance classes, singing lessons, it just fills my days. It's so hard and competitive. There's so much to learn. I guess it's selfish, but I know I'm doing exactly what I want to do."

"I don't think that's selfish," said Flor. "I think that's great."

"Thanks," said Cathy, with a smile of relief. "And I think what you do is great. Takes all kinds, right?"

"Takes all kinds," said Flor. "And there sure as hell are all kinds."

The last words Flor ever said to me in person were "No, Roger, it's OK, you sleep."

And she bent over to give me a warm, familiar kiss on the lips, her hair falling over my face.

And then, "Bye-bye, see you soon. I love you, *patojo*."

The door was open, the only light in the room coming from the hall, where a bellboy was lifting the last of her three heavy suitcases onto his cart.

But our last true conversation had taken place about two hours before, when I woke suddenly and euphorically and found her awake beside me, smiling at me in the dark and in a continuation of my dream. Except we were both fully clothed. I'd dozed off on one of her hotel room beds, but I still don't know (and of course never will) if she'd been lying there with me or if she'd just come over from the other bed.

"You were talking in Spanish," she said, as if surprised I hadn't forgotten how to. "And making such a commotion."

"I dreamed we were making love," I said, just like that, but then I yelped as if I couldn't believe it and buried my face in the pillow. But it had felt like wild, dangerous joy, and as innocent as if we'd just met and just had to do it—my heart was actually pounding.

She laughed is all. And rubbed her hand through my hair— when I was a child I'd make her do that for hours sometimes, and then she'd say, "OK, my turn."

"I really did," I said. "Crazy." But now I wasn't even sure that I actually had. Maybe it had been someone else I was making love with and then while I was still waking up she turned into Flor because I was trying to talk to her, in Spanish.

But then she put her arm around me and hugged me, and lay her head on my shoulder, and I felt her warmth seeping through me, and wondered if she could feel the state I was in, and felt sure that any second she was going to say something like *Well, in dreams nothing is forbidden and that's why I say dreams are just a bunch of* caca. Because I'd heard her say that before.

Instead she said, "Well at least you have those dreams about people you *know,* Roger."

"What?"

"It's better than having them about people you don't know at all, don't you think?"

"Isn't that supposed to be, I don't know, romantic—like maybe you'll recognize them somewhere later?"

"Maybe. But it's less mature."

Mature? "What do you mean, mature?"

"You know what?" she said. "I don't know what I mean. Sometimes I think dreams are really just a bunch of *caca*. In my opinion, anyway."

I suppose there were a million things I was dying to say, a million things I felt, or maybe just one or two of each, but all I could sort out to say for myself was something I instantly regretted for its daytime banality, returning me firmly to myself: "Did you like Cathy?"

"Cathy seems very nice, and I think she likes you a lot."

"She is nice."

"Well, you're still so basically unsure of yourself, Roger," she said. "It must be hard for you to feel confident about what you have to give."

"Thanks," I said.

She laughed quietly again, her head on my shoulder.

"Well what about you?" I asked.

"Me?"

"Who do you dream about, since your dreams are so mature?"

". . . Hah! I am in a big slump. Nowadays I have little orphan girls in my bed. They hold their own *lotería* to see whose turn it will be, and what can I say? If I say no now, I think I will incite a rebellion. So there I am, like a mother wolf with all her puppies. And some of them have very bad dreams, and I wake up in the morning in sheets wet with their *peesh*."

"Oh God, do you really?"

"Sometimes. All my pajamas have that faint ammonia smell now. It just won't wash out."

"Gross," I said.

We were quiet for a while, in the complete dark.

"Haven't you ever been really in love yet?"

"Really really?" She paused. "Of course. Once at least."

"Who?"

"You know who."

"Tony."

"Twice I guess."

"Tony and who else. Not Dr. Ben."

"Well Tony of course. But that was a long time ago."

"So who else?"

"You don't know him."

"You never told me?"

"Never told anyone, hardly."

"In Guatemala?"

"Uh-huh. I never told anyone because he is married and doesn't want to leave his wife. I really thought I wanted him to, but you know what? Maybe I'm relieved that he won't."

"What a jerk. You always fall for jerks, if you want my opinion." Not that it's really my absolute opinion.

"Well, maybe it's my opinion too."

The room was beginning to feel saturated with sleep again, with the dark and the retained warmth of Flor flowing through me too cozily for it to feel adamantly anything. Her alarm clock was set for a quarter to five. In another hour and forty-five minutes I'd be accompanying her to the airport. (Except she left me sleeping and went alone.)

"Well when I really fall in love it'll be with someone like you," I said. "Even if I have to go to Chiquimula and find an orphan and start over." It wasn't the first time I'd ever told her that.

"Hah," she said, her voice sweetly evaporating until she found it again somewhere damp between her chest and throat. "And when I next fall in love, I hope it's with someone who thinks as highly of me as you seem to, and can convince me that they're not just insane or something."

FIVE

My father and I didn't find any of our letters to Flor, or any letters at all, among what remained of her belongings in her second-story bedroom in the main house of Los Quetzalitos. I don't want to make too big a deal out of what isn't at all surprising: all her papers had been confiscated by the police for their investigation, even what private photographs she had. Any photographed face might lead to a suspect, a player in the baby trade. We understood that the police couldn't be expected to immediately distinguish the innocence of my or my father's face from that of a bearded, sad-eyed stranger with his arm around Flor's waist as they posed for an itinerant photographer in front of a painted backdrop of winged cupids at an Indian fiesta in Sololá—if there was, in fact, any such photograph as the one I've just reasonably imagined; I mean, if that's anything like what her "secret lover" looked like.

But the man who wouldn't leave his wife for her wasn't Flor's only lover during her four years in Guatemala. She'd had boyfriends, of course. Moya, I might as well tell now, was one of them, for a little while anyway (and he's *never* worn a beard).

"Did you ever give Flor a picture of yourself? Did she have any pictures of the two of you together?" I asked him on the Amtrak Minuteman train from New York to Boston, that six-hour journey—there was an hour's delay in New Haven—of bar car tale spinning, revelation, evasion, and resolve building, the end result being that here I am where I'd sworn I'd never set foot again, back in Guatemala.

Moya shook his head unsurely and seemed about to elaborate, but I cut him off.

"I'm only asking," I said, "because we didn't find any photographs at all in her room."

"Ah," he said, "*Pues.* She did own a camera. Though she never used it."

"I know," I said. "A Nikon, right? That was missing too." Well, what can you expect from police who don't even earn a hundred bucks a month? Even most of Flor's wardrobe was missing. I hadn't visited Flor during the years she was running Los Quetzalitos, but I know she used to have a jean jacket, a Boston Celtics jacket, a short leather jacket, the full-length leather coat she'd wear up on winter visits, and the striped ermine stole she bought during her overtly boom years of employment in New York. Even her perfumes and facial cremes and makeup, even that plierlike gizmo for curling eyelashes she was so funnily self-conscious about using that, when she did, she'd jump away from her mirror and pop out of the bathroom for just a show-time moment, grinning, holding the gizmo to her lashes and squeezing, just so you wouldn't think she was trying to *fool anyone,* you know. Well, she liked eyelash gizmos or whatever they're called and makeup and perfume and knew how to use them, of course she did! She'd grown up in a nuns' orphanage dusting her face with powder from the inside of the empty rice sacks in the kitchen, rice powder being a much more discreet cosmetic than, say, flour. The kitchen cooks would save her and the other girls the sacks. The nuns may have frowned on such vanities, but they didn't forbid them. Excessive strictness, they knew, was a good way to provoke teenage orphans into fleeing their provenance for the hard, corrupt, but freer life of the streets, a lesson Flor used to say she never forgot and applied even when baby-sitting me and, of course, later at Los Quetzalitos. Discipline and training, the *monjas* insisted on that, but they weren't inquisitorial. Flor had fun there, was the impression I always had.

She even played catcher on a girls' softball team that reached the Guatemala City schoolgirl semifinals.

So where were her cosmetics, her clothes? Imported cosmetics are expensive in Guatemala. Were they being sold in the smugglers' and thieves' black market in the Trébol? Or was there a policeman's wife sweating in an ermine stole and using the gizmo to curl her lashes in a hut made of sheet metal and cardboard in some poor slum barrio?

I had a terrible vision the other day of one of those donkey-drawn yellow trash carts bearing Flor's mattress like a giant blood-sated empress mosquito through the city streets to the vast garbage dump in Zona 13—But then I remembered that the orphanage, which of course has much daily refuse, would have contracted a private trash-collecting company. They use trucks.

The mattress had been taken away by the time my father and I found ourselves in that sunny, incriminatingly austere bedroom. Outside her window, a single star-shaped frond at the end of a willowy branch danced in a light breeze. The children were being kept out of sight, away from the room; we heard only the faintest infant cries and twitterings. One policeman, tiny and sun shrunken like a raisin in his dandruff-flecked blue uniform, sat on Flor's desk chair, on round-the-clock watch. *"Buenaaas,"* he singsonged when my father and I, let in by a politely disappearing nun, came into the room, and that was all. He just sat in that chair, daydreaming I guess, not even watching us.

Her closets were almost empty. The blond hardwood floor, freshly and rigorously mopped, gleamed. Her glossy rosewood desk looked derisively ready for its next occupant, all its scrap-littered drawers open. The walls had already been newly white-washed in seemingly random places so that now only white streaks marked Flor's final grabbings and gropings. Absent from the adjacent bathroom, with its jade-colored octagonal sunken tub banked with a small forest of densely growing ferns, was Flor's usual bathroom clutter. Even most of her likely underthings. The bookcase was full, and some of her music cassettes had been left behind, the ones that she'd taped herself or that others had taped for her, those with distinct handwritings inside the cases: *Merengues para Flor*. And sure, they'd left behind old shirts and pants, sneakers, a pair of mud-caked Palladium desert boots. On the walls, a few Guatemalan primitive paintings, a Caravaggio poster reproduction from the Met, and an autographed publicity still of Ozzie Peterkins, the All Pro NFL nose guard who adopted two little kids from Flor and who, while waiting for the legal paperwork to go through, built the elaborate hardwood jungle gym in the Los Quetzalitos yard. He ordered and paid for the wood and bought the necessary tools and everything and then built it all by himself. It was an incredibly nice gesture. And Flor had been thrilled to be able to tell my father all about it, of course. She'd phoned him right away and even put Ozzie Peterkins on, and Ozzie had promised my father that the next time his team came north to play the Patriots he'd leave free tickets at the gate and get him a locker-room pass and everything, except his team hadn't come to play in Massachusetts since.

"It seemed to me that a lot of her clothes, and of course her jewelry, were missing," I told Moya, on the train, though as far as I could recall what expensive jewelry she had could fit in one small, always very special, box.

"*Claro,*" he concurred, restrainedly enough, I mean, I appreciated his not attempting a verbal cataloging.

"And her safe. Apparently she had a small safe and the police took it. *That,* anyway, was on the list of confiscated things they gave us."

"Of course," said Moya. "Did they say what was in it?"

"Papers."

"My son," said my father—at National Police headquarters on Sexta Avenida, which looks like the Wicked Witch of the East's castle painted Miami Beach pink, with a monument and bust honoring now retired Colonel Chupina out front in a little palm grove—to young, gaunt, partially toothless *Sargento* Sandoval of the DIT (the police detective squad), a donkey-bristle crew cut atop his high, square forehead; Sergeant Sandoval was clearly perplexed by the situation his superiors, who must have decided it would be too impolitic to speak with us themselves, had placed him in. Flor, I was sure he believed, had been a base criminal, but our grief and concern had to be respected, after all we were Americans and all over the newspapers, and you could tell he wanted us to come away with a good impression of *him* at least—"is sure that Flor owned a stereo. But it was not in her room."

And I translated this, as I translated everything that was said during that seemingly pointless interview.

But what did this have to do with *Sargento* Sandoval, a desk officer? Couldn't we see that he was sitting behind his metal desk, a portable typewriter on top of it, in his own bare little office? Sergeant Sandoval can read and write, he stayed in school until he was fourteen, he is a *desk* officer, prestigiously detached from the more lucrative rackets of the streets. He simulated courteous professional thoughtfulness for a while. But his dark, yellowed eyes almost pleadingly beseeched us, Do you know what a cop earns in this country? What do you expect? Don't even think about it, *señores,* you're wasting your thoughts!

And then he folded his hands on his desk and smiled tightly, as if truly and bashfully chagrined over the disillusioning insight he felt professionally obligated to offer us: *"Ayyy, sí pues,"* he drawled. *"No sé, puede ser,* it could be. Many people have been going in and out of there since the event, no? *Las suecas? Se fueron, no?"*

The Swedes? They've left, no? Flor's Scandinavian volunteers. Young women from Sweden and Denmark—true, one had almost immediately flown home, shocked, terrified for her own safety, and the other girl had apparently taken refuge in the house of her boyfriend, a Brazilian working with an international aid organization. And the nurses, the *niñeras,* the kitchen cooks, and teachers had all been given at least a week off by the Los Quetzalitos Board of Directors, because the Sisters of the Holy Spirit had volunteered to move in en masse to tend to, quiet, and counsel the orphans, and would stay there full-time until the ordinarily aloof board of directors had appointed a new head of the orphanage and, assuming they were all cleared by the ongoing police investigation and were wanted back, regrouped the staff. For the board of directors, made up primarily of ladies from some of Guatemala's most distinguished families, some of whom had actually grown up with my mother, were not meddlesome: they sponsored a yearly charity ball and otherwise had given Flor wide sway, having left even the vital matter of overseas fund-raising in her hands.

So maybe it was the Scandinavian volunteers, or the nuns and *niñeras* and cooks, who had made off with all Flor's stuff. Uh-huh. Who were we to deny that human behavior can be disillusioning?

"Debe ser muy grave, muy grave para los niños, pobrecitos," said Sergeant Sandoval, several times, with heartfelt plaintiveness, whenever he found himself confronted with another of our appalled silences.

Which I cynically translated, even the second and third times, word for word and with blatant mimicry of his sentimental intonations. *He says it must be grave, very grave for the children* . . . And Sergeant Sandoval would nod along as if in solemn gratitude for my fidelity.

* * *

Two ladies from the Los Quetzalitos Board of Directors were kind enough to meet with my father and me in the coffee shop of our hotel, their commentary running along the lines of Such a shock. They'd never suspected. Originally, when they'd voted on Flor de Mayo's appointment, she'd seemed such an eager, well-educated young woman, clean, always smiling, one of those devoted to the welfare of the unfortunate among us but not at all resentful. They'd had no way of seeing through to her shortcomings if in fact she'd had any though of course they weren't saying that she had nor could they because that's why there are police, *verdad?* Though her past was most unusual, a girl from the servant class, wasn't that what she originally was? *Increíble, no?* But her credentials had seemed as good as those of her predecessor, a young Canadian woman who'd gone home to marry, and that had been good enough for the board. But then they'd begun to hear but of course had never believed. *Pues,* you know, just the sorts of terrible things idle people are always saying, that's what they'd thought at first anyway. "But in these terrible times, *ay no,* Señor Graetz, with so much subversion, which causes us all so much suffering. The Devil himself must have a perverted fascination with this country, I think sometimes that he can corrupt anybody. Not even a fine education guarantees protection because look at all the subversion we have here at our own university, Señor Graetz . . . ," said Señora Zambrano de Suero. The other woman, Señora Torra-Halbe de Ugarte, was wearing a shimmering, wide-shouldered dress of woven metallic blues and greens; fortyish, her round, silk-smooth, golden face framed by a luxurious mane of Irish setter red hair tied over one shoulder in a thick black velvet bow; her delicate wrists as embellished with bracelets as a harem dancer's and moving like that too, her fingers fluttering, invoking mysteries that had nothing to do with what we'd gathered to discuss; she had large hazel eyes and bright arched lips from which her sugary contralto and superficial inanities warbled like a blithe and senselessly charming seduction. Eventually it affected me that way, I have to admit—as if the exhaustion of so much bewilderment and grief inside me had suddenly left me vulnerable on the outside to the caresses of a gilded beauty and a well-meaning insincerity that seemed incapable of any feeling for death. I couldn't take my eyes off her face, her lips, her hands. Whenever she directly met my gaze, I looked away and my face reddened. Sensual delirium flowed through me, I spooned another dollop of papaya and lime sherbet into my mouth, begging inwardly for the meeting to be over so that my confusion could end. "You're Mirabel Arrau's son, aren't you?" she said to me, moistly smiling. "I am not sure that she will remember, but I met your mother at my older sister's wedding, oh, so long ago. Aida and your mama, they went to school together. That was in, well, I was still a girl, but I thought she was just so *linda,* so *dulce. Toda una dama.* Your father married one of the loveliest young women in all Guatemala." My father had a pretty confused-looking blushing reaction himself.

The three Espíritu Santo nuns my father and I spoke with when we went to Los Quetzalitos, only one of whom had known Flor when she had been a little girl under their charge, had stressed their own point of view that, if Flor had been doing anything illegal, then they were sure it had been under a misguided desire to do good. After all, it costs much money to run Los Quetzalitos and Guatemalans, lamentably, are not charitable—I already knew that from Flor, that even the annual Board of Directors' Charity Ball never raised more than a few hundred dollars. Three nuns in lean-fitting not billowing brown habits, with weighty, ferrous-looking crucifixes hung from thick chain-link necklaces, with bad complexions and slim, almost insipid smiles of formal piety. Flor had never claimed that Espíritu Santo was one of the more activist orders: they taught their girls to read and write, to crochet and work a sewing machine, to cook over a modern stove, taught them all the ritualized constraints of the Roman Catholic Church—Espíritu Santo girls didn't talk out loud in church to God (or gods) whenever they felt like it and so on. They were having a rosary mass in the convent chapel for Flor that night and invited us to attend. But it was later that same day that we went to meet with Ilya in the Swedish embassy, and by the time it was over the mass had already begun and all we wanted to do was go back to our hotel, phone my mother, and rest up a little before dinner at Uncle Jorge's.

Ilya was the Swedish volunteer who'd stayed. Consul Simms had contacted her at our request and arranged for her to talk to us in the Swedish embassy because she'd felt too frightened to meet us in any public place, or even in the U.S. embassy. She was a blond, heavyset girl—not the Scandinavian volunteer in that picture taken at the zoo—with pale, delicate skin and a timid, musical voice. The rims of her eyes and nostrils were bright pink, as if she'd been crying a lot or suffering from allergies, and it accentuated her natural features in a way that made her look something like a big, diaphanous, gold-dusted hen.

Ilya said that Flor, only five months before, had had to go into hiding for three days because the newly appointed *jefe de migración,* Colonel Ignacio Malespín, had demanded a twenty-thousand-dollar bribe in return for an exit visa for a little Indian boy who urgently needed a kidney transplant and was being flown for the operation to Stockholm, where a Swedish couple were ready to adopt him should he survive. We hadn't heard of this event? asked Ilya, with tremulous incredulity. No, we hadn't. *Coronel Malespín*—*"Ese salvaje bruto,"* that stupid savage, said Ilya, her quick strike into stingingly enunciated, slangy Spanish interjecting an oddly show-offy note amidst the otherwise restrained, quietly beseeching manner in which she'd been speaking to us, in perfect English—had said that if Flor didn't pay the bribe not only would he refuse to grant the dying child an exit visa but he would have her arrested for illegally trafficking in children, claiming he had the authority and proof to do so! Flor returned to the orphanage from her meeting with the colonel quite frantic. She told Ilya and the other volunteer all about it and then asked them to carry on without her and to not breathe a word of the whole mess to anyone. And then she went into hiding, Ilya didn't know where. That very night just one policeman arrived at the orphanage on foot and knocked at the gate with a warrant for Flor's arrest.

It was the Swedish embassy that finally resolved it, applying various discreet pressures and enlisting the help of other European embassies to save the child's life, of course, and also to protect Flor's health care abroad program, which the Swedish embassy had co-sponsored at her behest. Flor came out of hiding and said, Thank God that nightmare is over! And then she refused to say another word about it. About a month later Flor flew up to New York on her annual toy shopping for Christmas trip—her last visit—during which she didn't say anything to me about what had just happened!

But what could any of this have to do with a clandestine fattening house somewhere in the city? Well, even if any such place existed, Ilya had no way of knowing about it. Then Ilya turned sideways in her chair and lifted the back of her hand to her eye as if to hide from us what may have been oncoming tears. She was motionless for a moment, poised over her hand almost as if over a violin, and then she dropped her hand and turned to us again and dry-eyed blurted, "Oh Mr. Graetz, I am sorry, I am sorry, I do not know what to say, this country can make people so horrible, I do not know, I am so sorry. I trust no one here and am only remaining to be with my fiancé, Paolo, who is Brazilian and will be working here for Child Hope until the end of the year." But night after night she and Paolo had been wondering this: Colonel Malespín, had he known of an arrangement between Flor and the previous *jefe de migración?* Was that part of his proof? Why did he think he could ask for so much money? Twenty thousand dollars! This seems like blackmail, no? "I tell you the truth," said Ilya. "I have always defended Flor's honesty, though not always her organizational methods. She liked so much to do everything herself and would be so surprised when the clinic ran out of a medicine that for weeks she had been warned about. But when the bothering stopped, we suspected that maybe she had found the money to pay this. The child made it alive to Sweden, but just barely! And Colonel Malespín caused her no more trouble."

"Yes, that," said Consul Simms, when we phoned him right after: "The incident with Malespín, I knew she'd tell you about that. But I'm not so sure that any concrete conclusions or suspicions can really be drawn from it now," and, "No, I don't think it would do much good to speak with Malespín, assuming he agreed to, which I honestly don't think he would. He'll just deny the incident ever took place. He was fishing for a large bribe, no doubt about that. But did Flor finally pay him something? Well, there was a life at stake, after all. Or was the diplomatic pressure enough to back him off? As far as I know, it was. Under the circumstances, going temporarily into hiding like that was probably a very sensible thing for Flor to have done."

It was the previous night, after that excruciating first day of morgue, embassy, and funeral parlor, that I'd had the idea of checking out Lord Byron's, the so-called "gringo bar" in Zona 10. Why is it called Lord Byron's?—nobody seems to know; the long-gone original owner named it that, that's all. The gringo community, that part of it that regularly hangs out at Lord Byron's anyway, is tight knit.

And they are not parsimonious with gossip. Many of them are alcoholics or borderline, the usual expat scene, I guess. I knew, or at least Flor said, that in the last two years she hadn't gone there so much. But even back in '79 she'd spoken disparagingly of the place and the people there and liked to pretend she hardly ever went even though we were stopping in almost nightly, and she seemed pretty well liked by the regulars. I knew they'd be talking about Flor in Lord Byron's, and thought they would have heard everything there was to hear. I thought that I should go and that they'd recognize me right away and that then, if I could show them that I was willing to listen to anything no matter how hard it might seem for me to bear, that they'd tell me.

My father didn't want me going out by myself—Flor and even we had been villainized in the Guatemalan media, it seemed dangerous to risk provoking anyone with my presence. But I said that I'd take a taxi both ways, and that few Guatemalans went to Lord Byron's anyway. The truth is that I was impatient, driven by fury to try anything.

"There'll be U.S. Marines from the embassy guard there, Dad," I said. "And people who liked Flor. Nothing will happen to me there. I couldn't be anywhere safer."

So he went out to dinner with my relatives that night, telling them that I wasn't feeling well and had begged off. And I took a taxi the few blocks from our hotel to La Zona Viva, where Lord Byron's is located in the basement mall beneath a twin-towered condo complex. It's a very unelaborate bar. You walk down the stairs out of the pine-smoky air and into the bar's saturated stench of stale draft beer and wet dog hair. The dog, a mastiff-sized mongrel, is always sitting on the floor just inside the door, its ugly flanks mottled with mange. A dart board, a bumper pool table; the bar refrigerator plastered with bumper stickers (REAGAN-BUSH, U.S.M.C., M.L.N., names and logos of oil and oil exploration companies, et cetera); baseball or football betting pool schemes taped to the walls. It was a slow night, two women, three men at the bar, the tables all empty, when I walked in. No one recognized me, I didn't recognize any of them—I realize now, having recently been back there several times, that the Lord Byron's expats are the least likely to ever even glance at a Guatemalan newspaper or to watch Guaternalan news on television. That night the television over the bar was off, but in the last year they've had it hooked up to the satellite dish that brings American television to the condo towers: usually, these days, it's tuned in to Chicago Cubs games broadcast by the Chicago superstation, or the Armed Forces Radio and Television Network, or to a cable sports channel (once, when I recently happened to be in there, Harry Caray, the famous Chicago sports announcer, even sent greetings to "The Lord Byron's Cubs Fan Club in Guatemala City, Guatemala, all the way down there in Central America!").

The night I went there hoping to learn something about Flor, the woman behind the bar was a tall, large-breasted, but otherwise masculinely lanky mulatta from New Orleans named Crystal Francis (I know now, though I didn't then). She has tangled reddish hair, a honey-colored and freckled face, a wide mouth that is often friendly and extroverted when Wally, her oil company boyfriend, comes back to the city from the jungle, or deflatedly sullen when he doesn't. She owns Lord Byron's now.

Almost as soon as I stepped in I heard Crystal say to the other woman at the bar, ". . . Oh come on, Darlene, I've seen her be just as much a slut as you."

Darlene, I know now, owns a Zona 10 haircutting salon and is Crystal's best friend. She's from England, wispy and pale, pretty in a washed-out way. She turned her head sideways like a wan Madonna, rolling her eyes and lowering her lids, placing her thin hand over her chest, and said, "Me? Pfhuh."

"No one's sluttier than Darlene," said one of the men at the

THE LONG NIGHT OF WHITE CHICKENS

bar, middle-aged with balding hair and glasses, alcohol-ruined cheeks so pulpy and reddened they look violently scraped.

"Jake!" said Darlene, harumphing and swiveling in her chair, carrying on as if it were all joviality and idle flirtation though this Jake, a long-ago laid-off steelworker from Ohio, is a dour man, especially so since General Ríos Montt, an Evangelical Protestant, outlawed gambling. Jake used to own a large share of the poor people's slot machines you used to see all over Zona 1 in grimy little one-room arcades, and they made him a rich man by Guatemalan standards.

One of the other men said, "Give me one of those hotdogs" and gestured at the hand-drawn sign advertising all-beef Ball Park Franks. "Just a second," said Crystal, moving towards where I had just taken a seat at the bar. *"Bway-nas no-chays. Coe-moe pway-doe seer-veer-tay,"* she said. I felt the others looking at me, and, exaggerating my own Namoset accent, said, "I'll just have a draft beer, please," and watched her be mildly startled.

But I must have looked deeply disconcerted and disconcerting myself that night, like some kind of silent psycho, all my awry nerves showing. Crystal served me my beer without even a smile and popped a frankfurter into the microwave. What I'd instantly thought and been electrified by of course was that the "slut" they'd been referring to must be Flor. And I chugged my beer as if to drown out everything.

But then Jake said, "But I gotta say I wouldn't want to be her husband." And the other man said, "Zactly."

Crystal said, "Maury the Mercenary says he fucked her in Pana once."

Darlene said, "Maury says he's fucked everybody."

Jake said, "But not you."

Darlene dryly said, "Everybody needs a psychiatrist, don't you think?"

And Crystal exclaimed, "What!"

I sat there, my beer almost gone, my head spinning like a carnival ride.

A few moments later the man had his hotdog, and he took a bite from it and said, "Why don't you have cabbage and guacamole on these like the ones they sell on the street?"

"These are American dogs," said Crystal. "Go to the corner and buy one if that's what you want."

"There's no meat in those," said the man.

"Too bad," said Crystal.

"Why can't I have both?" said the man. "Cabbage and guacamole *and* meat. Like in Brownsville."

I paid for my beer without meeting anyone's eyes and left. Maybe their conversation would soon turn to Flor, maybe they'd already discussed her. I was there five minutes at most.

But one of the floral arrangements we received for Flor's funeral in Namoset was signed "With all our condolences and respect and fondest memories of Flor de Mayo, from Crystal Francis and friends at Lord Byron's." Of course they hadn't seen the request we'd had printed in the Guatemalan papers for donations to be sent to Los Quetzalitos instead of flowers to us. Apparently neither had the man who sent thirty-six red roses with a plain white card attached bearing a few lines of poetry in Spanish that Moya instantly recognized as being Rubén Darío's after I'd been wondering about it, and trying not to, for over a year (which I here roughly translate):

> *. . . and beneath the window of my Sleeping Beauty,*
> *the continuous sobbing of the running fountain,*
> *and the neck of the great white swan that questions me.*

"*Sentimental, pues,*" said Moya. "He thinks the swan is death or . . . something like this. There was no fountain under her window, *vos*. He thinks *he* is the fountain, but her window did not face the street." It wasn't Moya who sent those roses and the card. So it must have been the secret lover, the married one. Moya knows about him now, I told him, I had to, of course.

Moya had a brief love affair with Flor, one that ended, he says, about a month before her death. So all right, what am I supposed to say about it?

So maybe it was an inconsequential enough involvement, to her I mean, that she'd never thought it worth mentioning to me? Or maybe it would have embarrassed her to. Or she'd for some reason thought it would upset me to know. Whatever, Flor had every chance to tell me about it and she never did.

But his affair with Flor was just one of the things Moya came to Brooklyn to talk to me about, having decided that enough time had passed and that, for some reason, I really ought to know if I didn't. Actually, it was the main thing, probably, because he thought I already knew the rest of it anyway. So of course I never really let Moya get going on him and Flor because *not* in fact having known the rest of it, that's what I was excited to hear about. Now, I'm not holding back on that, Moya's information, his "revelations," for any reasons of suspenseful effect, as I think you'll plainly see when we get there, which won't be long from now. It's just that things have to come in some kind of order and there's so much else, like the funeral and the fifteen months after, to get through first, or at least to evoke, to establish as having occurred. There's Flor, the living Flor, my main assignment, to tell about her as I always have, as if none of this had happened. This, Moya likes to exhort me, is not going to be a chronicle of what it's like to be dead.

So "this" is another of the subjects Moya came to Brooklyn to discuss. He wanted my help, what only I, apparently, could give him. Who else if not me, *vos*? And this all began, Moya told me— if he had to point to the one moment when it really first came to him—one winter afternoon in Cambridge when, still sunk deep in his winterlong funk of gloomy, self-subverting thought, walking home from his nonfiction narrative class at Harvard, he happened to glance to his side and saw a child, a little Indian girl in a snowsuit, one of the orphans, he *swears,* from Flor's orphanage, playing with some other children in a snowy yard.

Eventually I had to say, "Kind of an interesting coincidence, but really, so what? Flor would have liked adopting a kid out to a professor. A Harvard professor? Are you kidding? No matter what else, Moya, she did do legal adoptions. There are children like that, from her orphanage, all over the world!"

But Moya somehow saw mystery, portent, and possibility in that little girl. She woke something up in him, he says, some big but shadowy idea. And soon, everywhere Moya went in Boston, he felt as if his actual shadow was snagging on Flor's shadow (his words), the actual and innocent shadow of her past. And her shadow seemed like a shadow of his big but shadowy idea as well. In pursuit of parallel shadows, he took out the newspaper article, never completed, completely unpublishable even in *El Minuto,* that he'd begun in Guatemala in a frenzy of private grief, fury, fear, and, I don't deny it, even heartbreak almost exactly a year before: an article on the circumstances surrounding Flor's death and the crime, which soon, in Cambridge, took on an ambitious but shadow-obliterating life of its own. Moya says his nonfiction prof was sympathetic to his overall aim, though totally put off by the shrill, overly subjective, hysterical, vulgarly generalizing slant of the thing. Where was Flor, her life? The prof found Moya's brief portrait of Flor's Massachusetts youth predictably allegorical: superficially and sardonically ridiculing of the United States, which of course was not how she really felt at all, and simplistically glorifying of her—apparently there was hardly any mention of me. Stranger yet, Moya says he didn't mention himself in it at all either, though really, he admits now, it was all about him, thus its failure.

"Did she tell you about the time she was lost in that snow-storm?" he asked me, in Brooklyn.

"Of course."

"You know that story well, *vos?*"

"Uh-huh."

"And the one . . . the one about your *abuela* and the monkey?"

"Moya, I know this stuff inside out, and tons more. Why?"—and so on. He hadn't thought of bringing me into it until he ran into my mother at that Latin American Society of Boston event.

It wasn't until we were in Namoset, after we'd taken the train from New York, that I told him about the secret lover. We'd gone downstairs into her bedroom in the basement and had both been sitting without speaking on her old bed for a while, but Moya's eyes had filled with quiet tears and suddenly I just blurted it out: There was a married man who wouldn't leave his wife for her but she did say that in the end she felt relieved that he wouldn't. By the way Moya gaped at me, and then briefly covered his face with his hands, and then quickly bolted to his feet and asked me to repeat what I'd just said—I absolutely knew then that it was the first he'd heard of it.

But I feel there's no need for me to hear any irrelevant details about whatever went on between Flor and Moya. If he had anything essential to tell me, I'm sure he would have by now. It goes without saying, of course, that I don't suspect him of being mixed up in whatever happened, and anyway, if he had been, it's logical to assume that my father and I would have heard about it because the police, or rather military intelligence (G-2), who basically run the police detective corps, probably knew all about their romance—much more than I know about it—for, whether or not they were spying on Flor during that time, they almost certainly were on Moya. And they hardly would have wanted to protect *him*. After all, it wasn't all that long after that Moya had to flee with his ever-whitening hair into exile, albeit into temporary and well-stipended Ivy League exile, though it was a brave enough choice he made, to come back. He could have stayed in Cambridge.

Moya says that when he returned to Guatemala a few weeks ahead of me he actually wore his Harvard necktie through customs—a none too discreet reminder to any and all interested on-lookers of what G-2's infamous computers could reveal with just the following finger taps on a keyboard: Luis Moya Martínez. "Six months at Harvard, *culerotes!*" On a special Save the Young Newspaperman Fellowship. He has many more influential and powerful connections now. Profs who can phone profs who can phone distinguished alumni senators and ambassadors who can phone *generalísimos* and say: Let that boy go! We know you've snatched him and do not harm another hair on his head or you can kiss even your nonlethal military aid good-bye! *"VE-RI-TAS, vos!"* Some general is going to call a bluff over just an honorable newspaperman like Moya? In the Art of War, not a good move. But you never know. He says they're still opening his mail, *vos*. Of course you can't go using up your U.S. Senate connections over a trifle like that.

SIX

Payaso cigarettes, Gallo beer, windows open and my sound box turned down low, Wilfredo Vargas lewdly, robustly growling, *"Miiii medicina eres túúúúú . . ."*
This is the bedroom I chose for myself: in the addition Abuelita had built over the rear part of the house, completed only a few years before the night she sat down in an armchair downstairs, let her head droop to the side, and went to sleep forever. "She passed away just like that, without any warning, just like a little bird," that's how my mother tells it. I'm sitting at the unevenly carpentered, untreated pine desk I bought the other day from an Indian vendor who was carrying it down the street on his back with four crude chairs stacked and roped between the upturned legs. "Just the desk," I said. Moya, when he saw it, said it reminded him of what the dictator Estrada Cabrera said long ago when after more than two decades in power he was deposed and imprisoned: "I have been like the Indian carpenters of Totonicapán, up at dawn and working hard every day of my life, forever making bad furniture."

Maybe it's just the absence of motor fumes and traffic uproar that makes breathing actually pleasant at night, that lets the mountains flow invisibly into the quiet of the city at night, into all its earthquake cracks. You imagine you can smell the infiltrated histories of soaked forests where the sun never penetrates, where a dead tree can remain standing perfectly mummified in the wet dark air for centuries, until someone comes along and just pushes on it with their hand or kicks or leans against it and *poof!*: it collapses into a pile of fine peat powder and drunken ants at their feet ("Sixty million years of constant photosynthesis!" I read that in a magazine article on the Guatemalan cloud forests). Every night smells quite a bit like leaf-burning season in New England, as if the damp smoke of faraway slash-and-burn farming fires mixes with the smoke from a million charcoal cooking and garbage fires lingering over the city's peripheral slum-ravines.

Usually, at night, at this time of year, it rains for at least a little while. You don't actually find Caribbean crabs scampering around the patio in the morning, but from the rain's clatter— heavy drops gradually quickening and suddenly subsiding, un- like the afternoon downpours, which come all at once—you almost expect to. What I do find in the central patio sometimes is the small antique fountain filled to the brim and moths or butter- flies floating, their wings washed absolutely translucent, anten- nae twitching like tiny oars. And once, sunk to the bottom and looking like a tiny medieval samurai buried in a limpid green tomb, a drowned hummingbird.

It's three in the morning and I'm nearly exhausted enough for sleep, though there's something about my nights here, this con- stant and more or less unfocused impatience and agitation I've been feeling, that keeps an echoing din going inside me, one that seems to grow louder the quieter it gets outside. Though this neighbor- hood, in Zona 1, with streets dark and deserted at night like a laby- rinth of canals, is never completely quiet. Sounds wake you in and out of sleep. The sudden squeal of faraway tires, backfires that sound like gunshots; the police who walk their beats in pairs, com- municating with each other across the empty blocks in the warbled code of a Maya whistling language, sounding like commando owls on secret missions into the night air behind enemy lines. This is the precise hour when the invisible city, as wide as the actual one, of crowing roosters starts coming to life, inciting the invisible city of howling, barking, yapping dogs. And when the light is deepest phosphorescent blue, that's when the soldiers of the Presidential Guard—the National Palace is only blocks away—come out for their predawn jog through the glowing mists, hundreds of rhythmically stomping boots against wet pavement and the occasional warrior druids' cry of some militant slogan being sounded off (Moya says his grandfather could remember when all military parades or processions were silent: "Because back then soldiers went barefoot, *vos!*"). Every 6:00 A.M. but Sunday I'm jolted back awake by the screeching transmission and thunderous idling of my neighbor's messed-up car in the echo box of his tiny garage, just over the wall on the other side of the narrow courtyard beneath my window. And one dozing spell later, from nearby or from farther away but always because it's always *somebody's* birthday, dawn's staccato explosions, strings of birthday firecrackers being set off, often accompanied by the fainter celebrations of mariachi bands singing *"Mañanitas"* . . . Then the uproar of the morning's first mufferless buses, and ambulant Street vendors crying out like professional mourners: *"Aguacaaaates"*—as if every avocado in Guatemala died yesterday. Ever hear a man pour all his plaint and grief into the word for eggplant? *"Berenjeeeeenas."* They pass in the street, stop by barred, shuttered windows or kitchen service doors to ring and ring, bleating out a name for whatever they're selling: *"Zapaaaatos"*—the ambulant cobbler. It's such an Indian sound: deep, resonant, ancient, the sound, somehow, that an immense, gnarled, and knotty old hardwood oak, ripped open by lightning, might make. But Indians have worked as street vendors in cities since Spanish colonial times, haven't they?—pitching their products as if embodiments of the Indian soul to people living behind high walls and barred windows ever since? The Spaniards could have forbidden it if they didn't like it, decreed a thousand lashes for the smuggling of excessive complaint or pagan anguish into the word for eggplant. Instead they must have encouraged this bathetic bleating as the key to good salesmanship! But why? (must ask Moya) . . . And then the *Bandas de Guerra,* the War Bands, public school kids practicing year-round for the Independence Day parade, marching through the streets in school uniforms, boys and girls playing rudimentary martial music on snare and bass drum, a few xylophones, a few trumpets. Also the daily Pan Am flight to Miami, taking off and shattering the morning in its thundering, straining, protracted reach over the mountains and volcanoes, rattling windows and walls. Time to get up.

I'd stayed out late (Lord Byron's) and was in the kitchen with a slight hangover, downing glass after glass of purified drinking water from the five-gallon jug mounted in a swiveling brace, while I waited for Chayito to finish preparing my morning orange juice. She insists on doing it herself, though it always takes her a long time, slicing green oranges in half with a knife that looks like Genghis Khan's sword at the end of her tiny arm, then pressing with both hands on the handle of the juice press as if drawing water from a rusty well pump. She always ruins it by putting in too much sugar, but I don't complain anymore because she's always made it that way and doesn't seem to hear anything I say anyway. Chayito was one of Abuelita's maids even during my childhood; I'm pretty sure she's the one who used to threaten to scorch me with her iron. She was living alone in the house, a pensioner maid tending ghosts, sleeping in the same old maids' quarters though all the other bedrooms were empty, when I arrived last month.

Suddenly the front doorbell, not the service door's, rang, so I knew it couldn't be for Chayito. Moya's the only person who has ever come here looking for me without any advance notice before, and never in the morning. So I was a little alarmed. But when I opened the front door there was just an old peasant-looking man out there, holding a dirty straw cowboy hat over his breast, and wearing an old buzzardlike black jacket with a frayed yellow shirt and thickly knotted tie. He was an Indian, or else heavily *mestizo,* and had the expression of a rain-drenched sparrow.

He asked to speak with my grandfather, but his presentation was much more floridly decorous than that: With your *pardon, joven,* could you be so kind as to inform *ml patrón* Don Rogerio Arrau that Chepito Choc Something of San Antonio Suchitepéquez is asking for just a little minute of his time and humbly awaits him here . . .

"But Don Rogerio has been dead for nearly twenty years," I blurted.

And he stared at me with birdlike, frightened eyes.

"But Doña Emilia, she finds herself in good health?" he asked.

"No, she has passed away too," I said, totally baffled of course. "Can I help you with anything?"

"And you, *joven?*" he asked. "You are of *la familia* Arrau?"

"They were my grandparents," I said.

"Sí pues," he said. "Yes, I see. Then you are their grandson. *Joven, permíteme* . . ." And as he went on with his speech a terrible pleading whine surged through what had so far been his demeanor of quietly desperate, befuddled dignity. His wife had died just the day before in San Antonio Suchitepéquez and he'd ridden the bus all the way to the capital to ask his old *patrón* for the money to pay for a coffin and a burial, just a decent pine coffin for his wife . . .

By the time he was finished telling me about it he was almost inaudible with grief and the plain fear, I saw, that he wasn't going to be able to bury his wife as he wished. But I told him to wait and closed the door, left him prayerfully blessing me there while I went up to my bedroom to get a twenty-*quetzal* note from my wallet, that amount being almost equal to the same in dollars. I felt moved, stunned really, by this encounter with an old man's pure grief and devotion and my inherited place in it. To have ridden the bus all the way from some faraway *pueblo,* arriving in the capital almost as if in another century, only to encounter his old *patrón's* gaping gringo grandson . . . Walking back to the door with the money in my hand I suddenly felt gratified, even excited over the whole incident, as if this old man was giving me a piece of information, an insight, worth far more to me than just the money I was giving him.

Then he said it wasn't enough. I saw all the hope go out of his pleading eyes in an instant; he even seemed a little angry. And I nearly became indignant. How often do you give a stranger twenty dollars and get told it isn't enough?

But his despair nearly drove him to a frenzy, roused him for one last desperate try. A decent coffin. A church burial. His withered cheeks were tear soaked. Fifty *quetzales* was what it would cost. He'd had no one else to ask but his old *patrón.* Bless you, oh bless you, *joven, ayudame* . . .

I was about to suggest that he go to my uncle at the store to see if he could get the rest there, when Chayito arrived at the door behind me.

"Chepito," she said, unsurprised sounding, a completely uncharacteristic note of sympathy instantly intact.

"Cesaria," he sobbed—the name he'd known her by in some remote past, I guess—and then he went through his story again. Chayito stood in the doorway consoling him while I rushed back inside for the rest of the money. Far away in San Antonio Suchitepéquez there was going to be a little funeral procession, a pine coffin, borne on the shoulders of villagers through muddy streets to a burial ground, that I had paid for.

Then Chayito and I watched him shuffle away down the long block, his hat back on and his head down, his shoes dragging like horseshoe crabs.

The family that lives in the small pink house next to the junkyard across the street run a dry-cleaning store out of their converted little garage, always with one of two almost fantastically pretty, always overdressed and bored young sisters, never the mother, working the counter—now I suddenly became aware of one of those sisters watching me and felt swept by the disquieting depth of tedium in her expression, in her strikingly Persian eyes. She looked back at whatever it was she was holding in her long-nailed hands, dry-cleaning receipts or something, and shuffled through them. Her purple dress had starched-looking, billowy sleeves; I could see her brassy jewelry glinting. I walk past that dry-cleaning counter, close enough to reach out and touch it, at least twice a day, always aware of either sister's furtive glance flashing-vanishing like a dark fish darting through coral. Sometimes I say hello but we never speak further. It would take a learned charm completely different from my own, such as it is, to know how to get past the iron formality, timidity, and stifled rage of those two bored, beautiful sisters.

Inside, in the parlor, I asked Chayito, "How did Chepito know my grandparents?"

She emitted a dry sigh. *"A saber."*

"But didn't he work for my *abuelo?*"

"Clara," she said.

"Well, as what?" I asked.

"A saber," she said, and shuffled back towards the kitchen . . .

I'd completely forgotten about Chayito's pink-plastic-frame reading glasses, forgotten that she even *used* glasses, until I came home late the other night and found her sitting in an armchair in the parlor in front of the glass-encased Virgin and the always flickering novena candles in the corner, reading out loud to herself in an old lady's monotone from one of Abuelita's old cowboy paperbacks. Just the sight of her made me cry out, and then I stood there, goose bumps rippling over my skin, patting my chest, grinning at her, and saying, *"Huy! Qué susto!"*

* * *

What my Arrau relatives believe is that the main reason I'm here is to sell this very house—that, and to take some time off to reacquaint myself with *la madre's patria* and, who knows, maybe even fall in love with and marry a *chapina* of good family (that's what *they,* albeit fondly, think) and then invest my fairly modest inheritance from Abuelita here (twenty thousand *quetzales,* not to be signed over to me until my wedding day, though if an irresistible investment opportunity were to suddenly arise, I'm sure I could talk Uncle Jorge into letting me have it)—this house which my mother solely inherited and tried, briefly, to turn into a hotel. But it received only a B rating from the tourist ministry, which meant she had to charge twenty *quetzales* a night, too cheap to draw a high-class clientele and too expensive for world-wandering hippies. Maybe, in three years, about fifty people, Central American traveling salesmen mostly, stayed here. So she quit the hotel idea.

That I should sell the house—though I'm certainly allowed to take my time—was about the third thought that came to my mother's mind when I told her of my plan to return to Guatemala with Moya. The first was "Oh Sweet Pea, oh no. But why? Those are ignorant and violent people down there now, and you're not a reporter. Your friend is, let him do it. Roger . . ." And I said, "Mom, don't you think the truth should be told?" and she said, "Of course I do. But not by my son!" Her second thought, once she'd accepted the inevitability and cautious thoroughness of our plan, was that I should be sure to bring nice clothes and not wear sneakers.

Moya and I meet in Pastelería Hemmings every morning, just after ten, for breakfast and to discuss our still evolving strategies, though often we end up just talking about Flor.

"You know what occurred to me the other day," I said to Moya there. "Why didn't Flor hate kids? You'd think she really would have hated them. I remember when she was in the fifth grade, and she was, well, at least sixteen by then. So her body confused the little boys in her class. They'd do stuff like chase her around the playground trying to grab her breasts and mooing—"

"—moong?" interrupted Moya.

"The sound a cow makes, you know? Until she had to start socking them in the face. And they were always trying to look up her skirt and everything. There wasn't much I could do about it. She'd already been jumped ahead a couple of grades" (though I used to do that kind of thing too, I'm sorry to say, though only at home, and only up to a certain age).

"Of course," said Moya, "running an orphanage, this is a great way to have revenge on children, no?"

"Yeah tight. Moya . . ."

"But she was always so reluctant to explain it, no? She said she was just asked to run Los Quetzalitos, and so she falls into it, just like that?"

"Well, I've heard you say you just fell into newspaper work, just like that," I said. "I mean, what were you doing in '79? Studying law. So look at you now?"

As for the street vendors, what Moya said is that back in the earliest days of the Spanish Conquest, when the Dominican friar Bartolomé de Las Casas was experimenting with peaceful conquest and evangelization and utopian community as an exemplary rebuke to the massacres being perpetrated by the conquistadors in the name of same God, king, and cause in this same *"reino de Guatimala,"* Las Casas summoned several of the Indian vendors who used to wander from village to village selling and convinced them to wander announcing the glory and redemptive martyrdom of Christ instead.

So maybe, reasoned Moya, ambulant Indian vendors have always pitched their wares with a certain fervor that would have struck the heroic friar, just as it had somewhat similarly struck me, as being appropriate for communicating the gospel to the Indians, who were pagan and idolatrous of course but considered the earth itself holy and everything that grew from it holy too?

"Interesting," I said, "I've read one book by Las Casas, but he didn't mention wandering vendors—"

"Or maybe this apocalyptic melancholy *did* infiltrate into the vendors' voices after the Conquest," said Moya, much more taken with all of this than I'd expected him to be. "*Saber.* Who knows. Strange that it is only *los ambulantes,* though. There must be no markets on earth quieter than the Indian markets, Rogerio. The women sit softly talking to each other in their languages, and, though also selling, they hardly call out a thing, no?"

"We may be in separate labyrinths, Rogerio," said Moya, another time. "But we are hunting the same minotaur, *vos.*"

That was the day we rather ceremoniously and symbolically inaugurated our investigation. All I did was go and look at Los Quetzalitos, nothing more than that, while Moya waited for me in the Café Fiori on the Avenida La Reforma. That was about two weeks after my return to Guatemala. (Given my emotional state when I'd been there with my father, I hadn't noticed very much, of course.) What could have been easier, more natural, than for me to have gone and looked at the orphanage on my own when the right mood took me? Something made me wait until Moya was ready, until even this could be made to feel like part of a coherent strategy.

Nobody in Los Quetzalitos, as far as Moya and I know anyway, has any idea that I've come back here to find out what truly happened to Flor. My father and I had those few days of media exposure here, but now, almost a year and a half later, no one has pointed at me in the street, shouting, *There he is!* Flor's "case" seems to have been forgotten, buried under so many other fleetingly sensationalized and inconclusive scandals. Even in those Zona Viva watering holes, I've recognized no one from that whirlwind summer when I did visit Flor five years ago. Some of them must be the same people, but I don't specifically recall any of them, nor they me. Even in Lord Byron's, Crystal Francis's eyes registered only the slightest glimmer of recognition from those few minutes last year when she'd served me a beer. Nevertheless, sooner or later people, even in Los Quetzalitos, may somehow get wind of my being here. Will that matter?

Couldn't I simply have gone to Los Quetzalitos, introduced myself, and asked to spend several days doing what the police never did, quietly and gently interrogating the orphans who were there that night, trying to draw out of them whatever they might remember?

Unlikely, said Moya, in the Café Fiori that very morning when we inaugurated our investigation. The new director, he said, is doubtless protective of the children and wouldn't want them reliving that already long ago—long ago to children, he meant—trauma. And we have to be prudent. It's not completely impossible that one or more of the orphanage employees really might turn out to be implicated in either plausible crime: the murder, the baby trade.

The new director's name is Rosana Letones. She's from Nicaragua, fortyish or maybe a little younger, supposedly the daughter of a Nicaraguan National Guard officer, one supposedly imprisoned now by the Sandinistas. But she went to college in the States—somewhere in California, thinks Moya—and has not lived in Nicaragua since. She's supposed to be *una tipa* good humored and fairly good looking, dark haired and featured (like Flor), but Moya's never seen her. He's just asked around.

"This is going to be next to impossible," I said that morning, feeling suddenly pessimistic. "We're not detectives, or child psychologists or seers."

That was when Moya said that about separate labyrinths, each of us pursuing the same minotaur. I have to admit I fall for this stuff, the heroic sentiment, even when it's that metaphoric. But I tried silently to explain it to myself, failed, asked Moya what he meant, and got a brief review of the mythology, which of course I'd forgotten, if I ever knew it. Theseus was after the minotaur in the labyrinth to free the city above it.

I laughed. "We're going to free the city, are we?"

"*Claro,*" said Moya, grinning.

By separate labyrinths I bet he meant that mine is personal, his political, national, or at any rate more than just personal, something like that. So OK, Free the city. Like Flor used to say, in dreams nothing is forbidden, and often enough during the last month or so this really has all felt like some kind of dream to me, though not necessarily a providential one. (One of the ways Guatemala City can seem the same as a dream: the only thing forbidden is waking up.)

Moya might be recognized by anyone in Los Quetzalitos, particularly the children, he said, so it wouldn't do for us to be spotted together outside, looking at it. There was much less of a chance that I would be, if only because the regular staff had been temporarily suspended in the immediate aftermath of the murder, when my father and I had gone there.

So I left Moya sitting in the Café Fiori with my *New York Times* and walked the several blocks to the orphanage, down the long, silent, wall-lined streets of Zona 10. Here, immense flowering trees rise from behind every wall, and the top floors of the more modern homes look like the superstructures of ocean liners in dry dock, satellite dishes like conning towers on every roof. Servants clustered, chatting, by service entrances as I passed. Gardeners on the aprons outside were busy pruning smaller trees and shrubs into neatly geometric or anthropomorphic shapes: quetzals, monkeys. Wild scoops of bougainvillea and orange trumpet flowers topped the walls, nesting in barbed wire and cascading down, hiding minibarricades of broken glass. I turned left, then right on 11 Calle. The large metal doors of a driveway swung open, pushed by two Indian maids in bright pink uniforms, and two black-windowed vehicles, a BMW and a customized Cherokee with gun portals in its sides, drove out and turned down the street—before the doors swung shut again I caught a glimpse of a yard lush with undomesticated jungle foliage, two turkeys strutting past the base of a fountain topped by a plaster reproduction of that famous European statue of a naked little boy peeing.

I turned one last corner and walked down the block towards an immense volcano looming on the horizon as if from just beyond where the walled, tree-bowered, narrowing street seemed to drop off into the sky. The volcano was a hazier, more subdued shade of blue than the sun-flooded sky around it. A single brilliantly white cloud was snagged over the crater.

LOS QUETZALITOS—the wooden plaque set into the whitewashed wall by the front gates still bore the hand-painted logo Flor herself had designed: a peaked roof with six happy quetzal chicks perched along it, rising sunbeams radiating from behind.

I stood for a while on the opposite side of the street, looking at the upper stories of the main house, where Flor's bedroom was. That part of the house is narrower than the rest, and the one side directly facing the street forms a white, windowless rectangle that, with its peaked, red-tiled roof resembles a church bell tower. The black barbed wire running in four taut and parallel strands from black iron rods set into the tops of the very high walls surrounding the property is new; later Moya said it wasn't there in Flor's time. That was all I could see: walls, the tower, the massive pines inside the yard, a barren but stately avocado tree, and one eucalyptus tree. I couldn't even see the roofs of the other buildings in the compound, or the top rungs of the jungle gym built by Ozzie Peterkins. Wind in the trees. Birds. All else was sunny translucence and silence broken only by the hollow clang of what sounded like a cooking pot dropped on concrete. Then I heard the far-off-sounding insect drone of a crying infant. It went on for a long time, then stopped.

The sheet-metal front gates have a small, sliding shutter for peeking through that can be latched shut from the inside, as it was now. But the gates are framed in the wall by two high stucco pillars, and in one of these pillars there is a mail slot, a slanted slice through stucco, mortar, and brick, with a dropoff chiseled into it from the inside to make a place for pushed-through mail to land.

So I crossed the street, thinking that I would run the risk of peering through the mail slot, and when I reached it I didn't hesitate, I just bent and did it: a walleyed view of grass and the gravel drive, concrete steps and a mop in its pail, tree trunks, and over there, straining my vision as far to the left as it would go, in front of the one-story structure that must be the classrooms, blurred by shadows and the shifting patterns of sun through the trees, a geometric edge of Ozzie Peterkins's jungle gym.

Then I heard voices to the right and looking over that way saw four girls coming into view, and a little boy crawling spastically after them with some kind of big white box strapped to his back. Another extremely thin boy was walking behind, with an expression too sunken and haggard for a little boy. The girls were about ten years old, two in pants, two in dresses. I could see now that it was a white wicker laundry hamper that was strapped to the back of the crawling boy—I saw its hinged door flapping open. The others glanced at him now and then, and glanced away. This wasn't play, exactly, no one was laughing very much. They were simply crossing the yard as if on parade, one boy crawling along with a laundry hamper strapped to his back. The procession crunched across the gravel drive and proceeded towards the jungle gym, the strange, thin boy lagging. One of the girls declaimed something, and I'd already stood away from the mail slot when it made sense to me.

"*Tortuga,*" she'd shouted. The boy with the laundry hamper on his back was pretending to be a turtle.

Through the barred gate of the service entrance across the street, an Indian man, holding a rake, watched me. I nodded towards him as I headed back down the street, on my way to the Café Fiori. "*Buenaaas,*" he softly intoned.

Is there, could there possibly be, any significance in the fact that it was quite possibly Flor's laundry hamper? I vaguely remember it as one of the few things the police had left behind in Flor's ransacked quarters. Moya thinks he remembers it too.

"So Rosana Letones wanted her own hamper. *Es lógico,*" said Moya, in the Café Fiori after I'd rejoined him there. "And for the children there, anything can be a toy. *Imagino pues.*"

He said, after I'd described him, that he remembered the thin, haggard-looking boy too. Apparently he's much older than he looks, and has a thyroid condition that has stunted his growth. Flor was always saying that she was looking for medical treatment for him in Sweden or elsewhere, said Moya, though she never managed to procure it because there were always cases that were more urgent or that had a better chance of being cured.

* * *

Here's an interesting story that Moya heard from another *El Minuto* reporter, who heard it from a doctor at Roosevelt Hospital just the other day:

In an unpopulated dirt field next to one of the new squatters' barrios that have sprung up on the city's outskirts in recent years, a woman and a little girl were violently struggling: the woman was slapping the girl around, apparently trying to drag her off, and the girl was resisting, shrieking for help, frantically trying to wrench free. The people from the barrio who witnessed this, mainly women too, were sure that the unknown aggressor was a witch who'd come to steal one of their children, and they rushed into the field to attack her with sticks, stones, and fists and would have beaten her to death if she and the child hadn't been able to make it understood that they were mother and daughter, and had merely been walking through that field on a routine errand when the girl stopped to urinate in some weeds, except she'd crouched right over an anthill and fire ants had swarmed up her legs, bottom, and into her dress, fiercely biting—thus the commotion of a mother trying to slap ants from the squirming body of a terrified child and to free her from her dress. The little girl must still have been being bitten as all this was being resolved, but it was her badly beaten mother who had to be taken to the hospital. She came that close to being killed, one more innocent victim of the hysteria and rumors spawned by the ongoing illegal baby trade.

Why did this strike me as an actual piece of evidence when I heard it, however indirectly it could be related to Flor? Because we have so little to go on and this simply *felt* like evidence, like the first in a long series of new clues that might ultimately exonerate Flor or even condemn her? A clue to the hysteria that had unquestioningly assumed her guilt, however rooted in the actual crimes of baby stealers and sellers; or a clue to the hysteria, provoked by an actual crime, that might have motivated whoever killed her.

* * *

Every day I remember this and remember it again now: Flor de Mayo, most recently a resident of New York City, sitting cross-legged on her sofa in the furnished Zona 10 apartment she'd rented after she'd moved out of the Pensiôn Aigle in Zona 1 (her job as director of the orphanage still in the future), recounting her first months in Guatemala City with the overexcited air of a small-town girl plunged into a true urban immensity for the very first time, telling me how really weird—actually she said *weer,* she always dropped that *d, really weer, Roger*—it was that Guatemala City seemed even bigger to her than New York, harder to know, somehow, but how could that be? Was it just terror and guerrilla and counterwar that made it seem bigger, made it throb invisibly out there, drawing all your sensations out into it? But not just that, she answered herself.

Not a city of East Sides and West Sides and deftly demarcated and marginalized neighborhoods but a city of straight wall–ruled and earthquake-cracked streets leading nowhere (down any one of which her killer might *always* be walking or driving, a secret lover passing on the opposite side . . .) and peripheral barrios springing up overnight so unknowable in their anonymous misery and secrecy that they're indistinguishable from the barrios that have existed for years; a city of *weer* and mysterious dwarfs and horse-faced women with fire eyes who only appear at night . . . and a census of rumors livelier and more visible than the names they're attached to ("The archbishop's chambermaid is pregnant!"). ". . . A city with at least one of everything, you know?" said Flor.

And I think I do know just what she meant now. Because a city with at least one of everything *feels* bigger than it really is—because if you can find anything you want, there must be many more things you don't even know about yet; and if there's *one* of something, why shouldn't there be another just around the block

or in another *zona?* One Lord Byron's . . . But that summer of
'79 we found one reggae bar too, one bar with a punk band, one
where the bar band plays only "Songs from the 'Sixties," one Al
Astra, a rich kids' discotheque in a credible planetarium, night
galaxies above and moonscape sculptures rising from the dance
floor, one Pandora's Box, the egalitarian gay discotheque (the
only place in Guatemala, Flor said, where rich and poor socialize
on a more or less equal footing), and one after-hours club she'd
recently heard about in a private mansion in Zona 10, restricted to
off-duty death squads and close allies in that netherworld only—
drinks and gambling after work, machine guns leaned against
chairs, and every single waitress in the place an adolescent girl
and completely, but completely naked, not allowed even to wear
shoes or jewelry (not that surprising in a city where as many girls
must work as strippers as they do as maids, but they wear G-strings
and stiletto heels at least); one public university run like a hive
of deadly secret societies; one exclusive rich kids' private university run like a temple to the worship of Milton Friedman (or is it
someone Asian now?) economics; one imitation Eiffel Tower;
one Street of Solitude, one Street of Forgetting, one Street of
Miracles, and one Street of the Rabbit; one Thai restaurant, one
Malaysian, one Japanese; one old hag street vendor called La
Millonaria, who held the last remaining Socialist politician's head
in her lap as he quietly bled to death in the parking lot he'd just
been assassinated in; one Hindu family, the women in saris, playing badminton in Parque Morazán on a Sunday afternoon, just
a few blocks from where I'm living now; one dark and musty
textile store that has, says Moya, the connoisseur of the city's
singularities, an ancient Chinaman at the counter who is fluent
in Yiddish after so many years of working for the even more
ancient and reclusive Polish Jewish immigrant couple who own

the place but never deal with the customers, preferring to sit in a back room behind a green curtain sipping hot tea from clear glasses, doing the accounts or reading and playing Big Band jazz records on an old-fashioned phonograph; one La Merced Cathedral, with its cracked bells tolling for half an hour before every evening mass, the oddly unresonant clatter carrying through Zona 1's dense, smoky air like the clumsily flapping wings of some hollow, tinny, mechanical bird; one most charitable Television Store Owner who tunes all the TVs in his display window to "The Three Stooges" every evening so that street kids can gather in the polished plaza of the store's entrance to watch but not hear, Indian street kids with lice in their hair and glue-sniffer eyes, dressed in castaways' rags, sitting there cross-legged, raptly watching and shrieking with laughter, punching and poking each other in imitation of the silent antics of Larry, Curly and Moe—this on Sexta Avenida, where the Arrau store runs the length of a block, the one avenue that at that hour and every night looks like a tunnel of perpetual flame with drifting motor fumes and smoke pouring from take-out caves and sidewalk braziers, everything illuminated by the Hong Kong–style canopy of protruding, bristling, blazing neon signs all along the avenue. Guatemala City seemed to Flor, back then anyway, and seemed to me and seems even more so now the biggest and most unknowable city on earth, one as particular in its inscrutable ways and strong flavors as any other—though I realize that this is probably one more illusion caused by the intensity and single-minded focus with which I now have to watch it.

In the newspaper today a photograph of an empty pair of loafers lying in a patch of weeds, left there during the night, no doubt, as if by a fairy-tale cobbler (not the ambulant one)—except that isn't the story. The loafers belonged to a previously disappeared university student whose *"cadáver manifestando señales de tortura"* had just been found in that same weedy lot. And so one of the papers, as if seeking a new angle on the same old story, ran a picture of his shoes.

PART TWO

THE LONG NIGHT OF WHITE CHICKENS

SEVEN

"The Namoset police! They were such handsome, rosy-checked, blue-eyed, big, strong boys. Not like in Guatemala. I'd see them and remember our police in Guatemala, those poor little guys, so *asoleaditos,* so tiny and sun shrunken, just like raisins, *ay no!*"—and she'd smile like a primly mischievous Japanese girl, or like some slyly ditzy ingenue on a talk show, all the while watching her interrogator try to fathom (though sometimes they were pretty dim and just said, "Oh") the surprising cleverness of her answer. Because that was how Flor liked to answer a question like "Well, what were your first impressions of life in the U.S. of A.?" And she had to answer that kind of question all the time.

"My first year in Namoset, when I knew too few people, I used to love to drive into the square with Ira when he went to buy his newspapers and bagels. Just so I could see a policeman, you know. The policeman would smile at me and oh! My face would turn all red!"

I was still in the last months of my quarantine for tuberculosis, back when Flor was first getting excited about the Namoset police. So much of my sense of that time comes from Flor's stories and reminiscences, though there are some things I vividly remember on my own, even from before she came, when I still spent most of the time on that sofa in the living room. I used to imagine, or maybe I'd just been told, that the healthy little children playing outside were my friends. Looking through a toy catalog with my mother, I picked out a pedal-driven fire engine with a ladder on the side with room for two that Keith Cleary, the blond boy my age who supposedly lived down the block, would ride in with me when I could go outside. Almost a year in Namoset, and all of it indoors! Keith Cleary was my best imaginary friend. I remember standing on the sofa inside the picture window, looking out at Keith romping in the snow with a fascinatingly big dog, a golden retriever with an orange coat as thick and lustrous as a circus bear's. My mother would tell me stories about Keith and me playing together: "Rogito *y* Keith have their own farm, the best and richest in Massachusetts, with all the prize cows and all the biggest pumpkins . . ." She was determined I not get too comfortable or accepting of my solitude. And she'd picked up somewhere the mythology of tuberculosis leading to a romantically morbid temperament: "What if he becomes a poet! *Qué horror!*" she has confessed to having feared, recalling the poets of her own youth, dissipated Rubén Darío imitators miming Parisian bohemian decadence, all spiritual opulence and spiteful wit, using cologne-scented verses and unspontaneous declamations to try to charm a generation of rich girls in love with Clark Gable or Pedro Vargas and then Frank Sinatra and whichever Guatemalan young men most looked like and best imitated them.

So who's to say? Maybe something like that really would have happened, if Flor hadn't come, obliterating my obsession with Keith Cleary: a rapt dread of the world outside, a solitudinous melancholy . . . Because for a long time the fire engine wasn't mentioned. And Keith Cleary wasn't outside anymore either, though I don't remember noticing. I didn't forget the fire engine though, it was still something I wanted, but whenever I brought it up my mother would tell me to choose something else. Why? Choose something else, Rogito. *Why?*

Then it was spring and I was allowed outside, and all the neighborhood kids despised me, because I was always clinging to Flor, because I was brown, chattery, spoke more Spanish than English, because I had then, I have to admit, the brattily effeminate and bossy nature of a Guatemalan rich boy spoiled by maids. But didn't I used to have a promised friend out here, Keith Cleary? My mother sat me down at the kitchen table. I retain the impression of an overcast afternoon, with fresh air blowing in through the window, and no lights on but what natural light there was filling the kitchen like crystal-clear water in a shadowy pool, so that everything—oven, fridge, Formica table, linoleum floor— had the glow of big white stones at the bottom of that pool. My mother was telling me about going to heaven and the little angels who were so happy. Keith Cleary had, a few months before, fallen through the ice on Sarah Hancock Pond and drowned.

Which is something that was always happening in Namoset: every year, it seemed, someone drowned, or died, or lost a limb playing on the train tracks. Anthony Borrelli, who lived fairly close by, lost a leg that way and was outfitted with an artificial one so that when he walked down the street, slapping his own thigh, he looked as if he was pretending to be a horse.

Keith Cleary became an angel. It was his little sister, Gail, who became melancholy. And I was terrified of their romping, excitable dog, Rex.

He, Keith, would have hated me anyway. At least at the beginning. To this day, though, whenever I hear the word *angel* or see choiring angels depicted on a Christmas card, I think briefly of that apparition, my first American friend. And I always hear myself saying his name, full of reverence and loyalty and pride and in a Latin accent, my tongue abruptly stopping against the hard *th*. I even used to feel like him, or have the vague sense of something never ending, when my parents bought me a German shepherd to help me over my fear of dogs, and we would romp together in the snow.

It wouldn't be until late spring that my toy chest, packed full, would be carried like a steamship trunk down into the basement, to that half of the wood-paneled room that would be designated my playroom, separated from your bedroom by an invisible line drawn across the tiled floor from the bottom of the stairs. The prettiness of your face hovering close by, my immediate addiction to your smile, cheeks, nose, eyes, your hair falling around me as I hugged you tight, your warm caramel smell, all of this is more of an eternal and safe sensation than it is a memory.

Just as exciting to Flor as the Namoset police were her journeys into downtown Boston on her days off during that first year, before my father put her in school, when she was still, of course, basically just our maid. She had a crush on the Paul McCartney look-alike who used to pose against the fountain near the Park Street subway entrance, lounging on the concrete basin with his long legs out straight and his Beatle boots crossed and his arms crossed too, basking in the bedazzled admiration and long-ing gazes of an encircling crush of star-struck, giddily bashful Latin American housekeepers who came into Boston on their days off to see him. Anyway, that's the way I've always pictured it from the way Flor told it and in memory have perhaps distorted it from the one spring day when, my quarantine finally over, Flor took me into Boston with her, and there he was, looking just like Paul McCartney, Beatle mop hair and the shades he always wore that must have been essential to the illusion, but he had the cheeks and nose and, most of all, that candied boyish smile. And it was his calling in life or something to lounge against that foun-tain being gazed at. I wonder if he even knew how to play the guitar, or if eventually, in the next few years, before he would have even had the chance to don Sergeant Pepper garb, he was drafted and sent to Vietnam—that would have been a strange twist in the life of a Paul McCartney imitator. Or maybe he was nuts. There must be thousands of people in Boston who remember him.

Did Flor really think he was Paul McCartney? It must have seemed completely possible to her: even Guatemalans knew about the Beatles and that the United States was a place where they actually walked around if they walked around anywhere. Maybe the first few times she was confused, and then it didn't matter. I was too young to comprehend celebrity, but I was quietly astounded, it expanded my sense of reality: here was the same fellow whose big face loomed from a poster on Flor's bedroom wall, and it all had to do with the music she played on her radio. (Within a year Flor would own her own small, plastic record player.) That same spring of my liberation my mother took me on the "Big Brother Show," I was part of the live, onstage audience, but when it came time to rise with Big Brother and recite the pledge of allegiance and raise our glasses of Hood's milk in a toast to President Johnson's portrait, I ran off the set crying to where my mother sat, shrieking in Spanish, not because I'd been instructed to just silently move my mouth along with the incomprehensible pledge but because I'd never in my life been able to drink a glass of milk without chocolate in it. All the rest of pre-school New England, including Flor, witnessed this routing of my composure at home on television. I'm not sure that I even remember the incident, but Flor rarely missed an opportunity to bring it up, even in later years, laughing delightedly and then sticking her arms out like a sleepwalker's and wailing, *"Mamiiii Mammmiii no puedo sin chocolate!"*

"Really? Guatemala?"

"Guatemala." And she'd smile, sitting up straight on her stool or leaning a little closer to whatever Boston beer commercial guy or whoever, anyway some guy in a rugby shirt, was working his pickup lines in some Kenmore Square or Comm Ave singles bar. He wasn't going to get anywhere though. But Flor liked attention. She liked telling her stories. The Irish like telling their stories too, so it wasn't an unusual thing to do in a Boston bar, especially in response to strangers' prying questions; it was Flor's own kind of blarney. We'd both be home for Christmas and we'd just go out but she'd never even tell them she went to Wellesley or later that she'd gone there and now lived and worked in New York.

"Wow, that's wicked far. All the way from down there, gee . . . You look . . . you look kinda like Bianca Jagger. Isn't she from down there?"

"Nicaragua. Like Bianca Jagger? Oh no. She has a sour mouth."

"Well I've nevah tasted it hah hah hah . . ."

—and she'd be smiling even more like a Japanese girl. I used to hate watching guys hit on Flor and two or three times, in later years, infuriated her by losing my temper, which I very rarely do. Then she'd have to use all her cleverness and charm to keep him, along with the *them* who usually lurked somewhere behind that *him,* from beating the crap out of me. Boston, as the whole world supposedly knows, is infamous for racial intolerance, outside the sanctum of its prestigious universities of course. But Moya has told me that even the Somalian student he befriended at Harvard, a political "refugee" like himself, when out walking in Cambridge had to put up with drive-by carloads of teenagers shouting "nigger." When some slightly more grown-up version of that sort of Boston boy finds himself thinking he might be on to an exotic lay, that's when you get the flip side.

"OK, you're prettier than Bianca. What'd you say your name is?"

"Purísima."

"*Pooreesahma?* That's a pretty name. That's neat."

"Let's go to Spit," I would probably interject here, talking just to Flor and referring to a rock club near Kenmore Square.

"Geez," the Boston boy would usually persist, dazedly shaking his invariably large head. "How long have you been living here?"

"Where?"

"You know, in the States."

"Fourteen years."

"So you're practically American."

"I am American."

"But you still have your accent, you know."

"I do?"

"So did you go to school here and everything?"

She'd nod.

"That must have been kind of tough, huh? Getting used to a new language and a new place and the snow and everything?"

"Oh, not so hard. Not exactly the Helen Keller story, you know what I mean?"

Not exactly the Helen Keller story, I must have heard that one a million times.

So questions like that. Did you move here with your parents? She'd just shake her head no. What do you do now? And she'd say something like "Oh, I work for Star Market, in the accounting department." And they'd say something like "That's very impressive," and then wouldn't want to hear very much more about it.

"What I always wonder is, OK—you're from down there. And you come here. And you're from that country and it's—don't get me wrong, OK?—it's poor, right?"

"That's what you always wonder?"

And he'd laugh, kind of shyly and kind of self-deprecatingly, this followed by an almost visibly surging inner determination, because he's *serious,* and just a second ago he was really getting somewhere here, wasn't he? But something in her attitude is beginning to rile him, because who does this squeaky beaner think she is, Bianca Jagger? *Star Market, big fucking deal!*—and his eyes briefly search out the jokingly glancing but envious eyes of his buddies at the end of the bar, and their eyes seem to say, *Nice tits! Go for it, Sully!*—OK, he will, he is, so she thinks she's hot shit, *he's* Sully, not a dope, not a wimp, not just some redneck. What's behind that smile of hers? *Foreigners,* shit, like she's Laotian or something . . . For some reason he has to swallow hard just once before going on . . . (And I'd be getting mad too, wondering why the hell you just couldn't find a polite way of asking him to get lost and yet knowing why.)

"So everyone wants to come here. It's poor there, hey, it's what it is, and there's money, there's work here. It's the American Dream, right? Who can complain? But it can be hard here too, I know, racism and shit, stuff. But you're here! But, like . . . What's it like? What was the first thing that really blew you away, made you go, you know, Wow, the USA! Different, but it's gonna be worth it. Or maybe not worth it, you know what I mean?" *Phew.*

"Boy, let me think about that a second, the first thing that . . . I know! The police!" All the time smiling, in my opinion anyway, something like a Japanese girl, that is, with a certain distancing formality and a certain seemingly naive playfulness and a certain coldness or even cruelty or maybe loneliness behind that sunny and accommodating smile.

Big disappointed nods, a sympathetic look, and he'd say, "The police, they hassled you—"

"Oh no! Quite the contrary! *They were great . . .*" Rosy cheeks, blue eyes, big strong not like raisins et cetera, he'd have to stand there and listen to the whole nutty thing, his own smile getting pretty frozen as he wondered if she was dumping on him or maybe he'd be thinking, Squeaky Weirdo, what the hell . . .

* * *

One of her stories—a version of which I imagine that guy in the bar having to stand there and listen to all the way through, one I know even Moya heard—was about both the police and one of her first trips into downtown Boston. She'd only been living with us about six weeks. And a blizzard hit Boston that afternoon. It was one of those once or twice a winter storms that always leave behind at least five feet of snow, completely burying the little statues of the Virgin attended by even smaller statues of rabbits and deer that the O'Briens kept on their front lawn, and that I could see from my quarantine perch at the picture window in the living room.

My father had already gone to work when Flor left the house that morning, and my mother had said nothing to her about blizzard warnings, though a light snow was already falling. Maybe my mother hadn't heard about it yet. She certainly doesn't remember having heard of it. She was treating it like any normal day, sitting with me in the living room, Flor could recall, doing her homework—my mother ended up not driving in to college that day, though. Her only class was scheduled for the afternoon, and by then . . .

Flor had long ago ascended the steps out of Park Street station, where the snow was already falling so heavily that Paul McCartney had abandoned his daily arena. But instead of turning around and coming right home, she'd wandered around. Of course she had. It was beautiful, and what did she know? The trees on the Common were turning white before her eyes; snow streamed like an endless parade of gauzy banners between the tightly wedged buildings of the downtown shopping district; shoppers hurried along the sidewalks as if too euphorically energized by the cold, clean carnival in the air to bother going into Jordan's or even into that bargain hunters' inferno, Filene's Basement.

And there were so many men out on the sidewalk; that *was* unusual, men looking very rigid and erect in their overcoats and whitening hats, rushing past her.

"You know, that should have been a warning, so many men on the sidewalks at that time of day, with their briefcases! Hurrying home! But what did I know?"

The buildings seemed to be dissolving, their shadows seeping over the snow and meeting in the middle of the buried streets and slowly darkening. The snow on the suddenly ever so quiet sidewalks was soon unbroken by any footsteps other than her own. By late afternoon the subways had stopped running out to the suburbs, and she was lost anyway. She'd strayed, it seemed to her, far from downtown Boston. Even the coffee shops were closed, as if for a day of national mourning.

For the first time that day she felt cold.

"Really cold, man."

She held her ice-beaded mittens between her chattering teeth as numbed fingers poked through the wet wool pockets of her soaked coat, descended like a cow's hoof into the delicate folds of her almost empty little plastic wallet, into the throbbing and empty pockets of her baggy corduroys. She'd lost the slip of paper with our phone number printed on it; maybe she'd left it at home in her bedroom! She didn't speak enough English to phone the operator, not even close to enough. Actually, she didn't even know about operators.

"Oh my. Now what?"

The snow seemed to breathe, seemed to be climbing up the walls of the black iron buildings pressing close around her. It crackled and flared like a swarm of self-incinerating mad white moths around the streetlamp's glare. Could you drown in snow?

"If you went to the ocean for the very first time, had never before seen a sunny blue ocean, would you immediately understand undertows?"

During her disappointment over the illusory shelter of a streetlamp's encircling glare on a deserted street corner in Boston, she'd suddenly remembered Petrona—one of the orphans at the Sisters of the Holy Spirit orphanage. One day, on an outing to the beach at Puerto San José sponsored by the Guatemala City Lions Club, poor Petrona had been pulled out into the ocean forever by an undertow. But that's *another* story. Roger knows that story. Roger used to think he knew all Flor's stories, right?

So what deadly and unsuspected property might snow have? She really was afraid. She had to think her prayers because her lips would not move, only her teeth. To make matters worse, she really had to pee.

"I was shaking like a washing machine gone berserk. You know how washing machines go berserk? Like suddenly they're possessed by some insane panicked demon going *thumpa thumpa thumpa!* Only you couldn't actually *hear* my bones shaking. But the police stopped because they could hear my frozen feet screaming. *Aieee! Help me!* They could hear this. 'You hear screaming?' They looked over and saw this snow girl shaking like a washing machine gone *berserk*. And my feet were screaming. *Aieee!*"

A Boston police car with heavy chains wrapped around each of its tires had come crunching down the street like a Soviet tank and to a slow stop where she stood beneath a streetlamp cowering and shivering and forever memorializing an anonymous street corner that in later years we decided must have been somewhere in the area of North Station.

The window of the police car came down, and a young, rosy-cheeked, blue-eyed policeman, so big and handsome and strong, not at all like our poor little police in Guatemala . . . This Boston policeman said, "Hi."

She knew *Hi* of course, she knew some words. But she could barely enunciate even *Hi,* her lips were so numb, her teeth so chattery. What should she say? It didn't matter. They were going to save her! The policeman had gotten out of his car. Boy, did he look warmly dressed! His mitten looked like a seal's flipper, and he laid it gently on her shoulder and guided her, very carefully and slowly, so that she wouldn't trip over her own giant throbbing feet or spill any of her brimming bladder, into the car.

"I have never, I tell you solemnly, been more in love with anybody or anything than with that policeman's seal-flipper mitten or the heat in that car. It was blasting! *Madre de Dios!*"

But she couldn't attempt to enunciate even in Spanish until the heat in the car had penetrated past her lips into her brain. Yes, even her brain had begun to freeze. You think she's smart now? Brain cells had been dropping dead like cows, like frozen to death cows!

Don't exaggerate, Flor . . . (or Purísima).

"I'm not! I'm not exaggerating!"

What was the name of the family she lived with? C'mon. She must know this. She should tell them right away!

"What is your name?" asked the policeman, enunciating so that every word floated clearly and separately towards her in the warm air of the car. There were two policemen in the car, both so rosy cheeked.

Oh yeah. "Flor de Mayo Puac."

"Puac?"

Could she nod yet? She could!

One of the policemen began speaking into his radio, pronouncing her name to the best of his ability.

"Graetz," she tried to say, though it must have sounded to them like *graze* or *grass* or *gretz* or *grease,* whatever.

"Nam . . . o . . . set."

They understood that. Namoset, that's pretty far, especially in a blizzard, the two policemen were probably saying to each other. Did she know her address in Namoset? Namoset? Her address there?

Time went by. With great effort, surviving cows in the thawing muck of her brain shook themselves awake, slowly pushed themselves up onto their legs and emptied their steaming bladders.

"Flor."

"I'm serious! Emptied their . . ."

They handed her a pad of paper and pen. But her fingers didn't work yet. Her fingers were full of bees. And the police car was slowly driving along now, which made it hard to write. She spilled the pen onto the floor, and the handsome young policeman smiled and bent to pick it up. Then he put the pen down on the seat and took both her hands between his own and rubbed them vigorously and she almost fainted with pleasure right then and there, with pleasure and, yes, completely rapturous love of uniformed blue-eyed humanity punctured only by the burning disconcertion and paradox of her bladder.

Finally she could write. She wrote her name. She wrote Don y Doña Graetz. She wrote 16 Codrioli Road. Of course she'd memorized that, but not her phone number. Who ever phoned her?

Not even Zoila, the Cuban maid on Pine Way, was her friend yet. Eventually Flor had friends, but it wouldn't be until later that same year that Father Milligan at St. Joe's in Namoset would introduce her to Zoila. And during Flor's second summer with us she would meet Ingrid Klohse, whose family had just moved to Namoset from West Germany, at the Girl Scout camp on Sarah Hancock Pond. And during her third year Flor, through the help-wanted listings at the Cuban American Institute in Boston, would find a maid's job in Chestnut Hill for Delmi Ramírez, her very best friend from the Espríntu Santo orphanage.

The police had been speaking on the radio. "Don Graetz," said the policeman, and he gave the address and waited for a reply. Everything wasn't computerized back then, you know. But eventually it must have come to this: "Well, there's an Ira Graetz at that address. And he phoned the station just a little while ago." And the other one perhaps slapped his forehead and said, *"Don*'s like *Mister* down there. *Duh.*"

Taking into account their general responsibilities as protectors of citizenry safety, the police couldn't very well command Ira Graetz to drive all the way into Boston in the middle of a treacherous blizzard. So they, in their powerful tank-tread car, drove Flor to Namoset, down the turnpike in a blizzard like in that nostalgic James Taylor song about the Massachusetts turnpike in the snow, past all the stranded automobiles belonging to commuters who, in just a few years, my father would always be pretending to be responsible for. What? Yes, responsible for, even on ordinary snowy nights! My father would stand at the open front door with his hand cupped to his ear, calling, "You hear them, Rog? Hear them, Flor? Chief Namoset and the Indians are hooting to me! They want me to come and help them dig cars out on the highway!" and he'd drop his hands to his mouth and hoot back so loudly that all the neighbors must have wondered.

"And really," Flor would reveal, "Ira was just going out to play cards with his friends. That's why Mirabel didn't think it was so damned funny."

But it was slow going even in that police car.

Among the three phrases my mother had made Flor memorize before allowing her into Boston by herself was "Where is the ladies' room?" and she'd already found that she could usually accomplish her mission whenever she had to say this. But where was there a ladies' room on the turnpike?

"What is the price?" and "May I have a hotdog and a hot chocolate?" were the other two, and, really, they were all she needed to enjoy herself on her days off. She knew how to take the bus from Namoset Square to Newton Highlands and switch there for the subway train to Park Street, and then how to get home. If it was too dark, or too cold, she could stop at the Brigham's in Namoset, ask for a hot chocolate if she wanted it, use the ladies' room, and phone my father and he would come get her in the car, but so far she'd never yet had to do that.

She needed to pee so badly she worked her hand under her coat and into the pocket of her baggy corduroys to hold herself in. Deeper and deeper went her hand, squeezing harder and harder. Feeling had returned to her fingers by then, and she touched the little slip of paper at the bottom of her pocket, all folded up, tiny as a fortune cookie's message. So she *had* brought her phone number! Oh well. No need to mention it now. They were almost home.

From Namoset Square, Flor could direct them to Codrioli Road, pointing and advising in Spanish, *"Por allá!"* The walk from our house to the bus stop, that she knew like the back of her hand.

The Virgin Mary, the rabbits and deer had vanished under the snow. Recently I'd learned that Chief Namoset and the Indians drove the snowplows, but it would be another year or so before I understood that my father helped them to dig out stranded motorists on the highways. For that they needed Indian snowshoes, and they'd always lend my father a pair. The police car with its twirling red light pulled up in front of our house, Girlie O'Brien's face appeared in a window, and I saw Flor and two policemen get out.

But she could barely move, not on her own. She was hunched over the squirming, boiling lobster inside her, biting her lips and feeling all mixed up: her elated anticipation of relief, a nagging sense of guilt over the little slip of paper. The police thought it was something else that was crumpling her, that perhaps being outside in the snow again was making her relive her recent trauma! One of them picked her up in his arms, stumbling a bit as he climbed up and over the immense barricade of snow the snowplow had built, and then he waded down our unshoveled walk to our front door. He'd spilled a little of her bladder, picking her up like that, stumbling. That was why, as soon as my father had shooed me back into the living room and then answered the front door, Flor, bent over, without even taking off her rubber boots or her coat, disappeared, staggering, bouncing off hallway walls as she made her way to the bathroom.

But the police thought it was something else, and it made them feel even sorrier for Flor, and angrier at my father. It was as if they thought Flor had run off to her bedroom to cry. So the police scolded my father loudly, with furious Boston accent and Irish brogue.

How dare he let a little girl go into Boston alone without even a phone number to call! On the day of a blizzard! She doesn't even speak English!

My mother said Flor was her niece, visiting from Guatemala, which is a very beautiful country, with a modern capital and sophisticated, educated, very well-off people living there, and not just the Land That Bananas Come From.

And the police, mollified by the reappearance of a blushing, grinning Flor, were pleased to learn a few things about Guatemala from my pretty and charming mother and to drink some tea with her before their long drive back to Boston.

My mother used to worry that someday police would discover Flor's true age and origin, and arrest her for employing an underage maid.

That night was the first time I ever heard my mother call Flor an idiot to her face. The police had left and we were all in the kitchen. Flor was having her soup, and then her dinner, and my mother was having a Kent with yet another cup of tea.

My mother didn't call her an idiot in an overtly nasty way. She sighed for about the hundredth time in the last ten minutes and said, almost as if to herself:

"*Ay Flor, pero cómo es que puedes ser tan idiota?*"

* * *

Before we left the bar she'd shake "Sully's" hand. If he made the mistake of asking for her phone number, she'd smile and say, with much graciousness, "I'm sorry. You seem like a really good guy. But I don't give that out." Usually there'd follow a brief, uncomfortable silence. Maybe he'd be thinking, Forget it, how was I supposed to get anywhere with her greaseball brother here anyway, or, That cock-tease! Or he'd be thinking that at least he knew where she worked and maybe the Star Market accounting department would get a phone call for *Pooreesahma*. Flor's friend Delmi Ramírez had actually worked there for a little while once, long after she'd left her maid's job in Chestnut Hill.

It might seem somewhat mystifying that Flor would even give the time of day to guys like that, in bars. But, believe me, she thought of it as play and did not think much of men who couldn't engage in it without hurting *themselves.* She had an exaggerated hunger for male attention anyway, which I trace to her childhood and youth: an all-girl orphanage, so many years in Namoset classrooms with children far younger than she. Her first boyfriend was Cuban. No wonder the blue-eyed police were such a big deal. Flor was beautiful, and had a cheerful disposition, which of course meant that at some point she had to develop her own way of handling men, but one which allowed her to go on rather methodically learning about them without entangling herself, or too quickly, harshly, even dangerously causing offense. Right up until she left for Guatemala in '79 she still hadn't outgrown an almost adolescent curiosity, an almost "boy-crazy" innocence and fleeting attention span. Flor was a bit of a loner, something of a stray cat, equally comfortable and uncomfortable with suave U.N. diplomats and Boston frat jocks or whoever.

Flor's stories became my stories too. Well, of course they did; I found myself using them almost as much as she did, though to somewhat different advantage. I mean, imagine you're on a first date with me and we get to talking, as one inevitably does, of origins, childhood, formative things. It's hard to be dry about it. When I was five a Guatemalan orphan became our maid . . . My father put her in school . . . like a sister . . . Once, there was a blizzard . . .

It was one of her best advantages almost right from the start, another tool, something almost exterior to herself, to be wielded deftly: her own life story! So what's left if you take away these stories? The truth? Why so skeptical now? (That's what I ask *myself.*) Yet it was amazing to see sometimes how quickly she could be provoked into a curled-up, almost crustacean silence. But there was no reason to do that to her. What did it accomplish? I'd always thought she had her own ways of letting you know. Even if she did seem somewhat trapped behind that Japanese girl–like smile and "Namoset Police!"—trapped by repetition and her mixed-up will to accommodate and her eventual disdain.

EIGHT

"... la polida de Namoset, pues," Flor de Mayo actually did say—on the twenty-third of October, 1982—when Moya, during the first extended conversation he and Flor ever had, *vos,* also asked her what it had been like, her first impressions, *pues,* to go from a convent orphanage in Guatemala City to that snowy, great land ...?

Luis Moya Martínez, columnist and reporter for the low-circulation Guatemala City afternoon daily, *El Minuto,* and Flor de Mayo Puac, *directora* of the privately funded orphanage and malnutrition clinic Los Quetzalitos, were seated in the walled patio of the Fo Lu Shu II, a Chinese restaurant in Zona 9; butane torches fluttered in each of the square little patio's corners, close to the vine-covered walls, and pastel paper lanterns were strung from the eucalyptus boughs overhead.

—like *raisins?* Had she really said that, that the Guatemalan police were like raisins?

When Flor had finished her little recitation, Moya had just looked at her, very straight-faced; he'd let a silence sit there, so that she for once would be the one wondering what that silence held. They hadn't even known each other for an hour yet, but already, *vos,* it was war of the softest kind. Flor had won the initial skirmish, within the first fifteen minutes, reaching out to turn off his tape recorder, challenging his ardent *venga acá* or come-on stare (his Russian-poet-deep-soul-soaring stare) with a much cooler stare of her own, then saying, "Moya, if you keep looking at me that way, *vos,* I'm leaving."

But then she had gone on about Namoset police and raisins, and so Moya had responded with thoughtful-seeming silence. Before this silence could become excruciating, just before *she* could find a way of turning his deft "nonreaction" to her advantage as she already had several other less pregnant Moya reactions during the course of this newspaper interview on the "orphan situation" that eventually became one then two shared bottles of Botrán rum along with several platters of fried wonton with sweet and sour sauce, this night that Moya met Flor and that eventually became known as the Long Night of White Chickens (or as the Night of Long White Chickens, or as the White Night of Long Chickens, or as the Never-ending Night of . . .), Moya broke the silence, his overall attitude conveying (he hoped) a very wry parody of certain well-known youthful emotions, though the words his tongue lugubriously and dramatically tolled were not those of a love poem, or of anything else obviously apt to the moment:

"*Aluuumbre, luuumbre de aluuumbre, Luuuzbel de piedraluuumbre, sobre la podreduuumbre.*"

Flor, of course, thought his behavior strange and just sat back, wonderingly looking at him.

"Asturias," she finally said. "So?"

(Because Moya's recitation had been from the opening paragraph of Our *Chapín* Nobel Laureate's most famous novel, may that bilious old turtle everlastingly fart in bitter peace in his ambivalent exile's grave in Paris.)

So what *had* Moya meant? Why Astumas and *luribre de alumbre? Saber.* Who knows! Love, which was already happening inside him, is this kind of dance, furiously fast, full of instant and instinctual decisions. But it really did have something to do with his sense that Flor had been speaking highly polished words (*"Namoset police,"* et cetera) that she'd spoken a thousand times in her life already, an impression confirmed when he got to know her better, however brief, and of course tragically ended, that relationship was. Then what was different about the Chicken Light of White Night? wonders Moya. Was it that no one had asked her to tell these stories, her whole life story in one night, for such a long time? Was it something in the way Moya had drawn it out of her? Something happening in her secret life at that time? Something in the *wonton dorado* and sweet and sour sauce? in the spectral Far Eastern mood of the Fo Lu Shu II? Why, on this night, did telling her life story leave her feeling so vulnerable to love and if not to love to what?

Moya had phoned Flor to ask for an interview on the "orphan situation," and though he'd come on a somewhat more disingenuous mission than even that, he had soon determined to seduce her, and was on the verge of having actually seduced her by listening to her stories, only, just when he'd thought he was about to succeed, the thing with the chickens. A week later he did succeed and then he had to wait nearly two months to succeed again, and by that time, *vos,* he really was in love with her. Five weeks later Flor broke off their relationship because, she said, she needed to be sure it was not inexplicable passion more than love because she had learned too painfully that the former never ended well and wasn't ready to go through that again. All in all it was, for Moya, an alarmingly feverish and disorienting period, full of many betrayals of the rigorous standards he'd always held himself to. Almost nightly they spoke on the phone. He had never in his life employed such impassioned logic as he did during those harrowing and epic conversations. He was certain it was explicable love and accused her of fearing the brilliant truth though he would never beg. Flor seemed to be coming around. Three weeks later, on the very night she died, he spoke with her on the phone and she said:

"*Arrgh!* I don't believe it! You may be right."

"Yes. I am! I will be right over."

"Give me through the weekend. What are we going to do? This is crazy. You're eight years younger than I am. I don't think I want to stay here anymore. Even if we went to Europe, what could you do there?"

"Go to a university."

"Yeah, right. And the first nubile little Parisian who comes along . . ."

"*No, no, mi amor* . . ."

"*Sí, Sí, mi amor!* You're totally Guatemalan, Moya, you can't change. And I don't want to live like an exile-bohemian. You see? I can't possibly be good for you. And I don't see you giving up on this place for long."

"But I am ready to! I . . . surrender!"

"I'll tell you one thing, no matter how much things *ever* change here, I'd never want to be Guatemala's first lady, that's for sure. My *gosh*, what a fucking nightmare that would be."

"*Cómo?*"

And then she had laughed so delightfully that optimism and a new kind of terror had concurrently flooded through him.

Where was Moya the night Flor died? At the newspaper office, and then he went home and phoned her. Had he believed what the newspapers said, that her "partners" had done it? A difficult question to answer. But for at least a few days he considered it a possibility, because so much can happen in secret, *vos,* and what was that compared with the shock of death? As for the prior rumors about her involvement, yes, of course he had heard them, but these he had ascribed, within minutes of meeting Flor, to the extravagant cynicism, envy, hypocrisy, and paranoia that pervaded and poisoned nearly every aspect of Guatemala City life like some biblical plague of maddened depravity. As for the shock of death . . . well, it wasn't the first time that someone he knew and even cared deeply for had died, or vanished, just like that, not that one is ever really prepared. Maybe one could never really be prepared, but a key to survival in that sad country was to live as if one always was for *anything.* Moya still quietly feels that after that ultimate shock he was never "quite the same" inside again, though of course he strove to hide and even to conquer this.

Why did Moya wait more than a year to contact Roger? Well, *vos,* several good reasons! What little information Moya had about the case, he'd just assumed Roger and his family had it too. Anyway, it had been twelve full years since they had actually been school friends. (Though he had seen Roger, briefly, in the summer of '79.) He was frightened of the indignation, disgust, and suspicion with which the Graetz family, and Roger especially, might receive the news that for a short while he had been Flor's lover. (Roger, in fuct, when he did fmally learn of it, was not thrilled, and fundamentally refused to hear any more about it.) And one thing more about Moya and Flor's love: they had agreed to keep it secret for the time being, it had been *"Un Amor Secreto,"* like so many others.

But Flor had loved someone else too, another Secret Lover, one she never told Moya about. Moya had to learn of the existence of this person from Roger. Flor was a mature woman, of course, in her thirties, free to do as she pleased, and Moya has striven, since his adolescence, to rid himself of the more childish aspects of machismo, though he has never stopped feeling that in love a degree of possessiveness is not out of place. But Moya had understood then, for the first time, why Flor had delayed the onset of their brief relationship for two months, and perhaps why she had broken it off five weeks later. Instead of in an uncharacteristic frenzy, he might have spent those two months allowing love to bring Flor de Mayo into such clear and persistent focus that he would have been able to prevent both the break *and* the murder—the murder that never allowed that break to reach its predestined resolution. In his heart of hearts, Moya believes this is not a farfetched supposition.

* * *

It all began that long-ago night in the Fo Lu Shu II; began, perhaps, at the precise instant when Moya noticed two small flames of incredulity in Flor's eyes and knew then that she had definitely registered his intention. Behind the superficial veneer of a woman animating herself for a newspaper interview that she'd felt unsure about assenting to in the first place, sat the actual Flor, getting ready to respond, Moya sensed, with patronizing teasing or outright ridicule, or stormy boredom. So he had to be careful.

He felt himself at several slight disadvantages, all but one of which he had immediately foreseen: the fact that he'd been an occasional friend of her "little brother" Roger was one, because wouldn't this make her think of him as "just too young"? Her mature and nearly intimidating beauty, of course, was another, though he had dared that situation before. It was the disadvantage that he hadn't foreseen that was unsettling: he'd anticipated that she might at first be distant, but that she would at least be respectful, that she'd have some idea of who he was, of his relative prestige. Instead it was as if no one had ever filled her in on the special dignity and worth of at least the Public Moya.

All the other foreign women who came to Guatemala and inevitably sought out Moya always brought a dignifying and even reverential air to their first meetings and, *vos,* this gave him much to work with. (And Flor was *like* a foreign woman now.) For in great American and European cities, at solidarity and university conferences and in editorial meetings, and even once, it had been inferred in Moya's presence, in the actual halls of Congress, Washington, DC, women (and men too, though fewer, and not quite in the same way) who cared for Guatemala and had been there or were planning trips there, spoke of Moya, and apparently said things like "Well, you must look up this Luis Moya Martínez. It's amazing, the things he gets away with in his newspaper, even despite the State of Siege! True, his paper is little read compared with others there. But he's very brave, and quite brilliant; I imagine that much of what he writes probably goes right over the heads of the secret police, if you know what I mean. Still, it's amazing he's alive. When you think of how many journalists have already been killed or disappeared there . . . So young too! Quite handsome in a funny way! Though his hair is turning white."

But Flor stabbed out her cigarette and turned off his tape recorder, then said she'd leave if he didn't stop looking at her that way. She sat back in her chair, both hands grasping the armrests, coolly returning his stare. It was as if, to Flor, Moya was just another Guatemala City newspaperman, and one she was only talking to because in boyhood he'd known Roger Graetz, in whose house in Massachusetts she'd commenced her *norteamericana* life.

At first Moya was too stunned to speak. Everything stopped, even the breeze that had been rustling the trees overhead, gently rocking the pastel paper lanterns and sputtering the flames of the butane torches in the corners of the patio, flames that had been sending glowing shadows waving across her face in an infinite series of variegated masks all modeled on the same person. It was still early evening, there were few customers. The waiters, who were not Chinese, stood chatting quietly by the archway that was an immense scarlet, gold-paint-embroidered dragon; the dragon separated the patio from the brightly lit, scarlet and gold dining area inside. The restaurant's sound system was tuned softly to a radio station playing Latin Caribbean dance hits, and, though Moya was not much interested in pop music or dancing, it seemed to him that every merengue ballad was telling something like an orphan girl's feisty and luckless story in Flor's own disturbingly thrilling voice. She was dressed in white white jeans and a loose-fitting white blouse that made the shadowy shapeliness inside almost unbearable. A violet sweater was draped over her shoulders.

Her almond brown cheeks were sun reddened from the outing to the beach she said she'd taken her orphans on the day before. *Vos,* it was like this: even the so smooth skin in the slight cavities of her collarbones, even her naked hands filled him with an almost frenzied desire to look brazenly under the table at her ankles and feet, though of course he did not do this. Her powerful, dark, nearly black eyes glowed like a gypsy fortune-teller's. And her dense, soft, meandering hair fell over her shoulders like, Moya suddenly thought, an Alice in Wonderland's, but black (as black as Flor's heart would have to have been if even one tenth of what they said about her after her death, or even before it, was true—).

"Flor de Mayo of Chiquimula, transplanted to the Land of the *Mayflower!*" that's what he'd said, and then he'd beamed a wide smile—a British woman had told him that even his teeth looked intelligent—and then widened it some more so that she would understand.

And she had turned off his tape recorder. "Moya, if you don't stop looking at me like that . . ."

Then, finally, she said, "All right. What is this?"

"Rum," said Moya. "Why don't we order rum, and Coke, and just talk." Though Moya rarely drank, he wanted to now. "And an order of *wonton dorado.* It is excellent here."

"I thought we were going to talk about the orphanage," said Flor.

Moya was used to a certain complicitous sympathy, and to being treated, *franidy,* as a kind of hero; and, truly, whether he fully deserved such treatment or not, he accepted it all gratefully. (There were many people far more heroic, and humbler, in his country, though not so many left in the city.) It provided him with an escape from deeper tensions, insecurities, doubts, obsessions. But it had given him new obsessions too, including an obsession with foreign women. Their eagerness to approve of Moya allowed him more easily to close himself, freed him to play. He played his role responsibly, he was helpful to his visitors, he dutifully exchanged bits of information with them, and often inspired them with daring and outspoken insights and analysis much blunter than anything he could ever actually get away with in his newspaper, where he was daring enough! He accomplished all this even while camouflaging his essential secretiveness with exaggerated eloquence and many pregnant pauses, during which he appeared to be making up his mind whether or not to go on, and then didn't. And they always paid the check.

But when this dynamic was absent, he felt cast out to sea. Did Flor even read *El Minuto*? Or any Guatemalan paper? She ran an orphanage; it wasn't possible that she could be living obliviously. He'd guessed that, especially in the context of a newspaper interview, ostensibly on the subject of orphans, she would be relieved not to be badgered about what they both knew was best left unsaid and was unprintable anyway (such as the reasons there were so many orphans) and would at least enjoy the distraction of his company. And he thought of himself as an expert distracter.

Wouldn't she find his audacity rather moving? Find even his undisguised advances moving, even if she chose not to respond? His interest in the story of her whole life moving? Didn't she know who he was, that there were people all over the world who were astonished that he was even alive! Death threats routinely came his way (over the phone, in the mail, slipped under his door, once a bloody handkerchief in a small black box). He endured that, and never released even a whisper of self-pity, and in fact didn't feel very much; he took full responsibility for the choices he had made in life and was not sorry about anything. But he frequently had a fluttery tic in his once otherwise healthy right cheek, and a weighty, perpetual storm in his gut, and sudden, unprovoked urges to whimper, which he always successfully defied. His hair was turning white. He certainly found himself moving enough—it was legitimate to admit that. He was twenty-five then, and didn't yet foresee going anywhere but Guatemala. But foreign women came here and sought him out and thought what he did was important. And he did his duty by them, and then let them breathe into him a sense of cosmopolitan dazzle, let them fill him with the teeming if temporary daydream that he could belong in such cities too, that someday, when he could be free from Guatemala for a while, he could go live in one of those urban paradises and be rewarded. But he'd begun to discover that when those women went home to their cities and left him behind, he often felt a bitterness, an unjustified contempt even, that he tried and mostly managed to subdue, though he carried a little bit of it, carried it one grain at a time in his heart, into his next encounter.

He always asked to hear about their childhoods in these places, which often they liked to talk about, though just as often they did so guiltily. But he pressed them to talk about it, because, no matter how many times they did, he always found something new to try to understand. Who were they? How had they gotten from there to here and why? Who was this gringafied Flor de Mayo Puac? Why had Flor left Guatemala and then, so many years later, come back to run an orphanage?

"Look, I know how it is with you guys, OK?" said Flor, suddenly pleasant, as if she were not chastising him but gently rebutting a point he had made in some high-minded discussion merely to prolong it. "You can't even go to the bank without trying to prove, to yourself of course, how easy it would be to make it with the teller. Oh yes, I know, *you're* not like that, *you* went to the Umversidad de San Carlos, the *compañeras* made dog food out of you if you tried. So you didn't pull this stuff on San Carlos girls anymore. Not pulling it became a new kind of game. Sexy stuff, right? So what's changed now?"

"... *Cómo?*"

She laughed. "You're all the same, exactly the same! You left the university and discovered that women liked the old way better, minus the more belligerent aspects. So now you overdo it, but there's a wink in there, an element of self-parody which you think adds to the charm. Well, maybe it does. Except when we're not interested. I came here to talk about what I do. I sent an editorial, oh, months and months ago, to your paper, to Celso Batres, did he tell you?"

"No," said Moya.

"He wouldn't publish it," said Flor, "but he met with me for lunch about it. Nice guy, actually. Which is what I'd always heard. He said the time wasn't right for my strong views, though he said he agreed with them."

"And what were these views?"

"I wrote that if the people with money in this country are going to support a policy of massacres in the highlands as a way of preventing revolution, then they have an obligation to look after all the abandoned and orphaned kids that policy is causing. Oh I know, they say they don't believe that massacre stuff anyway, they never go up there, it's not in the papers *here,* it's Cominie propaganda, well, who are they going to believe, their servants? So they'll adopt a baby parrot, a macaw, a monkey, a curlew, but an Indian orphan, *olvídate,* forget it. Not one Guatemalan has ever tried to adopt a kid from my orphanage. Not one."

Moya felt almost instantly heartsick over her naïveté: Why would any even middle-class Guatemalans adopt an Indian orphan when for the equivalent of thirty dollars a month they could have one as a maid, gardener, or houseboy?

"A curlew!" he said, forcing a laugh. *"Carajo!"*

"I know it sounds naive," she said. "It's *meant* to. It's wrong in every way, right? *Burgueses* adopting Indians? It would even and

189

probably especially infuriate the guerrillas. But, see, I do what I do, *pues*. Your boss Don Celso said that what I'm *really* asking for is for Jesus to come back and make everybody here act better. Well, my answer to that is, Isn't this the Devil's reign? *His* way must have sounded pretty farfetched too before he got control of everything. Think back to what it's like to live in a relatively civilized country, even this place was one once, for a while."

"Celso is very religious," said Moya.

"Well, I'm not, to tell you the truth," said Flor. "I guess I wouldn't mind a glass of rum."

"Of course we could never print something like that."

"So then what is there for us to talk about?"

"I would like to take a more indirect approach. Why did you come back to Guatemala?"

"Why?"

"In the United States you could be making much money, no?" he said. "You could have a great profession, a wealthy and intelligent husband, and not be bothered by the extreme and macabre situation we are living in in this insignificant little country. Instead, here you are making yourself crazy over the moral failings of *guatemaltecos* who will never adopt their own country's orphans. But if not for these failings in the first place, there could not be so many orphans. You are in a street with no exit."

But Flor seemed suddenly taken with the song coming from the radio inside, a woman with a throaty, feisty voice singing about a man called *Estúpido*. She smiled briefly to herself, then looked back at him. "What did you say?"

"No," said Moya. "Every time I look at *Time* magazine or the *New York Times* I find myself skipping over the articles on, for example, Ethiopia. Out of guilt I make myself go back and read them, imagining how uninteresting the same kinds of articles on Guatemala must seem to the average citizen of the world."

"I'm from here too, you know."

"Yes, but what drew you back, and then made you stay?"

She shrugged. "Oh, I don't know. A longing to see it again, I guess."

"Was your life in the United States so unsatisfying?"

"Not really. I mean, it was my life, *pues,* which admittedly has been pretty strange. So what made me stay . . . Well, what do you think? Why do you *think* I stayed?" She stared at him furiously for a moment, and then, suddenly, her mood seemed to shift again, and she grinned. "The way they make *wonton dorado* in Guatemala?"

Moya called the waiter. He ordered an entire bottle of rum with a bucket of ice and limes, and the wontons with sweet and sour sauce.

—*Luzbel. Lumbre de alumbre* . . . This came later. Somehow that particularly well-aimed and already affectionate joke of quoting Asturias helped to turn the tide, by making her want to protect and stand up for and insist on what was hers alone, *her* story. This was when he had begun to seduce her by listening.

Moya also has something to add regarding the tall, thin boy with the thyroid condition whom Roger spied trailing after that other boy who was pretending to be a turtle with Flor's laundry hamper strapped to his back.

The thyroid boy looked ten at most, but was something like nineteen. Quite intelligent, *vos,* though, because of his condition, often extremely lethargic. That unfortunate boy was too easily tired to ever be able to pursue a productive life, but he was not too easily tired to be continually sneaking into the girls' quarters to fondle and be fondled—a totally shameless *desgraciado.* Flor told Moya about that boy on the very Long Night of White Chickens, told him that she'd always suspected but had never been able to prove that he was the father of an infant girl born to a thirteen-year-old orphan just seven months after Flor had assumed the directorship of the orphanage. In the face of much evidence to the contrary, the girl went on insisting on the immaculate conception. Because the adoption laws forbade the separation of children from the same nuclear family—a law originally formulated to protect the integrity of the sibling relationship, of course, not that of mother and child—that girl and her infant daughter could only be legally adopted as a pair.

"So here was a chance," said Flor, in the Fo Lu Shu II, "for some couple to turn themselves into parents and grandparents at a single stroke!"

"How unusual!" exclaimed Moya, watching the ends of Flor's hair dangle over the bowl of sweet and sour sauce near her elbow on the table. If she leaned forward a bit more, he suddenly and capriciously reasoned, her hair was going to go right into the sauce.

"Needless to say, that couple never turned up. Not that I actually tried to find them."

By the time that girl was just fifteen, said Flor, she was working full-time in the orphanage kitchen and living on her own, at her insistence, in a rooming house near the bus terminal market, so that she could have the freedom she needed to find herself a husband, a father for the baby girl, who continued to live at Los Quetzalitos. But it wasn't long before she stopped coming to the orphanage altogether, either to work or to visit. A few months later Flor received a postcard: the girl had made her way to Houston, Texas, and had a job breading shrimp in a frozen food factory and would soon be sending for her daughter. She left no return address and Flor never heard from her again. And the thin, oversexed, essentially invalid boy with the thyroid condition never displayed the slightest acknowledgment or even awareness that the little girl—three years old by the time Moya came on the scene—was probably his daughter.

"Just another *machito,*" sighed Flor. "We don't operate in a cultural vacuum there, though I certainly wish we could sometimes." Later, when Moya began to spend time with Flor at Los Quetzalitos, it became obvious to him that she had never stopped feeling at least vaguely vexed by that boy—what was his name? He used to initiate and lead the boys in his quarters in masturbation sessions too. Flor was constantly threatening to expel him from the orphanage if he didn't stop, but she was never serious about these threats. What could she do? Was it so abnormal, she rhetorically asked Moya once, that the orphans, so hungry for love, would discover and invent on their own love's most obvious and greedy expressions?

"Bunch of horny buggers," said Flor. "Well, not *buggerers,* gosh, hope not anyway. Who knows what goes on down there when no one else is watching?"

"Let's face it," she said another time. "It could be a lot worse. In the state orphanages, Christ, it's the grown-ups who work there who molest those kids. That's one reason they're always running away, figure they might as well sell it on the streets instead of give it away for free, you know what I mean?"

Moya soon began to conceive of the orphanage as a subterranean hothouse generating aphrodisiacal fumes that floated like pollen through the windows, radiated through the walls and floors. And *putavos,* that, it seemed to him then, fundamentally explained a lot. Love explained even more, perhaps, and love has never been the same since. Though some of it, it seems to Moya even now, recalling his unforgettable five-week frenzy of *floramor,* must have been and must remain simply inexplicable.

Now Moya turns his attention to his photocopy of a certain notebook originally consisting of 160 bound and numbered pages, two-thirds filled with writing in Flor's own hand. One day well into his and Roger's investigation, Luis Moya had for seven hours buried himself in the basement archives of National Police Headquarters in Guatemala City; there, with the stealthy permission and advice of a friendly, stalwart, very bribed (with Roger's money) and only somewhat raisinlike police sergeant in charge of the archives, he'd searched for Flor's confiscated papers and records, held there among countless others in a moist, messy labyrinth of twined paper bundles and boxes. The case was not officially closed, and Flor's papers could not be returned until it was. That hardcover notebook was by far the most interesting item he found in that already rotting cardboard box of ransacked papers and unenlightening documents. In it Flor had jotted rudimentary records of adoptions, orphans, adopting families—omitting any mention of financial transactions, however—along with other memoranda regarding the daily operations of the orphanage and clinic.

Now Moya searches the notebook's numbered pages for the not uncharacteristic entry on Ozzie Peterkins, the gringo football player—that was humorous too, Flor explaining to Moya what is a guard of the nose—who built a jungle gym while waiting for an adoption to be finalized by the courts. Finally he finds it, on page 37, dated June 1981:

"Carlos and Moisés Fiallos just might be the luckiest little boys in the world! It really is incredible, they're going to grow up locker-room brats, Sons of a Man Mountain earning a third of a million dollars a year, and one who saves his money and invests it wisely to boot. Strange to think he's only a few years older than Roger. He showed me pictures of his house in Texas, just incredible, he built a lot of it himself, well, just look at what he's doing out in the yard right now. Where does he get that energy! He's so healthy and positive! He said, 'Flor, hon, what you need is a good ole jungle gym.' Before I knew it, he'd hooked on to that lumber exporter guy who claims to be a nephew of Lord Carrington, and now I have a truckload of top-of-the-line tropical hardwoods in my yard. It's like some ancient myth I don't quite get the meaning of is being played out here: For five days now he's been out there in his little yellow shorts and sneakers, wearing nothing else, showing off his truly stupefying muscles, hammering and sawing and sweating away, building the most elaborate jungle gym I have ever seen. I run back and forth to the family court showing off his financial statements, with my So what if he's a single parent, so what if he's African-American, *Look,* here are Polaroids of the jungle gym he's building for all the orphans! If this doesn't go through, I can just see Ozzie stomping down to the court building and kicking it over by himself—would serve the weasels inside right, believe me. At night he takes me out for dinner and he's so sweet, telling me all his dreams for Carlos and Moisés, we joke and say they're going to be a pair of Mayan-Warrior-Deity Outside Linebackers! Also he plays the guitar. All the children, who at first were terrified of him, now think Ozzie is a magical, friendly, gargantuan, talking and singing bear who "belongs" to us. But oh, are they going to be sad and jealous when he leaves with Carlos and Moisés quite literally under his arms, I'll have a lot of cheering up to do then. I phoned Ira, who of course loves this, he said Ozzie is a real crunching tackler. Also, I'm so glad he is not changing the boys' names. When I asked him why he's never married, he joked, 'I think there's enough of me here to be Mama and Papa both, don't you?' Said he'd marry me though. He's just kidding, I'm sure. But Ozzie seems in many respects a very mysterious man. So who knows! Oh no, Flor, not that. I told him I'm way too egotistical to ever be second banana to a famous football star."

NINE

Flor's thirteen letters and postcards offer no real clues. Weekend trips, brief excursions away from Guatemala, these often prompted her to write. Two of her letters were from Yucatán beach resorts, and another was written on a rainy evening at the counter of a Sanborn's in Mexico City while she was waiting to go to a *Bellas Artes* opera; one she wrote late at night, though the sky was still light, in a hotel room in Stockholm, when she'd gone on business related to the free health care abroad program. Sometimes she'd reminisce in a pretty obvious way about this or that: ". . . It's autumn up there. All our Autumns of the Patriarch! I keep feeling like it's time to get in a car and follow the changing foliage and the Harvard football team up to Dartmouth!" Or she'd try to analyze or exhort me in some more or less sisterly way: "Roger, what is it with you? . . ." Yeah, yeah, Flor.

Only two of her letters were really substantial, which isn't to say they were confessional or the sort of letter she might have written to a best lifelong female friend if she'd actually had one, to Delmi Ramírez, say, if Delmi had lived a life more in step with Flor's. But the two letters were important to her. Both were handwritten on unlined paper despite their length, and you could tell she'd held the pages over something straight to guide her lines across them, and her penmanship was even more fastidious and perfect than usual.

One was written in September '79, well into her very first year in Guatemala, when Flor finally found the courage or whatever it was she'd needed to take a bus out to Chiquimula to try to find out how or even *if* her father had actually died:

"Well, I went to Chiquimula. I almost said *home* to Chiquimula, but that would be a sentimental exaggeration, wouldn't it be? One morning I woke up and just knew I had to do it. I walked to where the buses are, thinking, Well, if there is any bus going to the *oriente*, if there's any bus leaving when I get there, if there isn't a bus, is, isn't, is, et cetera. *Fuente del Norte,* Fountain of the North, was the name of the bus I got on for this most formal journey. My attentiveness to the landscape was nil. Only once before in my life had I traveled this route, in the opposite direction, of course, an opposite clock: then it was evening when we went through the mountains, not sunny. I closed my eyes and tried to sleep so that the trip would go faster. I spent the night in a motel at the El Rancho junction and the next morning went on to the Chinaman's general store and from there retraced my childhood steps all the way out to the arid lands and through that chiaroscuro of candelabra cactus and agave. Not at all what you would expect, Roger. That walk, last executed by me when I was six, seemed even *longer* now and the land seemed even vaster and emptier than I remembered it from then, when it used to seem I knew the place of every cactus and invisible path. The horizon is still mountains. In stranded little settlements I asked everyone I encountered if they had any memory of 'El Negro' Puac, but nobody did. Several times I was sure I was lost, that I'd come in the wrong direction completely.

"Then a Toyota pickup pulled up in a cloud of dirt and dust, driven by the civilian *comisionado militar,* kind of like the local sheriff. Recently, I was to learn a bit later, he had actually shot himself by accident with his brand-new pistol in the foot, this was why he limped about. Well, he had no recollection of El Negro Puac either, but he said he knew an old woman who of course remembers everything that has ever happened around there, and he drove me to see her.

"But things have changed out there, Roger. People mainly grow tobacco for the foreign companies now, who teach them how and have brought in irrigation of a sort from the Río Motagua, which often doesn't have much water anyway. You see these little sprinkler systems, dancing weeds of water in the dust. So a lot has stayed the same too. The people out there must be even poorer than the Indians in the highlands because the land is so dry, but of course they would never admit it because they're so proud and practically consider themselves Spaniards. Maybe that's why they stay. Much more fertile valleys and plains are so close by, but the dry lands look something like the parts of Spain where only scraggly olive trees grow.

"So the Military C. drove me in his pickup. He was repeating, 'El Negro Puac, El Negro Puac,' as if something might occur to him, though I gardnered that he was just wondering about that Indian name and about me who could not have matched his typical notions of an Indian's daughter, I'm sure. I've learned that in the Izabal region there has always been quite a bit of intermarriage between Kekchis and the Caribs and mulattoes who've migrated in from the coast a bit, and I think that perhaps my father's origins were like that and that was why in Chiquimula he was called El Negro. Though for all I know he came from Honduras or anywhere and Puac was just a name he'd assumed since the Old Woman said that all he told about himself upon arriving in Chiquimula was that he'd worked in the town of Bananera loading banana trains and that his name was Puac. Which the old woman decided must be phony because why would the only tidbits of information El Negro ever gave out about himself be true? She just assumed he must be *huyendo,* on the run from who knows what. No one comes to live in the desert just like that, she said, not a big handsome *mango* like El Negro! She said this with such sudden old lady's gusto I almost blushed with pride. I'll never know, though, who my mother was, or where she came from or who nurtured me in infancy.

"Well, this *vieja,* my ancient oracle, was just there, in an *agua* stand she owns beneath a grove of dusty trees by a whitewashed little bridge over an almost totally dry riverbed. Yes, she certainly did remember El Negro and even his little girl, who'd sold eggs from a basket nearly as big as herself, and then she matter of factly accepted that it really was me (in jumpsuit and shades and baseball cap, picture it) and that, here's the stunner—she'd always believed it possible that it wasn't true that I had died along with my Papito!

"'I died too?' I gasped, from surprise. (Idea for a short story: the possibility that all my life I have been a ghost.) I couldn't help it, I started giggling like a maniac and, oh boy, that sent the MC into hysterics. He was bouncing around on his one good foot chortling, 'You died too! Ja ja ja!' and the old woman looking at me like perhaps I should have. 'No,' I said. '*Disculpe, señora.* It's just that I'm so surprised to hear that!'

"So this was all very weird. She really did seem to have an oracle's memory and omniscience. Which made it extra surprising, and spooky, and rather impressive that she had no recollection nor had she ever even heard of my father's lover, La Gatita. Which proves that he was *muy* tight-lipped and she was *muy muy buena* at sneaking around. Do you recall the man holding a machete on the tile on the wall in our old school library? Well, Roger, wait'll you hear this! It seems I may have some visionary capacities myself, though it is probably more logical to say that machete fights are about the commonest thing going out there and that as a little girl I knew it and it left an impression.

"I know I've told you many times what I remember of that fateful night and the day that followed, and that this all had something to do with Mirabel forbidding me to tell you any more scary or 'immoral' stories. How all I remember was Gatita coming back through the desert in the morning and my father gone, and how she just put me in her car without explaining, drove me all the way to the capital, told me my father was dead but not why or how, and turned me over to the *monjas*. The very first thing those nuns did was take away my sad, torn, red-dotted yellow dress that I loved like my own skin and had worn day after day for who knows how long. Later I saw one of the nuns using it to dust the pedestals of the saints in the chapel. Folded up, it fit into her hand like a sponge, the last visible evidence of my old life I ever saw until just a few days ago, when I finally ventured my return. Perhaps I should say next to last. The hard, callused soles of my peasant girl's feet dissolved too (in this, my first incarnation, my first layer of skin, I was a peasant girl! How easily one ceases to be one!), and I grew the soft feet of a convent girl, but this mysterious process I don't remember so well.

"Anyway"—

I should explain more fully here just what it was that Flor had told me so many times about what she remembered of that fateful night and following day.

By the time I was in the second grade and Flor was in the third, our conversational compatibility had greatly improved, unimpeded even by the school administrators, who had called my parents in for a special meeting to tell them that if Flor and I were to progress, then only English should be spoken at home, especially between the two of us. Several times a week we'd each be released from our respective classrooms for separate private sessions with a special education specialist who was determined to correct our accents:

"Say *mother*."

"*mudhair*"—because of my much younger age I eventually progressed much more rapidly at this than did Flor and by the end of elementary school would be speaking with a prolish Boston accent almost as strong and some would say as ugly as my father's.

Back then we spent most of our time together in the basement after school, Flor doing laundry and ironing or studying vocabulary flash cards and listening to the radio, me always hovering close by. Who else did she have to talk to, to practice her English with every afternoon? Maybe I'd also just reached an age, as well as a natural level of intimacy with Flor, where I could be a responsive and comprehending enough listener. We often broke the school's rule anyway, though Flor tried not to.

So this was when she first began to tell me about her father and La Gatita. The old woman in the letter remembered El Negro as a handsome man, and so always had Flor, though she hadn't seen him since she was six. "He was a very, *very* handsome man," she liked to say, in English.

But eventually Flor found a more exact way of describing him. Because on occasional weekend afternoons my mother would take us into Boston to see Mexican movies in mysterious places that weren't really movie theaters where we sat in folding chairs, and from where, the show over, we'd always tromp outside into a wintry dusk and the oblivious Boston streets feeling lonely and strangely, joylessly united in a way that we never did when we'd only gone shopping.

Flor decided that her father had looked just like a Mexican revolutionary in a movie, with skin the color of roasted coffee and blue-black hair and always needing a shave. A hard-muscled, hard-featured, and seemingly hard-hearted man, with eyes doing a constant slow burn, and who treated her with a terse, distant affection that of course filled her with love—

"—that of course filled me utterly, *utterly* with love," that's how Flor told it to Moya that long-ago night in the Fo Lu Shu II, her nearly whispering, all-pervading voice extinguishing the restaurant chatter and usurping the radio music. Moya was astonished by her carefully elaborating and unsentimental gravity, the sudden surge of near elation in her "utterly, utterly" and the way it had seemed to suddenly cast a spell, making the rum bottle and filled glasses and even the ice glow with colors that seemed to come from the timbre of her voice alone instead of the pastel paper lanterns and the butane torches in the scarlet-and-gold dragon-guarded patio. Moya asked, "Did he at all resemble you? Puac, this is an Indian name, was he Indian?" Flor mused over this for a moment, then repeated the information found in her letter to Roger about the interracial nature of the coastal departments; Moya, by the way, with a seagoing father and his father's seagoing father born in Puerto Barrios to mothers who themselves were the ambiguous offspring of mothers who for generations had intermingled with banana-boat loaders, sailors from everywhere, and North American fruit company clerks, shares that heritage. It is likely that Moya and Flor each have, had, an unquantifiable share of both Indian and even African blood along with Spanish-Moorish and who knows what else, *vos?*

Flor took a sip of her rum, smiled, and said, "I guess I've never thought of him as Indian because he seemed so big. But I was so little!"

Flor's father was peasant poor despite his mythic good looks, but La Gatita, his lover, must have had some money. Flor remembered her only as that, Gatita, little cat, but said she was thin, not little, in fact she was a few inches taller than El Negro. She used to drive over in the middle of the night in a dirty white convertible with a red top. And she had, said Flor, the whitest skin possible and straight black hair like an Indian and ash yellow eyes, big *gata* eyes, of course. Was she beautiful? She was strange, languid, very quiet, rarely smiling or speaking, but her nails and lipstick were always bright red. Flor thought she smelled like slightly soured milk. *"Micita de trapos,"* La Gatita used to call her, Little Rag Monkey. She even bought Flor a new dress that she refused to wear because it felt hot as an iron under the sun—not that Flor had ever yet seen an iron—and made of cardboard compared with the ripped, nearly worn to gauze, red-dotted and yellow dress that she'd worn day after day for almost as long as she could remember. We used to wonder if La Gatita could have been her mother but always decided that we didn't think so.

"—How can you be sure?" asked Moya.

"Intuitively," said Flor, "and rationally too, especially now. That old woman told me my father and I hadn't always lived in the desert, right? So was I conceived, born, in Bananera? Is my name really Puac? I don't know! Bet not, though. There's no record of a Flor de Mayo being born to a Puac in Bananera. You don't think I've checked? So maybe I was registered under my mother's name, who the hell knows, who says she and Papito were ever married? Gatita, I'm pretty sure, *was* married. Anyway, I don't smell like sour milk."

Flor's father would stay outside with Gatita in the hammock that was tied to one beam of a small wire chicken coop and to their one skinny cashew tree, and they'd leave the car radio on—that was probably the part my mother considered immoral—while Flor slept inside on the pile of cornhusk-stuffed grain sacks on a dirt floor that was their only bed. Then she'd wake with the last roosters and her father snoring beside her and smelling of slightly soured milk and of his own strong sweat, which in the sunrise heat always made the traces of lipstick still on his face dissolve into rosy little puddles.

But one dawn her fiither wasn't there beside her. When Flor looked outside, the car was, its radio still on, but the hammock was empty and they were both gone. Just that was an unpredictable enough event. She waited for what probably only seemed like hours. Suddenly Gatita came back alone through the desert looking like she'd spent a week wandering in it, and the very next thing Flor knew she was in Gatita's car, speeding through dirt clouds and then along the coastal highway. That was when she told Flor that her father was dead. Two or three times Gatita told her. What Flor always remembered was staring sullenly at the red dashboard, her hands folded in her lap, telling herself that she must be lying— Flor was only six!—or that a *duende* had possessed Gatita for the chance of stealing a little girl away. But Gatita was sporadically sobbing, looking sometimes as if she was about to take a frenzied, gagging bite out of the steering wheel . . .

Flor had never been out of Chiquimula that she could remember, but now they were on such a long and terrifying ride, climbing higher into the cold air of the mountains, fire-breathing trucks hurtling right at them down both of the cratered highway's lanes—she'd squeeze her eyes shut and, opening them again, discover that she was still alive, the trucks miraculously behind. Flor felt comatose with weightlessness and shock by the time they reached the flat, sprawling capital, and she'd already caught a cold from her too sudden ascension into the new and germy climate. Lost in the noisy delirium and smog, Gatita had to drive in circles for hours, it seemed, before she finally found the convent orphanage on the Avenida Simeón Cañas. There, in the parked car, Gatita, without a word, pulled a wedding ring from her purse and slipped it on. Which forever puzzled us, because it seemed that the opposite gesture might have been more appropriate, that is, for Gatita to have taken her ring off if she'd been wearing it before delivering a new orphan to a nuns' orphanage.

But what difference did it make either way?

"All it proves," Flor used to say, "is that Papito used to make her take off her ring when she came to see *him*."

Then La Gatita held Flor's hand and walked her in through the grated black iron gates and through the jacaranda-shaded small outer yard that was decorated with plaster statuettes of painted toadstools and grotesque laughing gnomes with long beards and pointy red Alpine caps, this being the nuns' idea of a toddlers' playground. There Flor stayed seven years, until Abuelita came and picked her to be our maid in Namoset.

"So this is what happened on the fateful night," wrote Flor in her letter, "according to the benign old oracle of the soda stand. Ours was a worthless piece of land, a piecrust made of baked dirt and so far from the river that to get water for us and our chickens my father at night would carry a pail across the desert to the nearest little *finca,* which belonged to a man named Soto who had only a small half-starved herd of cattle but a well, and from this well my father would pilfer water. This Soto had apparently been not much bothered by that, but he died and his son, who'd been working as a cowboy on Coronel Arana's huge ranch in Izabal, came and took it over. The old woman said that this *hijo de* Soto warned my father away from his well, though there's no verifying that now. But he caught my father taking water from it that night while Gatita waited in the hammock and with a machete decapitated him. Which, according to the seemingly lawless but actually quite strict and macho code of the desert, was a legitimate defense of property. Even if he had not warned my father, which I cannot believe he did, since it does seem my father was taken by complete surprise.

"When the old woman told me this, the mystery of my father's existence and death partially solved after so many years of, well of not exactly brooding on it but one does want to know these things, I almost had another fit of the giggles. I had to bite the inside of my cheek and think of something I'm accustomed to thinking of as sad (La Pobre Petrona, who always makes me sad). Remember how furious you used to get with me at serious movies, Roger, when your hero would get shot or something and I would have a laughing fit? That was during our first years together, and you thought I was so ignorant at times. What an uproar you caused when Ira and Mirabel took us to the drive-in to see *Von Ryan's Express* and at the end, when Frank Sinatra was shot in the back chasing his train and fell facedown on the tracks, I could not stop giggling.

"Of course my poor decapitated father was what Gatita had not wanted me to see or even know of. What an extraordinary and fast decision that woman made! Though it seems that perhaps in some deep down inner eye I somehow knew it anyway. It's not hard to gardner why Gatita, whoever she actually was, could not have taken me to live with her. By whisking me off to the nuns, she saved me from a truly awful fate, I am sure. As well as to your *abuelita,* I owe her everything! Who was she? Where could La Gatita possibly be now? I'm sure I would recognize her.

"So there were certain ironic complexities behind the blank-faced, I imagine, cheek-biting silence with which I returned the oracle's cataracted gaze. And she went on. When everyone saw that I had vanished, she said, they suspected that Señor Soto Hijo had hacked me to bits and buried me in far apart places, because people began to say they could hear me crying at night from several places in the desert all at once. But the old woman said she'd never heard it and so didn't completely believe it, and that those other people were probably just hearing baby hyenas and fantasizing.

"Of course, hacking up a little girl and strewing her about was considered repugnant behavior even in Chiquimula, and people spoke of avenging me and even ostracized poor Señor Soto Junior, who was, after all, innocent of any 'crime.' But the old woman certainly believes in my father's ghost. She says people have seen him in the blue light before dawn, you know, walking across the desert all the way to the river with a pail in his hand, trying to undo his fatal mistake. *Pues,* poor Papito, no?

"She said people call him El Sed now, the Thirst, and that they even leave tortillas and cups of coffee for him at night along his route and find them taken in the morning. Do you believe this? And the *comisionado* suddenly exclaimed, 'Oh him! El Sed. *Claro!* So that's El Negro Puac!' though later he said, *'Esas viejas* with their ghosts, they live in their mothers' centuries still. I don't believe any of it. Do you? *Yo no!* Though my mother . . .'" blah blah blah

"Señor Soto the Younger, you shall be happy to hear, was long ago riding in the back of a pickup fill of drunken MLN party militants on their way back from one of their fascist rallies in Esquipulas and it ffipped over. Earth receive an honored guest, Señor Soto Hijo laid to rest. His farm was taken over by a tobacco company, and the family who live where we used to now work in the fields there and live in a hut made of coarse boards standing up in the dirt, much like ours, though theirs is uglier, perhaps because my father saw to it that ours was neatly palm thatched and their roof is just more boards. The MC, rather a nice man actually, drove me there, returning to his chant of 'El Negro, El Negro,' and shaking his head profoundly. 'That's the way it happens,' he said. 'That's why they call it Guatemala's Wild West out here.' You know, even though it's in the East. I looked out at my old 'yard' from the pickup, didn't even get out. No more chicken coop, not even a trace of it, even the cashew tree is gone. Saw a couple of little kids standing around with just T-shirts pulled tight over their malnourished potbellies. Sometimes I used to go around with not even that much on, I'm afraid (we had no Evangelical Fundamentalists in the neighborhood then), the desert air my robe, the entire desert my diaper, until I was old enough to get what must have been my first dress, which was followed by the dress I mentioned earlier. And we always had enough to eat. I made our tortillas, and often there was something more. Gatita probably gave Papito money. Later the MC tried to put a move on me, but I threatened to stomp on his wounded foot if he didn't drive me directly to the bus and he laughed like a big macho house on fire and called me *pícara* and said that we *'pueblerinas'* from the desert never lose our scorpion sting *o algo así*. He waited with me for the bus, and when it came it was time for a Hollywood movie—ending witticism, something on the order of your adorable, when you were so nice to see me off at the airport before I came down here, 'Delta's ready when *you* are, Flor.' (No one ever gets why I thought that was so funny, I must have giggled in the air all the way here.)

"So I said, what else, *'Viva El Sed,'* and he laughed and said, *'Viva* El Negro. I am your friend forever.' Awww.

"It's getting chilly. I've been sitting on the patio of the Café Fiori, the place with the great cappuccinos and where all the private school boys and girls come after school? They've gone home for dinner now. Guess I'll walk home, sit out on my balcón tonight, and listen for far-off gunshots and squealing death-squad tires. Lovely. And yet, life is not really like that, is it? Not sure how long I'll be staying, it's conceivable I'm nuts enough to linger on quite awhile longer. So, are you really liking living in Nueva Jork? It will be fun, the two of us hanging out in the same city again when I get back. So glad you're finally turning into an adult, 'sort of.' I must say I miss you at the Tropical Room; you're the empty space at the end of every conga line.

"Adios, y con tanto Amor,
PUEBLERINA"

When I showed that letter to Moya in Pastelería Hemniings, he read it through without a word, then ran his fingers over the top page as if trying to smooth its neat creases and glanced at his fingertips as if checking to see if any of the ink had come off. He looked at me and said,

"She seems more sad about her dress than about her father."

"Well, it was such a long time ago," I said. "Like she says, another incarnation. My father was more like her real father."

"Chickens also truly touched something deep inside her, from back in that time, *vos.*"

I watched him keep a long, straight face—Guatemalans! This Guat irony on top of irony, whole indecipherable jungles of it hiding their raw, disturbed hearts.

He scanned the letter again.

"I like this," he said, "where she says that chopping up a little girl is repugnant behavior *even* in Guatemala."

"Even in Chiquimula, you mean."

"That's where you can see that Flor had an education," he said. "It was a fraudulent election *even* for Guatemala. Basest corruption, *even* for Guatemala. A repugnant murder, *even* for Guatemala. Just this one little word, *vos,* and we are weighed exactly."

In our basement in Namoset, in the unremodeled part where the utility sink and my father's workbench were and where in winter the heat from the furnace was just enough to keep icicles from forming along the poured concrete walls and naked insulation-stuffed ceiling rafters, Flor usually had laundry to do after school.

Back then we didn't have a washing machine or dryer. Clothes were hung to dry by the furnace or were carried out through the bulkhead into the backyard when the weather was warm. Ironing she did in her bedroom, which faced the playroom across a divide that was no less real for being invisible.

Flor's room became almost like a stage set, I watched her in it for so long, though of course so much that I didn't see happened there too; but it's almost as if I ought to be able to evoke her life in that room as if it was all one play: ". . . In the second act a German shepherd named Klink suddenly appeared, sitting on Flor's bed with sphinx paws and steeple ears. When, towards the end of that act, Flor made love to Tony for the first or second time, Klink was the only witness, and kept her secret until the end."

Most of the furniture had previously belonged to my already grown Graetz cousins and was there waiting for Flor the night of her first terrified descent into the basement: a bed with a white-enameled headboard decorated with pink roses and a matching dresser—in later years Flor would pray-paint both a glittery color called amber sunrise—a green pear–colored bedspread, a standing brass lamp with a warm orange shade, a glossy red desk. Maids' rooms don't often come equipped with desks, but my father must have thought no one could do without one.

Sometime during that first winter, when I was still quarantined in the living room upstairs, Flor discovered the shoe box on the shelf over my father's workbench where he kept his garden flower and vegetable seed packets. She secretly coveted those seed packets for months, so much so that in later years her coveting and the patience with which she waited for her chance to possess them came to symbolize her own innocent immigrant's wide-eyed greed even to herself. Alone, she would take the shoe box down and spread the seed packets out to gaze at the color pictures of flowers and vege-tables with the same exasperated longing a deprived boy might lavish on someone else's baseball cards. The simple logic of asking my father outright if he might please keep the seeds in something else so that she could have the packets of course eluded her.

Flor had already heard my mother joke about how my father seemed undecided over whether to turn our small yard on Codrioli Road into a farm or a forest, so excessive was his annual springtime mania for planting new trees, flower beds, and vegetable gardens. Using her Spanish-English dictionary, she labored at constructing the sentences she imagined would be necessary, and waited. In late March dump trucks arrived, depositing small mountains of rich wormy loam and peat moss on our front lawn.

One day soon after, Flor spotted my father carrying the shoe box full of seed packets out through the bulkhead door, and she followed him into the yard and stood quietly behind while he, on his knees, dug into the earth around the shrubbery in front of the house with a small hand shovel. The first seed packet he chose he tore open across the middle, decapitating the pansies depicted on the cover. Flor gasped so loudly he turned around with a worried look.

"Please, Ira, I like pictures flowers. May I have?" said Flor, speaking methodically and slowly.

Then from her pocket Flor pulled a pair of scissors. My father looked at her in confusion for a moment, then burst out in laughter that made Flor's face burn. "Of course, Floorie! Of course!"

But he only needed one more seed packet that afternoon, and let Flor cut it open carefully across the top with the scissors, and then let her keep it.

"*Ay gracias! Gracias!* Thank you, Ira!"

But she was privately disappointed that it was only one seed packet, and of pansies, not her favorite. Still, she went into her room and taped it to the wall over her desk.

My father must have seen it there. A few days later he came home with a whole manila envelope full of both common and exotic flower seed packets that he'd bought at a special nursery in Chestnut Hill for the express purpose of taking them to work with him that day, where with a penknife he cut tiny slivers in each packet's seam, and then poured the seeds into common mailing envelopes, which he labeled by hand if he thought he might use them later, or poured them out into the wastepaper basket if he knew that, lacking his own tropical flower greenhouse, he wouldn't. There were two dozen emptied seed packets in all.

Flor was stupefied by his generosity.

"I tell you," she'd say in later years, "it was as if he'd been growing a secret garden for me all that time just to make me happy. I understood why Mirabel had married Ira once and for all."

The twenty-five seed packets ended up taped in a five-by-five square to the wall over Flor's desk—the central spot went to the one depicting red, heart-shaped, yellow-stamened anthuriums, one of her favorite Guatemalan flowers—where they stayed for several years, until they began to fade and curl and she transferred them to the same scrapbook where she kept the reddest maple leaves from our biannual trips to Dartmouth.

Also in that room was the small table that her plastic radio and later her record player shared with a makeshift religious shrine: colored postcards representing the Virgin and the Sacred Heart, her little plastic scapularies. Attached to the wall behind it was the gaudy plastic crucifix she'd bought with her first saved-up earnings, with its impaled Christ on a lid that could slide open, revealing candles inside, a small vial of holy water, a sacred scrap of cloth. Here Flor did her evening patemosters and rosaries, her Gloria Patris, raptly whispering with sidelong smiling glances at me that became more and more frequent and comical as the grip her convent education had on her gradually began, inevitably I think, given the place and the era, to soften.

* * *

"—Mirabel and Ira are both wonderful people," Flor told Moya on the Long Night of White Chickens. "But to be perfectly honest about it—Hey! This is none of your business, Moya, really, the stuff you're worming out of me. Anyway, if they'd never met, where would I be now?"

"Here, *pues*."

"Oh no," she said. "More likely in Europe, a Spanish ambassador's servant."

"*Noooo . . .*"

"*Síííí*, that's if I was lucky. Spanish ambassadors had this thing about hiring Espíritu Santo girls, supposedly we made the best servants . . . But if Ira and Mirabel had never met, you would never have met Roger."

"And you would not have come to our meeting tonight."

"Well, that goes without saying."

"But destiny would have found another way for us to have met."

"You mean you would have been, what? A Spanish ambassador's gardener?"

"Yes, bringing you flowers every day!"

"I didn't want flowers. I wanted seed packets."

She told Moya then the story of her seed packets.

"Wasn't there a mayflower in your collection?" asked Moya when she was done.

"That's just any flower that sprouts in May, an anemone, for instance. I guess Papito named me that so I'd have a way of remembering my birthday after he was gone, like he foresaw it all, no? There's a girl in my orphanage whose parents named her Aspirina, imagine."

"She must have been a terrible headache."

"Hah hah. Or cured one. Can't let a kid go through life called Aspirin, though. Well, she was only an infant. She's Magali now."

"A pretty name. So you are a *benevolent* tyrant."

"A tyrant! Oh no, is that what you've heard?" And she smiled too brightly, showing her gums.

Moya's comment had aroused her suspicions in a new way. *Was* she aware that people did not always speak kindly about her, to say the least? But Moya had no desire to discomfort her now. Frantically his mind searched for a remedy. Then he remembered an English rhyme from his early Colegio Anne Hunt days and recited it:

"Old Mother Hubbard lived in a shoe. She had so many children she did not know what to do."

Flor's luminous dark eyes scrutinized his face, and, perhaps because she finally liked or at least trusted what she saw there, her smile relaxed.

"So what did she do?"

". . . *Pues,*" stammered Moya. "I don't remember."

"Mother Hubbard lived in a *cupboard,* Moya."

"You know what Doña Emilia told me right there in the mother superior's office?" exclaimed Flor, referring to Roger's *abuela* and the day she came to choose her; this was somewhat later in the Long Night, when she'd already from so much rum just begun to slightly slur her words. "She said, 'Now, Flor de Mayo, it is time for honest talk. I have reason to believe that God is angry at my daughter. As for the little boy, my firstborn grandson, I am worried that even his Guardian Angel will forsake him. I have been told that you may not be absolutely the most devout girl here, but that you are one of the brightest and stubbornnest, and that you have a laughing heart. So I am sending you to Boston to be bright, stubborn, and happy for me but above all for God. I want you to make sure that boy grows up a Catholic. This should not be difficult, he is very affectionate and, right now, truly lonely. I am not asking you to make him a priest. He has already been baptized, thank God. If he had not been, I think that would be the hardest thing.'

"That's what she said, Moya, just like that. Then she tried to explain to me what a Jew is. Was I scared or what? A Jew? *What did we know from Jews!*" Flor almost shouted, in English, her simultaneous laughter making her voice squeal, while her exaggerated accent was one that Moya had, in fact, heard some gringas speak naturally—such hearty, playful laughter caused Moya a brief pang of envy, followed by another of warm admiration.

"Listen, we had nuns that taught Jews as metaphors for evil, OK?" she went on. "Well, you know how it is here. Go up to an Indian town and tell them you're a Jew—not that I ever have, of course—and they look at you like you're out of your mind, or with terror, because they, some of them anyway, think the last Jews walked the earth a thousand years ago and only come back as devils, with actual tails, no less. Or they think Jews are what make volcanoes rumble, that they were imprisoned inside volcanoes as punishment for the crucifixion and there they remain. *This Jew,* Doña Emilia told me, has the heart of Job. He has suffered as much. My gosh, I was half-expecting Ira to be this poor guy covered in boils and sores. Then she said maybe I could save *his* soul too, and she and Sor Isabel just smiled at each other, like, Oh yes, wouldn't *that* be wonderful.

"That was that, she hired me, said she'd need a week to fix my papers. I was so sad and terrified that night that I couldn't sleep or stop crying. One of the other girls took me out into the yard behind the kitchen, woke up a chicken, and, you know, holding it like this, rubbed it up and down my body."

"*Qué raro,*" said Moya, watching Flor lean back in her chair as she waved her hands cradling nothing up and down in front of her chest.

"Well, this was a cure for fright. Though this was against the rules, such superstitions, of course."

"Did it work?"

"*Claro!* We were laughing so much and trying not to so the nuns wouldn't wake up, and this squawking, shitting hen. It was completely hilarious."

Both Flor and Moya had a good laugh over that. Flor poured herself a little bit more rum, squeezed *limón* into it, and took a bite from a long-cooled wonton.

"Of course this is not unusual, that an *abuela* would be concerned about this," said Moya. "But Rogerio is not religious, is he?"

"Ohhhh, I failed," said Flor. "He'd watch me do my rosaries and stuff, and I'd be thinking, I am putting on a show, but this isn't supposed to be like a show. I got myself so mixed up, Moya. None of the priests in Namoset spoke Spanish. I kept waiting for a miracle, for the Holy Spirit or the Virgin to speak to me in any language, but it was like they'd lost the trail of my soul in the snow. And I loved Ira so much I was practically waiting for him to invite me to be Jewish, you know? And what was I supposed to do on weekends, give up my Harvard football trips? Forget it! Eventually I just kind of said, Oh well, God forgot me. If he can't sniff me out here, it is because my faith is not strong."

"A theology of smells?" said Moya. "I see, true faith is always unwashed."

"Hmm-hmm," singsonged Flor, "*very* medieval. Though later me and Roger both really got into *Jesus Christ Superstar* for a while."

"But soon you fell in love with sin," said Moya, with jesting humor of course.

"Hah! That came later." And now Flor smiled with a disarming touch of bashfulness. "Ohhh, come on, I was a good girl. Most of the time."

* * *

Flor was pretty schizophrenic about religion, to say nothing of my own early and never quite resolved confusion. But there was desert anarchy and near paganism in Flor's early unreligious upbringing. And I think that wild empty space, that small desert world inside of her, was merely surrounded by her seven years in the convent orphanage; it was an outer layer of sorts but one she felt compelled to live in too, her second incarnation. Later love plunged her back into the small wild place: Flor gave herself to Tony—in the Namoset woods, just once in her basement room when no one else was at home, she'd finally tell me in later years—like a young desert girl who has never learned anything about making love except that everyone around her seemed to consider it a great and necessary joy. Then guilt and caution overtook her, and she made him wait nearly a year to do it again. But Tony was still a year or two in the future.

If in the desert Flor had barely even understood the need for clothes until she was four or so, seven years with the nuns had left her self-conscious enough. We almost always returned after school to an empty house, and I'd follow Flor right down into the basement, where I'd camouflage myself with mundane idleness in the playroom, shuffling over to my toy chest or turning on the television, while she changed out of her school clothes. Her back to me while she held her checked-flannel laundry shirt ready in one hand, she'd pull her dress off over her head with a sudden dolphinlike upward thrust of both arms: the sudden baring of smooth, cinnamon brown skin, black hair tumbling down around gracefully bladed shoulders, the slender arch of her long back and sapling waist, her high, rounded rear in girl's underpants, her pretty fourteen-year-old's legs taking a few steps in place; from behind like that, for those few seconds when she was almost naked, I always thought Flor looked just like Pocahontas. Next she'd have to disentangle her arms from the dress and then her shirt from it too. She'd toss the dress underhanded onto her bed and quickly dip one skinny arm down one shirtsleeve, then lean forward while her torso turned and her other arm reached across the small of her back to pull the checked-flannel curtain closed . . . Sometimes, in winter, she'd add another flannel shirt over the one she'd just put on. Then she'd don the oldest clothes she owned, which she wore only for housework now, the droopy sweater and skirt of her convent orphanage uniform. Sitting on the bed and facing me again, she'd smile as if saying hello, pull off her knee socks or tights, and in winter replace them with a pair of long, woolen, red ski socks that she tied on with shoelaces just above the knees.

Dressed for battle, she'd attack the laundry—or any of her household chores—with an energy that looked like enthusiasm and seemed to suggest she'd been born for nothing else, and always with the radio on, her voice evaporating when she tried to sing along to the higher notes, the sleeves of her sweater and shirt rolled up and her arms plunged into suds, her hair falling over her eyes and dabbed back with quick, sudsy taps of her fingers.

I still had a tubercular child invalid's absorption in all that was immediately around me, for I'd discovered that the basement, after a quarantine year of living above it and not even fully realizing it was there, seemed more full of possibilities and fascinations, especially with Flor in it, than all outdoors, where everybody basically hated me anyway. Building rudimentary Rube Goldberg contraptions out of whatever was at hand became a yearlong obsession. They were all theoretically designed to execute Flor, and she was my willing accomplice, holding the stepladder for me if I needed to climb up to some hard-to-reach place and so on. I remember running upstairs to fish the white lace mantilla my mother had married in from the plastic pouch in a bottom drawer of her dresser, where she kept my tiny, fake-pearl-brocaded baptism pajamas too. Downstairs I draped the mantilla over Flor's head while she sat patiently in my red wagon in her laundry uniform, her red-stockinged knees up and her arms wrapped around them. Then I explained that I was going to give the wagon a push and that it was going to roll into the T-shaped system of two-by-fours I'd laid out on the floor, knocking the stem of the T into the overturned laundry basket that had a metal bucket on top with a mop handle standing up in it, the mop handle suspended by string from a pine board balanced between two rafters, that board lashed by more string to another board positioned just over where the wagon carrying Flor was destined to stop, a Dixie Cup full of powdered ant poison balanced at its very edge.

"OK?"

"Bueno, mi vida," she said, looking extremely happy to be taking a break from laundry to go to her death in my mother's wedding mantilla.

I offered her one of my mother's Kents. She put it in her mouth and looked at me expectantly.

"Make a last wish."

"Just that you give me a little kiss good-bye," she said.

I gave her a kiss on the corner of her lips with both my hands on her cheeks, stood back, commanded her to cross herself, which she did, and then I bent over and shoved the wagon off with as much force as I could and watched as it slowly rolled forward while Flor, the back of her head covered by white lace, waved good-bye over her shoulder. I was already cringing with my eyes half shut and shouting "No!" when the wagon came to a complete stop a few feet short of the two-by-fours that were to set the demonic contraption in motion. Flor looked back at me over her shoulder with the unlit cigarette still in her mouth and a sorry expression, and then she pulled one foot out of the wagon, deliberately set it on the floor, looked at me a moment longer, and gave a hard push.

Everything happened more or less as it was supposed to though much less noisily, causing just enough commotion to nudge the paper cup of ant poison off the end of the board: spilling hardly anything, it plummeted to the floor, landing well behind Flor and off to the side, causing no more mess than a snowball.

"—I know this is ridiculous, but you know what I keep wondering?" said Flor, returning to the subject of her father, while a beguiled and already exhausted by longing and listening Moya leaned forward to position his head as close to hers as possible while she almost imperceptibly leaned closer too, a slow progress he'd been following as if by a nocturnal sundial: for some time the slightly curled ends of her hair falling in front of her right shoulder had remained suspended approximately four centimeters over the sweet and sour sauce bowl, but now that distance had been reduced by half. Now her ultimate tendrils were so close that even laughter or a sneeze might propel them briefly down to graze the surface of the sticky, lava-colored sauce. Moya's plan was already formulated: when she had leaned forward enough so that her hair had definitely descended into the bowl, he was going to say, "Flor, look, your hair is in the *agridulce* sauce!" Then he was going to take her hair in his hand and wipe it clean with a napkin or maybe he'd bring it to his lips and . . .

She said, "Do you think I have an obligation or something to hide myself somewhere along El Sed's route and wait for him to come along some night? *Hombre, imagínate,* here comes my father's ghost. Moya, what would I say? Papito, here I am, Flor de Mayo, all grown up and gringafied now? Oh, poor Papito, let me carry your pail. Won't you tell me who my mamita was?"

TEN

Here is the other of Flor's most significant two letters, which arrived postmarked from Guatemala one month after her final visit to New York, almost four months before that final seventeenth of February, 1983. It was the next to last written communication I received from her, not counting her annual Los Quetzalitos Christmas card. It began with a "Dear Roger" and then just plunged in:

"Maybe you are never so involved with a lover, so full of a sense of dramatic discovery about your lover, as during the days when you are trying to work up the decisiveness to leave him. Sensing the end, you begin to pull away, and resent him all the more because he makes it so difficult for you to finalize the break. In a way, I have come to realize, you don't live *in* a small country so much as *with it,* in a way comparable to how you might find yourself sharing your life with a not necessarily complex but completely involving and painfully demanding person. You pick up habits, gestures, and deeper attitudes. One day this relationship can end, and you will go your own way, but what you've picked up might remain a part of you forever, and no one who doesn't know that country personally will recognize these traits in you at all. Thus, in New York, someone well might say, 'Why, how very French of you' or how German, Japanese, or Russian, but how many people there will ever say, 'Flor, how very Guatemalan of you,' when faced, for example, with my strangely caustic delight over a news story about a wealthy young Colombian bridegroom honeymooning in New York who, while his virgin bride prepared herself for the consummation of their marriage in the bathroom of their luxurious hotel suite, jumped up and down on the bed out of happiness and anticipation. Jumped up and down so much, you see, from so much happiness and anticipation, that he became dizzy, lost his balance, and fell through the window that he'd apparently pushed the bed up against so that they could bask in the drama of the imperial view during the consummation. Eighteen stories he plummeted, dressed only in his leopard-patterned bikini briefs, gold crucifix, and Cartier watch, to his death on Park Avenue.

"Many *guatemaltecos* had the chance to laugh or sigh with caustic or lamenting delight over that story when it was picked up from a North American wire service and prominently featured in the country's most popular paper. But that same day's *New York Times* made no mention of it. I didn't see the *New York Post,* of course, but I would guess that if they did report it they stressed the possible suicide or murder angle. Perhaps they would have discovered that the Colombian bridegroom came from a loutish drug cartel family and the bride from a distinguished one fallen on hard economic times and for that or perhaps other reasons would not have been as inclined as the Guatemalans to take at face value the bride's story of how as she prepared herself in the bathroom she could hear the bedsprings bouncing. Perhaps this is simply a question of cultural aesthetics or even morality, the type of story each culture prefers. I happen to know that the North American wire service report not only made no mention of the social standing of the newlyweds' respective families, they didn't mention what the groom was wearing as he plunged to his death either, nor what the bride heard as she prepared herself or said later. In fact, there was no mention of the bride's actual activities before the fatal free-till at all. The wire service merely told that a young Colombian honeymooner had fallen to his death from the window of an elegant hotel in New York City, but an enterprising Guatemalan newspaperman had embellished those details in a way that his countrymen would especially appreciate. I am always surprised whenever a visiting foreigner expresses the opinion that we are a dour bunch with no sense of humor at all.

"So you can end up hating a small country just as you would a person. You cannot hate the United States, can you, with that sort of intensity without seeming a blind demagogue or extremist or plainly maladjusted—isn't the United States just too big, too full of situations and choices? (Needless to say, I have some not at all well-traveled Guatemalan friends who would disagree.) You live *in* the United States, amidst it, surrounded by it, and yet somehow always way off to the side with almost everyone else, spun out by a great centrifugal force, by that muscular, naked Idea of our Greatness holding the rest of us by the tail and spinning: the blur has become our nearsighted and *so* controversial focus. (Notice my slippery possessives: *my* Guate, *my* USA.) But isn't it true that certain abstractly peripatetic French philosophers count among our blessings particularly what so many prominent Latin American intellectuals denounce? Our theoretically blissful amnesia, our nation of Mr. Magoos driving through our neon Mojave of perpetually new *new*. Is that really the world I dispatch some of my quite historically prefaced orphans into? Is that more harmful than what the other side of the ocean offers them? Who am I to pass such judgments? But don't I remain here now because I trust myself to decide better than anyone else? Better to rely on the providential handshake and love springing to life in baby breath—charmed eyes than on eeny meeny miney mo, *cacara macara títere fue,* you to Sweden, you to Ohio, ho ho ho . . . ?

"You cannot really love the United States with the same focused particularity and compassion you might feel towards a small country either. You would not ever sum up your understanding of the United States over a cup of coffee or two and then find yourself weeping over it. Directing a black bitter laugh at the United

States, is this not like spitting into a rain cloud? Shouting *I love the USA* is not much more poignant than standing up and waving a big Stars and Stripes at a televised sporting event. *Triste*—this is much too flea sized a word to ever apply to the United States. Guatemala is bottomless grief in a demitasse. "That's really all I've been trying to say.

"Listen, the city is so silent tonight, and a cool steady wind, like a minstral"—I guess that here Flor meant mistral, the steady wind that blows out of North Africa across the Mediterranean, unless she meant minstrel, or else an intentional evocation of both—"is fanning the leaves outside. If the wind is headed in the right direction, then it might carry into hearing range the roars and growls of the jaguars and lions in the zoo, which is less than a mile away. The jaguars from our jungles, mythological to the Maya, the lions from Africa. They wake up in their cramped cages roaring for their breakfasts of raw horse meat or in grief over their shattered dreams of jungle empires, and sometimes the wind will carry it here. Some of the children, when they hear it, talk of nothing else the next day. I more quietly share their enthrallment. But we take them frequently to the zoo, where we hear and see these animals up close. So it is this wind, liberating and blending the roars of Guatemalan jaguars and African lions into 'last night's' single enchanted *tigre,* that seems magical."

Moya, glassy eyed as if from sleeplessness and his eyebrows raised, softly said, "Yes. This one. *Excelente, vos. Muy poética,*" when I confronted him with this letter in Pastelería Hemmings. His hand movements became a little jerky, touching saucer, cup, tabletop, teaspoon; he briefly and gingerly stroked his ear, straightened in his chair, and stuck out his chin, looking at me with pursed lips. I'd never seen him so disarmed.

"It's this bit about that reporter writing for the most popular newspaper that threw me," I said. I'd thought that meant the obvious Guatemalan daily, and Moya writes for *El Minuto,* a low-circulation broadsheet of never more than twelve pages owned by the extremely respectable Batres family. But the family really makes their money from *¿Dónde?* by far the most popular "newspaper" in the country, but it isn't a daily, and the Batres name appears nowhere in its pages. *¿Dónde?* comes out once a week and blankets the country at ten *centavos* a copy and to say that it's a Guatemalan *National Enquirer* is definitely an offense to the editorial standards of the latter. The paper specializes in the sensational, which isn't to say it evades the everyday reality. HE RAISED HIS GLASS IN A TOAST AND THE ROOF CAME DOWN ON HIS HEAD—the headline of a story on a man whose housewarming party ended with a fatal roof collapse. Infants born with frog heads, doctored photos to prove it, lots of that kind of thing. Instead of running a picture of a dead student's shoes, it's more likely to offer a close-up of his torture-smashed face—the Guatemala City firemen whose job it is to drive around the city at dawn picking up bodies make money on the side selling photographs of these victims to *¿Dónde?*—above hysterical prose lamenting yet another *ola negra* of violence sweeping over the country, further proof of God's displeasure with the prevailing amorality of the nation or something like that, and blaming no one else. Whenever Moya finds himself in a difficult situation at *El Minuto,* whenever he's written something that, however oblique, has still caused death threats like demented snakes to come slithering across the city to *El Minuto's* door, or has merely provoked phone calls to Celso Batres from the usual hyperventilating chorus of irate or curious military officers and prominent rightists seeking clarification, Celso Batres protectively banishes Moya to a pseudonymous byline in the pages of the scandal sheet until things have blown over. It was in *¿Dónde?* that

Moya embellished the wire service report of the bridegroom's plunge; it is during his stints there that he composes the prophecies of the Prophetic Rats of Barrio Prado Vélez, a regular *¿Dónde?* feature . . .

But Moya recognized Flor's letter because she'd read an abridged version of it out loud to him. So it was that kind of letter, thus its might-have-been-written-to-anyone tone. She'd been proud of it, he said, full of somewhat pretentious college girl pride over it. "Her manifesto," Moya called it, still unable to shake off his authorial sheepishness.

Of course I'd originally assumed that the lover in the letter was the other one, I mean, if that wasn't really all just metaphor for "the small country." But now I couldn't bring myself to ask Moya, So were you the guy she was trying to break up with? Some secrets you preserve by not really wanting to know, but if death seals more secrets than anything else, so does the will to keep them, and Moya certainly has that.

"Manifesto of what?" I asked him.

"I was never sure," said Moya, with a small, rueful smile. "Her manifesto of her right to hold long monologues with herself."

"Nothing wrong with that," I said. "I wish she'd done it more . . . She was trying to break up with Guatemala like it was a person?"

"*Pues,* we know she was thinking of leaving."

"I thought anyone doing what she was doing would *talk* about leaving, but that having stayed so long already was like a proof she didn't really want to. I thought this letter was more about why she was *staying*."

"I have to admit, Rogerio, I received it in another manner."

"That *you* were the guy she was trying to break up with?"

He looked at me expressionlessly for a moment, and then out the window.

"Well, let's face it, Moya," I said. "Maybe that *is* what she meant. Or she meant both. She just wanted to get away from *everything.*"

"Some days she wanted to go, and on others, to stay," he said, still gazing at the drizzling outside. "I was ready to go or stay with her, Rogerio, but I don't think I ever truly understood why one or the other. No, it is certain that I did not since I did not know, *pues,* that there was someone else."

"Yeah. Look, we were both in the dark about a *lot* of things."

Our silence felt like an extension of the dreary rain and view outside. Mingled with the usual traffic sounds was the faint, chugging music of the blind lottery-selling musician sitting on the sidewalk under the ledge beneath us, playing a *cumbia* on a cheap harmonica and supplying his own rhythm section with a coin-filled woman's compact case in his other hand—he's there almost every day and he's really very good.

Moya, I know now, lay at the heart of another of that letter's mysteries. Because it hadn't come to me in the usual Los Quetzalitos envelope with Flor's hand-drawn graphic of six happy quetzal chicks perched along a peaked roof and rising sunbeams radiating out from behind. This one came in a snazzy envelope from the Hotel Biltmore Maya—the snazziest hotel in La Zona Viva; one of the hotels, by the way and yet not at all incidentally, that Scobie Hunt and his wife, Anne, had been original investors in—and Flor had merely written the initials F.P. over the hotel's return address logo.

I've seen Moya do that, post his own Biltmore Maya envelopes, pseudonymously initialed though, in the mailbox in the hotel's lobby. Because ordinary Guatemalan envelopes are not usually addressed to such cities as Cambridge, Berkeley, West Berlin, or even London and so on, these can be expected to draw the at least slight attention of G-2 letter openers in the Guatemala City central post office. The hotel's mail goes directly to the airport, where, hopefully, the G-2 agents there don't sift through it, matching return address names and initials against a list of registered guests. No reason to trust in the integrity of the Biltmore Maya: the management there, says Moya, has collaborated with military intelligence in bugging the rooms for years.

Which is why he's always telling me to be careful of what I write in my own letters and of what I say over the phone. Moya says that even if you think the content of your correspondence is totally innocent, you never know how *they* might interpret it, because a lot of them must be real *ignorantes, vos.* What do I think, it's like the CIA, with at least a hundred great universities to go fishing in for young patriots seeking entry-level positions? What class of human being do I think G-2 finds to open mail? To listen in on international phone calls? Once, during a collect call Moya was making to the States, he could actually hear his eavesdropper having his or her lunch, the crackling paper of a sandwich or whatever being unwrapped, then the openmouthed and sticky chewing, the sucking peasant tongue searching out morsels hidden in rotted tooth crannies—So, sure, apparently they're not that hard to fool: "Aunt Irene" means Amnesty International, that kind of thing. But you don't want to draw attention to yourself; and you have to remember that you can never be really sure what will.

Moya's mother still does seamstress work for Anne Widow of Hunt. And Moya often visits his mother—especially when he wants her to sew him a new shirt or pants copied from one of the glossy fashion ads that Moya says he covertly tears from European magazines in fancy Zona 10 hair salons, ducking in without an appointment precisely for that purpose, sitting down to wait his turn for the *"it-will-never-happen-vos"* hair-coloring session and trim—"*I don't need to spend twenty quetzales to have my nostril hairs clipped, vos*"—picking up a magazine, sneezing violently like a movie detective to cover his filching tear of the Armani or whatever page, then jumping to his feet to announce the news conference at the Palace that he almost forgot about—"*. . . Ah la gran! I'm late! Perhaps another time. Hasta luegito!*"

Apparently his mother can sew anything. All Moya has to do is turn up with the ad and the bolts of fabric he buys himself from the textile stores in Zona 1. "*Guatemala produces famous textiles and cheaply, vos!*" It was on just such an evening a few years ago, when Moya was at his mother's for a triumphant fitting session, that Anne Hunt's chauffeur arrived at their door in a pouring rain with an umbrella and an urgent summons. After all these years, his mother still has no phone. Anne Hunt needed last-minute adjustments to an evening gown. "Why don't you come along?" said his *mamita,* whom I have never met. "It's been so long since you've seen La Doña."

Moya was in a happy mood. His pleated, olive green, cotton twill Armani pants and pale pink shirt fit perfectly. No seamstress like a *mamita* seamstress. Over his new outfit he wore the tight-fitting black Italian sweater that Edith, a West Berlin Green Party Angel, had brought him on her last research trip to Guatemala.

So he accompanied his mother to Anne Hunt's house, the new one adjacent to her school in a walled-in complex high atop an El Greco hill near the golf course—heavy rain, lightning, those walls glowing like a fortress of pink marble under the mercury vapor lamps as they rolled up the drive. He'd never been there, and was always eager for the rare chance to see how Guatemala's wealthiest lived.

"Oh Luis, what a lovely surprise!" said a smiling, fatter, flaccid-faced Anne Hunt when she finally came into the kitchen where he and his mother, having been let in through the service door, had been waiting at the servants' table. "Or *Don Periodista* Moya, I suppose I should say"—Don Newspaperman—this spoken, says Moya, with a polite but unmistakably insinuating chill. Her eyes widened a bit as she comprehended the fact if not the subtle, melancholy meaning of his prematurely whitening hair. Moya realized he'd never seen Anne Hunt without her makeup on, or dressed so girlishly gringa, in running shoes, jeans, and a Georgia Tech sweatshirt. He'd risen to his feet. She looked bad, *vos,* sad eyed, mean lipped despite the smile. That woman has suffered. Was he to kiss her on the cheek, a social equal? Of course not. She did give him her wide, damp hand, at the same time as she laid her other hand on his proudly and giddily beaming mother's plump shoulder. His mother then told Anne Hunt, would you believe it, that Moya had been just so happy and excited to accompany his mama for this chance of greeting his old headmistress, so dear to his heart. "I know that God decides what will happen to each of us, but that my son . . . the proudest moment of my life . . ." Moya felt his scalp scald as his mother went on about the night of the Colegio Anne Hunt graduation ceremony, when the graduating class had marched single file down the aisle joined by a soft, fragrant rope of white flowers borne over their shoulders, each carrying a white candle that each but one cupped against the wind, all the girls in white dresses with tiaras of white flowers in their hair, and Moya, the only male in the class to graduate on time and the first in three years, in a cheap white suit and white rose in his lapel and his candle blown out, while the Indian chamber orchestra, dressed in the same white suits, played "Pomp and Circumstance" on the wind-whipped, torchlit stage.

Finally Anne Hunt. fat ass quivering like flan in her jeans, led his mother upstairs to her dressing room, and did not reappear. Moya waited. After a while he got up from the maids' table, and, so as not to interrupt the one on duty maid who was sitting in a chair with her eyes riveted to the small black-and-white portable television where a Venezuelan soap opera was showing, he went into the adjacent room he and his mother had entered through. He wanted a soda, and there he had seen crates of empty sodas next to a storage refrigerator. In that room were washing machines and dryers, an ironing board, several five-gallon jugs of purified drinking water, bicycles, golf clubs. He opened the refrigerator, reached for a Coca-Cola, and then, in the cold light thrown by its open door, saw a large cardboard box full of envelopes on the bottom rack. Hotel Biltmore Maya envelopes. Well, these could certainly prove handy. Moya claims he'd never before stolen anything in his life, but now he did so guiltlessly and coolly. He stuffed fat handfuls of envelopes inside his belt all the way around his waist and pulled his sweater down over it and in that chilled paper tutu went back into the kitchen, sat, sipped his soda without risking the commotion of asking for a glass, and waited.

"—I have a present for you," said Moya, during those first few weeks after the Long Night of White Chickens when he was actively courting Flor.

"Envelopes, how sweet!" she exclaimed, puzzled at first.

Well, it was not as if he had so many other presents he could give. But he had this wealth of envelopes. And she *had* complained of some of her regular correspondence apparently never reaching intended foreign destinations.

But it was almost two months later that Flor, sitting cross-legged on her bed in Los Quetzalitos, had read him a version of that letter out loud from the spiral notebook in which she had composed it.

"But is this against me?" Moya bluntly asked when she had finished. Was Moya the lover whom Flor had compared to a suffocating, cloying, and polluting small country?

"Moya, I wrote this months ago, when I first started thinking of leaving, I hardly knew you yet. It's not about *you* or anybody, it's about Guatemala and the United States . . . You mean you weren't startled by my brilliant insights?"

"*Sí, Sí, mi amor . . .*"

"You weren't, were you? You didn't get it, oh gosh, maybe I should do it over again—" and with that she had torn the pages from the notebook, crumpled them between both hands—

"Florcita! Don't throw it away!"

"Oh, don't worry. I have like ten drafts of this thing in here," she said, and sighed.

ELEVEN

That letter, of course, had come ruefully and bitterly to mind several times during the ordeal of my and my father's two days in Guatemala. "Bottomless grief in a demitasse"—hadn't she written that *that* was really all she was trying to say? I hadn't been at all surprised when in the end she'd seemed to have decided to stay on and had never considered it my role to try to dissuade her.

Now we were flying home to Boston and Namoset with Flor in her casket in the morning. In our room in the Hotel Cortijo Reforma, my father was failing at trying to get an international phone line, his silent, agonized pacing punctuated by cajoling calls to the switchboard operator downstairs—he was in that concrete state of existence that Flor simply used to call "Guatemala Phone Hell."

In the hotel room, a soft breeze blowing in through the open sliding doors, I couldn't help but recall the evocation of the night air at the end of the second of Flor's significant two letters: I was thinking that this was the last night I'd *ever* breathe it, that I'd never come back here again, that this haunted night air belonged solely and forever to all of the ordinary and ordinarily malignant and spectacularly malignant inhabitants of this city that now seemed so vast, secretive, and unknowable, so apart from me. Yet it was also the air that belonged to as precise and totally unriddable a space as the coziest childhood memories: a space no larger than the central patio of Abuelita's house and the bedrooms off the covered passageway running around it, doors and shutters open, pastel walls like candied fruit in the warm yellow light, Flor on her bed that one summer she did come down with my mother and me, reading out loud to me from the book in her lap—*Breakfast at Tiffany's,* then an Agatha Christie—while I lay beside her watching moths and long-legged mosquitoes hover beneath the mildew-splotched ceiling. That was before Abuelita kicked her out, made Flor go home to Namoset with three weeks still left in our summer. Yes, Moya, the last straw was an "argument" they had over a certain very talented spider monkey.

But even during happy times, never mind the cataclysmic, origins such as mine—Catholic, Jewish, Guatemala, USA—can't always exist comfortably inside just one person. This isn't necessarily the biggest problem ever faced, far from it of course; it can even be pretty convenient when you're just looking for something to blame your own general confusion on; the easiest thing is to just ignore it, to not dwell on it at all. But what if you're not the ignoring type? Then you've been born into a kind of labyrinth, you have to pick and choose your way through it and there's no getting back to the beginning because there isn't any one true point of origin. Flor used to tell me to think of it as a great opportunity. Not exactly the Helen Keller story either, but lots of mixing and matching in the dark and dwelling on inner composition, the sketch under the painting. So that's one reason that during the years Flor was running her orphanage I read or purchased just about everything on Guatemala that I could lay my hands on. But I also told myself that by doing that I'd at least be living along an outer surface of her inner world there, and that I'd be able to better imagine her there, and so have more to say whenever I saw her. Even if Flor spoke little about it when we did get together—and often she seemed not in the mood to talk about Guatemala at all—I felt that I at least shared some of her new *gravity,* and that we spoke as two people well accustomed to it, keeping the conversation light. But this gravity, which I'd mainly acquired through reading—I hadn't been back to Guatemala since that summer when I'd visited her, though I was always making plans to go—had an allure all its own. I liked the esoteric solidity of a row of Guatemala books across my shelves. Political analysis, history, anthropology, human rights reports and solidarity publications, the travel writings of early explorers and missionaries; the *Popol Vuh* and *The Annals of the Cakchiquels;* the novels of Asturias, Cardoza y Aragón's *Guatemala: The Lines in Her Palm* . . . It was surprising, really, that there was so much to read about the little country that Flor, on crayoned schoolgirl maps, used to render as a flat-headed little duck looking back at its own tail feathers. I even owned a slim volume called *The Guatemalan Positivists,* about the influential circle of native scholars who, in the last century, proposed as a cure for the country's total backwardness a systematic belief in the progress of man through his own efforts and the study of logical philosophy. I'm not saying I read that book cover to cover, but just flipping through it you got the idea. The Positivists paved the way for the Liberal Reforms of the Great Reformer, General Justo Rufino Barrios, who discerned the export potential of coffee and took the logical next steps of terminating traditional Indian land rights and inviting ambitious German pioneers from across the ocean to come and own and operate the new, giant coffee plantations. Decades later another positivist dictator built imitation Parthenonlike temples to the Goddess of Wisdom, Minerva, all across the countryside. Guatemala has the highest illiteracy rate in Central America but also the oldest university, San Carlos, Moya's alma mater. And in the Strand bookstore I actually found a copy of a book written decades ago by a Cornell professor about nothing other than the history of that very university—which I've never actually gotten around to reading either, though I liked having it on my shelves among all those other brightly colored paperbacks with dramatic titles on the contemporary situation, its sober blue hardcover spine implying a deeper and more ironic take on Guatemalan history than I actually possessed and one that a working understanding of the contemporary situation probably doesn't even warrant. (In Brooklyn, Moya, stooping down to scan my bottom shelves before he'd even taken off his coat with what seemed a privately bemused eye, said that *Dracula* was the best book on Guatemala ever written.) Needless to say, much of what I did actually read was written from a leftist point of view or could easily be made to fit with one, but Guatemala has not tended to attract intellectual defenders of the right. Four hundred years of repressing the Indian majority, dictatorship after dictatorship, one decade of democracy ended by a U.S.-sponsored coup that issued in the current thirty years of military rule—understandably, the Rightist Latinist is likely to find more that interests him in, say, Cuba. I was definitely an impressionable enough reader, but it wasn't a political education I was looking for, nor was I necessarily trying to expand my worldview, which of course just reading about Guatemala isn't going to do for you. What it all added up to was nothing more than a new way through my personal labyrinth, or a new kind of gravity, one that went through me like a secret dye, deepening the hues of my already in place heritage. To keep it there, to keep it from fading, all I really had to do was carry a book like Fray Bartolomé de Las Casas's *In Defense of the Indians* around with me for weeks on end, opening it at random on subway rides into Manhattan and tuning back in to Las Casas's 500-page monologue and formal argument, originally delivered four centuries ago before the Spanish Court's Council of the Indies' out loud and in Latin, against the Holy Roman Church's and Bishop Sepúlveda's position that the Indians of Mexico and Central America were no better than beasts. Las Casas named the Guatemalan province where he lived and worked for a while Vera Paz, True Peace, and of course since he left it that remote and mountainous area has known little of that—

Meanwhile I went on living in New York, tending bar, neither happy nor unhappy with this way of life, good enough at it and sure that one day I'd get around to changing it all. While a separate part of me went on living in Guatemala with Flor and the ghosts of centuries.

After Flor died I of course stopped all that. All those Guatemala books turned instantly to hateful junk, slumped together now on the shelves' bottom tiers where Moya had immediately noticed them anyway, covered with the dirt blown over them by weekly, careless floor sweepings. I wouldn't even look at the *Times* anymore, buying only the tabloids. (Though now and then, as often as once every few months, I'd catch the grisly word on page 1 of the *Times* at a newsstand or someone would mention having read something or seen it on the news. There'd been another coup, I knew that. General Ríos Montt, who'd replaced Lucas García in a coup, was overthrown less than six months after Flor's death by General Oscar Mejía Victores, the portly brigadier, our current *Jefe de Estado*.) And I took down all those Guatemala artifacts—I'd been surrounded by this *tipico* stuff since childhood, and had only put it all up and out in the first place because I didn't know what else to decorate my apartment with: the carved Ancient Mayan Warrior lampstands that, removed from my mother's decorative Copacabana context, had suddenly seemed pretty cool; the long-taken-for-granted colors of Indian weavings on my walls that really had, with time, and reading, and dwelling so much on Flor and her heroic work with war orphans in Guatemala, begun at last to take on some of the mysterious life of the (I'd thought I really knew now) oppressed and devout Indian women who'd woven them; the wooden ritual dance masks of Spanish conquistador and Moor, jaguar, monkey, and deer the life of the Indian men who'd

carved and painted them just as their ancestors had been doing for
centuries.

My ancestors too! Because one of my great-grandfathers was
a fat and illiterate middle-aged Spaniard the day he arrived in
Guatemala City with no prospects at all, only to squander a number of years hanging around in the capital, where he made friends
with many powerful and positivistic people but stayed broke, until
he drifted out to the Pacific lowlands, where a mute card reader
signaled him his fortune by holding two fingers like horns up to
her head. Whereupon he guessed, "The Devil?" and she slyly signaled yes and no, guess again, and he said, "Cattle?" Which is how
he became a cattle rustler, riding all the way into El Salvador and
even Honduras with his band of lowland thugs and stealing entire herds, only a portion of which made it back alive to the lowlands village he'd turned into his own ranch, where the survivors
and offspring of his stolen herds proliferated on the lush, steaming plains. He became so wealthy that his friends in the capital
named him mayor. Peasants had to remove their hats when passing his veranda. And he provided slaughtered and roasted ox and
band music and fireworks every Sunday in the village plaza. He
built shrines to the Virgin of Lourdes throughout the province.
And he felt so obligated to spread his pure Spanish seed that Uncle
Jorge says that to this day everyone in that area is our cousin, an
anecdote my mother never includes in her phantasmic inventory
of Pride and Nostalgia. He married the prettiest Indian girl he
could find. His name was Francisco Medrano, and the pretty
Pocomil Indian was Josefa Coc, and he found her one day when,
out riding along the foothills just beyond the lowlands, he led his
horse down for a drink to the rushing stream hidden by jungle at
the bottom of a shallow *barranca,* and there, in a natural green pool
along the opposite bank, bathing naked, was the young brown
beauty with whom he began my ancestral line.

She was fifteen when she bore him his first child, and she died six years later while delivering his sixth child, but first daughter: Abuelita. That small and dainty-faced Indian girl who didn't even speak Spanish, born a decade before the turn of the century and preserved in no one's active memory but in one single hand-me-down photograph in my mother's album, dressed in a black Mary Poppins suit with choker, her ebony hair up in dowager's coils, was my great-grandmother? So that if she'd lived into old age I might well have visited her out at the ancestral hacienda and found her reverted to Indian ways, kneeling in the shade of a ceiba and weaving her own funeral *huipil?*

When Francisco Medrano died a decade after, it was of cancer of the tongue from so many years of licking his thumb to count out his money—telling that, you have to mime it like my mother does, thumb moving quickly back and forth between tongue and the invisible clump of bills in the hand.

The five sons inherited all the ranchlands and spawned five separate Medrano generational lines that apparently now have little to do with one another and almost nothing to do with we Arraus, city merchants, landlords, doctors, would-be venture capitalists. Abuelita, a ten-year-old girl, was dispatched with her ample dowry trunk to a boarding-finishing home owned by a Parisian widow in the capital.

My mother's father, the illegitimate son of one Colonel Rogerio Arrau and his nearrest, dearrest, lifelong mistress, had *mestizo* bloodlines going back to the Conquest.

Does any of this mean anything? I was trying hard to believe that it did. I had a URNG guerrilla poster that I'd picked up at a solidarity fair on my wall too, smiling young Indian *compañeros* standing on the crumbling, growth-tufted steps of a partially excavated Maya pyramid in a jungle clearing, their FALs and AKs exultantly hoisted over their heads. Looking at it, I'd sometimes attempt the feasible act of feeling moved by the notion that that was ancestral ground too and that ancient relations of mine really had lived among such pyramids as royalty, priests, warriors, slaves—their hearts ripped out by jade blades on the sacrifice stone, tripping their brains out from hallucinogenic water hyacinth enemas. I have a minority share in that *raza*. Well, you might as well have told me I had ancestors on Mars. Taking that poster down and rolling it up, throwing it into my closet with the rest of Guatemala, I petulantly thought that that "liberated" pyramid wasn't in Guatemala at all, but over the border in the safety of Mexico. That was when I was back in my apartment in Brooklyn, right after the funeral in Namoset. But it was already starting—*Guatemala no existe*—that night in our hotel room, when I felt so many of my embarrassing certainties, obsessions, gravity, and even love already seeping away, out through the sliding doors opened onto the balcony.

My father had finally gotten an international phone line and was saying, "Well of course we're bringing her home with us," his exhausted voice rising. I looked over at him from my idle slump on the couch. He was slightly bent forward, the receiver held to his ear, the fingers of his other hand over his wallet in his back pocket as if protecting it from pickpockets.

"Mirabel," he said after a while. "Aw Mirabel, be reasonable. Don't make it tougher than it has to be.

"I have money set aside, I can—Mirabel . . . Don't say that, she's family . . . Well, she was to me. And she certainly was to your son. He has been a great help, a great help, he's a brave kid, I am very proud of the way he's been here . . .

"Yes, Nelson's wife did phone and Jorge and Lisel have been very understanding . . . Mirabel, they haven't said anything about it . . ."

After my father hung up the phone, he stood over it for a moment staring down, his hand still in his back pocket.

"Dad?" I said. "What'd Mom say?"

"What?" he said, looking at me.

"How's Mom doing?"

"Imagine that," he said, after a long moment, in a tone of voice that made it seem he was beginning a new conversation entirely. "Your mother thinks we should have buried Flor here."

I found my mother's suggestion so shocking that my first reaction was to feel stunned by the logic of it, as if it really was the obvious thing to do and incredible that we had overlooked it.

"Didn't the consul recommend against it?" I said. While he had recommended against a public funeral and wake, he'd said nothing against a discreetly private service and burial in the General Cemetery.

"He absolutely recommended against it," said my father. He took a few steps towards me and spread his hands, then dropped them to his sides. "Sometimes your mother—Well, she gets things in her head."

"She has her own sense of proprieties," I said. "They're important to her."

"She is always so concerned about what people down here will think," he said. "She's under a lot of stress there, all by herself. She's all by herself, Rog. And people who knew Flor have been phoning, and she has been telling them that the funeral's down here . . . It must be terrible for her. Maybe we shouldn't have left her alone, but . . . ," and he shook his head. "We had to do it, Sonny."

"I don't think either of us could have handled it alone, Dad."

Minutes later the phone rang. Uncle Jorge was in the lobby, waiting to take us to dinner at his house. (". . . Ay, what a terrible event," said Uncle Jorge. "This kind of thing is always bad, bad for Guatemala." "Well, in fact, it isn't clear, not at all, Roger and I are not convinced of . . . " "What about what the Swede said, Dad?" "He was just after a bribe, Rog, and maybe she paid it to save that kid's life." "But where'd she get twenty thousand if she did—?" "Roger, what are you saying? Maybe she didn't have to pay *anything* in the end, because the diplomatic community came to her defense!" And Aunt Lisel interrupting, "Remember when *pobre* Chato, our *guardián* out at the chalet, was killed? He had a family, children . . .")

It was the previous afternoon that my father and I had gone to Funerales El Progreso to meet with Señor Acevedo, a portly, doll-faced man with recently sun-reddened cheeks and nose and a tiny, fastidious mustache. You wouldn't say that his small button eyes were merry, exactly, but they didn't even come close to achieving that butlerlike solemnity and discretion that you'd imagine would be instrumental to the demeanor of a highly successful funeral home owner, and Señor Acevedo was definitely that. Sharp and frank, that's what his eyes were like. He assured us that his security guards, "trained by Israelis at a private academy in Panama," were absolutely top-notch. Even if, before flying home, we wanted to hold a service so that people could come and pay their last respects, he guaranteed, money back, that there would be no troublesome intruders, either inside or out.

My father repeated Consul Simms's advice about how, in light of the uproar in the Guatemalan media, he did not think that would be best.

"One thing we've all learned in Guatemala," said Señor Acevedo, "is not to hold respectable families to blame for whatever their deceased might have done in life"—which I incredulously translated. "If this were not so," he went on, "I tell you the truth, almost no one would hold funerals and I would be selling *tamales* and *atol* in the streets."

Even now I feel the same slow chill spread over my skin as I did when I had to turn from Señor Acevedo to my father and speak those words. My father gaped at me as if I'd thought them up myself.

"No," said my father. "No. If you could just prepare her for the flight to Boston."

Señor Acevedo nodded lightly and said, *"Bueno,"* and switched to adequate English, speaking details and dollars and cents: Guatemalan funeral homes don't use embalming fluids as in the United States, so this costly process would have to be done in Boston, we'd have to contract a funeral hearse to meet us at the airport, you know at U.S. Customs they might open the casket, dogs will sniff for drugs, a funeral in Guatemala would spare us these expenses and difficulties, but as you wish. I sat there, in the funeral café, sipping my coffee and trying to work through a thought about Señor Acevedo being a kind of Guatemalan King Midas or maybe a younger King Cole the merry ole soul, ruling over his Kingdom of Violent Death with a necessary and frank good humor that his upper-class subjects had learned to emulate in order to make the transactions of daily life bearable and appropriately banal. (Just the other day when I joined Uncle Jorge and my cousins in Pastelería Hemmings during their morning coffee break, Uncle Jorge suddenly turned to my cousin Freddie and asked, "Isn't it true that Beto Cambranes was assassinated a few years ago?" "Yes," said Freddie. "Didn't he used to rent a warehouse from us?" And Freddie nodded yes. "Well then he's resurrected. Because he said hello to me when I was walking on La Sexta yesterday. *Ah la gran!"*—and then his thunderous, jolly conquistador's laugh.)

My father said later, when we'd left Funerales El Progreso, "A funeral home with a cocktail lounge inside it, imagine! And he talks about selling food in the streets! That fat pimp."

Moya says (though somehow I already knew it) that Funerales El Progreso, in recent years, had expanded into a brand-new building capable of conducting eight funerals at once. From the outside it looks like the corporate headquarters of any midsized high-tech firm on Route 128 outside Boston, a streamlined but monumental design. And inside it does in fact have a café and cocktail lounge with appropriately subdued lighting and classical music playing. Gleaming light green marble floors and walls and dark hardwood finishings, airport metal detectors inside the front doors, and a sign politely but firmly stating that *"Caballeros"* are required to check their weapons in the coatroom. During the worst of the urban violence, says Moya, it was not unusual for all eight of the funeral home's facilities to be in use on a single night. Many dutiful and well-connected people found themselves having to return there several times a week, or having to pay their respects to more than one family on the same evening, going first to stand briefly before the closed casket (or for as long as it took to say good-bye and then coolly flee the room without giving informers the chance to memorize faces or to report the telltale signs of suspicious bereavement, for example, overwrought and vicarious identification with the physical condition of the deceased, not despite but *because* the casket was closed) of the youngest daughter of a prominent family, a university psychology professor and volunteer social worker, reputedly tied to the left; and then next door for the wake of yet another assassinated wealthy Christian Democrat politician; and then, after an understandably relaxing cup of coffee or drink in the lounge, upstairs to where the young psychology professor's second cousin, a coffee plantation owner, executed by the guerrillas, lay in state. Outside, security guards stood with their Uzis, while others patrolled parked vehicles, poking bomb detectors that resembled long-handled dentist's mirrors under the fenders, exchanging hot-eyed stares with the personal bodyguards and chauffeurs of the mourners. In 1981, I'm sure, Señor Acevedo would not have bothered to solicit our business through the embassy. But in two years enough had changed in certain sectors of Guatemala City. Professors at the public university from prominent families and even not so prominent ones who had survived were living now in Paris, Madrid, Mexico City. *Finqueros* were no longer so defiant or foolish as to visit their own plantations, letting their administrators take the hits. The guerrillas' clandestine networks in the capital had been decimated to the point where they no longer had the capacity to carry out "armed actions" there. And if it was still dangerous to be a very wealthy but moderate politician, they had become so expert in their own security arrangements that it would take at least a small military strike force with grenade launchers and even a helicopter gunship hovering over to successfully ambush one of those armed caravans in traffic—which, of course, remembering Mayor Colom Argueta, has been known to happen in just that way. But if Funerales El Progreso is not quite as in demand as it used to be, the funeral parlors that cater to poorer people have remained busy. You see them all over Zonas 1, 4, 7 . . . like cheap Las Vegas wedding chapels, their signs advertising that they stay open twenty-four hours and other amenities.

Let Flor's funeral wait.

TWELVE

The party hadn't turned lively yet. Flor, Zoila the Cuban maid, Ingrid the German, and Delmi Ramírez and the handful of other Cuban girls who'd been delivered by my father from the bus stop in Namoset Square hours before were sitting on folding chairs in the basement, playing records, eating potato chips, waiting—Flor, no doubt with my father's encouragement, had persuaded my mother to let her have her own Friday night party in the basement as a substitute for the formal *quinceañera*, or sweet fifteen party, that of course my mother wasn't about to throw for her anyway. It was late winter, and Flor's sixteenth birthday was only a few months away. She'd already been jumped ahead to the fourth grade.

Zoila, barely eighteen herself at the time, had introduced Flor to the once-a-month Sunday afternoon dances at the Cuban Institute in Boston, and even Ingrid would go with them sometimes and then Delmi, having come up from Guatemala to take the job as a maid for a very wealthy family in Chestnut Hill that Flor had found for her on the bulletin board at the Cuban Institute, always did.

I heard car doors slamming and Latin male voices laughing, talking, and I ran to a window to see the boxy sedan pulled up in front of winter's perpetual snowbank and the eight Cuban boys who'd just gotten out of it. Teenagers, most of them, maybe a few were already in their twenties. They came clattering up the icy driveway, still talking and laughing, the red points of their cigarettes zigzagging in the dark. They didn't wear overcoats. They were dressed, every one of them, in sleek black suits, white shirts, and ties, their hair as exaggeratedly styled as their pointy, patent leather black shoes. Flor had heard them from the basement and was already waiting upstairs when they came in through the breezeway and into the kitchen on sixteen legs in a cold cloud of cigarette smoke and colognes, their hard heels dancing over the linoleum. And she stood there grinning ear to ear, in a white sweater and pink skirt, a pink barrette pushing back her hair.

Then she introduced them one by one to my parents and me—Flor knew all of them by name. While those mysterious shoes kept moving, fourteen shoes at a time, kept tapping, sliding, jostling, making it seem illusory that two shoes at a time were actually still for the brief moment it took to stand at the front of that impromptu receiving line—where the shoes' owners one at a time extended their hands in greeting:

"How do you do. Polite kids. Very nice. Your friends are polite boys, Flor." My father was chortling.

Except Domingo, the wildest one, squat and hyper, was all forward motion like a soccer winger breaking for the goal; even his jelly-rolled black hair seemed to be moving forward—"*Domingo!*" Flor actually seemed to sing his name out as if that were the only way to make it keep up with its owner. Domingo kissed my mother's hand while his shoes kept moving forward to the rhythm of the music playing on the cheap hi-fi downstairs, and before my mother knew it she was being mamboed across the kitchen floor. She let herself be led for a few startled steps and then exclaimed, "*Ay no!*" So that Domingo let her go. Klink, my German shepherd puppy, barked. My father chortled some more. My mother giggled. Domingo stood straight in the middle of our kitchen and, right there, began to applaud.

And Flor said, "This is Antonio."

"Toño," said a soft but manly voice. It wasn't until later that Flor began to call him Tony. He was, of course, the handsomest, the tallest, the suavest, with soft gray eyes, smooth cheeks, and a cleft in his chin, his thick oat brown hair brushed straight back over his high, golden forehead. *His* shoes glided like shadows under his long legs as he stepped forward to take my mother's, then my father's hand. Then he smiled for just a second at Flor, swerved suddenly to notice me, seemed to straighten even more as he looked down at me, smiled, nodded, said, *"Hola, caballero,"* and then he looked back at my mother:

"I've never before known what I know is true now, *señora.* Guatemalan women are the most beautiful in the world." He was proud of his fluency in English.

"You can say that again," said my father.

"Thank you," said my mother. "But have you met so many?"

"Flor, Delmi, and you, *señora."*

Flor blushed, his friends hooted. I gaped, for even I knew that this wasn't such a great thing to have said.

My mother's laugh dropped from an ice tray. "I don't think," she said, pleasantly enough, "that that is really a large enough sample for such a *strong* opinion."

A split second later, led by Domingo's war whoop, sixteen hard heels were stampeding down the wooden stairs to the basement. And Flor, like a Cinderella, what else, beamed at my mother as if unable to comprehend such excitement in her life and said, *"Gracias, Doña Mirabel, ay gracias,"* and then followed her friends down.

I spent that night, until I was sent to bed, crouched on a step midway down watching, while Klink whined and yelped and pawed behind the shut kitchen door—he was still too excitable to be allowed into the middle of a party.

Tony liked to wear the calm, serious expression of a discerning apprentice jeweler—he was nineteen and, back then, was working in a jewelry store in a shopping plaza in Watertown— but this was contradicted by his obvious high spirits. He danced with all the girls. But now and then he'd turn his gaze across the basement room at Flor, and whether she briefly returned the look or not he would smile the way you sometimes see someone smile just after they've received a shock that is about to make them cry. Then he'd spread his arms and shout, *"Niña de Guatemala!"* or "Girl Eh-Scout!" and stride towards her. Several times that night he seemed to relive that same epiphany of impulsive delight and delivery. And Flor, who hardly unclasped her hands from her belly all night, would look down at her shoes. So their conversations didn't last very long.

"I bet you are the only girl in kindergarten to have such a wonderful party," I heard him say, in Spanish, from where I sat, though I would hear Flor recall this conversation often, fondly or in self-recrimination, in the coming years. Flor kept her eyes on her shoes and said, *"Ay Toño! No seas tan malo!"*—don't be so awful!

"Malo? Yo? Aren't you in kindergarten? Or something like that?"

"You know I'm not," she bleated, glancing quickly from her shoes at me and then fmally right at him. "But if you're so sure, then there's nothing more to talk about."

"You are a beautiful beautiful flower," he said, cupping her chin in his hand. And then he went away. Minutes later he went through his act of discovery and exclamation all over again and came back. "Now I remember! Fourth grade! And what do they teach you in the fourth grade?"

"A otro perro con ese hueso!" she nearly shouted—Take that bone to another dog! And Tony went away laughing out loud to dance with blond, bird-faced Ingrid, whose German father was soon to ban her from seeing or receiving telephone calls from Cuban boys. Flor smiled up at me on my perch and waved excitedly for me to come down, while I made a big show of shaking my head no.

Flor didn't know how to mambo then, or was too shy to. The others danced mambos, rumbas, salsas, and, after I was sent to bed, made a conga line and held a limbo contest. Flor owned Chubby Checker's limbo single, and for weeks after we had to practice in the basement after school—the steps were pretty easy, you just had to bend backwards and walk-dance-stagger under the broomstick we suspended between the rungs of two chairs and kept lowering until we couldn't approach it without falling backwards onto the floor.

"—You must have had many boyfriends." Moya beamed, when it was still fairly early during the *Larga Noche de los Pollos Blancos.*

"No, I really didn't," said Flor.

"This I cannot believe," said Moya.

"Well, not serious ones. I spent most of my adolescence in elementary school, what was I going to do, date the Pee Wee hockey star? I had one boyfriend." And she looked at her watch. "Just one, really, when I was a girl. It's getting kind of late."

In a panic that she would leave, Moya blurted, "I remember seeing you, *sabes?* You came to meet Rogerio at the Colegio Anne Hunt, and I saw you." But maybe this was not a good tactic, because wouldn't it remind her of their difference in age? Yet he seemed to have recaptured her attention. "I thought you were so beautiful that I did everything I could to get Rogerio to invite me home with him so that I might have the chance of getting to know you better. But he never did. At night, I wrote you letters." Moya did vaguely remember seeing Flor, but of course the rest wasn't true, what he had really wanted was that electric train displayed annually in Arrau's Christmas window.

"Moya, gimme a break," said Flor, smiling in such a way that he knew that his arrow of flattery had finally struck that covertly ticklish spot inside. "You were just a little boy, you were Roger's age!"

Abuelita sent us Flor so that my mother's Codrioli Road penance wouldn't have to include housework too. But also because three Spanish ambassadors in a row had taken girls from the Las Hermanas del Espíritu Santo orphanage back with them to Spain—so claimed Abuelita anyway, scolding my mother in the tiny cement courtyard where she kept her caged canaries and finches during that one summer that Flor, seventeen, did accompany us down on our annual two-month visit.

But Abuelita must have had her own interpretation of the nuns' mission, because it really was as if she'd believed that God's and the Communion of Saints' and her own religious will, exerted and expressed through poor Flor, might somehow make us more like one of those families, like the family of one of General Franco's ambassadors from Spain—as if my father would suddenly start making money hand over fist, convert, join the Knights of Malta, all just to live up to the willful expectations of an Espíritu Santo girl.

Only my father, as usual, too coarse and unrefined a man to recognize his own offenses against dignity and order, had interfered in God and Abuelita's plan and distracted Flor from her mission, to which the tedium of all-day housework and narrowest ambition were essential, by putting her in school. And then everything that came after. Eventually he even let Flor take an evening job dishing out ice cream in Brigham's in Namoset Square. My mother said, "People will think we don't pay her. I mean don't give her money," and my father said, "Mirabel, she should start saving for college." And who was going to tell him any of it was wrong? Not even Abuelita, not to his face anyway.

She was a severe Catholic but an ebulliently severe one, one who seemed to take from her religion—especially in the years since my grandfather had died—a daily mandate to impose her ebulliently authoritarian nature on everybody else. But eventually she just had to resign herself to the fact that her mandate didn't extend beyond the borders of Guatemala. I mean, if life wasn't teaching Abuelita that, what was it? In Massachusetts the applauding company of her Saints died down. The spring that Abuelita came to visit us in Namoset, she saw what was going on, but what could she do? She pretty much just had to keep quiet about it.

That was a few months after Flor's party. Flor was still diligent about her housework—Abuelita would have had to notice that—*and* her studies. She wouldn't be allowed to date—that is, to let Tony or any other boy pick her up at home in a car and then go someplace in it—until she was seventeen. But by the time Abuelita came to visit, Tony and others were already phoning the house and even dropping by sometimes. And Flor was allowed to walk into the square with boys by then, to sit in a luncheonette or Brigham's, as long as it wasn't dark. Often my father had to go to the kitchen door leading to the basement and call down, "Flor honey. Someone else might need to use the phone."

Which is exactly what happened that evening when Abuelita was standing in the middle of the kitchen—she was restless and something of an egomaniac, and often preferred to stand and orate if everyone else was sitting. But my father at the door, calling down to Flor in so fond and undisturbed a way, really got to Abuelita—she turned into a statue, a squirrel-jowled, somewhat hunched and rotund statue with a live person trapped inside, staring with baleful disapproval through wide-open eyeholes at my father.

"Teenage girls and telephones, I bet it's the same in Guatemala, the same all over the world! Geez, the boys are crazy about her . . . ," he said, sounding hearty at first and then slowly trailing off. Then he left the kitchen, the Statue's eyes on him. Rolling Stones music was coming from the basement. My mother, sitting at the kitchen table, lit another Kent. I was there, on the floor and partly under the table, hugging Klink and feeling puzzled. Bounding steps on the wooden stairs: Flor's penny loafers, and then she was in the kitchen, grabbing a Coke from the fridge and opening it, leaning against the counter, smiling at Abuelita and at my mother and then at me and back at Abuelita. Klink's tail drummed against the floor.

"Did you buy anything nice today, Doña Emilia?" Flor asked brightly, in Spanish, referring to Abuelita and my mother's afternoon excursion to Filene's Basement in Boston. Abuelita's eyes seemed to widen just a bit more. And I had the thought—it felt just like learning the name of something—that it was disrespectful of Flor to have asked Abuelita if she'd bought anything nice, and I felt sorry for Flor for not knowing this too. My mother singsongedly said, "Yes, we did," but she seemed flustered. Flor said, *"Ah bueno. Me alegro,"* nodding, holding her can of Coke in both hands and staring down at the flip-top opening. She began to lift the can to her lips but then, as if she couldn't quite figure out how to, didn't. She headed back towards the stairs, whispering *buenas noches,* and, without kissing me good night, descended. Klink wrenched free, followed her down. Then the music in the basement was turned down a bit. "Roger, get off the floor," said my mother. I sat in a chair. "Nothing is hidden between heaven and earth, *mija,*" said Abuelita. "Would you like a cup of tea, *mamita?*" said my mother; she was glad, as always, to have cinnamon tea from Guatemala in the house again. The phone rang, simultaneously, at all its outposts in the house: the living room, my parents' bedroom, the basement. My mother shut her eyes. Mercifully it only rang that once. The music in the basement was turned down some more.

I perhaps didn't quite get that what had really turned Abuelita into a statue, more so even than my father's familiarity, was her specific realization that our "maid," whose salary *she* still paid, had her own phone in her bedroom and shared the line with the rest of us. But this was not a transgression that my mother could have easily explained away by revealing that the reason Flor had a phone in her room was that it was what she'd wanted for Christmas.

" . . . and she took me aside," said Flor, "and said, 'I see that you are happy, Flor de Mayo. You kept that part of your promise anyway, and I am happy for you. But I notice that, to my grandson, God is not too important.'

"Oh Moya, that lady, I was on the verge of tears, I swear. I told her I'd tried. Well, I had! Kind of. Well then she said, Don't worry, calm down, don't blame yourself, the U.S. has been disorientated ever since Castro murdered Presidente Kennedy, the whole world knows that. She said if Roger were a girl, well maybe *then* she'd be worried, but boys will be boys, they take longer, that kind of thing. She said, 'But I think I do see signs in little Roger of a spirit that one day might find its strength through faith. I mean to say when he is much older. After all, miracles have been known to occur in this family.' Then she told me about her Spanish father the rancher who was never religious either until he cured one of her infant brothers of cholera by giving him a drink from some shithole his cows drank from too, and this was the Virgin of Lourdes. Well I said, Yes, of course, I said, There really is something in Roger that God must like a lot, Doña Emilia, because he always wants to feed bread to the pigeons and ducks. Hah! Imagine? But you better believe I dragged Roger off to mass with me that Sunday.

"I was terrified of her. And you know what? I really had every reason to be—"

* * *

It was only when Abuelita went with us to Wellesley Square to watch the Boston Marathon runners go by that she really came forcefully to life again, the whitish light that always filled her eyes when she was full of her mandate rekindled. She charged out into the street in her orthopedic shoes waving a plastic Guatemalan flag, shouting, "*Andale! Andale, muchacho! Viva Guatemala! Viva Mateo Flores!*" at the inconsequential Guatemalan runner slumping by, while I took a freshly cut orange wedge from Flor and ran out to give it to him. Mateo Flores is the Guatemalan who'd won the Boston Marathon over a decade before, the most celebrated event in Guatemalan athletic history since gourd-headed Hunahpu and his brother outwitted the Lords of Xibalba on the Maya under-world ball court in the ancient *Popol Vuh.* "Just a poor little Indian raised on tortillas and beans and he outran the world's strongest men," I remember Abuelita telling me, bursting and just about apoplectic with ecstasy. "It was a miracle, I'm sure. Because that's what love of country can do, *mijito,* that's what made it possible for Mateo Flores to draw on the strength of every heart and leg in his country, even the poor cripple's! And when he came home, the government gave him a *house.* A modern house but with a dirt floor so that he could go on living like an Indian inside it, with his wife cooking his tortillas over the fire!"

It was the same government that had given Mateo Flores the house, the democratically elected but leftist government of Colo-nel Jacobo Arbenz, that just two years after the runner's victory, in 1954, Abuelita had personally helped to overthrow, defying the government-imposed blackout of the capital by lighting charcoal in a pit in her patio and fanning it while she stared up at the sky— waiting for the sound of Castillo Armas's National Liberation invasion force airplanes following a glowing path of patriotic grandmothers' anti-Communist fires through the mountains and over the darkened city to drop their bombs and strafe the National Palace, where Arbenz was shitting in his pants and preparing to flee the country.

Of course Abuelita had no way of knowing that those were CIA-provided and mercenary-piloted planes, that Castillo Armas couldn't have had less to do with them if he'd tried—not that she would have regretted it much, or at all. Because it is also true that an Arbenz magistrate had once summoned my grandfather and Uncle Jorge into court because of something or other a disgruntled employee had claimed, and fined them and even threatened to confiscate the family business if the employee's claims were not corrected. To which my grandfather had replied, "You'll need bigger balls than mine to get away with that, and I don't think you have them, *señorito mío,*" and then had started undoing his pants to taunt the magistrate with his balls. But he was restrained at the very edge of exposure by a grinning policeman's submachine gun perfunctorily leveled at him from across the courtroom.

The point being that Abuelita's patriotism was as ebullient as her feeling for God and absolutely inseparable from it. There was a Guatemala that God approved of and all the other possibilities which He didn't. And the Guatemala He approved of had everything to do with Order: orderly progress that was only possible through Order; and the indisputable degrees of respectfulness and deference due across the gradations of that order which kept the whole wholesome, law abiding, stable, positive, and right (and which made it inconceivable that any hardworking, dignified man would ever have to defend himself from unprecedented insults against family and property by threatening to display his balls in the atheist's courtroom).

All of this she believed deeply, with all the feeling for beauty, piety, and healthy vitality she was capable of. None of it translated too well to my father's USA, of course, though my mother in her very particular way has always believed in similar values and proprieties. This has found expression in her exaggerated fondness for Calvinist sayings such as "Idleness is the Devil's playground" and in her quiet, incremental rejection of the local Catholicism in favor of her search for a more individual version of Abuelita's symmetries and mandates. By the time I was in high school, for example, my mother was for a while quite seriously taken with the Carlos Castaneda books on the teachings of Don Juan, and though she never was about to ingest peyote in search of illuminating visions like the ones that Indian *brujo* and his scribe-apprentice had, she really loved the rhetoric of discipline and deference apparently expressed in those books, all that stuff about being a lonely Yaqui spiritual warrior, a *controlled warrior* in search of enlightenment in the modern world. "I am a controlled warrior," she would actually say, fighting down her frustration over one thing or another, even having to cook dinner, which she'd never in her life had to do on a regular basis until Flor went away to college.

The one summer that Flor did accompany us down to Guatemala she paid her own way from money she'd saved working part-time at Brigham's and the little bit on the side my father had given her for good grades. She was seventeen, and had just completed the sixth grade. Flor and my mother had agreed beforehand that in Abuelita's house no one would say she was a maid or try to treat her like one, though she would help out a bit with the housework.

But as soon as we arrived Flor learned that she would have to sleep in the maids' quarters. The explanation she was given was that I had my own room, my mother had hers, one room in the back had been converted into a temporary warehouse for thousands of Uncle Jorge's unsold imported Hula Hoops, and there was no longer a bed in the other spare room because Aunt Lisel had claimed the old four-poster bed in there for the brand-new house that Uncle Jorge had just had built in Zona 10. So if Flor wanted to go out and buy her own bed, mandated Abuelita, she was welcome to. But the extra cot in the maids' quarters was staying where it was!

So Flor went out and bought her own bed, and blew all her money on it and the delivery. And she pretty much stayed in that room from then on, reading and keeping the door closed, just going out now and then to check more books out of the Guatemalan American Institute Library, to visit old friends and mentors at the Espíritu Santo convent a few times, or to pick me up from the Colegio Anne Hunt, where, as always, I'd been enrolled for the summer.

Soon no one was speaking to anybody: Abuelita's maids weren't about to take this I'm-not-really-a-maid stuff from Flor, not when old Chayito and some of the others even remembered the day when Abuelita had gone to the convent orphanage to choose her. And Flor stopped speaking to them, not that she had much from the start anyway. And eventually the maids even stopped speaking to me, because they felt betrayed by my alliance with Flor. I stoked the bad feelings considerably by suddenly refusing to let any maid clear my plates after meals, carrying them into the kitchen myself as if instructively liberating them from their degrading labors.

Until Abuelita said, "You do that again and you can start shining shoes in the streets like any other *ishto bobo,* because I won't give you a thing to eat until you can pay for it, *mijito mío.*" And when I did do it again she grabbed my arm by pincer claws and dragged me right out into the patio and sat me down in front of a pile of her black orthopedic shoes with polish, rags, and a brush and said, "Get to work and God give you strength because you're not coming in until they're done and then we'll see, *mijito mío,* if you still think a servant's work is something to be disrespectful of!"

My mother could barely bring herself even to pronounce Flor's name anymore and sought any excuse to flee the house, her very existence on earth confirmed daily by the newspaper society-page photographs where her face was as ubiquitous as a postal stamp, always saying "cheese" at one baby or bridal shower baptism ladies' club fashion show and evening gala after another. She accepted every invitation to spend weekends at friends' coffee *fincas,* ranches, and beach houses, always bringing me along and leaving Flor alone at home with Abuelita and her maids to await the inevitable calamity of my return.

Because I always came back from those trips in bad shape, covered with mosquito and *chinche* bites, mottled with sunburn and rashes; limping from a fall out of a breadfruit tree, or with my hands swollen and on fire from the invisible spines growing all over a big green bamboo I'd grabbed onto as if it were a fire station pole; vomiting, dysenteric, and hallucinating with fever from the bad clams I'd eaten in Puerto San José, where I'd also been saved at the very last second from one of those implacable Pacific undertows by an anonymous German wearing just underpants who appeared out of nowhere and clasped my wrists when I was already vertical and rushing backwards on a long underwater journey—somehow those events along with my missing and worrying about Flor left alone with the maids and Abuelita always managed to reduce my emotional maturity to that of a five-year-old by the time we returned, to the endless annoyance of my mother and whoever we were traveling with. That was the summer I was endlessly being scolded to act my age, which was nine.

The long Sunday evening drives back from wherever we'd spent the weekend always became excruciating as soon as the highway winding down out of the mountains or up from the coastal plain began passing cliffsides painted over with political slogans and billboard after billboard standing in the roadside weeds advertising ladies' underwear, aspirin, French restaurants; the city at night suddenly visible through breaks in the landscape, a vast, intricate net of lights spread across the bottomless night far below, Flor just down there but still an hour to go because of the traffic stacking up behind trucks inching along like a circus parade of decrepit, flatulent elephants.

But finally we'd get there and a maid would let us in and I'd rush through the parlor, where Abuelita always sat watching television or listening to Chayito read out loud to her from a Zane Grey cowboy novel, and into the covered passageway along the central patio to Flor's room. Her only window faced the patio, light shining through the cracks in the old, flayed wood of the drawn shutters; I'd push the double doors open without even knocking. I was the only one admitted to the bare sanctum of that room—and the only one who wanted to go in anyway—where Flor passed her strange summer like a medieval princess awaiting the return of her promised one from a ten years' crusade, reading, thinking about Tony, listening to the radio, her head full of the same inane jingles repeated every three minutes on every station. Against the pale green wall where the bed Aunt Lisel took away had been and beneath the plain wooden crucifix and the framed painted eye radiating rays in all directions into painted clouds, angels, and the gilded logo *Dios lo ve todo,* God Sees All, Flor had parked her own bed of profligate but I think supportable pride.

And then she lay there day after day, defiantly and brazenly; inwardly mocking Abuelita's piety and striking some note of heretical triumph within herself; thinking scornful, wicked, hateful things and forbidden, frightening, intimate things; indulging herself in languorous daydreams to fill the hours when she wasn't reading; at times even enjoying this summer of hermit's hibernation from a more perplexing and complicated reality, and at other times bored out of her mind.

But those weekends spent alone in the house with Abuelita and her maids were Flor's true punishment for being herself that summer. She spent them even more reclusively than she did her weekdays. The younger girl still left inside her was just plain furious over being left behind, but that wasn't all.

Because the very first weekend that my mother and I had gone away, Flor *had* ventured out on her own that Saturday afternoon, and when she'd come home in a driving rain Abuelita's maids had let her stand out there ringing the bell until finally she'd had to retreat down the avenue to the shelter of a little *tienda,* a one-room cave of a grocery store with a steel shutter that was pulled down over the front at closing time. And that was where Flor passed the two hours that became her story of the two hours of somewhat opaque self-discovery that she would forever tell to explain *her* side of what happened that summer, and what she learned from it.

In front of the counter in that *tienda* were two small tables with chairs, and Flor sat at one, ordering nothing since she had no money, her arms wrapped tightly around her drenched self; while the men drinking beer and licking salt off their palms at the other stared, hissed, and clucked at her in the violating and weirdly tormented manner of Guatemalan macho amorousness, calling her "little brownie" and offering her everything they owned and would ever own though she knew better than to let them buy her even an *agua* and a *tamal.*

She sat there glaring through the rain and the thickening dusk, past the rectangular pastel facades of the simpler and smaller houses along the avenue at the higher, custard-colored and red tile–fringed walls of Abuelita's much bigger house. And she asked herself how it was possible to have gotten into so stupid and humiliating a predicament, with Abuelita's maids hating her so much that they wouldn't even let her come in from the rain. And then she decided that although she felt more scorned and rejected than she ever had in her life, there was not one thing she would have done differently to prevent it. And she contemplated every stealthy, riotous, or prosaic act of revenge she could think of, and realized that every one of her schemes might very well accomplish nothing but provoke Abuelita into using all of her power and authority to terminate her life with our family in Namoset forever—especially with my father not around to protect her. She concluded that she was so hemmed in by pride and circumstance that there was nothing, not another thing in the world for her to do but control her anger and get back inside that despised house and into her room and onto that bed and then stay there even more obstinately and uncomplainingly than before.

"*That* was the moment I became a United States citizen," she would say in later years, after she actually became one. It was right there, at that little *tienda,* that Flor decided once and for all that once back in Namoset she'd get her U.S. citizenship as soon as she could, which would put her beyond the reach of Abuelita's mandate forever.

Sunday nights I'd push open the double doors to her room and see Flor, as if in overlapping images, lying prostrate and sulking on her bed and already springing up from it like a surprised and rescued Pocahontas in the forest, and I'd walk in to mad squeals and hugs, wet kisses all over my face like I hadn't felt since we'd stopped playing Tunnel of Love in our basement in Namoset. If up in Namoset I was no longer the single most absorbing person in Flor's life, if she'd begun to treat me there, at times, with a true big sister's indifference and even impatience, that summer in Guatemala I must have seemed not only her one true friend on earth but her only reliable contact with the outside world as well.

"*Dame un beso,*" she'd squeal. Give me a kiss. "*Dame otro beso . . .*"

I'd lie on her bed beneath that All-Seeing Eye while she, thrilled at the diversion, rubbed lotions on my sunburns, jungle bites, and rashes, held ice wrapped in towels to my bruises and sprains, nursed my fevers—ran me, when I was really sick, to the toilet every few minutes and held her ear to my belly to reassure me that I didn't have worms.

"*Dime muñeco.*" Tell me, my doll.

And I'd tell her about my weekend adventures and calamities, trying to get it all in before my mother came walking down the reso-nating tiles of the passageway to rap on the door and order me out to kiss Abuelita good night and then to my own bed. Flor held me even tighter, cooed, "*Ayyy, mi precioso, Gracias a Dios,*" when I told her about my salvation from the undertow in that Aryan archangel's pair of outstretched hands. And then—after a few minutes of *Should I tell you? You won't tell your mother I told you? You promise you won't have bad dreams if I tell you?*—she told me, in a voice lowered to a damp whisper and unaccustomedly grave, about the Holy Week Saturday when the nuns had let the Guatemala City Lions Club take all the girls from the orphanage on an outing to that very same beach in Puerto San José, where a little girl named Petrona had been pulled out into that ocean forever, the endless rosaries for poor Petrona's soul in the chapel, how every night for weeks the girls fell to sleep weeping at night in the dormitory where poor Petrona's bunk stood heaped with flowers and a pile of penny candies on the pillow, and how every morning they'd find one empty candy wrapper and a wet, crumpled tissue which one of the older girls would hold to her own lips and then to all the other girls' lips in turn so that they could taste how the tissue was soaked with Petrona's saltwater *moco.*

Flor wrinkled her nose and spooned milk of magnesia into my mouth on another Sunday night while I burped and told her about the hundred baby bulls lassoed one by one by their hind legs then laid out in the dirt and steamy muck of an infernally hot Pacific Coast cattle ranch corral while a veterinarian used a silver knife to slice them open down there and reached in bare-handed to pull their testicles out by long blue cords then scissored them off and stuffed the cords back in and used a paintbrush to coat the wounds with purple iodine and then another brush to daub them yellow between the ears while ranch hands ran out with branding irons hot off the fire to add the stench of scorched rump hair and flesh to that of bull and horse shit. The incredible thing was that when it was all done the baby bulls would get up like nothing significant at all had just happened to them and saunter back into the swirling herd while the cowboys who lassoed them rode around on horseback eating bloody, slimy, pink-and-blue-veined raw bull balls like they were apples! To be like a cowboy I'd taken a big, chewy bite out of one too. Flor scolded, *"Bruto! Salvaje! Cochino! Qué grosero!"* And she rolled over on the bed laughing while I lay next to her on my side as if lassoed, doing my imitation of a baby bull at the decisive moment it got its balls snipped off, one eye fixed on the ceiling in placid panic and then just the tiniest gasp and a quick blink, that was all, and knowing what I was doing since I'd watched it done a hundred times.

And at a coffee farm on another weekend I'd driven off somewhere with my mother and a balding man with a thin mustache whom she called Pepe Ganús (rhymes with *caboose*) to look at a property he was interested in. But they left me alone in the car, parked on a jungle-banked, dirt road. And so there I was, sitting there, when suddenly a huge black tiger padded silently out of that jungle and then stood in the middle of the road staring at the car with mesmerized yellow eyes, a panther, it must have been, or maybe a jaguarundi. But it was there. In panic, my heart pounding, I rolled up all the windows, and when I looked back the tiger was gone. When my mother came back with Pepe I was crying, I swear out of fear that the tiger had eaten my mother and for no other reason, but Pepe didn't even believe that I'd seen a tiger at all and said I was too old to cry like that just to get attention, while my mother hugged me to her with her lips in my hair and said not a word.

Flor's face loomed over me, astonished, as I finished telling her about this. She'd pushed herself up on hands and knees beside me on the bed and, motionless now, seemed to be gaping at the green wall. Until I said, "A tiger, I saw it," and then she came out of her startled trance, smiled funny, kissed my brow, and said, "Of course you did," and then she sat crosslegged on the bed, almost pouting at that wall again, oblivious of me, her breathing charged with something slow moving but heavy, like private and quiet anger or deep revelation. And of course I realize now what Flor was probably thinking and getting so worked up about. Well, probably—I don't really care, to tell you the truth, I mean, I'm not at all surprised. But my poor mother, what a guy to pick, because that Pepe was really a *sleaze*.

Another time, at another farm he owned, Pepe was there, dressed as always in black trousers and a white *guayabera* shirt and a gold wristwatch and shiny black shoes that looked oddly tiny, like ballet slippers almost, on such a relatively tall, bulky man. But I got to go off two afternoons in a row with the *campesino* kids to wait in a sorghum field for the parakeets that came like clockwork at the same hour every afternoon to feed. The parakeets filled the big empty sky all at once, bursting from the faraway, spreading black branches of the banyanlike trees on the horizon, their reverberating chatter filling the air until suddenly they were plummeting all around us like an endless shower of gold and green arrows. Then it was the *campesino* boys' job to run through the sorghum lighting firecrackers from the cigarettes they dangled from their mouths and tossing them into the air—hundreds of firecrackers, gunpowder smoke and shattered paper bits and earsplitting explosions all over the place, until the parakeets finally moved off like the vastest, noisiest, green and gold magic carpet you ever saw. My mother had ordered me to just stand by and watch so I wouldn't blow off my fingers, but the second day one of the kids gave me one of his cigarettes—my first cigarette!—and a fistful of firecrackers, and I ran into the sorghum frantically lighting and tossing firecrackers up at the parakeets too until I tripped and the cigarette fell from my lips and I fell with my palm on top of it and got scorched. By the time I had it lighted again, the invasion was over.

That story made Flor jealous. She wished she'd seen it too. She sat on the bed looking as if the reason she hadn't gotten to see it was a very deep and perplexing mystery, but one that it was not beyond her capacities to solve if she concentrated really hard. Her lips quivered, she actually blinked back tears. And then she got off the bed and walked several caged circles, her hands fisted. She came back and sat down and gaped at me for the briefest second, then fell over with her face in the pillow.

"This," she said, softly and deliberately into the pillow, "has absolutely been the worst summer of my life."

It all finally came to a head because of the spider monkey Flor had always told me about, the one that could ride a unicycle and eat bananas off a plate with a knife and fork and that she remembered from her own childhood visits to the zoo with the nuns.

"Flor told me about that monkey, *vos,*" said Moya, excitedly, when we were talking about all this. "*Un mico sumamente dotado!*" A very talented monkey. And he laughed affectionately.

"Soom-ah-men-teh," I echoed, laughing a bit too, because that really is the way she used to say it.

But even back then Moya must have known all about Flor, because we were already friends at school and I would certainly have told him about her; though I was still too young then to be allowed to ride the bus home alone or with Moya. And he must have seen her too, when she would turn up in front of the Colegio Anne Hunt sometimes instead of Abuelita's chauffeur, Diego, to bring me home: Flor, in jeans and the light blue Columbia University sweatshirt she liked to wear, maybe carrying some books if she'd been to the IGA library first, waiting out by the front gate, and the older boys going, *"Ah, mira esa india rica, vos! Puta!* Why doesn't she come work for us! Listen to this little *indio,* he says she's his sister, *qué cerote, vos!* . . ."

I wanted Flor to take me to the zoo to see that monkey, and when I said so at dinner one night Abuelita was so instantly riled that she stood up from the table with her soft, rouged and powdered jowls trembling and her eyes full of white light and in a tone of triumphant outrage against all the disorder Flor had introduced into her house that summer shouted:

"Ya hace dos años que el mico ese murló!" It's been two years since that monkey died!

And she glared at me. It was more my fright at her anger than what she'd actually said that made me shrink down in my chair, face burning, tears starting. Abuelita sat back down, poutingly composing herself, resuming her meal of dark pigeon meat in raisin sauce and boiled vegetables. Then, looking directly at my still utterly chagrined mother with an entirely new expression of watery-eyed sentimentality, Abuelita smiled and let out a whinnying but dreamy laugh, and in a voice still quavery with turbulent emotion, said, "All of Guatemala was sad the day that monkey died, *mija* . . ."

It so happened that Flor was in the kitchen at that very moment, eating a solitary meal at the maids' table before the maids' turn and listening in on our every word—no one had ruled that Flor couldn't eat with us, I don't think, but this was yet another aspect of her stubborn stand in behalf of her own beleaguered dignity that summer. But suddenly there she was in the dining-room entrance, still holding her fork and looking something like a skinnier, darker Elizabeth Taylor in *The Taming of the Shrew,* wild eyed and taking deep breaths and looking like she might bite. Instead, in a voice I clearly remember as being shrill with adolescent insolence and hurt, she shouted:

"Of course they were all sad. This is a country of monkeys and that was the most talented monkey in it!"

That night there was shouting in the house for a long time after I was sent to bed, and phone calls to my father in Namoset. And the very next day Flor told me she was going home, though there were three weeks left in our summer vacation. She flew to Miami and then, to recoup some of her money, cashed in the rest of her ticket and rode a Greyhound bus all the way back to Boston. It was years before my parents stopped arguing sporadically about Flor's behavior that summer—and it was my father, of course, during one of those frantic phone calls, who had somehow prevented Abuelita from terminating Flor's life with us.

Though Flor did send Abuelita an earnest-seeming and oddly self-belittling note of apology, which my mother brought back with her to Namoset years later, after Abuelita's funeral, when I was in my first year in college and Flor had just graduated Wellesley and moved to New York. It was still in its envelope, postmarked Macon, Georgia, where Flor had mailed it from the bus station. The note was short, so I remember more or less exactly what it said:

"Dear Doña Emilia, Please forgive my bad behavior. You are right to demand nothing but respect in your house. I know that everything good that has ever happened to me I owe to you. Guatemala is a wonderful country and I will always be proud to be a Guatemalan. And you are a wonderful woman and grandmother and an example to me. I must try harder to understand pride. With all my respect and affection, Flor de Mayo Puac."

The only signs of defiance in that note were that Flor wrote it in English—which meant Abuelita probably would have had one of my uncles translate it for her—and enclosed her sixth-grade report card, which she'd brought with her all the way to Guatemala.

As for Pepe Ganús: I remember that when we were driving out of that very same farm where the *campesino* boys tossed firecrackers to keep the parakeets off the sorghum—it was the second time I'd been there, a weekend or two after Flor left—Pepe had suddenly stopped his pickup and, without a word to us, had gotten out of it and pulled a pistol from his *guayabera*-curtained waist and then aimed it with his arm out long and straight. He was aiming at a pig rooting in one of his fields, and he shot it dead. Actually his first shot missed—it was incredibly loud!—dirt flew up, but with the second and third shots the pig skipped a few times and fell over. Then Pepe got back in and we drove on, while he explained that the pig was from the village just beyond his property and that he'd warned the villagers to keep their animals out of his fields. My mother and I were both absolutely silent the rest of the drive home, our silent communication as exact and unequivocal as it might have been between two compatible adults on at least one matter: we both knew we'd seen something despicable. My mother didn't speak to Pepe again until we'd pulled up in front of Abuelita's. She stood by the open door of his pickup and said into it, in Spanish:

"My mother always told me never to trust a man with small hands and feet."

That was all she said. Which is why I remember so well that Pepe just pawed the air once with an extended and pointy little hand that resembled a delicate starfish, then reached across to pull the door shut, and drove away.

I live now in this very same house, where I take my meals alone at the very same long mahogany table above which the crystal chandelier still jingles as if from Abuelita's outbursts instead of from the shattering blasts of mufflerless buses passing outside or the occasional actual tremor in the earth; my meals cooked and served now by the last maid left, Chayito.

The other night I took Moya out into the patio and yanked up the tiles beneath which has been preserved, like a patriotic shrine, the blackened earth where Abuelita lit her anti-Communist charcoal.

This was distinctly meaningful to Moya, who is the sort of person who, say, when confronted with any fat non-Spanish dictionary will automatically begin leafing through it to see how many Guatemalan cities and towns and so on the compilers saw fit to include in the verifiable lexicon of that language; who, picking up a world history will flip to the index to see if Guatemala has its own listing; who passed up the chance of an Ivy League and cosmopolitan career as a professional political exile and expert on the murderous and stultifying little country that chased him out because he preferred to return and resume his oblique but heroic life as a newspaperman for a newspaper that hardly anyone reads (though everyone reads *¿Dónde?*). He looked down at Abuelita's charcoal pit for a long time, pinching his lower lip between thumb and forefmger, musing.

There was a clear, full-moon sky, the rain clouds having spent themselves that afternoon and been pushed off by a Caribbean wind sweeping over the desert and then the cordillera. Against that glowing sky the immense silhouette of a volcano, absolutely black and conical as a witch's hat, loomed even more impressively than it does by day.

"So much that Guatemala is living now," I said, "entered this country through this hole in my grandmother's patio."

Moya liked that idea. He gave me one of his flatteringly astounded looks and said, *"Bonita idea, vos."*

"It's like a witch's caidron," I said. "Except she couldn't really know what was in the brew."

"Sí, vos," he said. "So much that Guatemala is living, has lived these past thirty years, comes from this hole in your *abuela's* patio." I suspected then that he might already be developing this idea for a newspaper column. "So much, so many things," he went on. *"Pero tú y yo?—no.* Not you and I, Rogerio. Or any other *guatemalteco."*

Not him, not me, not Flor, or any other Guatemalan. I did realize what he meant by this. Hardly anyone entered Guatemala through the hole in Abuelita's patio. Tools were passed through it, that's true, such as killing tools for vile apes, all the tools they needed.

This was the idea Moya more or less went on to develop in one of his typically oblique newspaper columns, which I am proud to have contributed to in my way: Guatemalans must take responsibility for their own acquiescences and even defeats just as surely as they can take pride in the nation's victories and in their dreams of democracy, et cetera, et cetera.

THIRTEEN

The Park Street–bound Red Line train emerged from the tunnel and began to cross a bridge over the Charles River. Moya (he remembers now) sniffed loudly, drawing mucus back into his burning, stuffed sinuses. The flat gray light outside, the metallic brightness inside the train, hurt his eyes. Feeling sluggishly disinterested, he looked out at the view, the choppy gray river and the complicated mass of the city: the ancient-looking red and brown brick of the buildings, roofs of oxidized copper, domes, skyscrapers, the dead trees and the snow-patched dead grass along the river, bridges, sea gulls, the unbroken flow of traffic. He could not have felt more lonely, more acutely dissatisfied with or conscious of himself.

He wore a navy blue arctic parka with a hood fringed with neon orange fake fur, olive corduroys, and a long, red scarf wrapped three times around his neck, and socks that were too thin for the weather and made his ankles feel as dully distracting as a minor migraine, and the same black loafers that in Guatemala, where he could afford it, he used to have shined at least once a day by the shoe-shine men in the Central Plaza in front of the National Palace (the shoe shiners always knew the latest rumors about goings-on in the palace). The soles of his feet felt as chilly and wet as his T-shirt did under his armpits; his sweater itched. His hands, in shapeless leather gloves, were moist. He felt he had not chosen his winter wardrobe carefully enough. With his stipend money, he had rushed to the Harvard Coop, and feeling by turns impatient, intimidated, and wantonly enthused, had made all his purchases in one afternoon.

When, in his entire life, had he ever even worn bright red, never mind neon orange?—but the parka had looked warm, *vos*. He felt, now, like a bundle of dirty laundry.

Before coming to Cambridge, to Harvard, Moya had never in his life met a foreign woman, that is a European, North American, or Asian, who was not at least a little bit obsessed with what quite understandably obsessed Moya: Guatemala. Some of these very same women, of course, were indeed to be found in Cambridge, including the professor, Dr. Sylvia McCourt, who had arranged to have him come to Harvard in the first place, but in Cambridge there were so many more, millions it seemed, women who were not even a little bit that way. Here, in Cambridge, were millions of women who, if reading the news, were quite likely to skip over the occasional mention of the always revolting developments in Guatemala without feeling the slightest pang of interest or remorse. Yet these same millions, from what Moya could tell by eavesdropping on them in cafés, stammeringly conversing with them at the occasional gathering to which he was invited, sitting by them in classrooms and lecture halls, on the whole seemed— How did they seem? Alive, beautiful, healthy, opaquely serious. Fortune's favorite daughters. Totally mysterious. In Cambridge, Moya, at first, felt overwhelmed by a variety beyond his comprehension, and stupefied that he could have lived so long in ignorance of it.

Look at those two *chinitas*—but probably they were Japanese—sitting opposite him on the train, layered in contrasting black winter fabrics. They leaned into each other, chatting and smiling as if satiating themselves on the too rich scandal of someone else's love life. One wore a sickly blue shade of lipstick, the other brightest red. One had hair sculpted into an intricate mass of long, black barbs; she resembled an electrocuted bird with the radiant face of an obscene Oriental angel. Her face was painted like a Guatemala City whore's, and she wore the rugged black leather jacket of a corrupt Guatemala City motorcycle policeman. Yet look at the appealing propriety of her lap: her neatly ironed, pleated black skirt and the university textbooks piled there—*Advanced Immunology*—and her dainty hands primly folded on top in skintight, shiny leather gloves.

He looked over all the women on the train, students mainly, many of them standing. A girl yawning, her glassy blue eyes looking right at him yet not registering. Her quiet, composed, intelligent, somewhat tired expression looking right through him suddenly exhilarated him, as if he'd just understood that in Cambridge he would be allowed to remain invisible for as long as he wanted.

There was only one black on the train—the race problem, Moya had effortlessly deduced, was Boston's, and the United States', most pressing sociopolitical problem. But this *negrito* was with a white woman whose face was as composed and somewhat tired as the face of that woman sitting opposite. Not only were they sitting close together, holding hands, but they were both wearing headsets plugged into the same Walkman. Confirming an earlier insight: this other type of gringo, of which there were millions in Boston alone, often preferred any distraction to serious political discussion. Moya felt himself suddenly impassioned by a heated need to articulate, to expose; the subway train pulled into Park Street Station, and Moya, pretending to himself that he felt exactly like himself again but secretly despising or at least exhausted by himself; jumped up. In his heavy arctic parka, he walked like a penguin. The car emptied, and, accompanied by a hundred or so university students, only one of them black, he walked up the steps to the second level, where he spotted a Green Line train pulling in, which instantly made him feel the need to repress a soft inward sob. Why? Because the Green Line train was the one Flor used to take into Boston.

Why, everywhere he went in Boston, did he feel as if his shadow was snagging on Flor's, pulling him up short? Why Flor's shadow whispering indecipherably into Moya's?

"You will make a wonderful saint," he had teased her, much later on during the Long Night of White Chickens, after she had been somewhat drunkenly and certainly somewhat archly reciting the qualities, textures, and odors of impoverished and malnourished infants' *caca* and the endemic illnesses these revealed: ". . . yellow and stinky, that's giardiasis. Common diarrhea is runny, of course, and accompanied by much gas. Amoebas, bloody. Oh Moya, I see a lot of *caca*." But even these words had seemed beautiful to him, because by then everything Flor said seemed part of the long, slow Rapunzellike descent of her hair towards the bowl of sweet and sour sauce, which he had so raptly and suspensefully been following, watching the slightly curled ends of her hair descend ever closer to the sticky liquid as she leaned ever closer towards him. But then, with his teasing remark, Flor had immediately sat back in her chair, hoisting her hair far above and away from the bowl as she laughingly said, "Oh sure, Our Lady of *Caca*. Anyway, for his Holiness to accept me for canonization, wouldn't I need three miracles, or something like that? Well, so far, believe me, I haven't performed even one."

Here Moya's wit had failed him, as if it had fled into the new, daunting distance between hair and bowl. He had wanted to ascribe to her the miracle of having, in just a few hours, caused a springtime in his heart, but had immediately foreseen that there was no graceful and light way of disguising the rather complex emotion and condition such a remark implied. And while his mind stammered, the opportunity for a bright and affectionate rejoinder that her words had provided passed. Flor leaned forward on her elbows then, into the suddenly awkward silence, as if truly disappointed that she hadn't, in fact, ever performed a miracle. But her hair, the ends of her black, lyrically descending hair, now fell into the sweet and sour sauce. A small handful of Flor's hair now lay curled and partly submerged in the glowing, sticky liquid, and she did not notice.

Love, which was already happening inside him and he hoped inside of her too, is in this way furiously fast and decisive, aligned with both the miraculous and the rational: just when Moya's own confused ardor, shyness, and ominous lapse of wit had caused the wrong silence to settle between them, a silence awkwardly and gloomily after-scented with the problem of unhealthy infants' *caca* and Flor's failure to perform miracles, love had propelled her hair into the sweet and sour sauce, and Moya was free:

"Flor, *mi amor,* look, you have dropped your hair directly into the *agridulce* sauce," he said gaily.

And Flor, truly astonished, said, "Oh!" sitting up straight again with a light clap of her hands. Her hair followed her up, its sweet and sour sauce–coated tips sticking to her white blouse, just inside her breast. She said *"mierda"* and laughed, and reached for her napkin. But Moya gently took it from her. "Let me," he said, his face very close to hers now, his face glowing as warmly as one of the paper lanterns overhead as he felt her moist smile and breath so close. He brought her hair in his hand to his lips, and kissed it. She said, *"Moyyya,"* and laughed. He said, *"Qué rico,"* how tasty, and she laughed more softly and said, "You are really too much." And he said, "I wonder if the rest of you goes so well with sweet and sour sauce," and though she held herself perfectly still he could feel, even in the air between them, that her whole body shook with repressed giggles. *"Hah,"* she squeaked, barely able to get even that little sound out. "I don't require seasoning," she murmured, "I am sure." And he said, "Ah, no?" And then he said, "But I must clean this," and began to move the napkin towards the small stain in her blouse just inside her breast though she softly intercepted his hand. She held his hand briefly in hers, smiling at him, perhaps coyly, perhaps warningly, her eyes blazing. Then she took the napkin from him, dipped it into the ice bucket, and cleaned the spot herself.

"I feel it is a miracle," he said then, calmly. "I have not felt so happy in a long time."

The brief, barely lingering look they exchanged then was the bridge leading to everything that was to happen between them from that moment on.

"But my gosh," she said. "I've been doing all the talking!"

". . . So this was my first truly independent adventure, all the way from Miami to Boston by bus. Oh Moya, you should have seen it, I didn't have to pay for a single donut or soda all the way, and, by the time I got home, I had the addresses of seventeen soldiers to write to. Many of them going to Vietnam too. They were all so handsome and nice to me I couldn't believe my luck!"

"Seventeen soldiers! Did you write to them?"

"*Ay noooo.* Can you imagine what Mirabel would have said if suddenly I had letters from seventeen soldiers coming to the house?"

"Seventeen soldiers in Vietnam," said Moya and, being who he couldn't help but be, he shook his head portentously. "How many people know that twenty-eight Green Berets died in Guatemala in 1968. Plus the two thousand peasants killed in that obsessed campaign to destroy two hundred guerrillas."

"Really? Is that true? Twenty-eight? I've heard they were here but I've never heard *that*," said Flor. "Oh well, that figures." And after a short, distressed sigh, she added, "*Qué país, no?*" What a country, no?—Which one? Moya was about to ask—but Flor was already saying, "You know what I remember? We'd stopped for a break in the bus station at Macon, Georgia. And this gross, sweaty man came up to me and, well I cannot quite do a southern accent, but he said, '*Girrrrrl*, I *been* watching *youuu* and I can't figure it out. Are you *Filipeeno* or what?' . . ."

"How did you answer this racist man?" asked Moya.

"I said I was Guatemalan, *pues,* but soon to be American. He laughed like I had just proved his big ugly point somehow. But my soldier friends, some of them black by the way, chased him away. You know, in my Massachusetts family, we were always a bit judgmental against southerners; Ira had a tough experience down there in the army. But that horrible man in the bus station is the only adult who ever spoke to me that way in all my years in America."

"The only adult? You mean children—?"

"In Namoset! The teenagers there? Are you kidding! Spik this, spik that, spik spik spik, well, they thought they were being funny, you know, but they could not free this buzzing fly from their minds. The most provincial of the provincial. And such thugs! Ay, even poor little Roger tried to be like a thug, though he was never a convincing scary person—well, you knew Roger. Adolescence is a form of torture, in the United States anyway. Or so it seemed to me—"

FOURTEEN

"Before I met your father," my mother said suddenly, when we were sitting at the kitchen table over a bottle of sherry on the night of our return from Guatemala, after my father had already gone to bed, "I was in love with a man, a devout Catholic, a man who went to mass every day. And he turned out to be a very bad man, a liar, a drunkard, a womanizer. All my life I had been raised to believe that Catholicism made people good, Roger. But after that, I said, Catholicism does not make people good. And when I met your father I said, Look, here is a good man, and Catholicism had nothing to do with it. And that is why I married him."

This was the first time my mother had ever even alluded, in front of me, to her great girlhood love with the Italian who eventually married the coffee plantation owner's daughter, or spoken so directly about why she had married my father. I sat there pondering her reasoning for a while.

"Well, Dad *is* good," I said.

"He most certainly is."

"You think Catholicism makes people bad?" I asked.

"Of course not," she said. "But Flor was raised by nuns. Did this make her good?"

"Mom. Please."

"Look at the boyfriends she had. And did I think she was a good influence on you? I have held my tongue on this for twenty years. I was not as blind as I was innocent! And as far as you and your father were concerned, she could do no wrong. What about the time your father was in the hospital in New York and we sent you two back by train and she took you to that Cuban's apartment?"

"I wonder where he is now?"

"*Ach!* Probably in jail."

"Mom, Flor was upset, she thought Dad was going to die or something. And Tony was her boyfriend."

"And that African!"

"He was Nigerian. A Wellesley professor, a literature scholar. That's a pretty extraordinary person, don't you think?" Dr. Ben, from Nigeria, Oxford educated, a specialist in Melville and New England Transcendentalists—who knows where *he* is now. That was when Flor was twenty, twenty-one, in high school, and Dr. Ben boarded with Miss Cavanaugh in her house in Wellesley. She was an elderly Boston Brahmin feminist who, in the thirties, just out of Wellesley College herself, had undertaken a motorcycle journey with another young woman all the way to Chile. Miss Cavanaugh, who passed away a few years ago, founded the Latin American Society of Boston; she sat on the board of directors at the private school where my mother teaches and on the board at Wellesley College too.

"Miss Cavanaugh was aghast, my dear. That African lived in her house! She did not speak with me for a year. For a year I felt ashamed to show my face at Latin American Society meetings . . ."

"She was just jealous."

"*Cómo que* jealous? An opinion that perverted could only have come from Flor. Is that what she told you?"

"Miss Cavanaugh loved Flor! Hanging around her house, that practically saved Flor's sanity in high school. She helped her get that scholarship to Wellesley."

"She stole and sold my jewelry."

"That was Tony and you know it. After he found out about Dr. Ben."

"Oh sure, don't remind me—"

"And she never saw him again after that."

"Oh sure—"

"She never did, Mom. The guy was having problems."

"How do you know he didn't send those roses that came today?"

"Because they came with a poem attached, didn't they. She hasn't seen him for years."

"She never saw him again because he ran off to Miami with another woman."

"OK. Good. He went to Miami. Mom. Please. This isn't fair."

My mother's lips had closed into a little girl's pout.

"Mom. You loved her . . ."

"The saddest thing in the world is to die young, I would not wish that on anyone. She . . . mesmerized you for twenty years like a witch."

"She did not."

"My own mother saw this. She told me. Mirabel, she has your son under a spell like a witch. You loved her, and I thought that was good. Because you didn't get to see enough love in this house between your father and I. I don't know why I thought that was a good replacement.. . I was innocent but I was not blind."

"Mom, I had plenty of love . . ."

A one-day closed casket wake in McGee's funeral home; and then Flor's casket at the top of the aisle between the pews, in front of the altar, at St. Joe's, while a young priest who had never known her reached his hands into the enclosure Flor used to tell me was the actual Heart of the Holy Spirit and brought out the chalice and offered communion, which no one took, and then spoke a eulogy that was a brief outline of her accomplishments, lamented her terrible end without evoking the circumstances, all who knew her will so miss her. My mother wept as hard as my father and I. At the cemetery, in the snow, with the casket suspended over the hard rectangular cavity in the otherwise empty Graetz family plot, the priest dashed holy water like salt, wished her peace in the benevolence and forgiveness of God, and we, the few who had gathered, fled back to our cars. A few of her Wellesley friends were there, including that strange, malevolent girl with pink hair who, seven months later, would turn up all coked up or something when I was tending bar one night. Zoila, Ingrid, even Tony, lost to time, I wonder if even Flor had had any idea where they were now. Thirty-six roses and a poem at the house. Telegrams and cards. No past or even secret lovers in person among the mourners.

Delmi Ramírez arrived the day after the burial, on a Saturday, with her three young sons from Oklahoma, where she lives now. I hadn't seen her in about fifteen years. She looked older, much older than Flor. Her hair was dyed blond. She'd become a stern mother, of hawkish expression. She paraded her three Okie boys, bronze skinned and fair haired, stiff in their cheap new suits and bow ties, in front of my discomforted mother and father as if it were a visit to royalty, and boasted about how much money her mechanic husband was making in Tulsa—quite a lot actually—and said she owed all her happiness to Flor.

They were staying in the motel on the cliff overlooking Route 128, on the outskirts of Namoset, by the Industrial Zone. I went the next morning to have breakfast with Delmi in the House of Pancakes, and while we were sitting there, I guess it's pertinent to add, since it happened, Danny Ainge, the Boston Celtics guard, the Mormon from Brigham Young, drove up in a big car, a Cadillac probably, and came in for breakfast too, looking much taller than he does on TV among the real giants.

Delmi was full of nostalgia, and much more relaxed than she'd been in front of my parents. She went on and on about the convent orphanage days as if they'd been the happiest times anyone could imagine.

"Boys used to fly kites with messages for us over the walls. Sometimes they didn't even know our names. They'd write, For the *patoja* with curly hair. Or, For the one who looks like a beautiful rabbit. We'd argue over who they were for, and try to lift each other up over the wall to peek at them . . ."

But I kept thinking of the story Flor had told me four years before, in the one reggae bar in Guatemala City, a story that seemed so incredible and ridiculous that I'd thought she was just pulling my leg, dramatizing for the hell of it—I almost would have refused to believe any of it if Flor hadn't put so much effort into telling it.

"I know it's really *weer* sounding," Flor had said, "but I'm telling you, cross my heart . . ." Delmi, after a few years, had left her job with the family in Chestnut Hill, moved into an apartment of her own, and started working in the Combat Zone as a stripper. Then she became addicted to drugs.

"What drugs?"

"I don't know. Every drug." Flor never knew much about drugs.

And then Delmi had ended up in a lesbian bordello somewhere in Mattapan.

"A lesbian bordello? There's no such thing."

"No such thing! I was there! I went to rescue her! That lady had a whole house, and it was a lesbian bordello! Rogerio, you don't know the things that can happen to a Guatemalan girl living on her own in the city. She didn't have someone like Ira to protect her. It really was like the Devil got into her. I know, but that was what it was like."

Flor said the madam there kept Delmi stuporous and chained by her drug habit, completely out of it. Flor went in and slapped Delmi hard in the face several times and made a big commotion and dragged her outside and into the car where Tony was waiting. And then Tony kept her locked up in his apartment for three months, until her addiction was broken. This, if it was to be believed, had happened when for was in the ninth grade, and no one in my family had known a thing about it. That was back when my father's biggest worry was that Flor was going to blow everything by getting married to Tony.

Flor usually had a lot of tact, at least where I was concerned. Almost by natural disposition, she was incredibly protective of me. It wasn't until the last years that she started telling me things I'd never known or even suspected.

On one of her last trips to New York she told me that during her first year with us she'd thought often of leaving us because our house was so unhappy. Maybe the benumbed, comfortable giddiness of a day in the sun was responsible for this: we'd taken the train to Jones Beach together, and now we were having iced margaritas in the air-conditioned, pastel melon ambience of a Tex-Mex restaurant downtown. I'd said something about a college friend I'd gone to visit in Houston. And Flor brushed hair flayed by ocean winds out of her half-closed eyes, her pupils had a skittish black gleam, as if being buffeted by the uncontrollable thoughts slipping from a sun and margarita–sated mind, and she said, "Oh yeah, Houston—You know, I almost had a job there once. In Dallas. As a mayyyyd. *Fíjese.* This was during my first year with you . . ."

And it just came out. She'd even written to the Espíritu Santo nuns asking them to find her another job and they eventually wrote back to tell her of one in Dallas and she almost took it. Because it used to break her heart the way my mother would stay in bed on Sunday mornings, sobbing. I had never heard of this. Flor said she used to keep me downstairs, so I wouldn't hear it, my mother in the bedroom sobbing. It made Flor feel so helpless and lonely. But what would my father do? After a while he gave up. He'd go outside and do yard work, or he'd sit in his chair reading the Sunday papers, or he'd go into Boston to play cards. "And then the things Mirabel would tell me later, she had no one else to talk to, and I, who was I? What did I know?" There was so much sadness in the house, but that's why she'd stayed, because of me, to protect me from it and to love me.

Where do the what ifs stop and does a logic other than chance take over? (What if Señor Soto Hijo hadn't decapitated Flor's father? if La Gatita hadn't driven her to the Las Hermanas del Espíritu Santo? if I hadn't contracted TB? if my mother hadn't agreed to try to reconcile with my father? if Abuelita hadn't chosen Flor but another girl, even Delini Ramírez, instead?) With *that,* Flor's decision to stay with us in Namoset instead of going to Dallas (because of me), doesn't it stop being chance and become something else? It becomes Flor de Mayo, leading to everything else.

FIFTEEN

My mother had worried that I would not get to see enough love between her and my father, so she had thought Flor could provide a replacement, then Flor had mesmerized me like a witch. And as if that were all there ever was to it, with Flor's death the black (or white) magic spell that had held my family together dissolved. My mother, determined to start over, moved into an apartment in Boston, near the Quincy Market waterfront. And my father was left alone in the small house on Codrioli Road that Namoset teenagers had liked to call the Copacabana as if in celebration of all the happy illusions inside. Well, the house, now that all but one of those illusions were gone, couldn't just get up and rumba away, could it (leaving behind the gaping pit of the basement foundation where the beautiful demon from Chiquimula had conceived and raised herself)?

Like a true hero, in the face of all pessimism, my father was determined to hold on to the last illusion: he wanted to clear Flor's name, as if only by his doing that could some of life's old sparkle return. He wrote regularly to congressmen, who ignored him, and every other week phoned Consul Simms in Guatemala, who didn't, though the news was always the same, no news; no more was known with any certainty than had ever been known. We spoke frequently, of course, and sometimes I took the train up to Boston to see my parents separately on my days off. But I refused even to reminisce, to talk much about Flor. Guilt was my mask: like it was my fault, me who had originally convinced my father, arguing so passionately in defense of Flor's being in Guatemala at all. Of course back then my compelling arguments had little pleased my mother, because she'd always thought my so-called paralysis was a result of my feeling so thoroughly outdone by Flor that all I wanted to do was bask in the glow of our long association and that this was just the latest manifestation. Definitely an exaggeration, I used to insist.

It was my mother, who, in the months after Flor's death, displayed the most striking gift for survival and happiness. She just swept the past out of her way. She, who, after all, should have known her own country best, found a way to blame it for almost everything. Because of Flor, she felt she could no longer comfortably go back there, and said she didn't want to anyway. It was because of her own *"guatemalidad"* that she had remained innocent for so long after she was no longer blind, accepting what she shouldn't have out of life because she hadn't been able to get out from under Abuelita's mandates. Now she was occasionally heard to say that she was so ashamed of her native country's notoriety she was even thinking of renouncing her citizenship. As vice president of the Latin American Society of Boston, it was my mother who moved to cancel the annual Guatemala party in protest of the human rights violations there, though it is also true that the society had already canceled that party two years in a row for the same reason. But she still went on Channel 63 at Christmas as she does every year with some of her prep school Spanish class girls dressed in Indian *traje* to tell about Christmas in Guatemala, to sing a *posada* song accompanied by my mother knocking out the *tica-toca-tic* rhythm with a stick on a large turtle shell cradled under her arm. Certainly a sweet and harmless enough thing to want to do, I've always thought.

Before long my mother was seeing an Argentine heart specialist, several years younger than herself; who practices at Mass General—that is, they were romantically involved. But I'd first heard mention of him a few years before, as the so distinguished-looking clarinetist (who was also a surgeon) in the amateur Dixieland jazz band that every Tuesday night for years has been playing in a certain Mexican restaurant that my mother and her colleagues have long liked to frequent for margaritas and such following Tuesday night organizational meetings of the Latin American Society of Boston. My mother certainly deserves this kind of happiness; she said she'd only started seeing him recently, I didn't press the point.

She must have been thinking, though she never would have put it so blatantly, Well, now you are left with your own life, Roger. Get on with it. I knew that was true enough, and tried to behave, outwardly at least, as if composing myself to "get on with it" was just what I was doing. Of course no one could have expected that I wouldn't grieve deeply. I needed time to heal. But what exactly was there to get on with? To try to clean Guatemala out of my life had seemed a sane, if only symbolic, first step—Soon I felt I didn't even have a history. I didn't know what I was trying to heal. Had I lost a relative, a sister as it were? A best friend? A myth? A metaphysical lover? A lie? My own history?

There were too many questions. I couldn't handle it. I let my thoughts, my sadness and anger take a relentless course inside of me. If this was about the end of illusions, then I wanted to get on with that, smash them all up, be truthful and even brutal about it. Maybe that was how to heal. I told myself stories and learned that I could be made of the ones I chose to tell, not simply the ones that life had laid haphazardly around me. But now I chose to tell them silently, and only to myself. I wanted to purge myself of all the old stories, or at least learn to look at them in a new, mean way. *Remember the night my father had his two in the morning gallbladder attack in the Howard Johnson's Motel on Eighth Avenue in New York City?*—tending bar, where I was working six nights a week and taking as many double shifts as I could get, I told this and other stories to myself, corrupting every detail, nourishing myself on them like a ravenous ghost while as if in some separate dimension I went on amiably pouring drinks, bantering with customers; and even kept up my cheerfully tepid affair with Cathy Miller, who understood that my cold good cheer was a form of macho self-repression and denial, and that it was not the right time to press me for a commitment. But I wasn't repressing or denying anything, I thought I was doing the opposite, but silently, in that way of talking to yourself that isn't even quite inner monologue because you're hardly conscious of using words though of course you are. *That morning we saw Harvard lose to Columbia and their great quarterback Marty Domres at Baker Field and in the evening we dined at some fancy restaurant with an old boyhood friend of my father's named the Camel and his wife. Flor was nineteen and in the ninth grade. She was in her sophisticated stage and always asked the waiters for steak tartare even if it wasn't printed on the menu but they had it for once and I had the duck à l'orange because it was what I always ordered after Harvard games when we were on the road because though I really liked duck à l'orange I knew I would let my father down if I ordered anything else, had known it ever since that evening years before at an alumni-crowded restaurant after the game Princeton won because they had the great fullback named Cosmo with a long Polish last name beginning with K when a tall red-faced Texan who was actually wearing a cowboy hat and boots with his suit and Tiger tie stopped at our table on his way out to say that he'd been watching me relishing and devouring that ole duck à l'orange and that he envied my father for having a little boy with such a good hearty appetite, because his own son, who was evidently my age—and who stood behind his father limply glowering at me and who did, in fact, look kind of sallow and ill nourished—never ordered anything but hamburger and mainly, dang it, because he liked the french fries and licking catsup off the bun. This garrulous Texan had obviously had a few drinks, but still, his words had a great effect, everyone on earth soon heard of them. From then on I was little Roger who, after his Harvard game, just has to have his duck à l'orange, he picks the bones clean. The sulking sons of Texas millionaires ordered hamburgers, licked catsup off the buns, they made their fathers less proud. I would let mine down if I ordered anything else, not because of the dish itself or even what it symbolized though partly that but because it had become part of the ritual and this, Flor and I both tacitly understood, was what mattered most, my father's enjoyment of the ritual*—tending bar, bantering away and telling myself all this, my cruel stories, and trying to make them even meaner—*Steak tartare, oh yeah? Duck à l'orange! Oh sure. We've sure as hell lived up to all the shiny, lying promise of that fucking duck*—

Fifteen months after the funeral and one month after he had run into my mother at that Latin American Society of Boston event, Moya, then at Harvard on the special scholarship that saved him from death threats in Guatemala, came to Brooklyn.

" . . . "

"You mean you didn't know?"

"What do you mean I didn't *know?*"

"Oh Rogerio!"

"What? What didn't I know?"

"This was all a *fafero* job. Everybody knew that, within days, *vos!*"

"What? 'What the fuck's a *fafero?*"

"What's a *fafero!*"

"What's a *fafero!* C'mon Moya, don't dick me around!"

"*Ay no.* It's a reporter who takes *fafas, vos*—bribes."

". . . You mean Consul Simms knew this?"

"He must have known eventually. Within days, *vos.*"

"..."

"Or maybe not, *vos.* You know how it is, they don't leave the embassy so much. Some things they are the last to know."

"..."

"It isn't a consul's work to go around shouting *fafa* at Guatemala. Rogerio, do you know how unextraordinary this whole story was? Within weeks everybody forgot about it, forgot about Flor de Mayo..."

"..."

"Not *forgot* her, but, you know. I did not forget! But something like this is always happening. And who is going to make the big deal if it is common knowledge?"

"—Jesus. My relatives knew?"

"*Pues,* not *that* everybody."

"I don't—"

It was in the Brooklyn Museum café, just about the only place to get a cup of coffee in my neighborhood, that Moya and I had this conversation. And it wasn't even what he'd come to Brooklyn to tell me. Mainly he'd come to tell me about his love affair with Flor. He'd thought I already knew about the rest: about the *faferos,* and then the clandestine fattening house's true owners. This sounds like bombshell information, I know, but I've already warned that it isn't really. Of course I didn't really understand that back then, in Brooklyn, I mean at first, though Moya tried hard to make it clear enough.

So this was it, Moya's info: The police discovered, by accident, perhaps, a *casa de engordes,* a fattening house, a house for hiding children. So maybe, said Moya, some honest or corrupt but certainly *bobo* policeman found the house and thought he was going to "make a big bribe and then discovered that he was really made of shit . . ."

Because the house belonged to the sister and sister-in-law of López Nub. General López Nub who is now defense minister but at the time of Flor's death was *Coronel* López Nub in charge of a garrison in the highland department of Quiché, and then later one of the conspirators and beneficiaries of the coup against Ríos Montt—*"Un coronel muy poderoso,"* said Moya. "Anyone announces that, *vos,* prints that, about this house, and they are dead tomorrow. So the police are sitting on this like an egg they are too frightened to hatch. For how long? Weeks, days, something like that . . ." But the rumors were coming out, because even sun shrunken and tiny like a raisin *hobo* ambulatory police will talk, that a fattening house belonging to someone *más o menos importante* had been found—

". . . Then, suddenly, *puta,* a few days or even weeks after, Flor de Mayo is killed. And the police come out and say, See, we found this house *yesterday,* and now this woman is dead. It was *her* house. We captured this *niñera.* And the *faferos* begin to earn their money."

So there was Moya, in his navy blue arctic parka with its neon orange fake fur–trimmed hood, his pallor after a winter in Cambridge almost as yellowy and sickly as that of the Warhol print of Someone or Other on the museum café wall, telling me all this, which he'd thought I already knew and which, I'd see, didn't matter anyway because—I lit another cigarette and he said, "I haven't seen anyone do this for a long time. Smoke one cigarette right after another." I glared at him, frantic, and said, "Well what the fuck? The general, the army killed Flor?"

And he said, *"No, hombre,* I don't think so—But you will see—*Cálmate, vos* . . . You will see, it does not change things so much, Rogerio. Because—*pues,* why?"

The house belonged to López Nub's sister and *cuñada* (sister-in-law), a fact, if it is a fact, that Moya regarded as not even coincidental but as part of a ceaseless pattern, an ever-present camouflage that anyone else could have hidden behind (murderous *chafas,* colonels, and generals, reflecting the illusion of evermore as if in facing mirrors . . .)

"So who would dare to have put pressure on then *Coronel* López Nub to extort or embarrass him? Who else could have ordered police to that house, could organize such a plot to extort or embarrass except other even *more* powerful military men? But how many of these powerful *chafas* do *not* have relatives involved in criminal activities, *vos?* As long as it is just rumors and not an official accusation from a military tribunal, so what? So who is going to do this to a *coronel, vos?* Not even General Ríos Montt, unless a coup against himself is all he is wishing for. And *Coronel* López Nub, he is up in the Quiché waging *contra-insurgencia,* fighting guerrillas, burning villages—it is going to occur to this exceptionally busy man to get rid of this threat to his sister and *cuñada* and to his own family name in a country where no one expects a *coronel* to have a clean family name, by murdering this woman he has probably never even thought of so that she can be blamed? And to have her killed with a knife, a wound that with a little luck she survives?"

I said that I didn't get it and Moya insisted that he felt he was being lucid. I asked who paid the *faferos* and he said it wasn't necessarily what we really wanted to know, because *faferos* don't have to be paid by anyone in particular to say anything in particular. "We are talking about *un cierto tipo* who can survive as a journalist in Guatemala, *vos;* some draw a regular salary from the army and, for others, you can say even their regular salary is their *fafa. Fear, ignorance, and fafa are my shepherds, I shall not question or want,* yes?"

—But didn't I see how glad the police would be to rid themselves of this embarrassing problem caused by a *hobo* policeman who found this house he should have left alone?

Likelier though, he said, is that the whole mess evolved something like this:

The inevitable rumors were beginning, and so López Nub's sister and sister-in-law were becoming embarrassed. Because colonels can traffic in whatever they want, contraband, drugs, weapons, passports and immigration papers for Hong Kong Chinamen, you name it though no one publicly dares to; and all those government ministries, utilities, foreign-financed projects and nonlethal economic aid and newly accessible lands to plunder and grab, virgin ranches, oil and lumber concessions, their own fiefdoms; countless rackets more profitable, more macho, less arduous and less ignominious than the selling of Indian war orphans to clandestine fattening houses and abroad, a wimpy Corrupt Stork's racket for money-grubbing *caraculo* lawyers and witches . . .

But a colonel's *women?*—*they* go to tea parties and baby showers.

". . . So maybe other women are snickering at them, *vos*. Soon their children will be hearing comments in school, *vos*. López Nub's sister contacts her brother and says, Brother? Did you hear that the *directora* of Los Quetzalitos was found murdered yesterday? Can't you have the police say it was her house? And have them make a really big fanfare, *vos*. This woman was a stuck-up gringa-*chapina* . . ."

So here was a chance to put an end to embarrassing rumors about the sister and sister-in-law of López Nub and focus all hatred of baby sellers on Flor as well. Which excited the *faferos,* because here was *their* chance to make great patriotic rhetoric against baby sellers and make it sound like they were blaming the hypocritical gringo slanderers of Guatemala all in one murder, simply by accepting everything that the police said as true. In the end they would even feel justified and quite clever, because who would even be interested in the true rumors if not for the sensationalizing lies which they did not then realize were lies—*"Ja!"*—in the news!

And it was all so easy, because everyone said Flor was doing that anyway, profiting illegally off her adoptions.

"So what you're trying to tell me is that everyone in the Guatemalan press is a *fafero.*"

"Mostly everyone still alive, yes. Outside the morgue that day, *puta!* Our fafero Olympic team."

"You?"

"Rogerio."

"Well, why are you different?"

"*. . .*"

"You were there that day with the rest of them!"

"To see *you,* Rogerio."

Pssst! Oye! *The fattening house they were saying belonged to that gringa* chapina . . . ? *The archbishop's chambermaid is pregnant. The army ambushed a guerrilla column last night, wiped the shit out of them, and you know what? there wasn't a* chapín *among them, they were all Palestinians and Libyans,* vos! Who listens to every curlicue turn in the baroqueness of rumors that winds through Guatemala? Who believes them? Shopgirls, when privileged to hear them. If Uncle Jorge had heard, he would have thought, just a shopgirl's *chisme,* shopgirl talk. He likes the rumors about the Palestinians and Libyans. Choose your rumor.

"People were amused, Rogerio, this is all. Not amused about Flor, of course not. But one more murder in Guatemala *vos?* How many were going to say, 'This *one* murder! This is the most *outrageous* murder!' No, *vos.* Instead they said, Look how easily López Nub's sister and *cuñada* get away with owning a fattening house! What has *Coronel* López Nub been doing, flying them weekly loads *of bebitos ishtos* from the Quiché? Ja. Like this was funny. Do you see?"

"'No."

"Then this rumor, Rogerio. López Nub's sister did the murder, with her own hands. Because Flor was working with her but really she betrayed her. Because really Flor was with *La CIA*. She was pretending to arrange adoptions of stolen babies to nice gringo families but was actually bringing these children back to CIA hospitals so that their organs could be used for transplants to save the lives of rich gringos et cetera. *Increíble, no?*"

". . . His sister murdered—?"

"Rogerio! The sister of López Nub probably started this rumor herself. Because now that everyone knows she is a baby seller, she at least wants them to think of her as a baby seller *patriótica* and well-intentioned! I am not joking, *vos*. We are talking about some real *ignorantes*. This is a gross, stupid woman, Flor would *never* have let her into her room!"

"But what if they *were* partners, Moya?"

"Rogerio, no, *vos*. Impossible. Because in Guatemala there is this saying: Firemen should not step on each other's hoses. But sometimes I think this rule only rules *chafas*. If Flor was partner with a colonel's sister, then this other colonel, Malespín, could never have dared to threaten her, do you see? But all these rumors, Rogerio, what do they matter? The official police line is still that no one knows who did this murder, and for once maybe the official line is right."

"So who was the *niñera* at the house, then? The one who—"

"*Puta! Saber.* I don't know. A *niñera fafera*. I had no luck in finding her."

"You looked for her?"

"Yes."

"Oh. You mean you started investigating all this."

"Yes . . . Rogerio—"

"So you suspected from the start that something was . . . *not right.*"

"Not right, *claro.*"

"So who did it?"

"I don't know."

"You've told me everything you know."

"About that house, yes. It was not her house."

"So you *don't* think she was trading babies or whatever."

". . . I feel terrible, *vos.* I thought you at least knew about the *faferos.* Someone did kill her, Rogerio. Why?"

"So what do I do now?"

". . ."

"I mean what the fuck am I going to do about this?"

"I don't know, Rogerio, but I—But what I must first tell you is that Flor and I—*fuimos amantes* . . . Yes, lovers, a little bit, *pues.* For some months—"

"So what! So fucking *what!*" And an old Jewish woman surrounded by her coterie at the next table in the museum café rasped, "Keep yuh voice down, young man! Where do yuh think yuh are!"

So this, I felt sure, was the main reason Moya had come to Brooklyn to see me: to talk about Flor, about him and Flor, to get it all off his chest, thinking that perhaps enough time had passed and that for some reason I ought to know if I didn't, because it had bothered him not knowing whether I knew or not, and he'd thought that I knew the rest of it anyway. I never really let him get going on it. For some period of time—he said for a few months—they were lovers. Like what kind of lovers? A casual affair? *Lover* lovers? I couldn't bring myself to ask him this, let him tell it as it should be told when it is time for him to. Until a month before her death! *Claro,* given what I hadn't in fact known, he rapidly acknowledged, he could see why I didn't think it was so important that they had been lovers, *sí pues.* But, in Cambridge . . .

Eventually we got around to all of it, what I've already told. Her shadow in Cambridge. The girl from her orphanage in the yard. As for what the Swedish volunteer had told us about Colonel Malespín, it probably had been just another corrupt *chafa's* extortion scheme. Going into hiding like that really might have been good judgment on Flor's part, the only prudent thing for her to do, *vos.* Of course even when Moya knew her it would have been easy for him to miss some very hidden, even deviant side to her, he wasn't poking into everything she was doing, well, of course he wasn't—But in retrospect it's always easy to suspect that you might have missed something obvious. It was hard for me to listen, I was reeling under the overload of all he'd told me. It was really all too much to take in. It made sense that we collaborate, he said. If I wanted to. He went on about it. I guess I just sat there nodding— until the African immigrants who make up the staff of the museum café suddenly erupted at us in scolding tones from behind their push brooms and bus trays, telling us that the café was closing.

Outside, we went for a walk along Eastern Parkway. Of course we ran into the Guatemalan knish vendor's truck. It was parked in front of the little park next to the massive school for the deaf that I've never seen a single person go into or come out of, though there are always things like snowflakes scissored from paper taped to the insides of the upper windows. A strong, rain-portending wind was gusting around with more force up high than near the ground, ripping yellow-green leaves from the tops of trees, filling the sky with them. From a short distance the leaves, tumbling and twirling down, seemed to surround the truck like a tumult of parakeets.

"Knishes," I said. "It's a Jewish food"—after Moya had gasped in surprise at the sight of the thing, KNISHES CHAPÍN, quetzal birds, pyramid, and volcano painted on the panel. I'm sure it must have struck Moya as some kind of omen, though I suppose he would say he doesn't believe in omens, not Moya the Lucid. I told him, "It's always there."

We crossed the parkway so that Moya could get a closer look. A kid of about twelve, the vendor's son, was there too, standing on the sidewalk next to the truck with the visor of his leather cap pulled low over his eyes and a wooden handcart holding colored syrup–filled bottles to pour over shaved-ice cones, just like in Guatemala.

Moya mumbled, *"Pero increíble."*

I'd never stood so close to that truck before. It had first appeared in the neighborhood some months after Flor's death, and I'd just wanted to stay clear of it. I waited dumbly by Moya's side as he and the vendor began a short, cryptic conversation. The vendor said he was from Huehuetenango. Moya repeated *Huehuetenango,* and the man repeated it too, and then Moya, in Spanish, said, *Yes, it's been hard up there, hasn't it been?* And the vendor seemed suddenly nervous, brusque, his black eyes shrank. *Sí, duro,* hard, he said, and he turned sideways and slid some gyros onto the hot middle of his grill, though we hadn't ordered any. The meat sizzled softly. At the top of his wide, brown neck, along the underside of his wide chin, there was a long, crude scar. A scar near where Flor had hers, though longer and sealed with ugly, ruined skin—a machete scar, I thought. I saw that Moya, of course, had noticed it too. *You've been to Huehue?* the kid suddenly asked Moya, lifting his head to peer at him from under the visor. Moya said, *Claro.* And the kid turned to look at me, his tilted-up nostrils flared like an otter's, his Indian eyes a shinier, even blacker version of his father's. *And you?* he asked me. *You've been to Huehue?* I said not recently. *Ah,* he said, and looked back at Moya. *And how is it? Tranquilo?* the kid asked him. His father singsonged from inside the truck, *Sí, sí, tranquilo. Huehue 'sta tranquilo, verdad?* And the kid nodded, repeating, *Tranquilo, pues. Sí pues.* Moya shrugged and softly echoed, *Tranquilo.*

We bought a tamarind-flavored ice cone and a can of Coke. And after shaking hands and exchanging the usual Guatemalan courtesies—*A pleasure to have met you . . . A pleasure to have met you . . .* Gracias . . . No, jovenes, muchísimas gracias! *At your service!* . . . Gracias . . . *It looks like rain. Doesn't it look like rain? . . . Yes, it does. Well,* gracias. Qué te vaya bien . . . *Good luck with your knishes,* vos! . . . Ay gracias!—Moya and I walked on, both of us strangely shaken, I think, or mystified and briefly silent. I was licking the ice cone. The faint and artificial tamarind flavor, the grainy ice, the very idea of eating it there on Eastern Parkway was like a continuation of the melancholy and visceral (it had sent a shiver through me) ludicrousness of the conversation we'd just had at the truck.

"You want some of this?" I asked Moya, holding the cone out to him.

"*Gracias, 'mano.* No," he said.

"*Guatemala no existe,*" I said.

Moya raised one eyebrow. "*Verdad que no?*" he said. "*No existe.*"

He smiled sadly, and we walked on. Twelve years ago he and I had walked like this, to the bus stop after school every evening. Back then, on any one of those evenings, I might even have been carrying a syrup-flavored ice cone. I suddenly felt close to Moya then, on the parkway. What I mean is that for a moment this closeness really felt like a natural response to a mutual past, and not just a temporary illusion caused by a nostalgic ice cone and this sudden visit from a stranger, essentially a stranger—full of secrets, the secret origins of his prematurely whitening hair—but one full of perplexing news and connections to the present too, a *brand-new* present.

I really didn't know what else to say to him except "My father should hear what you've told me," and in response to his look I said, "About *faferos* and the fattening house."

He said, "I am going back to Cambridge tonight. We can go together, if you want."

Then that spell of closeness was broken as I kept running over in my thoughts all that Moya had told me. I felt my resolve growing, my heart turning to stone with hate. Total resolve, total and suffocating confusion and hate.

I just lost it, right there, with that stupid snow cone in my hand, for the first time in many months, I started to cry (for the first time in *seven* months, since that night when the girl who'd had pink hair at Flor's funeral had come in while I was tending bar to *reminisce*). And Moya—though I was as confused about him, because who the hell was this Moya and why should I tell him *anything?*—stood watching me for a moment, and then suddenly and stiffly threw his arms around me.

"You don't know what it's been like," I said. And he didn't, he didn't know the half of it. "Oh shit, you can't imagine . . . I'm sorry . . . I'll be all right . . ."

"It has been a nightmare, Rogerio, I am sure."

"And it hasn't ended. It's just going in a new direction, right?"

"*Sí, vos.* That's the way it is. But now you have a *compañero* in this."

"—You were almost my brother-in-law?" I think I meant this as a joke to dismiss my crying, or as a signal of gratitude for the way he was being, though I think the remark confused him more than anything else.

"*Ah pues,* not quite," he said after a moment, very solemnly, blinking.

"I'm sorry. When I'm ready, I just can't listen to it, you and her, right now. I've spent over a year being mad at her, and being—"

"It's not so important. I understand. You need to make friends with her in private again."

"That's it exactly," I said. "Except what you've told me about López Nub and everything, what does it change? She still might have gotten herself killed for trading babies. Isn't that what you're saying? It's like we're right back at square one."

"But don't you feel calmer now?" he said.

"Yeah, but why? Why should I feel calmer about it?"

"I don't know," he said. "Because somehow, in this grotesque, banal, and obscene comedy which I have today described for you—"

"—Thinking I already knew it!"

"*Pues sí.* In this labyrinth of obscenities, it is possible to believe in her innocence again, though perhaps this is just a fragile intuition to follow. Maybe we would not feel this if we did not love her."

"—So what if we find out we're wrong?"

"This is a risk, no? With the other hand I would say that, no matter what, we must never lose this again."

He walked with his arm around my back now, the way Latin American students who are good friends do.

I felt convinced then that he was some kind of genius and, though it embarrasses me to say it now, a savior. I felt fine being in the weaker position compared with where I'd been before, and ready to trust him with all my resolve and confusion. Like an earnest student, I said, "It being Guatemala, after all."

"*Pues sí,*" he said, lightly . . . which somehow means the opposite of "*sí pues*" though both mean "*well yes*" and both can mean "*Yes, well . . .*" But *sí pues* is more affirmative, *that's right! of course!* or it's fatalistic, as in *no kidding* or *you said it,* and with a question mark it's *Am I right or what?* But *"Pues sí"* is softer and has a short up-down melody, it's an open-ended and ambiguous punctuation: Well yes, and that's the least of it but just the beginning too, it being Guatemala after all, which, after all, doesn't even exist. (—and with a question mark it's a flirtatious little chirp, *"Pues sí? mi amor?...."*)

Personal involvement aside, how could he *not* have felt challenged. He, a Guatemalan journalist in exile enrolled in a course on nonfiction narrative—"A peripheral crime," he called it, on the Amtrak Minuteman train to Boston that very night. "But one that allows the weaving together of many threads, Rogerio. Because look at all the elements, *vos,* just the journalistic elements." And he listed them: the baby trade, war orphans, the war, the military and the counterinsurgency campaigns; the corruption, apathy, and ineptitude of the legal system, the police, and the press; a Guatemalan-born U.S. citizen with every opportunity to make a good life in the United States who mysteriously and dramatically returns.

He pronounces "Nonfiction Narrative" like any self-important, jargon-struck grad student, his whole nature seems to change, Moya's teeth turn to scissors for the few seconds it takes him to speak those words.

On the train, in the bar car, when I was feeling hyper and fervent and more resolved than ever, ready to drink and talk a streak and on the verge of committing myself to go in on all this with him, I'd almost said, *So go ahead, tell me about you and Flor, I'm going to hear it anyway, it's probably even essential to our investigation that I do.*

Because we'd been talking around and around it, dwelling on all the outrageous particularities of the crime and on Flor herself and me and Flor, but not on Flor and Moya. What our talk had so far most revealed about Moya, I'd thought, was an extraordinary generosity. He'd put his own immediate needs and obsessions aside, devoting himself wholeheartedly to helping me decide what I should do.

But now Moya was gazing with utterly lapsed expression out the window at the Connecticut seascape and had hardly touched his beer. The light from outside made him look even paler, dried out—losing his color from having no one to tell his love story to. It was my fault. It was, after all, what he'd come to Brooklyn to talk to me about. So I really was about to say, *Go ahead, tell me,* but the phrases that took shape in my thoughts dissipated on my lips. Instead it came out as "So who is this Sylvia McCourt? Just how did she get you into Harvard?"—because he'd already told me how, six months before, when it had become necessary for him to leave Guatemala for a while, a certain human rights organization had paid for his ticket out, and a professor named Sylvia McCourt had gotten him into Harvard.

Moya came to in an instant. Just the mention of the Harvard professor made him lift his hands to the tabletop and look at me with a wry expression. He sat up straight, took a fast drink of his beer, grinned, and said, *"Esa pícara, vos. Cómo me jodió."* About Sylvia. That *pícara,* meaning something like "that rascal," friendlier than "bitch," even admiring; *jodió,* "how she screwed, toyed, fucked with me." "How?" I asked, and ended up getting an episodic narration of the young adult Moya's political and amorous life, minus Flor—

SIXTEEN

Luis Moya Martínez does remember very well that long-ago train ride from New York to Boston. In Brooklyn and then on the train, Roger had given the impression that he did want to hear the details, any details, of what had transpired between his old friend, Luis Moya, and Flor de Mayo Puac. *Pues,* it almost seemed as if Roger didn't believe it, and so would not dignify this unbelievably tasteless joke or fantasy or lie by ever mentioning it again. But of course he believed it, or else why was he there, on the *El Minuto*–man train to Boston with Moya, headed to tell his parents of his decision to return to Guatemala?

But Moya did not actually need or desire a confessor, and the offering of such confessions and confidences is not exactly in his nature. (Secrecy is a church, *vos.*) He wanted something else from Roger, what only Roger was in a position to remember and tell; though Moya doesn't think it immodest to add that he also then believed he was offering his old friend a great or at least interesting opportunity. In truth, Roger's life in New York did not seem so stimulating, he seemed to have become something of a deadbeat there.

Flor had had sisterly concern about this, sometimes even saying, "Maybe Roger should come down here for a while. It might be just what he needs." Even at a time when she was often rhetorically asking herself, in Moya's presence, why she had ever come at all or stayed so long who needs this fucking heartbreaking hellhole I want to go someplace unpolluted is there any place like that Moya? Oh gosh, how would you know? . . . (How would Moya know.)

The true mystery of the life and death of Flor de Mayo Puac— Why she came? Why she stayed? As for Los Quetzalitos, she always claimed to have *just fallen into it,* just as, it is true, Moya could claim to have just fallen into newspaper work and thus all that came after.

Flor said, "Maybe you could help Roger get started in journalism."

Moya said, "Rogerio is going to come and work at *El Minuto* for forty *quetzales* a week? I don't see it, my love."

And Flor laughed, "*Ay Moya, por favor, no seas tan imbécil!* Maybe he could pick up a string or something. He probably thinks it's really hard to become a correspondent. I mean, *hah.* At least he speaks Spanish. And, after all, he is half Guatemalan."

"Whatever that means," remarked Moya.

"It can mean nothing or it can mean whatever he decides to make of it, this is the nature of the bicultural opportunity, you know what I mean?"

"Opportunity?" asked Moya.

"You know that famous definition of surrealism, don't you? The chance meeting of an umbrella and a sewing machine on a dissecting table?"

"*Ahá, sí pues.*"

"Well what about a gringo Russian Jew and a Guatemalan *fufurufa* Catholic on a dissecting table . . . ?"

After a moment, Moya said, "In a way this would be true of you too, *verdad? Puta,* quadcultural, in the sense that all *chapines* are at least tricultural, or at least, as you put it, there is this opportunity. Spanish, Indian, the synthesis."

"In a way, uh-huh. Culturally, I guess," she said. "Though for me, and I bet for you too, Moya, the synthesis, such as it is, is really all there is, and I wonder to what degree it actually *is* a synthesis, and not something else. How Indian do you actually feel, ever? Spiritually, that is. I'm not talking about toothaches, or the political ache. But even the average tourist probably sees as much of the highlands as you have in your whole life, am I right? So OK,

Guatemala, in what we like to think of as its deepest self, is Mayan. We, who aren't actually Indian, what is it we absorb? Not that supposed Indian lack of egocentrism, that community and cosmos first stuff, that's for sure. Oh yes, we can and should learn from it, but I don't think we do, much."

"A heavy spirit. A weightiness that feels Indian."

"Oh come on, you don't have a heavy spirit."

"But I do! This buoyancy surrounds it like a rag bundle that I am smart to never look inside of."

"Uh-huh. And the ancient wisdom is in there too, I suppose."

"No. What wisdom I have has been gained in this life, I am sure."

"At the Colegio Anne Hunt." She laughed. "As usual when we get on this subject, we soon begin to disguise our confusion and even guilt with the usual pretentious clichés."

"*Verdad?*"

Moya—who did detect in his boyhood friend a yearning for something beyond his bartender's life—offered Roger the chance to be a protagonist in a true-life adventure, one fired by indignation, repudiation, the desire for just vengeance or simply desire, and not without peril. Youth doesn't last forever, *vos*.

Truthfully, Moya thought his old friend "Rogerio" seemed like a really nice guy. And bartending had at least taught him the art of likability, which was not a bad thing to possess, it could open doors, even in Guatemala where—How should Moya put it? At Harvard one day, browsing in a bookstore in that paradise of bookstores, Moya happened to flip open an apparently much esteemed gringo novel, wherein his eyes instantly fastened on the sentence: "He had that Latin American likability."—*Puta!* Was that really a known generalization anywhere on earth, that Latinos, as opposed, say, to Germans, are likable? Likable to whom, *vos*? But Moya read it, in this book, which he then stood swaying and mumbling over like those Orthodox Jews with their Bibles he was to see later on a subway platform in New York. Because who especially likes Argentines? Or Peruvians, for that matter, those preening blond *hidalguitos* from the gilded seaside barrios of Lima (there was one in his seminar on the Romantics at Harvard and this pubic-hair-yanked-from-Lima thought he was Shelley, *vos,* for his oral presentation he actually pretended to *be* Shelley, and when he was finished the impressed prof actually said, *Gracias, Don Shelley,* and soon a certain exquisitely beautiful classmate named Ariadne was loving Shelley rather than Moya). Costa Ricans are the Argentines of Central America and Hondurans are too stupid to be hated by anyone except Salvadorans so Guatemalans hate Mexicans when they are taking a break from hating themselves and each other, but, *hombre!* of this Moya is sure, *guatemaltecos* are not especially likable—*vos,* the land of *mala sangre?* bad blood? a nation *not* born of the first *Malinche Azteca* but a nation unborn from a whole brood of humiliated and violated *malinches maya* impregnated by that genocidal lunatic, cheater at dice, and instigator of *La Noche Triste,* Cortéz's banished lieutenant, Don Pedro de Alvarado; to the north, a *mestizo* nation born of the love between a Malinche and a Cortéz, but down here a stillborn morass, not even a nation, *vos, ladino-mestizo* cities, Indian mountains, and not exactly a fraternal relationship between them. Sure, some are excellent, but the man who wrote of Latin American likability could not have met many *chapines, vos.*

But Rogerio, he was pretty likable, though *yanqui* as apple pie (an apple pie with a Maya nose). What pierced Moya about that likability was that it invoked Flor, made her seem close by. Roger and Flor were very different, but some things Moya had thought only Flor did, he soon realized that Roger did too. In Namoset, in the kitchen, Moya watched Roger peel a tangerine while they continued conversing. From inside the peel he stripped the white navel

and stringy white membrane, pinching it with his fingers until he'd
fashioned a small eight-legged white spider, which he set down
without comment on the table. Moya had seen Flor do that, on the
beach at Puerto San José, though she had marched hers from
Moya's chin all the way down his bare belly and past his navel—
Moya had quipped, "Innocent little spider." Then "innocent as a
spider" had entered both their vocabularies, and has lived on in
Moya's. "El Gordo was innocent as a spider, but they took him—"

On the *El Minuto*–man train, Moya prodded Roger. ("What
was it like, Rogerio, that one summer that Flor did come to Guatemala with you?") He knew Roger was still in something of a state
of shock; an immense new hole had just been opened up in Roger's
life, and in the bar car he seemed to be trying to fill it, draining
beer after beer. It was near sundown when the train rolled past a
long repertoire of waters: marshes, suddenly a beach in a cove
(adults strolling on that beach actually stopped and waved vigorously at the train, just as happy peasants in their maize fields like
to wave at anything that goes by), the horizonless vista of a bay. This
was when the conductor, an elderly Irishman with an alcoholic's
raw nose, came down the aisle speaking quietly though rhapsodi-
cally and as if only to himself about the bay at sunset, which he said
he had the opportunity to see almost daily and found more beautiful each time and that it was enough to make anyone believe in
God. The bar car's passengers all heard him and the effect was
unanimous: everyone looked out the window, filing reverentially
silent. Moya looked out at the soft yet brilliant blues, the dissolving pinks, the jubilant greens of sea grasses and trees along the
curving shore. After a while he reflected that with the exception
of there being not even one volcano on the horizon, this vast water-
scape could be Lago Atitlán at a similar hour. Except that lake
inevitably conjured thoughts of evil spirits and demons, of dervish
winds springing from the middle of the lake to pull Indian fisher-

men under, an unfriendly and forbidding lake that tourists often regard in an opposite way, comparing it favorably with those of Switzerland and Como, Italy. They say, that is the Indians supposedly say, that the wind that blows across that lake from north to south does so only when someone has drowned, because *La Dueña,* the Goddess of the Lake, doesn't want Indian corpses putrefying and befouling her crystalline depths, she just wants their spirits, so she makes that wind blow until those drowned Indian fishermen bob up amidst the reeds and floating pumice stones along the shore. What does Moya make of such myths? (apart from the recurring rejoinder: *Typical* of a goddess!) Water is water *vos,* gringos, *por ejemplo,* have sturdier boats, they don't toss their fishing nets in and fall in with them, they wear life preservers, and, most important, they all learn to swim. Here Moya feels totally ill at ease . . .

Moya does like to imagine a Guatemala so evolved from its present darkness that one day a future president, a cultured and worldly man, addressing the United Nations, might *choose* to do so in Tzutuhil Maya, his first, his native village tongue. And if Moya himself should ever gain such ultimate power, *claro,* what a sweeping land reform he would enact, returning, ipso facto, much ancestral land. Perhaps the most just Guatemala, or at least one expressive of the interests of the majority, would be one that Moya, no lover of farm life or of any form of ethnic nationalism, would feel compelled to flee, if only out of boredom—to Paris, with a clean conscience at last, *vos!*

Flor had been right: the average tourist saw as much of the Indian altiplano, the highlands, as Moya had; the same could be said for most Guatemala City *ladinos,* who rarely ventured beyond the tourist towns as well. But for Moya, trapped but always busy in his crowded urban grid, even travel to the tourist towns was risky, and to venture beyond them, completely proscribed.

The highways through the *milpas* (maize fields) and mountains were deserted. Military roadblocks were common. Sometimes men wearing black hoods with holes cut over the eyes were accompanied by soldiers onto the buses, and then people, peasants mostly, innocent as spiders, were pointed out by the black-hooded men, taken off, never seen again; the practical effectiveness of terror owes much to such theatrics. Out there Moya could easily be snatched, and by the time a foreign human rights organization heard about it . . . oh, too late; and no "witnesses," none that would talk.

Los Quetzalitos was home to many Indian orphans. In the yard, little girls played at being their past selves, kneeling in a circle, patting out tortillas from mud. The orphanage, of course, was conducted in Spanish, it had to be, and the children soon adapted. But with sudden bursts of Indian dialect and snatches of song, orphans often took Flor and even themselves by surprise. Roger had spied on a boy with a laundry hamper strapped to his back, pretending to be a turtle, but was that in any way suggestive of an indigenous atavism? Some private remnant of *son* and dance? A celebration of a *nahual,* a child's animal double and protective spirit? *Saber.* Who knows. Flor, who did know a bit about all this, once told Moya of an Indian belief that children separated from their villages had been separated from their souls. If they died, and were buried far from their villages, then their souls would forever wander, in exile from the world of the ancestors.

"Strange to think," she whispered, solemnly, "that under this very roof, then, are scores of little children who have been separated from their souls."

"So you are saying," said Moya, "that adult souls are portable, but children's are not."

"Apparently," she said. "And, believe me, nothing in the clinical orphanage literature tells you how to deal with *that.*"

"And when they go to Sweden or Paris to become Swedes and Frenchmen, do they remain separated from ancestral souls?" asked Moya. "Or do they then receive Swedish or French ones? Like that Indian boy you sent over to receive a Swedish kidney."

"Something like that probably takes place, yeah."

Flor could get quite carried away with these things, almost like a child trying to frighten herself. But of course, growing up in the desert, she'd been exposed to many superstitions, though she was ambivalent towards this aspect of herself. Once, during a trying conversation in her room, Moya said, "You have to trust me. I know you don't believe it, but we could have a great life together. My faith will carry both of us," and for emphasis he rapped his knuckles on the edge of her rosewood desk and she exclaimed, "Oh no! Don't tell me you're getting superstitious! That would be too much! I need you *not* to be!" Another time, in a more rational mood, she explained the tiny old man-monsters with beards called *los wins* whom some of the orphans apparently feared. "Well, think about it," said Flor. "They had corn *milpas* outside their huts. Ears of corn have beards. Looking into a *milpa* at night, they could imagine it was the *wins* out there, tiny wicked faces with beards, making the corn move and laugh. So you see where some of this comes from. Their mothers used to tell them about the *wins* to keep them from straying off from their huts at night." But once, standing in line outside a movie theater, Flor had met an Indian shaman, a *brujo.* He was well dressed though, fairly young, wearing a Swatch watch; he had once been a seminarian and then rediscovered *la vía autóctona,* the sacred Maya way. He worked part-time as a computer programmer. He claimed to have great powers. They went out for drinks. A few nights later he came and visited her at Los Quetzalitos. Outside, in the yard, sitting on rungs of Ozzie Peterkins's jungle gym, under the trees in the yard, he became very intense. He said, "You must trust me. If you don't trust me, it won't work. You must clear your mind of all suspicion you might have of me." He held both her hands.

"So you trusted him," said Moya, but Flor ignored the innuendo in his voice. Suddenly, she said, all the leaves on all the trees and bushes in the yard, eucalyptus and avocado up high, hibiscus and bougainvillea below, took on a buttery glow and began to rattle and shake in unison, not even as if from a strong wind, because there was no wind, but as if the night air had sprouted a tiny hand for every leaf high and low, which in unison were shaking them all up and down. Then it stopped. The *brujo* said, "You have stopped trusting me."

Flor laughed, "True, I had. He had one hand halfway up my arm under my sleeve, and another right inside my thigh. *Chapines,* even *brujos,* never just want to talk, do they? He said that if I went to bed with him then he would know I'd freed myself from all suspicion or doubt, and that then he would teach me everything. I said, Can't we just be friends? Oh well, he didn't want that. But he really did that with the leaves. Maybe I was hypnotized, Moya, but I saw it. Do you really think he could have taught me how to do that?"

Once, long before Moya knew her, Flor was staying in a chalet just outside Santiago Atitlán, on the lake.

"Who did this chalet belong to?"

"Just a friend," she said.

"Was he there too?" asked Moya.

"Just a friend. And no. And how do you know it was a he?"

Anyway, this was a really nice chalet. Most of the chalets on that side of the lake were no longer visited by their owners because of the proximity of guerrillas on the nearby volcano and mountains. Foreigners often rented these chalets from their owners now, and quite cheaply.

Here's a story Roger didn't know, though Moya did not reveal it to him. It was the kind of story that, outside the immediate

Guatemalan context, might cause extreme worry to loved ones far away. So of course she would have kept it from her Massachusetts family (as she often referred to the Graetzes—but then, who was her Guatemalan family?). It was a story that Flor only told Moya during an unprecedented moment of dense intimacy, confidence, and trust.

Every day while Flor was at the chalet, she jogged. So that day she went for her jog, through misty forests and *milpas,* on a dirt road here and there traversed by Indian farmers and sons carrying crude hoes over their shoulders or bent under impossible loads of firewood harnessed by straps to their foreheads and backs. At the sight of Flor in her maroon jogging outfit, the fear caused by unseen footsteps left their eyes; they even smiled as she went by. *"Buenas tardes." "Buenas . . ."* But at a remote bend Flor ran into three *judiciales,* civilian agents of the military. They were standing beside a black-windowed Jeep parked beneath the constant swooping and swirling of swallows from nests in the dirt cliff above. Well, these guys were always lurking around, armed of course, but it was most unusual that they would intrude themselves upon a foreigner or any resident of a lakeside vacation chalet. The three *judiciales* led Flor back into the forest and there ordered her to strip. She complied. She knew she was going to be raped and then almost certainly killed and anonymously buried there. None of the poor farmers she had run past would dare risk admitting to having seen her. Stupid of her to have gone jogging, to have forgotten she didn't really look foreign. It so happened she was menstruating. She pulled the tampon out by its string and tossed it on the ground between herself and the *judiciales. "Eso qué?"* They had never seen such a thing. Disgusted and frightened, they ordered her to put her jogging sweats back on. She was not to breathe a word of the incident to anyone or they would kill her. Now go, whore!

Indian and rural *mestizo* men alike apparently shared this fear and revulsion towards menstrual blood. Peasant women stuffed themselves with rags; some kept their periods secret. Flor had even heard it said that there were men who didn't even know women menstruated. It was considered a curse should a menstruating woman step over a hoe, or come in contact with any of a man's working implements.

When she told Moya, the incident was already nearly two years past. They were in bed, and had been talking for hours. It was only the second time that Moya had actually passed an entire night in Flor's bed in Los Quetzalitos. A brief silence held between them.

"You were very lucky, *mi amor,*" said Moya.

"Wasn't I?" she said. "And stupid to go jogging. Thank God for luck!"

It was to affirm the existence of luck, not to dramatically or warningly exploit a brush with the deadly monster, that such stories were usually told among intimates. "Thank God for luck!" You could never stop saying it in silence, but the company of a trusted intimate sometimes afforded the release of being able to say it out loud. Trusted, *de confianza,* that was key. Moya knew not to resume with questions such as "So what were you really doing all by yourself, if you were by yourself, at that chalet?" In the face of certain punishments and their manner of being applied, everyone is as innocent as a little white spider.

Moya will never forget the day he discovered that his own intelligence set him apart. This happened when he was ten, in Zunil, a village outside Quezaltenango, where his mother took him to pay homage to Maximón. Tricky doer of good and evil, sacred subverter and balancer, backwards and upside-down spirit, sexual degenerate, unsanctimonious and lax father confessor who just listens, Judas—all kinds of crazy stuff is the Indian Maximón, with carved wooden face and cigar in mouth, straw fedora and rainbow raiments, the most sacred relics of the ancestors and *cofradia,* or religious confraternity, bundled inside. But Moya's *mamita* took him to see a *ladino*-bastardized Maximón. In too tight necktie and itchy woolen suit, he rode with her on the bus through mountains and hills fill of sheep grazing and apple orchards to Xelajú, where they spent the night, catching another bus to Zunil in the morning. Maximón was housed in the large, dirt-floored front room of a crumbling mud-brick house in a mostly Indian town. Inside, pilgrims sat on benches along the walls, waiting their turn to prostrate themselves before the idol. Some had come all the way from Mexico. They all wore their best clothes and jewelry. Not an Indian among them. The *ladino* Maximón was a store mannequin with a painted mustache seated upon a throne. He wore mirror sunglasses, a bowler hat; in his mouth was a white, brass-tipped cigarette holder with burning cigarette. He wore a light blue suit, a yellow tie, saddle shoes. Around the throne candles and incense burned, and heaped flower petals festered among the offerings. Unlike the Indian Maximón, this idol did not receive drinks and splashes of *aguardiente.* From where he was seated, Moya could very well hear that every single pilgrim had the same request, for money. Make us rich, Maximón. They kissed the mannequin's hands, shoes, they took turns lighting its cigarette. They stuffed small bills into its clothes. Moya's mother, like all the rest, whispered and pleaded with desperate devotion. Make us rich, why not? She pinched Moya hard when he refused to kneel, refused to light the mannequin's cigarette, refused to utter a single request. Seated against the wall were three Mexican prostitutes in satiny red, yellow, green dresses, their rank perfume mingling with that of the candles and incense. They looked at him fearfully, at the blasphemer. He had a sudden desire to urinate on Maximón's saddle shoes. But he didn't. Reflected in Maximón's sunglasses he saw himself, his dark little face, radiating intelligence, and for a moment was stunned and silent, absorbed in the reflection. Moya loved his *mamita,* his doting and generous inferior. So he mastered himself. He took the idol's hand. Like an eloquent altar boy he spoke. He said, "Maximón, *cabrón.* Thank you for recognizing me." He picked up one of the tapered candles, held it to the cigarette. Then he took out his little wallet, removed the only *quetzal* in it, and placed the bill in the mannequin's bill-festooned suspenders. He winked at the three prostitutes, three winks, one for each. His *mamita* cuffed the back of his head and laughed. Everybody laughed. Moya turned and walked out of the idolatrous den, removing his necktie. Outside, he asked his *mamita* for an ice cream.

Moya's father was, of course, a sailor, but the last time either Moya or his mother heard a word from him, Moya was in his next to final year at the Colegio Anne Hunt; all of which is insignificant, because when his father left for the last time it was with an earful of Moya's gentle mother's shrill and fed-up wishes never again to have to *hear* another word from him. Fathers, especially among the poor, are not made to last in the tropics anyway, *vos.* This father could barely read, was a drunk, whimpered in his sleep like a depraved eunuch, was the sort of man capable of engrossing himself in an all-day bicycle race narrated over the radio, was full of *caca,* and when drunk only wanted to boast about the night he and his crew mates threw a sailor overboard in the middle of an equatorial Atlantic crossing because he was a bothersome, sneaky, hypnotizing queer, full of *maricón* black magic, so they threw him to the sharks, remorseless, with cackling pride—who needs a father with a mind and spirit inseparable from the worst filth all around?

On the *El Minuto*–man train, staring out the window at the ocean's vast, slow darkening, Moya thought of his father, of sailors in general, and recalled, with the same brief and clairvoyant sense of loneliness he'd first felt upon reading about him as he lay on his bed on a snowy afternoon in Cambridge, the Central American sailor who had burst in on the Nicaraguan consul in Paris one day almost a century before: *"I'm not here to ask for anything or to borrow money! I only wanted to salute you, sir, because you are my country's consul! I am a sailor, here in France off a boat from China, and next I go to India!"* The sailor said good-bye and left, having no idea that he had just saluted the immortal poet Rubén Darío, who years later recorded the episode in a slim memoir. A turn-of-the-century Central American sailor, wandering from China to France to Bombay, dropping in to salute his country's consul wherever one could be found. That's what Moya was thinking of when Rogerio interrupted his meditation on the train, asking about Sylvia McCourt. He was thinking that he would have to do something with that jaunty and uncorrpted little sailor in his annual Ode to Darío editorial, assuming he got his old job back at *El Minuto*.

Strangely, that haunted moment has lived on. Often, now, in his own voice and heart, Moya hears the lonesome ebullience of that world-wandering little sailor, late at night especially.

SEVENTEEN

S ylvia McCourt, only a year or two older than Flor, was already a tenured professor of political science at Harvard when she met Moya in Guatemala. She was prominent outside academic circles too: a frequent contributor of editorials and articles to influential newspapers and journals, invited to appear on televised panel discussions, a member of prestigious foreign policy councils and so on; Central America was her recent area of specialization.

"Curious choice for such a serious scholar, don't you think?" dead-panned Moya, when he first told me about her on the train to Boston. "She must not like to read very much, *vos.*"

"Oh, I don't know," I said. "I'm always surprised by how much there *is* to read, actually." But he was only joking, I think.

Moya and Sylvia were introduced at a happy hour gathering of Guatemalan journalists and political personalities held in Sylvia's honor by Teresa Truczinski, the U.S. embassy's press attaché, at her penthouse apartment in a Zona 10 condominium high rise.

There, a magnificently self-assured, aerobically fit, golden-haired, and tender-eyed Sylvia McCourt and Moya and several of the heartily cordial guests were all out on the press attaché's balcony enjoying the fresh evening air and the powdery-pastel vista of a typical, smog-abetted Guatemala City sunset. The horizon was a long, jagged line of dimming mountains, and, looming above, dominating the orange-pink sky with their irksome perfection and remoteness, were two immense volcanoes.

Before being invited to Teresa Truczinski's penthouse for the first time, Moya had never seen his city from the air. His flight to

Boston was his first in a plane, his return home his second—but all that was still in his future. Standing on the balcony, Moya gazed down, absorbed in studying the Zona 10 blocks below, an unlidded maze of high walls boxed around big houses and eerily unpopulated yards holding swimming pools, artificial waterfalls, blossom-splattered gardens, private aviaries; a maid took down laundry next to a giant satellite dish on a rooftop patio; in another yard a gardener stood over a small, whitely smoking pile of burning brush; a watchdog galloped along its side of the wall. Moya had once had a girlfriend who lived down there, in what seemed not just a long time ago but a whole other life.

Among the guests pressing themselves around Sylvia McCourt on the balcony were *Coronel* Lenz Méndez, the head of Army Public Relations, portly Pepe Arnulfo, director of the nation's largest newspaper, and Paco Palnia Passafarri, owner of the second largest paper and founder of his own political party. Also in attendance, most still lingering in the living room, were several of the country's more prominent *faferos*—and *faferas*—and Celso Batres, the suave and handsome and politically ambitious third-generation owner and director of the newspaper Moya worked for, *El Minuto* (*¿Dónde?* too, and much more profitably, though that was treated by everyone as a secret). One day not even two years before, Celso had come to the public university—*"La U"*—to guest-lecture at the law faculty and had ended up plucking Moya from an unknown fate, offering him a weekly column called "The University Student's Point of View" and full-time employment at *El Minuto,* mainly because of the sardonic, if respectfully delivered, insight Moya had offered during the question-and-answer session: "It's true, what you say, *Licenciado* Batres, that here in Guatemala there is a fundamental respect for freedom of expression. Here, anyone is free to say whatever he wants. And if someone doesn't like it, then he's free to kill you." Nervous giggles, beginning softly, swept the lecture hail, crescendoing into generalized laughter. Finally even Celso Batres, standing stiffly with his hand in the side pocket of his Italian jacket, had to let a boyish grin of mischievous acknowledgment undo his close-lipped, urban -*hidalgo* expression. So now here was Moya, by far the youngest person on the U.S. embassy press attaché's balcony, younger even than the two Indian waiters in white shirts and black neckties, balancing trays of cocktails wrapped in paper napkins in one hand while pulling out lighters to light the chain-smoking guests' cigarettes with the other. Teresa Truczinski always invited Moya to her gatherings when there was a visiting influential intellectual from the States in town. For one thing, she realized that Moya was one of the few working Guatemalan journalists who could hold his own in conversation with a visiting intellectual. Teresa Truczinski, pretty if bug-eyed, appeared to actually like Moya, but sometimes this seemed to conflict with feelings of annoyance that his presence aroused in her as well, a purely professional press attaché's annoyance perhaps, as when she seemed to wonder if maybe she'd erred in giving Moya and his opinions too easy access to some obviously impressionable yet not inconsequential visitor: Once, when Moya was leaving one of her gatherings in the company of a successful Hollywood screenwriter who was researching a movie—she'd been hired by an extremely famous Hollywood actress who wanted to play a young gringa widow who takes over her late Guatemalan husband's coffee plantation in a conflictive zone of the highlands—Teresa, smiling giddily and as if under the sway of emotions she couldn't quite master, intercepted them as they waited for the elevator that stopped right inside her penthouse living room; there she pinched Moya's cheek and held on to it as she said, "If it looks like a duck, walks like a duck, and quacks like a duck, then isn't it a duck?"

Moya had never heard this expression. In the elevator the screenwriter asked, "What was that all about?"

And Moya said, "Teresa thinks I am a Marxist. Or a Communist. A subversive, a guerrilla, a revolutionary, something like that. She was warning you, I think."

"I thought that was what she was driving at," said the screenwriter. "But I didn't want to say so myself Are you?"

"No," said Moya. "Teresa is afraid that by the time we finish dining tonight, I will have your gringa providing sanctuary for guerrillas on her farm, and giving all her land away to her Indian workers."

"Sounds good to me," said the screenwriter. "Maybe you're in the wrong line of work. Where does it go from there?"

Why did Teresa Truczinski think Moya was a Marxist or a whatever? Mainly because of his reputation as the country's one surviving newspaper columnist with some sting, however subtle, in what he wrote. She might not have had anything else to go on but that. Maybe she even thought his bright charm was sneaky and loaded, and that this was typical of young intellectual Marxists. But Teresa Truczinski also knew that whether Moya was actually a Marxist or whatever or not, visiting intellectuals from the States would often think he was too.

Which was usually fine with Teresa. She was glad to have Moya at her gatherings to give visiting intellectuals the idea that it just wasn't true that in Guatemala all such people were dead or in hiding or absolutely unwilling to show their faces at a U.S. embassy event. And she usually wasn't too afraid of whatever Moya might actually say to a visiting Sylvia McCourt, knowing that intellectuals tend to have a more inquiring and sophisticated take on the country than, say, visiting congressmen, and so are going to run across Moyalike opinions anyway, with or without a Moya. (She never invited Moya when U.S. congressmen were being hosted, there was absolutely no professional reason to.)

Teresa Truczinski realized, of course, that it is always a Sylvia McCourt, with all her prominent credibility, who is going to have much more influence than a Moya ever could on how some undecided congressman might vote on such issues as military assistance to Guatemala anyway. But, incredibly, a Moya might have some little bit of influence on a Sylvia. And there just wasn't much Teresa Truczinski could do about that. It was just one of the occupational hazards of a press attaché. It was often a thankless job, Teresa's.

Of course Moya had his own reasons for putting up with all this. One was his desire, even his duty, to meet and try to influence the thinking of all the Sylvias who came through Guatemala on what they usually and somewhat militaristically referred to as "fact-finding tours." Another reason was that Moya, for some time before his exile, had begun to suspect and hope that the army had finally begun to regard him as a relative untouchable because of his having been seen at so many events befriending the likes of Sylvia—that is, the army might have come to regard him as someone better left alone or even chased into exile than as someone to snatch, torture, rip open for his secrets, and then kill, realizing that to do the latter could very well boomerang, raising a hysterical outcry in the editorial and opinion pages of American and European newspapers all out of proportion to the damage he could do with his *mariconcito* propaganda dinners and screws with Sweet Sisters of Solidarity and the occasional Sylvia McCourt, a much tougher cookie than any knee-jerk solidarity or human rights type anyway.

The danger would resurface, Moya had always realized, if the press attaché ever decided that it would be frankly impolitic and insulting to the other prominent Guatemalan journalists and governmental representatives who attended her gatherings to keep

inviting Moya because he had finally become too "controversial."
But by having chosen to go temporarily into an "exile" sponsored
and even modestly publicized by an international human rights
organization; by having fled a country whose military regime and
civilian loyalists regularly denounce such organizations as fronts
for the Communist conspiracy to conquer the world; by having
allowed that same organization to arrange a few Guatemala-
tattling speaking engagements for him before solidarity and church
groups in the Boston area (to which the Guatemalan embassy in
Washington dispatched its own agents, and none too discreetly, *vos;*
they certainly stood out with their Mayan noses and bureaucrats'
polyester suits, with their soberly attentive and then, as Moya's
tattles mounted, turbulently rigid patriotic expressions)—by having done all that it is possible that Moya has finally crossed over
into what Teresa Truczinski and now her successor, Elsa Nardone,
would have to regard as the frankly impolitic, if not as an outright
admission of subversive association. Since his return to Guatemala,
the new press attaché hasn't invited Moya to anything, despite his
new Harvard connections and polish.

So there—then—was Moya, out on the *balcón,* inwardly arranging himself for the tricky combat of the next hour or two: be
noticed in just the right way, capture this Sylvia McCourt's attention in just the right way. He always employed the same method:
to be very cautious and subtle in what he actually said, while hint-
ing in various quietly vigorous ways that he would be able to say a
lot more in different, less guarded circumstances if he wanted to
(until Sylvia just *had* to get him alone).

Early on it was still time to hang back and let the others fray
Sylvia's attention a bit. Moya leaned against the smooth concrete
rail, neither drinking nor smoking, barely listening in, biding his
time, peering down over Teresa's potted geraniums and letting his
thoughts drift off with the view below, which was filling him with

a familiar, if always initially estranging, nostalgia for his Colegio Anne Hunt days, and for Anne Hunt girls, quite a few of whom lived, or used to live because every single one of them was married now, in the very houses he was now hovering over as if in a helicopter. *Hombre,* he'd come a long way in the six years since he'd graduated from that school, such abrupt changes in his life: *La U,* with all its hard-core political ferment, intrigues, and mortal danger, then the newspaper, his rapid and precarious rise to relative prominence there.

Back then, when he was a teenage scholarship student at Anne Hunt, instead of satellite dishes tuned in to every television channel in the sky, those houses had Betamaxes inside, and Moya found himself recalling the almost unbearable sweetness of the long-ago afternoon when he'd made out with Patti Mundinger in her den for the first time while a rented movie played: *The Hindenburg,* a burning Nazi blimp and Germans in flames screaming and leaping from it while his tongue played with Patti's in a rich delirium made up of her constantly replenished lipstick, her baby-clean breath, her perfume and the English garden fragrance of her freshly shampooed hair, her flickering gray eyes fixed on his with a startled, radiant studiousness that startled him right back. He held her delicate torso against him on the leather sofa, one hand playing with her buoyant little breasts through the fine fabric of her blouse and tenacious little bra for hours. Suddenly Patti's elderly urban-*finquero* father came into the room unannounced to say hello, receive a kiss on his cheek from his only daughter, and politely shake his visitor's hand. Moya stood and coped, wondering if the old *caballero* was noticing what felt like a stain on his pale woolen pants and the erection swelling beneath it, not to mention the lipstick smeared on his face, wondering how the old man couldn't, and realizing in the next instant that this was the kind of old man who made it a point of honor not to notice much at all.

"Mucho gusto," said Patti's papa, after he'd shaken Moya's hand. "Your father is Enrique Moya, the son of Violeta Rademan de Moya, no?"

"No," said Moya, smiling, showing all his teeth.

"Ah bueno, let us stay out of that labyrinth then," said the old man, who with another handshake left the room.

Later, breaking the lovers apart again, a bashfully smiling maid with a frozen shrug came in carrying a large silver platter holding chocolate cake and fresh-ground export-quality coffee poured from an antique silver urn into delicate china cups rimmed with actual gold and decorated with painted birds of paradise.

"Do you like coffee, Moya?" Patti spoke in a voice so sweetened by the excitement of love that it sounded to Moya as if she were asking if he felt the same about her.

"Of course!"

"Well, we own five plantations."

"Ajá."

She giggled delightfully. "I mean this is our coffee, from our *fincas,* that's all. We've got tons of this *caca."*

". . . It's delicious, *vos!"* It was the best coffee Moya had ever tasted.

Patti Mundinger! I couldn't believe it! "Almost pretty," insisted Moya on the train, suddenly seized by her again, all these years later. "Anyway, a certain something. And a little bit of a rebel, *vos,* truly." A *flaquita,* skinny, with ivory, gold-flecked skin and straight, reddish hair all the way down to her tiny waist and big gray eyes and kind of a rabbity nose and mouth, and that cheerful, fluttery nervousness, like inside she was full of butterflies. The summer that I was fourteen was my last at the Colegio Anne Hunt, so I hadn't set eyes on little Patti Mundinger in twelve years, but I instantly recalled that pretty and lightly borne nerviness, and the way she'd seem to set her attention down on any arbitrary thing and then get woken up from it in a startled panic. This, I'd thought then, was a true sign of unconquerable dumbness. We were eleven the summer that I watched from two desks away while Patti spent the whole morning in a trance, pressing and twirling and twirling a sharpened pencil against a fingernail on the hand she held flat against her desk . . . until finally she jumped up in stunned horror over the lead-smeared hole she'd drilled right through the center of her nail and the blood beading from it. With swooning steps Patti made her way up the aisle, not saying anything, on the verge of fainting, holding her hand up so the teacher could see. She was rushed to a hospital. And then Anne Hunt herself stormed the classroom, accusing all of us of having seen what Patti had been doing and doing nothing to stop it. Which was true enough. Though we all, Moya included, insisted in unison that we'd been paying too much attention to the blackboard to notice. Anne Hunt exploded, uncharacteristically blurting that it was because of children like us that Guatemala would always be a primitive country, completely uncivilized, because none of us cared, and if Patti died of lead poisoning it was our fault. It hadn't occurred to any of us that what we'd witnessed was a suicide attempt. I remember leaving school that day under a dark cloud, all of us feeling that we ought to rush off to church and pray for Patti. Even the most boisterous and sadistic of the *cabroncitos* were solemn. It all gave power and mystery to poor Patti's inscrutable little rite of self-immolation, so that we had to wonder what was really going on inside that cheerfully distracted, high-strung, and suddenly unnerving girl, and feel scared for her. Though I have to say I never saw her do anything that fascinating again.

But see, things did get to Patti, said Moya. The violence really started to get to her. That was during Moya's final year at Anne

Hunt, the year of the devastating earthquake of February '76 and the crackdown against the church reconstruction organizations and their volunteers, for the army and the Right knew that well-meaning city youth were easily led astray when they went up to the mountains or into the slums to help poor people; before long the guerrillas were strong again.

Patti was seventeen and falling in love with Moya, but soon the violence was all she wanted to talk about with him.

"Moya, last night I heard shots, and you know what kind of shots? Two. Just little seconds apart. *Pap* then *pap.* And then silence, do you know what I'm saying?" Patti's small voice would break. "Moya, yesterday morning our neighbor went out for his jog, and he ran by *three* bodies." She saw no humor in it. "Moya, you know what I thought during the earthquake, when we were afraid of the aftershocks and had to sleep outside? I thought, Look at us, the rich, shut out of instead of into our homes by fear for a change! Turning things inside out like that, I saw what we are made of. Fear! Is that crazy?"

She said she was afraid of dying. No, worse, she was afraid of getting used to it. So many people were dying and the worst thing that could happen to you, she speculated with touching uncertainty, would be to get used to it, close your eyes to it, because that would be a death in life, right, Moya?

Moya agreed. But he wasn't absolutely sure. Maybe there were worse things that could happen to you. *Vos,* this remains one of the big questions raised by life in Guatemala!

But none of the other girls at Anne Hunt ever talked that way. Maybe they were not as sensitive. They were not supposed to be, they weren't supposed to notice, they were raised to keep their eyes cheerfully closed to all of it. Meaning to impress, but slyly, they might say, "We should all do something to help the poor starving Indians," but then they'd let you know they meant the in *India*

Indians, and then they'd giggle, so cute, so deliciously sly. But look what happened to the Miss Guatemala who was disappeared! She'd had ties to the guerrillas, it was her lover who dragged her into it. You see what can happen even to a Miss Guatemala?

Patti wasn't like the others, even if she did have that inbred gift of playing the seductively chirpy and slyly clever *loquita* (little nutty one), the tried and true way for a girl like her to get what she wanted. But what did Patti want? For life to answer the questions she asked it, for it to turn itself inside out and show her. She'd made Moya her confidant. He was an outsider at the Colegio Anne Hunt no matter how many years he'd been there, so Patti thought she could tell him anything, thought she could safely open up and explore a whole forbidden inner life as long as he was there to listen. Except there was a peculiar sameness to what Patti kept finding; or maybe she just felt incapable of discovering anything else until she'd solved the basic riddle posed by what she kept finding, and so she just kept blasting away at that black-and-white, obsidian-and-diamond-hard riddle of social injustice, of just a handful of rich and everyone else poor, thus so much and so many kinds of murder.

Moya drank in all her words without regard for the bitter aftertaste of circular obsession because he was going in circles too: brooding over Patti's fruitlessly debated and resolutely maintained virginity while they made out for hours by the hippo pool in the zoo or progressed to various stages of undress in the Betamax den but with the door locked—her globe-trotting young mother off in Vienna or Martinique and wherever else it was she went with her art gallery–owning best friend or with her other friends, the cliquish members of the *No Tememos Tiburones Club de Buceo* (We Don't Fear Sharks Scuba Diving Club), of which the only member who actually ever dived was the owner of the two-hundred-foot yacht in which the members of the little club were transported about the Caribbean; her elderly father at home, though not in any active way. The old man could usually be found in his study, ineffectually double- and triple-checking his five farm administrators' accounts and sitting in a shaft of turquoise light from the pyramidal skylight overhead, which his wife had installed to prevent melancholy and as an inducer of pristine meditations.

"Moya, why everyone poor and we so rich?" "Patti, why don't you let me tuck my pigeon in? Why don't we raise a little dust?"— Patti growing increasingly fraught and almost anorexic, Moya gloomier and hornier, until finally, in the den, Moya did slip his pigeon in and *carajo!* that cheered them up for a while. Then Moya slipped his pigeon in over and over for months, they raised a lot of dust, *vos.* This was the first time in his life that Moya had been so in love. He worried that Patti might one day immolate herself into becoming a nun. He dreamt of the serene, strong, and happy woman that Patti, with his love and patient help, might someday become instead.

"Poor Patti"—that's what Anne Hunt used to say, in front of their American history class, whenever Patti, lost in a daydream about raising dust with Moya or just trying to catch a little nap after one of her sleepless, especially morbid nights, was unable to answer a question. "She doesn't get enough attention at home because her mother married a man much too old for her and so she has to go running around the world looking for excitement. Poor Patti has no one to talk to, no one to set an example for her. Do you see, girls, what happens when you marry a man too old for you?"

Why is it some people, no matter how they behave, quietly or extrovertedly, come wrapped in a poignant aura of loneliness and neglect and thus seem filled with the drifting black butterflies of delusion too, which even someone as ordinarily insensitive as Anne Hunt couldn't miss? But everyone knew that Patti's mother, who came from a good Guatemalan-Scotch-German family that had lost everything during World War II and never regained it, had married old Don Ernesto Mundinger for money. There were rumors that before the wedding, when Don Ernesto had by choice lived on one of his *fincas* in Alta Verapaz, he'd gone around wearing *traje* and had fathered children with Kekchi Indian women, that he'd been friendly with shamans and become fluent in Kekchi, that that was how he'd whiled away his life. Patti's mother had quickly put an end to that, moving him to the city. For the sake of appearances, of course.

Suddenly it even seemed conceivable that Moya, just turned eighteen, might one day marry the only daughter of a multimillionaire from a fine old family, descendants of illustrious German pioneer coffee planters. But then Patti's parents suddenly woke up, because Anne Hunt, not so insensitive after all, realized that if she didn't wake them up no one else was going to. Anne Hunt found a college in rural Ohio that would accept Patti immediately—after all, she *had* just graduated with passing grades—and off she went, without even a good-bye party.

For a while Patti wrote to Moya—describing field hockey injuries and ice-skating lessons, and the night she had to wait up until dawn in a freezing barn full of steaming cow shit just to take a stupid picture of a veterinarian delivering a newborn calf because it was her photography class assignment to do so, *qué putas, Moya!;* and the party she went to where she innocently consumed two hashish-laced brownies and ended up throwing up all over her dress after she'd devoured six bags of potato chips and pretzels all by herself; at college parties no one danced but just got drunk and drugged and stood around instead, everyone hated her Camilo Sesto records, she sure missed Moya and Guatemala.

It took about six months for Moya and Patti to lose interest in each other. Moya was becoming completely immersed in university life, truly wanting to purge himself of any association with the Colegio Anne Hunt, trying to act as if he'd actually spent his childhood at the *Liceo Javier* being taught by bearded Jesuit priests who'd had to flee into exile one after the other, or even at the *Escuela Normal* with the poorer boys and girls who were already in clandestine cells and spray-painting wall graffiti before they were out of puberty, or so Moya imagined. In political development, clarity, discipline, and even in his fundamental understanding of such pervasive euphemisms, he was still way behind the *patojos* who had actually gone to such schools, and didn't even understand the lesson yet of living as if not even your own shadow is in on what you are really thinking, *vos*. It took years to get that one down, to learn that a pose of complete apathy and silence could look stealthy and even more incriminating than outright subversive extroversion, the latter being the commonest tactic of second-rate infiltrators and spies. Playing *Dracula* had seemed to strike the right balance, but even that had gotten him into some trouble, but then he understood that *some* trouble could be the best defense against the *ultimate* trouble and was even preferable to no trouble at all when you knew that logically it should be there, which gave way to the common superstition that some trouble over and over again could inoculate against the ultimate. By the end of 1980 *La U* was a shell of its former self anyway, so many student leaders dead or in hiding or up in the mountains and much of the faculty dead or in exile; even protest marches through the capital had come to seem like mass acts of suicide, and so had ceased. Was it merely Celso Batres's lightning stroke that had saved Moya from his place in the deadly lottery, transferring him from one G-2 file marked "students" to the back of another marked *"periodistas"*? There was no way to know. Even the most innocent young spiders at the public university lived in constant danger.

It was early in his fourth year at *La U*—the very year that Celso changed his life—that Moya glanced at a newspaper society page and there, in the usual spread of tuxedoed and gowned *fufurufas* at a wedding celebration, recognized classmates from his past life at the Colegio Anne Hunt, and Anne Hunt herself and Patti's parents and, of course, *mamita mío,* Patti herself. Evidently she was back from Ohio for good and had just married Moncho Vasconcelos Grau, who the paper said had attended the American School, the University of Nevada at Las Vegas, and was now one of Guatemala's outstanding young Windsurfers. They were taking their honeymoon in Baja California. Patti looked skinny and like a spooked rabbit in her wedding gown—struck dumb, it seemed, by the photographer's flash. Moya felt—how should he put it?—*bad.* Something swept through him, an acidic and hollowing gust of *something* he'd never experienced before. It left a bitter aftertaste on his tongue, the old dried-flower taste of her voice. For a week or so after it continued to attack him at unexpected moments during the day, and woke him with clockwork regularity at a quarter to five, keeping him awake until dawn.

She really had been a little bit of a rebel, *vos.* Well, just her going with Moya proved it. And she used to love to go to the zoo, to see the hippopotamus couple there, though usually all they could see were two slimy humps protruding from the rank chartreuse water that was confettied with petals from the flower beds on the elevated banks inside the concrete wall ringing the pool. Once there was an Indian man there, just down from the highlands probably, looking at the paired humps. He lifted his amazed, delighted gaze to Patti and Moya and announced that those were the biggest snakes he'd ever seen.

Later, when Moya was already working at the newspaper, some little *patojo bobo* tossed into the pool a rubber ball, which the bull hippo swallowed; the ball got stuck in its esophagus. Despite the emergency operation performed by a team of veterinarians right there on the concrete sunning platform that arched the pool after zoo workers had dragged the choking hippo up onto it with ropes and pulleys, the hippo died. Its carcass was delivered to the immense garbage dump in Zona 13, and the very next day headlines appeared in the city's two main dailies announcing that the poor people who lived in the garbage dump were feasting on hippopotamus meat.

Naturally newspapers reach the garbage dump even on the same day they are published, and at least a few of its resident scavengers were able to read. Two days after the sensationalistic headlines, which *El Minuto* had nothing to do with, Moya was sitting at his Royal typewriter in the small second-story newsroom when a noticeably acrid and filthy stench came up the stairs, though nothing, not even the blank page of paper in his typewriter, moved. Then, from the reception desk downstairs, he heard a commotion of angered, affronted women's voices shouting *hipopótamo* this and *hipopótamo* that. He went down. Marta Andrade, the very pregnant secretary, and Natividad Molina, the less noticeably pregnant secretary, were standing rigidly a few feet back from the reception counter. And there, on the other side, reeking of nothing other than the garbage dump, that is, of an entire city's rotting vegetables and carrion and sewage and the toxic fumes of anything that can be thrown away and burned, all of it combining into a single stench that really did seem to have the solid abrasiveness of a hot blizzard of filth on a dry windy day at the dump, were about a dozen of the women who lived there. But for the wrapped, twined plastic leggings some of them perpetually wore for wading through garbage, they did not look that much different from the rest of the city's poorest people, in torn and stained dresses or shredded, smoke-smudged *traje,* boxy bellies protruding from so many years of parasite-infested diets and so many pregnancies, hair stringy and sticky because of the impossibly high price of even soap, brown faces too weighed down with premature wrinkles and toughened skin to be anything but impassive, open mouths displaying sporadic teeth that looked like wooden pegs hammered in at odd angles. But their eyes, despite whites reddened and yellowed from constant exposure to smoke and conjunctivitis infections, were livid black beams, irradiating all the fury and affront of what they seemed to agree was the greatest indignity yet inflicted on the poor who lived in the garbage dump—many of whom actually raised their children there, all of whom spent their days fighting with vultures and pariah dogs over the fresh leavings delivered by the donkey-drawn yellow trash carts and the big trucks of industry and private trash-collecting services, who fought over scraps to eat, junk to sell, and even boiled the carcasses of dead cats and dogs right there in iron drums to sell to the glue factories; and who lived in loose shacks made of junk erected on a terrain of compacted, sun-baked trash, which could spontaneously ignite into multicolored chemical flames at any moment during the dry season or melt into quicksand pools of putrid mush during the rains.

So it had been insult enough all the times television crews had arrived, hoping to film the eternal pariah dog said to be loping around the dump with a severed human hand in its jaws, or to record the discovery of yet another trash-swaddled abandoned infant (on its way to a private orphanage perhaps, destined to be raised by doting, wealthy, and cultured parents in Paris!), anything to sensationalize the domesticated hell the scavengers had to live in, to ridicule them as the lowest of the low, poverty's phantom clowns, circus performers already on the other side of life. But this was the worst yet.

"What do you think we are? Savages? Animals? *That we would eat* hipopótamo!"

"That ugly beast that we didn't even know was called a *hipopótamo?*" insisted the militant delegation of women from the thousands said to be living in and around the garbage dump. The

335

beast had lain there untouched even by dogs and vultures for all of that first day, and it wasn't until the third day that the sun had softened its hide and swelled its innards enough that it broke open on its own like a giant overripe melon, and then, yes, the dogs and vultures did feast on it, *"Sí, señores, but not us!"*

"Honestidad!" shouted one of the women.

"Honestidad!" shouted the others after her.

"Dignidad señores, por favor!"

They wanted Moya's newspaper to stand up for the essential and now ridiculed dignity of the garbage dump's residents, who hadn't swallowed a bite of hippo, though some had eventually boiled down its hacked remains to sell to the glue factories, *y porqué no?* They wanted *El Minuto* to denounce the other newspapers who had printed those slanders, and wanted those other papers to print retractions and apologies—they were on their way there next.

"Then, *señoras,* this is just the man you want to see," said Marta Andrade, still frozen in place behind her huge belly, her eyes running. She lifted one hand away from her nose to gesture at Moya, then turned and fled into the back patio, followed by Natividad Molina holding a handkerchief over her face.

Moya, eyes running too, listened, questioned, nodded in sympathy. It was rare in Guatemala City to find poor people standing up for themselves like this, even if their insurrectional anger seemed a little misplaced. He felt moved, convinced. He even felt a surge of relief, because the Essential Dignity of the Garbage Dump Women and the Slanderous Incident of the Dead Hippo was going to make a fine newspaper column, and he'd been really stuck, staring at a blank page all day. It was just right, just what he wanted to say and could get away with saying within the parameters of what was safely allowed in "The University Student's Point of View." (Moya still registered for, though never attended, one class a semester to keep this credential intact.)

Back upstairs, Moya set to work. During the next few hours, several of his colleagues arrived, alt of them cursing and muttering over the lingering smell that resisted even the bus fumes pouring in through the flung-open windows. He began his column by describing the hippo couple nestled in their stagnant, florid pool at the zoo, which he hadn't been back to in years; Cupid and Venus he named them, which he knew weren't their real names, but *El Minuto* didn't check such facts; he evoked their celebrated power to draw snuggling lovers from far and wide to the edge of their concrete pool, though he and Patti, specifically Patti, were the only lovers he knew of who had been affected by the hippos in that way. Of course he ended up thinking about Patti. Wherever she was and whatever she was doing on the other side of the city, she must have heard the news of the dead hippo by now, she must have remembered Moya.

He thought about Patti so much that afternoon that finally he had to make an arduous effort to summon all his concentration and rhetorical talents to finish his column. When it was done, Celso Batres liked it so much he said he wished he'd written it himself. But this was one column Moya was determined to see published under his own byline, on the chance that Patti would see it. Moya stood his ground. A staff photographer was dispatched to catch a bus over to the zoo to snap a picture of lonely and submerged Venus's solitary hump. Both the column and the photograph ran at the bottom of the front page of the next afternoon's edition. A week went by. No word from Patti. Well, of course not. Such is life in the tropics, *vos*.

"El Vergudo," Big Dick, was the name Patti had given to one of her stuffed hippo dolls and *"Chichas de Melones,"* Melon Tits, was another. *"Cara de Puta," "Pija de Mapache,"* "Woody Allen," and one, purple with yellow spots, was called "Anne Hunt." Patti's mother always brought her a hippo doll or figurine when she re-

turned from her travels. On the Amtrak Minuteman train, Moya recited the names of Patti's hippos. He was getting pretty emotional, looking back on his life, drawing lessons from it. Only days before, he'd made up his mind once and for all to return to his country.

Funny, he said then, how easily Patti Mundinger had slipped from his life, and how unexamined he'd let their parting be then. It had just seemed a law of existence, that he had to let her go without a fight. But couldn't it have been different? No? Maybe? Rich people have married poor ones for love in Guatemala before, *vos,* when that rich person was at least a little bit of a rebel, and as stubborn as his or her mate. But, like magicians, her parents had made Patti vanish, sending her away to Ohio until she came to her senses. And he, with all the complacency of a magician's audience, had been accepting of the fact that what magicians can put on stage they can make vanish—kind of impressive to watch, but completely expected.

Out on Teresa Truczinski's balcony, at her gathering of Guatemalan media and political elite and the distinguished visitor Sylvia McCourt, Moya felt stirred by his proximity to the mystery of power and his own insights into it. Which is what he always experienced at these events. Not that the guests included absolutely the most powerful people in Guatemala, but certainly Colonel Lenz Méndez, because of his high rank in the institution he served, and Paco Palma Passafarri, owner of his own newspaper and political party, and even Celso Batres were well on their way to becoming so. Most of the rest were ambitious *faferos* and comparatively potent enough—for all their diverse humanity, they were still very much like the actual voices through which the most powerful spoke to make it seem irrefutable that Guatemala was made up of many more assenting voices than just their own.

Power had always been a mystery, so ridiculously simple and brutally unanswerable that it seemed remote from ordinary human behavior. But what always really got to Moya at Teresa Truczinski's gatherings was his recurring revelation that even he, a sailor and seamstress's son, could probably end up just as powerful as anybody there (with the plausible exception of the monstrously handsome and up and coming Colonel Lenz). Moya felt confident that he could actually rise that high, even in Guatemala. If he wanted to, *vos*. On Teresa Truczinski's balcony it was all right there, just waiting to happen.

On her balcony, as at any gathering of wealthy Guatemalans, anyone would consider it extremely impolite to be offered a cold drink that wasn't well wrapped in at least a paper napkin. The middle classes, on special occasions such as *quinceañeras* (sweet fifteen celebrations), served drinks in paper napkins too, but only after the women had spent hours in the kitchen scissoring napkins in half to save money. Nearly everyone else in the country rarely even had the opportunity to endure cold fingers. Poor people's food stalls usually didn't have refrigerators; in their cantinas, men on binges passed out over warm bottles of *aguardiente* and beer. A significant portion of the population drank corn mush or coffee brewed from corn kernels or rainwater from hollowed gourds. This hierarchy of separate worlds seemed impregnable.

Unless one came upon a secret thread linking them, as Moya had—that thread in this case being Moya himself, his talents in combination with his fortuitous circumstances. It was all one world, that was his insight. Already, just being on the press attaché's balcony, he had a higher social position than he had ever aspired to or thought possible; from there, he could climb even higher. For example, he could move to one of the big newspapers (Paco Palma's or Pepe Arnulfo's), shut up and accept *fafas,* and with his rhetorical talent go on to become the country's foremost Greatest Living political columnist, elected and reelected head of the press association, a position he could then parlay into one of leadership in a political party, and then make his pact with the army and whichever necessary oligarchs, and then, it really wasn't at all unimaginable, even become a presidential candidate one day under a democratic system in which the army allowed civilian presidents to sit in the National Palace, which was the promised future both Paco Palma and Celso Batres were angling towards. Along the way he would feel obligated to partake of all kinds of illicit opportunities to enrich himself so as not to alienate others with a sanctimonious superiority. As president he would passively preside over so many lucrative rackets, so as not to alienate his democratic allies in the army high command, that for generations Moya children would be attending private schools in Switzerland and meeting their Moya parents for Christmas vacations in Gstaad.

That the corrupt and cynical route to power was much more decipherable and likely, and survivable, than an honest one was no surprise. Surely Celso Batres could never behave so scandalously. What was astonishing to Moya was that this future seemed at his fingertips, like a baited wallet protruding from Colonel Lenz's trouser pocket. Moya and the colonel and Paco Palma Passafarri and Celso Batres and everyone else were all part of just one world, one extending well beyond the borders of Guatemala. Already Moya was capable of infiltrating his voice onto the editorial pages of leading U.S. newspapers—in Lict, Sylvia McCourt would even quote him by name.

But on Teresa Truczinski's balcony, Moya understood that it was his particular fate, his obligation, his only viable choice, to have just the degree of access to the mystery of power that his being there guaranteed, and to manage it as well and as opportunistically as he could, and hope not to get crushed. He took one last, thoughtful look out at the city and the horizon. Out there, in the mountains, a scorched-earth counterinsurgency campaign; in the city, secret prisons, secret torture cells, secret courts, secret cemeteries, state of siege. Otherwise, everywhere in the country, as on earth, life went on as normal. The breeze fanned Moya's reddening face. The wild chatter of grackles seared the night air. It might have looked as if he was idly fingering the petal of one of Teresa Truczinski's potted geraniums, but really he was pinching it hard. He looked blankly at his scarlet-smeared fingers, put his hand in his pocket. Now it was time to fix a smile on his face and go into action, and that would be somewhat amusing, alternately elating and degrading, and later on, when he looked back on it, would produce surging feelings of melancholy that would last for days.

Colonel Lenz Méndez, in dress uniform, epaulets on his broad shoulders and candy trains of colored ribbons crossing his vast chest, had Sylvia McCourt's attention now. She must have found him kind of unbelievable to look at, though her expression didn't show it—her eyes were fixed on the colonel with a glistening, deep brown stare that seemed as frank and nonjudgmental as a healthy and beautiful dog's. Guatemalans were rarely as tall as the colonel, on the balcony only skinny Moya was taller, just barely. But the colonel was a massive stack of oblong muscularity, a military Michelin Tire Man, and literally monstrously handsome: with blazing blue eyes and close-cut, chafed blond hair and a pale Tecún Umán nose, he looked like a Paul Newman pumped up with helium. The colonel, like Patti Mundinger, came from German stock, though illegitimately, his mother rumored to have been an Indian servant on a plantation. If not for the name Lenz, Moya might even have suspected Patti's father of being the progenitor.

Sylvia was standing straight as a soldier herself, her napkin-swaddled drink held in two delicate-looking hands at her hip. Curly, golden brown hair was pulled back from her wide, angular face and tied into a fluffily cascading ponytail that stopped midway down her back. Moya could tell she'd spent the day in the sun—at the ambassador's swimming pool?—because the cut of her blouse bared her wonderfully rounded shoulders, and the warm reddish gleam of ripening mangoes suffused the firm, freckled skin there, and crowned her cheeks and nose. Then the cozy, perpetual creases of a slight and skeptical smile around her lips deepened, spreading new creases, not from anything the colonel had said but in generous anticipation.

And what did Colonel Lenz say?—this irrefutably capable man, nearly fluent in English, who had been chosen to head Army Public Relations during this difficult time when Guatemala was being treated as a pariah state on much of the world stage. The colonel said, "Do you know what I think, Sylvia?" and then he paused, looking down at her over his drawn-up chest, striking the pose of a confident and winning Military Animal refining a thought. "I can well imagine that you could have been a Miss America. You look like a Miss America!"

Puta, qué bárbaro, thought Moya, inwardly rejoicing over what a fool the murderous colonel had just made of himself

But on that balcony, only Celso Batres and perhaps Moya, by now, at last, had the sophistication and self-control to know never to use a line like that on a Harvard professor. If the colonel had been speaking to the sort of "gringa" he was most used to meeting—wives, girlfriends, secretaries, and aides of all those right-thinking pilgrims to the little land of Right makes Might: starry-eyed businessmen and congressmen, arms dealers, Texas billionaires, fantasy mercenaries on Soldier of Fortune paramilitary junkets—such a line might have come off charmingly and innocently enough. It was something almost any Guatemalan might have said. In fact several of the men on the balcony, including Pepe Arnulfo and even Paco Palma Passafarri, chuckled or nodded appreciatively.

Sylvia McCourt almost immediately blushed, her surprised, flustered, oddly delighted expression summed by an ever-widening grin that made it look as if she might ask, *What? Did you really say what I think you said?* But she didn't know *what* to say. It was the colonel who really looked flattered.

Moya guessed that Sylvia was thinking something like My God, there it is again, that hilarious, incredibly ingenuous and naive Central American masculine charm, even a combat-hardened colonel has it, you have to adjust your reactions, you need completely different standards when judging these people, but just wait until I get back to Harvard and tell my colleagues that a colonel said I looked like a Miss America!

Moya felt bitterly swept by pathos, and all tangled up in his divided self. Because he knew that in other circumstances he could sound just as naive as any of his countrymen, and that he could also be every bit as elitist and patronizing as the professor.

"Much more beautiful than Miss Jeane Kirkpatrick," said portly Pepe Arnulfo, the *fafa* king, jumping in with a deep, gravelly conquistador's laugh. He was the clever one, he knew exactly who it was Sylvia really wanted to be.

She gave in to it then, her laugh genuine and relaxed. "Oh well, that's the first time anyone's told me *that*. So thank you." She laughed again and said, "Though, you know, Jeane Kirkpatrick isn't a Miss." She beamed, enjoying herself now, at the colonel. "I *was* runner-up for high school homecoming queen once, though you don't want to know *when*."

Colonel Lenz Méndez's muscular cheeks colored. It had been getting around lately that the colonel was a particularly aggressive womanizer, which anyone might have guessed. But at a recent European embassy dinner he'd kept his hand on the knee of that embassy's chief political officer's gorgeous Laplandic wife throughout the meal, though she hadn't dared to mention it to anybody until later, when she told Celso Batres in circumstances Moya still wasn't very clear about, who told Moya, who told Rolando Mezquita, who was Paco Palma Passafarri's gossip columnist, who of course couldn't publish it but liked the story anyway. It was good to feed things like that to Rolando, because sometimes he'd repay you with something really interesting.

Colonel Lenz Méndez said that if Sylvia, unlike Jeane Kirkpatrick, was indeed a Miss, then she should spend some more time in Guatemala, she would find herself happily cured of that condition, he was sure.

And before she could figure out what to say to that, Paco Palma Passafarri, who wore an expression that seemed to be perpetually gloating over its own profound gloominess, said, "Oh no, Sylvia is married to her career, am I right? In Guatemala, you know, it is still very hard for a married woman to be married to her career too. Here it is like—"

"Hah! Bigamy," said Sylvia, finishing his sentence, her eyes flashing with keen interest at Paco Palma, because she knew he was an important man.

"Worse! Adultery," said Paco Palma. "And here a man will go out and hunt down his wife's lover if he has to, but how do you shoot a career! Instead the man gets very frustrated, and that is dangerous for everybody." And his face shifted into a thoughtful frown made up of many weighty and gloomy lateral folds while he nodded his head, which was his way of laughing at his own jokes.

The colonel, roused by rivalry now, said, "Guatemalan women don't have careers? When was the last time you set foot in the countryside, Paco? Washing clothes, grinding the corn, making tortillas, working in the fields, watching the children, weaving and sewing, feeding the chickens and pigs, going to market, I call that a career. A *campesina*'s work never stops!"

"And that has turned out dangerous for everybody," said Moya, from the periphery, and for the first time Sylvia's keen but tender eyes glanced his way, and their eyes briefly locked.

That night Moya and Sylvia went out for dinner and talked for hours, Moya so movingly that he actually brought tears to the politically influential professor's eyes. She was leaving for Nicaragua, the next stop on her "fact-finding tour," in the morning; and back in Cambridge she would quote Moya by name in her editorial, referring to him for all the world to see as "Guatemala's best young political analyst." At dinner in Guatemala City she had asked Moya for his definition of democracy. He had simply said that democracy is not a gift handed down from above but everyone's responsibility. In the context of the conversation they had been having, these words, so simple, idealistic, and hopeful sounding after such a pessimistic and apparently persuasive analysis, had brought tears to Sylvia's eyes.

"So why is she a *pícara?*" Roger quite reasonably asked, when Moya told him of it on the train from New York to Boston.

"Because she used these words to argue for military aid to the contras in Nicaragua. *Putavos!* That wasn't what I'd meant! So it wasn't so great for me." (Though that wasn't the only reason she was a *pícara.*)

". . . You mean it made trouble for you in Guatemala?"

"It could have. But, no . . . it didn't." (He let it be known, in certain circles, that he had been quoted "out of context" while, for his own protection, he pretended in other circles that he hadn't been.)

"Did you . . . Was she your lover too?"

"*Un poquito.*"

"What do you mean, a little bit?"

"Just that one night. We didn't make love, *vos*. She wanted me only to hold her all night long. Our talk, it had upset her somehow. But after, we stayed friends."

"So *are* you a guerrilla?" Roger suddenly blurted. "Look, I know, not a gun-toting one, obviously, but organized, you know, in propaganda or whatever?"

Moya peered at him for a moment over the can of Budweiser suspended in front of his lips.

"I just thought I'd ask. It doesn't make any difference to me, believe me. I just think I should know."

"*Bueno.* No, Rogerio. I am not."

Roger's face suddenly reddened.

"Rogerio," said Moya. "One thing you must be very clear about. When you are in Guatemala, you can never, ever ask anybody questions like that. No one would ever tell you anyway. And you can only get yourself in trouble by asking."

"Oh sure, I know that," said Roger. "But we're not in Guatemala now, are we?"

Sylvia McCourt had ended up feeling so upset—when that conversation in the restaurant had led to its continuation in her room in the Hotel Biltmore Maya (partially owned by Anne Hunt)—that she had needed Moya to hold her. The source of her anxiety might seem improbable, but Moya had been able to respect it. Sylvia really was a woman "married to her career," and at that moment her career revolved around searching for the most apt response to her own government's obsessed and often belligerent harangues on Central America, something that, without sounding at all extremist, would create a stir on editorial pages and in high-level foreign policy circles. She had wanted to propose an adjustment that in that highly calibrated and tense world would

rivet attention to her, just as the seemingly minor but unprecedented nudging of a pawn can explode like a bomb in a game of
chess between grand masters.

In general Moya believed that all political conversations, however passionate, were like games of chess between mediocre or even
very good players—nothing worth recording, nothing new ever said.
But Sylvia's great aspiration was to one day have intimate access to
the yielding ear of a future, probably Democratic, U.S. president,
and there was no reason to think that she might not attain it, if Professor Jeane Kirkpatrick, so many decades Sylvia's senior and no more
precocious, had. So Sylvia really was like a plausible Delphic Oracle,
a potential unleasher of war, plague, and famine; imagining what it
would be like to make love to Sylvia, Moya had pictured their synchronized orgasms combusting into a mutual vision of the isthmus
in flames in 1999. Moya had never found himself playing his own
game at such a high level, and he had wanted to plant a bomb too.

"If you want us to accept what *you* call democracy," Moya had
said, "which I admit would be an improvement, then you cannot
ask us to accept for ourselves what you *never* would for yourselves."

Because if democracy was everyone's responsibility, then
nobody could be immune from its most fundamental precepts. So
how can you suggest, Sylvia, that a small country such as Guatemala can have participatory democracy while forgoing, for example, the cleansing and inaugural rite of justice? Without it,
democracy would be degraded before it had even begun.

Sylvia McCourt admitted it was unlikely that the army would
allow elected civilians even to raise the possibility of trying them
for extrajudicial murder, or for any other crimes. She even agreed
that the absence of such trials would be one of the various and similar preconditions that the army would demand in exchange for that
promise to allow elections. After a long silence, Sylvia firmly suggested that one day the army might learn to stop torturing and kill-

ing civilians, that patience and pragmatism all around were what was needed.

Moya said, "Sylvia, you know in your heart that that isn't good enough. Anyway, they won't stop as long as there are civilians who are unhappy to live in a society that only an army can enforce. And how patient are we supposed to be? Oh Sylvia, if only countries like mine were given the chance to humiliate our own criminals. Maybe we would find the courage and coherence to do so, perhaps not. But, *puta,* as it stands now, even excellent friends such as you, Sylvia, essentially propose that we endure every human indignity because of the Soviet Union. Why don't you take your worries about Central America directly to the Soviet Union then, I'm sure you can work something out, and leave us alone!"

"Because that's not how it works, and those concerns are not frivolous. What's more, I do reject any notion of moral equivalency. Saving you from Communism is *not* an inhumane policy," she said, somewhat peevishly and defensively. The chessboard she had to play on was one of nightmarishly limited possibilities. He had wanted her to admit this, and she basically had.

". . . So what you're saying," she said then, in a softer tone, "is that because I think trading a higher level of aid for a promise of elections isn't such a bad deal, I'm some kind of apologist for murderers."

"No, Sylvia, you couldn't mean that!"

"What would you have me say then?"

"Absolutely no aid without trials. Trials are much more than a symbol. They are our only hope for becoming civilized. The army's power to terrorize must be ended."

"Hah! Not even Carter went that far. They'd think I'd gone completely off the map!"

Moya let himself smile warmly. "If my side doesn't win this one, Sylvia, we may never have the chance to win anything else, with or without elections. To me this is the only so-called ideological battle that matters."

Sylvia had a bit of a crisis after that. She was full of frustration, because she could not think of a convincing alternative to what Moya had suggested. Finally she said, "If only everyone down here were more like you, Moya. Idealistic, sure, but reasonable too; I'd even say wise. But it's not like that, is it, and you know that better than I do."

"Perhaps my reasonableness is my weakness," he said. "So let me say it. I would not be sony to see the blood of *chafas* running in the streets, yet I can do nothing to cause this. Some would say that even having this wish makes me as bad as they are. I hope that isn't true, since perhaps it is only a wish. Do you know that this hotel room is probably bugged?"

"Bugged, do you really think so?" she stammered. "Oh I don't care, I feel so . . ." Sitting on the bed, she held out her hands, inviting Moya to stop his antic pacing. "Let me hold you," she said, grasping his hands. "Hold me . . .

"I have to say," she said, when they had been sitting with their arms around each other for a while, "our ambassador is not a credit to my country."

"*Sí pues.* He has extremely small feet, did you notice? And his wife mocks him in public . . . I feel so . . . too."

". . . I don't know what to think. Believe it, that's troubling for me. You've made me feel so artificial, somehow. And that's because, well, we're on your home court here, aren't we?" (Here, Sylvia had to stop and explain "home court.") "If we were all exposed to the minute particulars all the time, we'd be incapable of deciding anything. And I'm supposed to resist that; I've been trained to think of what we do as close to a science, a human one, and yet the human element can come along and subvert everything sometimes, it's pathetic. But I know that when I'm back on my home court, so to speak, it won't seem like that anymore. And,

Moya, that's when I'll remind myself that the world isn't made of angels, and that political science most certainly is *not* the study of angels. And an angel is what I think you clearly are."

"Oh no, Sylvia, not me. Unless I am an avenging angel without wings, marooned on a soggy cloud. Anyway, angels are already—gone; they no longer live in the earthly dimension."

Pues, they kissed. There, on the wide bed in a probably bugged hotel room partially owned by Anne Hunt, Moya and the beautiful young Harvard professor kissed deeply, heaving against each other, both of them seeking a moment's transcendence in each other's roiling lips and tongues and warm breath, in the illusory promise of their bodies pressed together. For weeks after he felt drunk on the toasted almond smell of her skin, the intoxicatingly soft static of her crisp golden brown hair against his cheek, the lamplit mirage of her warm, arched neck. But truly, Sylvia was upset, and didn't want him to remove her blouse, she wanted only to be held. Sporadically kissing but always less passionately than the first time, they talked until dawn, about everything, including what Sylvia looked for in a man she might love. Self-knowledge was first on her list, a quality she clearly thought Moya possessed, though he felt he didn't, not in the least, mainly because his life, like almost all his countrymen's, had been constricted by such a lack of choices. He'd explored so few possibilities.

In Cambridge, back on her home court, Sylvia, a lioness again there, full of new arguments, formidably yet friendlily stuck it to Moya, which is the other reason he called her a *pícara*. It hadn't been fair, he'd felt ambushed, in no mood to defend himself, and anyway, he absolutely still stands by what he said the first time around. They never kissed again, nor, in Cambridge, was their having done so one night ever alluded to. And yet it was Sylvia who invited him to Harvard, and there remained his loyal and generous if occasionally antagonistic friend.

EIGHTEEN

And of course *I* believed him, and maybe I still do. What Moya truly is, I decided after just a few weeks here, is a first-rate Guatemalan newspaperman and columnist, practically one of a kind. Except his newspaper isn't just the one, or the two, that Celso Batres owns: Sylvia McCourt and almost everyone else he comes across, myself included, we're all supposed to be his "newspaper" too. He *works* on us, uses us. So Moya's a bit like Dracula after all.

It hit me this morning, just like that: Our investigation isn't meant to go anywhere. Like this is Moya's design, his original *intent*. Come and investigate a murder in Guatemala. It won't go anywhere! See? See what it's like here, America?

Could Moya really use Flor like that? What about Flor? Or am I the one who's just *losing* it now?

But listen to what he said earlier this morning—glancing around with his habitual and instructive caution at the powdery old women having coffee with four teaspoons of sugar apiece and angel cake here in Pastelería Hemmings—in response to my only halfhearted suggestion that we go public with at least the obvious allegations about the clandestine fattening house being owned by López Nub's sisters:

"Ah sí, vos, buena idea! Bueno está que nos atropellen, que nos ametrallen, que nos rompan la cara, que nos echen unos cien mil toneladas de mierrrda. Que nos culeen, vos, y no sé qué más, vos!"

What he was more or less saying was Oh yeah, great idea, man! Just great that they stomp on us, machine-gun us, break our faces, dump a thousand tons of shit on us, fuck us up the ass, *vos,* and I don't know what else, *vos!*

Moya obviously enjoyed this recitation, the violent salsa of it. He was beaming, the ruddiness flushing his face, making him look like he'd just come in from a healthy jog and almost boyish too, despite his salt-and-pepper hair, which can make him look a seriously lived decade older than his twenty-six years. He's back on *his* turf now. He can be downright raucous about terror.

This is the guy who, still frazzled by his several months of feeling lost in Cambridge, by his own querulous dismay over what he maintained was his sparse or by now just plain thwarted talent for self-expression in the face of what he called the bottomless North American "I," had said that being at Harvard had made him feel that "Spanish is a first-draft language or else the Guatemalans who speak it are a first-draft people." Of course he was dramatizing as well as ludicrously generalizing, and not being fair to himself, at least. But now his Cambridge internment is over. Guatemala can seem to provide all the self Moya needs, and, in his mastery of its relative handful of brutal nuances and complexities, he can dazzle, can seem as quick and intricate as a computer. Now I'm the one feeling totally out of it, as simple and tightly wound as rope.

I've been here nearly five months now, and so far we haven't uncovered a single concrete fact; we're not one bit further along than we were that day on Eastern Parkway, when Moya elaborated all that about *las hermanas* López Nub and the *niñera fafera*. I've felt ready for months to take some kind of stand—some kind of not too suicidal stand—but against whom? And how? Voice our dissatisfactions with the Guatemalan legal and media establishments in the free *fafero* press? Go to the Security Forces? (Moya insists that any such phrase as *rule of law* is just not in play here and debate over whether or not that is "really as true as it seems" is off the table. "Such is life in the tropics," he likes to say, as if winsomely, in English, and that's that.)

I was feeling humiliated, clownish, at a loss, utterly *softened,* sitting here this morning, watching Moya revel in our powerlessness with what struck me as such cynical glee; I have to distance myself a lot to get the idea that this behavior of his might be purely acclimative, that this is *his* way of kicking down the door and walking out something like a free man, because dwelling on it, seriously dwelling on it all the time would accomplish nothing but to make him feel so morose and so defeated that it would rob him of himself. He lives here, he's the one who had to flee into temporary exile and then came back, chose to. He's the one who actually gets death threats, I mean, in the past has actually gotten them. What bigger joke on life is there, I've heard him say, than feeling *fated to disappear,* thinking that first thing in the morning and then having to get on with your life, having to make this huge effort to fight off rational fear as just some narcissistic or even hypochondriacal (despite whitening hair, churning stomach, a sometimes tic under his right eye) indulgence. He needs to feel brave, so he needs to feel cheerful.

In fairness to Moya, it can't be said that he has ever actually practiced "investigative journalism"—but who in Guatemala actually does? Maybe he thinks we've tried everything possible and secretly is as frustrated as I am over how quickly we've run out of options. His idea of searching the lower-class *burdeles* was typical, because it made perfect and enticing sense on the surface and didn't reveal itself as ludicrous until I put it into practice. Off and on for weeks I haunted the poor people's brothels, carrying a photograph of Flor (not the too precious one of her at the zoo with her orphans) and another torn from an old newspaper of the *niñera fafera,* the alleged nursemaid who denounced Flor and then vanished.

Moya's thinking, then, was this: if Flor really had ever been involved in the illegal baby trade—and of course we were determined to prove that she hadn't been—then somewhere in Guatemala, most likely here in the city, there had to be a woman or girl, at least one, who would have worked for Flor, whose job it would have been, say, to take some illegally or ambiguously acquired baby into a municipal office and register it as her own, so that later she could turn up in family court with both baby and birth certificate and, still posing as the mother, give the baby up for adoption, that being the modus operands of so many immaculate conceptions and profitable deliverances. Similarly, the sister and sister-in-law of López Nub would have had to find a fake *niñera* if there wasn't a real one. Where better, *vos,* to look for women and girls who will rent their identities and faces than among the poorest who rent their bodies?

It's common knowledge, said Moya, that the low-class *burdeles* constitute the human pool that the foot soldiers of the baby trade are recruited from. And it has to be poor whores because no baby trader is going to hire one from an upscale *burdel* or a fancy *barra show,* because what if the family court judge already knows her personally or at least recognizes her? Anyway, no matter how appropriately distraught she behaves in court, she just won't look believable, won't *look* as if it is completely beyond her capabilities to find a husband or otherwise keep her child alive, and even the corrupt judges are sensitive to appearances. All of which made complete sense, because the girls I've seen from the upscale *burdeles* certainly look well fed and as if they go to dentists and hair salons too, and I happen to know that their employers even enroll them in aerobics classes at the same gymnasiums the *fufurufas* go to. Strolling around La Zona Viva in the afternoons, the upscale bordello girls, even in the way they dress and carry themselves, seem indistinguishable from the rich girls in every way—until they talk, anyway.

So I started at the level of the places that advertise themselves as "sauna-spas" in the newspaper classified pages and moved steadily downwards, all the way down to the appalling one-room shacks of the poorest people's *burdeles* along the railroad tracks at the edge of Zona 1, and hit many sorts of places in between. I always went alone, since Moya was always busy and has such a complete aversion to such places that he would have been useless. And usually I went late in the afternoon, just after siesta, because it was safest then, the lingering men less likely to be drunk yet or in predatory groups, though I still had to be careful, and knew to retreat quickly at the first signs of bleary-eyed macho hostility. I'd order a beer, try to strike up a conversation, all the time keeping my eye out for the *niñera fafera* and always *almost* finding her among so many scrawny, flat-chested girls with pocked complexions, orphan's haircuts, and stunned expressions over having found themselves stranded so soon in life among so many toothless, plump-shouldered, bawdy crones in bright-colored sliplike dresses. Eventually I'd bring out my photographs. "Have you ever seen either of these señoritas . . . ?" Then the silly comments would begin, the spurious claims, the women crowding around. I'd fold the photos away in my wallet, finish my beer with burning ears, and leave, ribald comments and mocking innuendos peppering me from behind as I made my way to the door.

Ridiculous, I know. Of course, one of the ruling suppositions of my mission was that I was never going to find a woman or girl who'd worked for Flor because there wasn't one—but that to be able to draw such a conclusion with any authority, the search had to be as meticulous and thorough as possible. What I really hoped was to find the *niñera fafera*. It was like a schizophrenic gambler's addiction, this desperate hope of not finding and finding at the same time. I was never going to be able to get to every *burdel*. Which is why what I was doing began to seem so stupid but also why it was so hard to stop. All I needed was one stroke of luck. What if I'd found someone who'd worked for Flor? Well then, that would have been the end, I would have packed up and gone home, there might even have been a secret sense of relief. But what if I found the *niñera fafera?*

It dawned on me, long before I gave it up, that it's so much easier to prove guilt than innocence. Innocence doesn't leave a trail. Not finding a girl meant almost nothing. (*Guate no existe.*) Yet what strange things I saw along the way: the run-down houses hiding "saunas," where old, bent Indian women wandered the dark corridors like medieval witches, carrying swinging censers heaped with the twisted stems of thickly smoking burning herbs even into occupied rooms to fumigate against lice and crabs and to numb the many hungers and terrors of stunned, scrawny girls; and the raucous place near the General Cemetery, where all the women were fat and wore bikinis, and all the men wore cowboy hats and western shirts, and the rooms had only curtains for doors and were all off the central bar area, and the men were all given sparklers so that after they'd accomplished their feats of love they could light them and hold them out through the curtains to whistles, stamping feet, and applause.

At times I feel completely puzzled as to why I've stayed on here in Guatemala. But this morning in the Hemmings I was feeling too sad, too soft, to feel any real anger towards Moya. He'd changed the subject anyway. Last night he was out with a young woman from Iceland, a radio reporter for Icelandic National Radio.

"*Fíjese,*" said Moya . . . But how to exactly translate *fíjese?*— a word so commonly used here and one so suggestive of a particular Guatemalan something or other as perceived by the Zona 10 gringos that some entrepreneur among them has even in the last year printed up bumper stickers that read ¡FÍJESE! which are for sale now in gringo-owned and -frequented restaurants and bars all over Zona 10, Lord Byron's, of course, included. "Just imagine!" is the translation my Spanish-English dictionary gives, though you can say that just as well in literal Spanish. "Fix on this" is the way I clearly recall Hemingway translating it in one of his stories, which is right too, more right than "just imagine" as growled by a hard-ass macho but all wrong for *fíjese* as chirped by some *chapina* secretary or maid. So why, here, wherever there are gringo-driven cars and Jeeps are there bumper stickers shouting, "JUST IMAGINE!" or "FIX ON THIS!" at the general populace? In Lord Byron's, among all the Reagan, U.S. Marine Corps, Chicago Cubs, et cetera bumper stickers stuck to the refrigerator there is now one reading ¡FÍJESE! and a stack of more for sale behind the bar—"What is it with all the *fíjeses?*" I asked the new bartender Crystal Francis has hired to work there now, a skinny, red-haired, leprechaunlike, small-town Kentucky, come to the Big Third World City kind of guy named Larry. He rolled his eyes and hooted, "Haven't been in Guatemala long, have you, buddy?" And a middle-aged man sitting next to me at the bar, who I later learned is the top executive here for an American food company, said, "I'll tell you what. Whenever I hear a secretary or *muchacha* say *fíjese,* I know the news is going to be bad and hard to believe. You know, like, *Fíjese, I would have dried the laundry if you'd asked me to, Don Pete, but you only asked me to wash it?* So there's my laundry, neatly folded and sopping wet, heavy as a brick, just in time for my business trip to Costa Rica." And Larry guffawed. "That's it! That's *fíjese!*" And he puckered his lips and batted his eyes like Betty Boop and went *"Fíjese! Ooooo!"*

(And the day that Consul Simms brought little Belinda Towne by the hand to Flor's orphanage, the abandoned little Texan was wearing a filthy yellow T-shirt with big red letters across the front screaming "¡FÍJESE!"—*"Fíjese!* You're telling me!" wrote Flor in her letter. "Her hippie parents just dumped her in Panajachel!")

So Moya said, *"Fíjese,"* and then, "There really is such a place as Iceland."

Worldwide interest in his poor, screwed-up little country turns up such wonderful surprises for him—so regularly that I guess it isn't so surprising anymore. Guatemala's the center of the world, no one can get enough of it, even Iceland is clamoring, dispatching her most affably articulate and insightful and of course politically progressive and let's not forget attractive media starlet, for smart Icelandic radio bosses somehow know that even the most cultishly secretive and murderous *generalísimo* can get diarrhea of the mouth when confronted with a pale European beauty proffering her little microphone like a peanut to Dumbo. Led by his dumb dick, this Sexy *Chafa*'s seduction attempt came out (as described secondhand by a gleefully whispering Moya in the Hemmings) as a boastful if somewhat sanitized avowal of the hard line, because, what the hell, it was only Señorita Green Party from Iceland, it's not like he'd say it on CBS: "Yes, we hit that town hard, but that's counterinsurgency, *chula.* Are not a few hundred dead Indians worth it if it means saving the country from Communism?"—in an editing room in Iceland, they will certainly cut that jaunty term of endearment, *chula.* What a great quote. But where can Moya use it? Not in *El Minuto,* or even in *¿Dónde?.* But he will copy her tape of it and play it for every foreign reporter or dignitary and human rights investigator who visits him. He'll infiltrate it out to the exile news organization in Mexico. His "newspaper" extends everywhere.

"We went," said Moya, "to the Cine Lux, for that new Star Trek movie. *Putavos!* It was excellent!" And then to a little Zona 1 café to drink muddy espressos and analyze the movie like a pair of seriously whacked out Parisian semioticians (Flor wasn't Moya's only involvement, he hasn't tried to hide *that;* he's been out with a lot of these European Green Party types and their *norteamericana* counterparts).

"You never go out with Guatemalan women anymore, do you?" I observed.

Moya, with his look of blown-away self-revelation, said, "This is true, *vos*. I am a bad son of the *patria*. I do not consume what the country produces!"

Now I look out the window from my perch here on the mezzanine and realize that it must be twenty past eleven, because Uncle Jorge and cousins Freddie, Mercedes, and Catalina have just emerged from the Hemmings, and are proceeding up the sidewalk. They'd been sitting downstairs for the last twenty minutes, and I hadn't even noticed.

Six days a week and seven during the Christmas season, for decades now, since the days when my grandparents ran Arrau all by themselves, when Arrau was just a ladies' hat store on the corner, since the days when Abuelito in dark woolen suit, fedora, immense waxed mustache, and carrying an umbrella first startled the downtown Zona 1 populace with his ability to walk with amazing rapidity over rain-flooded sidewalks on the very back edge of his heels with toes high in the air so as not to soak his shoes—Arraus have left the store every morning at exactly five to eleven and marched down 11 Calle to Pastelería Hemmings for their morning coffee break, a ritual repeated again every afternoon, though not as punctually, some time between five-thirty and seven, depending on the rain. Frequently Uncle Jorge takes his afternoon break alone now, since Aunt Lisel rarely comes to the Zona 1 store anymore, and Mercedes will be off taking classes in management and business at the Jesuit university, Catty home with her twins, Freddie off making his rounds of the smaller Arrau branches and boutiques in outlying zones and malls, or going to that fancy gym in Zona 10 that I go to also sometimes.

I watched them walk up the sidewalk, out of sight: Uncle Jorge in his gray Hong Kong suit, looking like a pharaoh with his balding coppery head and hawk's nose and flashing Arrau eyes, accompanied by his burly, curly-haired son and his two prettily contrasting daughters: brisk and hearty Mercedes in her box-kite two-piece suit and pumps, and sweet Catty, luminous green eyes and tea-colored skin though not the best complexion (Freddie teasingly and exaggeratedly likes to call her *"La Amenaza Pinta,"* The Spotted Menace), straight hair hanging loosely around her shoulders, in green blouse and faded jeans, pink sneakers. Even during the worst of the urban violence in '79–'80, Arraus daily dared the crowded downtown streets for the block-long march to the Hemmings for the morning coffee break, though they went accompanied then by a store security guard and Chus, the family houseboy and jack-of-all-trades, both of them armed with Uzis. It was Uncle Jorge's way of standing up for normalcy, I think, and even for the principles of democracy, the obligation of the hardworking if privileged Don Jorge Arrau to share the same sidewalks as his employees and mainly middle-class customers, just as his own parents always had, and to not even shelter his well-brought-up and close-knit family from them. Because even when I was at the Colegio Anne Hunt there were teenage girls who thought of Zona 1 as some faraway, disease-ridden, and murderous country, who were forbidden by their parents to go there and thought of their rare incursions as daredevil escapades.

Catty has told me that when she was in Montreal, going to college and falling turbulently in love with and becoming impregnated with twins by and finally marrying Ronnie the Skycap, every morning at five to eleven, no matter where she was or what she was doing, her thoughts would always travel back to that daily public procession of Arraus to the Hemmings for the morning coffee break. So that, even in Montreal, five to eleven was a break

for her too, the beginning of twenty-five minutes of secret tranquillity, a break from all the mixed-up fevers of love and home-
sickness and her constant fear of the guerrillas kidnapping her
father; a break from reading things in the newspapers like "upris-
ings threaten to cover the isthmus in blood" and not even being
able to say "Guatemala" out loud anymore without someone, even
Ronnie sometimes, answering "death squads," "massacres," "But
Catty, the guerrillas are going to win!"; when all her fears and
confusions were combining to keep her temperature at a constant
99.4 that never varied by even a decimal for all the time she was in
Montreal and put dark, melancholic circles under her eyes and
complicated her troublesome complexion and burned her ample
adolescent figure down to the almost boyish slenderness that has
been hers ever since, except during those culminating months of
pregnancy. Five to eleven meant security, because no one was going to stop her father from enjoying his tea and oatmeal cookies
ever, not when Catty could so clearly see him in her mind's eye that
she felt like she was right there in person, crowded into a booth
with her siblings and Papito just as they always had during the
Christmas season when they all worked together, even when she
was a little girl, when it first became her job to say, "Let me fix
your tea, Papito." Which is still her job, because whenever I see
them coming in from the mezzanine window and go downstairs
to join them, there's Catty fixing her father's tea:

"*Gracias, princesa,*" Uncle Jorge always says, and she, "One or
two teaspoons of sugar, Papito?" even though she knows that of
course he'll say, "Two, *mi amor,*" and then, "Let me taste it for
you—it's still too hot, Papito," and she'll blow across it softly and
taste it again and then, "Now it's ready, Papito," and he'll sip it
and say, "*Exquisito, mi amor. Gracias, muchísimas gracias,*" and then
dip the first of his two daily morning oatmeal cookies into it. Catty
in Canada could see it all so clearly that it didn't even hurt to ac-

knowledge her own absence, because over the phone her father had told her how that very first Saturday morning without her they had all gone to Pastelería Hemmings and Mercedes had felt too shy to assume her big sister's role so that Freddie had been the one to go, "Let me fix your tea, Papito," imitating Catty's voice and everything so that father and son had ended up laughing with so much hilarity and love that the laugh traveled all the way up to Canada and snugly buried itself in Catty's heart and sprang lovingly to life again every time she confronted the fact of her own absence from the morning coffee break. She'd just laugh right out loud, and Ronnie, if he was there, even Ronnie would smile and say, "It must be five to eleven."

Moya, walking down Sexta Avenida on his way home from the newspaper office, had paused on the sidewalk in front of the Picadilly's wide entrance and spotted Roger sitting alone at the bar in an aural halo of blaring electronic pop music, female voices chorusing, "*deenko dee deenko dee, deenko dee deenko DAH . . .*" Moya knew that his friend often did this in his loneliness and boredom now, drank in the Picadilly or elsewhere, and then went to where the only accessible women were (the well-fed-looking ones, eh?), often with his new friend from the gringo bar, that Larry.

But as soon as Moya reached the bar, before he even had a chance to sit down, Roger looked right at him and said, quietly and drunkenly:

"I get it, Moya. You really *are* in guerrilla propaganda or something and what this has *all* been about is trying to hide that it was the guerrillas who killed Flor."

Moya was so stunned he could only react, at first, with impersonal logic. "But no one has ever accused the guerrillas of that, so why would it even occur to them to try to hide it?" Then, still standing, hands in pockets, Moya felt a surge of anger. "Rogerio, *puta,* this is ridiculous and, to me, offensive."

"Or you killed her," said Roger, sounding more dispirited than actually accusing. "And you talked me into coming here and doing all this to cover yourself."

"If that were true, I would be both extremely clever but also insane to have dreamed up such a scheme. You are suffering," said Moya. "I know. And you have been drinking too much." And spending too much time in "upscale" *burdeles* and fancy *barra shows,* strip clubs, too, he thought to himself

"Then what is this? What is this, Moya? You've been fucking with me in some way I don't get."

Oh Moya, you didn't even suspect, you didn't think your old friend capable of actively holding such outrageous notions! Moya saw that his friend was distraught, and didn't really blame him. But surely he'd never intended to plunge Roger into such wounded and wounding confusion?

A sudden tear in Moya's eye was his only answer to his distraught friend. Did Roger, drunk as he was, notice that tear before Moya lightly wiped it away with his sleeve? Did he believe it? With something like martial rectitude, Moya straightened at the bar, with husky voice announced his departure, with comradely but stoic affection briefly laid his hand on Roger's shoulder, and said, "Go home, *pues,* Rogerio. You're tired."

"I don't want to go home. I can't sleep anyway."

You are becoming an addict to inexpensive sex and love that isn't love, Moya wanted to say, but stopped himself.

Instead he said, *"Bueno."* He did not further refer to Roger's pained but outrageous allegations, he simply went home, to his little room in the Pensión Bremen, only a few blocks away, where he sat up for hours matching his wit against the small computerized chess set he'd bought with the last of his stipend money in Cambridge.

But what a notion. That Moya would want to invent an entire chronicle of the life and death of Flor de Mayo Puac and the
ensuing investigation merely to cover his own, or the guerrillas',
tracks! Or that Moya would want to chronicle an entire life and
investigation only to show that it wouldn't go anywhere! True, he
had always known that it *might* not go anywhere, and that this
alone would not mean it was not worth chronicling.

That was in October. Roger lost faith and even seemed on the
verge of formally renouncing all participation in the investigation
and going home. Then things started to happen.

It turned out that Larry, bartender-*putero,* had earned a
haircutter's license in his native Kentucky before coming to Guatemala. By way of explaining the pungent anti-lice shampoos and
soaps he'd doused himself with before coming to work at Lord
Byron's one evening, he revealed to Roger that once a month, for
free, he cut orphans' hair in Los Quetzalitos, and had done so for
the first time that very afternoon. A charitable gesture, no doubt,
but even Larry admitted that the presence of the Scandinavian
volunteers was an inducement, a certain Norwegian in particular.
Roger saw his opening, and pretended an extreme interest in Scandinavian girls too. Larry invited him along next time.

At last, an unobtrusive entrance to the orphanage! It was by
far Roger's best piece of espionage work yet, *vos.* When they met for
the first time in over a week in Pastelería Hemmings, the two friends
reaffirmed their commitment to the project, yet Moya was left with
the feeling that Roger had still not overcome all his suspicions.

One new problem was that Roger now faced a monthlong wait
for Larry's next orphan haircutting day and another was that they
really didn't know what his plan should be, once he got inside.

"Try to make friends with Rosana Letones, without letting
her know who you are, of course," suggested Moya, referring to
the orphanage's new director. "Rogerio, who knows where it will

lead? Maybe she will let you take some of the children on an outing to the zoo or to the movies."

"A month!" exclaimed Roger. "I can't wait a *month!*"

Well, soon his three-month visa to stay in Guatemala would
expire again (actually, through a remote family connection in
migración, he'd twice received thirty-day extensions, but now Roger
had been told he could not have another unless he paid a certain
large sum to a certain recently promoted official whom the remote
family connection now worked under; an indignant Roger had
refused to pay it). He would have to cross into Mexico at Tecún
Umán, then cross back for a new visa. He decided to take a little
bus trip through the highlands and the tourist towns along the way,
mainly to help pass the time until the next orphan haircutting day.

Before leaving Roger gave Moya the money he would need to bribe
Flor's old notebook out of the police archives, in the basement of
National Police headquarters.

Roger, at the time, could easily afford it. The *quetzal,* for so
long on par with the dollar and in recent years nearly so, had suddenly plummeted to more than two to one and had gone on plummeting. Unfortunately Roger's inheritance from his *abuela* of
twenty thousand *quetzales,* which was to be turned over to him on
his wedding day, had never been transferred to an Arrau account
in Miami, and Miami wanted no part of *quetzales* now. So *tío* Jorge
Arrau decided to sign the inheritance over to Roger while it was
still worth *something, vos.* They went to the bank together to with-
draw a check for twenty thousand *quetzales,* worth nearly the same
in dollars only weeks before, and then took it to one of the heavily
guarded, black-market money-changing offices that had recently
sprung up in the blocks around the post office, and sold it for eight
thousand dollars in cash.

Mysteriously, the whole black-market trade in dollars seemed
to have something to do with the central post office, and it was the

post office that eventually played a main role in Moya's getting chased out again:

Soon after the *quetzal*'s slide began, everyone, Roger included, stopped receiving mail from the USA. But it wasn't until two armored mail trucks leaving the airport were hijacked within days of each other that rumors began to coalesce around the common suspicion that someone was stealing the mail. And there was only one logical reason for anyone to be doing that, *vos:* to get at the bank checks sent by immigrants in the USA to their loved ones and dependents at home, loved ones more desperately dependent than ever now that even half a dozen eggs could cost half a day's wage, though it was hard to see why even the price of eggs should be pegged to the dollar.

So Moya and an *El Minuto* photographer snuck into the post office mail-sorting room one afternoon during the siesta hours, pushed some of the heavy wooden counters aside, and photographed what they found: piles of envelopes sent from the USA, torn open and discarded. Celso Batres went ahead and published the picture on the front page of the next day's *El Minuto*. It was that rarest thing, an *El Minuto* scoop, one the boss thought they could get away with because on the surface it didn't seem to implicate anybody but the mail sorters. Except the mail sorters were taking their stolen booty directly to those money-changing offices near the post office. Some of these had originally been founded by ordinary merchants quick to capitalize on the new instability, which had turned dollars into the most hoarded and one of the most profitably speculated commodities in the country. But after a few Mafia-style rubouts, it had become clear to everybody that certain elements within the army were now in control of the black-market trade for dollars.

Which was why Moya, in his hastily composed column accompanying the picture of the envelope massacre, invented a decisive love letter, one that would have repaired the love between a

Juan Chapin working as a pharmacist's assistant in Los Angeles, California, and the girl from Barrio La Limonada who had resigned herself to never seeing or hearing from him again. Fearing eternal spinsterhood, she finally relented and married the army sergeant whose boorish threats "in defense of her honor" had chased all her suitors away, including the handsome young pharmacist who'd written to invite her to join him in California. She was never happy again. Moya signed off with this sentence: "The sergeant had an ally, *El Anticúpido,* who flies around with an Uzi instead of a bow and arrow, destroying love letters and even hijacking mail trucks to get at them."

Of course Celso Batres would never have consciously exposed Moya to mortal danger by publishing a column guaranteed to arouse the sharks' feeding frenzy, no matter how much glory it would bring the paper. That post office foray was a late-breaking story and Celso still had his own lead editorial to write and not much time to worry over Moya or even to notice the uncharacteristic lack of subtlety in Moya's closing line (though where did Moya explicitly say *El Anticúpido* was a military man anyway, *vos?*). The editorial, titled *Sin Razón,* No Reason, one of Celso's more frequently employed titles, was on the need to legalize the dollar black market so that it could operate in the open like the competing change bureaus familiar to all travelers in European capitals and even Mexico; which might not save the *quetzal* but would at least eliminate the degrading spectacle of so many hawkers in the streets around the post office, all those women in rags breast-feeding their babies while hissing "dollars dollars" at passersby, frightening tourists, leading them to illicit-seeming little back rooms; there was no reason that the act of changing money at the going rate should feel like a drug deal, was there?

So Moya's column appeared as written and on that first crucial day, in accordance with *El Minuto*'s small circulation, caused a small stir. But even the prominent dailies weren't afraid to follow *El Minuto*'s lead in waging a sensationalistic campaign against civilian post office employees and their gold rush fever, in fact *Anticúpidos* became the slogan of the entire campaign. Within days even the Miami-Cuban ambassador was forced to speak up, defending the inviolability of U.S.-stamped mail (if not the love between illegally immigrated pharmacists and their *novias* at home). And *that* was when the army must have realized that Moya had finally succeeded in actually hampering them a bit.

All of this happened while Roger was away on his short journey. While in Quezaltenango, on his way to the border, he happened to glance at the new issue of *¿Dónde?* and, flipping through it, found "The Prophecies of the Prophetic Rats of Barrio Prado Vélez," a regular *¿Dónde?* feature. This one was about a Quiché Maya Indian girl who had the ability to project her own world of experience far into the future, though she was in Hungary in the seventeenth century, a prisoner of the Bloody Countess of Transylvania, who all by herself tortured and murdered some six hundred clandestinely imprisoned young maidens and bathed in their blood, and, though the column was unsigned, he immediately recognized there the hand of his recently somewhat estranged friend Moya. ("The Bloody Countess is evil, but I am not," Moya had the girl say through the mouth of the prophetic rat. "We are almost opposites, though my temperament is not extreme. But her witch has warned that the blood of a brown-skinned virgin cannot restore her youth. I am the countess's unwilling servant and witness . . .") Roger correctly deduced that Moya must be in some trouble and phoned him at *El Minuto*. Of course they employed very guarded language over the telephone: "*Sí pues,*" said Moya. "I'm thinking I might have to visit Aunt Irene soon, if I can find the time. If you see some nice handicraft, would you buy it, something warm, a poncho perhaps, she likes that kind of thing and it's cold in Canada."

"Huh?" said Roger. ". . . Oh! Oh, *that* Aunt Irene! Moya, it's that serious?" Aunt Irene, of course, was a code name for a certain human rights organization sharing those initials. In an excessively panicked tone, Roger stutteringly said he was going to hurry his trip to Momostenango to buy a poncho but only if he could pay with his *Visa card.* "You know, my *visa* card?" he repeated. "See you soon then," said Moya, quickly hanging up.

Having craftily thrown the authorities off his border-crossing path (as if it was *he* who was in trouble), Roger soon returned to the capital with his new visa. There the situation quickly accelerated into one of ultimate danger: a death squad, waiting for Moya, as he and Roger were walking to a corner *tienda* for an evening beer.

But Moya doesn't want to talk about that, or about *them.* Why should he? He is alive, isn't he? Why give them free advertising? We know who they are, what they do and why they do it, don't we? Moya refuses to chronicle that encounter with a death squad.

NINETEEN

From approximately six in the evening until half an hour past midnight, Moya and Flor sat under the eucalyptus trees and the paper lanterns in the dining patio of the Fu Lu Shu II in Zona 9, in the glow of butane torches. She sat facing the arched entrance into the main dining room of the restaurant, a semicircle of wood carved and painted into a scarlet, gold-scaled dragon. Moya faced the vine-covered wall which during the course of that night had already undergone so many transformations: into the convent wall of the orphanage where she was raised; a Boston blizzard; a stuffy elementary school classroom where an adolescent girl sat squirming in her seat surrounded by children almost ten years younger; a Greyhound bus full of seventeen soldiers and an adolescent *gringa-chapina* rolling through the *norteamericano* Deep South . . . When Flor's hair finally descended into the sweet and sour sauce, love was already happening inside of him, perhaps for the first time since Patti Mundinger. But what made this night so different, that it led him back to love?

Because Moya had often done this, coerced foreign women (and Flor's citizenship, at least, was foreign now) into telling all about themselves. For him it was a form of travel, and something more. For them, it was often such a tender surprise that someone such as he should care. But who, in his position, wouldn't have? This goes to the heart of Moya, the curious role he played back then. They were inseparable, his heart and his role, like a heart-shaped cookie stuck to an overbaked cookie sheet.

His role was to tell his foreign visitors what they had come to hear, and sometimes even more; to enlarge his country, make it seem bigger, make it emanate, that was always his aim. Often all

he had to do was recite his country's folk sayings—some of them
of his own invention—with a certain dark élan: "In Guatemala,
vos, you can't even confide in your own shadow." "To be a Guatemalan of conscience is to live like a hunted animal." "In Guatemala, even the drunks watch their words, which doesn't mean they
don't make a lot of noise, *vos.*" "Oh well, *chula,* the dead to their
hole, the living to their *bollo.* What other choice is there?" (*bollo,* a
kind of sweetcake, rhyming with *hoyo*). They got the idea. Moya
had often pictured his women friends back in the cities they caine
from, addressing rapt audiences in church basements and university lecture halls or speaking over the radio with voices full
of dramatic emphasis, ". . . From so many death threats, his hair
is turning white! As he said on the night we met in the capital, *To
be a Guatemalan of conscience,*" et cetera.

With touching humility (not Sylvia McCourt, who had little,
but the others, the Sweet Sisters, the Angels) his visitors always
went out of their way to assure him of the seriousness and purity
of their intentions. As dryly and succinctly as possible, so that he
couldn't for a moment have cause to think they were in any way
seeking glory or reward for themselves from the suffering of others, they outlined their various projects and missions. What they
learned from him and others, they would take home and employ
in the fight against the deceptions of standard political discourse
and the mass media's parroting, against misinformation and indifference.

That was how they all saw it, *vos.* Even Moya had come to
see it somewhat that way, knowing that he could be a most effective "guerrilla" simply by allowing foreigners to secretively indulge
the fantasy that he was one, though of course this could never be
acknowledged between them, not even in the most seemingly intimate conversation (secrecy being a church, forced confession its
penultimate sacrament). He was always under surveillance, so his

first line of defense was to behave at all times as if he had no com-
promising secrets, as if he couldn't possibly be leading a clandestine existence as well. The moment it could be proven that he did,
not even his reputation as the country's last truly independent print
journalist (still residing in Guatemala, that is), with a network of
media-sophisticated girlfriends all over the world, would be able
to save him. Of course, Moya had always overestimated the effectiveness of what his friends accomplished when they went home.
But so did the *chafas*.

Few people in Guatemala read what Moya wrote in *El Minuto*
anyway. In a strange way, he wrote for foreigners. It certainly legitimized him for them. Then he, by paying attention to his visitors, by playing his role, legitimized them.

So just as Moya appeared to eschew clandestine ties, he had
no Guatemalan lovers either. He knew that he might endanger any
chapina who became involved with him. This sounds overly romantic, affected. So, put another way, it was certainly something
he had to consider. The last one had been Alma Mejía, the girl in
his theater group whom Roger had briefly met in Pastelería Hemmings in '79. She had fled to Mexico later that same year. There
she'd involved herself in exile work, a coordinator for the exile
theater groups that performed for solidarity audiences around the
world. She lived with a *compañero* without marrying him, they
gave their children names out of the *Popol Vuh*. Alma lived in the
organized *ladino* exiles' world of melancholy, heroic delusion: she
still believed in victory, in the transcendent logic of history, in the
inevitability of justice, in the poetic myth of one nation, on and on.

But Moya could no longer imagine himself falling in love with
a *chapina* who hadn't faced and made at least similar choices.
Wouldn't he want his woman to have a conscience, to be lively in
her heart, full of feeling and sweetness, to be at least a little bit
intelligent and capable? *Pues,* what would that bring her to? She

would have to lead some form of clandestine existence, if only in her heart.

Because by the time Moya met Flor, aboveground opposition hardly existed anymore. Where clandestine organizations survived in the city, it was as separate sections of a snake hacked up into many pieces, buried far apart and deep under the earth. It was hard to imagine a country more justifiably saturated with paranoia. The last thirty years of violent repression—not to mention the centuries before—had perhaps bred a new kind of human being, as if in a poisoned petri dish. Resolutely silent, suspicious, dishonest, full of denial, quick to believe the worst of anyone, guilty when guiltless, guiltless when guilty. Noisy in the cantinas, but, even then, the desperate noise of the stifled. And such capacity for delusion. Even the religious landscape had for many become one of confusion and delirium, because how to speak to the soul without addressing the terror so many felt there, and how to name the devil without increasing the terror? (But the Evangelical Protestants told the people that *they* were the devil, repent and be safe. So the army thought they had found a new ally in the shepherding of souls to replace the old one and said, Let there be more, and, from the gringo Bible Belt and California, the divine screamers poured down, warrior monks of the Conquest's unfinished business.)

He'd become a snob. Was that what it was? He didn't think any Guatemalan woman was good enough for him unless she also led *that* sort of existence? And he couldn't go near that kind of woman without risking both their lives because he was always being watched. And that kind of woman would probably mistrust him anyway. She would see through him, she wouldn't think he had it so tough, and of course he didn't. She would think he was merely some kind of *fanfarrón* (one who makes a great fanfare). She would even misunderstand him. And imagine the *compañera* who would also let him spend all his time running around with foreign women? (But, my love, it is all for the struggle to save the nation! *Síííí pues.*)

But it was part of the transaction, his modus operandi, for Moya to lure foreign women into telling all about themselves. All he had to do was listen and they were left feeling that a bond had been formed. To them it was all vitally important, of course: all the steps that had led to the decisive moment when they realized they cared so much about a far-off, suffering little country that they had to go there themselves, as something other than just a tourist. They never expected him to care. But he did, it fascinated him, he was detective, anthropologist, father confessor, and seducer all at once, listening to them outline their journeys in such a way as to make them seem somehow inevitable. Around them he was like a boy crazy for fairy tales: the little girls who wore wooden shoes and stuck their fingers in the dike, the sleeping beauties who woke up, the girls with peas under their piled mattresses, the princesses in their towers who let down their hair.

And with them, Moya had from time to time spent happy days and nights filled with scentless kisses and shockingly straightforward lovemaking. Then they went home. They always went home, and hardly ever came back; they busied themselves according to their needs and dispositions, and cultivated their nostalgia.

But Moya kept in touch. Almost as if using his hands to project ominous puppet shadows against a wall, he sent himself looming into the fond and concerned memories of others through the international phone lines. Usually, this was just to send greetings. The more familiar (to them) Moya saved his sentiments and ideas for the letters he posted in anonymously initialed Hotel Biltmore Maya envelopes. But a woman's readiness to accept a collect call in the middle of the night counted, *vos.* It was just such a series of calls, in an unprecedentedly urgent tone, one to his friend Laura Moore in Washington, another to Sylvia McCourt in Cambridge, that had so swiftly landed Moya at Harvard with stipend. (Where he, six months later, did the unexpected thing and went home himself.)

Even singular and exceptional Laura Moore (raised in Pocatello, Idaho, where her father was wealthy but an abusive alcoholic, and where she was a high school champion skier), the Queen human rights leaf-cutting ant, that intrepid two-legged bonfire of inexhaustible focus and feeling and will, went home sometimes. She went home with her suitcases packed with the cassette recordings and typed testimonies of victims who—and this was what truly amazed Moya—no matter how much their tragic tales resembled the hundreds of others Laura had already discreetly listened to and transcribed, always made actual warm tears slide from her reddened blue eyes, soaking her cheeks, the golden, angular face that others, mainly out of jealousy, regarded as being one of haughty and competitive scorn, but that Moya knew to be one of the most redeeming faces he had ever seen. Laura *always* came back. She was Moya's closest friend among the foreign women who came to Guatemala, but she had never been able to love him. They had not offered each other the slightest possibility of peace.

But none of his foreign women, his friends, offered that peace. They were too eager to submit. They only saw Moya in his role, and would consider it a betrayal to separate him from it. Eventually, a bitterness crept into Moya's relationships with the foreign women. Instead of arranging to meet them in restaurants with clean and credible food, he lured them to the poor people's food stalls in the market behind the cathedral. Even Moya, on just his *El Minuto* salary, could afford to eat somewhat better than that. He led them in by the butchers' stalls, the floors sticky and rank with old blood and flies, past the dried-fish sellers with their fly-coated offerings. At the food stalls he ordered chicken soup ladled from big pots into plastic bowls, a still feathery rooster's head submerged in the broth, or a whole claw. Or plates of beans with chunks of pig gristle. Warm sodas served with plastic cups washed and rewashed in tubs of cold, greasy water. Even Moya ended up with diarrhea.

"So what is it you look for in a man if you are to love him in a serious way?" Moya asked Flor de Mayo—this was still fairly early on in the Long Night of White Chickens, just after she'd told him that in fact she had not had many "boyfriends," adding a beat later, "Well, not serious ones." He hadn't even yet admitted to himself that he wanted to be that man, it was just one of his standard story-initiating questions.

And Flor didn't even pause to think. "Self-knowledge," she said brightly, as if she'd worked it all out long ago, and then she looked at him with her eyebrows raised.

Moya was astonished, because that was exactly what Sylvia McCourt had said just the previous year, when he'd held her in his arms all night, both of them fully clothed, in the Hotel Biltmore Maya. And self-knowledge, as Moya conceived of it, was perhaps his weakest, his least developed area—inevitably so, after years spent telling himself that even his own shadow wasn't in on what he was really thinking, *vos*.

It struck Moya, that night, as an extraordinarily superior thing to say, a standard that he had never before truly considered; now that he had heard it twice, the idea took on new authority, and for some time filled his inner life with self-doubt. Was it just a coincidence that two of the three most formidable women he knew had answered that way? The third formidable woman was Laura Moore, but she had answered the question with a caustic laugh and said, "I'll know him when I meet him.

Haven't yet." And then he'd felt her watching him from behind a mask of wry amusement.

Of course Moya didn't yet know Flor's habit of saying provocative and even somewhat pretentious things, often recalled at random from half-remembered philosophy and literature courses at Wellesley College, but spoken with spontaneous and unshakable conviction nonetheless. Having said one thing or another, she could often then defend it with rapid-fire chatty passion, spraying a mercurial logic all over the place. This habit eventually became very dear to Moya, simply because he learned to recognize it, and because he so liked her.

"*Sí pues,* self-knowledge, *aja,*" said Moya. ". . . But how do you mean this?"

"Gravity," said Flor immediately, as if she were being quizzed and had this answer ready too. "A stillness. That you feel not just comfortable with, but yourself stilled by. Stilled by? I mean, what do I mean? You don't just look for one thing of course, OK? I think love is two people separately looking in the same direction together. It's two people entrusted with each other's vulnerabilities. It's two people who are going to end up knowing everything about each other, as much as two people can know. So, self-knowledge. Gosh, who needs a guy who doesn't know himself?"

Sylvia McCourt had also answered this in a similar way, though more concisely. Solidity. Feet on the ground. A man who wasn't going to disappoint her by making ridiculous mistakes and decisions.

Moya asked Flor, "And so you have this, this self-knowledge?"

"Hah!" Flor had bleated after a moment. "I should hope that by now I've learned something." But then she leaned forward and whispered conspiratorially, "I'm somebody you phoned, remember? Supposedly for an interview about orphans. I came along because you're a friend of Roger's. Except now we're having this conversation." For a moment she held his gaze. "Except it's more like an interrogation."

"*Pero,* Flor! How can you say this? No one is insisting that you tell the truth, so it is the absolute opposite of an interrogation. I asked what it was like to go live in Boston, and you told me about policemen and snowstorms. *Luzbel de piedralumbre, pues.* Go right ahead! It is fun for me to figure out what you are really saying."

"But I didn't make that up, ask Roger, he knows that story— Cheers." Flor smiled, took a deep drink of her rum. "I'm not trying to *really* say anything."

"*Bueno, chula.*"

"You're pretty overbearing, you know that?"

"Yes, I know, you have already told me this. Would you like me to tell you about the Colegio Anne Hunt instead?"

"Hah! Absolutely not. Why would I want to hear about that?"

"I agree. But you were in school with little children when you were much older. And now here you are in Guatemala again, taking care of little children. Who would not wonder about this?"

". . . Excuse me? Wonder what?"

"Why do you not want to be with people your own age?"

". . . The two have nothing to do with each other, Moya. Back then I went to school because it was my best option. It was ridiculously boring, my very own excruciating road to *somewhere,* but I had to do it. Here I took the job because it was offered to me and it seemed an OK . . . *Oh!* Do you really think I had some mad, unconscious reason for taking the job at the orphanage? Why do people like me take jobs like that, I mean, isn't it always basically the same reasons?"

"I don't know, *pues* . . ."

"And listen, I didn't speak English at all when I arrived in Namoset, I didn't even read Spanish that well, so sitting in elementary school reading circles every day was necessary, and totally beneficial, however occasionally humiliating. Even the penmanship classes were helpful, believe it or not. But my life hasn't been this joke, Moya, and I'm no genius. I did the first three grades in one year, the next two in another. And by fifth grade the books were wonderful anyway, Jules Verne, *Tom Sawyer* . . . Oh yes, I also learned that time can move *very* slowly indeed. And it was a very illuminating experience, being this freak, who wasn't always sure if she was ten or fifteen, no? I realized my crush on a teacher was very different from a ten-year-old's; I think I went around spewing this chaos that everyone, myself included, was too puritanical to address, it being Namoset, Massachusetts, and not, say, Chiquimula. And math, *vos,* forget it, I was barely ahead of even the second-graders! You have to remember where I came from, Moya. The *monjas'* teaching methods were not quite jesuitical, you know what I mean? We had separate classes for sewing, cooking, sure. But religion spelling and math we received all in one class! 'Why does February have twenty-eight days?'—this is what our lessons were like—'Because this is the number of blisters Job had on his body! Spell *febrero!*' and we'd all have to recite F-E-B . . . 'Spell Job!' J-O-B . . . 'Count to twenty-eight!' *Uno, dos, tres* . . . 'Why does *febrero* have twenty-eight days?' Because Job Ecclesiastical 'Sesame Street,' you know?"

The reason Moya had phoned for de Mayo for an interview on the "orphan situation" in the first place was that, though he had no clandestine ties of his own, he sometimes wrote for the exile news service in Mexico (which was *practically* the same thing). What would be suppressed in Guatemala could be published there. Usually he didn't try to hide it; he used the telex machine in the *El Minuto* office to file if the story didn't seem especially controversial, or the telex in the Hotel Ritz if it did, and he never appended his name. Usually his dispatches were on his own initiative. Without their having to ask, he simply made a habit of sending the exile news service whatever couldn't be printed in *El Minuto.*

But the exile news service had only two regular ways of contacting Moya with their occasional requests. Highly trusted Sweet Sisters of Solidarity brought sealed envelopes from Mexico. And sometimes one of these envelopes suddenly appeared on Moya's desk, without his knowing exactly who had left it there.

Laura Moore had heard a rumor from a trusted source that someone who worked at *El Minuto* was an urban *subcomandante* for the "Egyptians," which was "Aunt Irene"—style code for the *Ejército Guerrillero de los Pobres,* the Guerrilla Army of the Poor. Though Laura Moore was extremely discreet and had an uncanny propensity for finding surprising sources, Moya was deeply disconcerted that someone had passed such a rumor on to her. But Moya knew that urban *comandantes* rarely fit the stereotype, that they had to be masters of circumspection and even disguise to survive in the city. For all anyone could really know, it might very well be Natividad Molina, the blithely unreliable receptionist downstairs, who was actually a deeply clandestine guerrilla *comandante,* and occasionally left envelopes on his desk. Laura Moore liked to indulge the fantasy—perhaps in the way of dreaming up her perfect man, the one she'd recognize as soon as she saw him—that it was Celso Batres, the very handsome and dashing and really quite intelligent and liberal-spirited owner of the little-read *El Minuto* and the ubiquitous *¿Dónde?.* That was certainly an amusing idea: Celso, Moya's boss and benthctor, leaving unmarked envelopes on his desk, directing him what to write for the exile news service. You never know, *vos.* But Moya told Laura it was even likelier to be Natividad Molina. He also told Laura he was furious with her for having told him about it in the first place, it was just about the last thing he wanted to know! (Secrecy being a church, forced confession et cetera, no one wanted a shadow that could be hauled out of himself like a bloody fishing net full of wriggling identities and names . . .)

One day, inside the unmarked and sealed envelope that had mysteriously appeared on his desk, Moya found a request for an article related to the illegal trade in orphans. Enclosed was a photocopy of a G-2 memo, on official Ministry of Defense stationery. The memo, beneath various bureaucratic subheadings, nonjudgmentally stated that there was at least one hospital in the United States, in Pittsburgh, Pennsylvania, that was purchasing Guatemalan orphans in order to use their organs for transplants to save the lives of rich gringos. Having served that purpose, said the memo, the orphans were then incinerated. At least one foreign-owned or -directed orphanage or clandestine baby-selling ring must be knowingly collaborating (said the memo).

In retrospect, this should give some idea of the credulous ignoramuses slaving away in the carrion-stuffed catacombs of the G-2 bureaucratic empire. But this should come as no surprise: Moya believed the memo too.

Eventually, when he went to Cambridge, he would realize that the United States was unlikely to allow such flagrant excesses to take place in a vigilantly regulated hospital within its own borders (though perhaps not as unlikely if a live orphan was worth much less in the marketplace than the sum of his or her parts). But back then it had seemed absolutely logical, in keeping with everything he had witnessed and been taught to believe and wanted to believe. Moya certainly understood why the exile news service would want a story on this scandal that seemed to him only marginally more lurid than so many others. But these sorts of stories were hard even for gringo reporters to substantiate. Not that the G-2 memo wasn't by itself substantiation enough for the news service. Beyond his willingness to contribute and apparent trustworthiness, it was Moya's lapidary rhetorical gift that the news service valued.

Inside the envelope, along with the memo, was a note written in an anonymous hand. It listed every U.S. citizen who owned or directed a private orphanage in the country. On this list, of course, was Flor de Mayo Puac.

From time to time Moya had heard Flor spoken of, and had always remembered her relation to his old school friend, Rogerio Graetz, who had betrayed him by staying atop a fence while Moya jumped down alone to face a vicious dog. Their friendship had, of course, ended over that incident; but Roger had never known how much Moya had looked forward to making up the next summer. He'd even evolved a plan, a little ceremony, whereby they, together, would toss poisoned meat to the dog from atop that fence, and thus renew the friendship. Moya hadn't known that Roger would not be returning for his annual two-month immersion in the Colegio Anne Hunt; often, when he felt lonely and sad, his *mamita* would even say, "But your friend the *gringito* will be here soon!" But it was not until 1979 that Moya saw his old friend again, and quite by chance, in Pastelería Hemmings—by then the dog must have been long dead, and was nearly forgotten. Roger was in Guatemala visiting Flor de Mayo, who for some reason had returned.

Since then, Moya had occasionally spotted Flor, had actually noticed her without having the slightest idea who she was. The very first time he saw her was one afternoon during the *refacción,* or snack, hour in the Hotel Pan American in Zona 1. A marimba band was playing, and she was sitting alone at the table closest to the Spanish-tile fountain and its continuous watery dribbling, reading a gringo paperback with a metallic blue-and-silver cover. She didn't touch her coffee, her pecan pie was half eaten. There was a pause in the music. Behind the long wooden keyboard of the marimba, the six musicians, in synthetic maroon suits, stood poised over their mallets like solemn waiters displaying six bottles of finest wine and then, all of them in unison taking a quick little bow, they launched into a sprightly rendition of the Wedding March, though no one in the room seemed to be getting married. Various customers and foreign hotel guests traded knowing smiles, rolled their eyes, or gaped at the sublimely straight-faced musicians bent over their expertly flourished mallets. But the attractive, dark, obviously Guatemalan woman curled up in her chair by the fountain went on reading, her expression not registering the slightest interest in the marimba band's perhaps unfathomable, though not atypical, decision to perform the Wedding March during the midweek afternoon snack hour. Nor did she glance up when the waiter, dressed in Quiché Maya ceremonial *traje,* with turban-like cloth headdress, britches baring his muscular peasant thighs, stopped at her table to refill her coffee. Moya's eyes were drawn to her sturdy if gracefully tapered brown ankle, the smooth arch of her heel and cheerfully naked foot: she had one leg crossed over her knee, and dangling from the very end of that raised foot was a black cloth loafer, lightly and continuously bounced away from her bare sole and then back, that light bouncing caused by a similarly repeated up-and-down exertion of her black-masked toes, both motions seemingly possessed by a rhythm that was not that of the Wedding March. She wore navy blue slacks, a loose-fitting and very clean white blouse, no jewelry that he could see, a subdued but arresting shade of red lipstick on her slightly pursed, musing lips. Her nose protruded with gypsy haughtiness against a backdrop of softly tumbling black hair. Lowered lids and the angle from which he watched partially obscured her eyes, which seemed fixed darkly and raptly on the shiny paperback perched on her thigh.

It didn't occur to Moya that he had seen her somewhere before, his memory didn't serve up the faded visage of a sweetly smiling adolescent in tight jeans and light blue sweatshirt with hair falling over her face as she bent to receive a kiss from little Rogerio racing towards her through the Colegio Anne Hunt's front gates, while the older boys clucked and hissed, *"Mira esa india rica, vos . . ."* But her hair was not straight and servants didn't go around dressed that way. Even back then she would have looked taller than she actually was, with longish legs, long, thin arms, a long if femininely rounded posture. But she was very brown, which was why the boys had called her *india*. Moya too was much mocked, back then, at Anne Hunt, for his own poor person's complexion, even by those boys who were not much lighter. But even such slight variations in hue allowed them to feel vindicated when taunting Moya. *"El moro,"* the Moor, *"Mulato," "Cara de mico,"* Monkey Face, they called him. At home he would weepingly plead before his *mamita,* "Why did God make me so ugly?" *Si pues,* that was when he was little.

The Wedding March came to an end, followed by a pretty and sentimental melody that Moya, never very musical, didn't recognize. One of her hands now hovered over the tabletop, groping in the air, while her eyes remained fixed on the book held against her thigh. Suddenly her hand dropped onto the half slice of pecan pie and picked it up, carrying it towards her lips. Moya watched as she obliviously worked the entire half slice of pie into her mouth, all the time still reading. She chewed; soon her long fingers were softly soothing her lips, apparently nudging sticky crumbs into the path of her flickering tongue. But then—perhaps it was a stifled laugh over what she'd been reading, or a bit of pie caught in her throat—crumbs flew from her mouth as she quickly hunched forward, hand scooped over mouth. Now he saw her eyes, large, nearly black, worried-looking disks darting around the room. The hand came away from her mouth, she sat back and resumed her reading. Could she be a prostitute? From one of the most upscale *burdeles,* perhaps taking a break before or after a visit to one of the generals in the nearby palace? But reading a book in English? No, it couldn't be. Should Moya rise and intrude himself upon her? No, she would rebuff him, she was certain to be *muy burgesa,* narrow-minded and petulant. Or maybe she was one of those former *barra show* girls, or the most beautiful flower plucked from some jungle backwater, who had married a colonel, accompanying him to some European capital while he served as military attaché in an embassy. There she had acquired her incongruous tastes for understatedly elegant clothing and vulgar novels, without ever shedding her bad table manners. What a funny world, all one . . . Moya went back to his newspaper, *El País* from Spain, borrowed from Celso Batres, who was as generous as he was handsome and liberal spirited and who always saved his *El País* for Moya; who would actually say to those who asked him for it first, "Ah, I'm sorry, I've already promised it to Luis Moya." So in that day's *El País* Moya read a Spanish reporter's account of languishing in a hotel in Ecuador with a raging fever from a bad bout of malaria when a local paper was pushed under his door, its headline proclaiming that Jesus Christ had reappeared in Guayaquil, the feverish reporter thinking, *Hostia! I'd better file . . .*

An absurdly high-pitched voice, in English, its *chapina* accent barely noticeable, full of bright and artificial formality and cheer, was saying, "Hi, Mr. and Mrs. Ferguson! My, you gave me a start. Are you enjoying your stay in Guatemala?"

The woman, all in one motion, had stood up and dropped her book on the floor, and was fumbling with delicate headphones and wire as if disentangling seaweed from her hair.

"Excuse me! I was just—It's not very patriotic of me, I know, but I just can't stand marimba." And then a squeaky, wheezing laugh. She stooped swiftly to retrieve the book, put it on the table, and shook hands firmly with the Fergusons, two middle-aged gringos who dwarfed her, accompanied by an officious little *chapín* wearing suit and steel-rimmed glasses. Flor, nearly two years later, when she was actually able to recall that afternoon, told Moya that the Guatemalan he'd observed was an adoption lawyer who had approached her on behalf of the Fergusons. She had decided then and there that even if a child were available—she couldn't remember if, at the time, one had been—they could not have that child. They'd seemed perfectly nice, said Flor, but not right, not what she looked for. Not that they wouldn't be loving parents, they had pleasantly homey if excessively narrow temperaments, her impression anyway. But she hadn't at all liked their description of their "All American" little town in South Carolina. Probably, just probably *not* the greatest place on earth to one day find yourself wondering why you're the only brown-faced-shiny-black-haired little kid in town. Another problem was that parents always want their children to think at least somewhat the way they do, *verdad?* Well, the Fergusons were Republicans, and proud enough of it to want it known. To each his own of course and far be it from me but in the South . . . Look, hadn't the South gone mad for Republicans and warring foreign policies? Weren't they all over Central America backslapping the killers now, donating helicopters and mercenaries and fundamentalist religions and army-plundered charity shipments to internal refugees to win "hearts and minds"? She assumed all that must be expressive of at least some degree of widely held community belief, however well meaning. No, she was sending no orphans there, impossible, *c'mon,* no fucking way— so many of them massacre survivors after all! The only gringo southerner she'd ever granted children to was Ozzie Peterkins, the black football player who built the jungle gym in her orphanage yard, a true sweetheart and something of a cosmic thinker, believe it or not, Moya. Also she didn't like it when people mentioned right away that they wanted a child under four years of age, in good health, as light skinned as possible, with full mental capacities, one that could be proven never to have suffered the potentially brain-damaging effects of severe malnourishment. They had every right, of course, every right, but she wasn't that kind of matchmaker. When she came down to it, she liked who she liked, *pues,* that was her right too. She tried to find parents she herself would have liked being raised by. She didn't do that many adoptions, and since there was no science to it, she simply interacted a bit, browsed through her own impressions and intuitions, until she decided. There was a *mística* to it. These were whole and often very complicatedly begun little lives she was signing over. It was important to have a sense of how the future would guide the past, you know what I mean? The power she had was incredibly intimidating; she said she needed nerves of steel sometimes, when faced with such a decision. It was just that she trusted herself to get it right more than whoever else might try to. It exhausted her. No one knew, she told Moya once, during the five brief and turbulent weeks that they were actually lovers, how often she had silently called herself a monster, how bitterly she'd derided her own conceits and prejudices—

"*No . . . !*" Moya had protested, and she, that night, had finally, for once, accepted his efforts to soothe her conscience, full of these strange dilemmas, rarely confessed, that he had never encountered before. She was telling herself, then, that she wanted to leave, and by then he wanted to go with her, only with her.

So apparently that was what Flor was telling the Fergusons and the tense and seething little lawyer, as politely as possible, that there was no child available, there in the Hotel Pan American, when Moya still had no idea who she was, when he had simply watched, dumbfounded by the squeaky gringo-intonations of her nearly ludicrous voice. He had been unable to comprehend another word of their conversation, trying to eavesdrop from several tables away through the strident buoyancy of marimba and dribbling fountain, other voices and silverware. It was over quickly. She stood and retrieved the crunched black cashmere cardigan that had apparently slid off the back of her chair onto the seat. Smiling, her gaze fixed with solicitous attention on the moribund Fergusons, she unfurled the sweater, put it on. She shook hands, even with the bowing little lawyer, and then walked rapidly out of the hotel, holding her paperback high in one hand against her chest and the Walkman by her hip in the other. It always made Moya feel sad to watch a vivid woman, one who obviously had pride and an earnestly lived inner life, walk with such self-possessed and somewhat self-conscious rapidity out of a public place. They seemed *always* to trail behind them so much undeserved rancor and suspicion. No one can watch a woman like that leave a room in that way without feeling dully left behind. He looked over at the table, and saw Mrs. Ferguson's livid blue eyes, her lips rapidly moving, Mr. Ferguson tiredly nodding along. The lawyer, meticulously working both knife and fork, delved into his chocolate éclair, his tiny feet in shiny black shoes poised on tiptoes on the floor beneath his seat.

The next time Moya saw her was at the front of the line at one of the other ticket windows at Cines Capitol, on Sexta Avenida. This night she was dressed in jeans and a short leather jacket. Moya and Rolando Mezquita were standing in line for *El Hombre Elefante.* Flor bought a handful of tickets for the Cantinflas movie, and went to where a dozen or so children waited in an orderly line with another woman, this one very blond, plain and plump, in her twenties. The children, boys and girls, were dressed variously, in untucked shirts, knee-patched pants, ill-fitting dresses, many of them with cowlicks, many of them Indian featured, many of them with runny noses. As soon as she reached them with the tickets, the little line dissolved, the children went sprinting towards the escalators laughing, screeching happily and frantically for popcorn, candy, *aguas.* The two women serenely followed.

A schoolteacher? wondered Moya, fascinated once again, not just by her beauty but by that beguiling air of distracted, pleasant, haughty something. He pointed her out to Rolando, Paco Palma Passafarri's gossip columnist. Rolando said, *Sí pues, La Flor. Esa gringa-chapina, muy rara,* very strange. Rolando unleashed a torrent of bilious invective, his eyes popping with steamy venom. A whore, a snob, *bastante creída.* Raised in *gringolandia,* with rich Jews, she went to be a servant but they gave her a fancy education because she used to screw that old Jew and look at her now, running an orphanage, a baby seller, sells her older girls to brothels too, she probably screws colonels to get away with it all, splits the profits with them, you know how they all are. Crazy woman, don't get any ideas, a nice-looking brownie but totally fucked up, she'll go with anybody for just one night, I think even Paco Palma has had her and probably his wife has too. They'd reached the front of the movie line, and Rolando said, "Why are we going to see this shitty Tarzan movie anyway, let's wait for the midnight show, it's from Sweden, I hear it's *chévere . . .*" Moya was accustomed to Rolando's hysteria, his hyperventilating purgings and regurgitations of all the futile gossip that ran like a virus through his overheated blood. It was as if the whole city spoke through him, but only in its most infecting, malicious, frivolous, resentful, dishonest, drunk with hatred and whatever else spirit. He vomited what he heard through razor-sharp, clenched teeth, got it out of himself, and then could be quite humorous and even gentle natured. He wrote poems, little poems, in sylvan *dariano* style, a Darío at his parodied worst, full of ornamental lacy weeping and laconic sighing over love's evaporating morning dew, and published them in the *El Minuto* weekly literary supplement under his late aunt's name. So Moya *más o menos* disregarded what Rolando had said about this Flor. What was her name again? Flor de Mayo Pulque, Pulpo, Puta, Puas, something like that, said Rolando. Picaflor. Flor Alambre de Puas, Flor Barbed Wire, that's what it is, *jajaja* . . . Could she be *that* Flor? wondered Moya, astonished. Maybe, yes, why not? Rogerio's "like a sister." So she had stayed in Guatemala! And ran an orphanage now? It must be her. *Qué raro. Verdaderamente.*

Now and then Moya saw her again, twice more taking her orphans to the movies. Each time he was left feeling more curious, even bewitched. He asked around about her. Some people actually said that she was *muy simpática,* very nice though very private, *muy fina,* with an absurd voice, poor thing. Others said she was a baby seller, but always in the tone of the usual rumor mongering. Moya even asked Celso Batres, who didn't even mention the editorial that Flor would later, on the Long Night of White Chickens, tell Moya that she had submitted to Celso. Though that wasn't surprising, since it would have led to a conversation, however brief, about why Celso had not published it. Celso said, "Oh yes. *La directora de Los Quetzalitos.* I've met her at their annual charity ball and here and there sometimes. A nice person, *muy simpática.* Well educated too. Taking care of orphans, *pues,* who could fault that? Can *you* fault that, Moya? No, I wouldn't believe the other things people sometimes say, which is why I assume you are asking me about her, *verdad,* Moya?" Despite the casual tone in which his boss had spoken, he was visibly angered, and glared at bewildered Moya with nearly violent contempt. Celso was, above all, a decent man, aloof from the pettiness and spite of bored reporters' *babosadas,* their doggerel, and it hurt Moya that Celso didn't understand that he held himself above that too. It especially stung Moya when, before walking away, Celso, all his suave self-control dissipated in an instant of schoolboyish blasphemy, snapped, "If my reporters had been there they would have been the first to speculate about how much God paid the Virgin herself for the

Conception, no, Moya?" Celso apologized for that remark, albeit briskly, the next day.

When Moya received the photocopied G-2 memo and the impossible assigmnent of writing a piece on the cannibalization of exported orphans for the exile news service, he didn't for a moment suspect Flor of involvement in such a racket. As for the more general charge of profiting illegally from adoptions, well, he understood the ambiguities of such a charge, the lack of legal guidelines and the general lawlessness that might make the simple will to get things done at least *look* improprietous. It was that way with everything, *vos*. He really wanted to meet this Flor de Mayo Puac, and his chest pounded, his eardrums throbbed, at the thought of phoning her out of the blue, arranging an interview on the orphan situation as a ruse for infiltrating himself into her life. It was crazy, it would never work, she might be gringa but she was *chapina* too, she would think of him as just another poorly paid little reporter, a forty-*quetzal*-a-week *periodista* with little more status than one of the sidewalk typists in front of the Palace of Justice, filling in official documents and titles for illiterates. But surely she would know who Moya *really* was, wouldn't she? And it would matter to her, wouldn't it? Finally he found the courage to phone her. Within the first few seconds of their conversation he realized that he already adored her highly individual voice. But she hesitated. He mentioned Rogerio, whom she called Roger; she agreed to meet.

And within fifteen minutes of knowing Flor de Mayo, there in the Fo Lu Shu II, Moya had dismissed all the rumors he had heard. Her eyes were too shiny, her smile too genuine, her manner too spontaneous, her initial skepticism of him too charmingly and frankly explained, for it to be true. She was *good,* he sensed this. She loved to talk, and nothing excited Moya more than a woman who did. He made her talk. He listened, doted, prodded, jousted, he led her into a verbal peregrination through her whole curious life. Yes, that night Flor told Moya quite a bit about herself (though almost nothing about that Cuban, or any other of her boyfriends), in that practiced yet previously highly reliable way in which she was accustomed to telling about herself. Moya was left charmed, transported, beguiled; full of dare, he finally kissed her hair and love exploded inside him. But she ended up in tears. That was just before two pickup trucks loaded with white chickens pulled up in front of the restaurant's gates.

Flor, from the very beginning, certainly saw right through Moya that night (remember that business about San Carlos girls, his ironic, winking machismo?). The extraordinary thing was that in doing so she bore him no particular ill will. Maybe that was because she felt she had been as buffeted by fate as he, only she admitted it to herself. In truth, they were both pretty spent, near the end of their ropes, the night they met, though he had hardly allowed himself to acknowledge that yet. But from the very first, in her frequently playful exposures of Moya, Flor really did introduce him to the game of recognizing himself a bit—or maybe it was more like bumping into himself, there on a train platform crowded with all his delusions and conceits—without letting it become tedious or traumatic.

And he wasn't *too* bad at seeing through Flor de Mayo, was he? Later he would tell himself that they had recognized each other very quickly that night, like two aliens from an unforgettable, infernally imbrued little planet. A planet that resembles this planet in almost exact detail and, in fact, overlaps it, so that aliens have to inhabit both at once. Which is why aliens often sounded a little nutty.

Everyone in Guatemala, she had declared, who could afford to should adopt an Indian war orphan. As if that were it, the ultimate moral and political solution that everyone had been waiting for. But yes, she knew, they would rather take in a curlew first! So Jesus should come down to earth and make everybody act better. Moya was appalled at her simplistic naïveté, until it dawned on him that what he was actually hearing was the exhausted yet lucid reasoning of a fellow alien. Moya realized he knew all he needed to know about how Flor had passed the last few years in her soul, for her to have reduced it all to this complex joke told with the straightest face and even the most serious intentions possible.

It was fragile but it was there, that stillness between them that she had spoken about, into which nearly everything could be confided. But in the end, Moya, very little was actually confided into it.

For one thing, though Moya didn't know it yet, Flor secretly loved someone else and never really had the time to love Moya instead, though he believes she would have, was beginning to. Which was why, a year later, he found her shadow tugging on his all over Boston and Cambridge, asking, *"Why am I a shadow? . . ."* Two forlorn, sadly empty, that is, not full enough, shadows . . . *Uff!*

This struck him, much later, long after the Long Night of White Chickens, as he again pondered the meanings of "self-knowledge." Flor and Sylvia wanted the freedom, the security, to be a total mess in the company of the man they might love, a very old-fashioned but entirely permissible desire, especially on nights when both women felt and ended up a mess. So "self-knowledge" had something to do with how they thought a man should respond. The distraction of the chickens saved Moya from the humiliation of taking Flor's mess so personally that she might never have forgiven him if she'd fully noticed. But the thing with the chickens would have distracted anybody, *vos.*

He had already kissed the sweet and sour sauce from her hair, and soon after, her lips, once, twice, three times, bouncing his lips lightly off the plush firmness of hers until the hard tap of her teeth against his made him feel like a man who has been groping in the dark but finally found the switch and thrown it, and the tangy rum and tobacco hot breath rushed in just ahead of her swirling tongue. Her tongue, this was unbelievable. He opened his eyes, saw hers resolutely closed, the glowing penumbra of her lantern and torch–illuminated cheeks just beneath his, her hair blazing coldly all around him. He quickly closed his eyes, returning all his attention to the merrymaking of her tongue in the flooded cavern of her mouth. Soon saliva dribbled wildly off lips, down chins, letting in noisy air as her tongue receded; he gave up his attempt to bring it back, parted; she watched him closely, eyes gleaming, the back of her hand brushed lightly over her chin.

"*Pues sí?*" she said after a moment. "Where was I?" She giggled, smiled almost mischievously, a little drunkenly, squinting. She looked down at her glass of rum and asked it, "*Pues sí, rum?*"

"*No sé,*" he said, I don't know, swallowing.

A moment later she amazed him, the sudden seriousness in her expression, her hands suddenly on the back of his head, the parting lips speeding towards him. This time they really kissed, *vos.* Well, hasn't Moya already told this? It was an almost successful seduction. When it was over, they sat back blinking at each other.

"*Vamos,*" let's go, whispered Moya.

". . . Have you been talking to other orphanage people?" she asked.

"Not like this, *claro,*" he said, smiling.

"No, *en serio,* have you spoken to Jim————?"—she named a gringo who was, of course, on Moya's already disregarded list. He ran an all-boy orphanage.

"No," said Moya.

She mentioned a few more names.

"You are the first," said Moya, his ears burning, as he felt himself growing dizzy with dismay and confusion.

"Well you really should talk to Jim," she said. "He's a pretty good guy, and his orphanage makes mine look like a bedlam. Except I don't think he likes reporters."

Before he knew it, she was confoundingly deep into a discussion of orphanages, slurring some of her words as she described this orphanage versus that orphanage. People said Jim molested his boys, she asked Moya if he'd heard that rumor. Moya certainly had, but said he hadn't. She said she found it hard to believe since his orphanage was so immaculate and the boys all seemed so happy well as happy as can be expected, trusting and industrious. Jim had such excellent programs, vocational training, workshops with every tool always neatly put away. They even had their own marimba band, hired to play at parties, and excellent teachers, well, he was a great fund-raiser, corporate sponsors in the United States and everywhere, some of the older boys even attended the public university while continuing to live there. And then there was that enlightened nuns' orphanage in Zona I where all the girls were Indians and were taught about their ancestral ways along with Catholicism by these real Mayanist nuns and the girls wore *traje* instead of uniforms and the nuns never did adoptions. Moya, what a great place, it always made her feel so inferior. But she just had to do *some* adoptions, it was the only way to finance the orphanage in general and the walk-in malnutrition clinic, where they actually *saved* lives, and, anyway, it was a great thing sometimes, to be adopted. But try as she might, a certain anarchy pervaded Los Quetzalitos and her children did not test as well scholastically as she wished they would. And you know what she had for vocational training, in one room set aside? A piñata workshop! Yes, her kids made piñatas, though the *niñeras* ended up doing most of the work. Go ahead, make fun of it, but they'd sold a few! On and on she went, mocking herself for the condition of her orphanage, laughing at herself, because what could one expect, she ran it all by herself didn't she, and had little funding, and she had always been well organized, but lately things were always slipping her mind, she kept running out of medicines . . .

Moya listened, distraught, feeling increasingly confused by her now. Why this, now? She seemed to be talking on and on out of some need that he could not fathom, in a tone of voice deliberate and alarmingly false, without conviction or even charm.

Earlier the Fo Lu Shu II, both inside and outside in the dining patio, had been almost full, but now Moya and Flor were the only customers. Inside, framed by the arched scarlet dragon, the Chinese family that owned and managed the Fo Lu Shu II sat at a large table, dining from heaping platters. *Chapín* waiters were desultorily cleaning up, folding white tablecloths, filling bottles of soy sauce. The fried wontons had long been finished off and the rum was gone too, there remained only the lime-clouded inches of liquid in their glasses. *La colita,* mused Moya—while she speechified on—"the little tail" is the name for those few inches of watery alcohol left in a glass but it's a name for a woman's *nalgas* too, her ass, also *culito,* though this type of *colita* or *culito de La culita* doesn't have to be and preferably isn't little; the poetry of the common man, what a culture, *vos.*

Flor was very quietly sobbing now, her face in her hands. Moya had no idea why. Why?

"*Qué, mi amor? Qué?*" he babbled.

"No no no, it's not you. I'm, I don't know what's come over me, it's not that bad an orphanage . . . I should get going."

"It sounds to me as if you do very well, everything considered," said Moya, lamely, for he felt sure it was not her orphanage that she was actually crying over. "I'm sure your children are as happy as could be. You take them to movies, I've seen you. A little anarchy, so what?"

"I don't just adopt my kids to anyone, you know," she said firmly. Then she stared at him, pouting, until she lunged back into speech, "I look for *great* parents!"

"Maybe someday those children will come back, like you did," he said. "Educated, determined—"

"Angry!" she interrupted. "I was extremely angry at what I found here, that's *why.*"

"Angry, *claro,*" he repeated. "They will come back and do wonderful things, like you did."

"No no no, that's not it, hardly. I just want them to have a chance to be—" and she sighed heavily—"they have a chance to become North American, Swedish, French, whatever, but for a lot of them, I think it will be how they come to terms with what happened here that . . . *Ach!* You know what I mean? For this, parents are important. If there is any poetry in my life, Moya, it's in the way I decide who gets to be the parents. No matter what else, I think I'm better at *that* than anybody!"

"A secret army of memories, sent out into the world!" he said, hopefully.

But she didn't even smile. "You're making fun of me."

"No! No I am not!"

He kissed the backs of her hands, and then her startling palms. She let him, but that was all.

"So I'm OK, *verdad?*"

"You are the most wonderful."

"Because what you believe counts. I can't be like an entire order of enlightened nuns, but, if not for me, where would my kids be? Out on the street? In a state orphanage, God forbid? Working as someone else's servant? Dead?"

"*Mija,* you don't need to prove yourself to me. Let's go somewhere," he said. "Let's go dancing," though he hated to dance, hated the way other men, often packing pistols, always cut in on whoever Moya was dancing with, and then they were always much better dancers than he.

"Why don't you come with us next time we go to the beach? I take them every week or two."

"*Claro!*" Why was she going on like this?

"I guess they won't serve us any more rum. Maybe we should go somewhere else."

"Whatever you want, *reina* . . ."

He tried to kiss her again, but she turned her head away, blinking rapidly.

Finally she said, "I don't know, it's nothing . . . It's not you . . . I just felt so vulnerable all of a sudden. I feel, I don't know . . . all surface, cold, like everything is on the surface."

"Surface? Superficial?" asked Moya, defensively. "Because of me, *vos?*"

"No, on my skin, in my nerves. As if my nerves are all there is." She shivered, and began to put her sweater on, wrestling with it. Her cheeks sparkled dimly with dried, wiped tears. She looked tired. Even her hair looked tired.

Moya heard clucking and looked up, saw three Indian men rapidly pass by, in straw cowboy hats, each carrying live white chickens by the feet in both hands. They carried the chickens through the dining patio and into the restaurant. Moments later, the men came back empty-handed. They went out through the front gates and then seconds later came back, hurrying by again, carrying chickens. From outside, on the other side of the wall, he heard the racket of a henhouse.

Flor laughed sharply. She drank the little bit of *colita* left in her glass. And Moya felt himself sunk in gloom, because they weren't going to even kiss anymore, he could tell—maybe never again. He couldn't bring himself to smile when she looked at him.

"Chicken delivery, obviously," she said. "Laying in the week's supply. Guess that's why they're letting us sit here."

"Poor chickens," said Moya, exhausted, his head feeling heavy with drink and the sullenness of dashed and bewildered hopes.

She lit her final cigarette. Already the hurrying men had made several more trips out through the gates, and then back in, carrying chickens.

"I'm sure Frank Perdue doesn't carry all his chickens to his slaughterhouse one by one. But everything gets done here in some stupid, slow, and inevitably cruel way, doesn't it?"

"Two by two," said Moya.

"Of course chickens always remind me of my childhood," she said. "Well, for obvious reasons, you know? My father raised them though only for the eggs. You're upset."

"No, *mi amor!*"

"Oh, you are. Don't worry about it, Moyyyya. I think maybe it was just hearing my own voice in my ears all night. You know? It was scary in a way, kind of awful, playing along with you like that. Pretending to tell you everything. I ended up feeling all on the surface."

"All on the surface," he repeated, still confused and even angered by the phrase. "I'm sorry."

"Oh no! Don't be, I've made a new friend, I'm sure. I really like you, Moya. I'm sure when I wake up tomorrow, I'll realize it's been an important night. Because it had a kind of coherence anyway, and it was fun. Like I got back in touch with something that is . . . perhaps not so useful to me. I've never been very good at explaining myself anyway, perhaps it's best to just let these matters rest. Perhaps. Let's go see what they're doing."

She stumbled a bit, getting up. Her white pants were nearly transparent with damp from so many hours of sitting. He could see the outline of her panties until she plucked the fabric loose.

Resting her hands on her hips, she arched her spine. She looked at him self-consciously, with unsure glittering black eyes, the pert lips twitching a bit, as if unsure whether to smile. But she did, and put out her hand, pulled him stiffly to his feet, and turned her back on him to watch the three men passing rapidly by, the hard soles of their mud-caked boots slapping the tiles, chickens dangling upside down from each of their fists, white wings partially extended and jerkily bouncing.

"But what do you mean you *pretended* to go along?" he asked, still baffled. "Pretended to go along with what?"

But Flor ignored him. She was standing at the front gates, looking out at the sidewalk, the two pickup trucks parked there, resonating with chicken noise. It, or something, made her laugh again, and with an awkward little step she turned and headed into the restaurant. Moya followed her through the dining room, past the staring waiters and Chinamen, into the kitchen. There, the entire floor of that cramped, reeking, damp, otherwise gray and dank kitchen, every inch was crammed with live, dumb, white, red-eyed chickens. Barefoot kitchen girls, Indians in shapeless gray smocks, were already at work, one of them wading through chickens, picking them up one at a time and snapping their necks, while another two stood over metal washtubs, plucking dead chickens.

It was a strangely arresting and riveting sight, and for that reason alone Moya forever referred to the night on which he met Flor as the Long Night of White Chickens.

But that long night was almost over now. Flor and Moya watched the feathery slaughter for only a minute or so, and then she turned to him with an odd smile. "They can't kill the chickens first before bringing them over here?"

Moya shrugged.

"We used to have live chickens delivered to the orphanage, to the kitchen of course, but I put a stop to that, it really isn't so much more expensive to get them plucked and cleaned, you know. I really have to be going," she said. "Are you going to stay and watch until they're done or something?"

"No, of course not," he said. "Flor, what's wrong? Why are you angry with me?"

"But I'm not," she said, and, while the kitchen girls watched them with looks of quiet astonishment, Flor kissed him hard and briefly on the lips and said, "Call me, OK?"

"Yes, *claro,* but—"

"Thanks for everything." And she turned and walked briskly out of the kitchen, through the patio where the paper lanterns had just been extinguished, and out into the street, where her Los Quetzalitos van was parked, though Moya had not yet seen it, since he had arrived first, and had waited for her at their table.

Flabbergasted, Moya shyly, meekly followed—But she was gone. He couldn't believe that he wasn't getting a ride home, though she had paid the rum and wonton tab. He couldn't believe the rudeness of her not offering him a ride home, though he guessed it had simply slipped her mind. He walked out through the front gates, past the two chicken-shit-reeking, now empty pickups, and looked down the otherwise deserted, tree-bowered, walled street. Not far from here, Roger had betrayed Moya atop that fence. He decided to walk the two long, empty, darkened blocks to Avenida La Reforma, where at this hour the *ruleteros,* the poor people's bus vans, were still running. He couldn't afford a taxi from one of the hotels.

A week later he did in fact accompany Flor and a vanload of orphans to the beach at Puerto San José. There, she later told him, she decided she really did like him a lot. It was his attentiveness to the smaller children as they strayed from the shaded cabanas onto the heat-searing black sand and there cried and screamed, paralyzed by their burning feet. Moya kept jumping up, darting over the coal hot midday sand, carrying children back into the shade. He was not ordinarily attentive to children, but the absurdity of the routine had captivated him. That night he slept with her for the first time, in the orphanage, in her bed—after she had chased out the brood of little girls who had been waiting for her there while Moya stood in the yard, under her window and small balcony, listening to Flor promising the whining and protesting little girls that they would only have to sleep away from her this one night. And it was true, Moya would not return to that bed for another two months, though he persisted in trying. Then they were lovers for five weeks, before she broke off with him again, saying it was over once and for all. Three weeks later, when he had felt sure he was on the verge of winning her back again, she was murdered.

Of course much that Moya never knew about was going on in her life throughout those months. Eventually she had even told him, rather vaguely, in a mood of defiant lassitude, about the incident in which Colonel Malespín had tried to blackmail her, driving her briefly into hiding. But it was also during that time, apparently, according to Roger, that she was breaking up with a man she deeply loved, who would not leave his wife for her. Moya didn't know Flor had another lover. But his mind is not so original: more than occasionally his vanity, his highest hopes, his embarrassing certainties were overruled by his suspicions. He voiced these more than once, over the phone, on those occasions when she agreed to meet him for dinner, those times when he impulsively dropped by the orphanage without calling ahead, once bringing a gift of Hotel Biltmore Maya envelopes. She said, variously, that no, she did not, that it was none of his business, that oh, come on, it's not that, and once she said, "No one else to speak of, but even if there was, come on, we've only made love once. Oh, I just can't handle a relationship right now, Moya. Please, just be my friend for a while."

Moya remembers that first morning, after he woke up in Flor de Mayo's bed:

"Every stroke," she said sleepily, sweetly, "feels like another, another piece of a fable, a fable that just goes on and on."

"Like another word in a fable, *mi amor?*"

"If a fable has to be made of words, *pues sí . . .*"

She was not referring to his pigeon, which now rested, salty and encrusted, wings folded, but to his hands, one of which was stroking her back and shoulders, the other stroking her *nalgas* as he held her against him. The room was warm with sunlight and love, and his touches, all the touches that were making up this one long prolongation of a sensual morning, every stroke felt to her like another "piece of a fable."

"What a pretty thought, Florcita," he said.

"On and on . . . ," she murmured.

Downstairs, as always, on and on, there was an orphanage. It didn't matter.

He stroked her *nalgas.* What pretty *nalgas,* what a pretty and perfect word, *nalgas.* One *nalga,* and the other *nalga.* Left and right *nalga,* one with a beauty mark right in the middle. Two *nalgas,* a milkier shade of brown. Very round and smooth and ample, decorated by one winking freckle right in the middle of a *nalga,* inviting so many kisses and soon delirious nuzzles. Didn't these wonderful *nalgas* express the radiant and robust side of Flor's nature, for she really was both of those things and these *nalgas* were too, warm and hearty like domed, clay bread ovens, like smooth hilltops with the sun just coming up behind, *Moya, ay no.* Her belly was charming, and her thighs smooth, strong, and long, and the triangular little puffs of flesh between her breasts and armpits always made him want to kiss them over and over before plunging his nose into the warm cow pasture clover of those armpits. As anyone can see, Moya was unspeakably happy that morning, stroking Flor's *nalgas,* prolonging her fable without words.

And then she made him wait nearly two months to do it again.

PART THREE

EL OMNI

The only ones daring enough to play are dead.

POPUL VUH

TWENTY

I'll be back in two days, I told Chayito before I left, and if I'm not, then don't worry, I'll definitely be back in five. It really was a small triumph of nerve and resolve that I was even able to formulate an illusory plan, I think, and one so specific at that— if not two days, five. That was three mornings ago. But I must have heard something less decided inside me, time rushing out like a tide and the possibility of going with it, because I packed extra clothing, four paperback novels (one for Zamara) and brought more than enough money.

I only said five days on the off chance that in El Progreso things would work out with Zamara in a way that we'd want to go someplace else to celebrate, maybe even here to the Hotel del Norte like we did the last time, or across the bay to Livingston. Except I felt so sure it was only going to be two days, I didn't even let Uncle Jorge know, figuring I'd be back before he even missed me, or that he'd phone and Chayito could tell him.

So I didn't dismantle and put away my homemade alarm and escape system either. It seemed especially unlikely that Uncle Jorge would drop by over the next few days and then ask Chayito for the key to the upstairs addition over the rear of the house, where of course I've been living all this time. But if by some chance he does, then he'll see it: empty soda and Gallo beer bottles stacked at the edges of chairs under the windows in the otherwise empty spare rooms facing the central patio; and in my bedroom, a coiled length of rope on the floor, one end tied to a side frame in the multipaned wall of glass, the windows on either side of it always left at least partly cranked open, the smaller square window that opens horizontally, and the long rectangular one that opens vertically—my escape window.

The steel door at the top of the stairs leading from the patio to the addition is secure enough, always left locked and latched when I'm inside. But someone could conceivably get up onto the roof, then ease themselves down the side like Dracula and work their way in through a window—but then they'd definitely knock over some bottles. (They wouldn't try it through my bedroom window because what if I saw them first and had a gun?) So I've always slept, lightly, with all the inside doors open to be able to hear anything in the other rooms. Even the crash of *one* of those bottles against the floor would have woken me, I hope, in a flash and had me moving with something like instinct: out of bed and dropping the rope into the narrow rear patio and letting myself down on it, scaling my neighbors' wall and then their neighbors' wall and so on, disappearing into the neighborhood like Spiderman.

I practiced it one Saturday evening when Chayito was at evening mass and my neighbors had all left early to assist in the preparations for a wedding party at their "Tío Humberto's" (nearly everything that gets said above a whisper in that house seems to carry into the narrow echo chamber between our windows—a hardworking middle-class family lives there), even their one maid, Juana, had gone with them, though strictly as a maid, of course. The first thing I did in preparation for my trial run was lower the blinds, as this would be a likely impediment in the case of a real emergency: I usually remember to lower them at night so that in the morning Juana, hanging laundry on their second-story rear patio, won't see me sprawled naked in bed in my glass exhibit case with a morning hard-on like she did the last time, peering at me from around the edge of a just hung towel, a clothespin in her mouth; I sat up, covering my lap with the sheets, and she ducked behind the towel and stood frozen there, hiding her face like a moose, until finally she just turned and scampered in her skidding flat shoes straight back across the small patio to the door.

On nights when I've felt especially paranoid, hardly ever for any concrete reason, I've at least remembered to keep boxer shorts on. But now I lay back on the bed fully clothed and listened for the imagined surprise of a bottle crashing and then I tried to move fast, up and out, slipping behind the blinds and flinging the rope out almost in one motion, stepping shoulder first through the window, and pulling the rope taut with my fists as I leaned out into the air, but then I hung there suspended for a moment, wondering which was best, to just boundingly sort of rappel down or to lower myself by the arms and shimmy down, which would probably be quieter, but slower—I ended up doing something in between, my knees and elbows banging off the metal window frame and the smooth concrete while I tried to stifle my *ouch,* the rope searing through my grasp before I caught it firmly; I was in better control when I reached the rough-surfaced stucco of the lower part of the house, walking myself down past the barred, curtained window of Abuelita's old bedroom. Then I ran to the wall and caught the top on my second leap and pulled myself up and rested there on my forearms, briefly studying my route: if I were to vault the wall at this spot, I'd land just behind their carport and have to run through their short, unkempt yard to the next wall. I let myself back down and stood there flapping my burning palms, bashed elbows throbbing. I knew I'd have to move faster if it ever counted. The small patio on our side used to be a garden with a flagstone path but now it's root-knobby dirt, a few drooping banana trees surviving down at one end, and some of Abuelita's finch cages, rusted now, stacked like empty lobster traps by the door in the corner. Using one of the rough-edged flagstones, I smashed a little foothold in the wall, widening an earthquake crack.

I felt it would give me half a chance anyway, though of course any number of things could and probably would go wrong. They might be able to chase me, but I'd be over the first wall before they got to my bedroom if I moved quickly enough, and then maybe someone along my route would offer to hide me, though I doubt it. The killers aren't always such nimble types anyway: I know because the four who were in the death squad that briefly displayed itself to Moya and me back in November were pretty beefy. Street kids, on the other hand, can probably flicker up and down the sides of walls like lizards. But I set up my bottles long before the first of those notes was slipped under the front door, when *los niños de la calle* were just about the last thing I was worried about.

Have I ever just come right out and said that this is an unbelievably sick and evil place? But that so much of it seems to happen with a certain genius, leaving behind almost nothing but invisibility and silence? All this with my rope and bottles was first provoked months ago, in January, by an incident that had absolutely nothing to do with me, when they broke in through the electronically wired windows of a relatively low-level, young Scandinavian diplomat's house without setting off the alarms, then raped her and used knives to so methodically mutilate her that she was left permanently disfigured in all her private places and will never be able to have children, though they didn't touch her face at all. Supposedly they did it because she'd become involved with one of the guerrilla organizations, she was passing information and embassy insiders' gossip to them or something. That's surely one of the reasons she and her embassy kept it quiet, as there was no way of raising the obvious charges without publicly admitting the indefensible diplomatic "misdemeanor," and no way of not sounding as if they were doing anything but voicing the most astoundingly paranoid and grotesquely undiplomatic insults ever voiced even if they did. Any way you looked at it, there wasn't much they could do or even say, and there was no way of proving anything. There wasn't even the galvanizing newspaper sensation of a Scandinavian woman in the morgue, and not even *¿Dónde?* has figured out how to translate silence. Of course she may have had the profoundest personal reasons for wanting to maintain her anonymity (*they'd* probably counted on that as well). She spent a week or so in the hospital and then was quietly flown home, causing far fewer ripples on the surface of things than even a declaration of persona non grata and a diplomatic expulsion would have.

Soon after the international aid organizations discreetly ordered all their foreign staff (presumably whether they'd ever cultivated guerrilla contacts or not) who still lived in individual houses to move to securer places, the Zona 10 twin condo towers over Lord Byron's, for example.

Which is how I first learned about it, from a Japanese girl working for UNICEF, Yuka, who'd just moved in over Lord Byron's and came down to have a drink a few times before the place grossed her out for good. She was really sorry to have given up her modern, glassy house in Zona 14 with the rear patio and hammock overlooking the primordial vista of untended tropical garden running lavishly into the maw of an immense and often fog-lidded *barranca*—with the volcano on the horizon behind it, oh, just so beautiful. Yuka said they'd all been cautioned that it was safest not to talk in public about what had happened to the diplomat but I seemed like such a nice harmless guy and why shouldn't I know? Then I suddenly understood why one of the new Scandinavian volunteers at Los Quetzalitos had suddenly flown home too, and felt pissed that not even Edvarga had told me about it. She's one of the other two new girls who didn't leave, and later, when I asked her about it, Edvarga said she'd been warned it was best not to talk about it too, both by Rosana Letones (your successor, Flor) and by the diplomats from her own country, who'd summoned their nationals for a secret meeting in the wake of the incident. Foreigners, after they've been here long enough, perversely love to be let in on this kind of secret anyway, I think. (My secret, of course, has been with me from the start.) It's as if they eventually learn or at least sense that the country can only be truly experienced through this particular kind of weighted silence; talking too freely about it, they might dispel both their own precautionary dread and sense of control, which could leave them feeling weightless again, outside reality, an utter foreigner again, not even nearly as well rooted as those Lord Byron's expats who blusteringly ignore and deny everything—another way of going native. Anyway, Rosana had assured them that she and the other girl had nothing to fear because— nervously tooted little Scandinavian laugh—there could not *possibly* be any government informers or active guerrillas among the orphans. Couldn't possibly be, I repeated, my face reddening because of other echoes the conversation had suddenly brought close (you). But Edvarga wasn't thinking of you at all, she smiled and blushed back at me as if responding to a flirtatious innuendo. I was trying to have a crush on Edvarga back then, so as to have one more excuse for dropping by the orphanage. But nothing ever happened, partly because the only love I was really interested in, even when I didn't want to be, was Zamara's.

That was when I put together my own alarm system, as Abuelita's house, unlike every other sensibly run household in the city with the means to afford it, has never been wired for security, not even downstairs, where only Chayito lives. If Uncle Jorge goes into my quarters he'll see it, bottles and rope, and worry. Or else maybe he'll draw panicked conclusions about what I've been up to here all this time (just one month shy of a year now), which he has certainly wondered about, I'm sure. Who knows what Uncle Jorge knows or suspects about my true life here? There's the little Chayito could tell, which she probably has, though I doubt Uncle Jorge would care that much about my having brought Zamara home a few times, though it certainly made Chayito treat me more stonily than ever. If Uncle Jorge were to ask her, *Eso qué?* Chayito's most characteristic response would be, Those are bottles on chairs under the windows. *El joven* puts them there.

Of course there's always been the excuse of the house—willed solely to my mother—and my supposed familial duty to sell it, but it's been sold for more than two weeks now, with little help from me, to an Evangelical Protestant ministry from Louisiana who agreed to pay in dollars rather than in ever-devaluing *quetzales,* so my mother is feeling very pleased and relieved about that, and both my parents are expecting me home soon because of it. The evangelicals won't be moving in until the first of July, seven weeks from now—Chayito, unless she stays on to work as a maid for the proselytizing heathens, will be living out her days in one of the boardinghouses my family owns near the Avenida Bolivar—by which time I'll probably be in Mexico or else back in New York. It was my plan to stop off and see Moya there even before the house was sold. But this new mystery and urgency of the notes, I don't know yet exactly what it means, or changes, or what to do about it. And I'm wondering if Chayito went ahead and told Uncle Jorge about that too, though I begged her not to.

The note Zamara slipped under the door before she went home to El Progreso came in a sealed envelope, my name crudely printed on the front, so Chayito couldn't have read that one. I mean the other two, from "the lost boy" (Lucas Caycam Quix is, or maybe was, his name). They didn't come in envelopes, but I'm almost positive I got to the first one before Chayito did; I came in and there it was inside the door, and I could hear a Catholic religious show droning on the radio from the kitchen. But Chayito definitely read the second one, a cryptic but more ominous follow-up that came four mornings ago.

She brought it to me in my room, wearing her pink-plastic-frame reading glasses and holding the note out between pinched fingers in one limp and twiny-looking old woman's hand. Like the first one, it was a full sheet of medium-sized lined paper that had been folded once, ragged along the edge where it had been torn from one of those staple-bound school copybooks.

I wasn't really surprised that another note had come, which isn't to say I hadn't been in a worried muddle about the whole situation, and I was dismayed that she'd found it first.

"*Mejor te vas de una vez mañana,*" she declared. Best to leave tomorrow. Home to the United States, I realized she meant as soon as I'd taken the note from her hand and looked at it and then up at Chayito again. It was kind of an extraordinary moment. I'd never seen her look so . . . lucid. Her expression was more cross than worried, behind the glasses her enlarged eyes were fierce orbs of implacable clairvoyance: it was the look of an *abuela* who has always known it but finally found proof that her grandson has turned out to be just as much of a reckless and gullible fool as his grandfather once was.

That's the conclusion Chayito's long life had suddenly brought her to—the burden of having outlasted everyone else in the only house she'd known since her remote Indian childhood in the mountains; the unsortable chaos of so many years and the populated fog inside her, which her ordinarily gruff demeanor barely masked—all of that had somehow been dispelled by this crisis of an anonymous threat against a family member slipped under the door, allowing Chayito to find the firm conviction that she was and maybe had always been Abuelita. That was what was behind her brusque command.

The note, scrawled in blunt soft pencil, merely said: "*Te vi. Venga el jueves o vengo por tí.*" I saw you. Come Thursday or I'll come for you. It was signed with a crude symbol, an upside-down tilted cross, I thought at first. Or maybe, no probably, some kind of dagger. This was totally idiotic and ignorant! Why would I ever agree to another meeting after a threat like that? Unless he, or they, really believed I was that desperate to meet face to face with Lucas Caycam Quix—your murderer, Flor? and now threatening to become mine? Come on!—and that I would deduce, since I'd been promised protection and trust in return for a cash payment, that the safest course for me to take would be to go along with the plan as prearranged. Did they think I was *that* stupid?

"*I saw you*"—that was Friday, when they would have seen me waiting on the Incienso Bridge before I changed my mind and retreated. Now it was Monday. Why Thursday? Why not tomorrow? Was it a ploy, phony precision meant to convince me of his, or their, seriousness? Buying time? For what? I could just walk away. They had nothing to gain in coming after me, it would just blow it for them. I folded the paper up and put it in my pocket, anger overcoming the fear trembling my legs. Because, in truth, I'd been expecting something like this note, though not that it would be so starkly menacing. Part of the anger I felt was at myself, for having become involved in this at all.

"Don't worry" is what I told Chayito after I'd put away the note. "I know who it's from. It's nothing, just *más porquería*. I was leaving tomorrow anyway . . ."

"Good. As long as it's tomorrow," she said, with a relieved, even forgiving finality.

"No, just to El Progreso, for two days . . . or five."

Then I went into an act, to reassure her, just as I imagined my extremely high-strung grandfather used to when he was in the kind of trouble I was going to pretend this was, which Abuelito often and scandalously was; at least until Abuelita forced him to give her sole dominion over their joint wealth and properties, to prevent him from giving it all away bit by bit to secret mistresses and even the fortunate whores he found during his sporadic but profligate bouts of madness. It seems I have a number of illegitimate half-aunts and half-uncles scattered about the city, some who became prosperous enough on their own (one owns a taxi company), others still living off modest Arrau-money retainers. A few of them were even invited to Catty and Mercedes's *quinceañeras*. (Uncle Jorge and my cousins, thinking it no big deal now and even a little quaint, have told me all about it; my mother, of course, never had.)

This note is from a crazy girl, I declaimed to Chayito. Obviously not a girl from, well, the type of background I understood that she and all my family would expect me to know, but we all make mistakes, Chayito, especially when we've been drinking and have too much money in our pockets! You know how I am, Chayito! Oh Chayito! What kind of girl would send such a vulgar note! What does she expect to get out of me that way!

Under my rant I was thinking: They wouldn't dare try and get into this house. And I'd been wanting to go see Zamara anyway.

Chayito seemed unpersuaded. Probably she didn't think it looked like a note even a desperate girl would write. But the lunacy of my onslaught had returned her to the fundamental fact that she couldn't really be Abuelita, because she didn't dare box my ears, or phone a travel agency to book my flight immediately and then place me under house arrest. That fierce light of grandmotherly omniscience had faded from her eyes.

"Please don't tell my uncle," I said. "He'll worry for no reason. And I am going home soon, I really am." She turned and shuffled out of the bedroom, and, addressing her tiny bent back and the long, withered braid hanging down it, I said, "Thank you for caring though, Chayito."

I left the next morning, carrying a nylon duffel fully packed with even more than I needed for five days. But I honestly don't recall even considering the possibility that I might not be back, or else why didn't I bring *all* my money? Before stepping out, I stood in the doorway for a moment, looking up and down the avenue.

A small herd of unattended goats was leashed by a single tether to the chain-link fence of the junkyard opposite, and our elderly mailman, hump shouldered from so many years of hauling around a fat leather bag almost bigger than himself was mopping his brow with a handkerchief while he urinated into the weeds by the crumbling salmon-colored corner of the little house next to the junkyard. Who was I looking for? A street kid, any street kid? One was passing by on the other side, but he was just a very small barefoot boy, in ragged black pants like a circus clown's and an even more torn white T-shirt, and he looked totally absorbed in the pale green slices of unripened mango he was devouring from the small plastic bag in his hand.

I hardly ever get mail anyway, I started walking even before the mailman was done peeing. I passed the dry-cleaning shop, its counter just a few feet in from the sidewalk, smiled and said *hola* to one of the beautiful bored sisters on duty there, and she smiled and said *hola* and then immediately went back to looking angrily stunned by life, trapped inside her strangely unapproachable beauty and the even stranger impression of an evaporating spirit which seems to surround her like an imploding halo.

At the corner I stopped and took another look around, and felt sure that I wasn't being followed. The Fuente del Norte bus line terminal was still thirteen blocks away, on 18 Calle, but I decided to walk, though there was no reason to. It didn't even occur to me that this might be the last time I'd ever walk this way, through this city that has become so familiar that right now I can shut my eyes and wander through its near replica inside me, hearing its mix of cacophonies and silences, smelling its smells, indulging myself in this weird beauty of an ugly city where you get to feel like an invisible angel just by roaming around in it not doing any harm to anybody.

So I didn't pause to notice specific landmarks and say goodbye to them; I didn't think, There's the little *tienda* where you decided to become a U.S. citizen because Abuelita's maids wouldn't let you in from the rain, Flor. Though only two blocks from the house, in front of the small private hospital with its two ancient ambulances parked out front, I couldn't help but remember, as I always do, that this was where a death squad intruded itself on Moya and me one especially pretty evening when the sunset was making everything around us glow with old-fashioned cigar box colors—we "escaped" it, of course, our reactions couldn't have been quicker. Though it was meant for Moya, not me. Which is why only he had to leave. (I'm invisible, or at least I thought I was.) That's another story, and seems almost another lifetime ago now. I have a lot to tell now, Flor. A lot to try and put in order. Six months since Moya left, and I feel like it's been practically a whole short, separate lifetime.

The dry season has gone on baking the city, and most of the countryside, almost a month longer than it's supposed to: the upper slopes of the volcanoes on the city horizon look almost faded to haze and the mountains are brown, streaked by dark green pine ridges and golden dirt roads. Downtown the traffic kicks up gusts of unwashed grit and litter, and puffs of undiluted black exhaust waft around weightlessly, hanging in the air like the ghosts of unsolved murders, breaking over pedestrians hurrying through them, eyes squeezed shut, hands cupped over mouths and noses. I stopped at American Doughnuts for coffee and a coconut donut, and while I sat at the counter looking out at a shiny customized van with gun portals in its sides stopped in traffic at a red light, I suddenly fantasized that inaugural rainy-season downpour finally falling, turning even that van's black bulletproofed windows translucent.

I've definitely developed a traffic phobia here (which might seem surprising since I never had one even in New York). Whenever I reach some downtown destination on foot, I feel limp with relieved tension and even a little proud and lucky to have gotten through it again. It's the way drivers speed around tight blind corners even on the most crowded streets; and the way some people seem to so exaggerate their pride in owning a vehicle and the elevated sense of hierarchy it brings them, that they think they own the space in front of the fender too and consider any pedestrian's intrusion into it a violation of private property and a slight against manliness. Even if you're just a few feet from the curb when the light changes, some of them come right at you, tires squealing as yet another mufflerless Toyota pickup explodes forward, and when you've scampered out of the way and whirled around what you usually see is one of those mustached *mestizo* faces staring hard from the driver's window, just daring or challenging you to do a *thing* about it. Even Uncle Jorge, with atypical scorn, has acknowledged, "You're right, Roger, the idea of pedestrian right-of-way was *never* exported to Guatemala!" Years ago Abuelito was knocked back onto a curb by a wildly careening bus (in fairness to the bus, Abuelito, even on foot, could be as heedlessly hurried as any Guatemala City driver) and treated for broken ribs by an old family doctor who dismissed the importance of the bump on the back of his head, which, had it been drained on time, wouldn't have hemorrhaged massively and killed him. That happened while my other uncle, Dr. Nelson Arrau, long before his nearly paralyzing stroke, was in temporary exile in England because of his persistent efforts to start a barefoot doctor program in the countryside; the then regime considered the idea of training students to be the rural Johnny Appleseeds of dysentery pills completely Communistic. My mother has always felt that, if Dr. Neli had been here, he would have diagnosed the bump, and Abuelito might still be alive today; he was six years younger than Abuelita. Subconsciously at least, I've probably been predisposed to a horror of the traffic here ever since.

But I'm not at all alone in this: Mariel, for example. She's a thirteen-year-old street girl, my best "contact" among *los niños de la calle.* She was telling me all about her terrifying life one day—razor fights with other girls over boys or the contested ownership of a pair of shoes; sadistic child molesters and their slickly baited ploys; police who round up vagabond girls just to sexually abuse them—but when I asked what scared her *most,* she didn't even have to think: "The traffic," she said, widening her glitter-painted eyes. "So many people get run over!"

And 18 Calle is where, I remember both Flor and my mother telling me, there used to be a famous *amate* tree—it isn't there anymore—that the Devil lived in, a tree with blossoms that supposedly only the blind could see. It's also the street where, in the afternoons and evenings, I could usually find Mariel. Or rather, all I'd have to do was walk up and down through the narrow space in the sidewalk left between all the contraband-vendors' tables and clothing racks until she spotted me from wherever she was lurking. It being morning when I passed through on my way to the buses, I knew she must still be asleep after one of her late thieving nights, crammed into a windowless room in some foul-reeking rooming house with six or so other kids to be safe from the police, sleeping with her shoes on to make it harder for any of the others to swipe them. I kept an eye out for her anyway, but it was more in that yearning way of revisiting the mixed emotions of the past, that futile attempt at telepathy (what's she thinking *now*)—as if it were years instead of months ago, when I was still playing detective, that we'd met here so that I could take her to lunch at Pollo Campero. I felt sure that if she saw me now, she'd hide. Whether from shame or fear or both, I didn't know, and probably never will.

The Fuente del Norte buses (the same line that transported you on your return trip to Chiquimula five years ago) leave from a lot crowded with the buses of other lines, an uproar of swirled dirt, engine racket, and the bayed chants of the *ayudantes,* the bus drivers' assistants: they call out the names of cities and towns for illiterates who can't read the signs over the windshields and then have to keep it up for the duration of the trip, hanging out the bus door baying, "Puerto Barrios Puerto Barrios" or whatever at every stop or every time the bus slows for people standing along the highway, most of whom probably aren't waiting for anything but are just standing there, which is why even express buses seem to take forever.

I bought a ticket for El Progreso in the tiny Fuente del Norte office, and though my "express" wouldn't be leaving for another forty-five minutes at least, I went back outside with my duffel and bought two cans of pear juice from the little girl who ran up to sell them, and a halved and peeled orange dipped in wheat germ and a touch of chili powder in a plastic bag from another, and the morning papers from the men selling those. I found my bus and got on, though it was still completely empty. It was one of those long-distance coaches with comfortable leather seats, though torn and patched, worn through to the straw in places; most of the reclining mechanisms didn't work either. This was total luxury compared with the knee-crunching peasants' buses I'd taken all through the highlands: squarish little boxes originally built in the faraway land where even children's school buses become obsolete and end up down here, refitted with chubby mountain- and mud-climbing tires and painted like colorful birds, kept running for-ever by ingenious mechanics who can conjure any spare part from any scrap pile; carrying whole bundled-up markets on their roofs and Indian peasants sitting four to a seat inside, children and even live poultry on their laps, the overfill squatting and stooping with stolid patience the length of the lurching aisle, the closed air thick with unsurprisingly unpleasant odors, not their fault, parasite-infested stomachs and intestines do that, turn people into nonstop farters and belchers.

I found a seat that was perfect, neither the window next to it nor the one up ahead was jammed. People here generally don't like to travel with the windows down—except when they're drunk and worried about vomiting—partly it's all these notions about chilly air giving you a cold in one way and hot air doing it in another; I *have* gotten colds traveling from infernal lowlands to cool higher elevations and vice versa, but as far as I'm concerned the stronger the breeze the better. Usually I have to fight these trip-long skirmishes, people seated behind me reaching over to close my window, me opening it again awhile later; it's the window ahead that's most important. But I felt pretty confident that by the time the bus reached the desert, people would want at least some air coming in—I left both windows partly open and sat down to wait. A certain coven of street kids, terminal glue sniffers all, like to gather at the far end of that lot, by the dilapidated row of food stalls and lime-trunked trees, but these weren't the kids I was supposed to be afraid of now. I could see two of them from the bus, slumped shoulder to shoulder on an abandoned tire in the shade, looking like gaunt, ancient opium addicts peacefully dwindling away. Now and then one or the other lifted a twiggy arm and brought the glue-soaked rag in his fist to his nose and held it there for a moment.

I ate both halves of my orange and saved the pear juices for the thirst of the trip. I couldn't bring myself to read the newspapers and just sat there staring out the window at the glue sniffers. It was then that it first occurred to me that I really should have put away my alarm system, like I always had whenever Uncle Jorge brought prospective buyers to look over the house. Eventually, slowly, the bus began to fill. The driver and his *ayudante* were in their separate front seats under the tinsel-wreathed portrait of St. Christopher, the engine was idling loudly. The *ayudante,* a middle-aged man, not a boy, kept having to get up and shout "Puerto Barrios" out the door, and now and then he clambered down to help someone with luggage. I'd left my duffel on the seat to discourage anyone from sitting there, but now I felt guilty and moved my bag up onto the rack. A few minutes later an extremely pretty girl got on, tall and slender like a young model, her fine-featured face full of that easy radiance that makes you think of healthy outdoor living, a loving family. She stood at the top of the aisle, holding her small suitcase in both hands and a folded umbrella tucked under her arm, her slowly blinking eyes scanning the rows of seats as if with innocently prim discernment before settling on the empty space beside me without meeting my eyes. She was one of those girls who fill you with a sense of wonder over what can happen even in deadbeat desert or banana plantation towns or a decaying and vice-ridden port (pretty much all this bus was going to pass through), places where so many of the men still live by such primitive codes that all their stories seem to end in violence, ruinous and drunken humiliation, or quietest oblivion when they're lucky; but sometimes they manage to provide the seed for a girl like this too, and probably nothing else. Her blue-green-striped dress looked brand new, as did the yellow plastic belt around her waist. Maybe she'd come to visit relatives in the city and they'd bought her the dress; maybe tomorrow she'd be back in a faded old hot-weather smock, washing laundry at an outdoor public sink or even in a river. Maybe on her visit to the city she'd learned how pretty she is, and now she was going to take this surprising knowledge home and wait to see what it meant. I didn't want to frighten her off so I pretended to busy myself in one of my newspapers, staring into it without reading, hoping she'd take the seat. From time to time I've lost my heart on the spot to girls like her and then have usually found them to be as ardently innocent as they seem on first impression, and so locked into their limited circumstances as to be almost incapable of construing anything else. Only outright abandonment or starkest desperation, both common enough, seems able to force an impulse towards freedom into their lives, and then only after they've already encountered the first bitter tastes of life on the move. I'm thinking now of Zamara, but of you too, of what might have been your fate if Señor Soto Hijo hadn't cut off your father's head in the desert.

When I glanced up again I saw both the bus driver and the *ayudante* remonstratively urging her to sit down between them on the shotgun seat. The *ayudante* was cleaning their belongings— jackets, blankets, the new issue of *¿Dónde?*—off the aisle side of the seat and pushing it under the dashboard while the driver, beaming and flirting from behind his wheel, took the small suitcase from her hands and then held it out to the *ayudante*. She was laughing, enjoying the attention, the special invitation to ride up front and watch the road unfold like a movie. She sat down and vanished from my craning sight.

It was near noon when we reached El Progreso, at the beginning of the arid lands. The town is just another of those heat-flattened desert towns that don't seem to serve a fundamental purpose any-more, though three or so centuries ago, long before it got the positivist-era name it never flourished under, it might have been a thriving mule caravan stop on the royal trade route to Panama, where the Spanish flotillas anchored. The bus, enough of its win-dows finally open now, hurtled down through parched, amber cactus hills and turned into an oven as soon as it pulled over to let passengers off. But the quivering heat outside and the dusty walk into town suddenly loomed ahead like a proof that I hadn't thought this through well enough and didn't know what I wanted to say to her after all. I sat back in my seat and tried not to have another thought about it until the hot wind was coming through the win-dows again. That was when I said my first good-bye, to Zamara, my lovely, pale, faintly olive-and-rose-hued Zamarita; feeling miserable because I knew Moya's prophecy on that last night we talked had probably come true (". . . her heart can break like any other, *vos*"). Except I'm so indecisive that now I'm not even sure it was good-bye. She was and must be still waiting for me, sitting patiently on that little stool in the shade of that one dusty mango tree, waiting for the willed surprise of my unresonant knock against the corrugated-metal door hung loosely on wire hinges to the stick fence enclosing the baked-dirt yard of her mother's house. But I hadn't told her I was coming, and had sent no message.

As soon as I decided not to get off at El Progreso, I thought I might go to Chiquimula instead, as if retracing your own previous journey had suddenly been revealed as my hidden intention. So often I've found myself doing that or imagining that I was: walking where you did, Flor, trying to see what you saw and know what you knew, even listening for your own inner voice in my thoughts and the silence all around . . .

When the *ayudante* came down the aisle collecting fares from new passengers after we left El Progreso, I paid again to go as far as Chiquimula, which made the *ayudante* and even some of the other passengers regard me suspiciously, as if there must be something wrong with me for not knowing where I was going. I spent the next hour or so watching the desertscape and the high, completely eroded peaks farther back, wondering if anyone ever went up there, even on horseback or mule, and for what reason. Somewhere in the desert, I'd heard, there is a prosperous and hermetic village where all the women and girls are blond and green eyed and spend their lives making the finest lace in all the Americas, just as their ancestors have been doing for centuries.

Then I didn't get off at the Chiquimula-Zacapa crossroad either, though the pretty girl, amidst much fanfare from the driver and *ayudante,* did. Opening her umbrella against the sun, she walked off into the Zacapa side of the desert all by herself, carrying her little suitcase. This time I voluntarily went up to the front to present myself to the *ayudante* and endure the embarrassment of changing my ticket again. He was still leaning sideways in his seat, trying to catch a final glimpse of the girl in the desert as the bus pulled out, his face and skimpy mustache drenched.

"I'm not getting off here," I said, holding the sweat-softened paper ticket out to him and reaching for my wallet.

"Este anda más perdido que el Judío Errante"—This one's more lost than the Wandering Jew—he said, grinning at the driver, who turned away from his driving to gape at me. All the other passengers were smiling as if it were all just too incredible. "This is the third time he's changed his ticket!" the *ayudante* boomed; and then a woman said, *"Ay pobrecito.* Can't you see that he's a tourist and doesn't know what to see?" And another said, "There's a dinosaur museum back there near Zacapa. Why don't you go see the dinosaur bones?" And I said, "No, I'm just going to Puerto Barrios." And then the *ayudante* grinned leeringly and said, *"Para las sirenas!"* for the mermaids, and the driver happily growled, *"Claro,* there's not one other reason to go to Barrios," which made some of the other women passengers look at me disapprovingly as I made my way back down the aisle.

Soon the desert was behind us, the landscape gradually turning a softly browned green: the vast cattle-feeding plains and stately trees of Izabal, and the ruined palm plantation with the oil-rich palms imported from Africa that refused to adapt to their new soil, row upon row of spear like trunks and fronds withered into floppy black mops that look like tribal Africa sorcerers' masks. And then, almost suddenly, the highway became a tunnel through banana plantation lowlands, the dense vegetation luminously green even in the shade, pushing the huts and small houses of occasional little settlements so close to the highway that the people who seemed to be perpetually sitting outside often had to pull their legs in to let the bus roar past. You could tell that life was different here because the air was so changed, not just hot but solid as it washed in through the windows, full of ineffable scents and a ripened viscosity that words and even innermost thoughts seemed to stick to: from outside the bus a young girl's voice haughtily piped, *"La cabronada es que . . ."* but the rest of her speech was carried off by the tearing of air as a speeding semi truck passed us going the other way; and then seconds later a young, shirtless man walking down the highway with his hands in his pockets and his eyes on the pavement mumbled, as if right in my ear, *"Huele ella así, pues, porque fuma como un turco . . ."* She smells like that because she smokes like a Turk. Only it was the woman sitting in front of me who burst out in laughter, screechingly repeating *como un turco* while the man beside her cheerfully snorted, *Así . . .* An evangelical radio preacher's voice boomed from the thick and seemingly unpopulated jungle outside, *"I Went under the Mountain and There I Saw the Big Dead and the Little Dead,"* and that's the last thing I remember hearing before drowsiness turned to sleep.

I woke up on the road into Puerto Barrios, where the air was no cooler or lighter but less haunted, stirred up by the hubbub of the perpetual parade of pedestrians and bicycle riders and the loud percolations of so many low-horsepower motorbikes bouncing along, driven by wiry brown and black boys, some with girls in colorful dresses and high heels riding sidesaddle on back, legs crossed at the ankles, toes primly pointed up.

And as soon as I stepped down from the bus a sun-bronzed blond girl on a scarlet stingray bicycle waved at me as she pedaled by, and then turned to smile brazenly over her shoulder. She was no more than thirteen, and looked as if she came from the secret village of the lace makers.

I hired a taxi to take me through town, down the long paved avenue to the oceanfront and the Hotel del Norte. And when I checked in I said I'd be staying for a week or two, maybe even three, and put most of my money away in their safety deposit box because the rooms there don't have locks. My life had changed again, but this was the moment when I first began to notice, because it was the first time I allowed myself to admit that maybe I wouldn't be going back to the city at all.

The last time I was here was with Zamara, in the middle of that spell-like stretch of months after Moya left when all I ever wanted to do and almost all I could think about was fucking Zamara. Same bus, same taxi ride. I should mention how simply and nicely dressed she was because of what happened at the check-in desk.

She was wearing one of those unadorned T-shirt-material dresses, purple, with a low back, and high-heeled gold-lamé shoes, the delicate kind, all straps, baring her painted toenails. I'd bought the dress. The cotton clung to her from the humidity and the long hours of sitting on the bus, but she looked remarkably fresh and neat, and the only makeup she had on was lipstick. Zamara has a wonderful stillness inside of her. Partly it's the way she likes to stop and stare at things—store windows, landscapes, people in the street; that stillness in her stare seems to beckon the world closer, as if quietly luring some timid creature. And after she's taken it all in and is almost ready to move on, she often doesn't say anything, communicating her reaction or appraisal with a quiet expression, as if words might frighten the subject of her interest off, even a store window full of delicately shimmering shoes. A suddenly bold, almost indignant widening of her dark, glistening eyes might mean, How ugly! But that expression of having just tasted something good, almost ruing a pleasure so ephemeral that there might not even be another spoonful for her: this can mean she wants something in the store window but doesn't want to come right out and ask. And a way of sighing, holding her breath and then letting it out softly and almost luxuriantly through her nostrils, the corners of her lips squeezed into a dimpled smile, her eyebrows slightly arched: this means, How lovely!

When we got out of the taxi she stared for a long time at the white balustraded seawall, the ornate stone benches, the green gazebo with its single bulb glowing like a pearl in the greenish evening air, the palms and seabirds, the clouds massed like faraway pink and yellow pyramids in the darkening sky, a majestic freighter as strung with lights as a used-car lot sailing diagonally out into the ocean, away from the new modern port nearby on the bay that has made Puerto Barrios practically obsolete as an actual port, though not as a center of seamen's nightlife.

"There go the *patria*'s bananas," I said, though of course I didn't know what the ship was really carrying.

"*A dónde?*" she asked.

"*A los japoneses.*"

A moment later she asked, "How do they keep them from rotting? You can't put bananas in ice."

"They're very green now, but I guess they'll be ripe when they get there. They have to time it just right."

I remember the way the breeze, drying her dampness just enough, lifted soft strands of dark hair off her partly bared shoulders, and that the soft, smooth-sheened skin was slightly blotched from the all-day heat, and tangy tasting when I kissed her there through the feathery drift of hair, one hand pressed lightly to the bared part of her back, feeling the almost humming warmth. Then she turned her head just enough to watch me from the corner of one gleaming eye, and when she'd sighed her happiness through her nose, she said, "They'll be yellow, like them," and giggled. I guess my look was blank. She widened her eyes and said, "*Los bananos . . . !*"

We walked up the waterlogged steps and into the hotel through the wide screened porch and into the office across the corridor from the bar—I was dying for a drink. A dapper man in a white *guayabera* who looked as if his ancestral roots might be in India stood behind the counter; at the desk a handsome, curly-haired woman sat behind a portable typewriter. They both looked for too long a moment at Zamara, then quickly at each other, and then the man asked me to step into the corridor, where he politely but firmly said that this is a reputable hotel and that guests aren't allowed to bring women from the town back to their rooms and that I'd find notices posted in every room saying the same.

I was amazed and felt awful for Zamara. Did it show like a mark on her face that only I couldn't see or what?

I knew I had to be careful, that if I challenged his sense of authority no reasoning or even a bribe would sway him. In these situations, it's always best to pretend not to speak much Spanish, just enough to earnestly argue in a single direction until hopefully the opponent gets bored.

"We've just come from the capital," I said, trying to look wounded and confused, as if I had no idea why women from the town weren't wanted there or why he'd mistaken Zamara for one of them. "We've never been here before."

"She is one of those from the Medellín," he said flatly, as if he'd had these arguments too often and wanted to get right to the point. The Medellín is the famous bawdy sailors' nightclub just down the road, and I knew for a fact that Zamara had never worked there or anywhere in Puerto Barrios, though her friend Paola does.

"The *where? Discuple,* but I don't know what you're talking about. She's my fiancée, we've just come from the city and I know this is a respectable hotel, anyone can see that. We're taking the ferry over to Livingston tomorrow."

"Señor," he said peremptorily, running one hand through his ointment-inked hair. "Anyone can see that you have only one piece of luggage."

I asked him, please, to wait there just one moment, I didn't want to embarrass my fiancée, and I walked back into the office with a breezy smile for Zamara, who was leaning against the wall glowering, and picked up my duffel—the clerk was already following me in through the door but I swept past him back into the corridor, and then I put the bag down at his feet and unzipped it. Zamara's things had all been packed on top.

"*Ve?*" I said. "Those are not mine." For emphasis I plowed my hand through her underthings, all of them new, and plucked out the top of the bathing suit I'd bought her just the day before. "Do you think this is mine?" I even pulled out her scrunched copy of *Vanidades* magazine, dog-eared from the trip. "Do you think I read *this?*"

The rooms in the Hotel del Norte only cost about six dollars a night and are almost as spare as changing stalls in an old-fashioned bathhouse and smell the same, with thick, glossy coats of paint to protect against salt corrosion and rot. I've heard the hotel was originally constructed as a United Fruit administrative building during the heyday of the U.S. fruit companies, though someone else said it used to be their malaria hospital. No one who works there now seems to know which, as if the salt air eats up memory when it hasn't been painted like everything else. But it makes a beautiful hotel, sitting like a giant, four-story Caribbean palace on the Bahía de Amatique, all wood, screened windows, and wind. The rooms don't even have fans, but don't really need them because at night, with or without rain, there always seems to be a breeze coming off the bay and in through the louvered, gauzily curtained double doors.

All night long you can hear wind in the long, verandalike corridors, evenly strained through the long screens, gathering whispered force in the maze of staircases climbing up through the middle of the hotel; then, as soon as the sun comes up, there's no breeze at all, and almost no air. Downstairs there's a large nautical bar and an even bigger dining room, screened in on three sides and surrounded by water, with white tablecloths, and black waiters in white waistcoats who stride with silent steps across the spongy floorboards carrying serving trays with all the dishes covered by silver lids (this is where I'm sitting now, at one of only two occupied tables, the gray, tepid water slurping at the pilings just outside).

In the open yard behind the kitchen there is a spider monkey, and a tree with a tire hung from a rope for it to play on. That evening, after we'd finally checked in, as Zamara and I climbed up the stairs on our way to our room on the top floor, Zamara paused on the first landing to stare at the monkey. It was pacing back and forth at the end of its long leash in that way spider monkeys do, looking like a long-limbed hillbilly with his thumbs stuck high into his suspenders. Then it climbed up into the tree and hung upside down, looking in our general direction and chattering. *"Ay, pobrecito el mico."* Zamara claimed the monkey was looking right at her and waved, though I doubt it could have actually made her out against the twilight and shadows.

"Zamara?" I asked her then. "Did *Teniente* López ever bring you to Puerto Barrios?" Until recently, the lieutenant had been her boyfriend, or at least she'd claimed he was. She nodded her head just once, and I asked, "Where did you stay?"

"At the naval base," she said, and I knew it must be true. Of course they would have gone to the Medellín and sat at a table with the base commander and his officers.

That night we went to the Medellín ourselves and sat at a table with Paola and the black Panamanian fire-eater who is the star act there. Then, long after we'd come back and fallen asleep, I woke alone in the single bed we'd been sharing though there was another one in the room, and saw Zamara standing in the light of the door she'd just pushed open. It was the beautiful, softly glowing blue light of a tropical predawn over the ocean, but I thought she probably shouldn't walk all the way to the bathroom stark naked like that.

"*Amorcita,* put something on," I said.

But she didn't even glance back before she stepped out. I got up and went after her with a towel, and found her just outside the door looking confused, blinking out at the immense bluish neon cloud that both the ocean and sky looked fused into.

"*Quiero ver al mico,*" she said. She wanted to see the monkey. "He was right here!"

"Zamara." I laughed softly. "*Estás somnambulando, vos.*"

I hugged her to me and walked her gently back to bed, and, when we woke again a few hours later, she didn't remember any of it.

I've been here three days. I really should phone Uncle Jorge, or at least send a telegram. People quite understandably worry and even panic here when they expect to know where someone is but suddenly don't and haven't heard anything: so many silences that last an eternity begin in just that way.

The newspapers say it still hasn't rained inland, but it does on the coast; the clouds pile up in great multitiered pillars, some of the rain sweeping in, a lot of it letting go out there, faraway wind-slanted or funnel-shaped commotions low over the horizon, probably capsizing fishing boats and shrimpers. I have an image in my head now of the last six months since Moya left having lifted off of me all in one piece, sort of borne up by the force of my meditations, hanging there like one of those heavy-bellied clouds. I can sit back, study that cloud, and begin to make decisions. Do I tell it in order? (my trip through the highlands and return to the city: Moya with the notebook, the death squad, then hiding out with Moya until he could flee the country; a week later I *infiltrate* the orphanage; two months later a nun whom I'd met on that trip through the highlands comes to the city with news of a lost boy . . .)

Or do I try to tell it according to some other logic? Because told in order, it wouldn't make sense: I didn't *understand* things in the order they happened, I didn't *foresee* what they would mean later; and I'm not supposed to be telling what happened to *me,* but about Flor.

I can't just let it out all at once either, but inside that fuming cloud that's the way it seems to be happening, all these charged particles slamming around: Lucas Caycam Quix. Sister Clarita. María de la Luz de Prey. Mariel, the street girl. Señora Mirza Lopez de Betz; her nephew, the lieutenant; even the *niñera fafera.* Rosana Letones. Celso Batres. This isn't supposed to be about me or even about Zamara, though she too plays a small role in what I have to tell now, the unfolding of your plausible fates. Moya, of course, was always supposed to be the chronicler of our investigation, but when he departed this land of wonders six months ago he was almost as innocent of all this—*almost,* I think, and still must be—as I was then.

Maybe I should start with the notebook and, if not with that, then the nun, Sor Clarita from Nebaj, who of course knew you. The first real lead came from her, and the notebook merely clarified it—confirmed by omission the ambiguous existence of a lost boy, Lucas Caycam Quix. Except I'm not sure that I can even tell the difference between what has actually happened and what didn't anymore, though the answers I'm seeking depend on my being able to: I don't even know if Lucas Caycam Quix is *real.*

If only there was a way to tell it all through your eyes, Flor. Then I could just be the passenger, bracing myself for the cruel impact I'd already know waited at the end of the ride (foretold but never foreseen right there in the palm of your hand, the indecipherably crisscrossed and layered one): Was your murderer, Flor, a vicious street boy who believes you "sold" his sister into French "slavery"? Or was it the general's sister after all? Or someone else entirely? And whoever it was, did you ever have a chance to understand or were you too distracted or muddled or defeated by something else?

Basta, mijito! Let the secrets rest, I can almost hear you pleading. Even exposing your murderer wouldn't get me to the bottom of anything but *that,* would it, and how can I expect to accomplish that in Puerto Barrios anyway? Why don't you just shake me awake as if from a dream and tell me to forget it? So here's one answer: I cannot because so far I have been unable to extricate myself from you, and I am tired, exhausted, of feeling haunted.

Wouldn't you rather hear all about Zamara, Flor? That happened, for sure. Or even about Moya and our "heroic" escape from a death squad? Oh Flor, she's so beautiful—though perhaps you wouldn't think so, you wouldn't think Zamara is *that* beautiful. With her soft pale cheeks and dark easily riled eyes and adorably expressive mouth, she really looks like she has a lot going on inside. She definitely has charisma, though she is often very quiet. She has black shoulder-length hair, cut in a wide, fringy bang over those eyes. Her voice is somewhat chesty and bleating, though in a much lower, that is far more normal, register than the voice I am obviously invoking. She's nineteen or else is lying about her age and is younger. She has a little son from when she was in the States three years ago, when she went to Los Angeles and found work as a maid for a family who didn't enroll her in elementary school and there fell in love with a half-Chicano, half-*grencho* (Zamara slang for grmgo) surfer boy named Rex, who impregnated and then dumped her. But she managed to keep her maid's job until her pregnancy became impossible to hide, and when she was fired she managed to hang on in L.A., illegal and with little money, brave Zamarita, until her baby was born so that he could be a U.S. citizen even if his mother couldn't. She named him Rex too, spent the rest of her money on the airfare back to Guatemala, and then moved in with her own long-single mother in El Progreso, also called Guastatoya now that everyone has tired of the stale mockery of the former. She languished there for about a year and then left her son behind with her mother and came to the city to work in the *ambiente,* though not in a *burdel* but as a *barra show* girl, as *"una artista de barra."* I met her soon after, in October, just weeks before I left on that nearly two-week trip through the highlands, the ostensible purpose of which was to cross the border into Mexico at some point along the way so that I could come back in with a new visa. Moya was already in trouble then, over his column about the post office and the black-market dollar trade, published while I was away. But he'd also managed to bribe your old notebook out of the police archives with the money I'd given him for that purpose—the notebook in which you'd preserved rudimentary details and sometimes startling anecdotes regarding the adoptions you arranged and the adopters (including Ozzie Peterkins, who'd wanted to marry you?); that very night of my return to the capital, November 4, after Moya and I had spent the afternoon poring over the notebook, the shit hit the fan, and we ended up hiding out in an *autohotel* called El Omni. Two days later I accompanied Moya to the airport for his second flight out of the country in a year, though this exile is probably going to last a very long time, if not forever.

I wrote to Moya yesterday and posted it from the hotel. I told him everything. I won't be surprised if it takes weeks to reach him, but I think it would be best if it got there just ahead of me:

TWENTY-ONE

I know; I'll start with your voice, recovered from this disorder of echoes inside me:

"All I want for Christmas is for Ira to get better"—do you remember that, Flor? In front of the F. A. O. Schwarz toy store on Fifth Avenue in Manhattan?—that's what you said again, so many years later, in Chichicastenango, during my trip through the highlands, when you spoke to me as if in a ghost story.

In Chichicastenango I picked up your trail again after having lost it completely during my search of the lower-class brothels of Guatemala City, in the frustration of looking for you everywhere where you couldn't possibly be and the despair that came after, when I came so close to abandoning our project for good. In the nighttime silence of a market plaza in Chichi, I heard your true secret voice. There, in that mountain market town or in the swooping patterns of bats in the chilly night air or simply in front of my stare, the secret logic of your life—*our* lives, because we remain linked in this no matter what—briefly spelled itself in the silence, almost as if in the suddenly decipherable lines in an impossibly crisscrossed palm.

When I got back to the city and found myself quickly holed up like an outlaw with Moya in the Omni, I even tried to explain it to him, though I'm not sure I really understood what I meant anymore, not in the same brief way I had in Chichi—it seemed an awful lot to hang on one seemingly innocent sentence spoken in front of a toy store window nearly *a* decade and a half before.

It happened in New York City, on a Sunday morning, seven or eight hours after we'd been woken in our hotel by the groans of my father's 2:00 A.M. gallbladder attack. We'd come to New York, of course, for the Harvard–Columbia football game and were staying, like we always did, in the Howard Johnson's Motor Lodge on Eighth Avenue. But the hospital my father was in was on the Upper East Side and that's where we were walking from, all the way back to our hotel, when we stopped in front of F. A. O. Schwarz to look at the windows. My mother had caught a dawn flight and was in the hospital with my father now, and we'd been sent back to the hotel to pack our things for the train home to Boston.

In front of the F. A. O. Schwarz window you asked me what I wanted for Christmas. I wanted Bauer hockey skates and gloves, and said so. I bet there was even a small note of indignation in my voice over your even having had to ask.

So see how much I'd changed by then? (Though of course so had you, nineteen and in your first year of high school, going around dressed like a French librarian, and me in the sixth grade.) Because for years, of course, all those prior years to the fifth grade, I mean, I'd been happier to spend my afternoons in the basement with you and as far as anyone could tell had been happily oblivious of any other possibility, though this seemed to have retarded me in some pretty obvious ways . . .

But it wasn't that hard to become a "Namoset kid" after all. I'd started tagging along and then just kept going, over and over, out to the frozen swamps, oblivious, or seemingly oblivious, as always, to whatever resistance I at first encountered. So I'd been accepted by the other boys at school almost as soon as I'd tried to be and not because they had finally become used to having me around, or because they no longer minded all the other ways in which I was different, or had decided to tolerate those differences. I really had become just like them, in every way that seemed to matter, I mean. And the ways in which I remained different seemed no more important than the ways in which anyone's personal history or idiosyncrasies might make him so, might expose him to continuous punishing ridicule, if he didn't know how, or lacked the essential enthusiasm and energy, to conform. So what if my house was called the Copacabana because of the funny accents they heard there, the funny decor they saw, the funny affectation of Spanish wrought-iron grill under the windows of our one-story ranch house? In Namoset there was always a lot of rough talk about ethnic and religious origins anyway, and, while there were plenty of fully Jewish kids around, there was only one Copacabana. I thought it didn't matter when I was called spik since anyone could see that I wasn't really a spik, I only sort of looked like one. Or I'd get stuck with temporary nicknames like Juan Valdéz.

Eccentricities, of course, attract a lot of attention in small towns, and Flor, especially by the time she was in high school, going around dressed like some uptight perfumed French librarian at the height of the hippie era and working in the Brigham's ice-cream parlor in the evenings, certainly attracted attention. By then she was starting to hate Namoset at least as much as my mother always had, but it was almost as if she expressed that by making the town love its own stereotyped if benevolent legend of her strangeness—because Namoset was never Flor's prison so much as it was the circus of her dexterity that had finally become the frumpiest little one-ring show, into which she still had to step daily for the performances of her interminable adolescence. Flor's story was so widely known and obvious seeming that people practically disassociated my family from it, as if she was a nearly permanent fixture of the town who bore the same relation to everybody. She was the pretty foreign girl who had started out as a nearly illiterate fourteen-year-old in the first grade and look at her now, nineteen, starting high school, straight A's, on her way to college!

Flor provoked a kind of baffled awe rather than maliciousness, because even though she was both cheerful and haughty, and seemed possessed by some unswayable and private sense of mission that *couldn't* have been only about wanting to go to college, she was always so dauntingly literal. All she wanted was to go to college, that's what she'd say over and over. In a town where, frankly, many people didn't think going to college was the be all and end all. It was as if behind this monomania, there was a secret that couldn't be communicated, perhaps having something to do with where she came from. As if she might be jailed in her native country if she didn't get to college. It was as if no one had ever encountered anyone so cheerfully single-minded and remote, which made her seem much more mysterious than she actually was. No one really knew a thing about her private life, about Tony. Every year she could count on the most self-regarding teenager in the senior class to contrive some spectacular play for her attentions, and at the climactic moment she might merely widen her eyes at most and say to him, *Are you on drugs or do you think this is one of those movies? You're just a boy!* Only I could have told them that this prudish and superior grandstanding was in one sense absolutely literal, but in the other simply a ploy. The myth of her own superiority and sovereign independence was her only defense against her own uncertainties, and her best weapon against Tony, whom she was as in love with as ever. And she was no prude with Tony.

With everyone else—outside of our family, of course—she was so literal it must have seemed *she* was the one on drugs. She wanted to go to college, that's all. Everything she did, every night she served ice creams, every book they saw her reading while she waited at the bus stop, was in the advancement of this cause. They all must have imagined that she went into Boston on weekends for the libraries, or for the art museum, or to case out the dorms at Radcliffe. She could have stood out on the corner with a sign saying, I NEED MONEY FOR COLLEGE, and I swear not a soul walking by wouldn't have dipped into their pockets. And if anyone asked her just what it was she intended to do with a college degree she was likely to answer with that same stupefying literalness and a smile that seemed to suggest an incomprehensible irony, *Oh well, we'll see, maybe I'll get married, the important thing is to get to college.* That was her late-Namoset persona, anyway. She wouldn't let anyone see her impatience and boredom, her deeper confusions. And on the sidewalks in Namoset Square, she was always so nice and friendly to the police.

I wanted new hockey skates and gloves, nothing else, and when in front of the F. A. O. Schwarz window I said so, you said, "Oh gosh, Roger, next thing you know, you'll be into cars." Like being into hockey was the same as being a greaser, when in fact, in Namoset anyway, the opposite was true. "You will be one of those little hoodlums who spend all their time trying to be scary, and then suddenly they have nowhere to go but the army or a gas station." The extraordinary thing was that your voice was suddenly quavery and high, like you were about to cry. "Roger, that would break my heart, do you hear me? I would feel like every minute I've spent with you has been a complete waste of time. Roger, you have to stop trying to be like everyone else. Don't you see where that will lead you? At dinner last night, in front of Ira's friends, when they asked you how you were doing in school, you went on and on about hockey. It isn't even winter yet! I could have died of embarrassment. We could all tell you were just making it up too—"

"I was not."

"Roger, you are not the star of your team. This is not even really a team, right? Teams of tough little boys from Boston do not travel all the way to the swamps in Namoset to play hockey against you and your friends."

I was silent for a moment, and then I giggled, and then, in response to your disappointed look, fell silent again.

". . . Well, what do you want for Christmas?"

You actually thought about it for a moment, but then you said, "All I want for Christmas is for Ira to get better," and there was a little catch in your throat, a tiny sob, and you exhaled a fluttery sigh . . .

That, and then the little catch in your throat, the exhaled tiny sob. It went *ping,* something in your voice, a note I can't exactly call false, because it wasn't quite that, but I've never forgotten it, and have never, until perhaps recently, fathomed its meaning to me.

There, in front of F. A. O. Schwarz, what I first felt was shame, because I hadn't said what you had, selfishly requesting hockey skates and gloves instead (no wonder you often seemed his favorite, you always knew *just* what to say), and then I felt a flash of confused anger, as if you'd tricked me. Well, we were tired, and of course you were concerned and still a little shaken, so was I. It had been a long stretch of nearly sleepless and frightened hours, set off by what still has to count as one of the principal shocks of my life: my father's bellowing moans suddenly waking us at two in the morning in our darkened room in the Howard Johnson's. You were in the other bed, across from my father's vacated one, and I was in a cot near the wall, and my father was in the bathroom with the door closed, moaning like some terrified, mortally wounded bear curled up in a cave. I'd never heard a sound like that, it froze me as soon as it woke me, that awful, surrendering sound of pure agony, but it stopped as soon as you ran to the door in your pajamas and shrieked, "Ira . . . ?" Then my father came out in his bathrobe with his hands over his groin and went silently to the closet and put his overcoat on and it wasn't until he sat down on his bed and reached for his shoes that the groans tore through him again. In a matter of seconds, it seemed, you'd helped him to get his shoes on and had rushed into the bathroom clutching your clothes to your chest and bounced back out dressed like a French librarian, with even the velvet ribbony bow tie neatly in place under the starched white collar of your blouse, tugging at the hips of your knee-length black skirt, slipping feet into black pumps and grabbing your houndstooth blazer and tossing your makeup into the pockets all in one motion while we were already following my father's moans and methodical steps out the door . . . Somehow he was able to tell the taxi driver the name of the hospital he wanted to go to. And there we'd waited, on an orange couch in a fluorescent-bright waiting room, terrified and feeling like orphans, disbelieving of the nurses and doctors who occasionally stopped by to assure us that everything was going to be all right, until my mother arrived from her dawn flight from Boston only five hours later, and was soon after let in to see my father.

When she came back out she said that my father didn't want us getting too worked up over what the doctors said was just going to be a routine operation, life should go on as normal, we had to be in school the next day. They couldn't have afforded the extravagance of keeping us in a hotel for a week anyway. Until my father was ready to come home, my mother would stay with an old friend from the Latin American Society of Boston, a Chilean woman married to an American business executive, Mr. MacKenzie, who worked in New York now. They lived in an apartment on the Upper East Side, only blocks away from the hospital.

And then my mother had given us money for the train to Massachusetts, and for the taxi from the Route 128 station to Namoset, as well as for a taxi from the hospital to the Howard Johnson's. But we'd decided to walk instead, so that we'd have more money to spend at the snack bar on the train.

It wasn't until we'd turned away from the F. A. O. Schwarz window and were walking down Fifth Avenue again, your words still echoing inside me, that I was able to briefly detach those words from the drama of the situation. That was when something went *ping,* a short and jarring little something, like an insight forming but then dissipating before it could be expressed. From then on whenever I remembered you saying that what you wanted for Christmas was for my father to get better, or whenever I found its echo in other things you said or even did, I'd relive that jarring little sensation of having felt on the verge of knowing something and then having lost it.

We caught the noon train from Penn Station, but, instead of getting off at Route 128 like we were supposed to, we went all the way to Back Bay Station in Boston. And then you took me to Tony's apartment, where we stayed until the morning. This was a completely obsessed and reckless thing for you to have tried to pull off, of course, and a big mistake in more ways than one, for it ended up wrecking your relationship with my mother, which had always been pretty tenuous, in a new and irreparable way. No matter what else, my mother had always felt that she could at least trust you to act responsibly in regard to me. But there was something else that the incident flushed out of hiding between the two of you, a rancor that was never overtly addressed and couldn't have been, having much to do with what you both felt about each other as women, I think, what each of you explicitly or intuitively knew about the other.

So you couldn't really have been all that surprised when, in the heat of the first face-to-face castigations following my parents' return from New York, my mother accused you of "acting like an ordinary whore in front of my son." But you gasped anyway, like it was one of the most unexpected hurts of your life, and whispered, "*Ordinaria?* . . . *Yo?* . . . Like a . . . in front of. . ." And gasped again and said, "*Ay no,* Mirabel." Then, silently, you stiffened and fixed my mother with a teary, accusatory stare of your own.

My mother may have, perhaps must have, found in that stare an allusion to her own love affair of two summers back with Pepe Ganús the hog assassin, which had also, arguably, taken place right in front of "her son" (though it is also true that they had been as discreet about it as possible, and the son, back then, had been quite uncomprehending). And perhaps in that stare my mother read another kind of sexual defiance, even more hurtful, that went deeper, and further back. You probably didn't think my mother had ever been a very good wife to my father. Out of blind loyalty or even out of an old Chiquimula predisposition, you tended to unthinkingly absolve my father of any blame in that, Flor. So I think it was at least partly because of my mother's trepidation and even panic over the silent messages in that stare that you escaped any punishment over the incident. (In fact my mother would actually seem even angrier over something that would happen the next year, when a Namoset High guidance counselor would summon her to a private conference and there accuse her and our family of treating you "like a maid.") In the end my mother—and my father too, for different, easier reasons—probably felt relieved to just accept the explanation, or alibi, that you tearfully kept insisting on: that your unprecedented lapse of judgment had been caused by your fear that my father might die.

That had to be accepted, you repeated it so forcefully, in a tone of voice much more shrill and adamant than I'd ever heard you use with my mother before. There was no echo now of the strangely innocent artificiality of your words in front of F. A. O. Schwarz. You were publicly forgiven, you even received some sympathy. My father, recuperating, in his bathrobe, his belly still stitched up, hugged you to him like a true daughter.

Even though you'd been exposed as a liar in another, though I guess perfectly mundane and adolescent way: for months you'd been telling my parents that it was finally over between you and

Tony, who my father had unapologetically been deriding as a "cannibal"—"What does that guy think he is, a cannibal? Oh Flor!"—ever since the last time he'd turned up at our house with his hair grown slightly longish and wearing an imitation tiger-claw earring and a necklace of shark teeth. I'd asked Tony that time if it meant he'd become a hippie, and he'd grinned rakishly and said that he was only pretending to be one, because "those white hippie girls, they really put out, man . . ." And you'd instantly shrieked his name and charged at him with pummeling fists until he grabbed your wrists laughing and said he was just *jodiendo* while you, trying to writhe free, seethed, "Oh sure! Fucker! Go back to your little hippie girls and their hairy armpits full of lice!"

That was the last time I'd seen Tony, but only I knew that you hadn't broken up once and for all. I spent much less time in the basement now, but I knew that you often spoke to him on the phone in the afternoons, though you always, always seemed to be fighting. I could tell whenever you, downstairs, had heard me come into the kitchen by the way your voice would drop to a harsh, tireless whisper. Later your eyes would often be red or angry or both, and you'd attack either your homework or housework in a highstrung way I knew to keep out of the way of.

You'd said we were only going to stop in at Tony's for a minute, and then we'd walked over from Back Bay Station without phoning to warn him. Maybe you were hoping to catch him with someone else or desperately hoping not to. But he was alone when we got there, in his pot-reeking, sparely furnished, though fastidiously neat apartment. Tony wasn't wearing any of his cannibal regalia, but his hair was still on the long side, falling around his collar, and the pierce in his earlobe looked like a tiny piece of lint stuck there. He wore a purple shirt with black polka dots, tight black jeans. Even though Tony rarely seemed as outwardly ebullient as he had that night when he'd first captivated you in our basement, he still had his quiet good manners and grace and his gray eyes still seemed to look at the world with a casual good humor that was contradicted by the obvious facts of his life and, often, by his moods.

He wasn't particularly surprised to see us, though my presence, which he seemed determined to ignore, made the visit unprecedented. Your explanation was brief: my father in the hospital, you were very upset and needed to see him. But the looks that passed between you! Yours suspensefully contrite, then worried and determined, Tony's grimly skeptical no matter what. It was almost as if our fraught weekend had been nothing but a brief interruption in an argument that had already been raging. Together you went right into Tony's bedroom and shut the door and soon I heard his voice rising sharply and yours defensively, both speaking at once in rapid Spanish. I had to just sit there on the couch watching television throughout the rest of that afternoon and into the evening, while, in the bedroom with the door locked, you and Tony alternately shouted and made speeches in passionate whispers so that I wouldn't hear, soothed, even wept I think, laughed or giggled sometimes, and eventually got around to basically fucking up as quiet a storm as you could before starting up the argument all over again. And often Tony forgot to whisper. Once I heard him referring to my parents in a muffled but sarcastic tone and felt unbelievably relieved when you angrily rebuked and shushed him. But nothing was more astounding than the way you suddenly and furiously began berating him just when the most recent silence had started to sound like peace at last, a tirade that only became comprehensible to me when your voice shifted into the chesty bleating of your most affronted anger: "—You think reading books and having dreams is an escape from reality? *Hah-hah!* Too bad books cannot be rolled up like marijuana and smoked, then you would like books, *verdad,* Tony? You think that being

447

intelligent and courageous makes *a* snob. Well she is twice the man you are! When Miss Cavanaugh was your age she went all the way to Chile by motorcycle and had romances with presidents along the way and wrote a book about it, but you don't even own a car! That's what American men do, isn't it, Tony? It's a matter of pride, it doesn't have to be a new one or at all expensive! They find some kind of car and take good care of it and then they can make wonderful romantic surprises! You could come by my house and say, Flor, I'm taking you skiing in Vermont! *Eh?* Just like that, Tony!" and you stopped yourself. And then Tony, in English, shouted, "Flor, a *car? Coño!* I can't afford a car!" Moments later you said, "Oh Tony, I think I am going crazy." And then Tony moaning, "No, I am a fuck up, OK? So what am I going to say? You are right. But *mierda, Florcita*, I'm trying to get it together, I am . . ." He sounded exasperated and deflated, totally wrung out; in the ensuing silence I pictured him spread facedown over his bed as if he'd just been squeezed like paste from a tube . . . "I just want you to realize you could be so much more. It's your choice, Tony. *Amorcito?* Only yours. You say you have put Cuba behind you, but you haven't put anything in front of you." And then more silence, and then other sounds. That's the way it went, until it had been dark outside for a while.

Now and then you came out of the room with your essential clothes back on, red eyed, gravely distracted or worried looking, and one time even looking as if you were trying not to laugh out loud over some delightful thought you were having. You'd hug and kiss me then and tell me we were going home any minute and that we'd only come here first because you'd been so worried about my father, and Tony, after all, was like your best and oldest friend not counting Delmi Ramírez (whom we never saw anymore anyway), and you made me promise that this would stay our secret, because I understood, didn't I, how worried you'd been about Ira? Well, see how much better you felt now? And then back into the bedroom, and soon that limited but unforgettable repertoire of sounds would start over.

That night Tony fmally came out and made hot ham, salami, and cheese sandwiches at the kitchen counter by pressing down on them with a clothing iron, wiping up the crumbs and grease right after. Holding the refrigerator door open, you smiled at me and said, "See? A giant lives here," because it was loaded with giant loaves of ham, salamis, cheese, bread, and whole cases of canned soda. Tony said he saved money buying his food at wholesale prices from his friend who was a produce distributor to delicatessens. He said it like this was a big-shot connection that only a very cool guy could have. Tony didn't work as an apprentice jeweler anymore. I didn't know what he did now, though he always seemed to have a job doing one thing or another, driving a taxi, or working as a salesclerk at Filene's during the Christmas season.

The three of us sat on the couch in front of the television eating our sandwiches and saying hardly a word, and when Tony lit up a joint I wasn't at all surprised, though I'd never yet smoked marijuana. You frowned at him, but this seemed just for show. He exhaled, waved the joint around a bit as if cooling it off, pinched it with his fingers, and dropped it into his shirt pocket, and then you asked if I was ready to go home. You went to the telephone and told us to stay quiet, though we hadn't exactly been conversing, and phoned my mother at the Chilean's house. I could tell it was a servant who'd answered, a Spanish-speaking one, from the way you said, *"Ah, bueno,"* and then went on in carefully enunciated English. Tony, from the couch, snorted, *"Pretenciosa,"* and you shot him a withering look and then switched to Spanish with the servant, leaving a carefully worded message. That is, you didn't say that we were at home, and didn't say that we weren't. You simply said you were very relieved to hear that my mother had gone out to dinner with the MacKenzies because that must mean my father was feeling better, and you sent love and good nights from both of us, and said we'd phone again after school.

Then you and Tony went back into the bedroom, where I could hear you arguing in whispers, and then both of you came out, all smiles, carrying sheets and blankets to make me a bed on the couch and to say good night.

Well, you *were* nineteen, after all, and even in the sixth grade there was a girl who was rumored not to be a virgin anymore. But I lay awake for hours, distressed and silently raging. It wasn't as if I was confronting that you fucked Tony for the first time in my life. It had been three years since I'd last watched you change out of your school clothes in the basement, since we had last played Tunnel of Love, like the carnival ride, the one we'd seen in a Hayley Mills Disney movie, closing our eyes and pressing our lips together, pretending we were in that movie, you running your hands through my hair and telling me I was Paul McCartney. It was just an orphans' game. Or it was the way the angels played. Well, you were only fifteen or so, a confused girl in a confusing body, stuck in a Namoset elementary school no less, so no wonder! Only twice had it progressed to a stage of touch these, touch this, aren't they like little rabbit noses, look . . . so that after you'd blushingly had to warn me that what we'd done was naughty though you promised not to tell. When other kids at school talked about sex, it sometimes amazed me to remember that I had once actually touched and kissed the rabbit noses on your small slippery breasts and that I could still remember it as if it had happened yesterday, though I told nobody. Sometimes it didn't seem to have anything to do with what everybody else meant by sex, or even with reality. Then, suddenly, it would, like when I listened to the faint rustlings of you fucking Tony on the other side of that wall. In a healthy light, of course, such memories should hold plenty of innocent sweetness. Tunnel of Love was no more wicked, no more unusual, than a nineteen-year-old's going to rather ludicrous and reckless ends to contrive a way of spending a night in bed with her boyfriend, was it?

I finally fell asleep there on Tony's couch, and in the morning I woke before you did and walked all the way to Boston Common and then across it to my uncle Judge Herbert's office in the courthouse, which is how my mother found out about it in the end. She'd phoned Judge Herbert only half an hour before I walked in, frantic with worry over where we were, because she'd phoned the house in Namoset, of course, meaning to catch us before we'd left for school.

All this is what I later found myself trying to get at with Moya in the Omni. Except what I'd always thought was going to be absolutely the most important thing for me to face just wasn't. Maybe you can't focus on one thing and say, This is it, the deep difficult truth that I've been evading. But there's this notion that speaking it out loud finally frees you, it all dissipates and you're changed, you climb out through a trapdoor in the ceiling into a new life. But it didn't, my confession just plummeted harmlessly to the floor like the paper cup full of ant poison balanced at the edge of a plank in my old "Flor trap" contraption in the basement.

That's what it was like when I told Moya in the *autohotel,* the Omni, in that red-velvet-and-satin room created for nothing else but adulteries and dalliances with whores, when I was telling him all this that I've been telling.

It just came out, I told Moya about the what never happened that came to seem as if it had—that *had come* to seem as if it had especially after what the girl with the pink-streaked hair said, the one who was at your funeral and who came into the Regina Bar & Grill one night seven months after while I was bartending (though her hair wasn't pinked anymore, it was dyed a lustrous auburn with black tips now). In the Onmi, my words just plummeted to the floor and lay there, no big deal, daunting me with the revelation that the truth, if there was one, lay elsewhere after all, or at least not only there, lay closer to that *ping* . . .

So there I was, sitting on one curve of the round, red satin–covered bed beneath the mirrored ceiling in our room in the Omni, Moya sitting on the other curve, trying to keep his mind off the terror of knowing that there were people out there who earlier that very day had tried to kill him—

". . . at Wellesley Flor used to tell the girls in her dorm that she and I, well, that we'd fucked all our lives practically, from the time I was twelve or so anyway. In the basement when no one was home. Like the incestuous enfants terribles of suburbia or something. But it never happened!"

"No, *vos.*"

"*Sí!* . . . So she didn't tell *you* that story anyway."

"No. Perhaps she outgrew this particular myth." And then he laughed, softly, but—Well, he'd had a nerve-shattering day, but still, I couldn't believe he'd laughed.

". . . Uh-huh," I said. "Anyway, that's what the girl with the pink hair said when she came into my bar one night. She was all coked up or something. That little story had really impressed her, it had stayed with her all right, back from when she was in college with Flor. I couldn't believe what I was hearing, though, I threw her out of the bar. I mean, not even a year after the funeral, imagine?"

"Flor could be very crazy, and *muy necia,* no?" he said, with no particular emphasis. *Necia:* pesky, naughty, mischievous . . . *Necia?*

"It never happened."

"*Ajá.*"

"But imagine its effect on me, Moya. I mean, I started to live in it like it had! Like it had happened, OK? Not even like I wished it had happened, but like it *had*. Because the thing is, it probably could have happened at least once, if I'd been different the one time, really just the one afternoon, when I *think* she gave me the chance to, except we never mentioned it again. Until that girl walked into the bar and said what she said, I don't think I'd ever really believed that maybe she *had* given me that chance, I thought it was more like my imagination, you know?"

"But what chance, *vos?*"

"It was when she was home that first summer after college. I came in from the yard through the basement and then into her room without knocking on the door except she'd just taken a bath, she had a towel on but she looked at me, and I said, Oops! Should've knocked, and Flor said, with just that look, You don't have to knock when you come into my room, Roger."

"... *Entonces?*"

"Nothing. I ran up the stairs."

"It never happened?"

"No. I thought she couldn't have meant that. Maybe she didn't—"

"Because of course you would have wanted it to. It's natural, *pues*. She wasn't your sister, not even your cousin. She was young y *todo*. If you had been in Guatemala it undoubtedly would have happened, *vos*, and you would have felt yourself scandalously in love for a little while, and then it would be just a nice memory of youth."

"... She never said anything?"

"Oh no. Of course she loved you very much, in that same way you always say you loved her. Like brother and sister, *pues*."

"... In my head, it started to seem like it had happened, Moya. That was the worst part of all that time after. I got secretly obsessed with it, trying to imagine this whole other life starting with that afternoon when it almost did, I think."

"Yes, I see, a missed opportunity. *Qué lástima, vos.*"

"A missed opportunity." This time even I had to laugh. "Is that all you think it is?"

"*Pues sí,*" he said. "Or—what else?"

Or what else . . . ?

"But she told the girls in her dorm at Wellesley that we had! But I mean, what an invention! *Why?* Well, to scandalize them, obviously, to make herself seem"—I shrugged—"the most interesting. She'd waited a long time to get to college."

"Yes, to scandalize them." Moya was silent for a moment. A moment later he said, "And then telling all these stories, she came home for summer, and thought one day, Well, why not? And you missed your opportunity."

"I wasn't even sure . . ."

"Maybe neither was she. That's what she was like sometimes, getting an idea in her head and then another one. You can see in her notebook that she considered marrying *el negro ése,* the football player. Maybe if he had asked her at the right moment, no, *vos?*"

"So what, is what you're saying. So what if I found myself in this really horrible head, thinking I was in—had been in love with her. So were you. Except, I don't know, it's more than that. It's been like my whole life."

". . . Yes, that is true," he said gloomily. "I didn't have a Flor in my whole life. So yes, *claro* . . . But the true question, Rogerio, is the same as always. Who was Flor? Truly, who was she? It was not so easy for her as for you to become 'just a Namoset kid,' eh?"

It was almost like he was saying, Who cares about *you*—about me, I mean. Especially since I'd never even let him tell *me* all about him and you, Flor. Though we did finally kind of get to that too, and to everything else, there in the Omni.

*   *   *

Even if my life during those first seven months after Flor's death was gloomy and privately estranged anyway, that was to be expected, it was what life was now. Then that girl, I don't even know her name, came into the bar while I was working one night; came in out of the blue, not pink haired anymore but artificially auburned and black tipped, on one of those hot early September nights, wearing a low-cut black minidress that set off her strikingly porcelain white skin, bared shoulders small cleavage and small yellowish eyes in such a way that she seemed to glow from within with refrigerated light. In her late twenties now, at least. She was by herself, and jittery seeming. Maybe she was on cocaine, and was on her way to something late-night and had stopped in for a drink to settle her nerves, or to meet someone, or just to pass the time. She had the brightly opaque gaze of some tiny animal creeping up to the edge of a clearing. We recognized each other right away.

"I know who you are You're—"

"Roger," I said. "You were at Flor's—"

"—funeral, uh-huh," she said softly, her eyes fixed too brazenly on mine. "We were friends at Wellesley." A moment later she giggled as if at a hidden meaning in our short exchange that had passed me by.

And I thought, Oh boy, what a wacko, that's all—though instantly and even bemusedly recalling an editorial that had run in a Guatemalan newspaper during the two days my father and I were here, which I remember almost word for word even now:

Wellesley College, world famous as a definer and inculcator of the most refined feminine values, the very same institution that prizes among its many distinguished alumnae Madame Chiang Kaishek of China, the star of the beloved movie *Love Story*, several Miss Universes, and Señora Fernanda Vieyra de Paredes, that *siempre bella exponente* of Guatemalan woman-

hood. To these very outstanding *damas* of Wellesley College
in particular one sympathizing editorialist wishes to convey
the assurance that one falling star does not dim the brilliance
of the constellation . . .

You see what happens to Wellesley girls? I practically sneered to
myself, though not out loud.

"Well, what can I get you?" That's all I said, coolly and
politely enough; she asked for a Stoli on the rocks. I got the drink
for her, didn't even charge her, and went on working. And because
I was aware of her unsettling eyes following me the whole time, I
made myself even more exaggeratedly extroverted a bartender
than usual, which was perhaps the wrong strategy, for I can see
now how that, along with the free drink, must have invited the
transgression.

She sat there sipping her vodka, watching me, smiling and
smirking away to herself as if over some bit of excited, sneaky cleverness. She was a little deranged or mad, and cocaine, if that's what
it was, wasn't helping her, that's what I thought. Then I glanced
at her and asked, a little exasperatedly, "What's so funny?"

But she just smirked and kept looking at me. I went back to
working my way up and down the bar. Finally I just stopped in
front of her and almost shouted, "What?"

And she laughed again, and softly said, "Oh, I was just remembering." Then I knew that she was about to say something
about you and felt dismally trapped since, after all, I had just demanded that she tell it.

"She used to talk about you a lot," she said, and it made her
feel so gleeful to say this that her bare shoulders wriggled.

"Uh-huh," I said.

"You were like my hero, one of my heroes for a while. I can't
believe it. Funny, isn't it?"

"I was your hero?"

"Well, you know how girls get in college, dorm talk, all night long, the big confessions," she said, leaning as close as she could to me across the bar, practically hoisting herself up on it, her slightly nasal, confusingly earnest yet ironical voice lowered to a near whisper now, her eyes fixed not on me but on something off to the side. "It was beautiful. And what a drama! All those years and your parents never suspected? So strange and secret, lovely and hidden, pure and very naughty at the same time. Was it like between mother and son, or servant and little master? Or like incest, but it wasn't really, because you weren't siblings and incest really is kind of fucked up and creepy anyway, and the way Flor told it was so beautiful. I was sad it was over, except on our floor it wasn't over, it was soap opera *número uno*—"

It wasn't true, and I said so. What else could I say? Well, imagine how I felt then, how this just impacted on *everything,* instantly. Stunned isn't enough. Poisoned! And for her to be so fliply sentimental, casual!

"It's not true," I said. It wasn't. I gave my head a little shuddering shake, as if to make her feel that she was just some kind of trivially bad dream. I didn't know what else to say. Nothing remotely like this had ever happened to me before (well, not since my Colegio Anne Hunt days, but that was just kids' stuff!). She's sick, just walk away, I told myself. But she, who was a most eloquent smirker anyway, who had as many smirks in her repertoire as Eskimos have words for snow, smirked as if she wasn't surprised that I was denying it.

"Flor always said you'd been sworn to secrecy or something," she said. "Oh, you poor guy! But, come on, we all thought it was pretty cool, pretty beautiful. We were scandalized too, you know, but trying so hard to show we weren't."

"Well, that was the point," I said, managing, really, to stay surprisingly calm. "To scandalize you girls. Impress you. Can't you see that? She'd waited forever to get to college, and I guess she figured out pretty fast what would make her the center of attention. That's all."

"But really, what was there to be scandalized about?" she asked, as if she thought we were actually going to have a conversation about it. "You weren't related, she wasn't adopted. She was just older—"

And then, just like that, I lost my temper, my voice became heated. "Look, what is this? Don't you think this is kind of disrespectful? Is this why you came to the funeral? You and Flor hadn't stayed friends. Because I know where you're coming from, Flor-corrupting whatever—" And *she* was blinking now as if my every sputtering syllable was *a* slap in her face. "You like evil. Like it's the very *coolest* thing, right? Look, I'm going to have to ask you to leave."

"Evil? I didn't say there was anything *evil* about it. God. Hardly. The opposite's more like it. Well, like I told you. Oh c'mon!" She seemed truly taken aback, this foolish girl. "We were friends in college, that's why I came to the funeral. I was . . ." She looked like she was about to cry.

But I went on. "Evil has caused a lot of hurt in my and my family's lives, I mean true evil, a murder, for example, not the kind you people find so hip and aesthetic. That's why you were at the funeral." I felt convinced, at that very moment, that she was very evil, and that she had come to the funeral to revel in it in some voyeuristic way, because she thought *you* had turned out to be evil too.

"*We people?* What—Oh please, man, take it easy. I just thought, you know, what are you so ashamed of?"

"I'm not ashamed of anything," I said. "I think you should leave. You are cut off."

"Look, I'm sorry. I can see—I'm totally indiscreet sometimes, OK? I didn't mean to—I thought. Oh—"

It surprised me that she was so upset, but it only angered me more, I'd really lost it by then. "Go complain to the manager if you want, but I want you out of here!"

"Jesus, I apologize, OK? Good-bye. Listen to me! Flor was great, we all loved her so much. This is so fucked up, I didn't mean anything by it. I didn't! OK?"

"What'll it be?" I said to another customer, who'd probably overheard the entire conversation, and then she left, she just turned and walked rapidly out of the bar, and left me there, kind of a different person now, again (kind of a different bartender too, in another fifteen minutes or so the manager would quietly relieve me of my duties for the night), flooded with a resurrected confusion, the long-buried, nearly buried, memory of one day during the first summer you were home from college, me fifteen, I'd just finished mowing the lawn, and then come in through the basement and through your door. You with a white towel around your torso, sitting in front of your desk blow-drying your hair. Oh well, you know, just the way our eyes met. Something solemn or dangerous beyond words. I said, "Oops! Should've knocked," and you smiled and in that voice, soft and atonal and somehow so like the voice in which a few years before you'd said that what you wanted for Christmas was for my father to get better, false but not false—you said, "Oh, you don't have to knock when you come into my room, Roger." And that look. "OK," I said, my face burning. And then I flew up the stairs. And it was never mentioned again. I thought it was all in my imagination, we always looked at each other with a certain affection, so what was new now? Nothing? You're turning into a handsome man, Roger. Well, so what? Even my mother said that sometimes. And you, with a college girl fantasy in your head, that's all—a game, a dare, a probing will to make a delicious fairy tale that had worked so well on your circle of admirers at college come true? What a splendid way to wrap up the actual story of your life with us! Or did you decide quickly that there was no need to, that *telling* it was good enough? Moya's right, who cares? Who would ever have cared if that girl hadn't come into my bar? Why would I ever have given it much more thought? Why should one striking though highly ambiguous declaration—which after all might simply have been meant in an innocently rhetorical way, as in, Oh, you don't have to knock! We're like family!—have come to so haunt me? Have come to fill me with the sensation of living *in* a secret and impermissible ghost story? Have come to give the what never happened a life of its own alongside what did? Why else, if not for the perhaps innocent or guileless—if also slyly malicious—indiscretion of one depraved and ditzy or just utterly voyeuristic once-pink-haired girl, would I ever have found myself wanting to make such a confession to Moya? And then it turned out not to mean that much, not to be the burdening truth I had thought it was at all! A missed opportunity, that's all . . . ? But not quite, because of how it lived on inside of me—

Well, I'd just come back from the highlands, and there is something about Indian towns that provokes a mood of thinking that the truth lies somewhere outside what you actually see and hear anyway, though what you see and hear is certainly there. Partly it's the pagan-mystical atmosphere of their religious practices, an impression enforced by the famous Indian reticence regarding that and almost everything else. And there's that widely repeated, and so often misproven, allegedly traditional Indian belief that "white" people aren't actually there, that we are part of the illusory world. And the silence of the mist-mountains, the silent solitude of Indian towns, at night especially.

I'd been traveling through the highlands for about a week already, full of silence myself, rarely exchanging more than a few words with anyone, when I stopped in Chichicastenango for the big Thursday market. It was there that a new kind of silence overwhelmed me.

The market, which used to be popular with tourists back when there were a lot of tourists, was closing down in the plaza. I was watching from church steps, surrounded by softly cajoling Indian incantations: the day's last worshipers swinging smoking copal-incense censers, splashing *aguardiente* over the small fires they built on the steps, talking in that very personal way to gods, ancestors, spirits. But what was most striking was the disconcerting quietness of the scene in front of me.

Indians from all over El Quiché were busy packing up their market in the dirt plaza at the end of just another unfruitful market day, that's all. They were dismantling their stalls, putting their unsold produce into baskets and sacks, wrapping big loads with tarp and rope. They were packing everything up and carrying it all off piece by heavy piece on their backs, unimaginable loads packed onto their stooped backs and held by straps around foreheads and other loads balanced on heads. Everybody seemed to be moving in slow motion. From the elevation of those steps, I watched moving patterns: the warm colors of *trajes,* black-haired heads, the whites of eyes strained upwards as if reaching to touch the protruding edges of the loads on their backs, and small clouds of kicked-up dirt under their feet. It was a melancholy scene, and very quiet. The creaking noises floating through the air sounded like they came from the strained rigging of a big three-masted ship in a strong wind, but this was only the creaking of so many loads and bundles strapped to the backs and heads of people carrying away their market.

But really it was the light that looked laid over them, over the plaza, that seemed like the actual place that this silence reverberated from, instead of from the people underneath it. An indescribable late-afternoon light was pouring through the white clouds, gauzy but evenly spread across the still-brilliant sky, and an orange sun was falling behind the mountains. The light was a most unusual, almost pumpkin-colored gold, but only just over the market, where it seemed to thicken semitranslucently, as if from the raised dust and drifting incense and even the shadows of the two bleached white churches on the plaza and the darkening mountains all around. It lay over the market, so still and golden, infusing every face and wretched posture.

I know what a religious painter would have made of it—the light of God accompanying the poor. It made their "suffering" stand out as if in a frieze, in a way that went beyond dignifying it. I could see how some people might think they were having a revelation at a moment like this. But wasn't it meaningless, just a natural accident, the light, I mean, not the people? Just a trick of shadow and dust and sinking highland sun. And not the suffering, of which there was evidence everywhere: the acrid rotting stench, the sweaty, shitty stink of poverty, the vista of so many bent, shuffling people consumed by the same staggering task, carrying their market on their backs to where buses waited on side streets, others facing long hikes home to mountain villages and *aldeas* miles away; stunted bodies of a race inverted and mocked by the healthier, brawnier, even chubbier physiques of the conscripted young Indian soldiers, who were well fed, barracks toughened and demented—I haven't mentioned that there were soldiers around the plaza, with their automatic weapons, strolling about in that aimlessly menacing way of soldiers in a garrison town. Well, there are always soldiers, everywhere. But it was only in the last year that the army had started letting nuns and priests back into El Quiché: right there in Chichi, a Peace Corps girl had told me at lunch that very day, they'd recently given back the Spanish priests' rectory on the outskirts of town that they'd requisitioned at the height of the war, except the Indians refused to go inside it anymore, not even to visit the newly returned Spanish priests, because of all the people they knew who had been tortured to death in the rectory when it had belonged to the army, so they were just leaving lighted candles for the souls of the dead outside the front door. (The Peace Corps girl, Cindy, from Wisconsin, had come into my nearly empty hotel for lunch and recognized me from her occasional weekends in the city, from the "gringo bar," Lord Byron's, and, though all that about the priests and nuns is the sort of thing no one would ever dare talk about in Lord Byron's, I'd managed, over the course of lunch, to convince her that "I'm not really like that," so she'd let herself talk—)

But if it hadn't been for that light and the way it had seemed to lay a separate dimension over the scene of the market closing up, a separate something that seemed to blend suffering, silence, faith—that light that looked like their companion—I know I wouldn't have felt so shaken, or maybe *moved* is the word, by what I'd seen, I might not even have noticed the silence. Maybe I would have thought, Poverty, soldiers, nuns and priests, torture, what else is new? Because if my months in Guatemala hadn't accustomed me to being at least aware of *that,* hadn't bred *that* silence inside of me . . . (Because who would want to listen to *me* go on about it down *here?* I used to talk about it much more when I was still *up there.* So that *down here,* when I find myself silently talking about it, I'm usually imagining someone listening *up there!*)

Then the light went away, and soon there was just the nearly empty market, with corrugated metal and plastic sheeting–roofed permanent stalls left standing, and steel gates rolled down over the fronts of the permanent shops along the plaza, and soldiers and the faint rotting smells mixed with lingering incense, and the silence that I couldn't let go of.

When I went back to those church steps after dinner and reencountered that empty silence—only it was even emptier now because almost everyone was gone and it was dark, bats twirling through that dark like fiendishly dancing roof tiles—after I'd been sitting there awhile, why did I think of my family and Flor?

Well, of course Flor was very much on my mind. Because of what Cindy had told me, I was trying to decide whether or not to take the long bus ride up to Nebaj, to see if I might find the nuns Flor had referred to during one of her earlier visits to New York. But there was something else that Cindy had told me. She said that whenever she tried to ride her bicycle out to the more remote *aldeas* in her jurisdiction and was approaching the entrance to one of those hamlets, Indians often ambushed her from the cornfields along the roads, throwing rocks and dirt clumps until she turned back. She'd been confused about why until a nun—"Believe me, only the nuns ever know what's *really* going down out here," Cindy said, exactly as you might have, Flor—told her it was because they'd all heard the stories about gringas coming to Indian villages to steal children. This anecdote had nothing to do with you, of course. You didn't do that. But it reddened my face anyway, as if it was an actual piece of damning evidence.

Sitting on those steps in the chilled night air, facing the plaza, I suddenly found myself trying to imagine what my family would have been like if you had never come to live with us. But I couldn't really imagine it. The frustration I felt was that same childish one of lying on my back in the yard trying to imagine the end of the stars. I had the thought that my family should never have happened at all, and then, as if in a silent panic, dismissed this nihilistic notion. But I could only imagine a silence, and then all of us as a product of that silence, our lives willfully built up and maintained around it, by you, Flor—somehow maintained by you. So that you could one day go to college.

That's when I suddenly remembered my father's gallbladder attack and your standing in front of F. A. O. Schwarz saying, "I just want Ira to get better."

That jarring little note was caused not by the artificiality of the sentiment, but by the unconscious truth that artificiality was essential to what we had, and lay like silence near the heart of everything, and made everything seem possible—made even lies seem not very different from nonlies. What 1 mean is, I realized you couldn't help it. That was your innocence. The love was real. But maybe you had no other way of expressing the life that had been given to you, or of really knowing it, except by pushing on the boundaries of that artificiality, trying to find where it began and where it ended.

But it was as if there was another life too, the one that would have happened if you'd never come to live with us. I had the sense of a true history developing, our true and invisible fate, always happening, unseen, alongside this other one, our silent companion, like the light I had seen over the market. And I wondered if maybe you had always or finally heard it calling you back.

TWENTY-TWO

"The de Preys are extremely wealthy . . . ," you wrote in the notebook that Moya bribed from the National Police archives while I was away on that same trip through the highlands; the de Preys being the French couple who'd come to Guatemala to adopt three-year-old María de la Luz Caycam Quix, originally from a small *cantón* in the municipality of Nebaj in the Ixil Triangle region of El Quiché, which I did in fact get up to, by bus from Chichi. ". . . Marcel, 35, is a businessman, and Nancy, 27, is a student and future full-time mother. Very loving, I believe, and so sophisticated, of course, and quite very beautiful. They are not overboard Catholics, but they intend a private Catholic education, as these are the best girls' schools in Paris. Nancy de Prey believes little children should begin learning Latin and to play piano even before starting school. This sounds farfetched, one of those things a well-meaning young mother will never get around to. I'd worry about them being overexacting, but come on, they're French, they want to be taken very seriously, but they are quick to laugh and are pleasantly surprised by the French restaurants here, thus capable of optimists' delusions despite themselves. They go quietly goo-goo whenever they see María de la Luz. They will be patient and loving with her no matter what, I know. They even intend to keep her name María de la Luz, or Marie de la Luz anyway."

And that was all, a typical notebook entry, in your own poised though somewhat bulbous print. It gave no other information except the date, February 3, 1983, which made it the last adoption you finalized. I realize now that means it happened sometime around the end of your affair with Moya, though he said he couldn't recall it or any other adoption, specifically. We'd only lingered over that entry, without even the slightest premonition of what it would come to mean later, because it was the last one, and because Nancy de Prey had given her occupation as student and is French. Moya thought that the de Preys might be the parents of the little girl he thinks he recognized playing in a snowy yard in Cambridge, because when the black-bearded man who was apparently the girl's father came out of that home's front door and picked her up in his arms, Moya heard him call her *"Poupon."* But the notebook named thirteen parents of both sexes who listed their occupation as student, three of them French, any one of whom might have ended up at Harvard and picked up that catchy French term of endearment, *Poupon.* Moya might just have *thought* that he recognized that girl and that she recognized him back, but any Guatemalan or Central American adopted orphan playing in a snowy yard in Cambridge might have provoked that hallucination.

But Flor, what a mess would have greeted you at Los Quetzalitos one afternoon (if you'd lived and stayed on . . .) when, just over four months ago now, in January, Sor Clarita came to the door with a Polaroid snapshot of an adult Ixil Indian couple in rags: Señor Caycam and Señora Quix de Caycam.

I realize, as did Sor Clarita of course, that you'd had no way of knowing that María de la Luz's and Lucas's parents were still alive, since Sor Clarita, when she'd turned the children over to you, had told you the parents were dead, believing it to be so herself, having even procured death certificates from the municipal authorities in Nebaj and encouraged you to find the children a loving home abroad if you could, since what future did they have here?

More than three years later the Caycams turned up alive— brought down by the army from the Cuchumatanes Mountains and interned along with the rest of their captured band of nomadic internal refugees in A'tzumbal, Camp "New Life" in Ixil, just outside Nebaj. Sor Clarita had found them there on one of her routine missions of charity and unofficial census taking through the model villages and military holding centers for refugees, which was why she was carrying the Polaroid, though the last thing she'd expected to photograph was a miracle. At first their surnames, Caycam and Quix, prompted no recognition; but by the time they'd finished telling how two of their four children had perished in an ambush during their flight into the mountains three years before, and that they'd never been able to establish the fate of the other two but that another internal refugee, formerly of their same *cantón,* claimed to have heard from someone else that the two children had been captured alive in the mountains and brought down to Nebaj and turned over to the nuns shortly before the expulsion of all Catholic priests and nuns from El Quiché, Sor Clarita knew exactly who the Caycams were. Tearfully, she confessed her own role in the transferring of María de la Luz and Lucas to a Guatemala City orphanage. The Caycams, of course, were overjoyed.

The next day Sor Clarita rode the bus all the way to the capital, a twelve-hour journey, and went directly to Los Quetzalitos to confirm her own worst fears: that she had found the parents of two children who you, through no fault of your own, had apparently allowed to be adopted abroad. Rosana Letones has no records of the adoptions you arranged and so couldn't tell Sor Clarita who in the world had adopted little María de la Luz and her older brother Lucas. But the Caycams, miserable as their circumstances now were, naturally wanted their children back. And what God makes, no one has a right to sever. Which was why cheerful and brave Sor Clarita was now kind of in hot water with her order over the screwup. She had no other recourse but to head off to the family court when it opened the next morning, hoping against hope to find a record of the adoptions in whatever bureaucratic mess awaited her there. But, as I'd already met Sor Clarita in Nebaj, and she alone knew of my connection to you, she phoned to tell me of the calamity. I told her to meet me right away in Pastelería Hemmings so that I could show her the illicitly acquired notebook, which so far had served no investigative purpose, and of course there it was: María de la Luz Caycam Quix, then three years old, adopted by the de Preys of Paris after having spent almost two full years in Los Quetzalitos. But no mention of her brother Lucas.

So where was Lucas, Flor? Why wasn't Lucas mentioned in your notebook?

"Ah pues. There must be some mistake" is what Sor Clarita said, of course. We were at one of the mezzanine tables in Pastelería Hemmings, having coffee and oatmeal cookies. Sor Clarita wears a grayish blue habit, cut like a nurses' uniform with the hem below the knees, and one of those modern headcloths with little more drapery than a French Foreign Legionnaire's cap. Pulling her hair back behind its tight band, the headcloth frames her round Indian face in a way that helps to lend her features a frank expressiveness. When Sor Clarita and I had talked about you in Nebaj, I'd only seen stubborn loyalty, even love, and a kind of friendly humor in those eyes, as if whenever she thought of you she remembered some risqué joke you'd once shared; I saw sadness in them too, of course. But a tragic and unjust fate, which she surely thought yours was, was nothing new to Sor Clarita. She preferred to save her laments for the scarcity of medicines and even corn among the little the military was allowing the nuns to distribute to the refugees. And because of her affectionate opinion of you, Flor, I'd left Nebaj feeling almost as secure about your true activities in Guatemala as I had when you were alive.

But now, over the notebook in Pastelería Hemmings, Sor Clarita's eyes looked suddenly clouded with perplexity and an even deeper disorientation. And my face reddened as it always does whenever, beneath the surface of whatever is happening or being said, your death suddenly reasserts itself like a haunting presence: a demon-you who won't go away, always still out there, forever reenacting the crimes that were attributed to you and taunting me with their obscure logic—because why no Lucas?

It's against the law, of course, Florcita, *niña perdida,* even in Guat, to separate siblings by adoption—prohibited in accordance not just with common morality but as a precaution against the mortal sin of accidental incest too. Did you tell the de Preys about Lucas? Had you ever spoken to Lucas Caycam Quix to ask for his permission to send his little sister to Paris or to tell him that he could go too? Where was Lucas, Flor?

"I'm sure that when I go to the French embassy, they will tell me that Lucas went with his sister to France," said Sor Clarita, collecting herself, a strained brightness in her voice. "La Flor forgot to write it down. She was like that, no? Once when I was visiting, *fíjese,* she forgot where she parked her van. *Uff,* we had to walk up and down streets—"

"Lucas is definitely not with the de Preys in Paris, Sor Clarita," I interrupted, quietly. "*That* she would have written down."

I thought then, We'll never find him. I knew it already. But there was never going to be a way to just dismiss the riddle of Lucas, because he had definitely been taken to Los Quetzalitos, and his sister was definitely adopted by the de Preys, and his parents were definitely alive and wanted *both* their children back, and Sor Clarita definitely found herself in a mess that would embroil her for months.

"Maybe he ran away," I said to Sor Clarita in Pastelería Hemmings. "Flor had some runaways, I remember her saying so. Maybe he didn't like being in an orphanage, or didn't want to go to Paris. And Flor went ahead and let María de la Luz be adopted because she thought it was best for her. Or best in some other way."

Sor Clarita put her hand over her mouth, as if to stop *me* from saying the unspeakable—that the *other way* might have been that the de Preys simply offered a lot of money. Of course it's always much more difficult to find adopting parents for a three-year-old Indian girl when she comes with a thirteen-year-old brother attached. But that still didn't explain what you'd done with Lucas. (I reject, out of hand, and did so from the start, any possibility that you could have "eliminated" Lucas to make his sister more adoptable.) Or maybe Sor Clarita covered her mouth because she'd suddenly foreseen what an exhausting and unrewarding quest she herself was now embarking on. It would have been almost impossible for her to say so out loud, I think, but didn't she have more important matters to deal with, so many people up there in the Ixil who needed her more urgently? But Sor Clarita had no choice now but to take responsibility for what she had innocently set in motion nearly four years before. Her mother superior had apparently seen to that, and with reason, because the reputation and even the security of the order's mission in Guatemala could be at stake. It would be a disaster if the avowed enemies of the Church, of nuns in the highlands in particular, were ever able to provide the press with a sensationalistic excuse to denounce Las Hermanas de San Vicente Paul as accomplices in the violation of adoption laws and even in the baby trade. It wouldn't even be beyond them to fly the Caycams, should they grow disgruntled enough, by helicopter to the capital for a press conference before the Constituent Assembly.

"Or maybe something happened to him," I said. "Maybe he died, Sor Clarita, and so it was perfectly legal for her to let María de la Luz be adopted. When you get in touch with the de Preys, they'll know all about it."

"Wouldn't she have written that in her notebook too?" Sor Clarita asked, her voice nuanced with hope. Her hand, perhaps instinctively, came up to grasp the plain wooden crucifix on her chest.

"Maybe not. It wasn't an official record or anything, she kept it just for herself, I guess." I slid the notebook towards her again, and her worried eyes followed as if it might suddenly jump up and bite. "But look at this, where Flor wrote, *No matter what . . .* Maybe that means something? Maybe Lucas is the *what?*"

And we both leaned close over the notebook, to look again at where you had written: "They will be patient and loving with her no matter what, I know." Here your enthusiasm had probably just bubbled over into an obvious banality, I thought. But I ran my finger back and forth under the small printed words as if trying to tease another meaning out of them.

Then Sor Clarita leaned back with a flummoxed sigh and stared gloomily at her oatmeal cookie as she dunked it rapidly in and out of now tepid coffee; fresh oatmeal cookies would be a rare treat in Nebaj, and she'd eaten her first one enthusiastically and without dunking it, smiling shyly as she chewed despite the business at hand.

I felt my eyes sting and searched frantically for something appropriate to say. This was real, not one of Moya's hypothetical scenarios, not another fabulation of silence, love, and shadows. A missing boy, and no one to implicate but you.

"We'll find him," I said, though I felt sure we wouldn't. "I'll help you any way I can, Sor Clarita."

"When I first saw that *patojo* carrying his baby sister in his arms, do you know what I thought?" Sor Clarita suddenly blurted. "That the soldiers must have captured them from wolves."

And then she told me the terrible story of what had happened to Lucas and María de la Luz in the Cuchumatanes Mountains, and I listened unaware that I was following the first footprints in a long trail that wouldn't reach an end until I stood on the Incienso Bridge nearly a week ago, waiting for a flesh-and-blood phantom to show himself at last. Up to that moment almost everything I'd been able to learn or deduce about your fate I'd found in what had come to seem the only worthwhile place to search: the ever-spreading silence and invisibility underneath everything here. Maybe that's another reason I left the bridge that day—not just premonitory fear: I didn't need a new explanation because I thought I already understood.

Moya, in his bitterest moods, used to say that one thing that went wrong with you was that you came back here, period. He thought that at Harvard he'd seen firsthand the life you gave up. Why fly away from the "American Dream" opportunities handed to you to go flitting around the dark side? What sense was there in that? But I'd *always* known why you did; I think now it was as simple as I'd always claimed. I knew why again as soon as I walked into Los Quetzalitos for the first time and encountered your clamoring horde of *peepee*-reeking orphans and I knew it even before that when I went to Nebaj from Chichicastenango, which was when I'd first met Sor Clarita, talking to her in the penetrating shadow of a military garrison surrounding the convent house that the order had only been allowed to reoccupy in the last year, recalling Sor Clarita from Bolivia. The garrison literally surrounded it, so that villagers had to pass two military checkpoints just to reach the convent door; inside the nuns could sometimes hear the screams of prisoners being tortured to death on the other side of the dining-room wall, they'd even made a tape recording of it to play for their bishop if he ever came to visit, not that there was a thing even he could have done about it. They'd held a little tape recorder like a stethoscope right up to that wall for that pain-and terror-maddened man screaming as if stranded all by himself at the bottom of a deep well, an unreachable well dug into the moon. Sor Clarita played it for me that night, a voice faintly screaming and howling between long gaps of silence from a small tape recorder atop a pine table in an austere nuns' dining room, not because she thought there was anything *I* could do about it, Flor, but because she had loved and trusted *you* and so just wanted me to know in the same way she would have wanted you to know, that's all. Four nuns were living there, in the little convent house called Medalla Milagrosa (Miraculous Medal) behind the church without a priest and an army garrison spread all around, but only one who had known you. And they only felt safe enough to talk when they were alone in the dining room upstairs, because who knew who might be an informer among the Indian girls in their beautiful red *cortes* who came to sew charity clothing in the dirt patio or the Indian men who came to chop firewood and the others who came for domestic advice or to ask for medicine or to confess or just to talk, or even among the catechists? So foreign visitors with prying questions were not their favorite kind of visitor, but luckily it was Sor Clarita who answered the door when I knocked at it, when I said, for the first time since I've been here, "My name is Roger Graetz, Flor de Mayo Puac grew up in my house in the United States." And Sor Clarita's bushy eyebrows went up in startled consternation. "Flor de Mayo, *la pobre,*" she said softly, and then put her finger over her coarsened lips. *"Pase,"* she said, and I came in, and spent the rest of the day with her, helping in her ceaseless chores, though all she really had to tell me then was that yes, she had handed over children to you before; she didn't really elaborate and there was no reason for her to then, because the Caycams hadn't turned up alive yet.

The mountains all around, with black pine–forested slopes darkened by the fog and mists spread over them like the tattered wings of predatory silver birds, concealed refugees who had fled into them to escape counterinsurgency, the notorious massacres, crop burnings, mass rapes, and pillagings that had already resulted in the complete unpeopling and abandoning of four hundred plus highland villages in five years. Tens of thousands of people had been living in and wandering the remotest valleys of the Cuchumatanes and the jungles of the Ixcan for years now, moving by night, sleeping in caves or in deep forest by day, living on roots, leaves, tiny forest creatures when they could catch them (which is how Lucas and his baby sister had survived too), sometimes stopping to plant some corn in the hope that the army wouldn't come before it could be harvested and burn it to prevent the guerrillas from eating; trying to evade army bombardments, for often the army did not distinguish between fleeing columns of guerrillas and those of refugees, believing them to be one and the same, especially since it was originally the guerrillas who had promised the refugees protection, declaring it a "liberated zone" like the so far unconquerable ones in the even smaller, neighboring country to the south. This one was conquerable, and the refugees were often abandoned by their protectors and sentries, even as they slept and an army incursion approached. They were bringing refugees into Nebaj by the truckload the two days I was there, jamming them into model villages for "reeducation," teaching them that they had actually fled into the mountains to escape the guerrillas and that they were forgiven now for the illogical error of fleeing guerrillas by going to hide where the guerrillas were, because they were just dumb gullible *indios* anyway but now they had a chance for a *New Life!* But the army was still turning the sickest children over to the nuns first because the nuns insisted. I saw a group of twelve when I helped Sor Clarita carry sacks of food and plastic plates from the market to the holding shed where the army had confined them, some still accompanied by their parents, their clothing in shreds and their hair falling out from malnourishment, their eyes liquid with infections, faces and limbs covered with sores and mountain leprosy; that's how Lucas and his baby sister had been brought down three years before, when they had been captured among the wandering remnants of a fleeing village that had been scattered by simultaneous bombardment and ambush on their way to Mexico. Lucas's parents (Sor Clarita had believed) and two siblings had been killed there, but in the chaos he'd managed to lift his infant sister, María de la Luz, from the cloth in which his dying sister had been carrying her on her back; later Son Clarita would insist that Lucas had been sure his parents had died too and the others with him had confirmed it, because so few had escaped that massacre, just as so few escaped so many massacres. Over time, Sor Clarita would realize that Lucas's story wasn't unique at all.

That day I spent with her in Nebaj, Sor Clarita collected from every one of her new refugees the same appalling story that, in the remote region they'd been marched down from, the routed guerrillas were so disoriented they were running around trying to sell salt to refugees for sixty *centavos* an ounce. But in the market, at the stall where Sor Clarita stopped to buy plastic bowls and plates for her new refugees, she asked the vendor to give her bowls and plates in every assorted color but green. "No green?" I repeated as I waited by her side, and then I knew why before she even answered, remembering the old no-war-toy policy you had revoked for G.I. Joes at Macy's that day. *"Es el color del ejército, pues,"* Sor Clarita whispered as we walked away from the stall, the color of the army, *pues* . . .

So what went wrong, Flor? I think I know why you stayed, and when I left Nebaj I thought I knew it better than ever. You could even have counted yourself as lucky, you didn't have to feel helpless, you were offered the directorship of an orphanage and malnutrition clinic. It was too late to go home because you'd already come and seen; you knew and had forgotten that *"Guatemala no existe"* and then lost "all perspective," living with a small country like it was a sick but curable person. So this felt right: an orphanage and malnutrition clinic was something you could put your heart and soul into, it was *you* all over. And though it wasn't righteous destruction and it wasn't social change, it *was* preservation—of little victimized lives. But preserving them for what? An inhuman question, only a demagogue would ask it, but there are plenty of those, and, anyway, a lot of these kids carried very important memories, memories that if well sheltered might even grow strong and hot enough to melt the fake movie snow of politicians, might even grow strong and audacious enough to lead a highly spiritual and vanquishing army down from the volcanoes. It was something to *do,* it could even be made to fit the big picture: the nuns turned endangered children over to you, you traveled right into the heart of the war zones to receive them sometimes, you involved foreign embassies in your health care abroad program and thus involved entire nations in the plight of little survivors. You did some adoptions but were fastidious about it, looking for the most healing and fertile soil for haunted and potentially very powerful memories—all that's fine, it's wonderful, even if a bit nutty, because, after all, later, not *one* of your orphans had any memory at all of Lucas Caycam Quix.

What I don't know is what went wrong or why, though I suspect now it wasn't so different from what Moya so feared in himself: the simple despair, hopelessness, and tedium, the germy dog bite of defeat. Which can always be overcome, because the strong persevere and heal, but there will always be that dangerous time when for a while it seems to blacken and *undo* everything.

TWENTY-THREE

"Cómo?" exclaimed Moya, in the Omni. *"Vos, cómo?* . . . You mean calling her back to Guatemala, *vos?"*

"No, not that exactly. I'm talking about who she was. At her most real, she felt artificial too, or something like that."

"Superficial?"

"I heard her say this once. All on the surface."

"Sometimes I think we sound like Rocky and Bullwinkle together."

". . . *Quiénes?"*

"Hey, Buliwinkle, you're right! Flor was never just a Namoset kid! She was *two* people!"

". . . *Una esquizofre'nica, vos."*

"No, because the other one was silent, invisible. Like when a guy gets his arm amputated but can still feel that it's there, still attached to him? He looks, and it's not there? It's as if he's two people, the other one still walking around with two arms, doing entirely different things, but where? He can't know. He just senses that he's happier or at least more complete somewhere else."

"Ah, bueno. So, today, the death squad did kill us. We are dead, *vos.* I can feel that this is so. Here we sit, in a hotel for *putas,* talking *babosadas.* But, *gracias a Dios,* we are happier than the dead Moya and Rogerio, who cannot see us."

"Yeah, something like that. But see?—*not* because Flor came from here and so could never really find a true Flor up there, and so had to come back here. That's not it. But because of what we were like, who we were . . . I don't know. I don't know what I mean."

* * *

Because of the way it happened. Because of the way we became almost a happy family. During that very first year, my unhappy mother poured her heart out to the silent, terrified, barely adolescent girl, though she would hate to admit that now. It was futile, what could that little girl say?—her disquieted eyes already imposing a silence on my mother, because what else did that girl know how to say and how else did she know how to say it but in the brightly atonal, hopeful, false but not false voice that said, "Ay Doña Mirabel. You will be happy soon, I am sure. Don Ira is so nice. Roger should have happy parents."

Before Flor knew it she'd become something like our idiot savant matriarch, our young foundling mother, daughter too. It's true, my parents, all of us, eventually found ourselves outwardly behaving as if living up to Flor's expectations of what we should be. Her personality was somehow stronger, soft-handedly molding us, showing us the way with none of Abuelita's stridence or mania for order. If Flor had never come to live with us, if my father hadn't put her in school and then everything else, would there ever even have been a normal conversation at our dinner table? What on earth would we have talked about?

Instead, we had Flor telling us about her trips into Boston, about what was on sale in Filene's Basement last week, about school, about the last book she'd read, about why she preferred the Princeton campus to the one at Cornell, about boys, about Tony when he was still considered "OK." And because Flor did all the housework and looked after me, this freed my mother to spend the time she needed on her college degree in Boston, and then on her job as Spanish teacher and Foreign Students Club and Romance Language Club director at Shreve Hall, the girls' private boarding school in Dover. Miss Cavanaugh was on the board of directors there (she was on the board at Wellesley College too), and that connection led to the Latin American Society of Boston, which

Miss Cavanaugh was the founder of, and to other social invitations where my mother never had to try to act American. That is, at Shreve Hall, she could be in her Empire of Nostalgia and the Kingdom of her Pride and earn a salary at the same time, and at the Latin American Society, be in it and socialize. Outside the house, my mother recovered her still youthful ebullience and developed her own will; it was as if *her* true life was out there, and then she could wear this new life home, where Flor helped her to sustain it by being just enough her Guatemalan maid.

Despite their rivalry, which became more pronounced over the years, Flor and my mother often seemed like old best friends together:

"Never, Flor, trust a man with small hands and feet."

"*Pero,* Mirabel. I have not met any. Tony's hands and feet are very big!"

Once Flor bought a Ouija board, the kind that came packaged like any other board game for children. That was soon after she'd turned nineteen, in the spring before that autumn of my father's gallbladder attack. In the basement Flor asked it, "Who am I going to marryy?" She concentrated very hard, with trembling fingers on the plastic Ouija disk. Slowly the Ouija roamed, spelling out "A-N-T-O-N-I ..."

"You're making it spell that," I shouted. Flor made a frightened face. "But I'm not!" And she flipped the board over angrily, then sat there with her hands in her lap, biting her lower lip. Moments later she set the board up again.

"Ask it again, it'll say someone else, you'll see."

But instead she asked it, "Who will Antonio marry?" This time it was me who flipped the board over, but then we both, to my relief, started giggling. But at dinner that night I said, "Flor's Ouija board said she's going to marry Antonio."

And my mother, in an instant, turned into a somewhat less convincing Abuelita. She put on her severest expression, looked at Flor, and said, "Those are sacrilegious because only God can tell the future."

"Mom," I said, "that's silly."

"No," said Flor. "Mirabel has a reason. I was stupid to buy this. Only God knows the future. It could be the Devil, trying to make me do the wrong thing."

"Has Antonio asked you to marry him?" asked my mother.

"No," said Flor meekly.

Now my father looked up from his food, but he didn't say anything. Flor said, "It was just a game."

"It was," I said. "And when it started to spell his name, she flipped it over."

Both of my parents were looking straight at Flor.

"I would never marry Tony," she said, as if reciting a memorized oath of office, and then she stared down at her plate as if she'd never before noticed the dismal surprise of her own cooking.

"*Ay no,*" said my mother. "I knew he would. What else does he know how to do? It would ruin your life, Flor de Mayo. Is that what you want, my dear, to ruin your life after you have put so much into improving it?"

"Aw, Mirabel, of course she doesn't," said my father.

"Yes, I know. My life," said Flor. "I know. My life. My life. If you want I will leave the table and throw that preposterous game which started all this away right now!"

"Flor, sweetheart, don't get upset," said my father. "We are just concerned for you. It's like Mirabel said, it would be perfectly normal for Tony to want to get married—"

"What else does he know how to do?" interrupted my mother. "Make babies so that you and the babies can starve together while he runs after women? He is a Cuban, no?"

"Oh!" exclaimed Flor, in that nervy state between laughter and tears. "*Y chapines, qué?*"

"My dear," said my mother (who had somehow picked up Miss Cavanaugh's way of saying "my dear" whenever she felt like getting up on Abuelita's high horse), "Guatemalans can chase after women all they want, but in this country they are not going to get anywhere, and do you know why? Because they are too short and not good looking. Unless they are from good families, in which case they are probably not in Boston but in Guatemala looking after their farms. Too many poor Cubans look the same as the rich ones, no? This has been the cause of Cuba's disaster, and if I were an intellectual I could prove it. But I do know this, you will not be the first young woman ruined by Cuban vanity and arrogance, *punto y cabal!*"

"Mirabel," said my father.

Flor just sat in stunned silence for a moment, with her hands in her lap, and then she lowered her head, and soon her shoulders were shaking with repressed laughter. "*Ayyyy Mirabel, pero qué horrible . . .*" But soon Flor started to cry. It was the first time she'd ever cried at the dinner table in front of all of us like this, with high-pitched braying sobs and squeals of bewildered misery. Her lips were twisted to the side, and, though her hair falling forward partly curtained her face, I could see fat, lusterless tears sliding down her face with astonishing rapidity, clinging briefly to her cheeks and chin and then jumping to her lap, and then she was gasping for air, hiccuping, whimpering, "*Tonyyy, mi pobrecito, ay noooo, nooo.*"

We all sat paralyzed for a moment. I had sort of caused this, of course, mentioning the Ouija, but I had the feeling that I shouldn't be at all sorry I had.

My mother sighed, but then said Flor's name in a sympathetic way. And my father got up from his chair and stood in an ungainly posture beside Flor until she finally propelled herself up and laid her head into his shoulder, and then my father cradled her head with his hand. Flor gaspingly asked that I be sent away, and I was, and then they talked for a long time.

"So this *one gusanito, este niño bonito,* this is who received all her love," interrupted Moya.

"But she had other boyfriends later," I said. "Dr. Ben, who boarded with Miss Cavanaugh in Wellesley, came next. And of course in college and when she was living in New York she saw people. I remember her mentioning a Brazilian who worked at the U.N., like she did for a while. She could have been a U.N. bureaucrat, you know, if she'd wanted to."

"Flor liked black guys, *vos.* I say this simply, well, because it just seems that she did."

". . . Well, Dr. Ben, a Nigerian professor, Ozzie Peterkins, a football player, there's not necessarily a pattern there, Moya. I didn't know the Brazilian. But, true, there weren't many white guys, I mean, you know, gringo white guys, that I can recall. On the other hand, you can say there were nearly as many white guys as any other kind."

"But in proportion to the general population? Far fewer, *vos.*"

"There was this one guy she was seeing in college for a while who used to call her his brown angel because before he met her it had never occurred to him that an angel could be brown. Some epiphany, huh?"

"I don't care what some fucking guy like that says," said Moya.

"Anyway, this kind of conversation, so what? It's just cultural. White guys usually don't grow up hearing *mi precioso, chulito, niño divino,* and everything in their ears all day long, that's all. Which probably makes it easier to be that way later, and Flor liked that stuff, right?"

"*Sí . . .*"

"Of course all that helps to make great romantic liars too, *machista* smoothies, so who says it's better? Anyway, what does this have to do with anything, maybe we should get some sleep."

But we just sat there, looking at opposite red-and-purple velvet walls, on the round red satin bed, under the fake-gold-marbled mirror on the ceiling, amidst the ineradicable scent of cheap perfumes, toilet waters, and colognes, the olfactory legacy from the female side of the room's history: adulteries, love for money, *amores secretos.* To protect customers' identities from employees and vice versa, there was a buzzer to press for room service or to pay the bill, and a revolving hatch, dumbwaiterlike, in the wall. And outside every room's door, a garage, that's why it's called an *autohotel,* just drive right into any open garage and the door comes down by remote control and not even a chambermaid ever sees you. Though Moya and I had come by taxi—as had Zamara and I about a month before, the first time I'd ever been in an *autohotel,* maybe in this very room, on this very same bed. On that first of our two nights in the Omni, six months ago, and following that brief silence after I'd suggested that we try to sleep, my thoughts really did turn to Zamarita, and the memory of our past lovemaking there. But I also wondered what she would have thought if she'd known that earlier that same day Moya and I had come out of my house and found a death squad, a black-windowed Cherokee with four murderers inside of it, four Freedom Fighting *matones* waiting for us, though in the very next instant we'd escaped them, because of *me,* my "heroic" reactions, putting, I even

joked later, a certain long-past incident and its persistent insinua-
tions to rest once and for all, because this was a death squad, make
no mistake about it, not just some pig-shit-worm-infested dog. And
of course I was dying to tell Zamara all about it.

Sitting there on the red round bed, I even imagined myself
doing that, saying, Zamara, you know what it's like when you
swim in the ocean and suddenly you imagine a shark circling? And
I imagined her widening her eyes at me like she always does and
saying, *Sí, mi amor?* And I touched her naked arm, affectionately
smoothed damp hair out of her eyes, and said (imagined), And you
half-expect to turn around and see the fin sticking out of the water,
circling you? But of course it's never there, and you think, God,
imagine if it had been there, what could be scarier than a shark's
fm circling? Well, that's what it was like when Moya and I came
out of my house this evening, Zamarita, though at first it seemed
like just any other evening. Some of the buses going by already had
their colored lights on inside. There were a few schoolgirls on the
sidewalk, I even noticed the way the powdery evening light made
their white blouses and even their white teeth glow kind of phos-
phorescently. Moya and I were going to the *tienda* on the corner to
have a beer there, but then I looked over and saw this black Cherokee following us. Driving along slowly on the opposite side, then
slowly veering into the middle of the street. I touched Moya and
we looked at it and froze, but the Jeep came to a stop too, and we
thought, No, it can't be, and started walking again, but then it
rolled along with us again . . . it was just like always having imagined what it would be like to see a shark circling and then there it
was, circling. Instead of running, we stopped again. Now all four
doors opened. They came out, three of them carrying Uzis, machine guns. You know, Zamara, the guys who are always described
in the newspapers as "four heavily armed unknown men"? So you
never read the newspapers, OK. Heavy *mestizo* faces, hard black-

beetle eyes—I can remember it so clearly. Only one wore sunglasses. Two in black leather jackets, one wearing denim, the other in jacket and tie. Big guys with big faces. All of this happened in an instant, right in front of that small private hospital just down the block. Where were the schoolgirls now, or anyone else? Why didn't anyone scream? Four murderers staring, just beginning to lift their guns like mariachi musicians lifting their instruments— I took Moya's arm and pulled him down behind one of the two parked ambulances there. That was my *first* split-second reaction, Zamara! And at that very instant the bus that had just turned the corner came chugging down the street, gears grinding as it fought for a higher gear, it passed right between the ambulances and the death-squad guys, and I jerked Moya up by the arm and we ran along with the bus like a shield between us and jumped onto it while it was still accelerating down the street! So that was my *second* split-second reaction, Zamarita! I saved us! Me, it was my reactions! Some of the passengers had seen *los hombres desconocidos* and now they looked at us, amazed, not saying a word, wondering if we'd been the intended target, hard to believe, wondering how it could be that we were there. The four *matones* got back into their Cherokee and then they sped away down the avenue, Zamara, past the bus and all the way down the long straight avenue and through all the red lights like a rocket soaring away sideways. Moya and I were still standing there by the driver, who had his own worries, what with his recalcitrant gearbox and shift. Over his windshield, taped sideways, was a girlie magazine foldout with the tits blackened out. Now we remembered to fumble in our pockets for change, since we still had to pay for this opportunity of having saved our own lives by jumping on a bus. And then we went and sat down in one of the empty hard seats. And Moya said, *La gran puta, vos,* and then he said, *Verdaderamente increíble,* and then he fell silent and monkey faced. That's when the adrenaline started coursing through us, when my knees and hands began to shake and I almost began to weep. We rode the bus all the way out to Zona 10, ourselves shaking and the bus, as always, shaking, its black fumes rising through the rust-tattered floor, until we got off near the Hotel Biltmore Maya (where, from the lobby, we'd immediately phoned Consul Simms, and he told us to stay someplace safe that night, and for me to come see him the next day, but to take a taxi and not walk *anywhere*).

So what do you think of your Roger-oger now, huh, Zamarita? Yes, she'd been listening (I was still imagining, there in the Omni), she'd taken this all in, her glossy pony eyes looked frightened now. She said nothing for a moment, just stared at me. Then she gave her head a cocky, affronted little shake like she always does. Maybe she grabbed for one of my cigarettes, like she usually does. She shook her head and looked at me almost poutingly and raised her chin and widened her eyes and said, *Bueno, te habés ganado mí respeto por lo heróico que sós,* and laughed. I laughed too and said, *No, en serio, Zamarita.* Now she bit back her own smile and acted huffy. *Acaso me crees bruta? Mentiroso!* No Zamarita, it's no lie, it really happened! We escaped and here I am in the Omni with Moya, maybe even on the same bed where you and I—Here I am dreaming of you, Zamarita.

Wondering what Zamara would have thought about it even filled me with the temporary certainty that she really did love me. Because I suddenly felt convinced that if something had happened to me it would have been a terrible loss for her, but one that she, like so many thousands of others, would have had to bear, silently and invisibly. Perhaps I had a pathetic right, on that one night only, in the Omni, to indulge myself in such ruminations.

But on the afternoon following our first night in the Omni, Consul Simms at the embassy would relieve me of my worst fears while at the same time dispelling that briefly glorious myth of our heroic escape by telling me that the death squad "could have splattered you two all over the sidewalk like tomato sauce if they'd wanted to. Those guys do *not* screw up. No, Roger, it was what we call a 'heavy-handed tail,' meant to send a message."

A message to Moya, of course, not me, and Moya certainly took it and was preparing himself, once more, to flee the country, so that even our holing up in the Omni, if they did know about it, was like a message back to them: *Moya is leaving, see? See how Roger also went to the Canadian embassy in the morning, trying to arrange the terms of Moya's political asylum and refugee status? So hold your fire, señores* . . . Because they would never come after just me, I could take the risk, had to, of coming and going from the Omni.

In fact Zamara didn't love me, not like that, not yet, and would not even have grieved for me that much if the death squad had succeeded in et cetera, if only because she already knew—I've tried to assure myself many times since—that she had nothing to gain from spending her emotions on me since I had already told her, with laudable honesty, that I wasn't likely to marry her or to bring her and her little son back with me to the States to live. Well, I wasn't. I said I didn't make enough money to support her and a kid in the States. I told her I was probably going back to school. I actually said law school. I told her I wished I could be two people, one who would be happy to spend the rest of his (lobotomized) life in a hammock with her and this other one who was so honest and who would be happy to go on spending time with her like a boyfriend until he had to go home (or until his obsession was sated).

I really don't think Zamara's life story would have turned out anything like Flor's even if the people she'd worked for as a maid *had* put her in a Los Angeles elementary school. And I don't think Flor's might have turned out like Zamara's had she gone to work for any family but mine, though of course there's no way of proving any of this. Zamara has had even less formal education than Flor received from Las Hermanas del Espíritu Santo, who nevertheless prepared Flor only to be a servant, albeit for the household of a Spanish ambassador. But it's hard to imagine Flor ever falling for some *chicano-grencho* surfer boy who would impregnate and then just blithely dump her, isn't it?

I picture her at least marrying Tony. But even Tony, with that Cuban *vanidad* and his jeweler's apprenticeship, might not have let himself fall for just a common house servant. One of the very first things that captivated him about his *niña de Guatemala* was the serious nonsense of that Flor-in-the-fourth-grade stuff. He couldn't possibly have foreseen, that first night in our basement when he teased Flor about being the luckiest girl in kindergarten, that he would lose her once and for all to a Wellesley College visiting professor, a Nigerian Melville scholar no less, when she was in her last year of high school and soon to be accepted on full scholarship to that same college.

A distinguished young man, degrees up the wazoo, Dr. Ben. But all that was necessarily hush-hush too, of course, they even tried to hide it from Miss Cavanaugh. I never doubted that it was a good relationship for Flor, it was about time she had a boyfriend she could admire and look up to, though it would have been even better if she'd had one she didn't have to keep secret. Miss Cavanaugh was wild about Flor and was always filling her head with notions of Third World pride and accomplishment, and here he was, a living embodiment of the excellence she preached. She even used to say things like "Flor, if it is your dream to be president of Guatemala one day or even your adopted country's United Nations ambassador, then don't let anybody call you a Don Quixote because El Quixote was a man and never had the opportunity to attend

Wellesley College!" Miss Cavanaugh was a feminist too, and in her youth had been an Amelia Earhart–like adventurer. On her famous motorcycle journey to Chile following her own graduation from Wellesley she'd had a love affair (she once confided to Flor) with a South American benevolent dictator and while it lasted apparently fell victim to the fantasy that she was actually going to marry and then reform him, democratize him and free the serfs, like a Boston Brahmin Evita Perón. Except this was during the thirties and the dictator had an ineradicable pen pal's enthusiasm for General Franco and Hitler. He used to summon a secretary from the German Mission to transcribe his letters to the latter, which is how Miss Cavanaugh learned about it, walking in on one of their sessions during siesta one afternoon. The very next day she got back on her motorcycle, rejoined her traveling companion, and off they went into the rest of the century. Miss Cavanaugh never revealed the identity of that dictator to Flor, who was too polite to insist on knowing. But Flor was once allowed a look at Miss Cavanaugh's constantly revised handwritten account of her journey, at the chapter including her traversal of Guatemala. I don't know why Miss Cavanaugh was never able to get it published, but I would guess its most obvious failing was a saturating gentility that erased all trace of her robust spirit: too many idealized descriptions of landscapes and picturesque customs and democratic prescriptions, no mention of her deluded tumbles in the hay. When Miss Cavanaugh finally did get a book published, it was an illustrated one on Christmas traditions in Latin America. Our inscribed copy was always kept on display on a coffee table in the living room with a bookmark at the page where both Mirabel Arrau de Graetz and Flor de Mayo Puac, in that order, thank Cod, received grateful mentions for their contributions to the Guatemala chapter.

Evidently Miss Cavanaugh was as convinced of the importance of holidays as she was about education and female independence, and looked like a physical manifestation of all her enthusiasms: titanic and pink, with enormous pillowy breasts and a handsome ship's-prow head slackened and spotted from age; her pale blue eyes almost always looked squeezed into a friendly John Wayne squint, and her hair, which she still wore long and tied back, was the same faded yellow and texture of an angel's on a Christmas tree ornament. Even her refined voice and laughter had a jolly, ringing timbre. Once a year she held an Easter egg hunt in her yard near the Wellesley College campus for the children of her many Latin friends.

I'd considered myself too old for years and had no interest in tagging along on the afternoon when Flor, soon to turn twenty-one and in her next to last year of high school, bicycled over to help Miss Cavanaugh color eggs and hide them around the yard. She loved going over to Miss Cavanaugh's in the afternoons whenever she had some free time, but she'd never before met her new boarder, who had just moved out of his apartment in Cambridge so that he could be nearer the Wellesley College campus, where he would be teaching Melville along with a course in modern African literature the following year. That afternoon Miss Cavanaugh coaxed Dr. Ben down from his attic room to help hide eggs in the yard and to meet the *guatemalteca* she was going to talk into choosing Wellesley over Radcliffe no matter what. Then it was a matter of minutes, not days or hours, before Dr. Ben began to win Flor's extremely flustered heart. Under a tree in Miss Cavanaugh's yard, while Flor was looking around for a place to hide the first egg, he sang her that song from *West Side Story,* "Maria, Maria, I just met a girl named Maria . . ." He knew all the words and sang it all the way through in a rich, deep, sensitive voice that he'd mastered in a boyhood spent in an Anglican Church school and its choir. First encounters like that one under the tree seem to have meant a lot to Flor. But Dr. Ben went off to Oxford and France for the summer, and it wasn't until he came back to Miss Cavanaugh's in the fall that things really got going between them.

Two months into that fall of Flor's final year in high school, my mother noticed that some of her jewelry was missing, including an heirloom from her father that she was saving for me, a gold, pearl-studded tiepin. A brooch was missing too, but this didn't matter nearly as much as the tiepin. Why would a burglar take the tiepin and leave the matching cuff links behind along with her few truly valuable pieces of jewelry? It was only because the robbery seemed to have been conceived for no other purpose than to hurt and madden my mother that her suspicions fell almost instinctively on Flor—though unspokenly, because there was absolutely no other evidence. I suspected one of my friends had done it and was miserable over the lack of respect this showed and terrified of the consequences. For a year, ever since the explosion over the guidance counselor, Flor and my mother's relationship had been at an all-time low, though each of them, knowing that by next fall Flor would be off to college, had been doing her best to keep from provoking the other. But that week following my mother's discovery of the missing tiepin was like a form of silent madness for all of us.

None of us knew a thing about Flor and Dr. Ben yet, and even I believed that everything had finally come to an end with Tony. Now there only seemed to be time for studying and visiting Miss Cavanaugh in her house near the providential campus, with its promise of a future that had finally begun to seem actual and attainable. But every morning Flor still had to wake up and confront the life that had been the same for too long, another day of high school, except the classes were actually hard for her now. It really was grueling, and I believe it did take a ton of inner fortitude to pull it off, Flor's last, long kick towards the finish line my father had stretched across her life nearly a decade before.

Which, of course, is one of the reasons her high school guidance counselor said he could easily imagine Flor inspiring a television movie one day. But he'd also seemed to have the idea that if that movie was ever made, my family would be portrayed as one more obstacle. He was under the impression that we treated Flor like a maid, that we "exploited" her, as he actually put it. That had happened in the fall of Flor's second year of high school, after she'd received the first C of her student career, in trigonometry, along with two rare Bs in chemistry and English. A huge deal had been made of this despoiling of Flor's invincibility; she'd gone around in a daze of angry disillusionment for weeks. What if she went on getting grades like that for the rest of high school? She was terrified it would mean kissing her full scholarship good-bye, despite her minority status and interesting individuality. Flor wasn't enduring this only to end up at Boston State or U Mass with half her high school classmates! *That* she could have done even if she'd moved out, married Tony, and gone to night school.

In her panic over that report card, Flor must have said something at school about not having enough time to study, what with her household duties and her evening job to save money for college (though as far as I could see, most of this was spent bargain hunting for French clothing in Boston) and in doing so must have set certain alarms off in the guidance counselor, who phoned my mother at Shreve Hall and asked that she come in to discuss certain private matters regarding Flor de Mayo Puac.

My mother came home from work earlier than usual that evening and went straight into the kitchen—where dinner, perhaps one of Flor's pot roasts, was simmering on the stove—and to the basement door where she called down to Flor in such a way that I instantly knew something was up. Then she stepped back and waited, demurely holding the collar of her raincoat closed under her chin with both hands as if against a chill. But her hands were trembling, and her fixed stare never wavered as we listened to Flor's footsteps scampering up the stairs. Flor came into the kitchen smiling a warm welcome, but a split second later her face fell.

"I spoke to your guidance counselor this afternoon, Flor," said my mother in an odd singsong. "He said that we treat you like a maid, and that this is affecting your ability to do well in school. He thinks it might be better if you went and lived with another family until you've graduated. What do you think, Flor? Would you like that?"

"*Ay no, Mirabel,*" whispered Flor, biting her lower lip.

"'Mrs. Graetz, I am *sorry* to be so blunt, but this is *not* Guatemala.' This is what that *heepie,* that jerk said to me! *Imagínate?* I had no idea. Do you feel like you are still in Guatemala, Flor?"

". . . Mirabel, I do need more time to study—"

"Unconshunabal—*Sin consciencia!*" shouted my mother, who proceeded then to orate her version of the guidance counselor's entire tirade, which included his opinion that it was unconscionable for my family to be taking advantage of the naïveté, generosity, and goodwill of such a wonderful girl, one whose life story he wouldn't be at all surprised to see made into a television movie. Mrs. Graetz, this is *not* Guatemala. Which he'd made a point of reading up on, he even delivered a brief recitation: exploitation of Indians on the plantations, the use of fatally poisonous pesticides banned in the USA but exported to Guatemala, the hemisphere's most inequitable distribution of land and wealth, and so on. In short, not just the land that bananas come from, but an altogether indefensible little place. The guidance counselor offered my mother profuse admissions of guilt over U.S. culpability. But he personally was not going to just stand by and watch such injustices perpetrated upon one student he was in a position to protect. If the situation could not be swiftly corrected, then he proposed that Flor live with another Namoset family, and suggested that the school board had the authority to enforce such a decision.

"—*Increíble!*" exclaimed Moya, almost gleefully. "So you do live with a small country like it is a person, no? It chases you like an angry little dog even up there. *Puta.* Here was this man, a guerrilla guidance counselor."

"Moya, the guy was basically ridiculous."

"But Flor was a political schoolgirl?"

"I don't think she had any idea the guidance counselor was going to go *that* far. She looked flabbergasted! And when my mother was finished doing her imitation of the guy, she said, 'Well, maybe it is a good idea, Flor. You would have more time to study, to visit Miss Cavanaugh, to sneak around with your boyfriends—'And then she exploded. She screamed, 'This is the gratitude of dogs! *Y yo que he aguantado todos los insultos de esta vida jodida sin siquiera levantar la mano!*' (And I who have put up with all the insults of this screwed-up life without even raising my hand!) Then she lifted her hand all right; she slapped Flor right across the face. Whack! That did it, that slap, she had a red mark for days. Flor screamed, '*Fuck your gratitude, fuck it!*' She ran downstairs hysterical and my mother was screaming, 'Go ahead, say your dirty words, say *fock!* say *sheet!*. . .' Oh boy, Moya, it was quite a scene."

"But Flor didn't leave your house?"

"Are you kidding? It all got pretty much worked out. With me and my father as referees, of course. From then on it was my job to vacuum the rugs and clean the bathroom once a week. It was already my job to shovel up Klink's shit from the yard every night and put it in the incinerator. No one was about to suggest I take over laundry and cooking too. She cut her Brigham's job to two nights a week. The way my mother finally put it to her was that she could go ahead and regard herself however she wanted, as an exploited maid if she wanted, or as a family member who had chores to do because the family wasn't rich enough to hire a full-time maid. My mother worked every day and nights too, Moya. She stayed at school late into the afternoons to run the Foreign Students and Romance Languages clubs and taught adult Spanish two nights a week at the Latin American Society because we really did need the extra money. My father, you know, never earned very much."

"But Flor *was* a maid, or felt like one, and resented it."

"Well, that's what my mother must have wished like hell she could have told that guidance counselor. Of course she's a maid! And an extraordinarily lucky one at that! That's what she would have *liked* to have said. I mean, after all, Abuelita *was* still sending up a salary of a hundred bucks a month, which isn't a lot but it's still four times as much as anyone pays servants down here. Which my father supplemented with rewards for good grades and everything, *he* called her salary an allowance. My mother didn't care what it was called as long as the housework got done. But sure, Flor started to resent it, or rather to resent my mother."

"Y *viceversa, vos.*"

"Because of course everyone else on earth treated Flor like she wasn't a maid."

"Like an aristocrat."

"I don't know if I'd go that far. As someone *very* special. Except, Flor thought, for my mother. Though, you know, my mother didn't actually treat Flor like a maid anyway. It was just this underlying thing."

"Guatemala, *vos.* This runs under everything."

"You don't think that was humiliating for my mother, sitting in that guidance counselor's office listening to *that*? Look, though she'd never said it to Flor's face, not ever, the fact was and always had been that at any moment, even after Flor had her U.S. citizenship, my mother could have given this ultimatum: Ira, enough of this charade, I didn't ask for a daughter, I need a maid. Do what you want with her but she's fired. I'll have my mother send up a good-natured *muchacha* who will be absolutely delighted to do her housework and go into Boston on her days off! In other words, Ira, *she goes or I go!* So why do you think it never came to that?"

". . . Because your father would have chosen Flor, *vos?*"

"No. He just would have refused to send her packing. And then what would my mother have done? It would have been her move, right? So OK, Mom was probably terrified of that and that was one of the things that restrained her, and I don't blame her. But she loved Flor too, and Flor loved my mother. But things just eventually got to a point, somehow, where neither one of them could admit that without undoing everything they felt they stood for. They were always challenging each other, like two gladiators. Their own myths clashed. The Empire of Nostalgia versus the, you know, the Wellesley-Bound—"

"Aristocrat."

"*Again* with the aristocrat?"

"I have experience of Harvard, *vos. Cómo no?* She, Mirabel Arrau's maid, Flor de Mayo Puac, was going to be like an *aristocrata* and have everything in *Los Estados Unidos* that Mirabel Arrau could not. In a few years more, if Flor had stayed, your mother might even have been teaching Flor's daughter at that school for rich girls, *verdad?*"

"That's part of it. Jealousy. Jealousy even of Flor's relationship with Miss Cavanaugh, the true Boston blue blood, OK. And also, like I said, what they knew or sensed about each other as women. Flor got to see Dr. Ben much more regularly than she'd ever seen Tony, who was basically like her childhood love. So her relationship with Dr. Ben was more mature, you know. Well, she was twenty-one, for Chrissakes. Miss Cavanaugh wasn't in her house all day every day, she was a busy woman, but it didn't take her long to figure out what was going on up in her boarder's attic. Who knows what Miss Cavanaugh really thought about it, maybe *she* was jealous. But no matter what she did with that dictator when she was young, she was, after all, a Boston Brahmin, nutty for Easter egg hunts. But by the time she got around to saying something to my mother about it—well, my mother and Flor were already at their wits' ends with each other. Flor, cool it with the African professor, Miss Cavanaugh can't take it, it's been centuries since she's had a lover—that's basically all my mother said. Later Flor said it was the first talk as true equals they ever had."

"And the tiepin, *vos?*"

"Oh. Well, after about a week, Flor just announced at dinner one night that it had *just* occurred to her what *might* have happened. Weeks before, she said, Tony had come to the house, uninvited of course, out of the blue, to try to win her back. In the afternoon when no one else was home. They argued in the basement, but she stood her ground and said no. Though she couldn't come out and say so, Tony had never really been out of her life, but Flor had finally told him about Dr. Ben and *that's* why he'd come to the house. So at the table Flor said that at one point Tony went upstairs to piss and that that might be when he'd stolen the jewelry. This time it was my father who got angry, but all he said was, 'Don't use words like that at the table, Flor.' Words like *piss,* he meant. And Flor actually went, 'Oh Ira, come off it.' She was exhausted, fed up, like I said, and she was miserable because she knew my mother was going to make her get the tiepin back. Which was just what Tony wanted, of course, I mean that must've been the *point.* So Flor went into Boston to see him one more time, and found him shacked up with some sleazy woman, and he denied taking the jewelry. Maybe he'd already sold it, or he just wanted to keep it because it really wasn't worth *that* much, beyond the emotional value of the tiepin to my mother, I mean, and maybe now in some twisted way to Tony too. In the end, my mother, every bit as sick of it all as Flor, just said, 'Well, now we know why Tony never succeeded as a jeweler' . . . But Flor came home from that final confrontation just totally devastated, over Tony, over the final waste of all those years of loving him, I guess. She felt so bad about it that things were never really the same between her and Dr. Ben again, though she really did like him a lot and respected him much more than she ever had Tony. Anyway, Dr. Ben was engaged to a Nigerian woman who was studying to be a doctor in France."

". . . And Flor did not know?"

"No, he told her."

"*Ajá!*"

And the next year you went to Wellesley and delighted and scandalized your dormmates with your enfants terribles fairy tale about us. Simply because it was that kind of fairy tale, and everyone who heard it wished it were true. Forget it.

Because there's another reason I've been telling all this. Moments later Moya, adopting his most formal tone, as if somehow it only concerned him in the most objective possible light, said:

"On that last night we talked, Flor de Mayo said, '*Vos,* I would never want to be Guatemala's first lady anyway. My gosh, what a fuck*een* nightmare this would be.' But I only mention this now, Rogerio, because of what you said about this Señorita Cavanaugh telling Flor that she could be president of Guatemala. And Señorita Cavanaugh herself, she thinking that she might be an Evita Perón *primera dama.* I wonder if this too might be a pattern."

"Moya, you're not about to suggest that Flor came back here because she wanted to be president or first lady someday, are you?"

But Moya persisted in pursuing his own echoes, and I believe now that they led him as close to the revelation of Celso Batres as he could get without knowing it for sure and speaking his name out loud; that is, if he didn't *already* know. Of course, back then I had absolutely no reason for suspecting any of this.

But on that last night that you and Moya spoke, which was also your last night alive, when Moya offered to go with you to France or anywhere, he said you answered that you'd never really wanted to be first lady anyway, which at first startled and thrilled him because it sounded as if you were on the verge of saying yes. He even thought your remark specifically referred to an old serious joke of his: that even he, Moya, could actually rise that high, could actually be *El Señor Presidente* one day, even in Guatemala, if he *wanted* to. It was only after you were already dead and he no longer needed his own optimism that he let his guard down and confronted what he'd felt pretty sure of all along but hadn't allowed himself to admit: his near certainty that he'd never confided any presidential aspirations to you, even jokingly. Apparently that was the first tangible hint Moya had ever had of another "secret lover," of someone else in your life of whom it could be said, at least jokingly, that he might one day, by marrying you, eventually make you Guatemala's *primera dama.*

"—So if not me, who, *vos?*" said Moya. "I mean, *puta,* Paco Palma Passafarri?"

So why did it occur instantly to me?

"Well, you always say Celso Batres might be president someday—You've never thought of that before?"

"But Celso is married, *vos.* And he is very religious. And his family is very powerful on all sides; if he divorced his wife, his father might even disown him, and his father-in-law, worse. And he would not ever get to be president, *vos.*"

"*So?* She *said* he wouldn't leave his wife for her."
Moya gaped incredulously.

"Well, you brought it up, Moya. I know he's handsome and everything, but, I mean, if Celso and Flor—wouldn't you have known about it?"

"*Claro,*" he said, but he still looked worried.

"But he didn't know about *you* and Flor, right?"

"Yes, he did, I am afraid," said Moya. "Celso is the only person I ever told, until you, Rogerio."

"So then it couldn't have been him. I mean, if he was with her, and you told him *you* were—"

"It was a boast, more than actually a confiding. Really, in a way, a terrible thing, a true moment of betrayal. Like some stupid macho, I made a boast. It was the only time I broke my promise to Flor to keep our love secret."

"You boasted about Flor to Celso?" I cringed inwardly, not having to hear the words to know what they were like, since aren't such boasts always essentially the same?

"*Sí pues.* I was angry and feeling bad, *vos.* This was soon after we after she had stopped seeing me. Which does not excuse it, *claro,* but . . ."

"OK, so you boasted about Flor to Celso. Then what? What'd he say?"

"*Nada.* He didn't say anything."

"So you see? Relax, it wasn't him, Moya. It couldn't have been. He would've punched you or something."

Seeing how chagrined Moya seemed over the revived memory of his indiscretion, I suddenly felt unbelievably touched, that's all. I understood that almost anyone might have done the same in the wake of an amorous rejection. What I thought was, What an inherently decent and even kind of innocent guy my friend Moya really is, to still be feeling so bad about a stupid boast. And also that he'd really loved you, and that you'd hurt him.

I said, "Look, you're reading way too much into this, Moya. One silly remark, come on. Of course it would be a nightmare to be first lady. And probably Flor *did* mean you. Anyway, you don't really believe that she ever actually worried about that, about having to become first lady, do you? Now I really think we *should* get some sleep because we're getting delirious here."

Later, after I found out about you and Celso Batres from Rosana Letones, Moya's boast, its possible and imaginable repercussions, became one more phantom key to your fate, which I pursued in much the same way I found myself simultaneously pursuing Lucas Caycam Quix, down an invisible trail made of my own speculations and "divinations," certain that in both cases I would never really know. So it seemed appallingly unfair to put any blame on Moya, despite everything else. I couldn't even bring myself to tell him what I'd found out since—never mind about the terrible but phantom scenarios I've been able to draw from it all—until the other day, when finally I put it into a letter.

That night in the Omni, Celso Batres invisibly and discreetly departed the room, like a ghost who has come much too early for a haunting. We thought we'd escaped certain death, and it had filled our blood and our heads with fireworks. We didn't even know yet that it had only been "a heavy-handed tail, meant to send a message," that they'd only wanted to *scare* us. I lit another Payaso cigarette; in my hand I held the square, poinsettia-red little pack, its portrait of an idiotically grinning white-faced clown. Then I put it down, exhaled, lay back, and looked up into the mirror where only three weeks before I had watched myself lying next to Zamarita, but now in that mirror I saw the grinning *payasito* on the red satin bed and Moya's hand reaching for it, heard him saying, "What the hell, I will smoke *one*." Though recently estranged,

Moya and I were good friends again. I was sure I'd even saved his life.

"*Una cosa más,*" said Moya suddenly, when he had finished his cigarette and finally seemed ready for sleep. "If your family was so poor—"

"I wouldn't call us *poor,* exactly."

"How was it you could afford all these travels with the Harvard football team, *vos?*"

"By betting," I said. "My father bet on every Ivy League football game, and that's all his winnings went to, our trips. He was really good at it."

And by the time I was done describing all the ins and outs of that, Moya had drifted off to sleep on the far curve of our round bed, and I switched off the light and lay back again, staring up at the blackened mirror. I thought about Zamara. I wanted to think about Zamara. Think about Zamara, I said to myself getting ready to feel almost happy, remembering Zamara as I'd seen her below and above me, on the bed and in the ceiling mirror, on that one night that she'd said was her first night in an *autohotel* too, though that doesn't mean much. But she hadn't been working as an *artista* for long, and they don't *have* to leave with the customers and most of the customers can't afford the hundred *quetzales* at least anyway (one night I saw Zamara write her price on a napkin for this American business type, she wrote "500," which is a price *no one* would ever pay and he laughed like it was a joke and she scolded, *En serio,* and he said, Forget it!). Thus the mythological or at least relative purity of *artistas de barra,* which perhaps only I, and certainly on that first night, wholly believed in—that first night that so resembled love that ever since I'd hardly been able to even go near her without feeling panicky symptoms, heart pounding, tongue tied—ridiculous, I know. And the only place I'd gone near her since was the place where she worked and where I'd first seen her, one of three fancy *barra shows* situated on the same block around the corner from the Conquistador-Sheraton in Zona 4: nearly pale, now multicolored Zamara (as I first saw her), eyes brimming with trepidation under the red, orange, and blue lights of the round, elevated stage, the yellow sequins of her tasseled costume's top and bottom flaring, her hips and thighs moving to the music and her elbows and hands lifted as if in a doll's embrace, her smooth shoulders and the tops of her skinny arms so slightly moving too, as if tingling from invisible kisses instead of nightclub drafts or something else spreading a chill over her skin, Zamara reflected endlessly in the light-spangled mirrors along the club's facing walls, her eventually bared, almost womanly, and impossibly pert everything moving but ever so delicately and modestly for a stripper.

Though I should make it clear that raunchily immodest dancing or patron behavior is not often seen at a reputable *barra show*. It's almost as if *artistas de barra* perform for genteelly degenerate princes instead of for the usual bunch of high school kids and young guys with jobs and off-duty junior military officers, and quietly high-strung cadets with their short Mohawk haircuts. Of course there are always older men too, variously respectable sorts with their paunches and mustaches. Only once in a while does a group of rowdy young Americans turn up—Peace Corps guys still new to the country, say—who forget or just don't know about the decorum of *barra shows* versus strip clubs in the States. So they yell and applaud too loudly when an *artista* removes her top and then her bottom, they gesticulate too wildly for her to toss her sequined garments into their outstretched hands from the stage. They don't know that an *artista* only tosses her things to a patron—though he will never wave his hands—when he has earned this by patiently buying her six quetzal fruit juices and watery whiskeys, for which she receives redeemable chips, and danced with her over and over on the club's small and always crowded dance floor. Only then might an *artista* toss her garments with a desultory flip of her hand to a patron and only then can he, for the amusement of his drinking buddies, hold her sequined and cheaply perfumed top or bottom to his nose and sniff it like a flower or wear it over his head, this being the only overt raunchiness permitted at a *barra show*, where the waiters will even glide over to the dance floor to deliver a chastening look to any *artista* dancing in the arms of a patron with too much pelvis grinding going on. Only later, and only if he has been buying her drinks and making her laugh with his jokes and danced with her and held hands with her and waited for her at his table when she has gone off to change because soon it will be *her* turn onstage again and then told her when she's returned how beautiful she looked up on the stage and how *sabrosona* she looks now, only *then* can a patron say, Let's go somewhere and *canchis canchis* or Let's go somewhere and fuck *mamita rrrrica* and then negotiate a price for an *artista* to accompany him to an *autohotel* or even for a whole weekend in a beach chalet or private *Jinca*—if he's wealthy, a junior military officer even, one who happens also to be the son of a general.

And because this is Guatemala and many of the polite young men, some of them junior military officers or ranchers or cocaine smugglers or even all three at the same time, carry pistols and are staring now at the backs of the wildly waving and uninhibitedly whooping gringo boys, the waiters, some of them pretty tough sorts themselves, with scars on their faces that can act like a warning third eye, come over to the gringos and tap one of them lightly on the shoulder and frown. And that's enough, and if it's not they gesture with their lips, in that precise way they have of slightly twisting their lips to one side or the other instead of pointing with a finger or even visibly nodding, they point with their lips at the table of hard-staring men with 9-mm pistols protruding from their belts or bulging in shoulder holsters under their jackets. And then the gringo boys settle down; even off-duty U.S. Marine embassy guards, who are of course prohibited from running around at night bearing arms, most of them really nice guys anyway who just want to party and don't want to be shot at any more than any of us do, learn pretty quickly not to mess with that.

So that's where Zamara was working when I met her, earning about a fifth as much as the girls in a fancy *burdel* like Marujas or the Valhalla but five times as much as she could doing anything else outside the *ambiente,* working in a shoe factory or as a shopgirl. She's one of the lucky ones in that respect, lucky to be pretty, that's all, and no father or brothers or even a boyfriend around to stop her. Most *artistas* even earn enough to hire Indian maids to look after their children, even though usually they'll all be living crammed into one room in a rooming house, the Indian maid unrolling her straw *petate* to sleep on the floor. But Zamara was lucky to have a mother who could look after little Rex. Almost every Sunday she took the bus to El Progreso to see her son and give her mother money, and then was back in time for work on Monday.

Zamara never tossed her things to anybody, ever. And that look she got in her eyes when her three-song set was finished and she'd been completely naked for about five seconds already but now had to walk that short, humiliating gauntlet past a few tables of staring men to reach the curtained entrance to the changing rooms in back, possessively clutching her sequined garments in one fisted hand down by her side, that thoughtfully riled and deeply perturbed what-are-*you*-looking-at look with which Zamara strafed the room; or that other look when she was still up there on the stage, when she was still in the second song of her three-song set and hadn't had to take anything off yet but was just moving her hips and *nalgas* and swiveling her high heels, watching herself watch herself ad infinitum in one of those facing wall-length mirrors, getting lost in an infinity of Zamaras watching Zamaras, every Zamara framed in diminishing arcs of colored lights—those looks are what told me Zamara has a lot going on inside. In my own boredom and drifting desire, I'd lose myself in that abstract Times Square of spangled lights and repeated dancing girl too, staring into that peaceful nighttime endlessness that seemed to have no surface. And on the very first night I ever saw Zamara I caught her eye right there in the mirror while she was onstage dancing and we smiled at each other like goofy adolescents—which of course is what she still is. A little later she snuck up behind me while I sat with Larry at our table and tweaked my nose! When I turned my head she was already dashing off with that country girl swagger of hers to sit with some of the other girls in a corner, dressed more plainly than the others that night, in just jeans and a plaid shirt, my lovely *pueblerina*. After she'd tweaked my nose and dashed off, Larry, with that Kentucky twang of his, with his bartender-barber's conviviality, said, "She's a frisky pony, that one." Usually he says things like "Tits you can bounce a quarter off" or "She's a racehorse, that one," though neither of those would apply to Zamara, who looks as if a quarter bounced off any part of her would leave an ugly bruise.

The song that always announced Zamara's appearance at the top of the lighted stairs leading down to the elevated stage was "I Wish They All Could Be California Girls." She'd come down the stairs to the Beach Boys, with careful steps and her hands on both rails, beneath colored lights and hanging ferns and against a backdrop of ultraviolet-lit fake boulders, and then she'd step onto the stage with that warning look already welling in her eyes and she'd lift her elbows and her hips would start moving almost as if against her will, as if they'd simply been trained to move like that to certain music. The second song was always *"El Mangu,"* her gaze floating away, mesmerized by all her gazes in the mirror, and the third Juan Gabriel's melting torch song . . . *miraaaa mi soledad, miraaaa mi soledad, que no me sienta nada bien . . . ,* her tasseled and sequined top coming off, then at the very last second the bottom snapped off, and then the short angry walk off the stage and past a short row of tables, before her startling, perfect, and rebuking white buttocks disappeared through a velvet curtain into the rooms in back.

Then came those first few nights of properly invested attention that I can't quite bring myself to call courtship, when I already had such a crush on her that all I did in Lord Byron's was bug Larry to close up early so that we could rush over, those nights of drink buying and dancing and hours of silly conversation and even a few quick kisses when the waiters weren't looking before I finally said that I would pay just this one time for us to leave the club together. (Larry, the expert, had told me that was the way to do it.) I felt as nervous as a teenager asking her out on a first date, but I made my little speech, I promised that we'd go on regular dates and everything but only this once would I pay for her as if she worked in a *burdel* and not as an *artista de barra.* She said yes, but in that way of hers, shaking her head no while saying yes and smiling as if this was very clever. We took a taxi to the Omni.

Less than a week later, not even minutes after Larry and I had arrived from Lord Byron's and had settled into our table, my eyes still searching the darkness and the double-rowed tables and banquettes and the dance floor, Larry nudged me so I wouldn't miss it, Larry who thinks nothing could be dumber than getting hung up on one *artista de barra;* but *artistas* don't have to turn tricks and some of them never do and some of them are hardly ever even asked to, but it's hard to say no to the money: so there went Zamara, wearing the Dodgers' baseball jacket she'd brought back from L.A. and looking remarkably like Linda Ronstadt in it, accompanying a patron I hardly got a look at towards the front door. He went out first, I just registered a yellow polo shirt and designer jeans, and she exchanged some quick, smiling remark with the doorman and then she was gone. While I sat there looking at the door like it was another kind of mirror, and Larry had a fit of yokel laughter over my crestfallen expression. It's not hard to steal love for free from this or that *artista* on a Sunday or even in the afternoons and evenings before they have to be at work, not hard even in a fancy *burdel* like the Valhalla, if you're foreign especially, and attentive and nice and funny enough, a friend, then it's not hard. Larry is practically the maestro at all that. Because of the way his face lights up as soon as he walks into the Valhalla and because of his red hair, the girls there call him *Fosforito,* little lit match, though before long Sofía, a *garifuna* black from the Caribbean coast, six inches taller than he, had exclusively claimed him, and the other girls had to keep away. Sofía works as a bank teller by day and in the late afternoons goes to beautician school, and she doesn't sleep in the Valhalla because she's already bought her own small house with a walled-in yard where she raises peacocks and ducks and she's saving her money to open her own Zona 10 hair salon, except there's the problem of trying to lure *fufurufas* into a salon owned by a *negrona.* But Larry is a *muy* convivial gringo, and he has a haircutting diploma too, so this is what Sofía offered Larry: a home and partnership in a fancy hair salon that she will pay for. All he has to do is marry her.

But I, up to that night in the Omni with Moya, had not been able to get anything for free from Zamara—who, the next time I saw her, disarmingly and affectionately smiled and said, "Buy me a stereo." I said, "I'll buy you an *elote,* " a roasted ear of corn like they sell on the street, and she laughed and said, *"Teniente López me compró un estereo."* She said it with a certain insouciance that made it seem like a very wittily ironic thing to have said indeed.

And I said, "Since when do lieutenants make so much money? I thought they had to at least reach major. Anyway, you told me you didn't like *militares,* Zamara."

Except she'd said *Lieutenant López,* a common enough name. But she was obviously dying to spill the beans, like she'd been out with a Kennedy or something, so it didn't take me long to get it out of her that she meant López as in López Nub, yes *that* López Nub, the general's, the defense minister's son, the nephew of the sister and sister-in-law, the women who according to Moya's scenario had instigated a defamatory newspaper campaign in order to drown out the rumors of their own involvement in a clandestine baby-fattening house. Moya's reaction to a López Nub relation suddenly turning up in the periphery of my life couldn't have been more blasé—he was supposed to be surprised that a millionaire general's son, a lieutenant, would turn up at one of the city's fanciest *barra shows* and choose the *artista* I claimed was prettiest? And what did I think, the lieutenant was going to spill all his family secrets to her and then elaborate? As for my competing with a general's son for the same girl, if that's what I was getting up to, well *that,* said Moya, was pretty much the way a certain Peace Corps guy got a bullet in his head a few years ago. No, you don't do it, Rogerio, *babosito,* you cede the territory. I knew he was right, of course, though I was as intrigued as I was, if not outright jealous, exasperated. I'd figured by the time I returned to the city from my trip through the highlands the lieutenant would have dropped her already, but I'd ended up in the Omni before having a chance to find out. It was ridiculous to feel hurt and angry at a *puta* for behaving like a *puta,* of course. But Zamara was an *artista de barra.*

But all that went through my mind as I drifted off to sleep at the end of that first night in the Omni with Moya was a repeat of that night's recurring thought that right here on this same round bed (it might actually have been the same bed) I'd made love to

Zamara, truly, had felt her soft belly and hips so sensually and naturally rolling beneath me, had felt her skinny arms around my neck and had watched in astonished adoration as private pleasure and mute desolation and even something like deepest wishfulness showed in the beautiful, long-lashed young face beneath me, the face turned sideways on the red satin pillow or looking open-eyed at me or past me into the mirror, where I guess the undeluded story was being told, but I couldn't stop smoothing her damp, soft hair with my fingers, kissing her, I felt overwhelmed with tenderness and even sadness, wishing at the same time for it to be possible for us to share something other than this and knowing it was impossible and not knowing, not comprehending that really it was her stealthy-as-a-panther spirit that was embedding itself in that place where one can love, that it was *that* and not her vulnerable abjection which moved me. I felt close to the source of something important that night, and I didn't even see it. Though I did kind of piss her off when I started babbling that I was going to save her, and she very haughtily scolded, "*Y vos quién sós, Jesucristo?*"

Vos. Guess what finally came in the mail?

Moya once knew a girl, born of Nicaraguan and Guatemalan parents, who had lived through two devastating earthquakes, the Managua earthquake of '72, and the one in Guatemala just over three years later, both of which occurred at night. Both times the wall behind Moya's friend's bed, as well as parts of the roof above, fell down upon her as she slept; both times her father's strong arms pulled her out through rubble in her bed just as she was waking up to the surprise of not being dead. Both times, exactly the same.

So it was for Moya, two rooms, two earthquakes (no strong arms): the first time in Flor's old basement bedroom in Namoset, when Roger said, "Moya, Flor had a secret lover," and the second in Alma Mejía's apartment in Mexico City, where Moya now lives on a sofa in the small living room, when, sitting on that sofa, he opened Roger's five-page letter, which had been mailed from Puerto Barrios, Guatemala, postmarked three weeks before, and read:

"Moya, I better just come out with it. Flor's secret lover was Celso Batres. Rosana Letones told me that they used to meet in a hotel suite that Celso kept in the Cortijo Reforma. That's the same hotel my father and I stayed in! Even the chambermaids knew! And Rosana knew because her grandmother, the mother of that Guardia Nacional colonel who's still in jail in Nicaragua, lives in that very hotel. Also Celso used to go with Flor when she had to go out of the country sometimes and probably vice versa, this confirmed by Rosana on her own orphan biz trips to Sweden and other countries, when people sometimes confuse her with Flor and even ask after Celso. Moya, let me get right to it, and, honest to God, I don't blame you, at least I don't think I do and pray that there's no reason to, because you didn't already know, did you, that night in the Omni when you told me about the time you boasted to Celso about Flor, you didn't know then, did you?"

Don't even confide in your own shadow, *vos*. Moya's country's folk sayings are nothing if not as apt to reality as folk sayings can be; he used to like to think this one ruled him, that even his own shadow was ignorant of his deepest secrets, thoughts, and anxieties since he never even whispered of these things in its presence. Keep your own shadow in the dark! (But cast a lucid gaze over everything.) *Bueno.*

Celso Batres, of course, had many qualities that Flor would have found endearing and attractive. Handsome, intelligent, wealthy, uncorrupted, even idealistic, no murderer, certainly an occasional reader of Darío.

She could be a little crazy, you know. It was as if hobgoblins, desert spirits, had stayed on inside her. Once there was a storm and Flor slipped silently from the bed. Moya woke, noticed her missing, and then found her standing naked with her arms out on the small balcony outside the window in a torrential rain that tasted of the Caribbean and wild and chilly mountain winds, lightning flashing in the shaking leaves all around. As Moya crawled through the window, all she said, in English, was "I love it here, Marco. I've never been so happy." "Moya," said Moya, thinking that perhaps she *had* said Moya. He stood beside her, naked himself; teeth chattering, amazed by the ecstatic gleam of her eyes. Back in the room, she calmly dried herself off, smiling at him without a word. Then she went out to make the rounds of orphan checking and came back chuckling because she'd found the orphan boy with the thyroid condition in the older girls' dormitory and had decided to let him stay there because both he and the girl whose bunk he was sharing were sound asleep, oh, so sweet. She immediately fell asleep herself, and in the morning claimed she only remembered certain fragments, she was certain they'd both shared the same dream, though she admitted that in 1979 she'd briefly had a relationship with one Marco Tulio, an architect who had suddenly and without explanation left the country, he's in Madrid now, well, you know how it was back then, he owned that chalet on the lake where—Did I really say his name? I really said *Marco*? How funny, I haven't thought about him in ages! Moya, you *can't* be jealous of some guy I went out with *four* years ago!

Clutching Flor in his arms after a bout of love during his five unforgettable weeks of not quite unrestricted nightly access (surreptitious late-night arrivals, dawn fleeings), Moya often had the remorseless feeling that he was presiding over the dissolution of the old Moya. It felt almost like an urge to die, a gambler's fearless but submissive faith in what comes after. He fell *totalmente* in love with her and soon lost all sense of familiarity with himself, a condition that challenged him all the more because she never once unequivocally declared that she was in love with him, though now and then she wavered; even her impassioned confusion seemed glorious cause for hope. Moya couldn't believe that he wouldn't eventually master both her indecision and his own unprecedented inner chaos, and emerge better for Flor from the struggle as well. In the meantime he went around in a feverish monk's rapture. Even by day, during those five weeks of love, he lived in a nocturnal carnival of watching her, smelling her, tasting, listening to, studying her. After they made love he wouldn't even wash, escaping with her salty film intact. He sat at his *El Minuto* desk humming her four-note love cry; the memory of her stilled-black-minnow gaze, her ever-scrutinizing and mysterious eyes maddened his afternoons. Moya had always been a robust lover, stunning his foreign girls with his unfailingly uncomplicated endurance; he had never been inventive, but he'd raised a lot of dust. But *floramor* was something else, like one of those fairy tales where the suitor has to perform ten perilous tasks first, *vos*. She said once that that was why she preferred older men, well certain ones, they were cheerfully perverse and had hearty and expert appetites minus the apologies or shyness of youth, they didn't give sex all those dumb meanings. In response to Moya's flabbergasted look she giggled. She said she was only *jodiendo,* that is, she was not being quite sincere, and then she turned her head to the other side of the pillow, laughing so deeply she ended up curled into a little ball. Another time Moya noticed Flor gazing at him with a chillingly premonitory sadness, but even before he could ask why, she said, "Someday, Moya, some other woman is going to get all the benefit of everything I'm teaching you." "No!" She had always known it was just temporary, and never pretended otherwise. Yet when Moya realized she was serious about leaving Guatemala, he said he would go too, despite the fact that she had already broken off their five-week "affair" and was now characterizing it as a beautiful but probably spent and needless passion. Moya persisted, argued, sought to prove—amazed that he was capable of pouring so many words over her doubts. How he entertained and amused her, even during those final weeks when she wouldn't see him anymore and might even have been secretly hating him (because of that boast) and almost all their conversations were over the phone. But at the very end, hadn't he almost convinced her? She said she'd never wanted to be *la primera dama* anyway.

One afternoon at *El Minuto,* only a week after Flor had broken off her affair with Moya, Celso Batres came out of his office to give Moya his daily copy of *El País* from Spain and found him sitting at his desk in a dark stupor. "Moya, why so *triste?*" asked Celso, cheerfully, the benevolent boss and benefactor, grandson of Don Celso Batres *el primero* and son of the visionary Don Rubén, in his shiny Bally loafers and Yves Saint Laurent blazer and slacks and monogrammed "it's from Jermyn Street, Moya, even better than your mother makes" shirt, and always just slightly mussed English schoolboy hair, and taller even than Moya, lean and broad shouldered and fit from going three evenings a week to tae kwon do classes with his two fair-haired little sons who always wore their white karate robes and yellow belts to the newspaper office where they ran around jamming the drinking fountains with bubble gum so that later the water sprayed out over Moya's *mamita*-stitched pants, *vos,* and sticking bubble gum mustaches on the black marble bust of Celso's illustrious late grandfather: Don Celso Batres *el primero,* once-upon-a-time Rubén Darío's worshipful young drinking partner and the founder of *El Minuto,* the most illustrious positivist paper of its day, though it hasn't increased a percentage point in circulation since. Though back then the patriarchal Don Celso certainly had not needed the money, *vos,* converting his indigo plantations to coffee, sheep firms to cattle ranches, Indian shepherds to cowboys. All that was eventually divided between four sons: two of those aging sons still living in Miami now while helping to fund their favorite extreme-rightist political party at home, *vos,* and another son living in Los Angeles, where he is a renowned interior decorator, and the oldest, the iconoclastic and visionary widower Don Rubén Darío Batres, living now behind high walls in Zona 15 on the El Salvador highway, in a secluded mansion compound said to be situated a full mile inside that pine-forested property, Don Rubén who inherited *El Minuto* as well and was its director until passing the reins to his only son, Celso (whom Flor had apparently—); a visionary and implacable and deeply religious old Don Rubén, always welcome at every papal nuncio's and archbishop's dining table, rumored to have been plotting his son's rise to political power since the day that son was born and named Celso, grooming him to be the aristocratic positivist savior and reviver of the reformist and nationalist cause of the '44 Democratic revolution once the power of those low-class military apes the gringos put in can at last be broken; a visionary Don Rubén who sent his son to the Colegio Austríaco and then to Ampleforth in England and to the Sorbonne for three years before returning him to the Universidad de San Carlos for one year to complete a law degree and begin learning his future as a man of the people; a Don Rubén who taught his son how to write courageously moderate editorials with smoke and mirrors so that a closer look would reveal they said almost nothing while creating a forceful and dignified impression and that the secret to maintaining a comparatively unfettered newspaper in Guatemala, one whose reputation for incorruptible independence would accrue to its owner and director, was to keep its circulation so tiny it could run without any advertising at all; a visionary and conspiratorial, if somewhat deluded, Don Rubén who for decades now has been cultivating junior military officers in secret, giving them seditious books to read and sending them to his brothers in Miami for advice with their investments, except none of those officers ever seemed to turn into anything but millionaire senior officers; an implacable Don Rubén with an unharmable son because fimily comes before politics and the old man with just a phone call to Miami would be able to summon a certain extreme-rightist party's private death squads like chariots from heaven should the apes or anyone ever harm his son; an astute old man who abetted his son's safety and even his social standing by marrying that son off to the daughter of his old school chum and founder of that same rightist party when that daughter was still in adolescence though Celso, enduring his sole year at the USAC, felt certain that he loved her anyway because he'd been told it was his wondrous fate to do so almost all his life and without a doubt she was charming and pretty, *vos,* that woman to whom Celso has been married fifteen years now but whom Moya has never seen anywhere but in the other newspapers' society pages, fitting her genteel gowns like packed-in cottage cheese but with a remarkable facial resemblance to her father, the same apple-cheeked face and the most beautifully cowlike eyes ever seen on a face that didn't belong to a cow, this being the wife of the same Celso Batres whom Flor had apparently loved, the same Celso who apparently had actually considered and maybe had even been on the verge of leaving his wife for Flor and who perhaps didn't really want to be president after all, who perhaps had been on the verge of committing either the most foolish or the most redemptive act of his life by running away from his preordained fate to love Flor forever?

Because why *else* had Flor suddenly dismissed Moya from her life, if not over this so-called Secret Lover whom Roger in his letter was now identifying as Celso Batres and whom of course, if it was true, Flor would not have been able to bring herself to tell Moya about, if only to spare him the humiliation, *vos*. Because what *if* Celso, after a separation of three or more months, during which Flor had briefly taken Moya as a lover despite herself, had actually and finally come back into her life, saying something like *I can't live without you, you've won, if you don't want to be first mistress someday then I will abdicate like that English king?* Because if Celso had actually divorced his wife to marry Flor he almost certainly would have been parted from his presidential future as well, because it is still a Catholic country, *vos* . . . And poor Don Rubén's only solace would have been that Celso, by inventing *¿Dónde?,* had at least fortified the family fortune and improved the national literacy rate just a little bit.

Cut the bullshit, Moya, did you know? That day, *vos,* in the *El Minuto* office, or even nearly two years later in the Omni when you confessed the boast to Roger, did you know?

This is what Moya forced himself to draw from the allusions scattered through Roger's letter: that Flor had taken Moya as her lover after at least two months of enduring her loss of Celso, which she had believed to be final, and after two simultaneous months of enduring Moya's blind and frantic persistence as well. Five weeks later, when Flor ended her *amor secreto* with Moya, perhaps she did so because Celso had unexpectedly come back. A week later Moya made his boast. Three weeks later Flor de Mayo . . . *pues*.

Rogerio, was it Moya's fault? Was it a *pendejo*'s jealousy and spiteful rage that made Moya say what he said? But how could it have been, if he didn't know? But during just that moment, when he betrayed Flor with his idiotic boast, did he somehow know it? He wouldn't even let his own shadow in on it but did his own shadow cast it up onto his lips anyway when Celso came out of the office carrying *El País* that day and said, "Why so *triste,* Moya?

Aren't any of your German girls in town this week?" Then Celso put the copy of *El País* down on his desk and smiled at his tormented employee.

Moya stared blindly at the newspaper on his desk, felt his face growing hot, and before he knew it he was answering with false, swaggering cheer: *"Ayyy, no sé, fíjese, la hembra esa, la* Flor, the one who takes care of orphans? *Me tiene bien enculado, vos! Pero es una mujer incansable!* She's inexhaustible! I just had an article on the orphan situation in mind when it started but, *puta,* I haven't had a full night's sleep since!"

For a moment Celso was silent, but he looked as if his eardrums hurt and as if this delicate yet anguishing pain was growing worse by the second: face slowly darkening, lips shrinking, eyes straining, fogging. After all, Celso had no way of positively knowing how Flor spent all her nights, so perhaps at that moment his mind was busily confirming fabricated past suspicions and jealousies of his own. His hand rigidly poised atop the copy of *El País* on Moya's desk, he rapped it with all his stiffened fingers and then lifted his hand into his blazer pocket and stammered, *"No me digas?* You don't say? *Pues. Aha . . .* There's a strange story in there today, a priest in Spain pulled out a pistol in the middle of mass and shot one of his own parishioners, *qué raro, eh?"* and he turned and headed back towards his own office while Moya hurriedly and plaintively said, "I love her, that's why I can't sleep, she loves someone else, I think, that's why she won't see me anymore," thinking that Celso wasn't even listening but he was because without even turning around he said, *"No te preocupes,* Moya, just play hard to get, I'm sure she'll come back. Women like that are all the same."

And then Celso went into his office and an hour later came out looking quite composed, saying good-bye to everybody without meeting their eyes, and he was back at work the next morning and then the next, everything normal, leaving at two in the afternoon and not coming back until six as usual, but for two days Flor wouldn't answer her own phone (*now* did Moya know it?) and when Moya phoned the orphanage office the Swedish girl who answered said she was in a meeting and on the third day Flor sounded very tired but not surprised to hear from him, *Qué tal, Moya,* but no, she still didn't want to see him, please listen, it can't be like that between us anymore, we'll be friends I'm sure, but please wait a bit Moya; though Moya went on persisting. Flor was too kind to blame him or perhaps still too stunned. Of course she didn't mention what had happened. Perhaps she was still hoping it wasn't final, and was probably hating herself, stupid Flor, getting mixed up with one of Celso's employees, one of his little *periodistas!* Maybe she'd always been terrified that Moya might say something to Celso or maybe believing it was finished between her and Celso had even secretly *wanted* Moya to say something even though theirs had been *un amor secreto* too and Moya wasn't supposed to tell anyone, but then when Celso came back it was too late and all she'd been able to do was pray silently that Moya would have the dignity to keep his promise?

So Moya caused it, he ruined their chance to be together, is that it? Flor was just with Moya to pass the time, or because she needed *someone* then, and then Celso came back. Celso had loved a "Wellesley College girl," one who, by loving Moya, from what undoubtedly would have been Celso's point of view, had returned herself to the desert.

Was it only the final illogic of despair and defeat that let Flor waver over Moya again at the very end? Or even indignation over Celso's snobby callousness, which had revealed to her the relative nobility of Moya, despite his crass boast? *Sure.* But she had liked Moya a bit, perhaps a lot, hadn't she? But it was the end. She was murdered, denounced everywhere but in *El Minuto* and *¿Dónde?*

as a baby seller. Celso Batres hid his own grief, shock, anger, and humiliation behind his suave pride. He approached catatonic, bewildered, and devastated Moya in the office and said he was sorry, a tragedy, take a week off, two weeks, he apologized for being so unsympathetic that day, she was a fine woman he was sure, he used to see her at the charity ball; that sensationalist outcry in the papers, it probably wasn't like that, was it? You were investigating all that with orphans, Moya, weren't you? We'll see when the dust settles, *pues,* time always tells . . . Celso was most convincing that day, *vos.*

And then Celso himself went away for a week, to the United States, to participate in a two-day forum on the nation's future at Georgetown University, for Celso's reputation as a moderate reformist democratic hope had spread among followers of Central American politics even without Don Rubén's manipulation, and at Georgetown he again met Dr. Sylvia McCourt, who later, at Harvard, told Moya that Celso's contribution had been most lackluster.

But when Moya returned to Guatemala more than a year after Flor's death, Celso most generously and decently rehired him, despite what Celso knew, despite how he felt, and it is not hard to imagine how he still felt, *vos,* over Moya having deceived his boss and benefactor, sharing his "mistress" behind his back, for he must even have suspected that Moya had known about him and Flor all along! Though Moya had not!

But hiring Moya back was no mere act of generosity. Undoubtedly, Moya's boast had given Celso the excuse he must have secretly yearned for in at least one-half of a divided heart, the excuse not to have to defy his own illustrious destiny and ravage his family for the pleasure of an outlaw love. Celso had hired Moya back because *caballeros* have no memories when it is the decent or prudent thing not to have them; had hired him back as his end of an unspoken gentlemen's pact to bury a dishonorable past by forcing a secret complicity upon a rival—one who hadn't even realized he'd been a rival—and who had no other source of employment or meaningful existence. Because it would never do for it to get out that Celso Batres had been the lover of the infamous *gringa-chapina* baby seller and that he had even been on the verge of abandoning his own wife for her, *vos*. Celso had the connections even to deal with the G-2 if it came to that, but Moya posed a different challenge. Better to treat Moya as a protégé, one who might share, in accordance with his position, in Celso's well-known destiny. Celso liked and respected Moya, Celso knew Moya had possibilities. Presidential secretary one day, Moya? Who knows, maybe even Ambassador Moya? Or Assistant Foreign Minister Moya? Such were the dreams of loyal *faferos*.

Moya never knew? Not even that night in the Omni, when he and Roger actually discussed the possibility that Celso might be the "Secret Lover," when Moya had been unable to disguise how perturbed he was by the possibility and seemed never to have even considered it before, though finally the two friends had dismissed it as too unlikely?

Honestly, sitting alone in the Omni throughout the day following that first night, in a red-walled whore room, on his way into exile again, this time probably permanently, because of one fucking column about the post office, that conversation with Roger about Celso barely crossed Moya's mind. He had other worries, *vos!* His fate was in Roger's hands; Roger, who at that very moment was running around Guatemala City having appointments and hopefully not sneaking off to see that *putita* of his: he was at the U.S. embassy learning from Consul Simms the seriousness of Moya's enemy's intentions, and he was at the Canadian embassy, trying to convince them that Moya deserved urgent action on his request for political refugee status ahead of so many others from through-

out Central America who made their way daily to that same beleaguered if fairly hospitable embassy seeking the same.

Picture Moya then, one peaceful spider waiting for so many
new surprises, sitting on a round red satin bed, with nothing to do
but read and reread the newspapers Roger had left for him that
morning. Well, it was his profession, it was what had brought him
to that room, after all. He read an editorial beginning "When
Guatemala City was a little cup made of silver, brimming with
peace, and the bands in the Hotel Palacio played Glenn Miller, so
that we called it the Choo Choo Hilton, after the Chattanooga
Choo Choo . . ." and turning the page, found a military spokesman saying, "These so-called disappeared, who are they? They are
people with no sense of responsibility who run off to Miami to seek
their fortunes without informing their families, abandoning wives
and children . . ." Deeper in the paper, he found the mundane news
that three separate bodies had been found by roadsides in three
separate departments, all showing signs of torture and missing
their heads. Moya knew that if he'd left Roger's house alone the
previous evening he might by now be missing his own highly iden-
tifiable head. He put the newspaper down. Now, in the Omni,
Moya wept. Quietly, *vos*. Since his return from Harvard he had
tried to be very careful in what he wrote, but that fucking post
office! He didn't want to go and live in Canada or anyplace else.

When Moya had collected himself, he recalled a prescient
conversation he'd had with his difficult friend Sylvia McCourt in
her office at Harvard only six or so months before. Sitting at her
desk lunching on yogurt and a can of tomato juice, Sylvia, by way
of trying to dissuade him from the imprudent martyr's folly of
returning to Guatemala too soon, had said:

"Moya, if I'm standing on a beach with a can of tomato juice
and I throw it into the ocean, do I then get an ocean mixed with
tomato juice? Or have I just lost my can of tomato juice?"

After a moment of reflection, Moya boomed, "Clever Sylvia! But this is the dilemma exactly! Well, which?"

"Actually," said Sylvia, blushing, "that's rather well known, I first heard it from a philosophy professor I had—"

"But ideas don't belong exclusively to anybody when people are discussing," interrupted Moya. "You said this yourself the last time we talked."

And she had, when Sylvia, exasperated by Moya's reticence during a long conversation that *she* had initiated—seemingly to prove how ferocious she could be now that she was defending her ideas on her own "home court" rather than in the Hotel Biltmore Maya—had said:

"Ideas aren't exclusively personal or incriminating, not in a discussion between professionals and friends, Moya. You don't have to hide. This isn't Cuba. Or Nicaragua, for that matter."

Which sounded like an insult to Moya, one that he could take personally or in behalf of *all* his countrymen. Sylvia had gone on pressing her attack.

"So what's the answer, Moya? *More* violence and dogmatism? Didn't the armed revolution in your own country fail because the guerrilla forces were, in fact, too ruthless? Don't they have to share the burden of so many civilian deaths caused by the army's counterinsurgency?"

"I don't know," said Moya, who was in no mood for this conversation. "I don't blame the guerrilla forces for that, for existing, if that's what you mean. Certainly not."

"They're blameless then?"

"I didn't say that. But if the armed movement had been stronger, Sylvia, perhaps they would have been able to create enough pressure for true negotiations and a true political opening," said Moya. "Isn't that realpolitik too?"

"Perhaps a strong and nonviolent mass movement, with no armed movement to muddle the picture, would also be able to create that kind of pressure, but much more effectively. And more cleanly. Grant it, Moya, there would still be . . . martyrs. But you have to admit, it hasn't been tried."

"*We did,* for ten years—"

"More than three decades is a long time ago, Moya. Conditions change."

"Not so much, I don't think."

"You've read *Le Rouge et le noir,* haven't you?" said Sylvia, trying another tact; Moya certainly had, though not in French. "You remember the scene between Julien and Comte Altamira, who led a liberal revolution in Spain that failed because he refused to cut off three heads? Julien thinks that's wimpy, doesn't he? To save four one must kill three! he declaims. To drive ignorance and crime from a country, man must pass through it like a whirlwind, violent, unafraid of poisoning himself! Is that what you think too, Moya?"

"No. But I've never been faced with such a choice, really," dissembled Moya. "Not when it mattered."

"You're faced with it every time you ask yourself what you would countenance in the name of change," said Sylvia. "Would you support and make excuses for any revolution, so long as it destroys what you already hate? Is that, finally, what you believe in, a politics of hatred and vengeance?"

"*Any* revolution, Sylvia? How many have I seen?" stammered Moya. "I'm sure there'll be adequate time for me to make up my mind before the next one comes along."

Moya, who wanted peace, justice, and liberty for his country (and a woman like Flor de Mayo, or even Sylvia, for himself) and who had recently decided that he was now a Socialist Parliamentarian Reformer (somewhat like Celso Batres was perhaps waiting to be), fell asleep that night dreaming of *whirlwinds*.

Then came the loneliest months, during which Moya hid, even from Sylvia. *Vos,* when other women had occasion to ask him where he was from, you know what Moya started doing? He found himself answering, "Mexico," or Spain or even Ecuador. Often the women knew much more about these countries than he and immediately recognized that his accent was incorrect. But Moya insisted. They went away convinced that he was quite strange. This was ridiculous of him, he knew, but, in his own experimental way, he was trying to get to know himself.

But instead of himself, Moya began to find Flor de Mayo. He found her everywhere in his lonely winter wanderings, during which he always felt dilapidated and sad, though eventually he began to feel dignified rather than frightened by his own sadness. Her shadow was everywhere, asking him why she was a shadow and whispering to him of the one period in his life when he had felt relieved of himself and on the verge of learning something else. "Boy wonder," her shadow teased him, and suddenly he felt full of pride and overwhelming embarrassment. Those solitary winter walks, when his shadow talked silently to Flor, both challenging and exhausting him, truly were Moya's first experience of freedom; so many opposites felt balanced within him: love and hate, to name the most obvious, but also high-mindedness and banality, bravery and cowardliness, vengefulness and forgiveness, loyalty and betrayal, absence and presence, guilt, no guilt—those walks when he knew he couldn't bring harm to anyone no matter what he confided to his own shadow or to Flor's or to anyone's.

One day, well into his stay at Harvard, almost exactly a year to the day after Flor perished, Moya saw a little *niña indigena* in a snowsuit playing in a snowy yard. His epiphany spawned an idea that spawned a conviction: a chronicle that, like that little girl, would be part of both the smaller world and the larger, one grafted almost seamlessly onto the other, and thus its actual range enlarged! That very night he pulled out his old and unfinished newspaper chronicle and spent weeks trying to complete it for his nonfiction narrative class final paper. But he failed utterly to abolish himself; it was as if Moya needed this story, along with all his stifling Moya-ness, to be adopted by someone else, someone living in an at least theoretically wider and more ventilated world. As has been told, he eventually thought of his old friend Roger Graetz. It was just an idea, and it was acted upon.

But, *vos,* it was never meant to lead to *this,* was it? The mad idea circuitously deposited in Roger's letter? That Moya's boast could in some way have had something to do with Flor's death, because it had so briefly plunged Flor into grief, turmoil, and maybe even self-destructiveness that she had given in to her wickedest invisible self or perhaps had just been so disoriented that she had sent one María de la Luz Caycam Quix to France without her brother Lucas?

"—because if you did know, and you lied to mc about that like you did about the guerrilla thing, or even if only your goddamned hair knew, Moya, and *that's* why it's turning white, well then is that what you wanted me to find out all along? You wanted mc to find out so that I could tell you not to blame yourself? Well, finally, Moya, I *don't* in fact blame you, OK? Not for *that,* just so long as it's not more important to you than knowing who actually murdered her. I don't blame you for that, and maybe I am just going crazy, because all I want to know now is, DID YOU KNOW? And when I get to Mexico, any day now, you will tell me, won't you?"

On that second evening in the Omni, Roger finally returned from his missions, knocking on the door. Water was running in the red heart-shaped tub in the bathroom. After scrubbing the tub twice with the cleaning implements he'd let the chambermaid pass through the revolving hatch, Moya was preparing a bath. He turned the water off, began putting his clothing back on, and shouted, "Rogerio?"

"Yup," answered Roger, drawing out *yup*'s vowel.

Moya hurried to unlock the door, and Roger came in, carrying a large envelope, which he tossed onto the bed before going directly into the bathroom to urinate. As he did so, he told Moya a little story: "That night I was here with Zamara, as soon as we finished making love she jumped out of bed and ran in here and took a shower. I mean as soon as we finished! I was kind of hurt, you know? But then she came back and we made love all night practically."

Then Roger came out of the bathroom, sat down on the bed, and looked at Moya, who was leaning against the red velvet wall and enduring an ulcerous cramp in his stomach, undoubtedly caused by stress and not the greasy fried chicken that had been served through the hatch for lunch.

"Are you going to marry her?" asked Moya, to break the silence.

"I already got my inheritance," said Roger. And then he sighed and said, "So you ready? You better sit down."

Moya decided to remain standing. Did Roger feel he had some new power over him simply because he'd saved Moya from a death squad the night before and now had spent the day arranging his fate? He sensed in Roger something he never had before, a capacity for petty cruelty.

Now Roger talked, explaining that Consul Simms had said that it was only "a heavy-handed tail," meant to send an unambiguous message, to Moya, not himself of course, they could have splattered Moya like tomato sauce all over the sidewalk while Roger just stood there if they'd wanted—

"You mean like tomato juice," said Moya.

"Whatever . . . So I didn't save your life."

"*Claro,* you *did,* Rogerio," insisted Moya. Was that what was bothering Roger? "Maybe just by being there."

"But it doesn't matter what I *did,* they were just trying to scare you."

"But that's good news, Rogerio!"

"Well, I guess," said Roger glumly.

"And the embassy, *vos?*"

"That refugee program is full. They say go to Mexico, to the embassy there, fill out these forms I brought you. The embassy here will recommend they take you if after a few months in Mexico you still want to go to Canada."

"And how am I going to get to Mexico? Did you say a few months, *vos?*"

"I booked you a ticket. Noon tomorrow. I'll give you some money to live on, it should last until you get to Canada, I hope it will."

"*If* I get to Canada," said Moya, who, in fact, never did and is in Mexico still. "In Mexico I will starve!"

"They're turning away an awful lot of people, Moya. The only reason I didn't have to wait in line for hours was because of that urgent action telegram from Aunt Irene. You know why they really won't let you come to Canada right away? Their policy is they're not going to give you all this money and an apartment and let you go to their universities and everything if in the end you're just going to come back here like some kind of addict next time things cool down. They know that's what you did the last time."

"But the last time I had not had such a heavy-hand message, *vos!*" The last time, on that day the previous year when he had phoned Sylvia and Laura Moore in Washington and set his first exile swiftly in motion, he hadn't been receiving anything more than the usual threats; what had become unbearable was the stifling nausea of helpless disappointment and regret he'd been suffering in silence ever since Flor's death.

"The guy did recommend that if you belong to any of the guerrilla organizations, then you should put that in the form, because, once you've admitted that, then you really can't come back. But I told him you don't. I was right to tell him that, wasn't I?"

"*Gracias,* Rogerio," said Moya, after a moment's silence. "*Eres un amigazo.* You are a great friend."

They were silent for a long moment. Then Roger stood up and said, "Crazy fucking world. Sorry, I can't just sit here another night." And then Roger went swiftly out the door again, saying, "Listen, Moya, you stay *right* here."

He came back at five in the morning, smelling freshly dusted with the same *putas'* cheap perfumes that lay faint and stale over everything in the Omni, and in something resembling a transcendent mood.

"She loves *me,* Moya, I can tell! I danced with her all night! And it's nuts, but I think I love her too, in a way. I mean she's just so . . . I don't know."

"You do not know, *vos.*"

"Oh come on, Moya, don't go getting all uppity *now.*"

"You have no right to do this, *vos,*" said Moya. "It is like colonizing a heart, making it your own banana *finca.*"

"Moya, for Chrissakes, not every flicking thing is politics—"

"Except she is going to believe that you love her. What she loves is the life she thinks you can give her, Rogerio. OK, *vos,* we all take our chances. But her heart can break like any other, so don't go telling yourself that it won't, just because she is a *puta.*"

"She's not a . . . Well, technically she is, but—Moya, I won't hurt her, I couldn't—"

"And that lieutenant of López Nub, *vos?*"

"The hell with Nub."

"Rogerio."

"She hasn't seen him in days."

"Rogerio, you cannot mess with—"

"Moya, I'm not suicidal. OK?"

So it went until nearly dawn, when the two friends finally managed to catch a few hours' sleep. Still ahead was the ride to the airport, that always dangerous stretch of highway into the airport where so many heavy-handed messages turned into the cruelest and most final hoax of all.

In the morning we phoned a taxi and rode back into the city so that Moya could pack some things from his room in the Pension Bremen. I'd thought that was unsafe, but Moya said it was a risk he was willing to take so as not to arrive in Mexico like some shipwrecked sailor. So we went to my house first, so I could change my clothes too, get some more money, and give Moya what I had to give him. Moya didn't want to say good-bye to his mother in person, though, it was better to leave her out of it, he said. He'd written her a letter, which I would mail for him, that would have to suffice.

Moya's room: cans of Doral *frijol negro* on the sill, bread rolls moldy in a humidity-fogged plastic bag; paperbacks piled in a corner, newspapers everywhere; no television, one plastic radio; his clothes carefully hung and folded in an old stand-up wardrobe; his chess computer; a desk with an old Royal portable typewriter on top, and drawers stuffed with papers, which he searched frantically through, making instant decisions, leaving some in the drawer, putting others directly into a large, tattered cowhide suitcase, including, of course, your old notebook, his photocopied version of it. He put on his Harvard necktie and paid a week's rent in advance (with my money), apologizing profusely to the Bremen's manager, who said he understood and would clean the room out himself.

When we came back outside, and his suitcase had been put away in the trunk, two large men stepped out from the doorway next to the pension's and got into the taxi with us without saying anything, one into the front passenger seat, the other in back. They were both young, in their twenties like us, both of them solid looking, one chunky, the other tall and strapping; one wore a denim jacket with large front pockets, the other a zippered windbreaker. The taxi driver's eyes, huge with worry, were fixed on mine in the rearview mirror. My first frantic instinct was to run, but I was sitting, stuck, in the middle—Moya leaned across me to shake hands and calmly told the driver not to worry. Then they were introducing themselves by name, which probably weren't their real names though I didn't catch them anyway; nor was I really able to focus on the small talk passing between them on the long ride out to the airport. Everyone fell silent and kept his eyes out the windows when we passed through the old aqueduct arch and into that long stretch of road running between a military base and the military airfields in the remoter stretches of the airport complex. The guy in back held one hand poised over his jacket pocket the whole way.

But it wasn't until we reached the terminal and it was decided that one would wait in the taxi while the other came in that I was sure. Because the one in back took off his jacket before getting out, and that was when I saw the hanging weight of a gun in that denim pocket as he laid it on the seat. The three of us went inside, and through the metal detectors, and then did everything else you do in an airport, including killing some time over coffee and sweet rolls in the upstairs café, where Moya tried to explain himself to me. When at last it was time for Moya to go through *migración*, we stood suspensefully watching from the other side of the fenced-off area, because sometimes they snatch people there at the very last second. The two of us watched until the official had checked through Moya's papers and finally stamped his passport; then he

was let through the glass doors, into the long murky corridor leading to the departure gates, where he turned to wave good-bye.

So Moya kept that one secret, the secret that justified all secretiveness, the one he must have always told himself it was the
most important to keep, so important to keep that he barely admitted it even to himself. He'd maintained only the most ambiguous and sporadic contacts anyway (he'd hurriedly and whisperingly
tried to explain as we sat upstairs in a deserted corner of the café),
since that's how they do it in the city now. He'd never before even
met the two *compañeros* who'd accompanied us that day, he'd simply phoned his contact from the Omni, speaking in a code. So did
I understand? "Rogerio, you too could be 'organized,' and even
though we work together, I might never know it." His duties had
required little more from him than that he be exactly as I'd always
seen him. Well, what could I say, then and there, in the airport café,
with his bodyguard listening in, occasionally contributing a softly
assenting *"Sí pues."* I just sat there nodding.

I never saw them again, Moya's *compañeros* in a nearly defeated army, who must have thought highly of Moya, to provide
an armed escort to the airport. To be honest, I was frightened of
riding back in the taxi with them. We shook hands, exchanged the
usual pleasantries, I gladly insisted on paying their fare to wherever they were going and told them that I just felt like walking.
It's a short walk, from the airport into Zona 10; I thought I'd go
and have a good lunch outside by the pool at the Biltmore Maya.

On that stretch of road leaving the airport there is a very long
wall that was obviously put there to keep people from seeing whatever happens in the military airfield on the other side. The wall's
entire length is decorated with murals painted by schoolchildren,
each one displaying a signature like "Colegio Santa Maria, Jocotán,
4th grade." Schoolchildren from all over the country were selected
to paint their happy and universal daydreams on that wall. Some

of the murals depict village *fiestas* without the drunkards, others circus scenes and animals; a fabulous white ocean liner in an ocean full of smiling sea creatures; farm scenes with roosters and pigs; happy families standing outside happy houses with happy pets. I didn't feel afraid anymore: if anything I even felt a little exhilarated, the ordeal and scary excitement of the last few days behind me, something new ahead. I knew I was safer, more "invisible" than ever now, with Moya gone. Browsing along that wall that informs travelers they are in a country that puts the happiness of children above everything else, ignoring the traffic behind and the varied air traffic overhead, I suddenly recalled the strange sensation of a remote childhood happiness of my own: those long-ago winter evenings, always just before supper, when I had to go outside and shovel Klink's puppy shit up from the snow, wrap it in newspaper, and put it into the small aluminum incinerator that resembled a funny little robot without limbs. I always struck more of the long wooden matches than necessary and stayed out there longer than I had to, smelling newspapers and puppy shit burning, watching damp white smoke pouring from the incinerator and floating up into the dark winter air. Except now I couldn't at all remember what it is I actually used to think about out there, or what it was exactly that had always made it pure bliss. But in my imagination I sort of painted myself onto that wall anyway, standing there beside a smiling little incinerator, puffy smoke rising into a sky the color of an old dirty nickel, snowflakes coming down, the Copacabana behind me and your light on in the basement, bright yellow in the small rectangular window just above the lawn.

Those were the first moments of the six-month stretch since Moya left, that whole separate short lifetime, which will definitely be coming to an end in another day or two, when I will take a launch to Punta Gorda, Belize, and from there make my way by bus through the Yucatán to Mexico City.

TWENTY-FOUR

S or Clarita was given dispensation by her order to spend as much time in the capital as necessary to resolve the fiasco of María de la Luz having been adopted by the de Preys of Paris minus her brother Lucas, two years before *los padres* Caycam turned up alive in the Ixil. With the help of the French embassy, she was able to track down the de Preys and write to them; two weeks later she received a typed and notarized reply in perfect Spanish. In that letter the de Preys maintained that you had merely informed them that María de la Luz was the only survivor of a family that had included three older siblings; you had not mentioned a specific Lucas. María de la Luz, only one year old when she was brought down from the mountains with her brother and three when she was adopted, has never, wrote the de Preys, shown any signs of remembering any member of her natural family. Surely, if she had a living brother, she would have at least spoken his name? The de Preys, however, were not going to damage "Lucecita's" fragile sense of security by dwelling on the subject of a missing brother with her, just as they had decided not to tell her what had happened to you. She was still far too young to be able to absorb such news or to comprehend its meaning, especially now that her past seemed safely buried beneath a five-year-old's absorption in and healthy adaption to her new life: the life, wrote the de Preys, that would be hers for the rest of her days and would never be re-placed by any other, the true life now of María de la Luz de Prey. As for María de Ia Luz's natural parents supposedly having turned up alive all these years later, missing all their children, the de Preys were skeptical. They questioned if the Caycams are who they claim to be, and wondered if they had invented the story as a means of

535

seeking financial gain. Though, of course, added the de Preys, if by some miracle a brother named Lucas is alive and found, and it can be proven that he is indeed María de la Luz's brother, they will do their duty and adopt him too.

"It's obvious that these are good people, to reply so scrupulously to just an ordinary nun with no legal power to do anything," said Sor Clarita, feeling confused by the news that the de Preys would adopt Lucas if we found him, since this was not likely to please the Caycams. "Because honestly, if there was a way to have left them out of this completely without doing an injustice to the Caycams . . . But instead, here is a faraway nun they wish they had never heard of, filling their home, a very good home I am sure, with so much undeserved doubt and turmoil. Have you ever heard of anything like this before, a nun whose work it is to spread unhappiness?"

More letters were exchanged, Sor Clarita reiterated that she had seen Lucas alive with her own eyes and in writing to them had merely intended to inquire if they knew of anything that might illuminate the mystery of his fate. As for the Caycams, she was fully convinced that they were indeed María de la Luz's natural parents. The French embassy raised the obvious point that the Guatemalan family court was unlikely to rescind the adoption on behalf of a poor Indian internal refugee family anyway, and that, even if they did, the French courts would undoubtedly refuse to extradite the child. Against her own better judgment and even wishes, Sor Clarita had to reply that God's law is higher. It was unthinkable that María de la Luz, now nearly five and French-speaking, should be taken from her wealthy and loving parents in France and returned to her natural parents to live in a zinc-roofed shed in a model village, though nevertheless the Caycams continued to insist that they wanted their one definitely surviving child back.

But when I last spoke to Sor Clarita, about a month ago now in Guatemala City, she had finally arranged a solution. Photographs of María de la Luz de Prey depicting all aspects of her extraordinary new life now decorated the rough plank walls of the resigned Caycams' shed in A'tzumbal. Soon, a substantial cash payment from the de Preys would arrive, which, along with the intervention of the French embassy, would liberate the Caycams from that model village and allow them to resume some vestige of their former life. They'd be much better off materially than before, though of course much poorer in family and community, since neither really existed for them anymore. They had also been promised a trip to Paris to visit their daughter; the de Preys were terrified that the authorities might confiscate María de la Luz if they were to bring her for a visit here. They were inviting Sor Clarita to come to Paris too, to act as translator and to provide spiritual comfort and even sanity on what promised to be a taxing journey for the Caycams.

"They are wonderful people, this family de Prey," said Sor Clarita, full of amazed emotion in the Hemmings. "At any step along the way, they could have refused to discuss it further and left it to the courts, and that would have been the end of it. Sometimes I even wished they would, I was prepared to accept all responsibility. But for it to end like this? *Es una maravilla. Fíjese,* these de Preys really do care about the poor Caycams."

"Well, Flor did choose them to be the parents," I said.

"Claro," said Sor Clarita softly. "No matter what else, she did that . . . *Ay no, pobre la Flor,* because truly, she was a love. I was always saying, Flor, why aren't you married yet? When is the wedding, *pues?* I was teasing, but perhaps if she had found someone good for her . . ."

"Yes, I know," I said, as we both fell into another of those silences that will forever, in my memory, seem inseparable from the Pastelería Hemmings mezzanine and the melancholy view outside.

"That little girl is already learning to play the piano," Sor Ciarita finally said. "Imagine what it will be like for the Caycams to see that!"

By then Sor Clarita had long ago given up her search for Lucas—which I'd sporadically helped her in—among the street children of Guatemala City, so many of whom had instantly claimed to be Lucas as soon as they'd sensed they might have something to gain. Eventually she'd come to believe that the likeliest scenario was that Lucas must have run away from Los Quetzalitos within days of having arrived, because that would explain why no one remembered him there. And that then, poor *patojito* of blackest horrors and misfortune, Lucas might have lost his life in any number of ways amidst the perils of the city streets, or even in trying to make his way back to the Ixil, driven by some suicidal mission of retribution. Though for all we could ever know, Lucas had walked all the way to the United States to find a better life, never intending to come back at all or even to send for his baby sister—which in the courts would probably have constituted abandonment of family. In that case, you would have been well within the law, "such as it is," arranging for the de Preys to adopt María de la Luz, since you had no way of knowing that the Caycams were alive. Though that still didn't explain why you'd neglected to tell anyone about Lucas.

Sor Clarita ventured the possibility, perhaps even the certainty, that because you'd decided that it was best for María de la Luz to become a de Prey, and because you had little or no more knowledge of Lucas's whereabouts or fate than we, you decided not to mention him, making his oblivion complete, so as not to risk any impediment towards swiftly legalizing the adoption; or to provide anyone, perhaps your most hostile nemesis, Colonel Malespín, the head of *migración,* with an excuse for seeking a large bribe.

But I thought, though I kept these ruminations to myself, that it was just as possible that you, quite simply, had forgotten all about Lucas, or that you were feeling too distracted to pay attention to the usual protocols and details just then, or that maybe in your rancor at life you'd even decided to defy them. Because if the adoption was finalized on February 3, 1983, that was right around the time of your breakup with Moya, and also right around the time that Rosana Letones's grandmother, Doña Hercilia Letones, noted, as did all the other gossips in the Hotel Cortijo Reforma, including the chambermaids, that you had briefly resumed your afternoon rendezvous with Celso Batres in a suite he kept for that purpose in that same hotel; which was also around the time that Moya made his indiscreet boast, which I'd bet anything is why for the last two weeks of your life you were no longer seen arriving on foot just before or after Celso at the Hotel Cortijo Reforma in the afternoons, nor was Celso. (And in Mexico I'll find out whether or not my friend Moya could possibly have intended that as the inevitable consequence of his boast . . . simply because I need to know, for myself now, and that's all.)

Of course none of this means that you were a criminal, Flor. Just because you at times liked to live a double or even a triple life; or because you could tell a monumental lie; or because you felt taunted by the secret unreality of your life; or because the defeat that was your own heartbreak compounded the encircling darkness of something or everything else—none of that means you were a criminal, or that you somehow saw or sensed the end coming and then for some reason decided to justify it in advance or to tempt it.

These were my obsessions. And it was I who became obsessed, though for just a while, with the absurd notion that Lucas Caycam Quix might have been your murderer, though this was based on nothing, on evidences as insubstantial as phantoms. I never forgot that I was developing my Lucas scenario almost in a last desperate attempt to make sense of the world for myself, trying to understand what it was in *you,* what might have been happening in you at that time that could have led him—or *anyone*—into your bedroom, carrying a sharp knife, on the fatal night. Not needing him to be real and not even wanting him to be real, believing he had *nothing* to do with you beyond an accidental involvement in an indecipherable but inevitable fate, I led Lucas Caycam Quix to you, Flor. He was the missing piece that allowed me to assemble an illusion out of phantom evidences, that's all. Because Lucas was small and light-footed enough to be the intruder who woke none of the sleeping orphans in his coming or going that night, but who left the one wide-awake orphan with the haunting memory of an easily dismissed noise amidst the silence. And Lucas had a motive, one implausible enough for an implausible murder. Most of all, I eventually understood, he was a murderer I could almost forgive, so that I could go on hating what had spawned him even more. But I should make absolutely clear that all of this, everything I was able to learn, fmd out, divine, about Lucas Caycam Quix, and even Celso Batres and the *niñera fafera,* happened during the first three months after Moya left. And then I gave up, because it was all contradictory, mixed up, inconclusive, but I felt I understood it well enough now according to my own needs and design. What came next was three months, basically, of Zamara, three months of something like live and let live, and Zamarita. Until, just a few weeks ago now, when Mariel the street girl claimed to have found Lucas and said that she could prove it.

When Sor Clarita first introduced me to the mystery of Lucas Caycam Quix that January morning in Pastelería Hemmings, I'd already talked to the one orphan who was awake that night, and it was soon after that Rosana Letones let Edvarga and me in on what she knew about you and Celso.

Because I'd already accompanied Larry to Los Quetzalitos on his haircutting day by then: stepping through those rust-speckled sheet-metal gates for the second time in my life and for the first time since I'd done so with my father, my heart hanging from a thread of apprehension and secret thrill as we made our way up the walk, Larry carrying his barbering tools in a brown paper bag, past Ozzie Peterkins's jungle gym and into the main house, where I immediately found myself swarmed by a clamoring horde of love-starved orphans in that first-floor playroom full of broken toys (where later I even found the same indestructible rubber spider you handed me on our last shopping trip to Macy's). I picked a tiny Indian girl named Francisca up in my arms because I had to pick somebody, so many were shouting and jumping up and down with their tiny hands in the air. She looked just like a baby brown Zamarita with the long bangs Larry had given her a month before; Francisca wrapped her arms tightly around my neck and then wouldn't let go, she kept kissing my cheeks and singing out happy little shrieks, and whenever I tried to put her down she just held on tighter, looking at me with the panic of a little girl being waded through deep water. Larry set up his temporary barbershop in the one-story schoolhouse outside the main house so as to escape the stampede, and I had no choice but to carry Francisca over there with me, and must have been holding her for nearly an hour already when I felt her warm pee dribbling over my arms. Larry cut thirty-nine heads of orphans' hair that day, which ended with both of us showering with antilice shampoo in the Scandinavians' bathroom (not *your* old bathroom, thankfully). True to his nature, he gave the boys military haircuts unless they knew exactly what they wanted instead, and indulged all the girls, employing every flourish learned in his Kentucky haircutting school and improvising others. *Niñeras* brought the younger children over from the house in groups of five—one of them picked up bawling Francisca and carried her away while I was still at the sink trying to wash the front of my shirt; when I put it back on, I left it unbuttoned. Only the older children were having classes that day, though these did not seem to be conducted with any firmness of purpose. Of the six windowed classrooms off the central area where Larry was cutting hair, two were in use: in one a middle-aged woman was writing the names of world capitals with chalk on a blackboard, and, in the other, one of the Scandinavian volunteers was sitting at her desk immersed in a magazine, some of the children bent over workbooks and others ambling in and out of the classroom to watch Larry. I soon found myself sitting on the floor with three of the older girls playing jacks and was positive I recognized at least one of them from the photograph of you outside the zoo, not so much by her features as by her laugh: the way, turning her head away to laugh, she held her knuckles to her lower lip; the lift of her eyebrow; light softly shining off the top of her high cheek. No one seemed puzzled over my presence there that day, certainly no one recognized me, and no one mentioned you at all. It was agonizing not to be able to ask them any of countless questions, to accept that all I could do was watch and listen, but this was weirdly enthralling too, to be a spy among children. The girls I was playing jacks with were too shy to converse with me, though they were quietly glancing at each other, shaking with giggles throughout. They were fourteen years old at most but already wore cheap lipstick, painted their nails, and were extraordinarily expert players, bouncing the ball and scooping up jacks with effortless sweeps of their hands. When it was my turn, they all ended up covering their faces with their hands.

Larry said, "Hey, Ed, where's Rosey?" Hand clamped around the back of a little boy's head, Larry was mowing away another Indian cowlick and exaggeratedly smiling and rolling his eyes at someone behind me; I looked over my shoulder and saw that one of the teachers, slim, blond, nearly diminutive Edvarga, had come out of her classroom. She said, "If it's Tuesday afternoon, she has gone to play cards with her grandmother and her friends. Her grandmother lives in the Hotel Cortijo Reforma," and she sniffily and confidingly added, "Rosana's father was one of Somoza's generals, they have much money," and then she smiled warmly at me. "So is this why you have come here today, to practice jacks? You are not a hairstylist too?" Then Edvarga, who hates being called Ed, abandoned her classroom to join in for several rounds of jacks. Apparently the schooling in Los Quetzalitos has always been fairly lax, from even before your time, Flor. I'm sure you did your best to improve it, but you couldn't do *everything* yourself.

One of the older boys who had his hair cut that day, exasperating Larry by insisting on a Michael Jackson cut, was Patricio, the eighteen-year-old whose incurable thyroid condition makes him look like an unnaturally elongated and emaciated ten-year-old with a wise old man's world-weary eyes. That long-ago day when I went to spy through the orphanage mail slot, he was the one I saw lagging behind that strange procession with the little boy who had your old laundry hamper strapped to his back. Patricio, according to Rosana, isn't expected to live for many more years, but he shouldn't have the sexual energy he apparently has either, though Rosana says he's much more of a tireless fondler, embracer, and smoocher than he is a tireless fornicator. But there's no stopping him, so as a precaution she gives him rubbers and he claims to use them, he's always asking for more, though Rosana suspects this is just an image-conscious ploy. I mention this mainly because it explains what Patricio was doing in the older girls' dormitory the night you died, when he was the one wide-awake orphan.

But I didn't meet Rosana Letones until the next time I went there, on my own, ostensibly to visit Edvarga. She really is quite a card, Rosana, fortyish, with a plain, friendly, brown face, a winning look of almost adolescent merriment in her eyes, and a lavish figure that, snugly packed as it always is into tight blouses, tighter jeans and hoisted up on high heels, seems always to be saying a gracefully timed if slightly lascivious good-bye to that manner of dressing.

One day during the Christmas season, Rosana let me take a group of six boys, including Patricio, on an outing for the first time. She trusted me well enough by then, without having any idea of our connection, Flor. But the orphanage is in this way like a lending library. Rosana never lets me take the girls, because everyone always wants to take the girls and the boys are always being left behind; the girls are cuter and better behaved, and the boys need big-brotherly role models. I took them downtown to Zona 1, to see the famous Arrau store Santa Claus, not having seen him myself in over twenty years. I'd warned my relatives in advance that I'd be doing that, ascribing it to a sentimental motive that probably didn't fool my worried Uncle Jorge. But there he was, standing on our blue-and-white tiled second-story balcony over Sexta Avenida, dressed as Santa, megaphone speakers mounted in the window behind him: the same small man who has been pantomiming along to my *abuelo*'s old tape recording for four decades now, never neglecting to open his mouth for a single one of the Belizean opera singer's booming *ho ho hos*. The block was closed off with barricades and police for the performance as always, packed with children and parents, and when Santa started raining candy and small plastic trinkets down, there was a mad, shrieking and roiling scramble. But Patncio clung to me, his cool sweaty palms grasping my arm and his head rested against my ribs. He is easily exhausted, very frail, he certainly didn't have the energy to join the mad scramble for candy.

"I've seen this before," he said dismissively. "La Flor brought us once."

That was the very first time I'd ever heard your name on one of your orphan's lips, Flor.

"Who?" I asked.

"Flor de Mayo," he said. "She died."

"How?" I asked.

"Murdered, *pues*." He clucked his tongue impatiently. "You didn't know that?"

"I've heard something about it," I said. "How did it happen?"

"Nobody knows," he singsonged, rolling his head against my side. I had to quickly return my girl cousins' waves now; they'd spotted me in the crowd from inside one of the mannequin-filled display windows.

"Did you like her, Patricio?"

"*Ah sí, claro, fue muy buena onda!*" he said, and then he giggled happily. "*Vos,* she liked making love." Then he imitated a woman's love cries, tremulously, not obscenely but mischievously, I understood that, but still.

"That's not very respectful, Patricio," I said, forcing myself to smile. "*Eres muy pillo.*" You're really an imp.

He giggled again. "The whole world likes to make love, she was no different, and she was lonely a lot. But when she wasn't, *ooooo!* Much noisier than Rosana." Some of the other little boys had come back, holding fistftuls of candy, pockets bulging with candy; one of them had a slightly bloodied lip.

"So you always know what's going on, huh, Patricio?"

He raised his small, wan face to gaze up at me. "*Claro.* But I wish I'd seen *el asesino.* I almost did, *vos.* Only I, because the rest were all asleep . . ."

On the night you died, Patricio, as he often does, had snuck into the older girls' dormitory, in a separate little bungalow next to the classrooms. He was lying awake in the arms of a soundly sleeping fourteen-year-old named Sarita in the top bunk closest to the window offering an unobstructed view of the front gates and the path to the main house. But the quiet rasp of the gate being unlatched and opened in one motion was the first sound he heard, and when he looked over the gate was already being quietly closed from the other side, he only heard its soft metal thump.

"Fue todo," that was all, said Patricio, there in the crowd in front of the Arrau store, while Tchaikovsky's bells boomed again from Abuelito's old recording.

That night Patricio had drifted off to sleep without giving it another thought, assuming it just must have been one of the full-time *niñeras* sneaking out.

So you didn't even scream—because you never had a chance to understand or because you understood too well? Your murderer severed your windpipe with a highly sharpened and medium-sized blade, maybe even a good kitchen knife, and then fled the room and down the stairs, silently, still carrying the never-to-be-recovered weapon, past mute dormitories of sleeping orphans and malnourished infants in incubators, and at least one wide-awake orphan, Patricio, who would have heard you had you screamed. Though on second (or millionth) thought, Why, if you understood too well, would you have kept quiet anyway? Pliant collaboration with your murderer, this hardly seems feasible, Flor, no matter what your despair or disgrace. Did he catch you by surprise, alone in your room? Were you alone because you wanted to be, and had shooed the usual brood of little girls away? Or were you waiting for some-body, or even for a late-night phone call you didn't want anyone to overhear? Or did you just need to be alone? Did he slash your throat and then suffocate you with a pillow so you couldn't scream? And then, your murderer gone, did you get up from your bed at least one more time, smearing bloody handprints on the walls as if groping all over for a light switch in a too dark and unfamiliar room, exactly as you might have groped on your very first night in our basement before making your way up the stairs to snack on a stick of butter? And then you went back to bed and died once and for all? This is too terrible! I'm the wrong person to describe this, I can't fake a coroner's detachment. But this is as close to a final report as we are ever going to get, Moya having departed long before he could get around to "chronicling" our investigation, as there was nothing for him to chronicle yet except maybe the secretive depths or shallows of his own perhaps misplaced guilt.

I had to stay away, of course, when, in January, only days after our first meeting in Pastelería Hemmings, Sor Clarita went with a French embassy official to interview all the orphans who might have been old enough to remember Lucas Caycam Quix during the short time he might have spent in the orphanage before running away, if that is in fact what happened. Talk to Patricio, I advised her. If anyone remembers, it will be Patricio. Only eleven orphans were qualified. Because privacy is hard to come by in an orphanage, the interviews were conducted in the room you set up as a piñata workshop, apparently so that some of the orphans could learn that useful craft; no one ever goes into that room anymore, though it remains cluttered with the wire skeletons of never completed *piñata animalitos,* cartons of crepe and tissue paper.

Patricio had only the shadowiest memory of it: he *kind* of remembered that there was an older Indian kid who promptly ran away, but kids were always coming and going, from the malnutrition clinic especially. But he also told Sor Clarita that there was another street kid named Lagarto who used to sneak *into* the orphanage to sleep with another of the older girls sometimes, very late at night, after you were asleep, until one of the girls complained and you threw him out and then Lagarto stood in the street outside screaming and throwing rocks at the gates and you went out in your bathrobe and shouted that if he ever came back again you would have him arrested. *You'll never get near one of my girls again if you don't lift your life up so you can come and visit in the day like a respectable boy!* Patricio claimed you actually shouted, which is possible, since your voice certainly carried, and it seems that everyone who ever knew her turns into Abuelita eventually. But street kids sneaking into the orphanage to make love to the girls? No wonder you always had a lice problem there. Except now with the new barbed wire atop the high wall outside, Patricio, as he puts it, has "the henhouse" to himself and no longer has to contend with outside rivals, but there's still a problem with lice. Rosana put that barbed wire up as soon as she was hired to replace you.

When I "just happened" to drop over to visit Edvarga later the same day of Sor Clarita's visit, Rosana said, "I think that poor woman was innocent because if she hadn't been, wouldn't she have thought of putting barbed wire up to protect herself? She might be alive today if she had, *verdad?* Or maybe she had men coming over the wall to see her too; nothing would surprise me anymore! But she was in love, you know. Oh yes, my *abuela* used to see Flor coming into the hotel where she lives. Everyone there knew about my poor predecessor and that newspaper owner, from that famous family, *los* Batres, no?"

Just like that, I found out, Flor. Rosana went on and on—rapt Edvarga providing the occasional little gasps and simple prompting questions that kept her going, so that I didn't have to say a thing—telling us that for a while her *abuela,* who after all didn't have much else to do with her bitter life as a hotel-dwelling exile but gossip with the chambermaids, had even become convinced that Celso Batres must be the murderer; until the chambermaids convinced her that it couldn't be, because he was such a gentleman, from such a fine family, there was nothing sinister in his having had a seemingly inextinguishable passion for his formidable mistress—seemingly because hadn't it been going on for more than two years without showing any signs of letting up? But when neither of you was seen coming into the hotel for months, everybody had been certain that the affair had finally ended, although Celso continued to pay rent on the suite. So no one had been surprised either when, about a month before you died, you and Celso started meeting there just as regularly as before. But one afternoon soon after, you and Celso had a fight: a chambermaid even heard his angry shouting, but it was over quickly because suddenly the door slanuned open and Celso fell silent as soon as he saw the chambermaid standing in the hail. You walked out and past her, swiftly to the elevator without saying a word, your head down and hair over your face as if to hide tears. You were never seen there again.

"—Practically the whole world knew about Flor and that Celso Batres," said Rosana, telling how even on her visits to Sweden and elsewhere on orphan-related business, people sometimes asked after Celso, and more than once had even mistaken her for you. "Honestly, that always gives me goose bumps, because: *huy no!* But that poor woman! I can't think badly of her no matter what. Of course it's all in the past now, two years ago already, isn't it best forgotten? But yes, Flor used to walk over to that hotel from here, in the afternoons. On foot, *fíjese?* She was in love, *es obvio.* Without a doubt, he's handsome. Intelligent, prominent, a newspaper owner, there are those who say he might even be president someday, I'm sure it's possible . . ."

We'd been sitting in Rosana Letones's new, air-conditioned, first-floor office, having coffee, all three of us smoking; but I was just staring down into my cup of coffee now, face throbbing. Edvarga set her cup down and picked up a clipboard and started riffling through its pages with what seemed feigned attention. "*Dios mío,*" Rosana said softly. "But it must be bad luck to talk this way." (Though she could hardly be superstitious, she even kept your old bedroom, simply because it *is* the best bedroom.) "Eddie,"

Rosana suddenly said, in English, "can you open the window please. Must let this smoke out!" Suddenly I blurted, "I'm supposed to be playing tennis with my cousin!"—and I got up, opened the door, and went out almost in one spastic motion, Edvarga exclaiming behind me, "You play tennis?" I walked all the way home, from Zona 10 to Zona 1, listening to you tell me how what couldn't plausibly have happened, very plausibly might have; and how none of it would have happened if not for Moya's . . .

It didn't take Sor Clarita and me long to find Lagarto through the help of the foreign social workers who work with street kids, one of whom, an Italian, does in fact remember you coming to them two or three times to report runaways, though of course you never insisted that the children be forced to come back and asked only for the chance to talk to them if indeed they were found. Lagarto didn't lift his life up at all, he's a complete glue addict now; the police caught him stealing automobile batteries one night so they'd poured glue all over his head, which was why he was going around with a shaved head, begging his few daily *centavos* by singing *"Cielito Lindo"* off-key on city buses. He's one of the glue sniffers who hang out in that lot where I caught the bus that brought me here to Puerto Barrios. But he'd never heard of a Lucas Caycam who'd run away from Los Quetzalitos either, but his mind was so glue fogged he didn't even remember *you.* None of the social workers has heard of any boy who ran away from an orphanage and then somehow learned that his sister had been "sold," though even if they had, they probably wouldn't tell me, as most tend to be somewhat romantic about *los niños de la calle* and very protective of them, with good reason, I'm sure, as the vast majority are harmless—and there are thousands upon thousands now, many of whom lost their parents in exactly the same way that Lucas believed he'd lost his. The police often kill street kids anyway. Maybe Lucas got involved in one of the *maras,* the criminal street gangs, many of these actually run by the police, and died that way (if he did die), at the hands of a rival gang. Maybe he was in a *mara* car-stealing ring or even, irony of ironies, the baby trade, snatching infants from their mothers' arms on the streets, and was killed for screwing up a job, or for some kind of double cross. Mariel the street girl knew a lot about all the different ways street kids can be preyed on or manipulated into being pawns in the lowest echelons of the rackets. I met Mariel during my search for Lucas, before I accepted that he must be dead or had walked to the States, and then gave up, even stopping my occasional visits to Los Quetzalitos. By then I felt so convinced of how you might have let yourself draw Lucas to your room that night, I didn't *need* it to be true.

Celso Batres, by the way, is the most self-disciplined liar ever or else has the coldest heart ever. I don't want to hurt you, Flor, but he denied any involvement with you when I went to see him at *El Minuto.* I didn't even phone for an appointment, I just turned up and asked to speak with him at the downstairs reception desk, where I gave my name, which he must have recognized; so it must have given him time to compose himself too, so perhaps it was a mistake to have given my name. (And what had you told *him* about us, Flor?) When I was let into his office he was sitting at his desk, family portraits and photographs of himself shaking hands with Latin American politicians and celebrities on all the polished ma-hogany walls. He asked what he could do for me, that's all, and when I told him who I was and that you had been like my sister and so on, he just tilted his head with perfect curiosity, like he was really puzzled about why any of this should matter to him, but was too nice a guy to ask out loud. And he really does *seem* like a nice guy, Flor, he even has some of Tony's elegantly good-natured airs, it isn't hard to guess that in other circumstances he'd be very charming and affectionate, I can even sense what you two had in common. But I also remembered you saying once that it is just one of life's injustices that the person who most deserves one's love is *not* necessarily the one who gets it (I even think it was before you met Moya that you said that, wasn't it?). So I finally said, *You* loved her, Celso, *you* sent that poem, *you* used to meet her in the Cortijo Reforma and so on and wondered to myself what crime I was actually accusing him of anyway. Still, he just sat there for such a long moment, looking so befuddled that I suddenly wondered if maybe Rosana Letones's grandmother had been utterly mistaken. But then Celso surprised me, pounding his desk once with an open hand and whispering seethingly that he'd had it with this zombie country where rumors are the walking dead, Moya's a Communist and is trying to poison his life, and he sat back, took out a navy blue handkerchief, and wiped his eyes, then looked at me with a steady gaze and said:

"I'm sorry about what happened to your sister, but I barely knew her. Believe me if you want to, or don't. The problem with this country is that everybody does everything in secret and, in the end, we all pay. I mean to say we all pay because everybody believes everything."

"You loved her though, I know you did," I repeated, staring at him. And the troubled look in his eyes as he stared back told me that it was true, and that he knew he was letting me see that. Or did I just imagine that too?

"I'll excuse your impertinence, but just this once, Señor Graetz," he said then. "Yes, your sister was a wonderful woman, I know. And terribly unjust things were said about her. But my advice to you is to find something better to do with your life than what you've obviously been doing. Find another way to honor your sister, if you loved her so much, instead of spreading rumors and indulging in this perversity. I have a family to protect. I don't have to tell you that in this country, when people spend their time plotting ways to harm people, they often end up getting hurt themselves. I should think that Luis Moya would have taught you that. I have nothing more to say."

Well, I really didn't persist in my "perversity," Flor. I gave up soon after and found another one, because it was around that time that Zamara fmally became my lover "once and for all," her thing with Lieutenant López finally behind her if it had always been as before her as she'd claimed—though without a doubt it took the *teniente* much longer to tire of Zamara than anyone had predicted. Zamara liked to insist that it was I who'd won her away from *him,* which I had a hard time believing, though I appreciated the attempted flattery. But I hadn't received a single threat of any kind, and I was never *that* invisible. For protection, I had nothing more than my bottle alarm system. I'd behaved as prudently as possible, during the months when 1 was "ceding the territory" to the lieutenant. But there had been many nights when I'd gone to the nightclub where Zamara works anyway and she'd always been glad to see me, had danced with me, had even returned my furtive kisses and nuzzles. Letting ourselves get carried away on those occasions, we'd even made promises to each other, though that I would marry her and bring her and her son to the States was never one of them. Zamara didn't turn tricks at the club anymore, not even for me on my boldest and most passionately persistent nights, but she was never there on weekends anymore, and all the other girls would say then that she was off with her lieutenant. Was she as frightened of him as I was? Was she just waiting for him to lose interest in her so that she could be with me? I can be a very romantic and self-deluding person. Because it definitely felt romantic— though admittedly sick to take any satisfaction from it—to go on wanting her while knowing that I could not have her because of her liaison with a most plausibly murderous and unprosecutable lieutenant.

One night I came into the club and as soon as Zamara saw me, before I even had a chance to buy her a fruit juice and thus establish my ritual right to at least sit beside her all night, Zamara rose from the corner table where she was sitting with the other girls and came towards me with a big smile. *"Hola, amorcito."* Without another word she led me by the hand to the dance floor, put her soft arms around my neck, her hips against my hips, and we both enjoyed my much improved dancing for a while—no longer did the other girls point at me and call out *"mucha ropa,"* too many clothes, during merengues and cumbias, so there's *one* accomplishment—and then she put her lips against my ear and said that it was over with the lieutenant, that I'd won her, she was all mine, and that we could meet tomorrow in the afternoon but only if I took her to that fancy new seafood restaurant in Zona 9 that looks just like a pirate ship; me murmuring in her ear, *Claro, claro, cómo no, mi amor, claro . . .*

If, as Zamara also claimed—though it is very possible my overly eager line of interrogation led her into it and she was just trying to both please and impress me and then later in her stubborn pride refused to retract it—but if it *is* true that *Teniente* López took her to his family's Pacific beach house in Likin one weekend, and that his Aunt Mirza López de Betz and her family unexpectedly turned up there with three of her own servants in tow, and that one of those servants was in fact the same girl who was photographed in the newspapers as the *niñera fafera,* if that is true—and Zamara said it definitely was, nodding her head and chewing her knuckle as she stared at the folded shred of newspaper in my hand; but maybe only *saying* it was true because I'd brought her back to the house and in my bedroom had pulled out that old newspaper picture and had asked her, Do you recognize this girl, have you ever seen her anywhere, for example, maybe when you were with the lieutenant on that day his *tía* turned up at the beach house?

So that maybe Zamara, thinking that it was a trick question and that I already knew, said it was true so that I would be sure to believe that she really *had* been to the beach house? But if that *was* true, and Zamara really *had* seen her there, well, what was I supposed to do about it and what did it really change? It only told me what I already knew and a little bit more: that Señora Mirza López de Betz was so secure in her impunity that she had ludicrously dispatched her own servant to perform the role of a captured *niñera* denouncing you, Flor, as the owner of an accidentally discovered fattening house.

It's entirely possible that the lieutenant took Zamara to his beach house. I've of course seen the undoubtedly contraband portable Sony stereo he gave her in Zamara's little room, and the Panama T-shirt he brought back for her from one of his "business" trips to Panama, undoubtedly undertaken on behalf of his *papi*. It's entirely possible that Zamara really saw the *niñera fafera,* but it's not that good a photograph and it is also possible that Zamara was just saying that to please or impress me and then refused to retract it because what did I think she was, a liar?

But if Señora Mirza López de Betz is mad enough to make her own servant play the *niñera fafera,* might she not have been mad enough to have contrived your murder too, her impunity like a limitless charge account for a free-spending madness, enabling her to take a life just to squelch an embarrassing rumor? Well, enough of these baseless speculations. I don't do that anymore . . .

Three months of Zamara, that's all, Flor. Three months of being able to say, Well this, anyway, was all I could do for anyone here, bring some love and happiness into one *artista de barra*'s life, and receive quite a bit more of it back. Three months of nights with Zamara and no more nights like those during the *first* three months after Moya left when I was without Zamara, when I used to sit in Cuatro Caminos, the little cantina next to the *barra shows* where

FRANCISCO GOLDMAN

the *artistas* often gather before and after work, drinking with Larry until the morning light was harsh, and the girls had all gone home, and only the drunken night-crawling scum remained, I sank pretty low, Flor. Three months of afternoons with Zamara, in her rented room in the ramshackle house around a concrete patio, making love in Zamara's windowless room, pictures from movie star magazines and *Vanidades* taped to the dirty pink walls, one bare light bulb in the ceiling; nights sitting next to Zamara, watching her yawning up into the smoky darkness behind colored *barra show* lights, plopping her head down in folded arms on the table and then looking up again, heavily sighing, *"Ayyy quiero morrrrir,"* from boredom, hate, this life of six nights a week from eight in the evening until five in the morning that if only I would rescue her from . . . but all I was ever ready to do was take her home, her place or even mine, despite Chayito's enraged stare—"This is my friend Zamara, Chayito," *"Mucho gusto, señora,"* and the stare; trips with Zamara, to the coast, where in Puerto Barrios we spent a night right here in the Hotel del Norte and a rainy afternoon in the house over a bar where the featured *artistas* from the fanciest sailors' nightclub live, playing gin rummy and smoking pot on her friend Paola's bed; and then across the bay to Livingston, where we stayed in the fanciest hotel and got to make love under a ceiling fan in our immaculate white room overlooking the bay, where at sunset we could see dolphins playing in the pink waves beneath all the swooping birds. What did we talk about? Hardly anything, though almost always amiably. Well, lots of things. Really, mainly, we fucked, and you know what that's like, when that's all you want to do and everything you do is part of that. But I treated Zamara pretty well, didn't I? I bought her dresses, I went with her to El Progreso to visit her mother and son in their poor persons' small compound of shacks around a chicken-shit yard and brought presents for them both; I took her to movies, restaurants and watched

556

her eat with her fingers, bought her real cotton underwear so that she could get rid of her poor person's sackcloth ones, and just lay in bed with her for hours with my nose buried here and there, smelling her hair, her neck, her armpits, faintly rose-and-olive-hued Zamarita. I told her drugs were bad for her and convinced her; I gave her a García Márquez novel, the easiest to read and shortest, the one about the colonel and the rooster, and she loved it, she took it everywhere with her and plowed right through it in about six weeks; I took her to the doctor and to the dentist and to the circus and on yet another of those nights when she'd skipped work because I'd agreed to pay her docked salary and the fine, I introduced her without fanfare or shame to my cousin Freddie when we ran into him and his *fufurufa* girlfriend in the Jaguar disco at the Hotel Biltmore Maya. I gave her one thousand dollars of my "wedding gift" to put towards her son's education. I tried to convince her to enroll in beautician school like so many of the other *artistas* do, but she wouldn't because it would mean too many afternoons away from me. And I was happy, I think, knowing this was temporary, and because our bodies really did love each other, and because my obsession seemed insatiable, and because she really does say a lot of funny things and has a wonderful stillness inside; because I stopped asking myself who I was or who I was turning into and didn't search for anything more inside her beyond that which I already knew about and, my God, what could have been more unfair than that? Because I still had five thousand dollars left and then three and then a bit more than one. Because my dancing got better and better and I even stopped reading the newspapers, because I just liked watching her, the way she watered the gardenias planted in Carnation milk cans outside her door in the afternoons before we went inside to make love; liked the way, on our walk to the General Cemetery one afternoon, she impulsively reached out and rang the bell attached to the ice-cream vendor's cart, waking the elderly ice-cream vendor dozing against a wall; liked the way she dragged me all the way to the General Cemetery just to see the famous spot where two illicit lovers are buried with their proper spouses, their adjacent tombs joined by the thickly gnarled, groping tendrils of a single dense vine. Two days after I told Zamara that I'd soon be going home (though to Mexico first), I received a letter under my door, full of misspellings, in chicken-scrawl print, telling me that I was a coward, a *putero,* a *vicioso,* a *borrachito,* one she loved anyway and had chosen over a lieutenant, one who was afraid to admit to himself that he had fallen in love with just a common *artista de barra* and because of that was going to turn everything into shit. When I went to the club to find her that night, her friend Lucy told me that Zamara had gone home to El Progreso to make her principled stand, certain that I would admit my error and follow her there. I was going to do that, wasn't I? Lucy was sure I was going to go, wasn't I?

Every night in the Medellín, here in Puerto Barrios, Paola asks me the same thing. I don't have to *marry* her, she says. Just go see her, anyway. You don't have to go back to the city. Take her to Mexico, why not? Zamara will land on her feet no matter what, *vos.* She's proud! Just go see her, *Rohyyer. Te vas, o qué?*

Well, I can at least do that, can't I? I want you to think well of me, after all. I haven't spent a year here only to learn heartlessness. By now I should have some idea of how to solve *my own* crime, anyway.

But first I have to tell about Mariel the street girl: her earnest endeavors to find Lucas on my behalf ended up inspiring a criminal mastermind with an idea for a trap that I almost walked right into, whether Mariel actually knows that now or not.

Fourteen years old, torn shoes, cowboy shirt knotted over belly, fake rhinestone–studded denim skirt missing most of its stones, and glitter smeared across her eyelids, the tops of her plump cheeks—at night Mariel sells sex too, in the cantinas off 18 Calle, slipping a cheap but potent mickey into her "suitor's" drink just before going to whatever sleazy room, and then making off with the usually paltry sum in his wallet. So she claimed, anyway, and showed me the pills, available in any pharmacy.

Manel came up from behind me one day on Sexta Avenida, grabbed my hand in both of hers, and said she'd found Lucas Caycam Quix. Again. This wasn't even a month ago, after I'd long stopped believing that he was even alive. But it was a practically once a week occurrence, Mariel snagging me on the streets of Zona 1, telling me she had news, so that then I'd buy her a meal, which I would have done anyway. Mariel had claimed to know of Lucas right from the start, back when Sor Clarita and I were initiating our search, but so did many of the street kids and usually for the same reason as Mariel initially did: not for money once they realized we weren't offering any, but simply to prolong our interest and attention. For a while I'd even formalized our agreement— Mariel was "my best informant"—taking her to lunch in Pollo Campero every Thursday afternoon, where I'd always let her win one *quetzal* at a time from me in macho bets over who could eat fried chicken with the most chili sauce heaped all over. Then I'd listen encouragingly while Mariel pretended that she knew about Lucas, but so far had been unable to find him, but was getting closer—I knew this let her feel that the lunches were part of an honest transaction, keeping up the illusion of a significant bond between us. My friendship was a big deal to her, I thought. I was nice to her, listened to her problems, and I wasn't even a social worker. And it was certainly always interesting to hear her totally appalling stories.

This time, when she pulled me off Sexta Avenida and into the Picadilly and then upstairs into a booth, we ordered pizza and waited for two boys who Mariel said would soon be arriving to explain everything. Then she got busy carving her initials into the tabletop with her fork. The extravagance of the whole ruse really was kind of touching, but I was in a bit of a rush that day too, with plans to meet Zamara for an afternoon movie. Just when I was trying to find the right way to say that it looked like they weren't coming after all, so that I could get the business of consoling her over the failure of the meeting out of the way—we'd just been served our pizza, and hadn't even had the first of our hot sauce bets yet—suddenly there they were, standing at the edge of our table with their hands in their pockets: two street boys, teenagers, with rolled-up sleeves exposing crude ink tattoos on their forearms—the skinny one, the boniest, with the harder yet handsomer face of the two, also had a solid black teardrop—the size of a peanut—tattooed just under the duct of his right eye, like it had been squeezed out in some moment of unprecedented pity or self-pity long ago, oily-inky, and then had just dried right there, before it could even roll down his cheek. That teardrop's effect, of course, was pretty sinister, since it seemed to signify the absolute opposite of a real tear, mocking anyone who might ever have expected or wanted him to shed a real one. But when I asked him about it much later his explanation wasn't so subtle: he said he'd gotten the tattoo when he was a little boy because someone had told him it would make people feel sorrier for him when he sang for money on buses.

No need to draw this out. They said they were Lucas's friends; I met with them twice more after that. They belonged to the same *mara,* street gang, and they knew all the right details: about Lucas's life, the adoption, his vengeful rage about it. They claimed he was one tough *indio.* Lucas did not earn his money legally, but at least they were *"una mara audaz."* What he'd believed back then was that someday he was going to earn enough to have his little sister María de la Luz, his last surviving family member, come and live with him so that they could start an honest life. But then you'd *sold* María de la Luz for thousands of dollars to France, where her organs were going to be removed and transplanted to rich people so that they could live instead, and that was why, in justifiable revenge, he'd killed you. I listened to this, but I was suspicious: I knew they could have put that whole story together just from what I'd already told Mariel, along with the usual rumors about the baby trade.

Then one of the boys said that Lucas had even kept your fur stole, his *petrecho de guerra,* his avenger's trophy, and even described it accurately enough, though he didn't use the word *ermine.* I asked for more proof, I wanted to *see* it. At the second meeting the boy named Gato Cinco—not Teardrop—pulled a delicate tonglike utensil from his pocket and laid it on the table and I thought, What's that for, boiling eggs one at a time? Then I realized it was an eyelash curler, not even rusted, shiny and silvery as if it had been preserved carefully and just polished; no makeup coated, tiny lashes stuck to it: *your* eyelash curler.

I told them that I had no desire to try to have Lucas arrested or to harm him, that I just wanted to talk with him. The first note slipped under my door, purporting to be from Lucas, affirmed his understanding of that. This crudely penciled but logical warning read: "If you are not being honest with me, this will come out bad for you." He would speak to me for five hundred dollars. Now Lucas's goal in life, according to his friends, was to earn enough money to buy his sister's freedom from France, rejoin his parents, and find a way for them all to live together someday in the city, or maybe Quezaltenango. I was to show myself on the Incienso Bridge so that he, from somewhere in the slum below, would be able to see that I had come alone. His friends would then come and fetch me on the bridge, and lead me down to him.

Is it so hard to see how I fell for this? But it baffles me now. I hiss: jerk, idiot, *payaso!* But sometimes things happen in a way that makes it seem that all your courage, resolve, or even intuition have succumbed to a dreamlike momentum outside of you. Then what saves you? Nothing, if you don't wake up in time. But if you do? An instinct? A warning from inside like one of those soft and silent premonitions that only pass between true lovers?

I didn't tell anyone about my important mission, not even Zamara, when I left on foot for the Incienso Bridge at the appointed time. So what did I think I was going to get out of "Lucas" for my five hundred dollars? Confirmation that his mad motive of revenge had been justified? Then what was I going to do, shake his hand? Of course I wanted to talk some sense into him about his plans to buy back his sister, and encourage him to rejoin his parents, who would be overjoyed to see him, and would soon have more than enough money to set up a modest home in the city or Quezaltenango, and begin a new and I hoped healing life. I wanted to tell him that we had *both* been cruelly wronged, and wanted to at least try to make amends with fate. I wanted to hear what he had to say for himself and look into his eyes and decide then what to feel about him once and for all. What if I found that I hated him for his brutal ignorance, despite the justification of his presumed motive and the horrors he'd survived? Maybe as a secret punishment I would later do what Zamara would probably do (and is probably doing to me right now): cut a *limón* into eight pieces and write Lucas Caycam Quix onto a strip of paper and then fold it back inside the pieces and sew the *limón* up again with red thread because the thread has to be red, and drop it into a sewer. But he wouldn't be the only one who deserved that hex.

The Incienso Bridge spans a vast, deep *barranco* behind Zona 1, a densely packed slum spreading down one steep slope, garbage perpetually smoldering all over the other. Five hundred dollars folded up in an envelope in my pocket, I walked all the way out into the middle like I was supposed to, and waited, standing on the pedestrian walkway inside the rail. The bridge seemed to sway underneath me whenever heavy trucks sped across. From where I stood, I could see all the way to the gorge's far end, where sheer rock cliffs looked as if they'd been split apart by a sharp ax of lightning: a thin, frothy stream ran out of the split and along the very distant, grassy, garbage-strewn bottom. Among palm trees that looked like pressed green daisies from that height and flame-flickering flowering trees were thousands of fiat tin roofs, weighed down with tires, boulders, cinder blocks, and rusted pieces of scrap, so that it looked like a factory had blown apart in the sky and landed all over the *barrio* in bits and pieces. Dirt paths shot down through that tumbling casbah of shacks; the people I could see walking on them were just specks. Perhaps one of these was one of Lucas's friends, climbing towards me now.

I waited for just a short time, listening to the way the walls of the gorge seemed to channel the *barrio*'s village sounds upwards along with the smoke from cooking fires and just as lightly: an airy, strangely inanimate repetition of barking dogs, demented roosters, infants crying, children screeching, radios playing, all of it amidst a soft-as-milkweed muttering that sounded like prayerful or vengeful old women whispering to themselves—probably just the wind and air reverberating in the hollowness of the gorge.

I didn't feel particularly nervous at first. I guess I was in a suspended state, waiting to see what would happen and knowing that I needed calm much more than fear to get what I wanted from the meeting. I wanted to know, is all, and wasn't it worth the effort to find out? But you know what I actually felt at that moment, Flor? You know what I was actually thinking? That I missed Zamara. I wasn't really thinking of Lucas at all, or even about this dangerous bait of five hundred dollars in my pocket. I had left her bed only hours before and still hadn't quite separated myself from the lingering coziness of her embrace, the bed, the dark little room; I still had the taste of her mouth in mine, and the cool dry air up on the bridge somehow made the damp scent of her in my nostrils even niore pronounced. Because I knew that this was the end and that it meant I'd be going home soon, and I just missed her already, that's all. And then I felt sad, as if instead of merely leaving the country, something much worse was about to happen to me. I probably even smiled to myself feeling nostalgic already, remembering how in bed that morning I'd told her some more about you, all about that time you were lost in a blizzard. Tiny, sun-shrunken, corrupt little raisins . . . like that the silent words came to me, on the Incienso Bridge. I've been trying to re-create exactly what it was I was thinking and feeling on the bridge and how it came to me, but it all happened in a matter of seconds, almost: *Tiny, sun-shrunken, just like corrupt little raisins, ay no* . . . By then I'd already begun to walk off. Casually, looking down, hands in pockets, as if really I was just going to pace back and forth a bit, impatiently, though what I was thinking now was Who else would have actually kept that eyelash curler around but a poor cop's wife? Some poor beat cop with control over a teenage *mara*. Five hundred bucks, a lot to some loser cop who'd probably keep most of it for himself sharing the rest with his two subservient punks, Gato Cinco and Teardrop. By then I'd already started running into Zona 1, and didn't stop until I'd reached the Avenida Elena, which marks the beginning of my neighborhood.

One of the last times I went home to Namoset I spent hours ransacking the house, looking for a certain old crayon drawing of a Christmas tree. I knew that the drawing had been kept around for years, and it seemed outrageous to me that anyone could have thrown it out, though maybe even Flor had done so, during one of her especially driven cleanings, not even pausing to reflect over its more than just sentimental value to me. I'm sort of surprised I haven't told this story yet.

One dim, wintry, and maybe even snowy day when Flor and I were in the first grade, we were all trooped into a sixth-grade classroom and lined up against a wall, in front of the blackboard, as if to face a firing squad. The girls from the school's fifth and sixth grades had already been assembled there and were lined up against the opposite wall, staring, scrutinizing us, their eyes excitedly jumping from face to face. What all the fifth and sixth grade boys were off doing that afternoon, I have no idea.

Then, on a teacher's command, the older girls literally stampeded down the desk aisles towards us, and I was immediately claimed by an excessively delighted sixth grader with curly, bobbed hair who must have really wanted a little brother and for some reason wanted him to look just like me. I will never forget the way she charged down the aisle, in a tartan plaid dress, her mouth open, one hand already reaching for me: I was flooded with pleasure and wonderment—for that moment I was all hers.

But of course no one chose Flor, who was even a little older than the sixth graders. The teachers had ignored this obvious dilemma. They thought, I guess, that Flor was the same, or even less developed, than a first grader, because her English, at that time, was only somewhat more advanced than baby talk. I glanced over and saw Flor still standing against the blackboard with a discomforted squint, a handful of hair pulled into her mouth so that she could chew on it. But the sixth grader was already excitedly pulling me towards her desk. I looked over my shoulder and saw Flor's eyes, furious, following us.

Flor solved this confusing situation quickly, though. She marched right over and snatched me from my girl and said something like, "I draw Christmas tree! Yes!" and began leading me towards an empty desk, though she stopped and turned to the suddenly bereft sixth grader and gestured for her to follow.

I guess the point of the day's exercise was that the older girls were supposed to crayon Christmas trees far more elaborate than those we were capable of, so that we could learn this skill and then take the drawings home to our parents as if we'd done them ourselves. I would also guess that the teachers' thinking included the idea that the older girls would get some practice at being perfect and attentive baby-sitters and little future mothers as well.

So the three of us ended up at the same old wooden desk where Flor, suddenly plunged into deep concentration and with her soft voice that mesmerized even the sixth grader, began crayoning in and explaining in Spanish—which I somewhat translated—the Christmas tree she said they'd had in her Guatemala City convent orphanage: she put white doves in the green boughs and flaming Roman candles and brightly colored mythological animals made of feather and straw that she told about as she went along, and she put a resplendent quetzal bird instead of an angel on top and set a parade of spider monkeys in cone-shaped caps riding unicycles around it on a floor carpeted with pine needles and tropical blossoms. Then came the eerily delicious minutes when there was nothing more to tell because for was filling in the picture's backdrop and occasionally yawning squeakily—the sixth grader and I as if hypnotized watching Flor's long, already womanly brown fingers curled around a series of crayons swished back and forth according to some dreamy pattern, until the sheet of paper was completely covered with the richly glowing sheen of stained glass. She let the sixth grader take it home with her, and then promised to make me another one later but only if I stopped crying.

That evening, at home, after she'd finished preparing our supper, Flor called down to me in the playroom where I was watching television, and when I came upstairs I found her sitting at the kitchen table, paper and crayons ready.

"*Bueno.* Now we will draw your tree, like I promised, Rogito," she said, with a somewhat forced smile. A bit mystified but eager, I sat beside her, and watched her do it all over again: the same *animalitos* and whispered anecdotes, slowly filling in the backdrop in the same dreamy way . . . Steadfastly, refusing to hurry, relishing and prolonging her perfect scheme, as if everything depended on its being a minutely exact replica of that afternoon's Christmas tree, Flor finally finished. Then, before I even had a chance to gasp in appreciation, she picked up the glossy sheet of paper in both hands and held it under the table—I heard paper tearing. She watched me with a bemused, expectant expression. My scream brought both my parents hurrying from the living room, where my father had been reading the newspaper in his armchair and my mother had been watching television and sipping domestic-brand sherry.

"You forgot all about me," Flor was saying, in Spanish. "This afternoon, when you threw yourself so happily on that girl, you left me all alone!" But she had already brought her hands back out from under the table, holding, intact, the spectacularly crayoned sheet. She'd hidden another piece of paper on her lap, that was the one she'd torn.

I stood there silently reeling as my parents came into the kitchen and suddenly, I guess because Flor started to first, we were both giggling, me so uncontrollably I finally had to lay down on the floor. My parents were very impressed by the drawing, and must have assumed that my scream had been one of delight, though my mother couldn't resist commenting with light disapproval on Flor's fantastical exaggerations.

So once upon a time, there were two identical drawings of that Christmas tree: mine and that sixth grader's.

Year after year, Flor brought mine out at Christmas and taped it to the refrigerator. And every time she taunted me with the memory of how I had supposedly rushed into the arms of the sixth-grade girl who had claimed me, and every time I succumbed to the same confused mix of hilarity and guilt and, of course, love, remembering how upset and then angry Flor had looked, left all alone, standing there against the blackboard with her hair in her mouth.

On the bridge, when I heard Flor's voice-that wasn't just memory. Her voice still exists, and that was proof. Memory is like a long conversation during which, at any moment, Flor might tell me something unexpected—as long as I, despite many other preoccupations, go on keeping up my end well enough, and listening.

When I spoke to Uncle Jorge on the phone, he agreed to wire me the rest of my money, which I'd been keeping in his office safe, when I get to Mexico. But it was a strange conversation. Puerto Barrios has sad associations for him, I know. That's because when my mother and uncles were young and still living at home, Abuelito suffered three mysterious bouts of certifiable madness, each of them three years apart. Suddenly he'd wake up one morning knowing entire Verdi operas by heart, singing at the top of his lungs. And then he would escape on his riotous sprees, buying expensive presents for his mistresses and whores, even signing family properties over to them until Abuelita had everything put in her own name. My uncles, teenagers the first time it happened, would have to track him down, and then they always had to take him, in a straitjacket, here to Puerto Barrios, where they'd book passage on a banana boat for New Orleans; there Abuelito would receive electric shock therapy and then be OK for another three years. Those gulf crossings with Abuelito in a straitjacket are Uncle

Jorge's most painful memories, and here I am now, leaving by launch instead of banana boat in a few days.

When I told him not to worry about the bottles on chairs he'd find in my rooms, he said yes, he'd already seen them, and that it made him feel very sad that my stay in Guatemala had ended this way.

"Tío Jorge, don't be sad," I said, kind of lamely. "Everything's fine, it really is. Though it would have been nice to see it raining there again." The rainy season had finally come to the city a few days before.

I didn't hear anything for a moment and wondered if the line had gone dead, but suddenly Catty was on the phone: "Roger, you didn't go to Puerto Barrios to get married to that girl Freddie saw you with, did you? Because if you did I am going to be *very* angry."

"What? No, Cat. Who told you that?"

"No one, it's just that Papi is very sad, and I thought—Well, he has been worried that you are going to do something crazy like that, Roger."

"Tell him not to worry about it, Catty. Really. Everything's great."

And then we said our good-byes: I wished Catty luck when she starts medical school next term and sent my love to everyone. But suddenly Uncle Jorge got back on the phone again to ask for my help in translating, into English, a strongly worded message he was sending to manufacturers in Taiwan regarding a certain missing shipment of toys that he'd already paid for. His voice was familiar again, booming: "The Taiwanese and I have exchanged twenty-seven telexes already, Roger! And neither of us still has the slightest idea of what the other is talking about!"

When I got off the phone I paid my hotel bill and walked all the way into town in the soggy heat to where the Fuente del Norte buses leave from. Just as I was about to board the bus, I looked up and saw a familiar face in the door, that same merrily bemused smirk, that very same bus driver's *ayudante* who'd made fun of me for not knowing where I was going. Grinning, he held his hand out for my ticket and said, *"Hombre,* all these weeks with the mermaids and still with a sad face? *Qué pasó?"*

ACKNOWLEDGMENTS

This would have been a different book if not for the friendship, and the guidance, of certain people, whom the author wishes to thank, while absolving them of all blame: Morgan, whose support from the very beginning, and patience, were integral; also Binky; Bex; Jean-Marie; Bob and Karen; Annie; los Andersons de La Mara Internacional, Ken and Jon Lee; Chuck; the Tintoris; my editors at Harper's; Anton; Webs; Aldo; my family in Guatemala, past and present; Tina, my best friend, The Not-So-Secret Sharer; and Julio, who cast a lot of light in a small country—that country is darker now, for me anyway, since he was forced to leave it.

A GROVE PRESS READING GROUP GUIDE
BY KATURAH JENKINS

The Long Night of White Chickens

Francisco Goldman

ABOUT THIS GUIDE

We hope that these discussion questions will enhance
your reading group's exploration of Francisco Goldman's
The Long Night of White Chickens. They are meant to
stimulate discussion, offer new viewpoints, and enrich
your enjoyment of the book.

More reading group guides and additional information,
including summaries, author tours, and author sites for
other fine Grove Press titles, may be found on
our Web site, www.groveatlantic.com.

QUESTIONS FOR DISCUSSION

1. What affect does Flor de Mayo Puac's arrival have on the Graetz family? Describe her relationship with Roger, with Ira and Mirabel. Discuss the role family plays in the lives of the different characters in the novel.

2. What does Flor discover about herself when she travels to Chiquimula? What is Flor's greatest challenge there? How are her memories transformed by her visit?

3. In what way does Flor identify with the maids in the story? How does she set herself apart from them?

4. Are there parallels between Flor and the other orphans? If so, do you draw any significance from these parallels? What do you make of the role of education in this story?

5. Was there any truth to what others thought of Flor? What did Flor think of herself? What did she believe in most? By what standards did she define herself? Do you place more stock in the opinion of others, readily adopting their perspectives over your own? Explain your answers.

6. Was Flor really guilty of conducting illegal adoptions, as the press and rumors suggest? Or was she a scapegoat, murdered to cover up the real "fattening house" of Mirza Lopez de Betz? Discuss if you agree with how the author chose to resolve Flor's homicide. Of all the possible suspects mentioned, who do you think is responsible for killing her?

7. Compare the reactions of Roger, Ira, Mirabel, and Moya to Flor's death. How does this event reflect on each of them?

8. "I don't even know if Lucas Caycam Quix is *real*" (p. 434). Are we meant to share Roger's confusion? Do you agree or disagree? Explain why.

9. "I dreamed we were making love" (p. 117). Why do you think Roger and Flor never explored a sexual relationship together? Do you agree with this decision? Discuss why you think Flor lied to her college friends about having an intimate relationship with Roger for years, unbeknownst to his parents.

10. Early in the novel what does the incident with the "demented" German shepherd say about Roger's character? Years later Moya tells Roger, "I would not want you on my side in a combat" (p. 47). Do you agree with Moya's opinion of Roger, or is he unfairly judging the man by his childhood cowardice?

11. Why do you think Roger waited a year to return to Guatemala to investigate Flor's death? Do you think during that time he believed in her guilt? If so, did this make you think less of him? Why or why not?

12. At what point, if any, does Roger begin to genuinely care for Zamara? Does he ever genuinely love her? What affect does she have on Roger?

13. Why do you think Roger needs to be seen as "heroic" to others? Does this need drive him to search for Lucas Caycam Quix and ultimately lead to the incident on the Incienso Bridge? Why or why not?

14. Why do you think the author chose to name the book after a night between Moya and Flor instead of one with Roger? What is the significance of the title in light of their conversation?

15. "So Moya kept that one secret, the secret that justified all secretiveness, the one he must have always told himself it was the most important to keep, so important to keep that he barely admitted it even to himself" (p. 533). What is the secret Moya has been hiding?

16. Discuss whether Moya's boasting was to blame for Flor's self-destructiveness and possibly her death. Do you think Moya knew the identity of Flor's "Secret Lover" before he made his macho declaration? Was his betrayal of Flor a justifiable response to his hurt and anger at being rejected?

17. Who do you think is responsible for the "unambiguous message" meant for Moya? Do you agree with Moya's decision? Would you have made the same choice? Think of a time that you have been threatened; what was your reaction?

18. What part does Maribel play in the story? Does her character change over the course of the novel? What affect does her "rejection of the local Catholicism" have on her family?

19. How is religion explored in the novel?

20. Why do you think Mirabel suggests burying Flor in Guatemala instead of Boston?

21. How does Guatemala function as a character in the story?

22. "One of the ways Guatemala City can seem the same as a dream: the only thing forbidden is waking up" (p. 150). What do you think the author means by this? Do you agree or disagree?

23. Describe how Roger's relationship with Guatemala unfolds throughout the novel. Why does he ultimately decide "*Guatemala no existe*" after Flor's funeral (p. 300)? Or, rather, why does Moya make this remark?

24. Discuss why Flor compares her relationship with Guatemala to that of breaking up with a lover.

25. In 1830, Stendhal wrote in *Le Rouge et le Noir*, "the drawback of the reign of opinion, which however procures liberty, is that it interferes in matters with which it has no concern; such as private life." Discuss this statement as it applies to Flor and the government of Guatemala.

26. Why is the memory of the "crayon drawing" of a Christmas tree significant (p. 564)?

27. "Memory is like a long conversation" (p. 568). Why do you think Roger feels this way? Do you agree or disagree? In what way does memory permeate the novel? How reliable is memory? Do you trust in the accuracy of your memories? Why or why not?

28. There are several compelling female characters: Flor de Mayo Puac, Mirabel Graetz, Abuelita, and Miss Cavanaugh. Compare how the author fleshes out the female and male characters. Do you think he does a better job with one gender?

29. Compare the characters of Flor and Mirabel. How does Flor serve as a foil to Mirabel? Who, if anyone, fills that role for Roger?

30. How do the men in Flor's life compare to each other?

31. How is Moya the book's coauthor, or even its secret or hidden author?

32. If Moya is the "secret author" of parts of the book, why does Moya refer to himself in the third person?

Suggestions for Further Reading:

The Brief Wondrous Life of Oscar Wao by Junot Díaz; *The Savage Detectives* and *Amulet* by Roberto Bolaño; *Senselessness* by Horacio Castellanos Moya; *Conversation in the Cathedral* by Mario Vargas Llosa; *Love in the Time of Cholera* by Gabriel García Márquez; *Paradise* by Elena Castedo; *Ways of Going Home* by Alejandro Zambra; *My Father's Ghost Is Climbing in the Rain* by Patricio Pron; *Riot: A Love Story* by Shashi Tharoor; *Silence on the Mountain* by Daniel Wilkinson; *Guatemala: Eternal Spring, Eternal Tyranny* by Jean-Marie Simon; *The Red and the Black* by Stendhal; *White Teeth* by Zadie Smith; *Dreaming in Cuban* by Cristina García